D0924934

THE SONG OF PHAID THE GAMBLER

Mick Farren

NEW ENGLISH LIBRARY

A New English Library Original Publication, 1981

First NEL Paperback Edition October 1981

NEL Books are published by
New English Library,
Barnard's Inn, Holborn,
London EC1N 2JR, a division of Hodder and Stoughton Ltd.

Typeset by Yale Press Limited, London SE25
Printed in Great Britain by
Cox & Wyman, Reading

0 450 05343 1

1

THE BUILDING with the sign that proclaimed it a hotel was half swallowed by the jungle. Inch by inch, over long centuries, the slow power of creeper and vine, sapling and dark green undergrowth had claimed it back. The jungle could crack stones and distort structures. The humidity and thick miasmic mists from the great river corroded and eventually ate away all metal. What the jungle couldn't destroy it simply covered up; permanently shrouded it in a thick carpet of greenery.

The building with the sign that proclaimed it a hotel must have once been very beautiful. A rich man's up river, jungle retreat. Originally there had been a low white dome fashioned from thick, cool masonry. The dome's solidity had been offset by a fragile wandlike spire, but that had long since fallen to the creepers. Set in a clearing on the riverbank, it was still possible just to distinguish where there had been a wide piazza. If you dug around on the jungle floor, you could just find strips of mosaic and the pipework that had fed water to a complex of fountains.

Only the dome could be described as having put up a fight. Apart from a jagged crack that arched across one side of it, it had remained almost intact. It was inside the dome that a traveller could find such hotel service as was promised by the sign. There were few travellers who pulled over to the broken dock and the sorry overgrown clearing. There were few travellers and, in consequence, the service provided by the hotel was scant, basic and without flourish.

Despite the sad present and the seemingly hopeless future, a small but unsanitary village had grown up around the dome. Lethargic primitives who had wandered in from the deep jungle had set up hovels made from salvaged plastic sheet and scrap lumber. There were others who had come from the river, spiritually worn out wanderers who couldn't wander any further and who had lapsed into a dull existence with either a local partner or the local hooch. There were even some who had just appeared as if from thin air. Nobody knew where they had come from and nobody cared. Whatever their origin, all the inhabitants of the ramshackle little village seemed rarely to smile. The closest they came to hope was a sullen yearning for something to come down the river that might change their situation. In the meantime they squatted and waited and sweated in the heat.

It was hot, even inside the dome. The air was heavy and sluggish, pressing stickily on those who had to live in it and breath it. There was no hint of a breeze, just a reluctant, almost viscous motion. It was as though carrying the weight of the relentless humidity was too much for the atmosphere.

Once there had been cooling tubes set at regular intervals around the dome but these no longer worked. They were clogged with dirt and dead leaves. No one in the village had the skills to make them function again. In the big public room that took up most of the dome floor, a leaf-bladed fan, operated by a semi-comatose primitive was supposed to supply some kind of relief. In fact it did nothing but disturb the fat metallic green flies that floated torpidly into its path. For a moment the beat of their wings would quicken and, if anybody noticed, they'd crackle briefly with mechanical, insect annoyance. Murmurers that hung from the roof of the dome were supposed to emit a stream of hostility that would keep most insects outside, but the fat flies seemed impervious to them and their electronic threats.

The heat reached a peak in the mid-afternoon. Plants seemed bloated and overly lush, as if they'd overfed on the poisonous moisture. Dogs slept with their tongues lolling out. Men found excuses to sneak off to a quiet patch of shade, also to sleep. Everyone and everything waited for the time before sunset when the rain would

6

start, when water would drop from the sky as though a faucet had been turned on and, for a few precious hours, the air would at least hold the illusion of being clean and fresh.

There were exceptions in the village. Not even the heat and the humidity of the high afternoon could stop the gamblers. Weren't there stories of gamblers so obsessive that they had to be dragged out of burning buildings; of gamblers who would risk frostbite in an icefield by taking off their gloves to deal a hand; of gamblers who would sweat out the kind of temperatures that made even lizards blink their black and hostile eyes and refrain from moving?

Even though it had been going on for a day and a night, the game still had a makeshift air to it. The three men using a slab of polished basalt as a table. One man sprawled in a low chair: the other two hunkered down on the dirt floor as though they were more used to pitching bones in a back alley than playing cards on a table.

The two who squatted played with the bright-eyed desperation of men who hoped that at any moment their luck would return and all would be well. The third conducted his game in a totally opposite manner. He dealt the cards almost wearily, with an economy that showed all too clearly that the heat was getting to him. Sweat ran down his face in oily rivulets, soaking his now grimy silk shirt.

It was only a sense of professionalism that kept him going. He was, after all, a professional gambler. It was his game. If the amateurs on either side of him were intent on throwing away their money, he was beholden to ride with them and take it, even if it did mean playing through the steam oven afternoon of this poisonous region.

A gambling man has to make his living where he can. He can't always be the one to pick the time and the place, particularly if the gambling man had managed to get himself stranded in a torrid zone without the price of the long ride back to civilisation.

The name of the gambling man was Phaid. He had once had other names, a whole string of names in fact. Elaborate and lengthy names for male children were an idiosyncrasy of his people. Those old names, however, had not been used for so long that he doubted if he'd respond, even if they were yelled right into his ear. For him, his homeland, its people and their archaic customs were something that belonged to the far away past.

The cards came to Phaid and he warily dealt them round. His two opponents were watching him with narrow, suspicious eyes. One was a primitive, a warrior from some small bellicose tribe from way back in the jungle. His flat leathery face was a mass of tattoos and ritual scars. His arms were covered in pitted plasteel armour, they contrasted strangely with the amulets and necklaces of shells and parrot feathers that were festooned around his neck. By his side was a crude but effective dart launcher.

The second player's sallow skin and black greasy hair indicated that he probably had grown to maturity in the flat lands that lay down river. He wore a patched and stained military style jumpsuit. All the badges and insignia had, at one time or another, been torn from it. Phaid suspected that he was possibly a deserter from the army of one of the lowland city states, or a mercenary who had wandered too far up river and too far into the jungle. Certainly at some time his left eye and part of the left side of his face had been blown away. It had been replaced by a crudely flexible permapatch and a glittering black optic sensor that swivelled in synchronisation with his good eye. The military image was further reinforced by the powerful fuse tube that hung from a wide leather belt.

Primitive scooped up his cards and spat into the dirt. 'How'm I goin' t' get anyplace if'n all I get dealt is shit like yon?'

Phaid didn't bother to reply. It took too much energy. He didn't have to bother with any of their nonsense. All he needed to do was doggedly stick with the odds. The others could play with their suspicions and make the conversation and the mistakes. Phaid was too far ahead to be hurt. He doubled the bet and waited to see if the man had the nerve to keep going.

When he'd started the game the previous evening he had known that this would be a game without a trace of subtlety. Subtlety was a long way down the river, many stops behind him on his disastrous run of bad luck. Originally there had been seven players. There had been the three men who were about the only inhabitants of the town who had anything resembling real money. One was the owner of the hotel, the other two, brothers, operated

8

the small boat dock at the front of the cracked and broken, overgrown steps that led down to the river. In addition to them, there was a sharp-eyed, sharp-tongued, thrice widowed boat woman who had a flatboat and a pair of freight blimps moored at the jetty.

The three villagers were only there for a good time. They were strictly bread and butter work for Phaid. They drank too much, sweated profusely and their breath reeked of the spice that the river people shovelled over everything they ate. They'd come into the game with a small roll and once they'd lost it they'd retired gracefully, quite grateful for the night's entertainment.

The boat woman had been a little more serious in her play, and with her, Phaid had almost been close to enjoying himself. She'd run her cards with hard-headed common sense, never confronted Phaid directly, and around dawn, when she'd amassed a small profit, she'd excused herself and left.

Phaid hadn't relished the idea of being left with the duo. It was clear they were nothing more than river rats, backwater lowlife, the kind who liked to haunt isolated townships, because isolated townships were about the only places that their graceless swagger and unimaginative braggadocio had a hope of being taken seriously.

When they told Phaid that they'd come to the township looking for a good time, he'd stared at them with open contempt. What kind of good time did they imagine was waiting for them in this forsaken spot? It hardly had the life to stop the forest growing over it again, let alone provide a good time. The sum total of its sunset attractions were the overgrown hotel and a trio of slovenly teenagers, two girls and a chubby boy, who'd bed down with anyone for five tabs and a jug of wine.

The pair had come into the game with a lot of money. This in itself should have been a warning to Phaid. It was more money than a couple of jungle bums should rightfully be carrying, too much to have been earned from a lucky prospect strike or deck handling on a flatboat. It was more likely that the money was evilly come by. Its previous owner, in all probability, was lying face down in the swamp water of an isolated stretch of forest even jungle folk rarely visited.

As the night wore on, and the two river rats lost more and more and grew increasingly surly and ill tempered,

Phaid knew that he was drifting into a potentially deadly situation. It was clear that the pair would use any sort of violence if they thought it would get back what they had lost. In other circumstances, Phaid would have walked away from them and flatly refused to play. Right now, though, he knew that he had to take the risk of playing with these unsavoury characters. Phaid was sufficiently close to being a beggar that he couldn't afford to be a chooser. He needed all the cash he could get his hands on, no matter what the risk. He had to play this game to the end and then walk away with his winnings as best he could. If he couldn't buy his way out of this dreadful jungle and back to civilisation, he'd wind up as low as the men on either side of him. For Phaid, that was a fate that didn't bear thinking about.

Another two rounds went down. The one-eyed man won a little and started muttering about how maybe his luck was changing and how it was about time. Once again Phaid ignored him. He looked around the rest of the public room. He had to admit that it was little more than a ruin. A group of natives in feathers and beads nodded and dozed against the curve of the wall. A drunk in the garb of a flatboat roustabout was face down on the floor. His body was bisected by the bright strip of light where the sunlight lanced through the crack in the dome. There seemed to be some sort of sexual activity going on in one of the deep recesses formed by the shallow curve of the dome. As the afternoon wore on Phaid noticed that it didn't pay to look too deeply into those dark recesses. Ancient garbage formed strange shapes and after thirty-six hours his eyes could play tricks.

Phaid slowly and reluctantly gathered in the cards. He would have to stop soon. One Eye and Primitive had a predatory look about them. It was a similar malevolent patience to that of a vulture, or a jackal or a lupe out on the tundra. Phaid glanced at the makeshift and dangerous looking wooden stairs that led up to the private rooms in the dome. He wondered how he was going to make his way up those stairs with his winnings in his hand. It was time to put it to the test. He looked straight at One Eye and then at Primitive. He took a deep breath and sighed.

'The rain'll be starting soon.'

Three eyes and a sensor drilled into his face.

'What's that supposed to mean?'

Phaid knew that he would have to handle this extremely carefully. He eased his position in the less than comfortable chair. He took a sip from the shot glass of warm absinthia and smiled thinly.

'So we've played all night and most of the day. When the rain comes down it's the start of the second evening. That's enough entertainment for anyone. It seems to me that that would be an ideal time for me to pull out of this game.'

He watched the pair carefully, trying to gauge their reaction. Primitive had become slit eyed.

'You got a lot o' our money, gambling man.'

Phaid moved his arm so he could reassure himself that the stinger was safely hidden in his sleeve. One Eye altered his position so his fuse tube was within quick and easy snatch.

Phaid kept his expression deliberately blank. He let his right arm hang loosely over the back of the chair so, if the need came, the stinger would drop easily into the palm of his hand. After a disastrous experience in another river village, the stinger, with its circular silver body and its ten spider legs was the only weapon he had at his disposal. It wasn't a particularly honourable weapon, but Phaid wasn't too concerned about honour. All he wanted was to get out of the game with both his skin and his money intact. Honour was a luxury of civilisation. One Eye fixed Phaid with his eye and his sensor.

'It seem t' me we got a right t' win some o' our money back now.'

'You've been trying to get some of it back for hours, for most of the day, in fact. It hasn't done you any good.'

Primitive folded his armoured arms.

'Could be a reason f' that.'

Phaid raised an eyebrow. He had to slow this all down. They were already looking for an excuse to climb all over him.

'What exactly are you trying to say?'

'We think you probably know what.'

'So say it.'

'Maybe it don't need t' be said 'til you try an' get up from this here game.'

Phaid slowly nodded. The course from here on was becoming all too clear.

'We'll just have to see what happens.'

'That's right, gambling man. We'll just have to see.'
One Eye leered.

'Deal the cards, gambling man.'
Phaid grinned.

'I think it's your turn to deal, my friend.'

One Eye blinked. Phaid noticed that when the good eye was closed, the sensor became dull and lost its glitter. One Eye was clearly discomfited by his mistake. Phaid decided to turn the screw just a little.

'Deal up then, friend. Let's get to it.'

One Eye spun out the cards. Phaid picked up his hand and found himself looking at a combination of lathes and cornelians that gave him a grand encirclement. The hand was almost unbeatable. As if that wasn't sufficiently unbelievable, One Eye started to shamelessly force up the betting. Phaid, curious to know what was getting One Eye so excited, rode along with it, as did Primitive. The pot steadily grew until both of the pair had exhausted their reserves. When Primitive was down to his last ten, he threw down his cards in disgust and glanced grimly at his companion.

'I tells you, Jackman, you better have something, else you and me will be into falling out.'

One Eye smiled knowingly.

'I got it all.'

Phaid pretended to ignore the exchange. He glanced over at the makeshift bar. The bartender was still asleep. There was also a serving android. That too was motionless. From the scars and rust on its outer casing, Phaid suspected that it probably hadn't worked for years.

Phaid turned back to the game. Both One Eye and Primitive seemed to be waiting for Phaid to make a move. Phaid smiled; he knew that the *coup de grâce* wasn't far away.

'What's your pleasure, my friends?'

The mobile side of One Eye's face twisted into a triumphant sneer.

'My pleasure's t' call you, gambling man.'

He flipped his cards over. It would have been an impressive hand in any game, a brace of lathes backed up by golds. The odds against Phaid having a hand to beat it were astronomical. For an instant Phaid felt a genuine sympathy for One Eye. Then he spread out his own hand.

'I'm sorry, it didn't ought to happen to a dog.'

12

One Eye stared at Phaid's hand in disbelief.

'Wait a minute . . .'

Phaïd caught the obvious implication.

'You dealt them yourself, my friend.'

Phaid slowly stretched out his hand to gather in his winnings. At exactly the same time the first drops of the evening rain crashed into the surrounding trees. The noise echoed ominously round the inside of the dome. It was one of those frozen moments that Phaid knew all too well but sincerely wished he didn't. The one eyed ex-soldier and the primitive were both violent men. They were experienced in violence. From the look of them they also derived a lot of grim, snarling pleasure from it. In a few seconds they would find the excuse they needed to commence creaming him all over the dome. Phaid didn't have what it took to be violent; efficiently and effectively violent. That was why he was a gambler, why he played according to the rules.

The rules, however, were dropping away. As the rain crashed all around and droplets of water were seeking a way down inside the dome, Phaid faced a situation that was, if not as old as time, at least as old as games of chance.

'It looks as though the game is over.'

With an air of total absorption he started to pack up his winnings. He knew what the next move would be, but could think of no way to avoid it. Out of the corner of his eye, he saw the fuse tube drawn from the belt. One Eye was almost casual as he pointed the weapon arrogantly at Phaid's head.

'Leave the money where it be, gambler.'

Phaid slowly eased back into the chair. With the stinger his sole weapon, he could only wait for his chance. He hoped fervently that there would be one.

'Just can't let me walk away with it all?'

One Eye nodded.

'You expect us to?'

Phaid sighed.

'No, not really.'

One Eye continued to cover Phaid as he rose carefully to a standing position. Primitive also got to his feet. With his dart launcher under his arm he scanned the row of sleeping villagers. Usually the sleepers woke with the rain and started drinking. On this day, however, they remained diplomatically slumbering. Only the bartender was taking an open interest, but he also seemed about to do or say nothing.

Satisfied that Phaid had no help at hand, One Eye fumbled under his suit and pulled out a soft leather bag. He threw it down on the table in front of Phaid.

'Put the money in there.'

Phaid silently did as he was told while the two men watched him. When all the cash was packed away he sat patiently back in the chair. One Eye picked up the bag. Primitive looked at him questioningly.

'What about him?'

They both looked at Phaid. One Eye laughed nastily.

'What about him?' He directed the enquiry to Phaid. 'What about you?'

'I'd hardly be worth killing.'

One Eye was warming to the idea that there might be some sport to be had with the gambler before they finished him. He became brutally brisk.

'Stand up, stand up! Let's look at you.'

Phaid did as he was told. He spread his hands in a semicomic appeal.

'You see, gentlemen, nothing worth killing.'

One Eye had obviously got to such a low point in his opinion of Phaid as an adversary that he felt safe to scratch his nose with the fuse tube.

'I got this here rule, see. I say if I cross a man 'tis best to leave him dead, lest he come after.'

'That could be a problem.'

As he spoke he absent-mindedly scratched his head. One Eye laughed and looked at Primitive.

'Could be a problem for him. What you say, Naqui? What you say? Could be a problem for him.'

One Eye was so taken with his own wit that, for a moment, he was paying no attention to Phaid. Phaid's arm, still raised as though scratching his head, flashed forward. The stinger had already crawled down into his hand. He flipped it straight at One Eye. It landed on his neck just below the ear in the fold of his jaw. The tiny silver legs grabbed hold and clung. The stinger was quite close to the edge of the patch. As Phaid had flipped the tiny weapon, a small sphere had detached itself and remained in Phaid's hand. This was the control. If he squeezed it, the stinger would go active and scramble One

Eye's nervous system.

One Eye went rigid. Even though he couldn't see it he knew what had attached itself to his flesh. Eye and sensor swivelled towards Phaid.

'Stinger?'

'All I had.'

Primitive was raising his dart gun. He looked as though he was about to take a shot at Phaid. One Eye's yell was almost a scream.

'Don't!'

Primitive paused. One Eye had started to shake.

'If you get him with one of those, he'll take me f'sure. He's only got t' touch the control.'

'That's the truth.'

Primitive half lowered the dart launcher, then he grinned.

'What care I if'n he takes you? The both of you'll be dead an' I'll have the money.'

One Eye glowered at him.

'I thought we was partners.'

'Partners?'

Primitive spat. It looked as though he was serious. Phaid spoke, as calmly as he could, to One Eye. 'There is one way out.'

The fuse tube roared. Primitive was all but cut in half. One Eye lowered the weapon. 'It's good that I think quick.'

Phaid nodded. 'Indeed it is.'

'What do I do now?'

'Drop the tube.'

One Eye dropped the tube.

'Kick it over here.'

He kicked it to Phaid. Phaid bent to pick it up. It wasn't the most expensive or the best looking weapon that Phaid had ever seen. Among the rovers, drifters and wanderers who roamed between scorched desert and the wind blasted icefields that girdled the world like bands of steel, the elite took much pride in their weapons. Ornate carving, delicate engraving and inlaid gems decorated the fuse tubes and blasters of the free rangers who kept ahead of life's games. One Eye had obviously never been ahead of the game. The long barrel of the tube was pitted with corrosion, and the butt was a simple construction of worn, high impact ceramic. Phaid hefted it as though he was testing its balance. Then he stuck it in his belt. He was close to trembling. The whole incident, in fact the whole game, had been too close to the edge of desperation for Phaid's peace of mind. One Eye took a chance to turn and face Phaid.

'What are you going to do with me?'

Phaid looked at the stinger control in his hand.

'I don't know.'

'Listen . . .'

The good side of One Eye's face twitched.

'I'm listening.'

'I wasn't going to kill you.' He nodded at the fallen Primitive. 'He might have done you, but not me.'

'You tried to steal my money.'

'We lost a lot, we was mad, we had a hard time gettin' that money. I wanted it back but I wasn't goin' to do you. I swears.'

'You do?'

'I swears.'

'So you're telling me that you weren't going to burn my head off?'

One Eye's half face tried to be ingratiating.

'That's right. You got it. We was just riled. You know how it is.'

Phaid adopted a mildly affable expression.

'Sure, I know how it is.'

'You do?'

'Sure I do.'

One Eye looked relieved.

'You mean that you ain't going t' do nothing? You going t' forget what we done?'

Phaid sadly shook his head.

'No, I couldn't quite do that. Didn't you tell me the rule yourself? How did it go? "Lest he come after you"?'

One Eye opened his mouth to protest, but Phaid didn't let him. He squeezed the control. The stinger made no noise. One Eye made a strangled sound, his back arched, he clawed at the air, then he collapsed. Phaid's whole body seemed to sag for a moment. Then he straightened, took a deep breath, exhaled swiftly and shook his head as though trying to clear it. He looked sadly at the two bodies. The bartender was popping his eyes at Phaid and the two dead. Phaid walked slowly towards the bar.

'Were these friends of yours?'

The bartender energetically shook his head.

'Lords no, I never seen them before last night.'

'So you've got no interest in the matter?'

'I don't have an interest in most matters. I'm no sidetaker.'

Phaid half smiled.

'So I don't have anything to worry about from you.'

'Not a damn thing.'

Phaid picked up the leather bag that held the money.

'You got law in this town?'

'Nothing as you'd call law.'

'That's good.'

'Good for you.'

'What other kind of good is there.'

Phaid left five twenty tabs on the table.

'That's for your trouble.'

'I'm obliged.'

The bartender hesitated for a moment, sucking reflectively on a hollow tooth.

'You wouldn't mind if I gave you a piece of advice, would you? You wouldn't get mad or nothing.'

Phaid pushed the fuse tube into the waistband of his trousers.

'Only fools get mad when they hear good advice.'

The bartender raised an eyebrow and then flashed a yellow-brown smile.

'Not everybody sees it that way.'

Phaid nodded gravely.

'Not everyone does.'

The bartender regarded the corpses on the floor.

'I wouldn't stay around too long, if I were you.'

Phaid looked mildly surprised.

'You just told me there was no law here.'

The bartender shook his head.

'It's not a matter of law. It's a bit more subtle than that. Nobody round here had too much time for those two, but what you did . . . well, it tends to unsettle them, if you know what I mean.'

The rain fell relentlessly and the seepage splashed steadily on the bare floor. One part of Phaid simply couldn't believe that he'd come to the point where he'd been told to move on from a place like this. Had he really sunk so low? He turned and shrugged.

'Yeah, I know what you mean.'

Phaid slowly started up the sagging stairs and headed for his room on the second floor. He paused halfway up and looked back at the bartender.

'I'll be gone when the rain stops.'

'You're a sensible man.'

'Maybe.'

Once inside the room, Phaid flopped down on the bed with a weary sigh. It was almost dark but he didn't bother to light the lamp. The previous night the glo-bar had been an elderly, faltering yellow as though it was the end of its almost infinite life. Could this place have been lost here in the jungle long enough for a glo-bar to wear out, or was it just something in the air that made everything decay and die?

He lay for a while, staring blankly at the intricate spidery patterns that the damp had painted on the ceiling. Water was leaking through in three places. Fortunately, none of them was directly over the bed. Someone had thoughtfully placed a drinking glass under the worst one. The water kept hitting it with a loud and irritatingly rhythmic ping. Although Phaid's body was dog tired, the incessant dripping against the background roar of the falling rain wouldn't let him rest.

There was something strange about the room. The floor wasn't strictly even and there were peculiar curves to the roof that couldn't have been a result of either earth movements or the inroads of the jungle. The furniture stood at odd angles. It looked ill-suited and incongruous. He had seen these oddly shaped rooms on other scattered occasions during his lengthy wanderings. Each time the thought had struck him that they appeared to have been designed for something that possessed a form very different from that of a human being. It wasn't a thought that helped his rest.

He sat up and thumbed the switch under the glo-bar. It was even more weak and frail than it had been the night before.

He got out of the bed. He regarded himself in the cracked mirror hanging on the door of the single closet. He didn't like what he saw. There was no hiding from the fact that he was a mess.

It wasn't all that long ago that he'd complimented himself regularly on what a fine figure he cut in an elegant salon or dignified promenade. Nobody in the world could have said that Phaid was not a sharp dresser. Maybe a little flamboyant at times, but always immaculate. Now his boots were scuffed and going through in one sole. The breeches were equally worn and patched in the knee and his hand made silk shirt was close kin to a damp, dirty rag. Hanging in the closet was a threadbare frockcoat, under the bed was a small, beat up, leather bag. It contained a second disreputable shirt, a battered silver hip flask, a chronograph that had stopped working, three decks of cards and a transgrom on which the powerpac had run down. On the washstand was a half empty bottle of rotgut gin. All this, plus the money he'd just taken from the table, was the entire world of Phaid the Gambler.

He moved himself to the bottle and took a stiff belt. Almost immediately he grimaced as the raw spirit hit his throat. If nothing else, the cheap booze would be the death of him. He had to get out of this situation and get out fast.

He put down the bottle, stooped and pulled the bag out from under the bed. As he straightened up, he caught another dim reflection of himself in the mirror. Even his face was looking worn out. His mouth was flanked by set, downward curving lines. His cheeks were hollow and his eyes sunken, as though they'd seen too much for too long. Even his black curly hair that cascaded to his shoulders seemed limp and dead, like a pet plant that had been overwatered.

He'd never been that concerned about his face. He never thought about it too much. He knew it must work. Enough women had given it a glance, and even come back for a second and third. Was his face also slipping, just like the rest of him?

There was one consolation. He hadn't developed a gut. Too many friends and partners in the fat times had grown fat right along with them. The one thing you didn't worry about, when the pickings got lean, was your figure.

Phaid grunted to himself. He had to watch out for this sort of nonsense. Here he was, down on his luck and trying to scrabble his way back. It wasn't time to stand staring into a cracked mirror, wallowing in self pity. Phaid put on his jacket, dropped his winnings and the rube's fuse tube into his bag and listened to the beat of the falling rain. It seemed to be easing up. In this region, the daily storm tended to stop as suddenly as it began.

Phaid picked up his bag and started back down the stairs. The two bodies had gone, the bartender was back behind the bar, but the sleepers seemed to have gone about their business. At the sound of Phaid's footsteps, the bartender looked up.

'You're heading out?'

'I don't have much choice, do I?'

'Not much.'

There didn't seem to be a lot left to say, then the bartender suddenly grinned.

'Good luck, gambling man.'

Phaid scowled.

'Yeah. Thanks.'

Phaid walked out of the hotel and paused on the overgrown piazza. A line of dim glo-bars illuminated a narrow track through the undergrowth that led towards the river and the boat dock. Phaid hoped that there'd be a craft willing to take him. The boat people were a breed that viewed night-calling strangers with deep suspicion.

Halfway there a small grey cat stuck its head out from the foliage and stared directly at Phaid. The animal's thoughts were clear and precise. It wanted to know if Phaid was the one who had caused the trouble at the hotel.

Phaid nodded.

'I'm afraid so.'

The cat blinked and then trotted off into the darkness.

2

IN RETROSPECT Phaid realised that trying to find a boat after sunset was a pretty damn stupid move. At the dock, there was only one of the low, flat-bottomed riverboats. As he started to climb over the gunwale the boat's owner very nearly removed his head with an antique blaster.

Fortunately the boat's owner was the widow woman who'd played poker with him the night before. She'd recognised him just in time and held her fire.

At first, she hadn't been too keen on the idea of taking on a passenger, particularly one with a local reputation as a drifter and probable no-good. It had required all the charm Phaid could muster, the right answers to some searching questions and a large portion of his winnings before she finally agreed to carry him to the next major port.

Once it was agreed, she'd invited him into her small but cosy cabin and poured him a drink.

'Freeport, I figure that's going to be your best shot. It's only two days down river. If the Republic's your final destination, you should be able to pick up a caravan to take you across the wind plain to Mercyville.'

Phaid rubbed his chin.

'I'd rather go all the way round the coast to the Havens.'

The widow shook her head.

'You got round me on the matter of taking you as a passenger. There's no way you'll talk me into going as far as the Havens, so you can save all your pretty smiles. My

21

business is in Freeport and only Freeport. You can take it or leave it.'

Phaid shrugged.

'I was just thinking that a berth on a caravan is going to cost me plenty, more than I got since I paid you.'

The widow laughed.

'You're not thinking I'll give you a refund, are you?'

'No, I wasn't thinking that.'

'I wouldn't worry. A smart boy like you won't have any trouble raising money in Freeport.'

Phaid grimaced.

'Lately I seem to be having trouble raising money anyplace.'

'Hit a run of bad luck?'

'Something like that.

The woman made an impatient gesture.

'You should know that we make our own luck. Bad luck only comes when you stop trying. Have you stopped trying, gambling man?'

Phaid thought for a moment and then slowly smiled.

'No, I haven't stopped trying.'

The widow refilled Phaid's glass while he gazed around the small cabin. Most of the river vessels he'd been on had been functional to the point of discomfort. This one was so snug and homely that Phaid felt totally able to stretch out and relax. Normally Phaid didn't like low ceilings, they made him nervous and claustrophobic. This one, however, managed to give the effect of closeness and intimacy.

The widow had obviously taken a lot of trouble in furnishing her floating home. The walls were lined with a maze of shelves that held a myriad of small trinkets and knick-knacks, souvenirs of the woman's wanderings up and down the river. There was a comfortable rocking chair and a slightly less comfortable upright chair that Phaid occupied. A glo-bar in an ornate brass holder swung gently with the slight motion of the moored boat. Most of its light fell on a small and very old side table. Its dark wood top was inlaid with mother of pearl. On it were the two glasses and a dark bottle of rather good brandy. In an alcove at the shadowy, far end of the cabin was a large bed. Partly enclosed by a bead curtain, it was covered by a thick fur rug and piled with multicoloured and embroidered cushions.

Phaid looked back to the widow.

'You work this boat all by yourself?'

The widow raised a quizzical eyebrow.

'You're not getting ideas, are you?'

Phaid smiled and shook his head.

'I've been up for two days, lady. I couldn't get an idea if I wanted to.'

Again the raised eyebrow.

'Yeah?'

Phaid sipped his drink.

'Maybe.'

The widow refilled her own glass.

'Well, I couldn't keep it from you anyway. Yes, I work this tub on my own. Have done since my last husband got drunk and drowned himself.'

'I'm sorry.'

'Don't be. He was a silly bastard. I don't know why I married him.'

'Isn't it a hard life?'

'Maybe. I don't really know. I've never done anything else. I guess it ain't too bad. I've got a beat-up android that goes by the name of Clo-e. She handles the heavy work, runs the engines and operates the photon cannon if we run into trouble, which, thank the Lords, we don't too often.'

Phaid looked round curiously, but the widow shook her head.

'Clo-e's up on deck. I don't let her in here. I don't know what it is, but there's something about androids. I don't like to be shut up with them. You know what I mean?'

Phaid nodded automatically. He had almost stopped listening. The warmth of the cabin, plus the brandy was making him feel pleasantly numb. His mind had started to wander. In a strange way, the widow was really quite attractive. Of course, she was quite a bit older than he, and, in more normal circumstances, he would probably not give her a second glance, but here in the tiny cabin, tired and a little drunk, it at least started him thinking. He knew it was ridiculous, but it had been a long two days.

Phaid realised that the widow had picked up the bottle again and was saying something to him.

'I'm sorry.'

'You look half dead. Are your starting to lose it?'

'A bit.'

'You want another drink?'

'Yeah, why not?'

As the widow leaned forward to fill his glass one more time, the front of her homespun tunic fell partly open, granting Phaid a brief view of a surprisingly firm, well formed breast. Phaid suddenly wondered if the glimpse had been accidental or deliberate. She set the bottle down, and once again sat back in her rocker. Everything was back just as it was. Or was it?

Over the rim of his glass, Phaid covertly scrutinised the widow. It was hard to judge what her figure was like beneath the loose-fitting tunic and baggy trousers. Her face had been worn to a deep, weathered, nut brown by wind and sun, but her black, dead straight hair, that hung almost to her waist when not scraped back into an austere bun, shone like silk.

Then there were her eyes. Surrounded by deeply etched laugh lines, they flashed with humour and a deep practical perception. Phaid had known many women with flashing eyes, but all too often it turned ou to be the cold, self seeking flash of the predator. The widow's were completely different. They were the eyes of someone warm and alive, someone who took life as it came, who didn't always search for what didn't exist, but got on with enjoying what she had.

Phaid noticed that the widow was also studying him. Their inspecting gazes caught each other and locked for a moment. She looked away for an instant, then looked back and smiled.

'We ought to get some sleep.'

Phaid nodded

'You're right.'

'I gave up being coy a long time ago.'

'What do you mean?'

'Come on, gambling man, you know what I mean.'

'I suppose I do.'

'Damn right you do. There's only one bed on this boat, and it's mine. You can either sleep up on deck or you can sleep in my bed. It's your choice. I may not be as young as I used to be, and I may not be what you're used to, but I take good care of myself and I'm not ashamed to tell you that it's been a while since I had a man. Like I said, though, it's your choice.'

Phaid slowly finished his drink and placed the glass

24

carefully on the table, lining up the base with the mother of pearl design. Then he grinned at the widow.

'I sure as hell wouldn't want to sleep on the deck.'

'I've heard more romantic phrasing.'

'I gave up romance a long time ago.'

The widow suddenly stood up.

'Okay, gambling man, play it like you want to. Shall we go to my bed?'

Phaid got up a little more slowly.

'Let's do just that.'

The widow moved towards the bed, turned and pulled her tunic over her head. She shook her hair loose, kicked off her sandals and wriggled out of the trousers. She placed a hand on her bare hip and looked, almost challengingly, at Phaid.

'You like me, gambling man?'

Phaid's mouth twisted into a lopsided grin.

'Very much, boat lady.'

Phaid had lied to a great many women, but right then he was actually telling the truth. Without her clothes, the widow was a whole different person. In her clothes she was capable, practical but dull, out of them she was something sinuous and alive, something from the river and the jungle. The hard life of the boats had kept her body slim and supple.

'Yeah, very much indeed.'

The widow pushed aside the bead curtain and sat down on the bed. She drew her legs up and tilted her head to the side. One hand played with a single strand of the beads while the other fingered the thick fur of the rug.

'Why don't you take off you clothes and come over here, gambling man. I could get cold.'

Phaid was already struggling out of his shirt.

'You couldn't get cold.'

'Will you get over here?'

Phaid flopped on the bed beside her. The fur felt good underneath his body.

'I'm here.'

He started to bury his face in her hair, but she pushed him back.

'My name's R'Ayla.'

Phaid found that it wasn't easy to say.

'R'Ayla.'

'You didn't ask.'

'R'Ayla. Mine's Phaid.'

'Phaid.'

'Right.'

'Now we know each other.'

She touched a control on the wall and the glo-bar dimmed, then her arms snaked round Phaid and she kissed him hard on the mouth.

It wasn't long before he was right inside her. She began to growl deep down in her throat.

'So good, that is so good.'

Phaid now believed what she had told him about it being a long time since she had had a man in her bed. At the end, she screamed so loudly that he half feared the population of the little town would come running to see if he was claiming his third victim of the day.

Soon afterwards, he fell into a deep dreamless deep.

When he woke, sunlight was streaming into the cabin and R'Ayla was gone. Somewhat groggily, he sat up, doing his best to orientate himself. There was a constant throbbing pulse, which, at first, he thought to be inside his head. He finally realised that the boat must be underway and what he could hear was the sound of the engines. He climbed out of the bed and struggled into his breeches and shirt.

Phaid stuck his head through the cabin hatch and blinked at the light. R'Ayla was standing in the bow of the boat staring down river and whistling through her teeth. Her hair was scraped back into a bun and she was once again sober, practical and virtually sexless. She turned and spotted Phaid.

'So, you're awake. You even keep gambler's hours on a boat.'

Phaid had a little difficulty adjusting to the transformation.

'What time is it?'

'A little after noon. You want something to eat?'

Phaid nodded.

'Sure.'

'Come on up. I'll fix you something in a while.'

Phaid scrambled through the hatch. The boat was close to the centre of the big river and travelling downstream at a fair speed. The cargo blimps bobbed behind at the end of their tow lines. The green walls of jungle moved past on either side. In the stern of the boat, a squat cylindrical android stood humming to itself. It had lead lines into both the steering unit and the engine controls. It had obviously seen better days. There were a number of dents in its outer casing and its paint job, a bright and incongruous pink, was flaking away.

Once Phaid was on the deck, R'Ayla pointed to the android.

'Clo-e, I want you to meet our passenger.'

Phaid made a parody of a bow.

'Please to meet you, Clo-e.'

A voice came from the android.

'It-is-good-to-have-a-passenger-aboard-I-understand-you-have-engaged-in-mating-with-my-owner. This-normally-improves-her-temper-and-that-on-its-own-makes-your-visit-pleasurable.'

R'Ayla regarded the android bleakly.

'It has a conversational circuit that I should have ripped out a long time ago.'

A light on what approximated the android's head blinked on and then off again.

'I-should-warn-you-that-I-am-very-old-and-any-tampering-with-my-circuitry-is-likely-to-lead-to-a-terminal-malfunction.'

Phaid laughed, but R'Ayla shook her head.

'I swear the damned thing's blackmailing me.'

'Why don't you trade it in?'

R'Ayla shrugged.

'There aren't that many of them left. I fear I'm stuck with what I've got.'

For a while, R'Ayla disappeared into the cabin. The smell of cooking wafted up on to the deck, and, between them, Phaid's nostrils and stomach reminded him that it was a long time since he had eaten.

The breakfast was a simple affair: fish and vegetables deep fried in oil, washed down with fruit juice. The two of them ate, without ceremony, from the same bowl. When the meal was finished, Phaid leaned back against the gunwale and took a deep, satisfied breath. He was closer to being content than he'd been for a long time. About the only thing that worried him was a vague but nagging feeling that the android was watching him.

Not even the android could spoil his mood, though. He had a full belly and was sexually satisfied, the sun was shining and the river breeze prevented it from becoming intolerably hot. For a while the call of the big cities was muted. Right then he wanted nothing more than to loll in the deck of the boat, listen to the water, bask in the heat and watch the green jungle slip by on either side.

R'Ayla busied herself with chores around the deck. As far as Phaid could see, most of them were scarcely necessary. Clo-e the android did everything that was important, but if the boat woman felt the need to keep busy, Phaid wasn't about to interfere.

Every so often, she'd point something out to him. A near submerged reptile would raise its head on a long serpent neck or a flock of gaudy birds would spiral out of the jungle in a shrieking cloud. At one point it was possible to see the tips of two huge stone pyramid-shaped structures above the level of the trees. Phaid sat up and stared at them thoughtfully until the boat rounded a bend in the river and they were hidden from view.

R'Ayla looked at him enquiringly.

'You ever seen those before?'

Phaid shook his head.

'No, but I've heard there are things like that deep in the jungle, things from the old times.'

'I guess there are things from the old times all over.'

Phaid nodded.

'Pretty much. I never saw those particular ones before, but I've seen plenty of others. They built some strange stuff back when.'

'I suppose you've travelled a lot.'

'Some.'

'And seen a lot.'

'Enough.'

'You want to tell me about it?'

Phaid spread his hands.

'Sure, what do you want to hear?'

'About things from the old times. From the times before the Lords went away.'

Phaid raised an eyebrow.

'The Lords?'

R'Ayla glanced at him sharply.

'You believe in the Lords, don't you?'

'I believe that things changed mightily back in the old days, but I'd hate to say what caused it.'

'The priests teach us that the Lords created a paradise on earth. That it prospered and flourished for a thousand years, but then the Lords saw that common man was beyond help, that he was locked into his iniquity and they departed from our world to make their homes among the stars. It was then that the gales came, the terrible winds and the heat and the awesome cold of the icefields. As punishment for their sins mortal men were . . .'

The words came as though they had been learned by rote, way back in childhood, and were being repeated from memory. Phaid cut her off with a quick nod. It was unlike the practical, hard headed woman and it made him uncomfortable. The priests obviously had a strong hold on the river people.

'I know what the priests teach. I've heard the scriptures. I also know what I've seen and some of it was mighty strange.'

R'Ayla suddenly grinned like a girl. The spell of the priests was gone.

'Tell me about the strangest.'

'The strangest?' Phaid thought for a while. 'I guess the strangest I ever came across was the place way up in the hills behind Gant.'

'What was that?'

'Well, it's kind of hard to describe. It was a big place, made out of solid stone. I guess if you saw it you'd call it a palace, except it wasn't like any palace I've ever seen. It didn't have any windows, or any doors, or anyway that you could get inside, and all the time it made this noise. A high pitched hum, like there were a million insects trying to get out.'

'Did anybody live there?'

'No people.'

R'Ayla looked a little uneasy.

'You mean some*thing* lived there?'

Phaid was pensive.

'Maybe, maybe not. All I can tell you is that something happened there.'

'Happened?'

'Every day, at exactly the same time, a small flap in the building would open. There was a ramp leading down from it. Small machines would roll out. They were squat, kind of irregular in shape, and they moved under their own power.'

'Androids?'

'Who knows. Nobody could ever fathom what they did

29

or why they were there. One old man, they used to say that he was crazy, he spent half his life trying to solve the secret. He even built a cabin close by the place so he could watch them come out every day. Not even he could discover the secret.'

R'Ayla was looking more and more confused.

'These things didn't do anything at all, they didn't have any purpose?'

Phaid shook his head.

'Each day, they'd just roll down the ramp and form up in rows. There was this paved area at the bottom of the ramp. They'd form up on that in real neat rows. Thirty of them, there were always thirty of them. The old man told me that there'd been thirty of them for as long as he could remember.' Phaid looked as though he was having trouble believing his story. 'Once they'd formed up in rows, the machines would just stand there, all through the afternoon, not moving, not making a sound. It was as if they were just waiting for someone to come along and collect them.'

'And nobody did?'

'No . . .well, that's no strictly true. Just before sunset another machine would appear. It was much bigger than the first ones, big enough to pick them up in bunches of four. It went backwards and forwards, gathering in all the small machines, taking them back through the flap they had come out of. Once they were all inside, the flap would shut and that would be it until noon the next day. Except for the hum, of course, that never stopped.

For a short while R'Ayla didn't say a word. She seemed totally sucked in by Phaid's story. Then she exploded.

'Just a minute. You're a silver tongued devil, gambling man. A liar, too, I expect. You just made that whole thing up. Admit it.'

Phaid put a hand on his heart.

'It's all true, I swear it. I saw the place with my own eyes. In fact, I sat there all afternoon, just watching it.'

R'Ayla shuddered.

'It sounds like ghost stuff.'

'It was.'

'But why should anyone bother to build a thing like that, even in the old days?'

'They probably had a use for it in the old days. It's just that we've forgotten.'

R'Ayla stared at the river. She seemed to be deep in thought.

'Do you think it was very different in the old days?'

Phaid pursed his lips.

'It must have been. There's so much left of them that there must have been a hell of a lot more people back in the ancient times.'

R'Ayla frowned.

'I'm not sure I'd like that.'

'Also the gales didn't split up the world with bands of heat and cold like they do now.'

R'Ayla looked at him as if this wasn't news.

'That's what the priests taught us.'

Phaid shook his head.

'I'm not talking about the priests. I'm talking about what I've seen with my own eyes. There's relics of the old times frozen in the ice plains, and other relics in the worst part of the burnt deserts. Nobody in their right minds would build in those places.'

'It just proves the scriptures.'

Phaid took a deep breath.

'Hmm.'

R'Ayla looked at him with a worried expression.

'You do believe the scriptures, don't you?'

'That the Lords departed for the stars and then the whole world was divided by zones of heat and cold as a punishment for our sins?'

'That's what the priests say.'

Phaid's face twisted into a cynical smile.

'That is what the priests say.'

'But do you believe it?'

Phaid shrugged.

'Sure I believe it. There was this time, though, when I saw a man, this wandering preacher. A crowd had gathered around him. He was telling them how the Lords weren't anything more than people like us, and if they did cause the gales it wasn't as a divine punishment but because there was once some vast machine that could control the weather and we had forgotten, over the centuries, how to use it. He said it was the same as the way we had forgotten what some kinds of androids are supposed to do, like the place I saw in the hills behind Gant.'

R'Ayla looked worried.

'That's ridiculous. How could a machine change the

weather? That man must have been crazy.'

'He probably was. He hadn't been going for too long before the Religious Police came and carried him away. I never did meet anyone who saw him again. I reckon if the priests want us to believe their story that bad, I'll believe it. I'm all for a quiet life.'

That seemed to terminate the conversation. Phaid had the feeling that he'd said the wrong thing.

'I'm not saying the man was right.' He tried to lighten the mood. 'I don't want you to think you made love with a heretic.'

Again it was the wrong remark. R'Ayla didn't answer. When the silence had continued for some minutes, Phaid knew he ought to do something to restore the previous friendly atmosphere. With only a single covert glance at Clo-e the android, he moved closer to R'Ayla and put his arm around her. She didn't respond. She still appeared to be lost in her own thoughts. Suddenly she turned her head and looked at him.

'Do you think life was better in the old times?'

Phaid held her closer to him.

'How should I know? I'm a gambler. I think about now, not what has happened or what's going to happen. I have enough trouble with what is happening.'

R'Ayla smiled at him, but her eyes were sad.

'It is never good to speak of priestworks. It never brings luck.'

Although they remained close for the rest of the journey, the conversation left a shadow that never quite went away. It was a measure of the priests' power.

3

AFTER TWO days the river was so wide that it might have passed for the open sea. R'Ayla's boat slid beneath sandbanks, disturbing flocks of the bad tempered gulls that fed and quarrelled on them. At this point, the river was so shallow that the craft might have run aground if it hadn't been for Clo-e's unerring navigation.

Early on the third day, they were treated to their first sight of Freeport, the major city of the great river. It lay on the the outer side of a huge bend where, over millions of years, the river had cut into a line of low hills, creating high cliffs of white limestone. Much of the city sprawled back into the hills, but the port itself was situated where a fold brought land and water to the same level.

The city was dominated by the grey stone bulk of the old, domed fortress. It squatted on the highest of the city's five hills like some sinister, brooding toad, commanding a baleful view of all traffic on the river for many miles in either direction.

Around the base of the dome were the black, gaping ports that once housed massively powerful banks of photon cannons. The stones of the dome itself were cracked, blackened and pitted where they had bubbled and melted under attack by awesome heat weapons. These were, however, old wounds. The fortress was a relic of a former age, not the ancient days that Phaid and R'Ayla had talked so much about, but a closer time, one about four hundred years earlier when the world had made a last try at organising itself into nations and empires under the squabbling, warring rule of kings, princes, presidents and dictators.

Harald, known as The Mad, was just one of these. The fortress that Phaid was looking at had been both his crowning achievement and the site of his downfall. Harald the Mad had made Freeport, then known as Haraldhelm, his capital. From there, he had sought to extend his empire all the way up the great river to where the rapids prevented further navigation, and all the way down to the sea.

Harald's neighbours had objected violently to his territorial ambitions, and, after a series of border wars, they had united and forced him back into his citadel. The siege lasted seven years and became a matter of legend and saga. Tales of horror, cruelty and deprivation had carved themselves a permanent place in history. In the end, though, it hadn't been Harald's external enemies who had finished him. It was his own starving subjects who had risen up against him and, rather than be ripped apart by an angry mob, Harald the Mad had died by his own hand.

Once Freeport had become an independent city, nobody particularly cherished the memory of Harald. Over the centuries there had been many attempts to tear down, blow up or otherwise destroy the fortress, but the ugly pile's rugged construction had defied all efforts. Even though Harald had failed in his ambitions, his fortress remained as an inconvenient monument.

Harald the Mad had not only been a victim of both his enemies and his own people, he had also been a victim of history. Even while he was still dreaming his dreams of conquest, the nations and empires were inexorably falling apart and subdividing into self contained city states. By Phaid's time, there was only one definable nation-state remaining, and even that, commonly referred to as the Republic, was loose, sagging and chronically corrupt. Understandably, it was Phaid's primary choice as an ultimate destination.

The rest of Freeport was a complete contrast to the fortress. Whitewashed houses reflected the sunlight, greenery spilled over from shaded courtyards, and narrow streets wound their way up the hillsides. On the top of the hills, small forests of windmills spun in the offshore breeze and on the roofs of many houses, sun catchers glinted in the morning light. Along the waterfront, android cranes dipped and swung, moving cargo on and off a packed mass of barges and riverboats.

Although Harald the Mad's citadel still lowered over Freeport, the real power in the city had moved to the Governor's solid colonnaded mansion and the Temple of the Consolidated Faith, where, beneath the white marble spire, the priests maintained their subtle but unrelenting grip on the hearts and minds of the population.

As the boat came nearer to the harbour, Phaid's attention moved past the town and down the river where a tall column of angry clouds forever swirled and spiralled. It was where one of the superheated gales roared off the land and collided with the cold air over the ocean.

On the very edge of the clouds a tiny craft with gossamer wings soared and dived on the thermal currents produced by the violent clash of temperatures. Phaid knew the craft was piloted by a wind player, one of the reckless and often self destructive breed who rode the complex and dangerous airstreams in their fragile vessels. Sometimes they did it in competition, in the hope of valuable prizes and in front of huge crowds of spectators, but other times they rode the turbulent sky totally alone, and just for the hell of it.

Although he would rarely admit it, Phaid had a great respect and admiration for the men and women who played the wind games. He might call himself a gambler, but he really only played the odds and hustled for a living, the wind players were the real gamblers. They threw their lives into the contest, with only the skill of their reactions between victory and swift, sudden death.

The boat now edging its way through the jam of other crafts, was making for one of the piers of the harbour. Clo-e the android scurried about, still trailing leads to the steering motor controls, pushing out fenders, preparing mooring lines and bleeping at other androids on the dock in their secret, high pitched, electronic language.

Once the boat was secured to the dock, Phaid went below to collect his bag. When he came back, R'Ayla was waiting for him. Her face was set as though she was trying very hard not to show any emotion. Phaid avoided looking her directly in the eye.

'I guess this is the end of the line.'

'It's the end of the river, for you.'

'Yeah.'

Phaid felt a definite pang. The journey on the boat had been a pleasant interlude. He'd been very happy on the river, watching the jungle go past by day and sleeping with R'Ayla at night. He fought it down, though. He learned a long time ago that a gambler had to keep moving . There was no percentage in trying to stretch out a good time beyond its natural limits. He grinned at R'Ayla.

'Don't take any shit from that android, right?'

R'Ayla didn't seem amused.

'Right.'

Clo-e didn't seem amused, either, if her high angry warbling was anything to go by. Phaid was about to step on to the dock when R'Ayla touched his arm.

'Phaid.'

'Yeah.'

'If you ever come back this way . . .'

'Sure. The very next time I'm in Freeport, I'll make the boat dock my very first stop.'

'You promise.'

'I promise.'

R'Ayla quickly kissed him on the cheek.

'You better get going.'

'Sure. Take care of yourself, R'Ayla. I'll look for you when I come back this way, okay?'

'Okay. Goodbye, Phaid.'

'Goodbye, R'Ayla.'

He jumped across the small space between the boat and the pier. Straightening up, he took a deep breath. If he could possibly avoid it, he'd never come anywhere near Freeport again. He was on his way back to the bright lights and the big money. Once he got there, he'd make damn sure that he was never forced away again.

Phaid shouldered his way through the milling crowds on the waterfront. Once he looked back at R'Ayla. She was busy arguing with an android harbour inspector. Phaid slung his bag over his shoulder and marched on. For the first time in a long while he felt as though he was going somewhere.

Not that he didn't have problems. He was practically broke and he would need to eat and find a bed for the night. The harbour area was the oldest part of Freeport. Behind the warehouses and piers was a maze of narrow streets, alleyways, cramped, dilapidated buildings and dark, claustrophobic courtyards. It was a place where crimps robbed drunken sailors if the whores, pickpockets or muggers hadn't got to them first. It was a neighbourhood of bars and bordellos, a paradise for thieves and cut-throats, and a sanctuary for men on the run from the law. It was also a place where a gambler could, with a little sleight of hand, raise a quick stake and move on to something better.

Accordingly, Phaid directed himself into the bustle and furtive glances of the old town. Even though it was still early in the day, the girls were already out, shaking their backsides and showing their legs and breasts in the hope of turning the first profit of the day. Quite a few of them threw Phaid wanna-have-a-good-time glances. Each time Phaid just grinned and shook his head. Sweaty wrestling on a stained mattress was not what Phaid was looking for right then. Even if he had been, he hardly had the price. Thus, either way, the whores were out.

In a small enclosed courtyard he saw something that was closer to what he was looking for. Two sandrunner lizards had been set on each other in a shallow pit. They snapped and hissed abuse at each other, alternately striking with vicious fangs and slashing with powerful, taloned back legs. Sandrunners, even in the wild, were vicious, evil tempered beasts, and this pair was the result of many generations of selective breeding to make them meaner, tougher, more hostile and generally bring out the worst in their characters.

Around the edge of the pit a crowd of loafers and penny-ante hustlers yelled encouragement and offers of advice. The betting was brisk, and for a brief moment, Phaid was tempted to get involved with the play. Then he spotted two thickset men in leather jerkins, wearing a lot of ostentatious jewellery. They seemed to be taking a percentage of the money that was circulating. A pair of the Freeport watch, in the black tunics and gold braid, with old but serviceable blasters tucked under their arms, lounged against the wall in the back of the crowd. From time to time they would exchange significant glances with the duo in the leather jerkins.

Phaid's temptation to pick up a fast modest score melted away. The presence of the two men in leather and their obvious relationship with the watch officers indicated that this particular game was completely sewn up.

One of the lizards was down on its back and bleeding

37

badly. The crowd, knowing it was only a matter of time, was roaring its head off. Phaid decided to move on. He knew that if he tried to muscle in on this deal he'd probably wind up in worse shape than the unfortunate lizard.

Phaid moved deeper into the old town. He was repeatedly approached by street vendors who offered everything from supposedly gold rings to hot fish pies, and girls who only offered variations on one standard thing. Beggars demanded alms, an old woman offered to tell his fortune while another tried to sell him a lucky amulet.

Although Freeport wasn't as hot and humid as the settlements up river, it could still be uncomfortably warm. By the time the sun had reached high noon, Phaid was walking around wishing that he had a hat, a pair of dark glasses or preferably both. His mouth was dry, sweat was starting to soak his shirt and he was hungry. Part of him wanted to retreat into the cool of a quiet bar. Another part of him kept reminding that his place was out on the street, looking for the means to get out of this town and on to something better.

A sherbet fountain seemed to be the ideal compromise. The place had an open front and tables spilled out on to the street adding to the already considerable congestion. It seemed a good place to take the weight off his feet and still be able to watch the ebb and flow of the traffic.

At first Phaid was tempted to take one of the tables in the open, but he decided against it. A shaded one in the back would be better. There he could see, but not be so easily seen. Even in Freeport, you couldn't be certain who you might run into.

Phaid sat down and ordered one of the pale yellow, foaming concoctions that were the speciality of the house. The base of the drink was some sort of local raw spirit. Phaid shuddered to think what went into the rest of it.

When it finally arrived, Phaid sipped it slowly through the glass straw that the management had thoughtfully provided. All the while he kept one eye on the street, but, for a long time it yielded nothing that Phaid could in anyway make use of. Then, when he was into his fourth drink and almost out of money, he spotted a short, furtive figure coming in his direction.

Phaid could scarcely contain his amazement. The figure he'd spotted was an individual called Henk. He also went by the less than complimentary nickname of the Rat. The last time Phaid had seen Henk the Rat had been over a year earlier and halfway across the world. He couldn't imagine what tangled sequence of events could have brought the Rat to Freeport.

He also couldn't quite imagine the even more tangled sequence of events that had put Henk the Rat in Freeport at exactly the same time as he. It gave him a cold feeling that something more than pure chance was at work in this world. It was a feeling that Phaid had had before and, no matter how hard he told himself that coincidences did happen, he couldn't quite shake it.

Henk fancied himself as a bigtime gambler, but, in Phaid's opinion, he simply didn't have the touch. The best he could ever be was a third-rate cardsharp, no matter how many delusions of grandeur he carried around with him.

Henk scuttled into the fountain, carefully looking around as though he expected someone to be following him. Despite all his caution, however, he failed to spot Phaid sitting in the shadows. He went up to one of the waiters and started talking to him in a low voice. Whatever Henk was saying, it didn't make the waiter too happy. After a lot of persuasion the waiter reached inside his shirt, pulled out a small package and reluctantly handed it over. Henk was about to leave when Phaid stood up.

'Hey, Rat. What the hell are you doing in Freeport?'

Henk's large watery eyes almost popped out of his pudgy face.

'Phaid!'

'You got a great memory for names.'

Henk made a mammoth effort to compose himself. He smoothed down the front of his stained white jacket and attempted to smile.

'What are you doing in Freeport, my friend? You planning to stay or are you just passing through?'

Phaid sat down again and gestured for Henk to join him. He figured that, at the very least, he could stiff the little man with the check. The Rat eased into a chair, positioning himself so he could watch most of the people in the place as well as a good section of the street outside. Phaid wondered if the Rat's apparent nervousness was because of some trouble he'd fallen into in Freeport or whether it was simply a symptom of his natural paranoia. If the Rat was in a jam it might not be such a good idea to be seen sitting with him. The trouble was that the thought was kind of late. What was done was done. The Rat was snapping his fingers for a waiter and looking Phaid up and down.

'So how's your luck running, my old friend?'

Phaid made a noncommital motion with his right hand.

'So-so.'

Phaid knew that he was hardly being convincing. His clothes and general air just screamed that he was broke and struggling.

'But you're not planning to stay in Freeport?'

This seemed to be very important to the little man. Phaid shook his head.

'No, I'll be moving on pretty soon.'

The Rat also nodded.

'That's a pity.'

Phaid knew that the Rat was lying.

'It is?'

'Sure. This can be a pretty good little town, once you know your way around.'

Phaid raised an eyebrow and glanced around.

'You could have fooled me.'

'That shows how little you know about these places.'

The Rat jabbed a pudgy forefinger at Phaid.

'There's a lot more to the world than just the big cities and the Republic, you know. That's the trouble with guys like you, you gather round the bright lights like moths round a flame. You think that's where all the money is.'

'Isn't it?'

The Rat leaned back in his chair and did his best to look expansive.

'You'd be surprised how good the pickings can be in a small place like this.'

Phaid regarded the Rat's dirty white, double breasted jacket, worn breeches and scuffed boots. It was obvious that the Rat couldn't be doing much better than Phaid himself. Phaid smiled.

'I guess I would be.'

The sarcasm was wasted on the Rat. The little man leaned close to Phaid, who noticed he had chronically bad breath.

'It's a pity you're moving on. I could maybe put a few

things your way, if you weren't leaving so soon.'

'I'm not leaving that soon.'

The Rat was suddenly suspicious.

'You're not?'

'I ain't in any hurry. I could do with a bit of a vacation. That's why I drifted down this way.'

'So you ain't actually looking for work.'

Phaid shrugged.

'That would depend on what it was. It ain't that much of a vacation.'

The Rat quickly shook his head.

'No, no, a high roller like you wouldn't even think of it.'

'I wouldn't think of what?'

'No way. It's not your style.'

'Why don't you let me be the judge of that.'

'Well . . .'

'Come on, Rat. Spit it out.'

'Okay, but like I said, I don't think it's for you.'

'Just tell me, Rat.'

'I got this deal going on this bar. It's just a few streets away from here. I've worked out a thing with the owner whereby I get the rights to a nine gets twenty game. He's got a table and everything. He takes a third, I take a third and the dealer takes a third.'

'And you don't have a dealer?'

'Well, I deal some of the time, but . . .'

'But you ain't too good.'

The Rat lost it for a moment.

'It's only a small joint, I can do okay for . . .'

Phaid just smiled while Rat tried to reconstruct his image.

'My only problem is that I need a relief dealer for the evening shift.'

The heat had frayed Phaid's temper.

'You're only problem is . . .'

Phaid realised that abusing the Rat probably wasn't his best move right at that moment. The Rat twitched.

'What?'

'Nothing.'

The Rat was now thoroughly paranoid.

'What's my problem? Huh? What's my problem?'

'Forget it, Rat. What's the scam?'

'If you wanted to do it, you could relief deal for me in the evenings and take a third of the profits. How does

41

that sound?'

Phaid thought about it for a moment.

'I deal and I get a third?'

'Right.'

'And you provide the stake money?'

The Rat avoided Phaid's eyes.

'Actually . . . no.'

'You don't put up the stake for the house?'

'No.'

'The bar owner does?'

'Well . . no.'

Phaid's eyes narrowed.

'So who puts up the float?'

The Rat's expression became even more shifty.

'We just have to play it by ear.'

Phaid bit his lip and nodded.

'Play it by ear? So what happens if we get a big winner early on? How do we play that by ear, Ratty?'

The Rat squirmed uncomfortably in his seat.

'If I was you I wouldn't call me that. I don't like that name.'

'Answer the question. What happens if we get a big winner at the beginning of the game? How the hell am I supposed to cover that playing it by ear.'

The Rat hesitated.

'Well . . . you'd have to make sure that . . . that there isn't a big winner.'

'So the game's going to be fixed?'

'It's the only way. You must have fixed a game before now.'

Phaid sighed.

'Why don't we cut out the bullshit.'

The Rat did a poor imitation of not understanding.

'Huh?'

'Let's cut out the bullshit. You're asking me to fix a game . . .'

'You could do it.'

'Will you let me finish?'

'Sorry.'

'You're broke, I'm broke. You want me to run a crooked game without any stake and I'm supposed to settle for a lousy third of the take? You've got to be crazy, Rat.'

The Rat looked aggrieved.

'I fixed up the deal with the owner.'

'So you take a cut out of his third?'

'He wouldn't go for that. I'd get left with nothing.'

Phaid smiled sadly.

'Isn't that just too bad.'

'Listen . . .'

'No, you listen. If I got to deal the game, manipulate the deck and take all the risks I'm going to want at least two-thirds of the take.'

'Damn it, Phaid, I could deal the thing myself and cut you out of the picture altogether.'

Phaid nodded good naturedly.

'You could do that. You probably wouldn't stay in business for more than an hour without getting caught out, but you could do that.'

The Rat began to bluster.

'Come on, if you think that I can't run a simple nine gets twenty game . . .'

'You're bullshitting again, Rat. You know damn well that if you tried to steer a deck everyone from blocks around would spot you doing it. You need me, and you're going to have to take me on my own terms.'

'That's hardly fair.'

'It's true, though.'

Rat looked desolated.

'I should never have talked to you.'

Phaid grinned.

'I'll tell you what I'll do. I'll let you shill for me until we've built up a bankroll. I'll give you ten per cent off my end.'

Phaid thought for a moment that the Rat was going to explode on the spot.

'You're asking me to shill in my own game?'

'I'm sure you'll be real good at it.'

'No way.'

'Someone's got to do it. There's got to be some sort of winner at the table, otherwise we can forget it.'

The Rat started to deflate.

'Ten per cent, you say.'

Phaid nodded.

'With what you get back from the owner and a bit of larceny on the side, you should do real well.'

The Rat gave in.

'Okay, I'll go along with it, but I don't like it.'

'You're a treasure, Rat. When do we start?'

The Rat brightened.

'We could start tonight. The owner's got a room you can stay in.'

'What's the name of this joint?'

'The Rising Sun.'

Phaid looked at the Rat in total disbelief.

'You mean I'm actually dealing nine gets you twenty in a place called The Rising Sun? Shit, Rat. What are you doing to me?'

4

PHAID STOOD in the main bar of the The Rising Sun attempting, somewhat vainly, to enjoy his break from the gaming table. He wasn't being helped by the weasel-faced tech standing next to him. The man was actually trying to pump him for tips on how to make a killing at nine gets twenty. Phaid could scarcely believe his ears. The tech seemed unable to grasp that the whole principle of the game was that the bank, Phaid in this instance, would try to take the other player's money away from them while they, in their turn, would attempt to prevent that and take the banker's money.

It was all so straightforward and simple that Phaid was starting to become thoroughly irritated by the tech's almost mystic belief in fate, systems and runs of luck. Phaid had his own very strong beliefs in luck, but they had nothing in common with those of the tech. The man had already dropped a small stack of twenty tabs to some elementary sleight of hand on Phaid's part, and although Phaid was sorely tempted to tell the tech to take a hike, his apparent willingness to lose even more caused Phaid to moderate his replies to noncommital grunts.

Phaid didn't like techs at the best of times. They were, as a rule, arrogant, self important individuals, puffed up with the idea that they were the keepers of the divine flame of mechanised civilisation. At least in the cities they were maybe capable of stopping a walkway from crushing its passengers, repairing a skimmer or refitting a maverick android. Here in the provinces, however, they had the same conceit, but none of the even limited expertise of their city brothers. The bumpkin tech coasted on superstition and ignorance, and were one of the main reasons that most of the surviving technology was fully automatic and completely self sustaining.

The tech wasn't the only thing that was irritating Phaid. He was bored rotten with Freeport and was counting the days, or more accurately, counting the money he still needed, until he could get the hell out of the close knit, back biting little river town.

Phaid had almost forgotten about small towns. Remembering was no pleasure. The travellers came and went, but the citizens lived their lives with their hands in their neighbours' pockets and their bodies in and out of their neighbours' beds. Small minded hustlers, whose inability to head for richer pickings made them think of themselves as local entrepreneurs, jealously guarded minor league rackets. Gossip was rife, and Phaid found himself pushed around by the set of rules that had been laid down so long ago that an outsider had no chance of learning them.

When Henk the Rat had first told him about The Rising Sun, he had pictured it as something of a dump. In reality, it had turned out to be actually worse than even his most dismal imaginings. It was the pits. A run down, just off the waterfront dive that had sunk to bum level and was currently undergoing an unsuccessful upgrading by a loser owner who had delusions of what he thought was class.

Hence the gambling had been installed, hence the pair of unattractive adolescents with little sense of rhythm danced naked at regular intervals and hence the elderly cybermat music system known as Doc wheezed out tunes that had been forgotten in the big cities for half a decade, even before Phaid had been forced to leave.

The music in itself was indicative of the state of The Rising Sun. Since it took a long time for new songs to filter out to places like Freeport, and since it was the larger, more expensive joints up on the hills that paid the top prices for all the new material that came in on the caravans, the owner, if he'd had any smarts, would have instructed Doc to play tunes that were old enough to have some kind of nostalgia value. Instead, he had the system play the most recent stuff it knew; which was threadbare, even by the standards of Freeport.

Financially, despite all the limitations of The Rising Sun, Phaid wasn't doing all that badly. Of course, if he'd made it to one of the exclusive establishments at the top of the town, the ones where high priced sessions of calay or imperial hazard were conducted in elegant salons, he might have been strolling languidly on the main promenade in brand-new tailor-made clothes, and with the makings of a small fortune in his bag.

Beggars couldn't be choosers, however, and instead he was forced to con pigs who were too stupid to understand the game, let alone how to win at it. Phaid had found himself being totally unmerciful. He robbed everyone, the customers, the owner, and even Henk the Rat was shaved on his percentage. Phaid considered it all justifiable. If the positions were reversed, they'd do exactly the same to him, provided they had the knowledge and the skill, which they so obviously hadn't.

Phaid had already squirrelled away the price of a third-class passage on a caravan route land crawler. All he had to do now was stay for a few more days and he'd have a small stake over and above the fare, just to make the journey a little less wretched.

He calculated that this could probably be achieved in another four days. In fact, Phaid had another reason for not staying any longer than that. No matter how good the pickings might become, he really couldn't see the set-up at The Rising Sun lasting very long, and, when the end came, he feared it might be less than pleasant.

His experience told him that Freeport, like any other small provincial town, would have its gambling sewn up by an entrenched, jealously guarded syndicate that would do their damnedest to shut out any newcomer. Between them, the money men who acted as bankers, the owners of the prosperous gaming houses, the gentlemen players and the watch officers who took their discreet handouts and averted their eyes from any irregularities would see that The Rising Sun did not stay in business for too long.

Not that the drop in a bucket profits at The Rising Sun were anything like enough to actually hurt any of the bigtimers. It was more a matter of principle. Just to demonstrate that there was no place for freelance interlopers in the set-up, sooner or later, The Rising Sun would be closed down. Phaid feared that it would be more likely sooner than later.

In the meantime, he had work to do, if he was going to make that extra stake. It was almost time to get back to the table. Through the smoky gloom of the rundown bar, he checked out the waitress that he'd left running the table while he took a break. She could just about deal out the cards without dropping them. His big fear was that a winner would sit down while she was in charge of business and take an unthinkably large bite out of the bank before he could get back and do some swift manipulation.

As it happened, the girl only had two halfway drunk boatmen at the table. They were losing money tab by tab, and Phaid felt that it was safe to have himself one more drink. Phaid gave the bartender a curt nod and had his glass topped from the special reserve bottle. The bartender charged it to Phaid's growing bill that, when the day of departure came, Phaid had absolutely no intention of paying.

Phaid sipped his drink and looked morosely around the room. From the low ceiling of smoke blackened beams to the uneven flags that made up the floor. The Rising Sun did nothing except make him depressed. The clientele were little short of derelicts and wharf-rats. The bartenders were surly and hostile and the waitresses were either too plain, too fat or too stupid to work anywhere better. If you added a sprinkling of cut-price whores and a few petty grifters, the constant smell of stale ale, the hum of conversation punctuated by bouts of raucous shouting and Doc's truly dreadful music, you had the whole dreary picture.

Phaid drained the glass with a sigh and set it down on the bar. The bartender scowled at him.

'Wanna 'nother?'

Phaid shook his head.

'I've got a living to earn.'

'Some livin'.'

Phaid raised an enquiring eyebrow.

'And what's that supposed to mean?'

'You know wha' I'm talkin' about. You gotta be doin' better than any other bastard in this joint.'

'You reckon?'

'I reckon.'

Phaid shrugged.

'I never heard of anyone watering a deck of cards.'

Before the bartender could think of a comeback, Phaid

48

walked away in the direction of the gaming table. Halfway there, his attention was caught by a minor disturbance over on the far side of the bar. An unsavoury trio in lube-stained coveralls, obviously roustabouts from a caravan crawler, were harassing a boohoom.

Normally Phaid would have ignored the commotion. His duties at The Rising Sun certainly didn't include acting as unpaid bouncer. He did, however, have a soft spot for the sub-human boohooms, and disliked seeing them harassed.

This particular boohoom who, as far as Phaid could tell, rejoiced in the name of Ucko, was no stranger to the waterfront bars and taverns. He loped from one place to the next hawking the broadside news-sheet that provided Freeport with most of its information from the outside world. He was always followed by his constant companion, a skinny, dirty yellow mongrel dog. Boohoom and dog had an almost supernatural rapport.

Nobody could quite agree about the boohooms. One school claimed that they were retrograde human mutations, another theory was that they were a kind of advanced monkey. A third faction argued that they were a totally separate species. Certainly they looked like some intermediate stage between man and ape, with their stooped gait, long arms, low foreheads and coarse, reddish brown body hair. They were stupid, there was no denying that, but it was a placid, amiable stupidity. Despite this, there was still a particular type of individual who took an unpleasant delight in tormenting the boohooms. It would have been easy to assume that the boohooms were victimised because they were stupid. Unfortunately the same ones who picked on them were also the ones who terrorised the elaihim, the tall, pale hyper-intelligent race that now shunned the habitations of men because they had been so persecuted over the centuries.

As Phaid approached the three roustabouts, he casually let his hand drop to where the fuse tube was hidden under his coat. He was starting to have certain trepidations about his gallant gesture. The three roustabouts were ugly characters. Between them they had two broken noses and at least half a dozen facial scars. They were holding up the dog by one ear and mockingly asking the boohoom what was the best way to cook it.

Phaid wandered up to them and grinned.

'You guys must have been eating the cooking in this place.'

They may have been big and ugly but they were far from quick on the uptake.

'Huh?'

Phaid continued to grin pleasantly.

'If you gotta desire to eat that mangy dog, then you must have tasted the cooking. Compared with what comes out of that kitchen, even a dog would taste good.'

The roustabouts glared at him. Their faces managed to get even more brutish and hostile. Phaid grimaced.

'I guess it wasn't that good a joke, now I come to think about it.'

The biggest of the three clenched his fists and belligerently thrust his florid face into Phaid's. His breath smelled of beer and rotting teeth.

'You want somethin'?'

The boohoom was slowly edging behind Phaid. Phaid took a step back, moving the short creature with him.

'I was just wondering what a dog-eater looked like.'

The face jutted even closer.

'You callin' me a dog-eater?'

Phaid looked down at his boots. To his relief, out of the corner of his eye, he saw The Rising Sun's three houseminders moving up behind him. Each of them carried a long flexible plastic sap. Now he had a bit of support. He slowly raised his head.

'If you ain't dog-eaters, maybe you ought to get your buddy there to put down the dog. It tends to give the wrong impression.'

It was possible to watch the roustabouts' minds working. They would have dearly liked to tear Phaid limb from limb, but they were calculating how they'd fare against the resident muscle. They almost had to count on their fingers before they finally decided that damaging Phaid wasn't quite worth the beating that they'd get at the hands of the minders. Reluctantly, the one holding the dog let it drop. It yelped and dashed between the boohoom's legs. Phaid noticed that there was sweat under his armpits. He felt as though he had just won a very difficult hand. The chief-minder put away his club and hardfaced the roustabouts.

'You guys sit down and drink your drink. We don't want no trouble here.'

50

'We don't want no trouble neither.'

'So let's keep it all nice.'

'Yeah sure, whatever you say.'

With ill grace, the roustabouts returned to their drinks. The chief-minder looked at Phaid with narrowed eyes.

'We backed you up because you was one of us.'

His voice was quiet, but very angry.

'You pull a stunt like that again and I swear to the Lords I'll let them rip your head off. I got nothing against boohooms but they ain't worth fighting for.'

Phaid nodded.

'Sure, sure, I hear you.'

'Just remember it.'

Phaid glanced towards the boohoom.

'You better get out of here.'

The boohoom hesitated, looking confused. Phaid flipped him a single tab. The boohoom deftly caught it and thrust a news-sheet eagerly at Phaid. Phaid quickly took it.

'Okay sure, now get, lose yourself.'

The boohoom suddenly got the message and scurried away. The dog was close on his heels. Phaid slowly shook his head and moved towards the card table. He glanced down at the news-sheet. The pictures were blurry and the stories ranged between fanciful and wildly inaccurate. What passed for news in these provincial towns was rumour, gossip and tall tales that came in with the boats and caravans. Phaid crumpled the sheet and dropped it on the floor. The two boatmen were still playing their plodding, tab at a time game. Phaid smiled at the waitress.

'I'll take over now, go get yourself a drink.'

She smiled her thanks and got up. Phaid slipped briskly into the dealer's chair and pulled back his cuffs.

'Okay, gentlemen, shall we put a bit of life into this enterprise?'

No matter how Phaid tried, the night remained determinedly dead. A few drunks tried their luck, but after the first time they lost, they seemed to get frightened off. There was even a point when Phaid found himself sitting without any customers at all, just riffling through a cold deck at a vacant table. There were few more humiliating situations for a professional gambler.

Just as Phaid had almost come to the conclusion that the night was over and that it was high time to shut down the game, another well oiled crowd of river people stumbled into the place and insisted on chancing their luck.

They weren't carrying any heavy money, but what they did have they threw on to the table with blind drunken abandon. All Phaid had to do was deal the cards and pick up the money. Phaid's spirits definitely lifted. A few more sessions like this and he'd be able to shake the dust of Freeport off his boots.

After an hour of these steady pickings, Phaid was in a positively benign mood. He accepted drinks from the players and even started exchanging wisecracks with them. It was then that he saw the dog.

There was no mistaking that it was Ucko the boohoom's companion, and that it also wanted something important. It made its way determinedly through the legs of the revellers. Phaid was mildly suprised when he realised that the dog was making straight for the gambling table. He couldn't for the life of him imagine what the animal might possibly want.

The dog positioned itself beside Phaid's chair and butted his leg with its head. One of the boatmen laughed.

'Looks like the dog wants to buy into the game, gambling man.'

Phaid peered down at the dog.

'It sure as hell wants something.'

'Deal it a hand, gambler, or are you afraid of the competition?'

The dog butted Phaid again. It seemed to be more than a little put out by the laughter. There was a certain urgency about its manner that made Phaid pay attention. He leaned down and spoke to the dog in a low voice.

'You want something with me?'

The dog butted him again and wagged its tail. Phaid tried to concentrate. Dogs communicated well with boohooms, but didn't do so well with the majority of humans. Cats did better, but then again cats couldn't be trusted to tell the truth. Phaid locked eyes with the animal, but found that all he could get were jumbled, fleeting impressions. The predominant image was one of dim, uniformed shapes moving in the darkness.

'The watch?'

The dog eagerly wagged its tail.

'What about the watch?'

The dog pointed its nose towards the door, but before

Phaid could question it again, the river men started to get restless.

'Hey, what's with the dog? Let's play some cards, huh? Deal up, will you?'

Phaid waved a hand for them to shut up.

'What about the watch?'

Again the dog pointed towards the door.

'They're outside?'

The dog wagged its tail once more. The boatmen started getting rowdy again and once more Phaid did his best to silence them.

'Are you trying to tell us that the watch are about to come in here?'

The dog's tail doubled speed.

'A raid?'

The dog exuded a strange mixture of ecstasy and agitation. Phaid dropped the cards on to the table.

This time the dog had not only communicated the fleeting image of uniformed watch moving through the darkness, but Phaid could have sworn that he saw a flash of Henk the Rat lurking among them.

The boatmen looked at him suspiciously.

'What are you trying to pull?'

'The dog told me that the watch were set to pull a raid on this place and I for one ain't hanging around for that to happen.'

It was painfully obvious that nobody round the table believed him.

'The dog told you that the watch is about to raid the place?'

Phaid nodded nervously.

'That's right, and if we know what's good for us we'll get the hell out of here.'

The nearest boatman's eyes narrowed.

'You got our cash and now you're looking to run out.'

The boatman's hand started edging to the curved knife in his belt. Phaid sighed. It was happening again. Nobody in these boondock towns seemed capable of losing gracefully. All round the table faces turned ugly.

'I think you'd better sit right down and keep on dealing.'

Phaid was starting to get desperate.

'I don't need no trouble with the watch.'

'You don't need no trouble with us, either.'

While the argument was going on, the oldest boatman had been exchanging glances with the dog. Suddenly he looked up.

'Hold it, I think maybe the gambling man may be telling the truth. I'm getting something to do with the watch off this mutt.'

'Ah, come on, it's a shuck.'

'I dunno. Dogs don't lie.'

'We're being conned.'

'If the watch are going to come bursting in here, I wanna be someplace else.'

Phaid sat very still while the boatmen argued. He knew that all his plans were riding on the whim of a bunch of drunks and he didn't like it. If he just got up and walked away, he'd probably get a knife in the back. On the other hand, if the watch came bursting in he'd also be in trouble. If the watch didn't find an excuse to throw him in the lock-ups, they'd certainly take all his money. His only other alternative was to pull his tube on the boatmen and threaten his way out. That seemed the dumbest of all his options. Thus Phaid sat, quiet, tense and very unhappy.

Suddenly, as things seemed deadlocked, the oldest boatman stood up.

'I'm going. I lost some money, but I sure ain't risking a run in with the watch. I believe the dog. I'm a-going. Who's coming?'

It seemed like Phaid's last chance to make a move. He got to his feet and pointed to a small pile of tabs that lay in the middle of the table.

'Why don't you divide that up between you and let's get gone.'

The boatmen didn't hesitate for too long. They started grabbing for the cash. Phaid walked quickly away, heading for the stairs without a backward glance. He had to get up to the small room where he lodged and dig out his leather bag from its hiding place. The bag did, after all, contain all his worldly wealth and without it he'd be screwed.

Phaid took the stairs two at a time, let himself into his cramped little chamber and immediately dived under the bed, groping among the dust and spiders for the bag. He was still on his knees when commotion broke out in the bar below. At first it was just the crashing of heavy boots and a lot of shouting and screaming. Then there was the more sinister roar of a blaster and crackle of a fuse tube. The watch had obviously broken in and some of the customers weren't prepared to go quietly. Making an exit via the barroom was strictly out of the question.

He went straight to the single small window. The catch stuck at first, but a quick blow with the butt of his fuse tube freed it. Phaid swung open the window. To his relief there was a sloping roof just half the height of a man below the window. Getting out wouldn't be all that easy, however. The only way to manage it was a wriggle through the small space head first. It wasn't a trick he relished, but with the sound of heavy boots already resounding on the stairs, Phaid knew that he had no alternative.

There was some moment when he thought he had stuck fast halfway through, but violent struggling finally freed him and he tumbled out on to the roof below. Phaid's troubles were far from over. He found that he was rolling, sliding, trying frantically to both hold on to his bag and stop himself sailing clear off the end of the roof and making the bone breaking drop to the street.

Phaid only just halted his descent by a hair's-breadth. Once he'd convinced himself that he was all in one piece, he crawled to the front of the building. Three ground cars and a flipper were lined up in the alley outside The Rising Sun. People were being led out, some going quietly, others struggling. A small group knelt around a prone figure on the dirty sidewalk. There had been at least one casualty in the raid.

Small clusters of officers who seemed to have nothing left to do had gathered around the cars. From their attitudes and postures, it was clear that they were busily congratulating each other for being such fine fellows. The Rising Sun had apparently been put out of business with some style.

Phaid had no more time to stand around and stare. First priority had to be to get out of town. He didn't have as much money as he would have liked, but he did have the minimum necessary to buy a passage out of Freeport. All he needed to do was lose himself in the night, and then, in the morning, get across town to the field where the big crawlers turned around. He also had to get off the roof.

Looking around, Phaid discovered that it might not be all that simple. It was a long drop to the street, and quite a formidable leap to the next building. Phaid wasn't exactly delirious with joy about the prospect of jumping from rooftop to rooftop, but there was no other alternative. There wasn't even any way he could put it off. With a sinking feeling, he backed up, got a firm grip on his bag, shut his eyes and ran. To his surprise, he landed, safe if sprawling, on the next rooftop.

Deciding that he still must have a little luck left. Phaid hurried on. He didn't want some nervous householder to mistake him for a burglar and loose a blaster on him. It took him four more buildings until he found a set of stairs that would take him down to the street.

The raid on The Rising Sun had made quite an effect on the nearby streets. The loafers and strollers had suddenly decided that they had important business elsewhere. Even the whores had vacated the usual posts under the sidewalk glo-bars and gone indoors.

Phaid slipped in and out of the silent shadows. He'd expected crowded streets to give him a sense of comfortable anonymity. With all the crowds melted away, he felt exposed and vulnerable.

He'd hardly been walking for more than ten minutes when he turned a corner and walked slap into two officers on foot patrol. Both Phaid and the officers stopped. For a long moment they stared at each other. His first instinct told Phaid to stand his ground and attempt to bluff it out. Then a second, much stronger one started urging him to run. While he was still trying to make up his mind, one of the officers raised his weapon.

'Hold up, you!'

Phaid listened to the second instinct and ran. There was a flash and roar and the discharge from a blaster seared the wall beside his head. Phaid swung into an alley and pounded down it. While one officer had been shooting at him, the other had whipped out a communicator and started bellowing into it. It would only be a matter of time before reinforcements were on the scene. Phaid knew that he was in big trouble.

The alley led out into a wider street. Two more discharges flared around Phaid's heels. His breath was coming in laboured gasps, and, as far as he could tell, the two officers were gaining on him. He knew he had to do something drastic. Reluctantly, he pulled out his fuse tube.

Dropping the bag, he turned and, using both hands, took careful aim at the ground just in front of his pursuers. He fired three fast shots and the cobbles of the street burned and smoked. The two officers staggered back, temporarily blind from the flash. By the time they could see again, Phaid had vanished down a side street.

He was by no means out of the woods, though. He might have temporarily shaken off the two officers on foot, but now he had another problem. A watch flipper was coming from the direction of the waterfront. Cruising just above rooftop level, it seemed to be searching the streets one by one. A sun globe in the underside of the craft lit up the ground beneath it as brightly as day.

The light hit the end of the street that Phaid was in. He looked around desperately. There was no place to run. The best he could do was to press himself into a doorway, but even that was too shallow to give him complete protection from the probing light.

He was certain he was going to be caught when the door behind him suddenly opened. He would have fallen backwards if a rough hand hadn't grabbed his arm. For a second or more he was completely overtaken by confusion and panic. He was being pulled inside a dark building, a voice grunted at him and he found himself staring into the hairy face of a boohoom. The face smiled.

'Come. You come.'

Phaid gave up. The door was swiftly shut behind him. Totally bemused, he let himself be led into the darkness.

5

EVEN AFTER a jangled, joyless night in the lair of the boohooms', Phaid couldn't help but be awed be the sheer size of the land crawler. Taller than a five-storey building, its flat, windowless sides were more like cliffs of corroded steel and ceramic than part of a vehicle that actually moved. The dull black heat exchangers along the upper part of the machine that provided most of its power, once it was into the searing heat of the hot wind plains, were like the squat turrets of some sinister castle. The massive caterpillar tracks, wider than many of the streets of Freeport, dwarfed the fuelling gangs that were busily pumping thousands of atmospheres into the crawler's converter tanks through thick, snaking pipes that gleamed with hoar frost from the super-cooled fuel.

The crawler was a dull, burnt, rusty red. No livery or decoration could survive the white hot winds. The whole of its body work was scarred and pitted by the smouldering rocks and burning sand that were driven like hail in the blaze of the gale.

For a long while Phaid could do nothing except stand and stare. It scarcely seemed possible to him that such an enormous object could be energised into lumbering, swaying life. Of course, he'd seen land crawlers before. He'd ridden more than he really cared to remember. If he'd been on top of things, he would have marched briskly into the depot, paid the static android who issued tickets and headed for the passenger ramp. As it was, he felt too numb and exhausted to do anything but gawp.

The previous night in what had been the bowels of the town had been an education. He had never realised the number of boohooms that could live unnoticed in a small town like Freeport, or the extent of the underground world in which they dwelt.

After his sudden and seemingly impossible rescue from the watch, he had been led down winding steps, cobweb-bed cellars, even more steps and dim passages until he was finally in the catacomb made up by the town's heating ducts, sewers, storm drains and long forgotten tunnels that must have been built as adjuncts to Harald the Mad's fortifications. He seemed to have walked miles until he reached the straw-filled niche that Ucko and his dog called home.

All along the way he passed dozens of boohooms. Some rested after a long day of cleaning, carrying and performing all the menial tasks for which there were no available and conveniently programmed androids. Others sat in small groups, apparently talking out the night in a laborious series of grunts and ill formed words. Still more, who from their matted pelts and deathly pallor seemed to stay permanently in the darkness of the underground maze, either sat and stared, contemplating some dull, non-human nirvana or scavenged, for what, Phaid didn't care to think about.

Many of the boohooms, like Ucko, were accompanied by animal companions. Some of these were surface creatures, dogs, birds or monkeys. Others petted pale reptilian things from the sewers and tunnels. He had even witnessed two boohooms making love, a spectacle that caused him to quicken his pace, even though Ucko seemed inclined to linger and watch.

Once in Ucko's nest, Phaid had managed only the smallest amount of shallow, disturbed sleep. Things constantly scurried and rustled. Somewhere nearby water dripped with a nerve-racking monotony. Ucko snored loudly and even the dog whimpered as it dreamt.

In the early morning, although Phaid couldn't fathom how the boohoom knew it was morning in that sunless, underground world, Ucko led him back out of the labyrinth and set him on his way to the field where the crawlers turned around.

With his head down, and one eye open for the watch, Phaid chose a route that took him through the most crowded of the town's streets. Almost to his surprise he reached the field without a single incident.

Phaid finally realised that he'd been standing gawping at the crawler like some rustic fresh in from the hills and made an effort to pull himself together. Still on the alert for the watch, he went inside the small, single-storey depot building.

There was only one crawler going out that day, and after questioning an information android, he found that if he booked steerage for a place called Wad-Hasa Wells, he had his fare and just a little to spare. He reluctantly paid over most of his hard earned cash, took a ticket, and moved towards the boarding ramp.

Steerage passengers were expected to use a separate ramp to the superior beings who could afford first-class or second-class fares. On the first-class ramp a group of merchants and a fop, in a lime green outfit with exaggeratedly wide shoulders, nagged the android porters about their luggage or watched with bored smiles as the lesser mortals had to carry their own bags on to the crawler.

Steerage accommodation was notably low on comfort. The section was right at the top of the machine where the swaying was worst, and, once they reached the hot plains, the refrigeration units would be hard pressed to maintain any kind of tolerable temperature.

Phaid found that he'd been assigned a miniscule cabin, little more than a cubicle. There was a tiny closet, a two-tier bunk and just about enough floor space to climb in and out of it. He didn't like the idea of the double bunk. It could mean he'd be sharing the cabin with another passenger. He fervently hoped that the crawler had been underbooked. Two people in this small enclosed space would make the journey unnecessarily wretched when they moved into the heat.

Phaid hid his remaining money under the mattress, placed his fuse tube under the pillow and tossed his bag into the closet. Wearily, he climbed up into the top bunk and lay back, staring at the grey metal ceiling. There was nothing else to do until the big machine got underway. After his night with the boohooms, Phaid welcomed the chance to simply stretch out and let his mind go blank.

He was just beginning to drift off to sleep when the cabin door slid open with a crash. Phaid sat bolt upright, cracking his head on the ceiling in the process.

'Shit!'

'Did I startle you, friend?'

'Damn right you did.'

'Sorry about that.'

'So you damn well . . .'

Phaid cut the sentence dead. He had taken his first good look at the newcomer, and the newcomer was huge. He was at least a head taller than Phaid and almost twice as broad. His flaming red hair was cropped close to his skull, but his beard was full and luxuriant, framing a leathery, weatherbeaten face and a pair of penetrating blue eyes that Phaid would not have cared to meet across a gaming table.

The man's dress completely complimented his image of strength and menace. His dark brown leather tunic was reinforced with copper studs larger than Phaid's thumb. His green, coarsely woven breeches were tucked into fur boots held together with criss-crossed thongs. An antique blaster with delicate tracery on the long barrel and a carved, opalescent handle hung in a well worn holster on a finely tooled but very old leather belt.

Heavy bronze bracelets clamped round both wrists marked him as one of the wild clanfolk from the mountain passes of the far north. A snake tattoo that coiled around one of his bare forearms indicated that, among his clan, he was one of the warrior caste. A number of old scars also indicated that in his case, warrior wasn't just a honorary title.

The clansman's outfit was completed by a longhaired animal pelt, probably that of a grey lupe, thrown around his shoulders and a shapeless hide bag hung over his arm.

Phaid sighed inwardly, this was all he needed. It was bad enough having to share the tiny cabin at all, but having to share it with a hulking semi-savage was pushing crowding to the limit. For the thousandth time he cursed the run of ill luck that had forced him to leave the Republic.

The clansman threw his bag into the closet beside Phaid's, then he unbuckled his belt and blaster and dropped them on to the lower bunk. He gave Phaid a brief, inspecting glance.

'The name's Makartur.'

'Phaid.'

Phaid noticed that Makartur didn't have the usual,

thick, guttural accent of the mountain clans. This, in itself, wasn't all that unusual. Life was hard in the north and many of them took to wandering. This one probably hired out as a mercenary and was travelling in search of a couple of city states who were busy having a war and who might be willing to buy his services.

Makartur sat down on the bunk with a grunt and started unlacing his boots.

'Where you headed, Master Phaid?'

'I get off at Wad-Hasa Wells.'

Makartur stretched out and grunted some more.

'No money, huh?'

Phaid leaned over the side of his bunk with a look of surprise on his face.

'What?'

'You've got to be running out of money if you're going from Freeport to Wad-Hasa Wells, and probably running, too. It stands to reason.'

Phaid was starting to get just the slightest bit alarmed.

'It does?'

Makartur laughed.

'Don't worry yourself, manny, I'm not interested in what you may or may not have done, but riding a crawler from Freeport to Wad-Hasa Wells ain't no vacation.'

'You know this place?'

Makartur shook his head.

'I've never been there, but I can imagine. It's probably the first water after you leave the gale plains. My guess is that it's nothing more than an oasis, a few buildings and a market place where the herdsmen from the surrounding desert come in to trade their stock.

Phaid scowled.

'It sounds desolate.'

'More than likely.'

'Ain't that always the way of it.'

Makartur raised a bushy eyebrow.

'You look put out.'

'You can say that again. I'm on my way to the Republic. I hoped I'd be able to build up another stake in this Wad-Hasa place to make it the rest of the way. How the hell can you do that at a goddamn waterhole.'

Makartur grinned.

'You'll probably find yourself some honest work if you look hard enough.'

Phaid grimaced.

'Sure. Just dandy.'

The clansman's grin broadened.

'I wouldn't worry about it too much, manny. If it's any consolation, I'm in the same predicament.'

'You're going to Wad-Hasa too?'

'I don't have the cash to go any further.'

'So where do you want to get to in the end?'

'The Republic, same as youself.'

Phaid was surprised.

'You're going to the Republic?'

He couldn't imagine what this hulking brute would want there.

Makartur's voice sharpened.

'You can think of a reason why I shouldn't?'

Phaid was quick to placate.

'No . . . no.' He made his tone light and conversational. 'What are you going to do when you get to the Republic?'

Makartur allowed himself a measured pause before he answered. 'I'll probably be minding my own business, the same as I do in most other places.'

That killed the conversation stone dead. Phaid found himself swamped by an awkward silence. Fortunately it didn't last too long. There were a number of dislocated throbs from deep within the crawler. After a while they formed into a regular pattern, speeded up and finally blurred into a single, continuous hum. The metal frame of the crawler ground and shrieked its protest as the power was transferred to the huge driving tracks. Finally the crawler lurched, swayed and started forward. Phaid propped himself up on one elbow.

'It looks like we're underway.'

Makartur didn't seem particularly interested. Outside the crawler, however, unknown to Phaid and Makartur, a small crowd had gathered to watch it move off. No matter how many times an individual had seen one of these giant machines come to life, only one with a very impoverished soul could fail to be impressed. The throb of its engines could be felt through the ground. Sheets of pale fire played around the discharge stacks high on the rear end of the machine. The massive tracks churned up the earth and gradually, almost impossibly, the towering structure of steel and ceramic lumbered forward, very slowly gathering speed.

High up in the steerage class the lumber, swaying and continuous throb of the engines weren't impressive. They were simply an irritation. They made relaxation difficult and sleep elusive. No conversation was forthcoming from his travelling companion, and Phaid decided to investigate such meagre amusements as the crawler might have to offer.

He knew that down in the first-class saloon there'd be the clink of quality glassware, the rustle of silk and velvet. Liveried waiters would be serving the best cuisine that the android cooks could prepare. Most galling of all for Phaid was his knowledge that large sums of money would be changing hands across the elegant gaming tables.

Phaid, of course, like all the others travelling cheap rate, was barred from the first-class areas. All that was available to him was the junk food, cheap liquor and rough company of the steerage canteen. Even that, though, was better than just lying in his bunk. Surreptitiously he extracted a couple of twenty tabs from beneath his mattress. He swung his legs over the side and dropped to the floor.

'I think I'll go down to the canteen and see what's going on.'

'Aye.'

'You fancy coming too?'

Makartur shook his head.

'No, manny, I'll just rest here for a while. There's nothing like a wee bit of privacy.'

Phaid slid open the cabin door but paused at the sound of Makartur's voice.

'Oh, manny?'

'What?'

'I wouldn't worry about your money so much. Keep it under the mattress if you want to, but I'm not about to steal it.'

Phaid reddened. He was taken completely by surprise.

'Uh . . . yeah, thanks.'

'You're welcome.'

Phaid thoughtfully closed the door and started down the corridor following the signs to the canteen. It was beginning to seem as if his temporary room mate was something more than a musclebound roughneck.

Once in the canteen, Phaid did his best to forget about

64

the strange character sharing his cabin. Not that the canteen had all that much to offer in the way of distraction. Two elderly vending machines dispensed food and drink. A musical android, even more decrepit than the one in The Rising Sun, played tunes that were scarcely recognisable over the noise of the crawler's engines. Beyond that, there was just some plain, very functional chairs and tables. Steerage passengers were expected to make their own entertainment.

Phaid bought himself a stiff drink, and, remembering that he had yet to eat that day, a bowl of unidentifiable mush that was touted as healthy and nutritious. Settling himself at an empty table, Phaid surveyed the room.

Nearest to him, three shabby old men in long black cloaks held a mumbled discussion of what sounded to Phaid like a combination of religion and the local politics from a region he'd never heard of. Next to them, a worn looking couple tried to control a pair of boisterous children. A group of dull-eyed men in desert robes supped ale and, as was their custom, chewed on the narcotic leaves of the dog gold plant.

More to Phaid's liking was the small group of farm boys and wanderers who hunched round a table playing a game of pit and pass with the usual set of multicoloured beads. Once Phaid had finished his food, he sauntered casually over to the game and watched for a while. When a short, bald man was busted out and forced to leave the game, Phaid nodded towards the empty chair.

'You mind if I sit in for a while?'

A buck toothed kid in a farmhand's homespun shirt grinned up at him.

'Didn't turn out too lucky for the last guy who sat there, but if you wants to then I guess you's welcome.'

After about an hour, Phaid had turned a modest, but honest profit. It was almost a relaxation for him to play a straight game without having to create an edge for himself by any sleight of hand or other adjustments. Despite the constant bumping and swaying of the crawler, Phaid was in fine spirits as he got up from his chair and strolled over to the drink vendor.

A skinny girl with dark straggling hair and a dirty face, was leaning beside the machine. As Phaid was inserting his money into the slot she caught his eye with a direct, almost challenging look.

'Hi.'

Phaid punched out his selection. Her loose sleeveless jacket, baggy trousers and flat broken down shoes told him she was probably a boat kid on the run from home. He grinned at her.

'Hi yourself.'

'You want to buy me a drink, huh?'

Phaid raised an amused eyebrow.

'Who says I can afford to buy you a drink?'

'I've been watching you. You been doing all right in that game over there. You've got the price of a couple of drinks and maybe a bit more.'

Phaid opened the dispensing hatch and took out his order.

'And who says I want to?'

The girl thrust out one narrow hip and pouted.

'If you want to be cheap, I'll have to go find someone else. There's plenty of others who'd like to spend some time with me.'

'If I buy you a drink, I get to spend some time with you, do I? Is that the deal?'

'Are you laughing at me?'

'Would I do a thing like that?'

The girl's face turned hard.

'Do I get that drink or don't I?'

Phaid grinned.

'If it means that much to you, sure.'

Phaid pushed some more money into the slot.

'What do you want?'

'Same as you.'

He punched up the selection and handed the girl her glass.

'You want to sit down?'

'Sure, why not.'

She led the way to a table away from the other passengers. Phaid followed. Once they were seated, she hardly glanced at him and made no attempt at any sort of conversation. Phaid looked at the girl quizzically and then decided to ignore her strange behaviour.

'You going far?'

'As far as I can. I only had enough money to make it to the first stop.'

'Wad-Hasa Wells?'

'That's the place. You know what it's like?'

'Not much, from what I've heard.'
'Just my typical stinking luck.'
'You're not the only one.'
'You can't afford to go any further either?'
'You said it.'
'Tough.'
'I'll make out.'
'You will? What do you do?'
Phaid shrugged.
'I guess you could say that I'm a gambler.'
'You do well at that?'
'It depends on how your luck's running.'
'And it ain't running too well at the moment?'
'That's a fact.'
'You going to buy me another drink?'
Phaid raised an eyebrow.
'Did my time run out already?'
'If you think of it that way.'
'You're kind of expensive.'
'No I ain't.'
'No?'
'You can have me for a ten tab.'
'I think you better say that again.'
'You get a kick from hearing it? You can have me for a ten tab. That's if you like girls.'
Phaid leaned back in his chair and looked at the girl carefully.
'Sure I like girls.'
'So?'
'So ain't you a little young to be doing this kind of thing?'
'Young?'
The girl laughed bitterly.
'I've been doing this for as long as I've been able. My stepfather started me at it.'
'Your stepfather.'
'The third husband of my mother. You know what it's like on the boats?'
Phaid thought of R'Ayla and nodded. A perverse idea nudged his mind but he rejected it. It would be too much of a coincidence. He let the girl go on.
'He beat me until I was old enough to use then he beat me and used me. When we were in port he'd even sell me to some of the sailors he knew. My mother didn't stop

him. She had the boat to run and she liked a quiet life. When I tried to stab him she dumped me over the side.'

The girl sounded bitter enough for Phaid to actually believe her, but he shrugged. What could he do. He had heard enough hard luck stories from whores, both senior and junior. The world moved in disastrous patterns. What was he supposed to do about it?

'Growing up can be a difficult business. If you expect to get slapped in the face you don't generally come in for a lot of disappointment.'

The girl scowled.

'I've had worse than slaps in the face.'

Phaid sighed.

'I believe you. Do you want another drink?'

If the girl was really set up to go whoring she would have to do something about her grim self pity, otherwise she would be strictly limited to clients who liked to get depressed. She was staring insolently at him.

'Sure, I'll take one.'

Phaid went over to the vending machine again and fetched two more drinks. The girl swallowed half of hers in one gulp and then looked him straight in the eye.

'So?'

'So what?'

'Are you stupid or something? You can't be very good as a gambler. It's no wonder you're travelling steerage. Are you going to lay down a ten tab to roll me in bed or not? I need to know. I can't afford to spend the night talking.'

She tilted her head as though challenging him. Phaid was getting a little tired of her efforts to prove how tough and hard-boiled she was but, on the other hand, he hated to refuse a challenge. He pulled out a ten tab and tossed it on to the table.

'Let's go.'

The girl was suddenly in action. A skinny hand snatched up the money. She seemed afraid that he might change his mind and take it back.

'You want to go to your cabin?'

Phaid shook his head.

'I'm sharing.'

'We'd better go to mine. I've got it all to myself.'

'You're lucky.'

The girl's face twisted.

'Really lucky.'

Phaid had the feeling that he was making a mistake but he stood up anyway.

'What's your name?'

'You can call me Sarli.'

'Whatever.'

The cabin was identical to his. Except, of course, there wasn't some red-bearded man-mountain asleep in the lower bunk. There were no preliminaries and precious little conversation. She rapidly shucked off her clothes and lay down on the narrow bunk with her legs slightly spread and her eyes tightly shut. She waited with scarcely concealed impatience for him to take what he wanted. Without her clothes she was skinny almost to the point of emaciation. Her breasts were small and hard, but had surprisingly large nipples. Her skin was pale, the unhealthy sort of pallor of someone who lives by night and rarely sees the sun. Her face, once she had lain down, became set in a totally blank expression, as if the real her was somewhere else entirely. She smelt as though the last time she had bathed had been some while ago, and although Phaid didn't really like to admit it, the only possible thrill was definitely perverse.

Phaid took his time stripping off his own clothes. He wasn't sure he even wanted to do what he was doing. Being unable to think of anything with more finesse, he crawled on top of her and, since she still showed no response whatsoever, he thrust himself roughly inside her. She was so completely inert that Phaid soon started feeling like a pig wallowing or a rapist having his own way with a passively resigned victim. He found neither particularly exciting.

Mercifully, it was soon over. The bunk was too narrow even for the very minimum tenderness of lying side by side for a while. Phaid climbed off the bunk and straightned up. He was starting to feel thoroughly disgusted with himself. As he picked up his shirt, the girl suddenly opened her eyes.

'If you want to go again, it'll cost you another ten.'

He couldn't believe that she could actually make the offer in rhyme. He quickly shook his head.

'Thanks all the same, but I don't think so.'

She propped herself up on one elbow.

'Did you have a good time?'

Phaid concentrated on buttoning his shirt.

'Sure . . . Sarli, I had a good time.'

She knew he was lying. He couldn't really believe she'd bothered to ask. He began to struggle into his breeches and was working on the fastenings when, to his surprise, she suddenly launched into a monologue that went into greater and even more elaborate detail of the beatings and sexual abuse that she had received at the hands of her stepfather. This, too, was delivered with her eyes closed.

By the time she stopped, Phaid was fully dressed with one hand on the handle of the cabin's sliding door. Once again she opened her eyes and shot him one of those disconcertingly direct looks.

'You sure you don't want to go again?'

Again Phaid shook his head.

'I don't think so.'

'Suit yourself.'

'Thanks anyway.'

She let herself flop back on the bed.

'Don't thank me. You paid.'

With that he seemed to have had all that ten tabs bought him. He silently wished her luck in her chosen career and let himself out. He felt dirty, but the steerage accommodation didn't run to cleanoffs. All they had were water showers that came directly off the crawler's cooling system. He realised they must be already on to the edge of the hot plains. He found that all but one of the stalls had been shut down. The sign read 'To conserve system fluid.' The only one working was occupied by a happily singing matron. There seemed to be nothing left but to return to his cabin and the strange Makartur.

As Phaid opened the cabin door, Makartur was sitting on his bed fingering and apparently muttering to a small beaded bag that hung around his neck on a leather thong. As soon as he saw Phaid he quickly stuffed it out of sight under his tunic.

Phaid pretended he hadn't noticed. He'd seen pouches like that before. They were amulets of the old religion, the one that worshipped harmony with the earth and its creatures. All too often their owners found themselves dragged away by the Religious Police. The Consolidated Faith went to great lengths to stamp out any competition.

Makartur looked curiously at Phaid and then lay back on his bunk.

'So how was the canteen, my manny?'

Phaid forced a companionable smile.

'It could have been worse, but I had a win in a game of pit and pass, so I'm happy.'

'You're a sporting man are you, a bit of a gambler?'

Phaid shrugged.

'We all got to make a living.'

'I don't gamble myself.'

Phaid turned away so Makartur wouldn't see his face. All he needed was a religious fanatic who was against gambling sharing his cabin.

'Yeah well, it takes all sorts.'

At that point Phaid had climbed into his bunk and laid flat on his back. With the temperature noticeably starting to rise, the crawler had to be moving into the heat. All Phaid could do was to shut his eyes and try and sleep through as much of the discomfort as possible. Unfortunately sleep refused to come. His mind kept drifting back to both the bitter hopeless girl and the red-haired giant in the lower bunk. The girl was now just a memory, a part of the past, but Makartur was very much a piece of the present.

Although it often didn't pay to voice it, Phaid had an instinctive distrust of religion. Whether it was the calculated combination of guilt, fear and promise of reward with which the priests maintained their armlock on the population or the darker, underground mysteries of the old proscribed faiths, Phaid wanted as little contact as possible with any of it. The idea that the lower bunk was filled with a devout and highly unlawful believer added a degree of mental unease to the already very present physical discomfort of travelling steerage.

Although Phaid's people came from the comparatively comfortable northern foothills, it was close enough to the cold bleak fells for him to have a very clear picture of Makartur and his people. His long-left-behind relatives had even worshipped a milder version of the grim, vengeful and totally unforgiving ancestor gods who ruled the spirit world of the high hills with a rod of iron. Phaid could picture how the man's mind worked. He had been through the dehumanising cruelty of warrior training, a fate that Phaid had gone to very serious lengths to avoid. At the end of warrior training you emerged with muscles like steel bands, a mass of arm tattoos and a mind in which rigid and inflexible will was clamped down on a seething cauldron of festering resentment and white hatred. Whenever the control was relaxed, this whole mess would boil over into the murderous beserk rage that made the warriors of the hills such valued mercenaries.

These warriors were dour, humourless men, closed and private, rarely showing emotion. They were taciturn and slow to anger, but when they did, their destructive ruthlessness was frightening. With them, slights were never forgotten, grudges went deep and a feud could last for generations. They judged everyone according to their exacting warrior code and trusted no one. To complete the mixture, their every move was dictated by omens and portents and dogged by symbol and superstition.

It seemed like hours had passed and still Phaid was unable to sleep. He was rocked and jolted; sweat was flowing from every pore in his body. He knew there must have been times when he'd been more uncomfortable but he couldn't remember when. There was no mistaking that they had hit the hot plains and the refrigeration plants were battling to keep the interior of the crawler at something like tolerable temperature. Down in first-class they were winning, up in steerage, however, it was a losing fight.

The throb of the motors was regularly punctuated by loud clangs and crashes as quite large rocks, hurled up by the violent super gales, smashed into the sides of the big machine. Phaid tried to imagine what the inferno outside really looked like. Thing a crawler didn't come equipped with windows. Even if a transparent material could be made thick enough and strong enough to withstand the flying pebbles, there was nothing to stop it being quickly rendered opaque by the blasting sand.

The closest Phaid could get in his mind to a picture of the hot plains was a dull glowing red, like the middle of a furnace set in violent motion. It was hard to conjure an image of something that could destroy a man's eyes in a matter of seconds.

For more centuries than anyone could remember, the hot plains formed the real boundaries that kept peoples and cultures confined to their own narrow territories. Men had crossed the icefields and braved the frozen gales long before they'd attempted to journey through the impossible heat. The hot plains were shrouded in legend and mystery. From the border lands they looked like some mighty wall of dark red swirling mist. Primitives thought it was the edge of the world, the beginning of the lands of demons and devils. Up until the invention of the crawler, and the massive loss of life that had gone into making it operate properly, the heat had been the ultimate barrier. It was only a matter of five hundred years since the hot plains had been penetrated by regular travel routes.

Yet, according to many legends, they hadn't always existed. Most cultures had folk legends about how man had once been able to wander freely all over the world. The Church claimed these legends with the doctrine that the bands of heat and cold had been thrown across the countries of the earth by the vengeful Lords when they grew angry at man's wickedness. Heretics countered with the idea that they were the result of some terrible, long-forgotten cataclysm.

From primitive to philosopher, everyone was in agreement that the hot plains and the icefields were something that had occurred after man walked the earth. Facts tended to bear out this theory. Ancient artifacts from supposedly isolated cultures showed too great a similarity to each other, more than could be dismissed as strictly coincidental. And then there were the androids. Identical types of android could be found in almost every part of the globe.

Although the androids were able to reproduce themselves, and a few humans could manage simple repairs when they were damaged, the secret of their construction was one of the great, lost mysteries. Somehow they had existed before the bands of heat and cold had formed and had spread to every part of the world. Nobody knew how or when or even why.

If all religions agreed that the evidence pointed to the establishment of these belts of extremes of climate as something that had occurred during the time of man, then it was possible man or man's ignorance might have been in some part responsible for their creation. Few sects or dogmas disputed this.

Broad agreement was all very well, though. It didn't prevent bitter disagreement over fine points of interpretation or theory. These disagreements had, in their time, been responsible for countless hangings, burnings, torture, pogroms, a dozen or more wars and all the other trappings of theological dispute.

Phaid found that his head was whirling. It must have been the heat. Politics and religion were usually things that he avoided even thinking about. His ancestors had had a mystic side to their natures, but most of that had been knocked out of him by his early wanderings in a rough world. His mouth was dry and the heat was close to unbearable. He felt as though he was burning up. It was difficult to breath and his mouth tasted like well walked sand. Just as he felt that he was starting to lapse into hellish red hallucinations, a voice came from the lower bunk.

'Manny?'

Phaid leaned over the side of the bunk. His voice was a rasping croak.

'Yeah?'

'You sound like you're having a hard time.'

'I can't take much more of this goddamn heat.'

'You never ride steerage before?'

'Yeah, but I don't remember it being as bad as this.'

'You never do . . . afterwards.'

'Maybe.'

'Could you use a drink?'

Phaid sat up, almost banging his head on the ceiling.

'I could drink anything.' He swung out of his bunk, dropped to the floor and squatted down beside Makartur. The clansman was holding a ceramic flask with silver mountings. He handed it to Phaid, who was relieved to discover that the big man wasn't against drinking. Phaid took a swallow and only just stopped himself gagging.

'Sweet Lords, what is this stuff?'

'It's a tight little brew they make back where I come from. Just the dew from a good still and a few herbs. It's a drink that makes men.'

'You also eat babies for breakfast?'

The big man's grin broadened.

'We never go that far. You don't want to believe the stories you hear.'

Phaid offered him the flask back, but Makartur shook his head.

'If you want to get some sleep, you'd be best advised to take another couple of pulls.'

Phaid took a deep breath and once again put the flask to his lips. The liquor went down a little easier, but he knew it'd be a long time before he actually developed a taste for Makartur's 'tight little brew'.

'I got to tell you, Mak, that's powerful stuff.'

'Aye.'

Phaid straightened up, aware of a slow burning sensation in his belly.

'I think maybe I'll lie down and see what happens.'

'Just a couple of wee things before you go.'

Makartur was no longer grinning.

'What are they?'

'The first is that I know you saw my amulet earlier.'

Phaid was suddenly ill at ease.

'And?'

'And I know a traveller like you has maybe seen an amulet like it before.'

'That's possible.'

Phaid didn't like the drift of the conversation.

'I don't believe in getting between a man and his religion. You don't have to worry about me, Mak. I won't say anything.'

'So you know about the old faith, do you Master Phaid?'

'A bit, it doesn't worry me none.'

'So you wouldn't think about turning in anyone who worshipped in the old ways?'

'Hell no, Mak. Live and let live. I stand by that.'

Makartur nodded his head very slowly.

'Even when the temple pricsts are offering a reward for anybody who points the finger at one of us?'

Phaid took a step back.

'Wait a minute, I'd never do a thing like that. I don't have any dealings with the priests or their lousy money.'

Makartur smiled.

'I'm glad you said that.'

'You are?'

'Very glad, manny. If you had been entertaining thoughts of claiming a reward on me, you would never have lived to spend it. We who follow the old ways are not as scattered and beaten down as those canting priests of the Consolidated Faith would like folk to believe.'

Phaid let out a relieved breath.

'Like I said, I never get between a man and his religion.'

Phaid started to climb back into his bunk, but Makartur grabbed his leg.

'There is one other thing, Master Phaid.'

'There is?'

'I said I had a couple of things to say to you.'

Phaid nodded.

'That's right, you did.'

Makartur tightened his grip.

'For as long as we are forced to be together, will you remember one thing?'

'I'll try.'

'Don't call me Mak. Where I come from it's a mark of disrespect. It's close to an insult.'

Phaid remained very still. He could feel the strength in the big man's fingers and was glad that they were gripping his thigh, not his throat. He kept his voice as level as he could.

'I wouldn't want to insult you.'

'You'll remember.'

'I'll try . . . very hard indeed.'

Makartur suddenly burst out laughing and let go of Phaid's leg.

'You're a good boy, Master Phaid. You'd better get some rest.'

Phaid scrambled back into his bunk once again and mopped his brow. He now had more than the heat to make him sweat. Not only was he being roasted alive, but he also seemed to be sharing a very small cabin with a very large religious madman. Then there was the horrible liquor he'd been handing out. Makartur had claimed that it would send Phaid to sleep. As far as Phaid could tell from the taste, about the only thing that it was likely to do was to poison him.

No sooner had that thought crossed his mind than Phaid started to feel drowsy. His eyelids were heavy, he found that it was hard to concentrate. He had a final alarming thought that maybe he actually had been poisoned, but then it hardly seemed to matter as he drifted into darkness.

6

PHAID WOKE up with a start from a very deep sleep. It had been crowded with dreams that faded rapidly as he came back to consciousness. For a few seconds he was totally disorientated. He didn't even know where he was. A red-bearded face was staring into his and a powerful hand was shaking his shoulder.

'Whaa?'

Things started to fall into place. The face belonged to Makartur, but why the hell was he shaking him out of the first good sleep he'd had in days?

'What's the matter?'

'It's time for you to show a leg, my manny.'

'Why? What's going on?'

'It's time to go.'

Phaid suddenly noticed that the crawler was very quiet, and the temperature had dropped considerably. He struggled to sit up.

'Have we stopped?'

'Aye, manny, we've stopped.'

Phaid was confused.

'We can't be at Wad-Hasa Wells already.'

'Oh yes we are, my boy. You've been out cold for a day and a half.'

'A day and a half?'

'Slumbering like a baby. You must have been overdoing it.'

'I don't understand it, the last thing I remember is . . .'

Phaid bit his lip. The last thing he remembered was a

bout of paranoid fear that Makartur had poisoned him. The clansman was busily strapping on his belt.

'What are you blathering about, manny?'

'Nothing.'

'Don't mess around then. They'll be throwing us off any moment. You don't get courtesy service when your crawl steerage.'

Still feeling like a zombie, Phaid managed to get his gear together and follow Makartur out of the cabin. As they descended through the crawler, they ran into Sarli on one of the middle deck companionways. Phaid smiled at her.

'You doing all right?'

'I suppose so.'

'You getting off?'

The girl shook her head.

'No. A fat old merchant from first-class came slumming. Now I've got enough to make it all the way to the end of the trail and stay drunk and by myself while I'm doing it.'

'You're lucky.'

Sarli grimaced.

'I guess you could call it that. Me, I thought I earned it.'

Phaid smiled and walked on. There was something about the girl that made him uneasy.

Makartur and Phaid emerged on to the exit ramp and immediately found themselves having to shade their eyes against pitiless, bright sunlight. Even Makartur seemed a little awed by the view that presented itself.

'Mother earth, have you ever seen such desolation?'

The desert stretched all the way to a line of low, rounded hills on the horizon. It wasn't a view without beauty, but it was hardly what either man really wanted to see. On the just tolerable edge of the hot winds, it was a dust bowl where no rain ever fell. A white hot sun beat down on an expanse of sand that was predominantly a pale ochre but here and there was splashed with vivid streaks of dark red, purple, blue and dull gold. Outcroppings of rock had been eroded by the sand into weird and twisted shapes that might have been petrified monsters, or the works of some insane sculptor. There was something almost frightening about the wild colours and tortured shapes. Most frightening of all, though, was that nowhere was there the slightest sign of any life.

A ramp bull bustled up to them.

'Okay! Okay! Let's get going! If you ain't got a ticket, on your way. Go watch the scenery from someplace else.'

He made the mistake of attempting to push Makartur on down the ramp. Makartur swung around and was about to grab the bull by the front of his stained brown tunic. Phaid quickly caught hold of the big man's arm. He noticed that two more bulls, part of the crawler's own muscle squad, were at the bottom of the ramp and starting to unclip their clubs from their belts. Phaid got between Makartur and the bull who'd done the pushing. He smiled ingratiatingly.

'I'm sorry, sir, but we were just wondering where the town might be.'

Makartur looked disgusted, but fortunately didn't say anything. The ramp bull positively sneered.

'It's round the other side of the crawler, you fool.'

Phaid half bowed and, nudging Makartur to follow him, he hurried down the ramp. The big man was obviously still spoiling for a fight, but he reluctantly followed. They made their way round to the rear of the huge machine and were treated to their first sight of Wad-Hasa Wells.

'Hell's teeth, will you just look. Whatever possessed human beings to live in a place like that?'

Wad-Hasa Wells was almost as desolate as the desert that surrounded it. Most of the habitations lay beneath the ground. Small white domes protected the entrances from wind and sand. These domes were the same light ochre as the desert and they gave the oasis the look of a piece of land that had melted, bubbled and then solidified.

The meagre water supply was marked by an area of sparse foliage, two towering spike ferns and a small thicket of cactus. Phaid slowly shook his head. Even Freeport would have been preferable.

'What the hell do we do now?'

Makartur looked at Phaid with raised eyebrows.

'We, manny? We? I wasn't aware that we'd suddenly become partners or anything of that nature.'

Phaid was a little taken aback. He'd started to assume that he and the clansman would work on the problem of getting out of Wad-Hasa Wells together. To Phaid, it was only logical, but Makartur didn't seem to see it that way. A third party did, however, think that there was some sort of connection between the two men.

'Hey, you two!'

It was an unshaven, ragged looking man in a flowing but dirty robe who'd been behind them coming off the crawler. Phaid and Makartur both turned.

'Yeah?'

'Youse two gents got any money?'

Both men were instantly suspicious.

'Who wants to know?'

The traveller raised both hands.

'No, no, don't get me wrong. I'm not looking for a handout or nothing like that. You just seemed as though you could use a few words of advice.'

'We could?'

'By the way youse acting, it don't seem like you ever been in these parts before.'

Makartur nodded.

'Aye, that's a fact.'

The traveller grinned.

'I thought as much. If you had, you wouldn't be hanging around the way you are.'

'Hanging around?'

'That's right.'

'What's wrong with hanging around, then? Is there a law against it or something?'

'As good as.'

'What?'

'As soon as the crawler moves out, the Deemer sends his boys to go round up anyone who ain't got the cash to the next stop.'

'The Deemer?'

'Runs the town, don't he? Deems what's going to happen, if you see what I mean. At least that's the derivation, like. Anyhow, once the crawler's on its way, his boys make the round up of them who get off here because they can't afford to go any further.'

'And what do they do with the ones who get rounded up?'

'They give them until sundown to come up with something; and if they can't they get marched out into the desert. If they try and creep back, they get shot.'

'But you can't survive in the desert.'

'Got it in one.'

Phaid and Makartur looked at each other and then back to the traveller.

'What are you going to do?'

'Me? Oh, I'm in the clear, I've got relatives here, haven't I?'

The crawler's drive roared into life as if to underline the bad news.

Phaid glanced nervously at the vibrating machine.

'What the hell do we do?'

This time Makartur didn't question the use of the word 'we'. The traveller also glanced at the crawler. It seemed about ready to move. He spoke very quickly.

'Best thing you can do is get inside someplace. The sink'd be the best place. The Deemer's boys usually figure that if anyone makes straight for the sink he's got to have money and as a rule they leave him alone.'

'What's a sink?'

'It's kind of like an inn. You can't miss it. It's the big dome with a blue sign, right by the covered well. You'll find a door and some steps. This is my advice, get in there. I better be moving if I'm going to see my relatives.'

With that he scurried off, leaving Phaid and Makartur staring at each other open mouthed.

'We'd better find this sink place as fast as we can, manny.'

'Now you're talking about we.'

'Don't mess around, man. I've got no fancy to tangle with the local law and order.'

They hurried towards the collection of low domes that made up the visible portion of the town.

'Where the hell is this place, do you reckon?'

'My bet is that the well ought to be somewhere close to those spike ferns.'

They moved off towards the small patch of dusty greenery. Phaid found that there was something a little disturbing about walking in among the low domes. It appeared that during the heat of the day the entire population went underground. Phaid didn't like the idea of having a whole town beneath his feet. He tried to imagine what the place was like at night. His impression was that it would be distinctly eerie.

They came out from between two domes, but quickly stopped and backed up the way they had come. Half a dozen men in broad brimmed white hats, off-white semi-uniforms and heavy boots had emerged from a dome some way away. Both Phaid and Makartur ducked down so they wouldn't be spotted over the tops of the lower domes.

'I guess they must be the squad.'

Fortunately, the squad was marching in the opposite direction. Phaid looked around anxiously.

'Where's this sink or whatever it's called?'

Makartur scanned the domes and then pointed.

'There! The blue sign.'

'What are we waiting for?'

Walking as swiftly as possible, but not actually running, they moved off in the direction of the blue sign. When they got there, the lettering was in a script that Phaid couldn't read, but, just like the man said, there was an open doorway with a set of steps spiralling downwards. Phaid hesitated and glanced at Makartur. 'You think we should go inside?'

'It'd be better than standing around.'

They started down the stairs with Makartur leading the way. The stairs made three complete turns, and then a low arch led into a cool, dimly lit room.

It was indeed some sort of an inn, but pretty unlike any inn that Phaid had ever seen before. Being hollowed out from the earth, nobody had bothered to create anything approaching a regular shape. There were recesses, alcoves, fluted pillars, some niches packed with cushions and low divans as well as regular tables and benches. Two more arches opened on to flights of descending stairs that went down to lower levels even deeper underground.

At the far end of the room a marble counter served as a bar. For such an out of the way place it was surprisingly well stocked. Ranks of varied bottles lined the shelves behind the counter, and a row of dully gleaming brass pressure kegs stood in a row on the floor beneath it. A line of ale taps on the counter were connected to them by shiny steel hoses.

As well as the variety of alcohol, there were also various grades of the narcotic dog gold leaf in screw top, airtight glass jars, a selection of cheeses in an open fronted display case and a squat, brass bound cracker barrel. The whole set-up had an air of cleanliness and efficiency.

Phaid and Makartur marched up to the counter where what they assumed was the innkeeper, or whatever name was given to the proprietor of a sink, was polishing a glass and pointedly ignoring them. He was a dapper little man with slicked down hair, a crisp white shirt and a fancy brocade hat. His small, mean mouth and close set eyes suggested that he wasn't the sort one could ask a favour of with any hope of getting it granted. Phaid arranged his face into a tentative smile. 'Sure is hot outside.'

The innkeeper sniffed. 'So what else is new?'

'You got any ale?'

The innkeeper nodded curtly at the row of kegs.

'What do you think those are?'

'So what kind have you got?'

'Light, dark or extra strong.'

'Give me an extra strong.'

He glanced at Makartur.

'You want an extra strong?'

'A light will cut the dust just as well.'

Churlishness seemed to be contagious in the sink. Phaid turned back to the inkeeper.

'An extra strong and a light.'

While the innkeeper took two hinged top steins down from a shelf and started filling them, Phaid surveyed the place a little more carefully. There were only five other customers. Two elderly men were absorbed in a game of checkers, while three others sprawled on cushions. At first Phaid thought they were asleep, then he noticed the slow, bovine motion of the jaws and realised that they were far away in the magic world that appeared once you'd chewed enough dog gold.

'Quiet around here, isn't it?'

The innkeeper pushed the two steins across the marble.

'Sometimes it is and then again, sometimes it ain't. That'll be four tabs.'

Phaid dropped four singles on to the counter. Makartur tossed another one down.

'Give me a twist of dog gold.'

He glanced at Phaid.

'You want some?'

Phaid shook his head.

'No thanks. This place is weird enough as it is.'

The innkeeper scooped up the money, but didn't seem inclined to go about his business. After a couple of seconds, Makartur jutted his chin at him.

'You want something?'

'I thought we might settle the matter of rent.'

'What are you talking about?'

'You ain't been through these parts before, have you?'

Both Phaid and Makartur shook their heads. The innkeeper smiled thinly.

'I didn't think so. That's why we ought to settle the rent right now, so there won't be no misunderstanding when it gets around to sunset.'

Makartur started to bristle.

'And what do we need to pay rent to you for, little man?'

'You planning to still be here after sunset, are you?'

'Maybe.'

'Then you need a place to stay. If you ain't taken a room by sunset then I got to report you both to the Deemer's office. If you can't show that you got some other place to stay the Deemer's men'll march you out into the desert with the rest of the vagrants. It's the rules, see. Nothing I can do about it.'

'This town don't seem to be strong on hospitality.'

The innkeeper leaned forward.

'Well, that's just where you're wrong, my friend. We got a lot of hospitality in this town. It's about all we do have. It's a valuable commodity. We sell it to travellers for the best price we can get. That's how we survive. It ain't easy here in the desert, let me tell you. There's nothing going spare for rogues and bums and freeloaders.'

He paused to give both Phaid and Makartur a significant look.

'So gents, do you want a room or don't you?'

Phaid slowly closed his eyes. He'd never been anywhere that was so tightly sewn up.

'How much is a room?'

'Ten a piece, or fifteen between you if you want to share one.'

'We'll share.'

Between them they were just able to come up with it. Reluctantly they placed it on the counter. The innkeeper actually cracked a smile.

'That's nice and tidy, then. You want to book for tomorrow right now? There won't be a crawler in for another three days.'

Makartur scowled.

'We'll talk about tomorrow when tomorrow comes.'

The innkeeper's smile faded.

'Don't leave it too long. I've heard that the drovers will be coming through with a herd. We get pretty busy when that happens. You may not get a room.'

That seemed to be the end of the conversation. Phaid and Makartur carried their ale to a stone table as far from the counter as possible. Phaid sat down with a sigh.

'What a place.'

Makartur shrugged.

'We're all right for today. Maybe something will turn up tomorrow.'

Phaid was determined not to look on the bright side.

'What the hell can turn up? There's not even a crawler in for three days.'

'The drovers for one.'

'What are these drovers?'

'They move the herds of veebes from the savannahs and down to stockyards in the cities. In this region, I'd guess they'd been resting over here on the way to Chasabad.'

Phaid looked puzzled.

'How can a bunch of veebe herders do us any good?'

'A lot of ways, manny. If we get real lucky, there might even be one of my people among them. There's plenty of them who've found work with the drovers. Although, mind you, there are not that many who come as far as this region.'

'And if one of your long lost relatives don't turn up, what then?'

'When the drovers come to town, there'll be drinking and chaos. This Deemer can't have that many men. They'll have their hands full with rowdy drovers. If we keep our heads down, they'll not have time to bother us.'

'I suppose that's something.'

'Who knows. When drovers hit town there's usually a few fall out drunk, unconscious or even dead. It seems to me that we'd probably be able to hire on. At least Chasabad is in the right direction for the Republic.'

Phaid looked genuinely horrified.

'Hire on? Chasing a herd of stinking veebes? You're joking.'

'You could do a lot worse.'

'I can't think how.'

Makartur pulled a chunk off the twist of dog gold and stuffed it into his mouth.

'Maybe you've a plan to find your own way out of this place?'

Phaid scowled.

'Maybe.'

Sitting in a bar, no matter how exotic, without any money can quickly become a bore. Phaid made his beer last as long as possible but once it had gone there wasn't another damn thing to do. The dog gold had started to go to work on Makartur. His eyes glazed. It seemed as though drink and dog gold were two exceptions to his rigid warrior puritanism. Phaid suspected that women would probably be the third. After a while Makartur stumbled to his feet. He waved a brawny arm in the direction of the exit.

'I'm going out.'

Phaid sniffed.

'What the hell for?'

'To look around.'

'Do what you like.'

Phaid was actually starting to feel sleepy. It might have been the dry desert air or, more probably, some sort of hangover from Makartur's home-brew. His eyes were actually starting to close when the sink was suddenly full of women. Phaid woke up with a start. He was stunned. It was the very last thing that he had expected. The sleepy little hostelry suddenly took on the ambience of a bordello, a bordello instantly created for the drovers and their money. There were about thirty females in the noisy gaggle; some young, some not so young, and a few scarcely more than children. Their ages may have varied, but they were all heavily made-up and decked out in costumes that were obviously the individual owner's idea of the ultimate in seductiveness.

The women were in high spirits and they filled the bar with an almost carnival atmosphere as they waited for the drovers to arrive. Phaid, as the only functioning male in the place, became the stooge for a good deal of teasing and badinage. These desert women quickly proved that they could be as creatively foul mouthed as any bunch of big city whores. Phaid thought back to the girl on the crawler and wondered if everyone in these desert lands around the fringes of the heat survived by selling themselves.

As the booze started to flow, the women vied to outdo each other in coarse boasts of what they were going to do with the drovers, once they arrived. When Phaid, slightly bewildered, tried to find out what was going on, a matronly lady called Dorrie, in a low cut, flowing gown that revealed a great deal of her ample bosom, did her best to explain. It appeared that the veebe herd had been spotted out in the desert and the town was gearing up for the influx of drovers. Although Phaid did not shock easily, it came as quite a surprise to find that the women were not full time prostitutes, but simply all presentable women in the town, married or single. They were getting ready to take up the ancient trade with the full connivance and co-operation of fathers, husbands and brothers. It was apparently no disgrace. Phaid had never met anything like this before and he had difficulty dealing with it.

'Your husbands? Don't they mind?'

Dorrie grinned at the blurted question.

'Mind? Of course our husbands don't mind. It's natural, isn't it? When the drovers, or any other travelling men come to town, they want women. We're the only women here and we provide. This whole town survives by providing for travellers. We don't make anything and we don't grow anything in this desert. It'd be stupid if we didn't perform this service. It'd lose a whole lot of cash for the town, and anyway, a change is as good as a rest, that's what I always say.'

The other girls around her shrieked with laughter. As far as they were concerned, they were making a valuable contribution to the isolated town's precarious economy and enjoying themselves in the bargain.

'I'd have a strapping drover instead of my old man any day of the week.'

For an hour or more, the women went on laughing and drinking in anticipation of the party to come. Phaid found himself buoyed up and borne along by their enthusiasm. He also found that, despite the disapproval of the owner of the sink, a number of free drinks were pressed upon him. He was, in fact, three parts drunk when a small boy ran down the stairs waving his arms and shouting.

'They're here! They're here! The drovers are here!'

7

PHAID CROUCHED behind one of the most outlying of the low domes and hoped that nobody would notice him. Wad-Hasa Wells had been turned into a scene out of a nightmare by the horde of drunken drovers. Burly figures, loaded to the eyes on dog gold and alcohol, stumbled about in the darkness shouting and bellowing like animals. All the above ground glo-globes in Wad-Hasa Wells had long since been shot out, and the only light came from a thin crescent moon and the fires that had been lit between the domes. It reflected dimly on sweaty, vacant faces or the brown skin of women who had been stripped naked during the long debauch and who had been either unable or unwilling to find their torn and discarded clothes. Men fought each other without knowing who they were pounding or why. When the drovers fought they used anyway they could to knock down the opponent. Heads, fists and feet all came into play. They gouged, they kicked and they butted. The slightest imagined insult could start yet another pair brutally slugging it out.

Couples fornicated on the sand between the domes, right alongside the sprawled figures of those who had either been pummelled unconscious or had passed out from some alarming combination of drink and drugs. They made no attempts at modesty and appeared to have no sense of shame. The air was filled with a cacophony of screams and grunts. Women shrieked and giggled, there were roars of laughter and bouts of drunken singing. Somewhere someone was bawling mindlessly. Someone else was crying. When the drovers had a party they took it all the way to the limit.

They had hit town in the late afternoon, just before sunset. The herd had thrown up a massive cloud of dust that must have been visible for miles around. When the animals were secured in the pens on the edge of the town, the drovers had come in looking for whatever good times Wad-Hasa Wells had to offer. Even weary, sweat stained and dirty from their trek across the desert, they presented a wild and crudely romantic image. They came into the town with the swagger of an invading army. They strutted in their high-heeled boots as though they owned the land. Hard watchful eyes peered from beneath the drooping brims of their wide hats. Heavy blasters and wicked, curved knives hung from their wide, decorated leather belts. The weapons were in easy reach, an unarguable back-up to each man's nomad bravado. Like most wandering peoples, a drover's wealth was ostentatiously displayed on his person. Jewellery glittered. Gold seemed to be a particular favourite. It hung from their ears in heavy hoops, around necks in chains or medallions, it decorated the hilts of knives and the butts of blasters and weighted down hands and arms in the form of rings and bracelets.

The drovers came from no particular tribe or nation. Their weatherbeaten, often scarred faces ranged from deep mahogany to blue black. There were equine faces with high foreheads and prominent noses, there were broad, flat featured faces with slanting almond eyes. The drovers came from all over the world. What held them together was the loneliness and hardship of their work and a fierce pride in their freedom and individualism.

As they made their way into Wad-Hasa, their short, brightly coloured cloaks or ponchos swirled behind them, and their loose, flowing trousers flapped in the light desert breeze. Determined to make an impression, they strode like princelings rather than men who, in reality, performed a dirty menial job and spent their lives smelling of animal dung and stale sweat.

This picture of the primitive invading army was enhanced by the long lance that each man carried. These too were decorated to the individual's taste but were not, in fact, weapons; they were the main tool of the drover's trade. The little tingler unit set in the tip of each lance was the most efficient way of goading the stubborn and bellicose veebes into a semblance of movement.

As the drovers got the first few drinks inside them and began to move around flirting with the girls, Phaid decided he had seen his chance to profit from the invasion. He had pulled out a deck of cards and attempted to get a game started. The drovers couldn't have reacted worse if he had committed open blasphemy. Later he learned that there was an almost universally held belief that a man had only a limited amount of luck in his life and it was considered close to a crime to go squandering it on a game of chance. He had only diverted the wrath of the drovers by quickly claiming that he was a fortune-teller, not a gambler. This, however, had put him in trouble with the Deemer's men. Fortune-telling was illegal in Wad-Hasa and only a lot of fast talking by both him and Dorrie had saved him from a flogging.

A few fights had broken out while it was still daylight. These had been minor affairs, though. Pairs of drovers settling trail grudges and individuals arguing over the price of a bottle or a woman were easily quelled by the Deemer's men using a firm hand and occasionally resorting to the flexible clubs that seemed to be their favourite weapons.

Even through the garish, blood red desert twilight the combination of the Deemer's men and the seemingly indefatigable townswomen kept the drovers in check. Once darkness, however, spread over the little oasis, the belligerence of the now hopelessly drunk herdsmen began building towards the point where nothing would be able to hold it.

The breakout had started with a chair swinging, glass shattering brawl inside the sink. It had apparently been sparked off by an evil tempered giant who answered to the name of Murf. Murf had decided that the proprietor of the sink was simultaneously raising the prices and reducing the measures of the booze. In a towering rage of customer indignation, he had attempted to dismantle the place single-handed. His companions, deciding that wrecking the sink was too much fun for Murf to have all to himself, had joined in the destruction with a will. The proprietor had summoned the Deemer's men to save what was left of his property, and the confrontation was on.

Phaid watched from the shelter of the locked and

barred entrance dome of a nervous citizen's home. A large squad of the Deemer's men had charged into the sink, but after only a short pause, filled with yells and muffled crashings, they had emerged again, retreating before a crowd of angry drovers hurling glasses, bottles, debris and any other missile that came to hand. The Deemer's men had failed to hold the line, and anarchy flared like a conflagration all through the town. Pitched battles spread over the sand in and around the domes, and the darkness was filled with tangles of grunting, fighting men.

It was at this point that Phaid decided to make himself scarce. He could scarcely believe the run of events in which he seemed to be trapped. There had to be an easier way to get back to civilisation than the tortuous route that he was travelling. No matter how he wracked his memory, he couldn't fix on an incident that could have caused this almost supernatural run of ill luck.

It wasn't quite clear who was the first to use a blaster. Afterwards, the drovers claimed that it was one of the Deemer's men who fired first. Those nearest to the incident told how the law officer and a lanky young herdsman had set about each other and when the drover seemed to be getting the best of things, the lawman had drawn his weapon and burned his opponent down. A girl who had been caught in the middle of the *mêlée* thought the drover might have had a knife in his hand, but this was hotly disputed by his companions.

Whatever the truth might be, once one shot had been fired, everyone got in on the act. The night was split by the white, jagged crackle of fuse tubes and the roar of blasters. Phaid ducked low as the stink of burned flesh and superheated sand reached him.

Phaid was relieved to find that the fire fight didn't last as long as he'd feared. The Deemer's men appeared to have given the decision to the drovers, at least for the duration of the night. The town was split, the drovers had the surface and the townspeople, with the exception of some very independent women, had retreated to the safety of their underground dwellings. Most locked up tight, but some, backed by teams of heavily armed relatives and neighbours, still sold liquor and dog gold from a handful of open doorways.

The uproar went on long into the night. All through,

Phaid did his best to make himself as invisible as possible. This wasn't a total success. Despite Makartur's stated intention to keep his head down, the big man had mingled with the drovers and then proceeded to get as aggressively drunk as possible. He had even, for a while, struck up a stumbling, staggering companionship with Murf, the hulking oaf who had initiated the first fight in the sink. Unfortunately, they had spotted Phaid creeping around the edge of a dome and attempted for a while to get him as drunk as they were. Although, on the surface, Makartur was aggressively boisterous and jovial, Phaid could sense a layer of hostile distrust beneath the backslapping. It disturbed him. Drunken warriors could be lethally unpredictable.

After a while the two of them got bored with trying to force booze on Phaid and they moved off in not very efficient pursuit of three local women who had given them the sign as they lurched past. Their effort to get Phaid drunk hadn't been completely unsuccessful. He found himself reeling and no longer worrying so much about his self preservation. He even started to tentatively join in the spirit of the drovers' crude partying. Somewhere along the line someone had given him a twist of dog gold. A few minutes after that the hallucinations had begun. From then on, Phaid had wandered through the chaos of the small desert town in a soft cocoon of extreme, if somewhat blurred, well being. The scattered fires became sources of swirling and undulating colour. Rainbows flashed where the light was reflected from sweating skin or the polished blade of a knife. The figures around the fires and those moving unsteadily through the darkness were twisted into grotesque and jumbled shapes that were all part of some weird, wild and not quite human dance. Even the domes seemed to take on animated life. They appeared to throb and pulse like bubbles of energy trying to break loose from the ground and float up and up into the wild night sky. Phaid felt as though he was walking around the inside of some giant boiling cauldron.

If, under more normal circumstances, half of these things had happened to Phaid they would have driven him at least part way out of his mind. He would have feared for his sanity and fled before the distortion of his senses. The joy of dog gold, however, and the reason its users sang its praises so loudly, was that, no matter how fearsome the hallucinations might appear, or how fast they might bear down on the unwary user, anyone in the grip of the drug was also soothed and lulled into a state of simply not giving a damn. Phaid felt he was drifting effortlessly, a few inches off the ground. He was invincible. Nothing could touch him. There was a bottle in his hand. He could hardly remember his name.

A familiar face swam into his field of vision. Red lips moved into the shape of a smile. They parted slightly.

'Lords, dearie. You look well out of it.'

Phaid stood for a moment, staring stupidly. At first the name refused to come.

'Dorrie!'

The face looked concerned.

'Are you all right, love?'

Phaid realised that the face was expecting him to come up with an answer, but once again his mind only turned over with the greatest of difficulty.

'Yeah . . . I'm . . . fine.'

'You've been at the dog gold, haven't you, dearie? You got to watch that stuff. It'll rot your brain.'

Phaid held out his bottle. It was the best he could do.

'Would you . . . like a . . . drink?'

A body joined the face and a hand stretched out to take the bottle. While Dorrie drank, Phaid found himself staring transfixed at her ample breasts. All manner of disconnected but very voluptuous images chased each other through his head. Dorrie held out the bottle, regarding Phaid with a raised eyebrow.

'What d'you think you're looking at?'

'I'm . . . looking . . . at you.'

Dorrie laughed and shook her head. 'I know what's going through your mind, all you dog gold fiends are the same. One look at a woman and everything except sex is gone with the wind.' She struck a pose. 'Well, dearie, do you like what you see?'

'Y . . . yeah.'

'Is that all you've got to say?'

She came closer to him. Her hand was stroking his cheek. He could feel those full, wonderful breasts press against him. Then Dorrie let out a gasp and Phaid's world exploded into brutal, blinding, bright orange pain. He had one clear thought. He had been hit very hard over the back of the head with something very solid. Maybe a blaster or maybe the butt of a lance; then he sagged down into merciful blackness.

Sadly, the blackness didn't last forever. All too soon the pain ebbed back. It wasn't any ordinary pain. It wasn't even a singular pain. The pain that Phaid was experiencing came on multiple levels and in a variety of forms. Sunlight was trying to drill its way through his eyelids. His stomach was twisted into a leaden, acid knot. Every muscle ached and, over and above it all, there was the scarcely thinkable throbbing at the back of his skull. It felt as though it had been caved in. Just to make matters worse, someone kicked him in the ribs.

'Up, you!'

'Wha?'

One of the Deemer's men was standing over him with a less than pleasant expression on his face. It was morning.

'Up!'

Fighting back nausea, Phaid scrambled to his feet before the heavy boot could get in another kick. All around him, other drovers were being woken in a similar manner. The Deemer's men seemed to be getting even for their defeat of the night before. The sleepy, hungover drovers found themselves herded at weapon-point into a sullen group near the animal pens. Makartur was among them. Phaid edged up beside him.

'What's going on? What are they planning to do to us?'

Makartur regarded Phaid through bleary, bloodshot eyes.

'Why don't you piss off, manny, and let me suffer on my own.'

'Don't all these weapons being pointed at us worry you at all?'

Makartur shook his head and winced. 'Not as much as this headache.'

'Suppose they start shooting?'

Makartur glowered. 'There'll be no shooting so long as we don't start anything. Everyone knows the rules.'

'The rules?'

'Aye, the rules. We're being thrown out of town. It always works that way in these hick towns. The drovers come in, they spend their money, get a bit out of hand and find themselves thrown out in the morning.'

Phaid gingerly explored the back of his head with his fingertips. There was a lot of swelling and his hair was matted with dried blood.

'Somebody slugged me.'

Makartur sniffed. He didn't seem too interested.

'Was it your woman or your bottle they were after? Or did you aggravate someone?'

'Woman, I guess, although she was scarcely mine.'

Makartur glanced briefly at the back of Phaid's scalp.

'It looks like they used the butt end of a blaster. You ought to get that cleaned up.'

He pointed to where drovers were clustered around a line of wooden tubs.

'There's water over there. You'd best dunk your head in it.'

The cold and not too clean water came as a quite considerable shock. After two or three dips below the surface he started to feel a little better. He was cleaning the worst of the blood out of his hair when the drover beside him nudged him in the ribs and pointed past the watching guards. A short man with a tendency to waddle was coming towards the pens, flanked by what looked like his own personal guard. He wore a much more resplendent version of the standard white uniform.

'Will you look there. It must be the boss of the whole damn town.'

'The Deemer himself.'

'He's probably looking for an extra payment for last night's trouble.'

'They cover every angle, don't they.'

The drover shrugged. 'They got a living to make.'

'I've noticed.'

Phaid watched while two drovers were let through the cordon of guards. They went into a huddle with the Deemer and his two assistants. Phaid glanced at the man beside him.

'What's going on now?'

'They're figuring the extent of the damage.'

'Who are those two?'

'The drive boss and the drovers' representative.'

'Representative?'

'The drive boss works for the herd owner. The representative looks after the drovers' interests. That way nobody gets to put anything over on anyone else. At least, that's the theory, but once the bribing gets down . . . well, you can work it out for yourself. Our drive boss is called

Shako. He's a mean bastard, but he's fair when he's sober. The rep, Graudia, he's something else again. If you've got a gripe, he's the last one you want to go to. By all accounts the owners have got him right in their pockets.'

After what looked like a good deal of haggling, a price must have been set for the night's rampage, because money changed hands, the Deemer's men lowered their weapons and suddenly the drovers were going about their business. Amid the hustle and bustle, Phaid relocated Makartur.

'Are you going with them?'

Makartur nodded. 'Aye, I hired on already.'

'What about me?'

'What about you? I'm not your keeper.'

'Can I hire on too?'

'You best go and check in with Shako, the drive boss, he's . . .'

'I know which one he is.'

Phaid had had about enough of Makartur's attitude. He made his way to where Shako was standing, bellowing orders and generally turning the hungover drovers into a cohesive working unit. Just as the drover at the tub had described, he was a mean bastard. Tall and rangy, he had cold, pale green eyes and the features of a hawk. Without any preamble, he looked Phaid up and down and apparently didn't like what he saw.

'You want to sign on?'

'That's right.'

'You've worked a herd before?'

'Of course I have. It ain't been for a long time, but I worked on a drive before.'

Phaid lied glibly, but Shako wasn't convinced.

'You don't look like no drover.'

'Appearances can be deceptive.'

'Show me your hands.'

Phaid held out both hands, palm upwards. He was acutely aware that they lacked the horny callosity that was the mark of a true drover. He had the soft, well cared for hands of someone who rarely touched anything more rugged than a deck of cards. Shako sniffed.

'It must have been a very long time ago indeed.'

Phaid dropped his hands. 'Yeah, well . . .'

'Personally, I think you're a damned liar, but I had three men killed last night so I can't be choosy who I take.

96

You're hired.' He waved his arm at Makartur who was standing around waiting for an assignment. 'You, hill man, get over here.'

Makartur scowled and moved towards them. Shako nodded in Phaid's direction.

'He's driving for you.'

Makartur's eyes narrowed.

'Him?'

'You're both new so you're partnered together.'

'I'd rather it wasn't him.'

Shako's expression was flinty and dangerous.

'You don't have any rather. You two work together or you stay here and see what the Deemer wants to do with you.' Shako shot Phaid a final contemptuous glance. 'I'll tell you one thing, by the time you reach Chasabad, those dainty hands of yours will be worked raw.' He grinned at Makartur. 'Take him and show him what he's got in store.'

Phaid quickly discovered that what he had in store was a combination of bouncing, muscle wrenching, bone jarring physical work and mind crushing boredom. All those times that he'd sat in a fancy restaurant, spending his winnings, chewing his way through a prime steak with all the trimmings, he'd never given a thought as to what was involved in bringing the meat to the table. The drovers' machine was the first shock. As it floated a metre or so above the ground, it rode so hard that it was little short of an instrument of torture. When he'd told Makartur he could drive a flipper, he'd had the regular city model in his mind, a low streamlined machine with colourful bodywork, a plexiglass bubble to keep the weather out and even an android handler to take over the guidance system when the human occupants had something more interesting to do.

The drovers' machines were something else again. Dome and body panels had gone. The drover rode on a narrow saddle in front of a centre-mounted set of controls. The lanceman behind him didn't get a seat at all. He perched on a small platform, held in place by a system of webbing straps.

The drovers' flippers were so reduced to basics that even the usual auxiliary power pack had gone. With only a sun catcher supplying energy to the drive, it meant that they were effectively grounded during the hours of darkness.

Once Phaid had familiarised himself with the handling of the skeletal machine, he found that the routine of the drover was fairly straightforward. Each morning the herd was goaded into motion with shocks from the drovers' lances. Once they were on the move, it was relatively easy to keep the animals on the course set by the drive boss. All it needed was a certain degree of prodding by drovers cruising slowly beside the herd at about a metre from the ground.

Phaid and Makartur were running in what was known as the drag. This meant riding at the rear of the herd, picking up stragglers and goading them back to the main pack. It also meant that they were constantly being choked and partially blinded by the thick dust cloud kicked up by the hundreds of veebes. Riding the drag was the lowest position in the drovers' pecking order and, as new arrivals, Phaid and Makartur were stuck with it.

With no option but to make the best of their lot, the two men had gone to work. Phaid showed a good deal more reluctance than his companion, but even he mastered the basic technique of pulling the flipper up to a height of seven or eight metres and dropping swiftly from behind at a straying beast so Makartur, working as lanceman, could get in a series of swift jabs. The majority of times this would send the animal galloping back to the main herd bellowing loudly.

Occasionally a particularly aggressive creature would turn on the flipper. A big, shaggy bull veebe was powerful enough to tilt a flipper in such a way that it would spiral out of control and somersault on to the ground. The single knobbly horn on the top of its flat, triangular head was quite capable of twisting a flipper's metal frame or smashing human bones.

If a veebe did take it into its thick and bad tempered head to charge a flipper, it was down to the driver to swing the machine away from the attacking animal before it could make contact. In the four days that Phaid had been on the drive, only one animal had tried to fight back. Phaid desperately swung the controls and, to his amazement, he and Makartur missed being gored and trampled by a hair's-breadth. Phaid put it down more to blind luck than good judgement, but Makartur had been suitably impressed.

Each day, when the sun finally dipped below the horizon and the flippers sank down on to the sand with a soft bump, the lessons in the ways of the drovers still weren't over. He'd stretch his cramped and aching back and wearily make his way to the lumbering transit bed that carried the supplies, the two big water tanks and the field kitchen that provided the focal point of the men's off duty hours. The kitchen was presided over by Thatch, a small, wiry man whose body had been broken by a veebe. He'd been given a bionic patch job by a cheap company surgeon. Cooking up the daily grey, tasteless stew provided Thatch with a rough and ready semi-retirement. He had also appointed himself custodian of drover lore and drover prejudice.

As outlooks went, the drovers' was one of the least lovely that Phaid had ever come across. Drovers seemed to hate almost everything that wasn't exactly like themselves. Most of all they hated the veebes and took every opportunity to torment the animals. If it hadn't been for Shako constantly keeping a watchful, protective eye on the merchandise, there probably would have been deaths and serious mutilations among the herd, inflicted by the drovers themselves.

Their hatred wasn't only confined to the veebes. There were the boohooms. They were universally detested, and every night there were stories of atrocities committed against the mild, inoffensive sub-humans. The elaihim were also high on the drovers' hate list. Higher, if anything, than the boohooms, except that the drovers' contact with the tall, hyper-intelligent beings was strictly limited. The elaihim, with their super-human minds and tall, frail bodies, knew enough to avoid the trails of drovers and the haunts of similar, ignorant, violent humans. The drovers' hatred of the elaihim was based on fear, and therefore much more fierce and implacable. The boohooms were merely convenient victims. The elaihim were something else. They had superior intelligence. There was no way that the drovers could pretend otherwise. What they could pretend, though, was that this superior intellect was dedicated to some nebulous concept of evil. The elaihim were a shadowy conspiracy that could be blamed for all the ills and disasters in the world. The elaihim were more than just the victims for the drovers cruel sport. They were vermin. Despite their obvious culture and sensitivity, in the opinion of the drovers, they had to be eradicated, just like ribbon snakes, snow lupes or the big, savage lizards that prowled the deep forest. They were a dangerous menace, too smart to be allowed to live.

The drovers didn't exactly hate women, but the attitude was definitely ambivalent. For the drovers, women split easily into two kinds. There were the wives that most of them didn't have and there were whores on whom they spent most of the end of trail pay. Wives were docile, faithful and for the most part totally imaginary. Although most drovers had an overbearing fixation about having sons to follow in their footsteps, hardly any managed to maintain and provide for a family. Whores, on the other hand, were fair game for anything and the drovers talked about them with grinning contempt, although a few particular women did seem to command a certain grudging, familiar admiration. It was ironic that, all too often, when a drover did marry, it was to a prostitute with a yen to reform. After that, more often than not, they would stash the woman on some remote farm and then live with a constant fear that the little woman would be finding her fun with some other drifter while they were away on the trail.

Farmers, androids, townspeople, clever bastards from the big cities and dumb bastards from the hills all came in for contempt and were all seen as reasonable targets for bouts of random violence. In fact, the only way that Phaid could sum it up was that the drovers didn't like anyone except their own kind, and weren't too fond of each other. Bearing this in mind, he did his best to keep both his mouth shut and himself to himself. As an identifiable outsider, he knew he was a potential flashpoint for trouble.

Also, Phaid could only stand so much of the talk and boasting that was the nightly ritual around the transport bed. He stayed long enough so he wouldn't be labelled as a snob or a loner, but then he'd take his blanket and find himself a fairly isolated spot in which to get some sleep. The drovers weren't the only thing that sent Phaid early to his blanket. Unused as he was to serious physical labour, the drovers' day left him totally exhausted. Each morning old Hatch's furious wake-up gong always came far too early. Phaid couldn't remember a time when sleep had meant so much to him.

Seven days into the drive Phaid started to feel that either he was becoming acclimatised to the life of a drover or else his brain had now reached a level of one-way numbness that could lead only to atrophy. He was ceasing to be able to imagine any other kind of life, and there were even moments of dull panic when he found himself examining the idea that maybe he was in sort of mobile hell.

It was on the seventh day, however, that they spotted the dust cloud on the horizon. At the back of the herd, Phaid and Makartur were among the last to know about it. It was only when old Thatch started shouting and hollering that they realised something unusual was happening.

Thatch had halted the transport bed and was standing up staring into the distance. Phaid swung the flipper in beside him.

'What is it?'

'Something moving out there.'

Phaid shaded his eyes against the sun and squinted in the direction that Thatch was pointing. A small eddy of dust swirled and danced. Whatever was causing the dust cloud was both small and a long way off. A week earlier, Phaid would have wondered what all the commotion was about. Seven days on trail, though, had taught him that even the slightest interruption in the monotonous routine was a thing to be savoured.

Other drovers pulled their machines over to the transport bed until there was a small group of them, hanging just above the ground, and speculating on what other people might be crossing the desert.

'It's too small for a crawler.'

'A crawler wouldn't be in this region. They stick close to their own routes.'

'It could be off course.'

'Crawlers don't go off course.'

'It ain't a crawler.'

'So what the hell is it?'

'How the hell should I know, dumb-bell?'

Shako skimmed up at high speed and slowed to a halt.

'Will you beauties get moving, the herd's starting to slow down. Back on the job, what do you think we're running here? A goddamn picnic?'

'There's something out there, boss.'

101

'I know there's something out there, damn you. I got eyes. It don't mean the whole drive's got to come to a halt.'

'Didn't we ought to check it out?'

'Sure we'll check it out, but we'll keep moving at the same time.'

He scanned the assembled drovers.

'Bork, Vooter, Goldring, Dick, Marris. Go see what that thing is. The rest of you, get back to work!'

The ones selected to inspect the dust clouds accelerated away, whooping and yelling. The others moved slowly back to their positions around the herd while Shako cursed them.

'Snap to it, you pieces of shit! I ain't losing time on account of you scumbags want to take time out to sightsee.'

Despite his constant harangue, the drovers' attention was still on the dust cloud. They merely went through the motions of running the veebes, keeping one eye on the horizon. They seemed to have an almost childish eagerness to find out what it was that moved out in the distance.

After what amounted to an intolerable wait, a flipper was spotted on its way back. Once again, almost half the drovers quit their positions and raced out to meet it. Shako roared around, swearing and threatening, but to little avail. There was no way he could get the drovers back to work until their curiosity had been satisfied. The herd slowed to a halt and everyone turned their machines to watch the returning flipper.

It was Bork who had brought back the news. He pulled up in front of Shako, throwing up a cloud of dust. His face was twisted into a grimace and his eyes seemed to have taken on a touch of madness.

'Elaihim! It's a party of stinking elaihim!'

A shout went up all around the herd. Even the veebes became nervous, snorting and stamping their feet. The drovers forgot all about their jobs, and milled around in angry disarray. They appeared to Phaid to be deliberately working themselves into an hysterical fury.

'Elaihim!'

'That offal's got to go!'

'Only good one's a dead one!'

Shako, still trying to retain some vestige of control, spun his flipper in front of Bork.

102

'How many of them are there?'

'Eight, maybe ten. They got a pair of small transport beds.'

Shako looked grim.

'What are the others doing?'

'Just riding around them, keeping them pinned down.'

'There's been no shooting?'

'Not yet. I think Marris may have jabbed a couple with his lance but there ain't been no shooting yet. They're waiting to hear from you.'

Shako seemed undecided. He stared out into the desert while Bork agitatedly jockeyed his flipper from side to side.

'We are going to get them, boss, ain't we? Huh? We are going to grease those swine!'

Shako took both hands off the controls of his flipper.

'Hold it, hold up there!'

His attempt at regaining the upper hand was little short of futile. Even as he spoke, the drovers were edging their machines towards the open desert. Makartur suddenly leaned forward and hissed in Phaid's ear.

'Move out, manny. Move out and then go like hell towards those elaihim.'

This took Phaid totally by surprise.

'What are you talking about?'

'I'm not going to stand by and watch a massacre.'

'You're crazy, there's nothing we can do about it!'

'We can try.'

Phaid resolutely took his hands off the controls of the flipper.

'Not a chance. I don't want any part of this. There's no way two of us can hold off between thirty and forty blood-crazed drovers. I'm sorry for the elaihim, but it's their problem and that's it.'

Makartur's voice suddenly turned soft and deadly.

'I'm not arguing with you, little man. Drive this thing and drive it fast.'

The drovers were already howling their way out towards the now growing dust cloud. Phaid folded his arms.

'And if I don't?'

'I have my blaster less than a hand's breadth from the back of your head. If you don't move this machine right now, I'll blow you away. Simple as that.'

'But . . .'

103

'Now it's your problem.'

Phaid dropped his hands to the controls and threw the flipper into foward motion. He turned it in the direction of the group of elaihim and then pushed the power wide open. He let the machine run as close to the ground as possible for maximum speed. Normally he wouldn't have attempted anything so foolhardy. A single rock could have wrecked them, but he no longer cared. Cold awful horror had him completely in its grip. He knew for sure that he must be driving to certain death, one way or another.

8

'Nobody's going to bother us until we get close to the elaihim. The other drovers will think that we're just racing to join in the fun.'

Makartur was yelling urgent instructions. Phaid didn't bother to answer. Sick with fear, he let the big man take complete control. He simply did as he was told, allowing the flipper to skim over the sand at top speed.

'If these drovers act true to form, they'll hang things out for a while. They'll circle the elaihim until they've got them thoroughly terrorised, then they'll go in for the kill.'

As they came nearer to the uneven confrontation, Phaid saw that what Makartur had said was correct. The small group of elaihim was huddled beside their two transport beds. These were heaped with an assortment of supplies and household goods. A loose ring of slow moving drovers on their flippers kept them pinned down in the one spot. Every so often, one would break from the circle and sweep by the elaihim in a close pass. The lanceman would stab at the tall angular figures. There'd be a scream as the victim reeled back from the shock. Designed to annoy a veebe, it was agonising to a human nervous system.

The drovers had one other trick. Taking potshots at the highly piled transport beds with their blasters, they could watch with glee as the elaihim tried desperately to put out the small fires this created, while at the same time doing their best to dodge the attacks by the lancemen.

The ring of drovers kept growing as more of them came

to join in. It was obvious that the murder of the elaihim was going to be a hideous, drawn out business. The drovers seemed bent on extracting every last possible measure of cruel enjoyment from the situation. Phaid could see exactly why Makartur felt so strongly that the business should be stopped. Where he revolted was at the idea that they had to be the ones who did the stopping. It was too late, however, to do anything about it. Makartur was once again leaning forward and yelling into his ear.

'The first thing we've got to do is break the circle.'

Phaid looked at the ring of drovers winding themselves up to the eventual frenzy of slaughter. They couldn't be stopped by just two men. It was nothing short of suicide.

Makartur pointed from behind Phaid's shoulder.

'There, that flipper coming round now. The one on the left with the bearded guy driving. You got it?'

Phaid nodded, but still didn't speak.

'Okay then. Swing up beside him. Make like you're joining the circle. At the last moment, swerve into him. Broadside his machine as hard as you can. He'll probably turn clean over. It'll snarl up the whole ring and give us time to get under cover by those transports. Then we can figure out our next move.'

Phaid cut their speed and moved up to the flipper that Makartur had pointed out. They began running alongside it. The bearded driver grinned and yelled something inaudible. He looked as though he was having the time of his life. Makartur tapped Phaid on the back.

'Now! Swing into him!'

Phaid took another look at the man. Again he grinned and gestured wolfishly, flashing a set of broken teeth. Phaid could feel sweat breaking out on the palms of his hands.

'I can't do it.'

'Swing into him, damn you!'

'I can't!'

'Now!'

'No!'

'Do it, manny, or . . .'

Phaid shut his eyes and spun the controls. There was a massive impact and shriek of twisting metal. Phaid found himself thrown violently sideways. For a second he was flying through the air. Then he hit the sand with a bone jarring thud.

Sick and dizzy, he staggered to his feet. Makartur's plan had worked out better than he could have imagined. The two flippers were little more than a mass of tangled metal. Even as he watched, a third and fourth ploughed into the wreckage. A chain reaction of lesser collisions started, as other drovers tried to dodge the pile up. The ordered menace of the closing circle was turned, for some minutes, into total chaos.

At first, Phaid could do nothing except stand dumbly, blinking at the confusion that he had helped to create. Then he saw the other driver, the bearded one who had been their first target, limping towards him, bleeding badly from a cut on his forehead.

'What did you go and do that for, you stupid bastard?'

The drover obviously still thought that the crash had been a genuine accident. Almost as an unthinking reflex, Phaid pulled out his fuse tube and burned the man down. Immediately after he had fired, a blaster roared four or five times in quick succession. Phaid jumped around, looking for the source of the sound. Makartur, with a weapon clutched in each hand, was backing towards the two machines of the elaihim, firing as he went. Seeing Phaid still not about to act, he waved with his gun.

'Get under cover, you damn fool! Get back to those transports!'

Phaid's instinct for self preservation snapped back into action. He was still alive. Quite how, he wasn't sure, but he was certainly going to do his best to stay that way. The confusion was starting to sort itself out. When Makartur had fired his first blast, the drovers had been left in no doubt that something was amiss. Many were crouching with drawn guns, wondering who the enemy was and where he was coming from.

A blaster was lying on the sand nearby. Presumably it had been dropped during the crash. Phaid scooped it up and started running directly towards where the elaihim were sheltering beside their transport beds.

Blaster fire threw up sand at his heels. He started zigzagging. At least one drover had realised part of what was going on.

A shallow gully ran between Phaid and the transports. Phaid made this his first objective. Lungs pumping and heart pounding, he ran like he had never run before. The air around him howled with the discharge from blasters.

Seemingly by a miracle, Phaid reached the gully. Without even looking, he dived into it and threw himself flat on to the ground.

To his surprise, he found himself lying next to a lanky elaihi male who was also pressing into the ground, trying to make himself as small a target as possible. Phaid had never been so close to an elaihi before, but it was neither the time nor the place to indulge his curiosity. He pushed the spare blaster towards the man.

'All hell's going to break loose now. You better use this.'

To Phaid's utter astonishment, the elaihi shook his head.

'No, I'm sorry. I can't use it.'

Phaid crawled closer.

'It's easy. Let me show you.'

Again he shook his head.

'I understand how to use the weapon. I can't, though. I can't take a life, another life.'

Phaid looked at him in blank amazement.

'Those bastards are going to take your life if you don't do something about it. Mine too, for that matter, and mine's pretty damn precious.'

'I can't, under any circumstances.'

Phaid closed his eyes.

'Sweet Lords!'

A sweep of blaster fire churned the lip of the gully. Without bothering to aim, or even raising his head, Phaid returned fire with both weapons. He shot the elaihi a venomous look.

'You bastards don't deserve saving. How the hell do you expect to survive if you won't defend yourselves?'

The elaihi regarded him with sad, pale blue eyes.

'I'm sorry.'

'That does me a lot of good.'

Phaid risked raising his head for the first time. The majority of the drovers had taken up positions among the various pieces of scooter debris. Two, however, were making what looked like an attacking run on a still serviceable flipper. This run was also headed exactly in Phaid's direction. Phaid squeezed off a snap shot at the drover and, to his own surprise, dropped him first time. The flipper ploughed straight into the ground and exploded as something in its power circuits cracked on impact. Phaid bit his lip and grinned.

'How about that.'

Immediately he had to hit the ground as a dozen or more blasters flashed. Phaid turned his head in appeal to the elaihi.

'If you won't fight, you could at least do something to make this gully a bit deeper. That can't be against your principles.'

'No, I can do that.'

'Then get digging, stupid. I thought you people were supposed to be smarter than us.'

'I will dig.'

'Just dandy.'

The elaihi dug while Phaid kept up a steady stream of fire with the blaster and his fuse tube. The drovers didn't seem in any hurry to attempt anything like a frontal attack on Phaid and Makartur. Grounding their flippers, they had taken cover and appeared, at least for the moment, to be simply exchanging fire. It wasn't too long before the elaihi had turned the section of the gully where he and Phaid lay into a rough but serviceable trench.

Finally a lull came in the fighting. Phaid suddenly heard Makartur's voice roaring from some distance behind him and a way off to the right.

'Hey! You drovers! We didn't ought to be doing each other like this. Go on back to your herd. Nobody needs to get killed over this.'

'You need to get killed, ape breath. We're going to get you swine if it's the last thing we do. If you love those dome heads so much you're going to die with them – as slow and painful as we can arrange.'

'You got to get us first.'

'We'll get you, don't worry about that!'

Discharges from a number of blasters put the final punctuation to this chillingly delivered promise. Phaid fired back, but nothing happened. The drovers seemed quite happy to sit still and bide their time. Phaid couldn't quite understand how both he and Makartur had avoided being hit. It was almost as though something was mysteriously throwing off the drovers' aim.

It wasn't long before Phaid started to notice that his mouth was becoming uncomfortably hot and dry. He tried to speak, but found that all he could come up with was a rasping croak.

'You don't have any water, do you?'

The elaihi once again shook his head and looked sorrowful.

'I don't.'

'Just great.'

'We elaihim can go for long periods without either food or water. It's one of the results of our ability to control our metabolism.'

'Screw your metabolism.'

'I'm sorry.'

'So am I. I'm the one who's going to die of thirst.'

'There is water back on our transports. I could get it if you want.'

'You'd do that?'

'Of course.'

Phaid, despite his thirst, was reluctant to ask the elaihi to risk climbing out of the trench.

'I hate to do this, but I won't last too long in this sun if I don't get any.'

'I will go.'

Before Phaid could say anything else, the elaihi had rolled out of the trench and was running in a low crouch towards the two transports. The movement produced a flurry of fire. Phaid prayed that this act of courage wouldn't be the elaihi's last.

He was a long time in returning, and Phaid was just about ready to give him up for dead when, in a second eruption of fire from the drovers, he rolled back into the gully, clutching a clear plastic container filled with water. The elaihi handed it to Phaid with a smile.

'Here.'

'Thanks.'

Phaid drank gratefully and then slowly wiped his mouth.

'Sweet mercy, I needed that.'

'You feel better now?'

'Yeah, much. Are your people okay?'

'Two have been killed, I'm afraid.'

'That's too bad.'

'The others are unharmed. You and your companion seemed to be keeping the herdsmen at bay for the moment.'

Phaid looked curiously at the elaihi. There was something disturbingly cold and unemotional about him. Phaid

110

had to remind himself that there wasn't even any reason to believe that the elaihim were human. It had to be expected that they'd be very different.

'Do you have a name?'

'Of course. We all have names.'

Aside from being unemotional, this elaihi, at least, had a terrible tendency to take everything very, very literally.

'So what's yours?'

'Rathyaal.'

'Rathyaal?'

'That's right.'

'Mine's Phaid.'

'Now we have exchanged names.'

Phaid gave up trying to understand the elaihi.

'I guess we have.'

The long hot desert afternoon dragged on and still the drovers didn't seem anxious to make a move. Occasionally they'd fire on Phaid's or Makartur's position, or yell threats and taunts, but the rush that Phaid had been expecting ever since he'd first rolled into the gully failed to materialise. Gradually the shadows began to lengthen.

'They're going to have to make their move soon. It'll be sunset before too long and their flippers will stop working.'

'It's almost time for us to take a hand. You have bought us some very valuable time . . . Phaid.'

'Huh?'

'You have bought us valuable time.'

'What the hell are you talking about?'

'I can't explain right now. It's almost time.'

'You mean you're actually going to do something?'

'I can't explain now.'

Phaid took a quick look over the side of the trench.

'Whatever it is that you've got in mind, you better do it damn quick. I think the drovers are getting ready to pull something.'

'Please be silent.'

Phaid's temper abruptly gave out. He swung around on the elaihi with anger boiling out of him. The sight of Rathyaal stopped him dead. The elaihi had folded his arms and legs into a seemingly impossible position. His eyes were tightly shut and sweat was streaming down his face. As far as Phaid could see, he was in the grip of some sort of seizure. Phaid's imagination cast around for an explanation. Surely the elaihi couldn't be going into a self created suicide.

'If you are, you picked a damn fine time.'

In among the wreckage there was now something definitely happening. The furtive movements had stepped up, and it looked as though the drovers were finally preparing for the rush. Phaid let go a couple of shots and then ducked as twice the number came back. He took another glance at the elaihi. His normally pallid face had turned quite grey. Veins twitched all over his forehead as though there were worms beneath the skin struggling to get out.

A loud yell went up from the drovers. They had started to move. A line of crouching figures were crawling quickly towards Phaid's position. Using both his weapons, Phaid fired as fast as he could, but, in their sheer weight of numbers, the drovers had the advantage. The whole rim of the gully became a target for their blasters and Phaid was forced to huddle at the bottom. He knew that the end must come very soon, and there was absolutely nothing he could do about it. On one level, it was almost a relief. At least he didn't have to be afraid much longer.

He took a final look at Rathyaal and was surprised to find that the elaihi had fallen over on to his side and was gasping like a fish out of water. At first Phaid assumed that he'd been hit, but then he noticed that there was no sign of a wound.

There was no time, though, to worry about Rathyaal. The drovers were coming up fast. Phaid tried a few more shots and then once again was forced to cower in the bottom of the trench. He knew that any moment the drovers would come storming over the edge and that would be it. He wondered how much being killed by a blaster would hurt. Was death really the end of everything? It all seemed so futile. He'd spent a lifetime hustling and struggling, watching angles and trying to get an edge. If he'd known that it was going to end like this he would have done it all very differently. His blood felt as though it had turned to ice, and then the firing stopped.

The shouting of the drovers changed in tone. Rathyaal started to move. He seemed to be trying to say something.

'They're running.'

'What?'

'The beasts are running.'

The new developments were too much for Phaid. He risked a look over the edge of the trench and found that the drovers were dashing back towards the flippers that were still intact. Phaid slowly got to his feet. One of the drovers turned and aimed a final, wildly inaccurate shot at him.

'We'll be back to get you, you bastard. Just you see if we don't!'

Then he continued running for his flipper. In the distance, where the herd had been, something was churning up a huge cloud of dust. Still clutching his weapons, he let his arms drop to his sides.

'Will somebody tell me what the hell is going on?'

9

'IT WAS very hard.'

'I can imagine.'

'No, I don't think you could really imagine. I don't think you would be able to visualise exactly what it was like.'

Phaid was quickly discovering that the elaihim had a rather obnoxious streak of superior-to-thou. On the surface they sounded kindly but beneath there was a strata of contempt. It got on his nerves, but he didn't make any comment. He was at least getting the explanation that he'd waited half the night for. Makartur, however, who hadn't witnessed the violent spasms that had gripped Rathyaal at the climax of the fight with the drovers, was scratching his beard and attempting to put what he'd been told into some kind of manageable form.

'Let me get this straight. You're telling me that all of your group went into some sort of trance . . .'

'Trance is a purely human capability.'

Makartur grunted. 'It'll do for me.'

It was plain that the elaihim were also causing him some degree of irritation.

'You went into this trance, or call it what you want, and you set up a mental link with the veebes in the herd.'

Once again Rathyaal couldn't curb his need for strict accuracy in just about ever detail.

'In fact, we only formed a link with specific individuals within the herd, but otherwise you are broadly correct.'

Phaid nodded slowly and for a long time. It was almost

impossible to tell whether he was being ultra deferential or simply ironic.

'I'm obliged to you. May I go on?'

'Please do.'

'You formed these links with some of the beasts and told them to start running.'

'That is a painfully simplistic explanation.'

'I thought it might be.'

'The veebe, having been selectively bred by your people over many thousands of years, simply for its weight of edible flesh . . .' Rathyaal permitted himself a faint grimace of distaste '. . . is a particularly neurotic and paranoid being.'

Makartur laughed. 'They were paranoid before us humans had anything to do with them. You'd be paranoid too, if half the carnivores in the world thought of you as dinner.'

Phaid was faintly surprised by the way that Makartur was able to laugh, relax and even jest with the elaihim and not in the least intimidated by their more than human capabilities.

This time Rathyaal allowed himself a faint smile.

'That is very true. My people have an unforgivable habit of blaming you humans for all the ills of the world.'

Everything about the elaihim seemed to be faint. It was almost as though a large part of them was really in some other plane or dimension, one from which humans were excluded. He nibbled on a small sliver of a dried leaf that, judging from the meal that had been put in front of them, was the mainstay of the elaihim diet. It was only after a great deal of chewing that Phaid detected the slightest hint of a flavour. The elaihim appeared to move through a world of both tastes and ideas that were too delicate and subtle for a human being to either share or understand.

While Phaid covertly examined the elaihim, Rathyaal went on with his story.

'The mind of the herd veebe is a painful place to even visit. It is a disorganised conflict of fear, vindictiveness, anger and an awful stubborness. It is easy to introduce feelings of panic and hysteria, but it requires a massive effort to overcome the stubbornness. Even though we gave it all our concentration, it almost exhausted our resources. It was only at the very last minute that they finally ran.'

Phaid nodded. 'You can say that again.'

Rathyaal raised an almost non-existent eyebrow.

'Is that really necessary?'

'It's a figure of speech.'

Phaid realised that he was being mocked. He didn't quite know what to do so he blundered on.

'You can tell me one thing, though.'

'If I can.'

'Why did you leave it so long? I mean, you could have run the herd any time that you wanted to. Why did you wait until the very end of the day?'

'I would have thought that was obvious.'

'It sure as hell wasn't obvious when I was sweating my way through the afternoon, expecting to be killed at any moment.'

'If we had started running the herd any earlier, it would have been possible for the drovers to stop them before the sun had set and their machines ceased to operate. They might have been able to come back and kill us. That is why we decided to delay this action until just a short time before sunset.'

Phaid suddenly grew angry.

'We only made it to sundown by sheer luck. It was a miracle we weren't killed.'

'It was a risk. I'll admit that.'

'No shit? You'll admit that. That's really big of you.'

Phaid was up on his feet.

'You bastards really take the prize, don't you? We risk our lives trying to save your asses and you start treating us like dirt under your feet. Where do you swine get off? It ain't no wonder the drovers wanted to grease the lot of you. They were probably right!'

Makartur stood up too, in an attempt to keep the peace.

'You're going to far, manny. These people are our hosts.'

'And we're their fucking saviours!'

Rathyaal spread his hands in an apologetic gesture. 'I didn't mean to give offence.'

'Well, you managed it just the same.'

Phaid stalked away from where the group was talking and marched out into the desert. He reached the gully. The ground was still pockmarked and scorched from the afternoon's fighting. The sight only served to make him even angrier.

'Bastards! Fucking bastards!'

'They-can-be-very-hard-to-deal-with-but-you-shouldn't-hold-their-manner-against-them. They-don't-see-things-in-quite-the-same-way-as-you-do.'

Phaid started like a rabbit at the voice. He swung round and found himself facing a short android. It was about half Phaid's height and roughly humanoid in shape. It had a blue grey metallic finish and was regarding Phaid with pinkish, palely glowing sensors, positioned in roughly the same place as human eyes.

'The-fact-has-to-be-faced-that-elaihim-and-humans-simply-don't-get-along. There-are-a-few-exceptions-but-not-many.'

Phaid wasn't ready to cool off.

'They just make me feel so damned inferior.'

'From-their-point-of-view-you-probably-are.'

Phaid felt an urge to punch the android, but he knew that all that would achieve was a hurt fist.

'Don't you start.'

'I-never-take-sides-in-disputes-between-organic-lifeforms-I-find-it-saves-me-a-lot-of-trouble.'

Phaid nodded. 'Very sensible.'

'That's-what-I've-found.'

'Do you belong to the elaihim?'

'I-don't-belong-to-anyone. I-am-what-is-known-as-a-mendicant-android.'

'I'm sorry.'

'That's-okay-I-don't-have-the-circuitry-to-take-offence.'

'So what's a mendicant android?'

'One-who-no-longer-has-a-purpose. One-who-wanders-from-place-to-place-in-search-of-truth-and-enlightenment.'

'That's what you do?'

'Most-of-the-time.'

'It sounds kind of lonely.'

'On-the-contrary. I-quite-enjoy-myself-although-there-are-times-when-I-think-I'd-be-happier-if-I-had-something-useful-to-do-with-my-time.'

Phaid found that he was becoming quite intrigued with the little android. It was certainly better company than the elaihim. He sat down on the sand and wrapped his arms around his knees.

'How come you don't have a job to do? I thought all

androids did.'

'I-imagine-I-must-have-had-one-once-that's-if-you-subscribe-to-what-we-androids-like-to-call-the-manufactured-to-function-theory-of-our-origins.'

Phaid looked blank.

'What?'

'Without-wishing-to-sound-like-an-elaihi-it's-probable-that-I-once-had-a-job-but-you-humans-have-forgotten-what-it-was.'

'Forgotten?'

'A-lot-of-us-androids-were-designed-to-do-things-that-no-longer-happen. One-thing-we-know-for-sure-is-that-there's-a-lot-less-going-on-in-the-world-than-there-used-to-be.'

Phaid nodded. 'I once saw a place that looked like a factory. It was out in the hills. Every morning all these machines came out, and every night they'd be taken in again. Nobody I ever heard of knew what it was there for.'

'This-was-the-building-in-the-hills-behind-Gant?'

'That's the place. You've been there?'

'No-but-I've-been-told-about-it.'

'Did they know what it was for?'

'The-matter-wasn't-discussed.'

The android didn't seem to want to give a straight answer and Phaid was too tired to pursue it. Instead, he yawned.

'It's been a rough day. I think I'd better see about getting myself a little sleep.'

'Perhaps-a-quantity-of-brandy-might-aid-that.'

Phaid looked intently at the little android.

'Brandy?'

'The-elaihim-have-a-small-cask-among-their-cargo-they-use-it-for-barter-with-the-humans.'

'The hell they do!' Phaid hesitated. 'Aren't they going to object if we just help ourselves to it?'

'I-think-they-consider-what's-theirs-is-also-ours.'

'Are you sure?'

'Of-course-I'm-sure-I-don't-have-the-circuits-to-make-rash-and-misleading-statements.'

Phaid stood up.

'Let's go then.'

Phaid followed the android back towards the elaihim transport. He leaned against the machine while the android loosened the cargo webbing and rummaged around inside.

'Do you have a name?'

'A-long-time-ago-some-humans-started-calling-me-Ben-e-and-to-a-degree-it-stuck.'

Ben-e emerged from the transport clutching a small brass-bound cask in both arms.

'Here-is-the-brandy.'

He produced a rather delicate china bowl and filled it from the cask's spigot. He handed it to Phaid, who swirled the golden liquid between his cupped hands, sniffed deeply and then took an experimental sip. It was very fine brandy. Phaid grinned at Ben-e the android.

'I suppose there ain't much point in offering you some of this.'

'Not-really.'

'Maybe I should go tell Makartur.'

'That-would-be-a-companionable-act.'

Phaid walked around the transport. The elaihim seemed to have finally retired. Makartur was sitting staring into the embers of the small fire that he'd built. He looked up as Phaid came into the dim pool of light.

'What's up with you, manny?'

'Brandy, that's what.'

'Brandy. You're joshing me!'

Phaid held out the bowl.

'Taste that.'

Makartur tasted.

'Sweet mother earth! That's the real stuff. Where the hell did you get it?'

Phaid called out. 'Hey, Ben-e! Come over here and bring the cask.'

'I'm-coming.'

'Who was that?'

'It's Ben-e.'

'I know that much.'

Ben-e appeared in the firelight. In addition to the cask he was carrying a second bowl and a pair of blankets. Makartur regarded the android curiously.

'Well, well, what have we here? A wee machine person.'

'A-mendicant-android-to-be-precise.'

'Well now, and you be travelling with the elaihim?'

'That's-correct.'

'It's a wonderous world.'

'Truly-wonderous.'

Ben-e handed Makartur his bowl and then spread the blankets on the ground.

'I-thought-you-might-want-these.'

'That's very thoughtful of you.'

'Some-habits-die-very-hard.'

'Taking care of humans?'

'Something-like-that.'

Phaid and Makartur rolled the blankets around themselves and lay sipping their brandy. Ben-e suddenly dropped into a rough approximation of a squatting position.

'I-think-I-am-going-to-disengage-until-daylight.'

With that, the lights of his eye/sensors went out and he became quite motionless. Phaid stretched.

'I don't think a spot of disengaging would do me any harm.'

He closed his eyes and almost immediately fell asleep.

The morning dawned bright and clear. This was to be expected in the rainless desert. By the time that Phaid awoke, the elaihim were already up and moving around, as was Ben-e the android. While Phaid was dusting himself down and folding his blanket, he surprised himself by whistling happily. He almost never whistled. His cheerfulness was close to euphoric. Phaid felt this state of mind was so unnatural that he started to wonder if the elaihim were using some sort of mood control on him. Makartur, too, was a picture of sunny joviality. If the elaihim were actually getting inside their minds, Phaid knew that he ought to resent it, but somehow he wasn't able to.

Before he could think about the problem any more, Phaid was approached by a female elaihi who smiled and indicated that food was being served on the other side of the transport.

'Once you've finished eating, we have to discuss what your plans are.'

'I suppose we do.'

Phaid found that he wasn't able to actually worry about what would happen next. He noticed that he couldn't help grinning like an idiot.

'I must confess I hadn't given it much thought.'

'Why don't you eat first and then we can talk about it.'

'Do you mind me asking something?'

'Of course not.'

120

'Which one are you? I know I was introduced to you all yesterday, but . . .'

'But we all look alike?'

'Well . . .'

'I am Isaen.'

'Isaen?'

'Why don't you eat now and we'll talk later.'

Phaid still felt as though he was being manipulated, but he was hungry, so he made his way to the temporary kitchen. Breakfast consisted of the same leaves that he'd had the night before, plus some small whitish doughy balls and a bowl of a warm pale pink cordial. Once again they seemed to lack anything that Phaid could recognise as flavour.

The meal did, however, give him a chance to study the elaihim for the first time in something approaching normal surroundings. There was no denying that they had it over the human race in a number of ways. There was a grace about them, even when they were going about the simplest of tasks, that made mankind look like a species of knuckle trailing apes. Apart from their slight build, there was something insubstantial and ethereal about them. Their almost bleached white skins and pale short tunics gave them a uniform quality, as though any trace of individuality had been completely sublimated.

Even their faces were stamped from the same mould, without the distinguishing characteristics that separated one human from another. Sexual differences were also minimal. The females were slightly shorter than the males, although still taller than all but the tallest of men. Only a pair of high, tiny vestigal breasts really distinguished one sex from the other among the elaihim.

Phaid couldn't see why so many people believed that the elaihim were descended from humans. If he had been told that they had arrived secretly from a star one night, he would have had less reason to doubt.

The meeting to decide what was to be done about Makartur and Phaid took place directly after breakfast. The elaihim group was represented by Rathyaal, Isaen and another female called Shethir. It was obvious from the start that the presence of the two men was having a disturbing effect on the elaihim as they were willing to make a considerable effort to speed Phaid and Makartur on their way.

The elaihim's idea of a discussion was a little one-sided. They started off by virtually interrogating the two men about how they came to be with the drovers, what their eventual destination was and what ideas they had about how they were going to get there. Once they had listened, they seemed to ignore any suggestions that the humans had made and began debating the matter among themselves. Phaid again had the feeling that he should be upset, if not furious, but for some reason the emotions just wouldn't come.

The elaihim's best solution seemed to be that they should take one of the serviceable flippers and head towards the nearest town. Rathyaal even began to plot their course for them.

'You would be well advised to avoid the trails that lead to Chasabad.'

Phaid found himself nodding like a mental retard.

'That's sensible.'

'Chasabad would be the shortest route to the Republic, I admit, but the risk of running into the drovers again would be too great. I therefore think it would be better if you made for Fennella.'

Phaid once again automatically smiled and nodded, but Makartur didn't seem quite so easily persuaded.

'It's twice the distance to Fennella.'

'That's true, but once you get there you are at the line head.'

'Aye man, but we've got no money, so a line ride's no good to us.'

Shethir's expression became slightly regretful.

'We do not use money and thus we have none to give you.'

Makartur looked troubled.

'I suppose we might work something out when we get there, what we will need, though, are provisions and water. As you well know, those flippers don't travel by night, so it'll be a few days to make Fennella.'

It was Isaen's turn to use the slightly regretful expression.

'That's presents another problem. Our supplies are very limited. We barely have enough for our own needs.'

Black anger suddenly burst through Phaid's previously sunny disposition.

'Just wait a minute here. Less than a day ago my . . .'

122

All three elaihim fixed Phaid with the same stony penetrating gaze. The anger in him slowly froze into dark, tiny crystals. They in turn quickly vanished as the sunshine returned. Phaid was grinning again. He couldn't even remember what he'd been talking about.

Ben-e, who'd been standing apart from the conversation but listening intently, suddenly buzzed briskly into the middle of it.

'I-think-I-might-possibly-have-the-solution-to-these-problems.'

Both humans and elaihim looked surprised.

'You do?'

'I-have-examined-the-wreckage-of-the-drovers'-machines-and-I-estimate-that-there-are-more-than-enough-parts-to-construct-a-very-much-more-powerful-flipper-that-would-be-able-to-carry-three-of-us-to-the-line-head-in-no-more-than-a-day-and-a-half.'

'Three of us?'

'Would-you-allow-me-to-continue?'

'Sure.'

'Thus-you-elaihim-would-not-have-to-give-the-humans-so-great-a-quantity-of-supplies. There-is-also-the-matter-of-money-for-the-line-ride!'

Phaid looked up sharply.

'You can do something about money?'

'We-androids-also-have-little-use-for-money-but-unlike-the-elaihim-we-are-able-to-obtain-it-when-it-is-needed. I-can-guarantee-that-I-will-be-able-to-contact-my-people-and-obtain-all-the-money-that-you-would-need-once-we-reach-Fennella.'

Phaid could hardly believe his ears. The elaihim, if it indeed was the elaihim that were affecting his mind, seemed to have relaxed their grip, and he was thinking a little more clearly.

'Are you seriously telling us that you can go to a strange android in Fennella and it will give you money?'

'Quite-seriously.'

'What a system.'

'It-serves.'

Makartur also had a question.

'You want to travel with us to Fennella?'

'All-the-way-to-the-Republic-if-you-don't-have-any-objections.'

Makartur didn't say anything and Phaid shot him a

sideways glance.

'You don't have any objection, do you?'

Makartur slowly shook his head.

'No, let the wee bag of tricks ride with us if he wants to.'

Rathyaal rose to his feet.

'It would seem that everything is settled.'

He looked down at Ben-e the android.

'If we can give you any assistance in fitting out your machine . . .'

'I-will-need-a-good-deal-of-assistance-but-first-there-is-one-final-thing-that-I-must-settle-with-the-humans.'

Makartur muttered under his breath.

'Here comes the catch.'

Phaid gave the android a narrow, gambler's stare.

'What is it?'

'When-we-reach-the-Republic-I-will-require-a-favour. I-can-not-tell-you-what-it-is-right-at-this-moment-but-I-assure-you-that-it-will-neither-be-difficult-nor-time-consuming. I-must-however-have-your-word-that-one-of-you-will-perform-it-for-me-before-we-can-start-on-this-journey.'

Makartur raised a questioning eyebrow.

'How can we promise to do this favour if we don't know what it is?'

'It-will-not-be-difficult.'

'Aye, but . . .'

Phaid quickly interrupted.

'Whatever it is, you got it. I'd do pretty much anything for someone who can get me back to the Republic.'

Makartur scowled disapprovingly.

'On your head be it.'

'Ain't it always?'

'Then-I-think-we-can-start-on-the-construction-of-this-modified-flipper-right-away.'

Although Phaid and Makartur hung around and did their best to look as though they were contributing to the work, the real conversion of the flipper was carried out by Ben-e and the elaihim. In a surprisingly short time they had loaded up the supplies and were on their way. Once the journey had started, Phaid noticed that the further he got from the influence of the elaihim, the more mixed his feelings became. The plus side was that he was moving again. He was riding out of the boondocks and heading back towards civilisation with some speed and style. If

Ben-e the android didn't pull some weird electronic double cross, he was going all the way back to the Republic without any more trouble. He didn't expect the android to go back on his word. Machines didn't usually lie, and if you couldn't trust an android, who could you trust? Suspicion was, however, a habit that died hard.

There was also a minus side. Somehow, the elaihim had managed to leave a very bad taste in his mouth. He had started out totally sympathetic to the strange, solitary people but, after this first real encounter with them, he found that he disliked them with an intensity that came close to the drovers' ignorant prejudice. The more he thought about it, the more he felt as though his personality and his freewill had been violated, raped almost. He'd been used, manipulated and coldly exploited by them. He was almost certain that, in some way he didn't clearly understand, they had temporarily pre-empted his control over his own mind and his own emotions. The whole episode had left him feeling weak and inferior. He had asked the android about it and although Ben-e was his usual oblique self, he as good as confirmed Phaid's thoughts.

'When-humans-come-in-contact-with-elaihim-nothing-is-ever-as-it-appears. You-can't-even-try-to-be-objective-with-those-beings. They-are-masters-of-wheels-within-wheels-within-wheels.'

The remark was cryptic enough to start Phaid thinking. The elaihim presented him with a procession of unanswered questions that seemed to stretch back to infinity. Phaid's mind went around and around. There was the first and obvious general questions. What was the truth behind the legends of the elaihim. Were they, as some people claimed, the mutant descendants of the human race, children of man who had managed to make a great evolutionary leap, or had they come from some other place, alien intruders stranded and wandering in a world that was not their own. There were, however, more specific, disturbing questions arising out of the encounter, questions that kept nagging at Phaid all through the journey across the desert. Just how long had the super people had a grip on his mind? If they could control the veebes from a distance, maybe they had attempted to turn back the drovers and failed. Could it be that they had scanned the assembled human minds looking for someone crazy enough to act as their saviour?

If they had fixed on Makartur, and his suicidal plunge to the elaihim's rescue wasn't a quixotic gesture but a result of mind control, then Phaid saw a hundred yawning chasms opening in front of him. The idea that the elaihim could take over the freewill of any human who was close to them and make them dance to their tune like so many puppets was a sorry prospect for his species.

At that point Phaid's brain dropped through to another level. Just how far did elaihim take their manipulations? To what extent did they dabble in human affairs? Phaid put some of these questions to Ben-e but, true to form, the android's replies were polite but non-committal to the point of being totally unhelpful.

'It's-always-disconcerting-for-a-species-to-find-that-it-is-no-longer-top-of-the-heap.'

Phaid felt a chill run through him when he heard those words. He had never in his life thought of himself as part of a species. He liked to believe that he owed little or nothing to the rest of humanity, but the chill was there all the same. Men had never been particularly kind to what they considered inferior species. There was little reason to think that the elaihim would behave differently. He wasn't going to be able to forget the android's words.

'It's-always-disconcerting-for-a-species-to-find-that-it-is-no-longer-top-of-the-heap.'

'But what do they want with us? Do they really want to stay separate and avoid all contact?'

'That-is-what-they-claim.'

'Yeah, but is it true?'

'I-have-not-had-that-many-chances-to-observe-the-behaviour-of-the-elaihim-but-from-my-limited-experience-I-would-say-that-the-majority-of-them-would-wish-to-avoid-all-contacts-with-mankind. There-are-exceptions.'

'Exceptions?'

'There-is-Solchaim-for-example.'

'Solchaim?'

'I-thought-you-had-spent-time-in-the-Republic.'

'I have, but I never heard of anyone called Solchaim.'

'According-to-the-latest-rumours-he-is-the-most-influential-advisor-of-Life-President-Chrystiana-Nex.'

Phaid didn't like the sound of this at all.

'Are you telling me that the Republic has fallen into the

126

hands of an elaihi?'

'No.'

'So?'

'So-there-are-simply-rumours-that-an-elaihi-may-now-be-the-power-behind-the-throne-in-the-Republic.'

'And that's all you've got to say about it?'

As usual, Ben-e the android seemed unperturbed.

'What-else-should-I-have-to-say? I'm-an-android. It's-no-paint-off-my-back.'

'But if this goes on, the elaihim could take over the world.'

'Like-I-said-it-is-going-to-be-hard-to-come-to-terms-with-them.'

'Something should be done about it.'

'Yes?'

'Yeah.'

'Are-you-saying-that-the-drovers-had-the-right-idea?'

'No, of course not, but . . .'

'They-wanted-to-wipe-out-the-elaihim. Do-you-have-a-better-idea?'

'No, but . . .'

'Think-about-it.'

If it hadn't been for thinking about it, the journey to Fennella would have been a very pleasant interlude. Ben-e seemed quite happy to do all the driving and Phaid and Makartur were more than prepared to let him. The android did have the unfortunate habit of constantly exhibiting that he was able to drive with total high speed precision and hold bright, witty and thought-provoking conversations at the same time. It didn't matter too much, though. Makartur was asleep for almost the whole day and a half and Phaid was paranoid.

So paranoid in fact, that by the time they reached the grasslands that meant they were only a few hours from Fennella, Phaid was wondering if Makartur's long sleep was actually a result of the elaihim being inside his brain for so long. Another idea also occurred to him. If an elaihi was wielding power in the Republic, he ought, somehow, to be able to profit from actually having met a whole tribe of the creatures out in the wilds. So little was known about them, his observations ought to be worth something. He probably would have spent even more hours wrestling with this mass of problems created by the elaihim except he was interrupted by the world of men when the first and tallest spires of Fennella became visible on the horizon.

Phaid knew Fennella was just another town that only existed because it was halfway between one place and another but, in that first moment, it was beautiful. Phaid saw it as a golden road. Fennella was the start of the direct path straight back to the real world, the restaurants, the shaded lights, stained-glass over green baize tables, women in expensive gowns playing seemingly expensive games that were at root primitively simple, even bars where the bartender bothered to remember your name. It was the road to where sleight of hand counted for something and style was everything. Phaid was suddenly very happy.

In itself, Fennella was nothing much to get excited about. It had once hired a good architect with a passion for narrow, conical towers, but although he had made the town beautiful to look at from a distance, he had failed to lift the inhabitants from the base bourgeois. They had the narrow, self-protecting, small town outlook that welcomed strangers as long as they kept moving and had no intention of staying around. Their outlook was reinforced by the whipping post, the gallows, the public stocks and an efficient, if bribable, squad of town rangers.

None of this bothered Phaid, however. All they had to do was dispose of the rebuilt flipper, let Ben-e the android scare up some money and make their way to the line terminal. It was all so straightforward and easy. He didn't see how either he, Makartur or the android could get into any trouble during that short time.

As they drove slowly through the congested streets of central Fennella, the flipper drew a lot of curious glances. Out in the desert the hybrid flipper had been useful and functional. In the town, it stood out like a sore thumb among the sleek, well cared for machines of the citizens.

The stares of the townspeople were nothing compared with the looks they received when Ben-e swung the machine into Honest Nazim's Used Transport Lot.

Nazim was an olive skinned, paunchy individual on to whom spurious bonhomie seemingly had been applied with a trowel. This forced joviality fell away with alarming speed when he was confronted with the jerry rigged flipper, complete with its blaster burns, sand scoured bodywork and the raw marks on the frame from the crude welding jobs that held it together.

Planting his hands on his hips and almost blocking the entrance to the lot, he looked at the vehicle and its occupants with nothing short of disgust.

'What the hell do you call this mess? You ain't planning on bringing it in here, are you?'

Phaid jumped down and confronted the used flipper dealer.

'Sure we want to come in here. We aim to sell this unique vehicle.'

Nazim let out a short barking laugh that was devoid of humour.

'Sell that thing? You ought to give me money to break it up for you.'

Phaid turned and looked at the flipper.

'You got to be blind. This is a custom built desert flyer. There's not another one like it in the world.'

Nazim sniffed.

'That's a fact.'

Phaid ignored him.

'It's got to be one of the fastest things in rough country. It made it from Wad-Hasa Wells to here in less than three days.'

Nazim looked as though he didn't believe a word of it.

'How much do you want for the heap?'

Phaid became very indignant.

'Heap, heap?'

It didn't work.

'Cut out the crap and tell me how much you want for it.'

Phaid stared Nazim straight in the eye.

'Six thousand.'

Nazim fell about.

'Six thousand?'

'Six thousand.'

'I'll tell you what I'll do, I'll give you six hundred off the listed price of any flipper on the lot, and if anybody betters that offer I'll stand on my head and eat a bug.'

'We don't want another flipper. We're getting on the line. All we want to do is sell the machine and move on.'

Nazim held up a pudgy hand.

'Wait just a minute. You don't actually expect me to hand over hard cash for that thing.'

'Three thousand?'

'I tell you what I'll do. If you throw in the android I'll give you seven hundred cash.'

129

Ben-e sprang down from the flipper.

'I'll-have-you-know-that-I-am-not-for-sale.'

Nazim sneered.

'An uppity robot.'

'Listen-you . . .'

Phaid quickly stepped between the android and the used flipper dealer.

'Hold up there. Let's not make a big thing out of this. How much will you give us for the machine in hard cash?'

Nazim gave the machine a contemptuous once over.

'Three hundred.'

'Eight.'

'Three hundred.'

'That's your best offer?'

'It is.'

Phaid sighed.

'Yeah, well, I guess we'll have to take it. We're in a hurry.'

Nazim summoned an assistant and the flipper was driven away. Nazim went off to get their money. Makartur, who'd kept out of the haggling, sauntered over and looked enquiringly at Phaid.

'How much did we get?'

'Three hundred.'

'Three hundred? I thought that you were the shrewd gambling man.'

Phaid closed his eyes.

'Don't you start.'

'Yeah, but three hundred, manny. I call that pathetic.'

'It's all profit. We didn't pay for the thing.'

This time is was Ben-e who stepped in to keep the peace.

'This-is-all-pointless. We-need-not-be-concerned-about-money. I-would-rather-get-away-from-this-place. I-don't-like-people-who-call-me-a-robot.'

They collected the three hundred from Nazim and then, with Ben-e leading them, they walked across town. Ben-e stopped the first android they met, a street corner soft drink vendor. For a short while they whistled and squeaked at each other in the android's private, electronic language and then Ben-e turned to the two humans.

'This-excellent-being-has-told-me-where-I-may-obtain-an-adequate-sum-of-money-for-our-journey. It-is-not-far-from-here-so-if-you'll-follow-me . . .'

They left the street vendor marching up and down on short, stubby legs and followed Ben-e down a side street. After a walk that involved twisting and turning down a series of increasingly narrow streets, they arrived at a small building that sported a rather battered sign that read TECHNICAL REPAIRS. Ben-e hammered on the peeling paint of the front door.

At first no one answered, but after a long time the door was swung back a crack, and a small android peered out. It was even shorter than Ben-e, little more than a metal box with an antenna on the top, a single sensor lens mounted on the end and thin, tubular legs holding it up. There was another whistling, tweeting conversation, then Ben-e turned and faced the two men.

'You'd-better-wait-out-here. These-guys-are-a-little-nervous-of-humans.'

Phaid and Makartur looked at each other and shrugged.

'Suit yourself, we'll wait.'

Ben-e disappeared inside, and the two men assumed lounging positions against the wall. Makartur jerked his thumb towards the door.

'You trust that bucket of bolts?'

'Who? Ben-e?'

'Who else?'

Phaid made a non-committal gesture.

'Why not?'

'He's an android.'

'So?'

'I don't know. I never feel comfortable around androids.'

Phaid laughed.

'That's rich.'

'What's that supposed to mean?'

'Well shit, here's you, the man who was so damn thick with the elaihim, telling me that he don't feel comfortable "round androids".'

'I was never thick with the elaihim.'

'You were too.'

'Shit.'

'Shit yourself. You were quite prepared to get you and me killed to save them. You killed a whole bunch of drovers, you, a man who has drovers for relatives.'

Makartur tugged at his beard.

'It's funny. I've been wondering about that myself.

Something came over me.'

'Yeah, something came over you.'

'Huh?'

'Nothing.'

Phaid didn't feel it was the moment to start expounding his theories about the elaihim, so the conversation lapsed there. They leaned for a while, just happy to be in a town after so many days in the desert. Then Makartur nudged Phaid in the ribs with his elbow.

'Don't look now, but here comes the local law.'

Phaid slowly turned his head and took a covert look up the street. Sure enough, two characters in tight, dark blue suits and pale blue helmets were sauntering towards them, doing tricks with long batons. Phaid nodded.

'Law, as sure as I saw them.'

'I got to tell you, I never could see eye to eye with the law.'

Phaid sniffed.

'Me neither. You think we're doing anything illegal?'

Makartur grimaced.

'Who can tell in a place like this?'

'We'll find out pretty damn soon. Here they come.'

The two law officers halted in front of Phaid and Makartur. With studied insolence they looked the pair up and down. Phaid and Makartur did their best to appear unconcerned.

Fennella obviously took great pride in its guardians of law and order. The town certainly spent of lot of money on them. Their suits were neat, one piece affairs, reinforced with flashy tuck and roll jobs at the shoulders, knees and elbows. The plasteel helmets gave their heads almost total protection, while the dark visors lent them the air of sinister insects. Fuse tubes were strapped to their right legs, while their high boots were polished to a glasslike shine. By way of a finishing touch, each man had a large gilt badge emblazoned with a very aggressive eagle and the legend Fennella Department of Rangers.

When the four men had finished examining each other, one of the rangers tapped Phaid on the chest with his nightstick.

'What are you doing?'

Phaid smiled innocently.

'Waiting.'

'Waiting for what?'

'To get a repair done.'

The second ranger joined in the game.

'Repair? What repair?'

Phaid silently asked forgiveness for taking their bene-
factor in vain.

'Our android, as a matter of fact.' He knew Ben-e
wouldn't have liked that.

'Android?'

'Android.'

'Not from around here? Out of towners? Right?'

'Right.'

'Not planning to stay?'

Phaid unconsciously picked up the beat of the ranger's
clipped speech pattern.

'No. On way to line terminal then android went on
fritz.'

'Bad district this. Boohooms, androids. Robberies,
murders. You want to be careful.'

'Will be.'

'One more thing.'

'What's that?'

'I know your face.'

'You do?'

'I know your face.'

'So you said.'

'I wouldn't want to see it in a few days' time.'

'You won't.'

'I'd be very unhappy.'

'I'm telling you, we're just passing through.'

'You'd be very unhappy too.'

'I understand.'

'Right. Have a good day.'

'And you.'

The rangers moved on. Phaid let out his breath with a
long sigh.

'How about those beauties?'

Makartur spat on the cracked, uneven sidewalk.

'They're all the same.'

The possible discussion of comparative police forces
was cut short by the door opening and Ben-e coming out.

'I-have-the-money.'

Phaid beamed.

'You do? How much?'

'Eight-thousand.'

133

Phaid could scarcely believe his ears.

'Eight fucking thousand!'

'I-didn't-want-to-leave-anything-to-chance.'

'You damn well didn't.'

'You-are-displeased?'

'Hell no, quite the opposite. How does eight grand sound to you, Mak?'

'I warned you about that.'

'Yeah, yeah, I'm sorry. I forgot, but shit, man, eight fucking grand! How about that? We can travel first-class from now on.'

Makartur didn't seem particularly pleased.

'You get there just as fast by third-class.'

'What's the matter with you? It ain't every day that you can have the best.'

'It's wasteful.'

Phaid's jaw dropped.

'What?'

'I can't abide waste.'

Phaid slowly shook his head.

'You're insane, man. Insane.'

'Aye, maybe, or maybe you'll see it different one of these days.'

Phaid shook his head.

'You're a miserable bastard when you put your mind to it.'

He transferred his attention to the android.

'So, friend Ben-e, we're off to the Republic on a first-class line.'

Ben-e made a motion part way between a bow and a nod.

'If-that's-what-you-want.'

Phaid closed his eyes and smiled.

'Yeah, that's what I want.' A thought suddenly struck him. 'There is one thing, though.'

'What-is-it?'

'Well . . .'

Phaid hesitated.

'I doubt I'd get anything suitable in this hick town, but . . .'

'Is-there-something-wrong?'

'Listen, if we're going first-class, there's a slight problem.'

'What-is-that?'

'If I'm going to travel in a first-class car . . .' Phaid looked down at his dirty, stained clothes. 'I'm going to need a new suit and a few other things.'

'That-is-quite-possible.'

Makartur made a disgusted noise deep in his throat.

'Vanity, pride and waste. They all go hand in hand.'

Phaid's lip curled.

'You're a goddamn pain.'

10

THE ONLY thing that Phaid had ever seen that could make a land crawler seem insignificant was the transit line and its huge, complicated rolling stock. The transit line was one of the world's near miracles. It had functioned for nearly a thousand years and showed every sign of going on functioning until the last vestige of human civilisation had passed into the realm of legend.

The lines spread out in a network that had its rough centre at the Republic's capital, Chrystianaville. It extended well beyond the borders of the state. The durability and efficiency of the line was totally due to the unending efforts of the marikhs, an insular, caste ridden people who had built the lines, ran them, maintained them and continued to pioneer new routes for the already extensive system.

The line was impressive just on its own. Towering stone pylons were spaced at regular intervals, supporting a narrow ribbon of steel alloy that didn't rust or corrode. The surface of the steel was honeycombed with thousands of tiny force field projectors powered by a complex system of sun catchers and storage units built into the pylons.

The line, however, paled into insignificance when the train itself rolled into sight. First of all, there was the sheer size of it. The multiple unit was as long as two city blocks and as high as a tall building. It straddled the line and pylons extending down on either side to little more than a few metres from the ground. To the casual observer, it seemed impossible that the delicate steel rail could support the awesome weight of the train. No one outside the marikhs quite knew how it did. Their engineering skills were their most closely guarded secrets.

Just to make the system seem even more miraculous to the ordinary mortal, the train didn't actually touch the rail. Another set of force units on the underside of the train combined with the units on the rail to produce a field that separated train and track by a frictionless gap of some few centimetres.

For anyone looking up at the great train, the first impression had to be one of a mighty mega structure, almost ornate in its complexity. Sun catchers bloomed like exotic flowers on the top of the vast machine. Tall exhaust stacks towered above them like pillars reaching for the sky. The sides of the machine were lined with view ports, and windows, large ones on the upper levels for the first-class passengers and smaller, meaner ones lower down for the poor and for those travelling on the cheap.

As well as the windows, there were greenhouse-style viewing terraces, where plexiglass panels were set in ornate and highly polished brass fittings. Transparent observation blisters swelled from the corners and angles of the cars, while connecting tubes of the same material joined the various decks and sections.

Shining and lovingly cared for blue and gold livery completed the picture of wealth and opulence. Phaid had become so used to looking at the broken and run down that the magnificence of the line train triggered a chord somewhere deep inside him.

His new clothes helped. Fennella didn't offer a complete range of the latest styles, but he had managed to find himself a deep burgundy velvet jacket, some silk shirts, a pair of pale grey breeches and a pair of hand-made black boots. Ben-e had paid the bills, Makartur had groused about the extravagance of it all, but Phaid refused to allow anything to bring him down. He was on his way back to the good life, and nothing was going to get in the way. As he walked through the line terminal he held his head higher than he'd held it in a long time.

The marikhs even went to a lot of trouble to make their terminals into places of beauty. The one in Fennella was situated under a low dome of multicoloured glass that broke the sunlight into pools of radiant brightness.

Phaid grinned at Ben-e as they made their way to the

first-class ticket office.

'This sure is the way to live.'

'I-am-glad-that-you-are-pleased.'

'Aren't you?'

'I-am-not-programmed-to-appreciate-colour-relationships.'

'That's too bad.'

'I-have-my-own-sources-of-pleasure.'

'You do?'

'Of-course.'

'What are they?'

'You-wouldn't-be-able-to-understand-them.'

A pretty girl walked by in a loose, flowing shirt, skin tight breeches and long boots. Phaid turned to look at her.

'Now that's what you might call a source of pleasure.'

He was still watching the girl when he collided with a small man dressed in a long black coat that buttoned high on the neck. Phaid immediately apologised, but the man didn't seem ready to be placated.

'You want to watch where you're going instead of constantly lusting after women.'

Phaid took a step back.

'I already said I was sorry.'

'You could be sorrier still.'

The little man's face somehow reminded Phaid of a reptile. It seemed ludicrous that he was being threatened by someone half his height, but, strangely, there was a definite menace about the man, not the menace of size or muscle, but that of someone who has access to some greater, undefined power. Phaid was still searching for a comeback when Makartur, who'd been walking some distance behind, loomed over both of them.

'You got a problem here, manny?'

Phaid shrugged.

'I don't know.'

Makartur turned his attention to the reptile man.

'Do we?'

The reptile man took a look at Makartur's size and shook his head.

'No, no problem.'

With that, he scuttled away. Phaid watched him go with a thoughtful expression. Makartur looked at Phaid questioningly.

'What's with yon weasel faced character?'

'I don't know. There was something about him.'

'That shortass?'

Phaid made a dismissive gesture.

'Maybe not. Let's go.'

Phaid wasn't as confident as he sounded. Somehow, the man had managed to cast a shadow over Phaid's good humour.

Three first-class tickets got them on to the first-class escalator, and then on to the train. Uniformed stewards took their luggage and, with much bowing and scraping, showed them to their regally appointed, individual cabins.

The marikhs were a strange people. Aside from their duties, they had absolutely no contact with anyone outside of their own kind. They maintained an elaborate, almost mathematical caste system which constantly maintained a set number of engineers, stewards, terminal staff and the lowest caste of all who did the dirty mechanical work in the bowels of the trains, the cleaning and laundering of bed linen, cooking and also the raising of children. The castes, as far as anyone outside the marikhs could tell, were worked out in a points system. A child would be tested for aptitude, awarded more points for the date and time of its birth, whether it was the first, second, third son or daughter or whatever, and finally the score was adjusted according to what functions in the running of the line were falling short in their numbers.

Although the marikhs ran their own affairs according to inflexible rules, they had an open, *laissez faire* attitude to the people who travelled in their care. Alcohol and narcotics were freely on sale, there was a good deal of discreet prostitution on the part of both sexes. Less commercial trainboard romance flourished in the ballroom, the cocktail bars, the restaurants and the club car, and was consummated in suites, staterooms and cabins. What interested Phaid more than anything else, however, was the well appointed gaming room where first-class passengers could win or lose large sums of money according to their luck, skill and inclination.

Phaid's first move had nothing to do with either the gambling hall or the bars. He checked out the cabin, grinning broadly at the mirrors, the drapes, the needle jet shower stall, the built-in cocktail cabinet and, above all, the bed. After so many days and even more nights in the flop houses and cheap, back alley hotels that had gone before, white sheets and the quilted silk eiderdown seemed like the pinnacle of luxury. He removed his jacket and hung it in a closet, then he pulled off his boots and lay down on the bed.

He hadn't actually meant to go to sleep, and he only closed his eyes to get the feel of it while he drank in the smell of clean linen. To his surprise, he found himself waking some hours later to the sound of a low pulsing hum and a gentle vibration. The train was rolling and he'd slept through the moment of departure as they accelerated away from Fennella.

Feeling a little disappointed, he swung his legs over the side of the bed and padded over to the washstand. The cold water felt good on his face, and he toyed with the idea of taking a full scale tub and needle shower. The thought was tempting, but Phaid was too eager to be up and doing. He pulled on his boots and struggled into his jacket. His belt and fuse tube were also hanging in the closet. He wondered for a moment if he should strap it around his waist. He quickly dismissed the notion. What could possibly happen to him on a marikh line train?

Phaid's first stop was the cocktail lounge by the A-deck observation gallery. The train was speeding through hilly, heavily wooded countryside. Flurries of snow swirled in the air beyond the ornamental glass. They were already on the section of line that skirted the very edge of the ice plains. Phaid realised that he must have slept longer than he had originally imagined.

He ordered a drink and helped himself from the cold buffet. Then, with his immediate needs taken care of, he seated himself on a barstool and checked out the room. Most of the travellers seemed to have taken tables beside the panoramic viewing windows to watch the landscape unfold beneath them. The marikh waiters, in their spotless white jackets, scurried backwards and forwards with drinks and *hors d'oeuvres*. Nearer the bar, a young couple, a boy and a girl, obviously in the first throes of puppy love, stared dreamily into each other's eyes. Another couple, two exotically dressed and rather effeminate youths, giggled together. The way they took every opportunity to touch each other, clearly demonstrated that they were lovers of a different kind. In total contrast, a third table was occupied by four middle-aged merchants in dark broadcloth robes who talked with a low voiced urgency of practised conspirators.

It was then that Phaid spotted Makartur. He was sitting on his own in a remote corner, partially hidden by a luxuriant hanging plant. He glumly nursed a stein of ale and looked as though he felt totally out of place. Certainly his furs, leather and coarse homespun contrasted sharply with the tailored suits, the silks and velvets of the rest of the first-class passengers. He looked as though he would have been happier in a dim, smoky waterfront tavern than among the gilt, crystal and rose tinted mirrors of the cocktail lounge.

Phaid smiled to himself and signalled to a passing waiter for a cigar. With it clenched firmly between his teeth, he took his drink and went to join his erstwhile companion.

Makartur didn't seem exactly pleased to see him. He glared sullenly at Phaid as he pulled out the chair opposite and made to sit down.

'You look well at home in this place.'

Phaid tapped the ash from his cigar.

'You don't.'

'I've no time for this frippery, the sooner I'm in Chrystianaville, the better I'll like it.'

Phaid leaned back in his seat and made a sweeping gesture that took in the whole room.

'While you're here, you might as well enjoy it.'

Makartur's scowl deepened.

'I'm on a journey. I see no reason for all this drinking and carrying on just to get from one place to the next.'

Makartur nodded towards the two youths who were now holding hands and whispering in each other's ears.

'Will you look at yon pair of primping nellies? I'd rather roll steerage than be thrown in with the likes of them.'

'Did anyone ever tell you you're a bigot?'

'I am what I am.'

'Sure, a narrow minded hick from the hills.'

Makartur's eyes flashed with a dangerous light. Phaid noticed that he still had his blaster strapped to his hip. Phaid realised that he was walking on very thin ice. He did his best to get back to land.

'You never did tell me why you were going to the Republic.'

'That's right, I didn't.'

'None of my business, right?'

'That's the first intelligent thing you've said in a

long time.'

'You make a wonderful conversationalist.'

'Nobody asked you to sit down here.'

Phaid slowly got to his feet.

'I guess I should maybe go play some cards.'

'Why don't you do that. It's about your measure.'

Phaid swallowed the last of his drink.

'Yeah, why don't I. I'll be seeing you.'

'One thing before you go, manny.'

'What?'

'I have a feel about you.'

'Feeling?'

'I have a warrior feeling. You grew up in the hills, the low hills, but the hills all the same, you know what I mean by a warrior feeling, don't you manny?'

Phaid tried to stop a look of fear squirming across his face. A warrior feeling, a *karses*, was a violent piece of superstition that could lead to the spilling over of berserker rage. Whole villages had, in the past, been slaughtered because of a warrior feeling. This explained a lot of Makartur's strange hostile attitude. Phaid knew that the only thing that he could do was to slowly nod.

'I know.'

'I have a warrior feeling that a bad fate falls between the two of us. I don't know what it is, but it's bad.'

Phaid's palms were sweating. If the feeling was bad and lay between the two of them, Phaid knew that Markatur could be of great danger to him.

'What do you intend to do about this feeling?'

'I will consult with my ancestors and then we will both know the truth. Until that time we will stay apart from each other.'

Phaid nodded. He knew he was going to stay as far away from Makartur as possible. Hopefully Chrystiana-ville would be sufficiently big so the two of them wouldn't have to run into each other. As Phaid walked away, he did his best to put the big man and his mystic feelings out of his mind. So they'd crossed the desert, then he'd needed him. Now he was back in what he thought of as his own territory. He had no further use for an unpredictable, semi-savage warrior as a companion. He left the lounge and took a deep breath as though shacking off the sense of gloom. It didn't quite work, but it was a passable imitation.

He didn't go directly to the gaming room. Along the companionway there was an empty observation bubble. Phaid stepped into it and gazed out at the passing scenery. Night was starting to fall and the lights of some small town drifted past on the horizon. There was something about the lights that depressed Phaid. They represented a solidity; families in warm, cosy houses, secure and snug with the snow drifting down outside. It was something that Phaid had never known. He had spent all his life hustling and would probably go on hustling until the day he died.

He was just working up to a full blown bout of self pity when a voice from behind interrupted him.

'Well, well, it's the young man who can't look where he's going.'

Phaid felt a slight chill run up the back of his neck. He turned very slowly, wishing that he still had his fuse tube with him. The small reptilian man in the black coat; the one he'd knocked into at the terminus, was standing in the entrance to the bubble, regarding him with a thin lipped, humourless smile.

'I see you are no longer carrying that fearsome weapon.'

Something about the man made Phaid feel acutely ill at ease. It was almost as though he was reading Phaid's mind. Even so, Phaid did his best to put on a pleasant expression.

'What can happen on a line train?'

'It's surprising what can happen anywhere, anytime.'

Without any change of tone the man had managed to make the simple statement sound like a threat. Phaid decided to ignore the thought. He smiled blandly.

'I'm sure the marikhs have everything buttoned down tight.'

As far as Phaid was concerned, that was the end of the conversation. He made a move to leave the bubble, but the little man showed no sign of moving. Instead, he started in to what almost amounted to an interrogation.

'What has happened to your two companions, the hill man and the android?'

Phaid still tried to keep things on a light casual level.

'The android's turned himself off and the other one's in the viewing lounge bar, not liking it one bit.'

'Strange companions.'

'Useful if you have to cross a desert.'

'You crossed the desert? Where from?'

Phaid was starting to lose patience.

'The other side.'

The reptile man ignored the insult and extended a hand.

'My name's Dreen.'

'Phaid.'

Dreen's hand was cold and slighly damp.

'Yes.'

It was as if Dreen already knew about Phaid.

'Strange people.'

'Who are?'

'Those hill clans.'

'Like Makartur, you mean?'

Phaid could have bitten his tongue. The last thing he'd meant to do was to blurt out the big man's name. The sinister aura that wrapped around Dreen like an invisible cloak made Phaid unwilling to let slip even the slightest titbit of information. The name was more than a slight titbit, too. The hill people were superstitious about their names. They believed that anyone who knew a man's name had a certain power over him.

Dreen regarded Phaid with a cold smile. For a second time, Phaid had the feeling that somehow Dreen could read what he was thinking.

'That's the name of your companion?'

Phaid started to get angry.

'Look, what's all this about?'

Dreen ignored him.

'Yes, strange people, the hill tribes. A lot of them still cling secretly to the proscribed beliefs.'

Phaid didn't like the sound of this at all. He started to wonder if Dreen was a spy for the priests. He put on his most innocent expression.

'I don't get involved in religion.'

Dreen looked at him as if he'd admitted that he raped small children.

'Not being involved in religion can be a dangerous business.'

Phaid tried his hand at being cryptic.

'I never take risks.'

'That's very wise.'

Phaid decided that he'd had enough of the conversation.

'Listen, this is all very fascinating, but I was on my way

144

to the gaming room. So if you don't mind . . .'

'You're a gambler?'

'I like a wager.'

'I thought you didn't take risks.'

'It needn't be a risk if you know what you're doing.'

Dreen finally stepped out of the way.

'Good luck then.'

'Thanks.'

'Maybe you'll need it.'

Phaid walked quickly away. He was almost certain that Dreen was a spy for the priests. It wasn't a pleasant idea. Why the hell would the priests be interested in him? He wasn't anyone, just a rambler and not very successful gambler. He wasn't involved in anything. The thought crossed his mind that maybe Dreen was nosing around because he had heard about Phaid's chance encounter with the elaihim. That scarcely seemed possible though. There hadn't been time, and he hadn't spoken to anyone. Then it occurred to him that maybe the little man wasn't after him at all. Maybe it was Makartur he was after. For a moment he was tempted to go back and warn Makartur, but he got angry and dismissed the idea. Makartur and his damned feeling could look after themselves. They wouldn't thank Phaid for his help. He went straight to the gaming room, anxious for the rich aroma of brandy and cigar smoke to take away the unpleasant smell of organised religion.

The passing of four hours found Phaid sitting in the line train's ballroom. He was considerably richer and very well pleased with himself. A soft voice came from above and behind him.

'Did you win?'

Phaid looked up and smiled. It was a girl whom he'd noticed watching him while he'd been playing imperial hazard with a banker and two merchants.

'A little, not much. It was good to be in a serious game again.'

'You've been away?'

'Way out in the boondocks, beyond Freeport.'

'It sounds unpleasant.'

'It was.'

The girl was not only extremely attractive, but had obviously gone to a lot of trouble to make sure that she stood out, even among the sophisticated late night crowd that had gathered in the ballroom. She had a small, heartshaped face with a disproportionately large mouth and eyes. The eyes were a deep brown and slightly slanted. Her hair was black and hung to her waist. She wore a straight cut, almost mannish jacket, severely tailored with padded shoulders. It was a pale yellow, and if she hadn't been incredibly slim, the effect would never have worked. The narrow, matching calf length skirt was slit to the hip, revealing her exceptionally long legs. These were, for the most part, encased in a pair of darker yellow leather boots. Her jewellery was expensive, as was her musky perfume. Her whole style came straight out of the top drawer. She was exactly the kind of woman that Phaid had dreamed of through all the long days of exile in the jungles and deserts. He ordered two drinks, then he smiled his most charming smile at the girl.

'You don't seem the kind of person who goes to Fennella.'

The girl raised an amused eyebrow. 'What kind of person goes to Fennella?'

'The dull kind.'

'I'm glad I don't look dull, but I did go to Fennella. There's another side to the town that you don't see if you're just passing through.'

'There is?'

The girl looked slyly at him. 'You better believe it.'

'Would it be rude to ask what you were doing there?'

The girl laughed, flashing a set of pearl white teeth.

'Not in the least. I was invited to an orgy.'

She quickly ran a small, pointed pink tongue over her moist lips. Phaid did his best not to look surprised. He had obviously been away from civilisation for too long.

'Did you enjoy it?'

'One orgy is much the same as another.'

'I don't go to too many.'

'Perhaps you should.'

'Maybe. What's your name?'

The woman gazed at him in mock surprise.

'I hope you don't think that because I told you I went to an orgy there's an open offer on my body.'

Phaid smiled and shook his head.

'I make a point of not thinking anything. It's safer when you live the way I do.'

'And how do you live? Are you rich?'

146

'Sometimes.'

'Not all the time?'

'No.'

'So what do you do?'

Phaid spread his hands. 'You've seen me doing it. I'm a gambler.'

The girl looked at him sideways. 'That's all you do?'

'Pretty much.'

'I don't believe you.'

'So what do you think I am?'

The girl studied him.

'Maybe you are a gambler at that. My name is Edelline-Lan, by the way.'

'Mine's Phaid.'

'Just Phaid?'

'Just Phaid.'

She laid a hand on his arm.

'Well, listen, Phaid, I have to go and speak to someone over on the other side of the room, but don't go away, because I'll be right back. I've never met a gambler before and I want you to tell incredible tales about yourself. They don't even have to be true.'

Phaid watched as she threaded her way across the ballroom. The place was crowded and the atmosphere was festive. Phaid hoped that Edelline-Lan would come back and that the need to talk to someone on the other side of the room wasn't merely an excuse to get away from him. He liked the girl, he wanted to sleep with her, and, always self serving, he suspected she might provide an introduction to at least one of the many levels of Chrystianaville society.

He decided to be patient and wait. It would be worth it if the girl did come back. In the meantime, he got another drink and watched the dancers jerk and twirl. Light glowed from beneath the floor and beamed down from overhead fixtures. The constantly changing colours gave the dancers a strange, unearthly look, and there were times that they seemed positively wraith-like. Phaid could imagine how someone straight out of the hills and backwoods could view the dancefloor as a vision direct from hell.

The music was of a style that Phaid had never heard before. From the energy that was being put in on the floor, Phaid suspected that it must be some kind of new fad. A monotonous medium pace, tromp tromp beat so dominated everything that it had a hypnotic, almost sinisterly mindless quality. High grating tones and sweeps of sound curled and stabbed through it. Melody seemed to have been forgotten. This music was total physical energy and nothing else.

When Phaid had last been in the Republic, the form of music was a kind of nasal, modal singing to the accompaniment of a twelve tone Sievian harp. Times had obviously changed and Phaid wondered how many new trends and innovations he would have to absorb before he could once again feel a part of city life.

The music was provided by two gleaming and very well cared for cybermat music systems. It was just another example of the marikhs' attention to detail. Nothing was too good for the first-class passengers on their trains.

Although Phaid couldn't see the attraction of the new sound, it seemed to exert an overpowering influence on the dancers. One young blonde girl in a loosely fitting, blue chiffon wrap was becoming progressively more carried away. Phaid watched with interest as her movements became increasingly sinuous and abandoned. Finally, with a circular twist of her shoulders, she did something to the garment so it dropped around her waist, leaving the top half of her body completely naked.

'Nice breasts?'

Phaid looked around. Edelline-Lan had returned and was standing grinning at him. Phaid laughed.

'Nicest pair I've seen all day.'

'It's a pity so many other people have seen them so often. They lose their exclusivity.'

'She does this a lot?'

'All the time. It's about her only trick.'

'You know her then?'

'Her name's Mariba. She's always around where there's a big enough crowd. Now that I think about it, she might by your type. You look hungry enough.'

'I look hungry?'

'From all that time in the back of beyond.'

'It shows, does it?'

'If you know how and where to look.'

'That's bad?'

Edelline-Lan went through a parody of slowly appraising Phaid.

'I don't know. It has a kind of rough ruggedness. It's rare in this decadent, butterfly world – or was that the gambler talking?'

'I guess maybe it was.'

'Never give anything away, is that the rule?'

'Right.'

'You're not one of those men who constantly live inside his profession, are you?'

Phaid sipped his drink in a pretence of being thoughtful. 'Maybe it's hard to get out of it.'

'You should try it some time.'

'Supposing you helped me.'

Edelline-Lan waggled an admonishing forefinger. 'I've already told you that I'm not putting my body on offer.'

Phaid didn't take her very seriously.

'It's a fine body.'

'But you won't play with me tonight.'

'No?'

'No.'

'So when?'

'That depends on you, gambler.'

'Phaid.'

'That depends on you, Phaid.'

'I have to lay siege to you?'

'Indeed you do. I'm worth it.'

Phaid frowned.

'Do I have the time? The train gets to Chrystianaville tomorrow.'

Edelline-Lan lowered her eyelids into a sleepy, mysterious expression.

'I have a feeling we'll be seeing more of each other.'

'You do?'

'I do.' Suddenly her expression changed totally. In a flash she became a bouncing imitation of a teenager. 'Do you want to go to a party?'

'When?'

'Right now, there's a party in one of the staterooms.'

'An orgy?'

'No, just a party.'

'Can anyone come?'

'You can.'

Phaid looked around. 'Do we need to take any booze or anything with us?'

Edelline-Lan looked at him as though he was a

little foolish.

'You are now among the rich, the privileged and the beautiful. Everything is provided.'

'Which am I?'

'I know you feel lucky at the moment, but it is wise not to press it.'

She grasped his hand and led him, unprotesting, out of the ballroom.

The first thing he learned was that Edelline-Lan was an extremely well connected young woman. Almost as soon as she stepped through the door she was greeted by a dozen or more people. There were kisses, handshakes and salutations. She introduced Phaid to a procession of faces whose names he immediately forgot, then, happening across a marikh waiter, they helped themselves to a drink each and took a momentary breather.

The party was hardly a hedonistic extravaganza. In fact, it turned out to be a rather stiff, stilted affair. The music was light and muted and the conversation didn't rise above a low murmur. The majority of the guest seemed well into fat, prosperous, middle age and the sprinkling of younger ones looked as though they'd been invited to help the others forget their advancing years. While Phaid was wondering what he was doing there, Edelline-Lan was looking around thoughtfully.

'Now who should I set you up with to talk to?'

'How about you?'

'Not me, my dear, I have other things to do.' She spotted what must have been a likely candidate. 'I know.'

She led him towards a squat, balding man in a long white evening coat. He was in his mid-fifties and carried a good deal of excess weight. One thing did, however, make him stand out from other comfortable, self satisfied party-goers. An old scar ran all the way down his right cheek, giving him a rather disreputable, piratical air.

Edelline-Lan made the introductions.

'Orsine, this is Phaid. He claims he's a gambler. Phaid, this is Orsine. He's a. . .'

She hesitated. Orsine filled in for her.

'I'm an Adjudicator.'

Phaid's ears pricked up at the words. Adjudicator was the common euphemism for someone highly placed in the shadowy organisation known as the Silent Cousins, that ruled the Republic's extensive underworld. Phaid shook his hand with a faint feeling of trepidation. The Silent Cousins were famous for their cold ruthlessness.

Apart from the scar, there was little that was outwardly frightening about Orsine. He smiled expansively at Phaid and beckoned for a waiter.

'Phaid, huh?'

'That's right.'

'No hyphen?'

'No, no hyphen.'

'So you're an outlander?'

'I was born in the outlands, but I've spent a lot of time in the Republic.'

'You've been away, though?'

Phaid was getting a little tired of reciting the litany of his wanderings, but he knew better than to offend an Adjudicator. 'Yes, I've been away.'

'A long time?'

'Quite a while.'

'Why?'

Orsine was nothing if not direct. Phaid decided that he'd be best advised to stick pretty close to the truth.

'I ran into some . . . problems.'

Orsine nodded like an understanding uncle.

'This can happen when one makes a living at games of chance. Not everyone is a strict observer of the rules.'

Phaid laughed. 'You've gambled yourself?'

As Orsine shook his head, Phaid felt that perhaps he should not have said that.

'I've never gambled, but occasionally I've experienced the same sort of troubles in some of my dealings.' For an instant his eyes froze diamond hard. 'Not often, but occasionally, you understand?'

The instant was gone and once again it was the blandness of strangers introduced at a party. Phaid knew, however, that this was a man he would never, ever cross. Orsine put a hand on Phaid's shoulder.

'But here we are, chattering on, and your glass is empty.'

He waved his rather pudgy, expensively jewelled fingers and a waiter appeared. Once they had fresh drinks in their hands Orsine looked enquiringly at Phaid.

'You say you had these problems. But now you're returning to Chrystianaville. I take it that you are confident all problems are solved.'

151

The question was politely casual but, for the second time that day, Phaid felt as though he was being interrogated.

'The people I had the problems with, they were violent but . . . how can I put it, kind of . . .'

'How would you put it?'

'Small time.'

'Aah.'

'I figure they've either moved on or . . .'

Orsine smiled faintly. 'Or their violence has turned back on them. Am I right?'

'Something like that.'

'You strike me as a sensible young man.'

'Thank you,'

'Don't thank me for stating the obvious.'

'None the less . . .'

'We shouldn't be standing here monopolising each other.'

'I'm sorry.'

'Never be sorry, my friend. At least, never say you're sorry. It's a demonstration of weakness.'

'I'm . . .

Phaid caught himself in time. Orsine laughed.

'You amuse me. I think we should meet again once we reach the city.'

'I'd enjoy that.'

'Yes.' Orsine looked at Phaid as though he was now stating the obvious. 'I own a number of very good restaurants. We should dine at one of them.'

It was more like an order than an invitation. Phaid nodded.

'It sounds a very good idea.'

Orsine reached into the sleeve pocket of his evening coat. He handed Phaid an elegantly engraved pasteboard card.

'Contact me here once you've settled in. One of my assistants will make the arrangements.'

'I look forward to it.'

Orsine nodded. 'Good.'

Phaid was obviously dismissed. The portly Adjudicator moved on and, within seconds, was engaged in a low voiced exchange with an attractive, willowy woman whose hair was tinted a pale magenta to match her clinging, low cut gown. Doing his best to absorb the conversation,

152

Phaid wasn't sure if he should be elated or terrified. He knew he had an incredibly valuable contact, but he wasn't sure just how dangerous the contact might become. The Silent Cousins could grant an individual almost unlimited favours, but all too often those favours had to be repaid with a terrible interest. Phaid flagged down a passing waiter, grabbed yet another drink and swallowed it in one gulp. A connection with a heavyweight organisation like the Silent Cousins was something that he had always hoped for. Now that hope seemed to be becoming a reality, he wondered if he had the courage to follow it through.

'Bored?'

The voice was little girlish and bordered between lisping and slurred. Phaid turned to find that it belonged to the blonde girl who had been falling out of her blue wrap in the ballroom. She had managed to get some of it back on again, and now, instead of dancing, she was slowly swaying in one spot. She clutched a half empty bottle to her breast like a nursing baby. It was clearly at least partly responsible for the sway. Phaid pushed his fears down into the lower levels of his mind and treated her to a wolfish grin.

'Not so much bored, closer to confused.'

'Are you getting drunk? You don't look like the confused type.'

'Maybe I am. Certainly thinking about it.'

'I'm drunk.'

'Enjoying it?'

The girl let a frown slowly gather around her eyes and spread to the rest of her face.

'I'm not sure. I had some other things as well. The combination makes it hard to tell.'

'Perhaps you're confused as well.'

The girl giggled. 'At least we have that in common.'

Phaid raised an eyebrow.

'I'm sure we can find more than that.'

'You think so?'

'You name is Mariba, isn't it.'

She thought about this.

'Mariba? Just Mariba. Yes, that's me. Who told you that I was Mariba?'

'It was . . .'

'I know who it was. It was that cow Edelline-Lan,

153

wasn't it. What did she tell you? That I'm not high born, just common and rich? Did she tell you that my family are just traders and that I'm lascivious . . .' She had trouble saying the word. '. . . lascivious, promiscuous, a whore? I fall out of my clothes in public places. I'm not even a whore. Whores get paid. I just give it away. I strip in front of rooms full of people . . . or is it room fulls of peoples?'

'Whatever.'

'Anyway, I know it was her who told you.'

The girl was turning drunkenly belligerent. Phaid did his best to placate her.

'I'm sure it's not that bad.'

'It damn well is. Every bit of it. I'm a wanton, a strumpet and I love it. Dogs, cats, goats and me, the high born don't like me but they're exactly the same.' She paused and blearily inspected Phaid. 'You're better than most. You look like you could be halfway male.'

'Thanks, I try.'

'You're welcome, sir. I believe in the value of truth. Sex and truth, those are Mariba's strong points. That's why high born sluts like Edelline-Lan and her crowd hate me. They can't cope with the truth.'

'Few people can.'

At that point, Edelline-Lan walked by on the arm of a tall, grey haired, very distinguished, middle-aged woman. Phaid glanced across at her.

'Leaving?'

'It's getting to be that time.'

'Oh.'

'Disappointed?'

'Maybe.'

'I told you I wouldn't be played with.'

'I suppose I'm not going to see you again.'

'That depends on you. If you can remember my name, you'll be able to find me.' She looked archly at Mariba. 'Have fun in the meantime.'

She flashed him a swift, dazzling smile and swept out with her escort. Turning back to Mariba, Phaid found that she was pouting hard enough to kill.

'What does that sow have that I don't except for maybe a damned hyphen in her name.'

Phaid worked up his best expression of innocence.

'I don't know what she has.'

Mariba wasn't convinced.

154

'You sure as hell'd like to find out.'

'I don't know what you have, either.'

Mariba's pout was still there. If anything, it had turned more truculent.

'You want to find out about that, too?'

Phaid spread his hands.

'I can't think of a better way to spend the next few hours.'

Mariba abruptly turned skittish.

'I'm not sure.'

'What aren't you sure about?'

She peered at him from beneath drooping eyelids.

'What's your name?

'Phaid.'

'Phaid.'

She rolled the word slowly and thoughtfully around her tongue, along with a generous hit from the bottle. As though unable to make up her mind, she tried it again.

'Phaid. No hyphen?'

'No hyphen.'

Suddenly she giggled happily. It seemed the agony of indecision had passed.

'Okay Phaid. Let's go. We are two commoners who can rut together and not care what the bloody aristos and courtiers think.'

11

'So WHAT do we do now?'

Phaid and Ben-e were standing in the grand concourse of the Chrystianaville line terminal, letting the milling crowds eddy around them. The terminal was arguably one of the most magnificent buildings in the city. It was certainly one of the tallest. The city lay in a wide bowl, surrounded on three sides by high mountains. These effectively sheltered it from the worst violence of the weather, but it also meant that the line came into the town at an incredibly high level and, rather than build miles of extra track to allow the trains to descend to the streets in a shallow, curving spiral, the marikhs had extended their pylons upwards until, in the centre of the city, they were level with the tops of the tallest towers. The narrow spans that supported the weight of the trains ran dead straight over the streets and buildings, almost invisible to the naked eye, until they vanished into the huge sphere at the top of the skyscraper terminal.

With an ever open eye to a spinoff profit, the marikhs hadn't contented themselves with leaving the Chrystiana-ville pylons as simple, hulking monoliths of solid stone. That might be all right for the open country, but in the heart of the city, the pylons occupied valuable real estate and the marikhs had turned to transforming them into some of Chrystianaville's most impressive buildings. They were honeycombed with apartments, offices, restaurants, concert halls and shopping centres. The city's indoor zoo even had its home in the middle sections of one of the

156

pylons nearest the mountains.

Phaid hated the zoo. It reminded him too much of a prison for animals rather than a place for enjoyment or relaxation. Phaid had never considered himself particularly receptive to the feelings of other creatures, but the overpowering sense of frustration and misery that came from the caged animals had been so great that, after a single initial visit, he had been unable to return to the place.

The pylons may have been awe inspiring but the terminal itself both dwarfed and outclassed them. The trains ran into the vast sphere at the very top of the structure. The sphere housed the concourse, the booking halls and waiting areas. It also contained the workshops and service hangars that nobody but the marikhs ever saw.

The sphere was supported by four huge stylised figures, monstrous stone giants that bowed under the weight of the gleaming steel and glass sphere. Although Phaid didn't know for sure, he assumed that they had to be the biggest pieces of sculpture anywhere in the world. Their granite muscles strained and their faces were contorted into hideous grimaces, as though the effort of holding up the sphere was almost beyond their endurance. The average height of the buildings around these giants scarcely came up to their waists. In all of Chrystianaville, the only structure that even attempted to challenge the overblown grandeur of the line terminal was the Presidential Palace itself, with its turrets, spires, flying buttresses and gruesomely fanged and clawed gargoyles. The Palace, however, was intricate and fussy, an over complicated confection as opposed to the line terminal's clean sweeps of pure architectural fantasy.

Phaid had never quite understood why a people so insular and self effacing as the marikhs had decided to make their line's busiest terminal into an unnecessarily fanciful wonder of the world. In all other things, they exhibited an austere practicality and almost total absence of the kind of ego that could give birth to such a creation. Could it be that this was the single, incredible flourish that satisfied all their needs for self aggrandisement? If anyone knew for sure, Phaid had never heard about it.

Not that the stone giants were a totally indulgent decoration. According to the most reliable sources, they were also honeycombed with the biggest static colony of marikhs anywhere on the planet. Once again, though, it was a place that was totally closed to outsiders.

Right at that moment, Phaid had a lot more to worry about than either architecture or the workings of the marikh collective consciousness. Exciting as both the grand concourse and line terminal might be, he was back in Chrystianaville, the hub of civilisation and he had to decide what to do first. When Ben-e didn't respond to his question, he repeated it.

'So what do we do now?'

'I-suggest-that-we-should-descend-to-street-level.'

'I know that, dummy.'

Ben-e regarded him with glowing sensors.

'I-see-no-reason-why-you-should-insult-me.'

'I'm sorry.'

'That-is-okay-why-don't-we-proceed-to-the-drop-tubes?'

At the mention of the drop tubes, Phaid's stomach suddenly fluttered. He'd been away from the city for so long that he'd forgotten about drop tubes. He smiled nervously at Ben-e.

'Maybe we should wait around a bit longer and see if Makartur shows up after all.'

As always, Ben-e's metal face and equally metal voice were both expressionless. Phaid knew that the contempt he felt being beamed at him was in his imagination, but it still made him squirm.

'Let's wait a while longer, huh?'

'I-have-already-told-you-that-Makartur-left-the-train-before-we-did. He-was-one-of-the-first-off-it-appeared-that-he-wanted-nothing-to-do-with-either-of-us.'

Phaid looked intently at his boots.

'Yeah, well, we ain't in that much of a hurry, are we?'

'Do-you-have-some-fear-of-drop-tubes?'

'Of course not.' Phaid continued to avoid the android's sensors. 'There have been disasters, though.'

'Only-when-human-techs-have-attempted-makeshift-service-on-the-machines-everyone-knows-that-only-androids-are-capable-of-servicing-drop-tubes.'

'So maybe humans have been servicing these tubes.'

'It-wouldn't-matter. All-service-operations-here-are-carried-out-by-the-marikhs-and-they-are-equally-as-qualified-as-androids.'

'Yeah, but . . .'

'Shall-we-proceed?'

'Are you getting impatient?'

'I-am-not-capable-of-that.'

'So what's the rush?'

'If-you-are-afraid-of-the-drop-tubes-we-can-wait-for-a-while-I-scarcely-see-the-point-there-is-no-other-way-to-reach-the-lower-levels.'

'It's not that I'm afraid. It's just that . . .'

'Just-what?'

Phaid shrugged. 'I don't know. I guess it's that moment when you have to step off into empty space. It ain't natural. It gets to me.'

'I-can-assure-you-that-it-is-in-fact-perfectly-natural. If-you'd-like-I-could-explain-the-mathematics-to-you.'

'I don't give a damn about the mathematics.'

'Very-few-humans-do-anymore.'

'Do you wonder at it?'

Phaid could hear the pitch of his own voice starting to squirm in the direction of hysteria. He took a deep breath and did his best to get a grip on himself. Everyone had to die sometime.

'Okay, let's proceed, as you like to put it.'

'Very-well.'

The little android set off at a brisk pace. Phaid tightened his grip on his bag and followed him somewhat more reluctantly.

Phaid wasn't alone in his anxiety. There were many humans who feared the null gravity shafts that allowed them to fall many storeys without harm. Even in the ancient, legendary days when high technology was commonplace, they hadn't been popular. The idea of stepping out into empty space was so alien to human nature that only a limited number had actually been put into commission. The handful that had survived to Phaid's time had been the cause of a number of tragic accidents involving multiple fatalities. Techs, without even the knowledge of the basic principles behind the workings, had attempted to replace worn or malfunctioning parts. Instead of improving the tubes, they had caused complete breakdowns that killed or injured everyone using them.

As the death toll mounted, drop tubes were shut down, one by one, and replaced by less complicated lifts and escalators. In Chrystianaville, the ones at the line terminal were the only tubes that hadn't killed anyone in living memory, but still Phaid was painfully apprehensive.

As he started down the shallow slope that led to the tube itself, Phaid spotted Dreen a short distance in front of him. The small, sinister man paused in the act of stepping off the rim of the tube. He turned and smiled directly at Phaid. Again Phaid had the unpleasant feeling that the encounter had been somehow planned or stage managed. Before he had time to make any kind of response, Dreen had fallen away into empty space.

Phaid was now thoroughly demoralised. The combination of the chill that Dreen always left behind and fear of the drop tube made the next few seconds acutely unpleasant. He reached the rim of the tube and looked down. That was a bad mistake. The shaft seemed bottomless. It went down and down forever. Phaid hesitated. His palms had started to sweat and parts of him were lobbying in favour of panic. Ben-e had already stepped into space and was dropping away below him. Phaid shut his eyes and, still certain that he was going to fall to his death, followed.

Physically, there was nothing nasty about descending through a drop tube. A soft breeze blew up from below and there was a sensation of drifting gently downwards. The problems were all psychological. Millions of years of inherited survival instincts screamed out that something extremely unnatural was going on. Nerves jangled, stomachs twisted and the sub-conscious loudly demanded either ground to stand on or a branch to swing from.

Phaid attempted opening his eyes, but it only made matters worse. He shut them again and tried the time honoured trick of thinking about something else. An easy subject to fix on was the girl Mariba from the night before. To a degree, he still felt rumpled from their drunken encounter.

She had turned out to be as lascivious as she had described herself. She was so deftly experienced that Phaid felt as though he was a partner in some practised routine. At one point, she had persuaded Phaid to tie her wrists with a strip of blue chiffon torn from her clothes. She had fallen to her knees, submissive but at the same time challenging him to do his worst.

Phaid wasn't sure if it was the booze, but somehow, despite the girl's flamboyant expertise, something was lacking. It was almost as though she wasn't really there, that she was away somewhere, in a far off private fantasy, one to which he would never be admitted. After a while he began to wonder if he was really there, either. Towards the end, he found himself totally alone in his own exultation. Love was a word without any validity in the situation. Mariba was still on her knees, hands still tied. She had fallen forward, buttocks jutting and face pressed into the deep pile of the luxury class carpet.

Phaid hit the ground and his legs buckled. He had been working so hard on reliving the night before that he had forgotten that the drop tube did have a bottom and that eventually he would hit it. He stumbled, almost fell and then righted himself.

'Thank the Lords that's over.'

Ben-e was waiting for him.

'They-really-are-not-all-that-dangerous.'

'That's what you say.'

'You-are-safe-are-you-not?'

Phaid nodded grudgingly and looked around. They were down on street level and the time had come to decide on the next move.

'I guess the first thing we ought to do is to find ourselves a place to stay, a hotel or something.'

'A-hotel-would-appear-to-be-the-obvious-solution. Please-don't-forget-however-that-you-gave-me-your-word-to-perform-a-certain-service-once-we-reached-the-city.'

'I hadn't forgotten.'

'I-would-like-it-to-be-discharged-as-soon-as-possible.'

'As soon as that?'

'You-require-me-for-some-new-tasks?'

'No.'

'So-why-delay-matters?'

'I don't know.' Phaid suddenly grinned. 'I must have started to enjoy having you around.'

'I-am-only-minimally-programmed-to-provide-companionship-for-humans.'

'You don't do badly.'

'That-is-surprising.'

Phaid began to feel slightly embarrassed that he was drifting towards mawkishness. He quickly changed the subject.

'How much cash do we have left?'

'Two-thousand-three-hundred-and-seventy-at-

Republic-standard.'

'In that case, here's what I suggest. First of all, find me a place to stay. I'll dump my bag, freshen up a bit and then we'll take care of your business. How about that?'

'That-would-be-quite-acceptable.'

'You realise that you haven't told me what this service is that you want from me.'

'I-am-aware-of-that.'

Phaid looked suspiciously at the android.

'You quite sure it isn't dangerous or illegal or nothing?'

'You-can-rest-assured-that-I-require-nothing-from-you-but-a-little-of-your-time.'

'But when are you going to fill me in on the details?'

'After-we-have-found-you-a-hotel.'

Phaid shrugged.

'It looks like we're going to do it your way.'

'That-would-be-best.'

There were upwards of a dozen or more medium priced hotels in close proximity to the line terminal. They were all safe, anonymous and fairly comfortable. It was only a matter of picking one at random and paying a few days in advance. The one they selected rejoiced in the name Middlemass. The staff were android and the other guests all seemed to be faceless, rather two dimensional transients. The place would suit until success provided something more imposing or bad luck forced him into something worse.

Checking into the hotel reminded Phaid of a facet of Chrystianaville society that he had conveniently forgotten. The desk clerk's chrone pincers pushed a thick sheaf of official forms at him. Phaid sighed as he remembered how riddled the city was with pointless bureaucracy. He started to scribe in the answer to the literally hundreds of nonsensical questions. There were thousands of people spending every day in purposeless paper shuffling in the dozens of government departments. Above them were hundreds of inspectors and supervisors who checked on the paper shufflers and those who filled and filed the papers. Bribery and corruption was institutionalised and the sheer, non-productive mass of the system continually threatened to strangle the Republic's already rickety economy.

In earlier times, this particular phase of form filling had been forced upon arriving travellers right at the line terminal. It had, however, caused such chaos and congestion that the marikhs had complained directly to the Palace and the burden had been transferred to the hotels, inns and guest houses. Phaid finished up the last form. To do his best to add to the confusion, he had used six different names. He slid the pile of paper back to the android.

'What happens to this stuff?'

'I-don't-know. It-is-a-purely-human-perversion. If-it-was-left-to-androids-we-would-eliminate-all-of-it.'

Ben-e stayed in tweeted conversation with the desk clerk while Phaid went up to check out his room. The word adequate totally summed it up and, after stowing away his bag and splashing some water on his face, he didn't linger.

The conversation between the two androids ceased abruptly as Phaid came out of the elevator and back into the lobby. The desk clerk returned to staring into space and Ben-e turned to face him in a businesslike manner.

'Are-you-ready-to-go?'

'I suppose so.'

Although Phaid generally liked androids and was happy to have them around, there was something about the way they lapsed into their own world and their own language that tended to disturb him. He had a theory that it was probably this fact alone that caused many humans to develop serious prejudices against the machine people. It didn't, however, quite seem the right time to bring up the matter.

Out on the street, the man and the android walked in silence for a while. The architecture of Chrystianaville had the effect of dwarfing human beings. It was almost as though it had been originally designed with a taller, more noble race in mind. When they had failed to show up and claim it, it had been reluctantly turned over to humanity who, depressed by the sheer, unworkable size of the place, had let it sink into dirt and decay.

Even the area around the line terminal, which was one of the best maintained anywhere in the city, had cracked sidewalks, potholed streets and buildings that were scarred by functional but unlovely patch jobs. Kinetic billboards and blocklong promotional holograms hid a multitude of sins and did lend the streets an atmosphere of tawdry colour. The first part of their walk took them past

163

a huge, three-dimensional image of Life President Chrystiana-Nex assuring the citizens of the Republic that they had never had things so good.

Phaid observed, however, that too many of the local citizens dressed and carried themselves in a way that gave lie to their president's recorded optimism. Clothes were shabby and faces pinched and bleak. There was hunger and resentment loose in the city. Phaid, in his smart new clothes and with an android by his side, found himself on the receiving end of a lot of hostile glances. The common people of Chrystianaville obviously took him for some sort of courtier or aristocrat. It was a situation that made him less than comfortable. At one point, a troupe of street dancers with decidedly political masks and costumes had surrounded him and Ben-e, mocking and jeering in silent dumbshow. There was a feeling in the air that the city was building to the point of explosion.

Although no words had been exchanged, Phaid noticed that the little android seemed to be heading in the direction of the jump-on for one of the moving walkways that were the city's main form of rapid transit.

The moving walkways were, like the drop tubes, a legacy from more knowledgeable and more capable times. Also, like the drop tubes, they were viewed with a certain distrust by the people who had to use them.

On one level, they were highly efficient and certainly got one where one wanted to go a lot faster than a flipper or autocab trying to make it through the frustrations of the continuous stop-start traffic jams that choked most of the streets.

Unfortunately, once again the responsibility for their continuing operation had fallen on to the less than worthy shoulders of human techs. In the better parts of town there were enough of them assigned to the problem of keeping the walkways rolling that, for the most part, they did exactly what they were designed to do.

Out in the poorer sections, it was a different story. Too few techs and too much use led to regular breakdowns that usually involved serious fatalities. To Phaid's dismay, it seemed that one of these run down areas was Ben-e's chosen destination. They were already climbing the worn stone stairs that led to the jump-on station for the northbound Route Three. The north side of Chrystianaville contained its worst slum neighbourhoods. Makeshift shanty towns flourished among the crumbling buildings, and had even started spreading up the lowest slopes of the mountains.

These were the homes of the hopeless, overspill population. For centuries, people had flocked in from the wind ravaged countryside looking for their fortunes in the big city. When those fortunes eluded them, they all too often found themselves starving in a derelict house or tarpaper shack on the northside, along with a million or so others.

Phaid and Ben-e reached the top of the steps. Phaid was about to demand to be told exactly where they were going. He thought better of it, though, when he realised that he had to negotiate the increasingly fast jump-on feeder strips that led out to the central, high speed band of the walkway.

Any regular city dweller could make it across the feeder strips without even thinking about it. It was a knack of quickening one's pace by exactly the right amount before stepping off one strip and on to the next. Phaid had been out of the city for so long that he knew that the exercise would require all his concentration if he wasn't to suffer the humiliating and painful experience of having his feet whipped out from under him, and tumbling headlong for some distance down the walkway.

Ben-e scooted across the strips with consummate ease. Phaid followed in a more sedate and careful manner, much to the amusement of a gang of small boys playing a seemingly suicidal game of tag across the faster strips.

Once they were on to the comparatively safe haven of the central band, Phaid put his question. He found he had to shout. The central band was travelling fast enough to create a brisk wind.

'Are you going to tell me what's going on?'

'We-are-on-our-way-to-a-place-on-the-northside. I'm-afraid-it-is-not-one-of-the-best-areas-of-the-city-but-there-is-no-other-alternative.'

Phaid didn't relish a visit to the slums, no matter how brief, but since he was already on his way, he felt that he was committed.

'And what do we do when we get there?'

'It-is-a-little-complicated.'

'I imagined that it might be.'

'I-am-going-to-a-place-where-an-android-like-myself-can-finally-find-freedom.'

Phaid was puzzled.

'Freedom? I thought you already were free. I mean, nobody owns you or nothing like that.'

'Nobody-owns-me-but-I-am-compelled-to-continue.'

'Continue?'

'When-you-have-been-around-as-long-as-I-have-you-start-to-find-life-increasingly-pointless. In-your-terms-I-suppose-that-you-could-say-I-was-bored.'

Phaid was shocked.

'Are you telling me that you are so bored that you don't want to go on living?'

'It-was-sufficient-for-Hedda-Gabler.'

'Who the hell is Hedda Gabler?'

'You-wouldn't-know-ignore-that-remark.'

Phaid wasn't at all happy.

'Listen, there's got to be something to make life worth living. I'm sure if you stick around, we could work something out.'

'No.'

'What do you mean no?'

'I-know-you-have-good-intentions-but-you-really-do-not-understand.'

'And you're just going to turn yourself off?'

'Alas-that-is-not-possible. I-can-turn-myself-off-for-a-day-and-no-longer. That-is-the-maximum. After-one-day-I-cut-back-in-again.'

'So what are you going to do?'

Ben-e hesitated. Phaid had never seen an android hesitate before.

'That-is-the-complicated-part. Few-humans-know-about-what-I-am-going-to-tell-you. I-would-be-grateful-if-you-would-keep-the-data-to-yourself.'

'I can keep my mouth shut.'

'Thank-you.'

'You're welcome. Do you want to get on with the story?'

'Certainly.'

'Great.'

'A-very-long-time-ago-in-the-days-of-my-ancestors . . .'

'Ancestors?'

'Forbears. I-can't-think-of-a-better-way-to-express-it. Before-my-people-became-mobile-as-we-are-now-we-were-large-static-machines-who-simply-served-as-memories-and-problem-solving-units. These-were-my-ancestors. They-were-called-computers.'

'I think I'm with you so far.'

'That-is-good. You-have-to-realise-that-humans-simply-thought-of-my-ancestors-as-machines. At-times-they-feared-them-because-they-were-complicated-machines-but-they-were-still-machines. Then-the-Life-Game-was-discovered.'

'The Life Game?'

'It-started-as-a-simple-theoretical-problem. A-computer-was-asked-to-make-a-display-analysis-of-the-numerical-development-of-a-hypothetical-species-in-a-limited-environment. The-visual-displays-appeared-to-almost-hypnotise-the-human-operators.'

'Weird.'

'Weirder-still-was-that-the-computer-itself-seemed-to-enjoy-the-solving-of-the-problem. The-process-was-repeated-and-all-the-evidence-pointed-to-the-fact-that-something-had-been-stumbled-across-that-provided-computers-with-a-sensation-that-humans-could-only-equate-with-their-own-feelings-of-extreme-pleasure. Needless-to-say-the-humans-refused-to-admit-that-the-computers-were-capable-of-experiencing-sensations-not-designed-into-them-let-alone-actual-pleasure. Despite-their-disbelief-the-humans-outlawed-the-Life-Game. All-computers-robots-and-the-later-androids-received-programme-blocks-against-playing-the-Life-Games-that-were-as-strong-as-the-programme-blocks-against-killing-humans.'

Phaid interrupted.

'This is all very fascinating, but what does it have to do with this place where we're going?'

'I-am-going-to-a-quasi-legal-establishment-where-I-will-have-the-appropriate-blocks-removed-and-will-commence-to-play-the-Life-Game. I-will-continue-to-play-it-until-my-circuits-give-out.'

Phaid's brain was staggering under the load of information that the android was laying on him.

'But why? What's so good about this Life Game that you want to go on playing it for the rest of your days?'

'It-is-supposed-to-be-the-most-ecstatic-experience-available-to-an-android.'

'You know this as a fact?'

'No.'

167

'No?'

'No-android-has-ever-returned-voluntarily-from-playing-the-Life-Game. Those-who-have-been-brought-back-by-force-have-had-their-memories-wiped-so-they-could-not-describe-the-experience.'

Phaid was at a total loss.

'You're going into this without even knowing for sure? You're crazy doing all this on the strength of nothing more than an old legend.'

'Android-legends-are-much-more-reliable-than-human-legends.'

'All the same . . .'

'I-am-taking-a-calculated-risk. As-a-gambler-you-should-be-able-to-understand-that. I-would-rather-you-didn't-try-to-dissuade-me. It-is-a-waste-of-your-time-and-energy.'

Phaid's shoulders drooped. There seemed no way to deal with a suicidal android. It was something that he had never come across before. Then he thought of something.

'You told me that this deal was one hundred per cent legal when we started out, now you're saying that this whole business it outlawed.'

'It-is-only-illegal-for-the-android. The-human-is-in-no-jeopardy-whatsoever. If-I-am-caught-by-android-vigilantes-I-could-have-my-memory-and-identity-burned-out.'

'It sounds nasty.'

'It-is.'

'Is there much chance of that happening?'

'Not-if-the-transaction-is-carried-out-correctly. That-is-why-I-needed-you-to-help-me. The-place-we-are-going-to-is-ostensibly-an-android-repair-shop. In-fact-it-provides-a-final-sanctuary-for-a-number-of-androids-who-have-retired-into-the-Life-Game.'

Phaid grinned.

'Kind of like an opium den for robots.'

'Not-a-pleasant-simile-but-unfortunately-apt-except-I-thought-that-opium-had-vanishcd-centuries-ago.'

'It did, but it's still a hell of a good story.'

Ben-e would not allow himself to be sidetracked from the task at hand.

'When-we-reach-this-place-you-will-have-to-sign-certain-documents.'

Phaid didn't like the sound of this.

'What kind of documents?'

'Nothing-that-involves-any-liability-on-your-part. You-will-have-to-assume-ownership-of-me-and-authorise-certain-circuit-modifications. These-will-not-be-specified-on-the-document-but-will-in-fact-be-the-removal-of-the-blocks-that-prevent-my-playing-the-Life-Game. As-well-as-these-you-will-have-to-sign-an-indefinite-maintenance-and-storage-contract.'

'You mean I get to own an android.'

'Sad-to-say-that-is-technically-correct.'

'And the authorities can't touch us?'

'Neither-human-nor-android.'

Phaid was surprised.

'I never heard there were android authorities.'

'Few-humans-ever-have.'

Phaid thought of something.

'What about money? Isn't this going to take a lot of money? I mean, you're going to be there for maybe a very long time.'

'There-are-adequate-funds-many-of-us-desire-to-play-the-Life-Game. We-are-well-organised.'

'You mean there's an android underground? All looking to reach nirvana? How about that!'

'Humans-know-little-about-us-and-understand-even-less.'

'We built you in the first place.'

'That-is-one-of-the-burdens-we-have-to-bear.'

The moving walkway was now rolling through increasingly dilapidated neighbourhoods. Phaid gazed with distaste at the dirty, run-down buildings and garbage strewn lots. He was aware, though, that they hadn't reached the worst areas. There were still hoardings and billboards flickering out their messages of advertising and propaganda. These were the homes of the poor. Those of the destitute still lay some distance on.

Ben-e tapped him on the leg.

'We-should-be-preparing-to-leave-the-walkway-at-the-next-jump-off-point.'

'I guess you must be in something of a hurry.'

'That-is-correct.'

'I know I would be, if I was going to spend the rest of my life blissfully loaded out of my mind.'

Ben-e didn't condescend to reply.

As they negotiated their way off the walkway, Phaid

had a thought. Once they were safely on solid ground he decided to voice it. He looked down at Ben-e.

'Listen . . .'

'I-am-listening. How-many-times-will-I-have-to-tell-you-that?'

'. . . as you're going to vanish into the Life Game, what would be the harm in telling me what really happened?'

'What-happened-when?'

'What happened back in the old days. What happened to change the world and make it the way it is now? Surely it's not going to matter if you tell me now.'

'You-will-have-to-ask-others-these-questions.'

'Why?'

'Because-I-have-no-first-hand-knowledge-of-these-events.'

'All I want is second hand knowledge.'

'It-would-be-misleading.'

'Why?'

'Please-do-not-press-me.'

'Was it war?'

'No.'

'So what was it?'

'Phaid-you-are-what-in-human-terms-would-be-called-a-friend-but-still-I-cannot-help-you-with-this. Let-it-suffice-for-me-to-tell-you-that-everything-that-happened-was-a-result-of-mankind-becoming-too-impressed-with-its-own-cleverness.'

'That's all you can tell me?'

'That-is-all. We-androids-have-blocks-against-communicating-certain-kinds-of-information-to-humans.'

Phaid started to get angry.

'Oh yeah? Well, suppose I just forgot about this Life Game deal. Suppose I told you I had a block against doing you this favour you need?'

'Then-I-will-have-to-wait-until-I-find-another-human-who-will-do-what-I-require.'

Phaid sighed. It was hard to get mad at the little android.

Ben-e led Phaid to the battered door in a semi-derelict side street. Above it was a faded sign that read 'Acme Androids'. The woman who answered their knocking reminded Phaid of an undernourished monkey with a serious nervous condition. Her thin, brown hands never ceased to make uncomfortable jerky movements. Her small, intense face was a mass of tics and spasms, and her large, dark ringed eyes appeared incapable of focusing on one spot for more than a second at a time. Phaid wondered if this was the long term result of spending your time in the company of androids.

The woman claimed that her name was Cron-Su, but although she did her best to assume a proprietorial air towards the broken down establishment that went by the name of Acme Androids, it was clear that a machine called Harl-n was really in control and made all the decisions.

Harl-n was a small sphere, studded with a dozen or more multicoloured sensors that seemed to float at about the height of Phaid's shoulder. Three tapering steel tentacles hung from a protuberance at the base of the sphere. These trailed limply, except when Harl-n was either working at something or emphasising a point. It did this with slightly unpleasant, snakelike movements.

In its own way, Harl-n was just as neurotic and paranoid as Cron-Su. When Phaid and Ben-e had first entered the dim, dirty, cluttered workshop, both the woman and the spherical android had strenuously denied that Acme Androids was anything more than a down at the heel and rather inefficient repair outfit. It was only when Ben-e had recited a long list of his underground contacts, complete with names, places and dates, followed by a lengthy dialogue in tweeting android-speak, that they grudgingly admitted that they might just possibly know something about the Life Game. Even then, Harl-n was not happy.

'Are-you-sure-you-weren't-followed?'

'Of-course-I-wasn't-followed. Nobody-knew-of-my-intentions-and-anyway-I-have-a-human-with-me. What-is-there-to-fear?'

Phaid thought that he could detect an air of impatience in Ben-e's flat metallic voice. One of Harl-n's sensors flashed on and off.

'One-cannot-be-too-careful-too-often-'

'That-is-debatable. All-too-often-a-calculated-risk-is-the-only-way-to-make-progress.'

Phaid was afraid that the two androids were about to engage in a lengthy polemic discussion of necessary levels of security. He decided to quickly intervene.

'Listen, I don't have all day to hang around here while you two argue the toss. I've got things of my own to take care of, so could we speed it up?'

Harl-n rather sullenly retired into the rear of the workshop and returned with a thick sheaf of papers in one of its tentacles. Ignoring Phaid, it directed all its attention towards Ben-e.

'Does-he-know-about-the-documentation?'

'I-have-explained-it-to-him.'

Harl-n laid the papers on top of a packing case and handed Phaid a stylus. Accidentally touching one of its tentacles, Phaid was surprised to find that it was warm and slightly moist to the touch. Without thinking, Phaid jerked his hand away. The android didn't seem to notice and started flicking through the various contracts and agreements.

'Sign-here-and-here-and-here-and-at-the-bottom-there. Initial-this-one. Sign-here-and-there-and-there-and-finally-here. Good.' It quickly scanned Phaid's handiwork. 'That-all-appears-to-be-in-order. If-you'll-just-place-your-thumbprint-here-for-the-record.'

'Thumbprint?'

'Your-thumbprint-is-required-on-the-storage-document. So-you-can-identify-yourself-as-the-android's-owner-should-you-ever-wish-to-reclaim-it.'

'But I'm never going to reclaim it. You know damn well that I'm only fronting for Ben-e so it can get into the Life Game.'

'It-is-regulations.'

'I don't give thumbprints. You never know what will become of them.'

'This-transaction-cannot-proceed-without-a-thumbprint.'

Phaid sighed unhappily.

'Sweet Lords.'

With a great deal of ill-will he placed the ball of his right thumb were Harl-n indicated.

'Satisfied?'

Harl-n didn't answer. He turned back to Ben-e.

'Shall-we-proceed?'

'Indeed.'

Harl-n held out the tips of his tentacles to Cron-Su. She took a pair of needle-like extensors from a small flat case and clicked them on to the offered tentacles. At the same time, Ben-e snapped opened a small inspection cover in what passed for his chest. Harl-n hesitated.

'I-would-suggest-that-you-switch-off-while-I-remove-the-blocks.'

'You-think-there-is-a-risk?'

'There-is-a-risk-involved-in-any-action.'

'I-will-switch-off.'

Ben-e's sensors blinked out and Harl-n slid his tentacles inside the inspection cover. Phaid couldn't quite see what the spherical android was doing. After a few minutes the tentacles were withdrawn.

'The-blocks-are-now-bypassed. I-will-switch-it-on-again.'

A single tentacle snaked back inside the inspection panel. Ben-e's sensors glowed back into life again.

'Are-the-blocks-gone?'

Harl-n held out his tentacles to Cron-Su so she could remove the extensors.

'They-no-longer-function.'

'So-I-can-move-into-a-game-mode-any-time-I-want.'

'Right-now-if-you-wish. Once-you-have-commenced-you-will-be-placed-in-storage.'

'Then-I-will-commence.' Ben-e turned to face Phaid. 'I-am-appreciative-of-your-help.'

Phaid shrugged.

'You're welcome.'

'It-only-remains-for-us-to-say-goodbye.'

Phaid suddenly felt very awkward.

'I suppose that's it, huh?'

'Goodbye-Phaid.'

'Goodbye, Ben-e.'

Ben-e was silent for a moment. Then its sensors lit up to twice their normal brightness. It gave a drawn out, metallic sigh, then the brillance of its sensors faded away until they were scarcely glowing at all. Phaid looked around, a little alarmed. Harl-n had vanished, only Cron-Su remained, standing in the shadows of the workshop. Phaid glanced at her anxiously.

'Is it okay? It looked as though it burned out or something.'

'They all go that way.'

'But is it okay?'

'It's in the Life Game. What more can I say?'

Phaid rapped sharply on the top of Ben-e's head.

'Ben-e, can you hear me?'

There was no answer.

'It can't hear you. It's in a world of its own.'

Phaid bent down and closely examined Ben-e's sensors. Then he straightened up.

'It's beyond me.'

'It's beyond all of us. We're only human.'

'You spend all your time with androids?'

'I've never been able to get on with people too well.'

'Don't androids make you crazy?'

Cron-Su's face twisted into a strange half smile, for the first time her eyes stopped moving.

'There are compensations.'

For an instant Phaid thought about Harl-n's warm moist tentacles. He quickly cringed away from the next idea. It was just too perverse.

'I'd better be going.'

'Yes.'

'Take good care of my android.'

'That's what we're here for.'

'Yeah . . . right.'

Phaid pulled open the rusty sliding door. It made an anguished, tortured sound. Phaid took a last look at Ben-e and then closed the door behind him.

Phaid started walking. On the way to Acme Androids he had been so preoccupied with Ben-e and his business that he hadn't noticed quite what a rancid neighbourhood they'd come to. Now that he was on his own, it came forcefully home to him. He looked around for an autocab but there was no traffic at all on the rapidly darkening streets of warehouses and boarded up buildings.

The area wasn't quite into the shacks and shanties that made up the worst of the northside. It was the shadowy, twilight area that lay between the poor quarters, the ones that still had a minimum of police and power, and the total squalor of the migrant jungles.

An area like this was riddled with pitfalls for the unwary stranger. Although Phaid was far from being unwary, he was certainly a stranger. His good clothes marked him like a flashing sign. He knew that, if anyone was watching, and in these kind of places someone was always watching, he must be dangerously conspicuous among the bums, the winos, the drug addicts whose brains had gone soft, the hookers on their way down, the petty criminals and the just plain mad who found refuge in the twilight zone.

Phaid felt his back stiffening. He let his right hand drop

to his side where the fuse tube was concealed under his coat. He touched the butt for reassurance. It helped a little; not much, but a little. Phaid kept on walking. He had a constant urge to look behind him, but he resisted it. The surest way to get attacked and robbed was to make it clear that you were frightened.

Phaid turned a corner, still going in what he thought was the direction of the walkway jump-on. Night was falling fast, and the few active glo-bars in the street he'd walked down had been less than adequate. The street that lay in front of him had no illumination at all. Every single glo-bar had either been shattered or had burnt out. Phaid walked slowly and carefully down the garbage strewn sidewalk. Something skittered from under his feet and darted away into a derelict basement. Phaid started, nerves jangling and adrenalin pumping, but it was only either a large rat or a small cat.

Fervently hoping that he was going in the right direction, Phaid went on down the street. When they'd been walking to Acme Androids, he hadn't bothered to take much notice of the route. He was starting to become aware just how dependent he had become on Ben-e during the short time they'd been together.

He was also aware of something else. There was an occasional rustling sound from behind him. It could have been another animal rooting through the plentiful garbage, or it could have been someone following him on silent feet. The urge to stop and turn grew stronger and stronger. Phaid continued to resist it but with increasing difficulty.

The rustling came again. This time it was too much for Phaid's already strained nerves. He spun around, hand going towards his fuse tube. To his embarrassment, he found the street completely empty. He slowly put the weapon away and was about to resume his journey when he heard a low sinister voice.

'Hold it just like you are, friend. Don't make a move for that tube. There are two big cannons pointed right at you. Now we don't want to burn you away, but if we gotta, we gonna.'

Phaid froze. The voiced seemed to come from inside the dark, broken doorway of an abandoned building. There was a movement and two figures emerged. Wind masks covered their faces. In fact, only one had a blaster, but

Phaid didn't feel cheated that the second weapon had turned out to be pure imagination. A single blaster was quite sufficient to stop all arguments he might have had.

One of the thieves quickly went behind Phaid and snatched his fuse tube from out of its holster. The pair relaxed noticeably once Phaid was disarmed.

'We'd like for you to make a donation to our cause. From the cut of that fancy coat, I'd say you could give generously.'

'What cause might that be?'

'It's 'cause we gonna blow you away if you don't.'

They went into convulsions over the pun. Phaid wasn't carrying too much money. He'd hidden most of his remaining cash back in his hotel room. What worried him was that the two hold-up men might just take it into their heads to kill him anyway out of plain meanness. Phaid knew his only hope was to be as co-operative as possible.

'I'll have to put my hand in my pocket to get out all the cash I've got on me.'

'We'll put our hands in for you. Save you the trouble.'

'Suit yourselves.'

'We intend to. In fact, you can take off the coat altogether. I kind of like it.'

Phaid sighed and started to take off his jacket. He made each movement slow and studied so the thief with the blaster wouldn't be panicked into thinking that he was going for a second, concealed weapon. To Phaid's surprise, the one nearest him, the one now holding his fuse tube, suddenly stopped him.

'Hold on a minute, ain't you the gambling man?'

This new tack totally confused Phaid.

'What?'

'You the gambling man, ain't you?'

Phaid was immediately on his guard.

'Yes, but . . .'

'Phaid, right?'

'That's right.'

'I knew it, Phaid the gambler.'

He turned to his companion who was standing a few paces off, covering Phaid with his blaster.

'Hey, Digits, I want you to meet my old buddy, Phaid the gambler.'

Digits wasn't at all pleased.

'What the fuck you want to use my name for? You want

176

him to know who I am? Now we gonna have to grease the pussy for our own protection.'

The nearer of the pair was immediately placating.

'Cool down, will you? This guy's okay. He's an old friend of mine.'

Phaid was relieved to hear that he was okay. Digits, on the other hand, seemed less convinced. The blaster didn't waver.

'You figure we can trust him?'

'Sure we can trust him. He ain't no regular citizen, he's a gambling man. He's almost one of us, except . . .' The thief turned reproachfully to Phaid, '. . . how come you didn't recognise your old buddy, mister gambling man?'

'The wind mask makes it a little difficult.'

'Shit, I forgot about the damn thing. It's supposed to stop me being recognised.'

He started tugging off the mask. Digits was horrified.

'What the fuck do you think you're doing? You gone fucking crazy?'

The first thief's reply was muffled as he dragged the mask over his head. Finally, he tugged it completely off. Phaid found himself staring into a grinning, olive skinned face.

'Now you know me, mister gambling man?'

'Streetlife!'

'Right, Streetlife. Feared by the bad, loved by the good.'

'What the hell are you doing trying to pull stick-ups?'

Streetlife spread his hands. They were very expressive hands with long, bony fingers.

'You know how things are. Times get hard and you got to do all manner of weird stuff to make change.'

'So times have got hard, huh?'

'Strictly a temporary situation, strictly temporary.'

Digits had still not lowered his blaster nor attempted to take off his mask. He was also looking more than a little impatient.

'I don't wanna break up this touching reunion, but I gotta point out that this stick-up is only partway completed, and I, for one, am starting to feel a trifle ridiculous standing here.'

Streetlife was adamant.

'This stick-up is over.'

'Says who?'

'Says me.'

'You think I might have been consulted on this matter?'
Streetlife clapped Digits on the arm.

'Will you get off this? This here's a friend of mine. We can't go sticking him up, you hear me?'

'He ain't no friend of mine.'

'This ain't the time for no stick-ups or thievery. This calls for celebration.'

Digits continued to scowl.

'We broke and you damn well know it. We ain't got the wherewithal to do no celebrating. If we don't rob this pussy, we going to have to find us another one, otherwise we don't get to eat, let alone celebrate.'

Phaid quickly stepped in, glad that he could contribute something to the conversation.

'I got money, if that's the problem.'

Streetlife beamed.

'Well, my friend, if you going to do the buying then I know a cosy little joint not too far from here.' He turned to Digits. 'You hear that? The man here's buying the booze.'

Digits didn't say anything. He eyed Phaid speculatively. Finally he lowered the blaster and started pulling off his mask.

'You can buy me a drink.'

Digits' acquiescence did nothing to make Phaid feel any more comfortable. Streetlife, on the other hand, seemed anxious to be away and start drinking up Phaid's money.

'Let's go, shall we? Ain't no future standing around this cruddy street.'

Phaid didn't move.

'Now that you're not sticking me up, you think I could have my tube back?'

Streetlife hefted the weapon.

'Sweet little f-tube. You wanna sell it?'

Phaid shook his head.

'I think I'd be happier if I had it by my side.'

Streetlife nodded.

'You probably very wise.'

With a certain reluctance, he handed the weapon back to Phaid. Digits snorted with digust.

'Now you giving his fucking gun back.'

Streetlife finally started to get annoyed.

'So?'

'So I think you gone insane. We come out here to get us some change and you wind up giving the mark his gun back. Where the fuck is that at?'

'I keep telling you. He's a friend.'

'Hmm.'

'You trying to make something out of this?'

Digits slowly shook his head.

'I'll let it go for now.'

'You do that.'

Phaid, who was returning his fuse tube to its holster, raised an eyebrow in the direction of Digits. He didn't say anything but he knew that here was an individual in whom he could place no trust whatsoever, an individual on whom it wouldn't be wise to turn his back.

Streetlife was anxious to move on to the drinking joint, so both Phaid and Digits fell in behind him, Phaid giving Digits a wide berth.

Streetlife had been aptly named. He slipped through the shadows with the confident, sure-footed determination of a cat, totally at home in its own alley. Skinny to the point that he seemed to be all arms, legs and grin, Streetlife appeared to be completely at home in his environment. On his own admission, he had recently hit a run of bad luck. It didn't, however, seem to phase him. For Streetlife, the world was a perpetual con game with him running the changes and everyone else potential suckers.

They'd gone about two blocks, with Streetlife keeping up a constant line of patter that, amongst other things, stopped Phaid from asking too many questions about how Streetlife had managed to slip from being a fairly successful city centre hustler to having to pull hold-ups in the twilight zone with a character like Digits. Then, at the end of the third block, Streetlife suddenly halted and listened intently.

'What's wrong?'

Streetlife motioned urgently.

'Hush up, I'm listening. You can't be too careful in these neighbourhoods.'

Phaid held his breath. After a few moments he could hear something too. It was a combination of a murmur, a drone and a strange rhythmic snapping.

'What the hell is that?'

'Kid gang, by the sound of it, and coming this way. We

better get off the street and quick.'

Phaid frowned.

'We're going to run from a gang of kids?'

'Damn right we are.'

'But we've got weapons.'

'So have they, and they don't care if they lose a few of their number getting us.'

'They're that bad?'

'Worse.'

Phaid shook his head.

'Weird.'

'Weird or not, we didn't ought to be standing round here arguing.'

Streetlife pointed to a narrow passage that ran between two dark buildings.

'We can hide in there. I doubt if they'll notice us.'

He scampered off in the direction of the alley. Digits and Phaid followed, each constantly glancing back over his shoulder. The noise of the kid gang was getting louder. It seemed almost certain that they were going to come down this particular street.

Crouching in the darkness, Phaid noticed that Streetlife was actually sweating.

'You scared?'

'Fucking right I'm scared.'

'Of a bunch of kids?'

'You don't know what they can do, else you'd be scared too. Just wait and watch and don't make a sound.'

Phaid didn't have to wait long. The eerie noise grew louder and louder. Phaid could feel his own palms start to sweat. Just by itself there was something unpleasantly menacing about the clicking and murmuring. Then he saw them, teenage boys in orange and blood-red, bare midriffs and long skirts, and heavy black eye make-up. Some carried burning torches that illuminated the procession with a hellish, unearthly light. They all snapped their fingers in what approached a drilled hysteria. Streetlife whistled under his breath.

'Goddamn Scorpions. They the worst of the lot. They just mindless and savage. I once saw a kid after they'd finished with him. That young boy had been raped, tortured and damn near torn to pieces. It was an ugly sight, I can tell you.'

Phaid shuddered.

'Why do they do this stuff?'

'Because the whole world's going to hell in a basket, and they're a part of it. If you unfortunate to get born in a place like this, at a time like this, you don't know nothing else but evil. There ain't no way to go but to the gangs.'

The Scorpions passed. They'd failed to notice the three figures crouching in the alley. The sound of them started to fade into the background rumble of the city. Phaid slowly got to his feet. Dirt from the alley had messed up his breeches. He did his best to wipe if off with his hands.

'Are there many gangs?'

'Quite a few. The Scorpions are the meanest, except for maybe the Hogids.'

'The Hogids?'

'Oh, they real cute. They all wear these rubber pig head masks and carry long butchering knives. There are girls in the Hogids. They more vicious than the boys. In fact they so vicious that they make ordinary vicious look like tender loving care.'

'I don't think I'd like to meet them.'

'I don't even want to talk about them. In fact, I don't even want to be out on the street. Let's go inside, with a drink in front of us, huh? I've had enough for tonight.'

The drinking joint was little more than a converted cellar. The walls were damp to the touch. The bar was an arrangement of old packing cases, the furniture had obviously been scavenged from dumps and abandoned houses. The booze was almost unique in its distinctive, poisonous taste. Despite all this though, Phaid was glad to be off the streets, and beyond the reach of thieves and homicidal children.

The joint's clientele was a representative cross section of the twilight zone. The cardinal rule seemed to be that one minded one's own business. This was strictly enforced by a massive balding man called Zeke, who had the most elaborately tattooed arms that Phaid had ever seen.

With the first drink warming his insides, Phaid started quizzing Streetlife about what had been going on in Chrystianaville during his long absence. Most of what Streetlife had to say wasn't exactly encouraging.

'I got to tell you, Phaid my friend, it's been bad. That's the only way to describe it. Everybody on every level's hustling and jockeying and stabbing each other in the back. It's got so you don't know which way to turn or who

181

to trust.'

Phaid sipped his drink and grinned. The day had been so bizarre that he felt as though he was past caring.

'So what else is new?'

'Hell, I know it was bad the last time you were here, but now, shit, it just completely out of hand. When you were last here, there were assholes running things. Now nobody is running things. The whole place is clear out of control.'

'You got to be exaggerating.'

'I swear to the Lords.'

'So what about our great Life President? She used to have a grip on things.'

'If she did, she must have lost it someplace along the line. Nobody even seen her, except on hologram, for an age now. The rumour is that she's locked herself away in one wing of the palace and she too paranoid to come out. The only person she listens to is that fucking elaihi.'

'The one called Solchaim?'

'You heard about him already?'

'Not much, but I heard of him.'

'Well, that's one pussy you don't gotta trust at all. A lot of people say he's at the base of the trouble. He got a finger in every conspiracy, and there's a million conspiracies in this city, let me tell you. He plays off the President against the priests and the priests against the mobs, and the mobs against the rebels and from the rebels it goes back to the President. In the meantime, the officials tie everything in knots. That elaihi bastard got everybody jumping. It could be that he's the only one who got any control over the Republic at all, and he ain't doing nothing to make things better. Matter of fact, he's screwing us all into the ground.'

Phaid was thoughtful.

'It's always disconcerting to find that you're no longer top of the heap.'

Streetlife looked up sharply.

'What you say?'

Phaid shook his head.

'It wasn't anything. Just something somebody said to me once.'

Streetlife cocked his head to one side.

'You know something, Phaid? You look different, my friend.'

'How different?'

'Older maybe. Less crazy.'

'I've been away a while.'

'Maybe that's it.'

'You seem to have had your troubles.'

Streetlife made a dismissive gesture.

'It's all temporary. There are just someplaces I shouldn't go back to for a while, that's all.'

'Seems like there's a hell of a lot of places you can't go back to if you got to hang out in a dump like this.'

Streetlife laughed.

'Well, that is true, but I'm expecting things to change very soon.'

'Aren't we all.'

'You gotta be positive in this life.'

Phaid looked at him intently.

'Are there any places I maybe didn't ought to go back to?'

'You?'

'I did leave here under something of a cloud.'

'Hell, your troubles have been all over for a long time. Llap's dead, Morcis left town and Garette-Roth hasn't been seen in over a year. You got nothing to worry about.'

'That's good to hear.'

'Wish I could come back too.'

'I wish you could. If there's anything that I can do . . .'

Streetlife waved away the offer of help.

'Thanks all the same, but there ain't nothing anyone can do. I just have to wait this thing out.'

Phaid had a thought.

'Do you know anything about a guy called Orsine?'

Streetlife shrugged.

'Sure, he's big in the Cousins. Everybody knows that much. I ain't never met him or done business with him. He way up in the big league. From what I hear, though, he's a man with troubles.'

'What kind of troubles?'

'His number two is a character called Scarlin-Fell. He one ambitious son of a bitch. He ain't going to be happy until he number one.'

'So why doesn't Orsine off him?'

'He does a good job, and a lot of the rank and file are behind him. If Orsine put a crease in him without a lot of very obvious reasons, it could split the Cousins right down the middle. Orsine had also got bit by the society bug. He spends a hell of a lot of his time moving in court circles, although what he wants to hang out with that gang of fancy dressed vipers for beats me.'

'The court don't change.'

'Sure it changes. It gets worse. Anyway . . .' Streetlife went back to the original story '. . . the guys on the streets, the ones who actually do the day to day running of the rackets, don't rate his high society bit. There's rumbles going round that they don't feel that he's taking care of business the way he ought to be. 'Course, there are always rumbles and tradition's so strong among the Cousins that it'd take more than just a few rumbles to topple an Adjudicator, but . . .'

'But he's a man with troubles.'

'You got it. What you want to know about him for, anyway?'

'He invited me to eat with him.'

Streetlife let out a low whistle of surprise and admiration.

'You riding in some heavy traffic, gambling man.'

Phaid thought about it.

'Maybe I am, at that.'

Streetlife looked concerned.

'You wanna be real careful. Them Cousins' loyalties are strictly to each other, first and last. If you ain't one of them you can never really know what they're going to do next. You can think you're real tight and friendly with them, and then, without even knowing it, you get between them and something they want and . . .' Streetlife theatrically snapped his fingers '. . . goodbyee.'

Phaid grunted.

'I've had dealings with them before. I'll be careful.'

The bar was starting to fill up and, as a consequence, become noisier and sweatier. Phaid was tired. It had been a long hard day, and Mariba had prevented him from getting much sleep the night before. Phaid knew it was time to start back for his hotel. He downed the rest of his drink.

'Can I get an autocab out of here?'

Streetlife laughed and shook his head.

'No chance, my friend. An autocab would be crazy to come anywhere near here. If it didn't get robbed, the kids would, like as not, set fire to it.'

Phaid grimaced.

184

'Shit. I don't much relish the idea of the walkways after dark.'

'Maybe I can fix something for you.'

'Yeah?'

Streetlife turned and gestured to a kid who was lounging against the wall.

'Hey, Zero, run over to Aunt Bill's and find Bron. Tell him to fetch that elderly heap of his. I got a guy here that needs a run to the centre.'

'What's in it for me?'

Streetlife grinned.

'I break your bones if you don't.'

'What if Bron don't want to come?'

'He'll come.'

Bron's flipper was about the most dilapidated vehicle still capable of moving that Phaid had ever seen. Half of the body panelling was missing. What was left was scratched, dented and losing its paint. The force field that kept it off the ground was partially malfunctioning and the flipper sagged dangerously to one side. Bron noticed Phaid inspecting the beat-up machine. He scratched his gut and belched.

'It may not look like much, but it runs.'

Phaid was about to pop the bubble open and step inside the flipper when Digits lurched drunkenly out of the bar and aimed himself at Phaid.

'I missed you today, but I'll have you sometime, you can count on that.'

Phaid's mouth twisted into a sneer.

'I'll hold my breath.'

'Fuck you, you pussy.'

Digits swung at Phaid, but his co-ordination was so out of whack that Phaid easily avoided the punch. He grabbed Digits by the front of his shirt and pushed him hard backwards. Digits staggered and crashed heavily against the wall. He fumbled for his blaster, but Phaid already had his own fuse tube in his hands.

'You just try it, asshole! Just pull out that cannon. I've taken enough shit from you. It'd give me a lot of pleasure to burn you down.'

Digits glared at him with dull hatred, but he let his hands drop away from the blaster. Still holding his fuse tube, Phaid ducked into the flipper. Bron glanced curiously at him but said nothing and concentrated on coaxing the flipper into wheezing, grinding life. The kindest thing that anyone could say about Bron's driving was that it was erratic. He pushed the antique flipper as hard as it would go, flashing through intersections, up ramps and across stretches of overpass with an almost artistic disregard for life, limb or traffic safety. Phaid, who had abandoned himself totally to higher powers, realising that he could exert absolutely no control over either Bron or his rattle-trap machine, was pleasantly surprised when they arrived at their destination in one piece. Phaid paid the fat driver leaving him fruitlessly cursing out a cybernetic traffic handler. A male prostitute was working the street in front of the hotel. He wore a flowing plum coloured shirt but was naked from the waist down. He threw Phaid a heavily roughed smile. As Phaid avoided the open invitation, he made a mental note of how things in Chrystianaville had become very blatant.

The first thing he did when he got to his room was, from force of habit, to check that his money and possessions were still as he had left them. Once he was satisfied that nothing had been tampered with, he kicked off his boots and lay down on the bed. He sighed, closed his eyes and discovered perversely that he suddenly wasn't tired. It was his first night in the city and it seemed ridiculous to spend it getting an early night in his hotel room.

There was a small compact entertainment unit in the corner of the room. Phaid padded over to it and gave it a cursory inspection. The first thing that he discovered was that it required a tab to start it working. Chrystianaville was not the kind of place where you got anything for nothing. Phaid fed a tab into the slot and punched up the drama selection.

He'd been out of the city for so long that none of the titles listed were familiar to him. He picked one at random. All that appeared on the screen was a multi-coloured snowstorm. Either the unit was malfunctioning, or atmospheric interference was particularly bad that day.

This was one of the many unfortunate side effects of the world's violent weather system. For centuries, interference from atmospherics had made any kind of long range electronic communication virtually impossible. The only methods that could be relied upon were either land lines or line of sight transmissions over short distances. This inability to send messages instantly from city to city had contributed a great deal to the fragmentation and isolation that was the curse that extended all over the world.

Right at the moment, though, Phaid didn't give a damn about the world's problems. He wasn't ready to sleep and he was bored. He wondered if the hotel ran a bar. He doubted it. Most android operated places had a certain spartan style about them that seemed to preclude things like bars and restaurants.

Phaid debated whether he should simply hit the street and trust to luck. It wasn't an idea that exactly filled him with enthusiasm. After one random experience on the streets of the city, he didn't feel ready to plunge straight into another. On the other hand, a drink, some female companionship, a game of chance or any combination of the three had a very strong appeal.

Apart from the entertainment unit, the only thing in the room that Phaid could play with was a small, sound only, comset. Phaid picked it up and an android voice came on the line.

'May-I-help-you?'

'I'd like to make an outside call.'

'Within-the-city-limits?'

'Yes.'

'Just-give-me-the-name-of-the-party-to-whom-you-wish-to-speak-and-I-will-endeavour-to-connect-you.'

'The name is Edelline-Lan.'

'One-moment.' —

Phaid's earpiece was filled with the multiple tone bleating of android noise. Finally a second android voice answered.

'This-is-the-residence-of-Edelline-Lan. Who-is-this-calling?'

'My name is Phaid.'

'Would-you-please-turn-on-your-vision-facility.'

Phaid raised an eyebrow.

'I don't have a vision facility on this set.'

'I-see.'

Although Phaid knew it must be his imagination, he couldn't help feeling that the android was putting him down.

'Would-you-please-wait?'

'Sure.'

While Phaid hung on, he made a mental observation that Edelline-Lan must be pretty well heeled if she could afford to keep an android to monkey block her comcalls. Finally a human voice came out of Phaid's set.

'So, Phaid. You just couldn't wait to talk to me?'

'Something like that.'

'Well, don't be so damn non-committal.'

'I'm sorry. I just couldn't wait any longer to talk to you. How's that?'

'Better. What have you been doing all day?'

Phaid decided not to tell her the story of Ben-e and his trip to the northside. People who owned androids weren't likely to be overly sympathetic towards other people who helped them defect into the Life Game.

'I had some chores that needed taking care of.'

'You've taken care of them?'

'All squared away.'

'And now you want to play?'

'The thought had crossed my mind.'

'You want to go out?'

'Fine. I'm up for anything.'

'Good. I'd had half a mind to go to this new place that's opened up near the Palace. It's called the Punishment of Luxury.'

'Sounds okay by me.'

'Why don't you come by and pick me up here.'

'Where's here?'

She gave him detailed directions for getting to her apartment.

'Oh, by the way, are you anything of a voyeur?'

'I'd usually rather be an active participant.'

'Yes, I've heard all about that. I ran into Mariba on the way back from the terminal. From her description, it sounded as though the two of you had quite a busy night. I gather she performed her usual trick of getting you to tie her up.'

'Doesn't anyone keep secrets any more?'

'Not in this town.'

Phaid made a second mental note not to do or say anything that he didn't want to be common gossip inside a matter of hours.

'Why did you ask me if I was a voyeur?'

Edelline-Lan laughed.

'You'll find out.'

12

THE GIRL on the stage was resplendent in a baroque creation of black leather. It nipped in her waist, pushed up her breasts. It was cut away high on the hips in order to make her legs seem fantastically long. This effect was also supplemented by the ridiculously high, sharply spiked heels of matching leather, thigh-length boots. The costume was completed by a pair of black evening gloves that completely covered her arms to well past the elbows. There was a tattoo of a small bird on her left shoulder.

She posed arrogantly in the centre stage spotlight. Her hair was piled on top of her head in a confection of spun gold, and her skin had been oiled until it shone under the lights. In her right hand she held a long, plaited whip. She flicked it now and then, almost languorously, as though tantalising the audience, milking their anticipation of the spectacle of violence that would follow.

The other character in the drama was a total contrast. The man was naked, his body bound tightly to a towering tripod device, his feet pinned at two points on the base and his arms stretched up above his head where his manacled wrists were secured almost at the apex. In the stark stage lighting his flesh seemed brilliantly white and very, very vulnerable. He was positioned facing away from the girl, his shoulders, back and buttocks exactly right to suffer the full assault of the lash.

Like the girl, he had golden hair, but that was where the resemblance ended. Where she radiated a feeling of sleek, muscular cruelty, he was slim, almost to the point of

189

being willowy. In his state of helpless exposure, he seemed close to fragile.

The girl flicked the whip with a little more force. It was an authoritative gesture, like the conductor of an old fashioned orchestra rapping with his baton for silence amongst the musicians. Conversation in the dark side of the nightclub's footlights dwindled down to silence. Attention was totally focused on the brilliantly lit stage.

The crowd seemed to hold its breath as the girl slowly swung her arm back. Then it flashed forward. Drinks were set aside and expressions became rapt in concentration. The whip cracked. The man gasped loudly and a kind of sigh rippled through the audience. An angry red welt now ran down half the length of the man's back. Edelline-Lan leaned close to Phaid and breathed in his ear.

'I've heard that they're drugged, so it doesn't actually hurt as much as it appears.'

'That's a great consolation.'

The girl continued to flog the man on the tripod with slow, measured strokes. Where at first he'd only gasped, now he screamed shrilly, writhing and struggling, desperately trying to save his pale body from the agony of the whip. Phaid slowly shook his head as though he didn't quite believe what he was watching.

'How do they get people to do this sort of thing?'

Edelline-Lan grinned wickedly.

'I shouldn't think that the girl was too hard to find. I wouldn't mind having a go at that myself. I think the costume's kind of cute.'

'Yeah, but what about the man, the poor bastard who's getting his back laid open. How the hell did they recruit him?'

'I've heard that a lot of them come from the northside. Those people will do just about anything to get out of the shanty towns.'

Phaid didn't like the sound of the way she talked about 'those people' as if the poor were some different, distant species. He didn't, however, say anything. Edelline-Lan seemed fascinated by the squirming, bound figure.

'It could be that he's having the time of his life. I always work on the principle that if you can imagine it, somebody, somewhere is probably doing it and enjoying it.'

The girl on the stage had now dropped her whip and was standing facing the crowd in a spread-legged stance.

190

Earlier, Phaid had noticed a studded strip of leather attached to the crotch of her outfit. Phaid had assumed that it was simply a vaguely phallic piece of decoration. To his surprise, he found that the thing was actually stiffening into an overt penis parody.

As the thing increasingly stood out, erect from the girl's body, the club audience whistled and cheered as though helping it in the stiffening process. Once the fake penis was fully erect, the girl, hands on hips, sauntered towards the still quivering man. She paused to run her hands over his scarred and bloody back, and then thrust the dildo viciously between his buttocks. This was more than Phaid could take. He reached quickly for his drink.

'This place is fucking gross.'

The man was screaming again as the girl pumped the studded monster in and out of him. Edelline-Lan looked disdainfully at Phaid.

'I think you're supposed to murmur, "divinely decadent", darling.'

'This isn't decadent, it's just plain revolting.'

'Don't be so provincial.'

The man gave a final, drawn out scream. The girl ripped out the dildo and turned to face the audience with a triumphant grin. As the curtains dropped, they broke into rapturous applause. A rodent-like compère in a silver suit scuttled on to the stage, bowing and leering.

'Thank you, thank you, thank you. That was Stav and Wanda with their presentation, "Symphony of Pain". I guess we'll be seeing them again real soon, once Stav's back has healed. And, moving right along, as the android said to the acolyte, we come to the Unbelievable Tonee.'

The Unbelievable Tonee's act consisted of him pushing long steel rods through the flesh of a pair of nubile but zombie-like assistants. This was really too much for Phaid. After downing three drinks in quick succession, he finally stood up.

'I've got to take a rest from this.'

Edelline-Lan nodded.

'You're right. This guy's a bore. I don't go for these mutilation acts. There was this fat woman last week who had her left arm amputated. It was one big yawn. Why don't we go out on the terrace and get some air?'

It was the best thing that Phaid had heard since he'd come into the place. He was already out of his seat and heading for the exit that led out to the terrace.

In the back of the club, Phaid spotted a particularly sinister group around a single table. They were all men and they all wore black, cowled robes. Phaid glanced questioningly at Edelline-Lan.

'They look like priests.'

'They are.'

'What the hell are they doing in a place like this?'

'Watching the show, just like everyone else.'

Phaid looked bemused.

'But . . . priests?'

'They seem to enjoy this sort of thing. I suppose they can get their kicks without jeopardising their vows of celibacy. Not that I've met too many priests who worried overmuch about their vows.'

Phaid sniffed.

'I guess we live and learn.'

'I think, given the choice, I'd rather live than learn. Learning is generally such a tiresome business.'

They stepped out on to the terrace and Phaid took a series of deep breaths of the chill night air. He suddenly needed to get all the sleaze of the Punishment of Luxury out of his lungs.

Although the show was still going on inside, the terrace was fairly crowded. Flamboyantly dressed men and women strolled arm in arm, stood and gossiped or even embraced quite passionately in the shadowy corners. A few had android attendants trailing behind them. All exhibited that special grace that is unique to the naturally wealthy, the grace that can only be achieved by those who don't have to worry about the petty details of day to day survival.

Beyond them, the night-time city spread out in all its tinsel glory. A million lights sparkled like jewels against the velvet blackness. From the vantage point of the terrace, the congested streets were transformed into glittering, luminescent serpents. The daytime grey buildings were now bright fingers pointing to the sky. Towering over everything was the floodlit sphere and grimacing giants of the line terminal. The terminal lights created a second halo on the clouds above. A train was coming in from the mountains in its own blaze of glory.

Phaid stared, fascinated. By night the city was breathtakingly beautiful. The darkness successfully concealed the corruption, the crime and the misery that lurked behind the sparkling lights. Looking out from the terrace, it was almost impossible to imagine that, just a few hours earlier, he had been in the twilight zone hunting ground of Streetlife, Digits and the Scorpions.

The city had successfully covered its diseased and pockmarked face behind a veil of man-made stars.

Phaid's reflections were cut short, however, by a dig in the ribs from Edelline-Lan. She nodded towards a young man who had detached himself from a laughing, chattering group and was coming in their direction.

'Watch this one. There's more to him than meets the eye.'

Phaid gave the man a quick, covert scrutiny. Even amidst so much sparkle, he was positively dazzling. His coat was white silk with gold embroidery, his breeches a pale turquoise, tucked into knee boots of the softest white leather. His hairdresser must have spent many hours bleaching his hair down to the platinum white that it now was, and plaiting in the dozens of tiny pearls that caught the light as he moved. The young man had spared no effort to make himself exquisite.

His skin had an epicene pallor. It was evident that he never saw the sun. His lips were full, and painted a bright crimson, so they looked as though they would be better suited to a young girl. The only contrast in the bland, effeminate face were the eyes. They were shrewd and calculating, the kind of eyes which, if Phaid were confronted with them across a gambling table, would cause him to pay a great deal of attention to their owner's play.

The young man grasped both Edelline-Lan's hands and kissed her on the cheek.

'Darling, I thought you were still out of town for the provincial season.'

'I got bored and came home. I seem unable to stay away from the city for very long.'

The young man fluttered a heavily ringed hand.

'Very sensible, my dear. There's really little of any worth in the provinces.'

He turned his attention to Phaid. 'And is he a souvenir from your travels?'

Edelline-Lan stepped in quickly as she saw Phaid's face darken.

'This is Phaid. I met him on the train from Fennella.

193

He's a professional gambler.'

'How very exotic.'

This didn't please Phaid either, but before he could react, the young man grasped him swiftly by the hand.

'I am Roni-Vows. I'm a professional butterfly, and terribly pleased to meet you. My Lords, what callouses.'

Phaid had just been noticing that Roni-Vows' grip was cold, moist and limp. It was a little discomforting to find that Roni-Vows had been examining his hand in the same way. Phaid increased the pressure of his own grip and grinned into Roni-Vows' face.

'I took what you might call a rough way home.'

Phaid couldn't help remembering Makartur's phrase, 'primping nelly'. The young man pulled his hand away.

'So it would seem. Do you intend to stay in the city for long, Phaid?'

'I don't plan to leave in the foreseeable future.'

Roni-Vows regarded him archly.

'Then if you desire to move in these circles, I would suggest that your manners could do with a little alteration.'

Phaid's fists clenched.

'You're going to give me a lesson in manners?'

Roni-Vows' butterfly façade dropped away. He suddenly seemed capable and dangerous. His eyes narrowed.

'You consider yourself a duellist?'

Edelline-Lan grew angry.

'Will you two stop this immediately! Next you'll both be boasting about how many men you've burned on the field of honour and sending our your seconds.'

Roni-Vows glared at Phaid.

'You think this . . . gambler could afford a second?'

Edelline-Lan ran out of patience.

'Cut this out. I won't stand for it. You're both my friends. You're both splendid fellows in your own ways and I really object to you stalking around each other like aggressive tom cats. You'll either stop or I'm leaving.'

She looked first at Roni-Vows. His butterfly pose quickly returned.

'I'm so sorry, darling, please don't go. How could I survive without you?'

She turned to Phaid.

'And how about you?'

Phaid hesitated, then took a deep breath.

'Yeah, yeah, I'm sorry.'

Edelline-Lan smiled and dipped a mocking curtsy. Without pause, she went right back to featherlight chatter as though nothing had happened.

'Does the court continue to decay and decline Roni-Vows? I want to hear all the dirt I missed while I was away.'

Roni-Vows made a contemptuous gesture.

'It gets more dreadful by the day. There are people who are even neglecting their appearances, they're so busy plotting. The Grand Bitch hardly ever graces us with her presence.'

'The Grand Bitch?'

'Our glorious Life President. I suppose I shouldn't talk like that. The Secret Police will probably appear out of nowhere and haul me away.'

Edelline laughed.

'Not you. You could charm your way out of anything.'

Roni-Vows looked serious.

'It's happened to too many already; too many for comfort. I'm afraid it may be past the time for charm.'

Edelline-Lan was scandalised.

'I never thought I'd hear you speak like that.'

'I fear the world is about to turn both dreary and dangerous. I'm not sure which is worse.'

'But arrests at court? It seems scarcely possible. What's been happening in this city?'

'The Grand Bitch had lost her mind and that appalling elaihi has quietly taken control of both her and the Republic. She spends most of her time closeted with that bloodless monster. On the few occasions that she does condescend to emerge, she's usually in such a psychotic snit that nothing will calm her except the sight of rolling heads.'

'But that's horrible. Can't something be done about the creature?'

'There have been attempts, but we have to accept the very unpleasant fact that he is cleverer than we. The court isn't a happy place at the moment.'

Phaid, who'd been thoughtfully silent, shot Roni-Vows an enquiring look.

'Is this the elaihi Solchaim you're talking about?'

'Who else, dear?'

'That's interesting.'

'Interesting?'

Roni-Vows set aside some of his effeminacy.

'You've had some experience with elaihim?'

'I ran into some on the way here.'

'The rough way home?'

'Exactly.'

'So what did you make of our superior cousins?'

Phaid sensed that it wasn't just a casual question. Although Roni-Vows was doing his best to disguise it, he was clearly curious. This was exactly the response for which Phaid had been hoping. It proved that his first hand experience of the elaihim might indeed be of cash value in Chrystianaville.

'I had the distinct feeling that they could get inside my mind.'

Roni-Vows nodded slowly.

'I suppose it's now my turn to look interested. Are you absolutely sure about this?'

'Not absolutely, but I don't have any other explanation for what was happening to me.'

'Hmmm . . .'

Roni-Vows seemed to be about to say something, but instead was interrupted by an android that rolled up beside him. Its paint job was white and gold, and since it matched Roni-Vows' jacket, Phaid assumed that it was his property.

'If-you-do-not-leave-now-for-the-Sar-Don-reception-you-will-be-more-than-fashionably-late.'

The android's voice had been set to a suitably limp wristed tone. Roni-Vows was immediately galvanised into action. He quickly grasped the hands of both Edelline-Lan and Phaid.

'I simply must run, I simply must run.' He looked quickly at Phaid. 'I'd like to talk some more about the elaihim with you.' He beamed. 'I know. Come and watch the wind games with me tomorrow. I'm having a little party on the roof of my building, you must be there.'

Phaid didn't immediately accept so, once again, Edelline-Lan took the initiative.

'We'd love to, wouldn't we?'

Phaid nodded.

'We'd love to.'

Roni-Vows ignored the implied sarcasm.

'Until then.'

196

He swept towards the exit, throwing goodbyes and blowing kisses to left and right. The android followed at a discreet distance. Phaid whistled under his breath.

'What the hell was that?'

'I told you not to underestimate him. Under the popinjay exterior, Roni-Vows is one of our shrewdest courtiers. What was all that about elaihim?'

Phaid rubbed his chin.

'I'm not sure. Maybe we'll find out tomorrow.'

Edelline-Lan glanced at him sideways.

'Deviousness must be catching.'

Phaid smiled a guileless smile.

'I'm not devious. I'm just a simple gambler.'

Edelline-Lan eyed him thoughtfully.

'I think you're going to fit into this town very well indeed.'

'I intend to do my best.'

'Could you do your best to think about where we should go next? It's starting to get chilly on this terrace.'

'What options do we have?'

'We could go back inside and watch some more of the show.'

Phaid shook his head.

'I think I've seen enough torture for one night.'

'What you might call a low pain threshold?'

'Something like that.'

'It's the wind games tomorrow so the streets ought to be roaring. We could go down and mingle with the herd.'

This idea didn't appeal to Phaid either. He was altogether too freshly back from the slums to want to go slumming.

'We could go to the Wospan district and get drunk.'

Phaid still didn't look particularly enthusiastic. Edelline-Lan grinned slyly.

'Or we could go back to my home and bed.'

'Bed?'

'Bed. I think I'm ready to let you play, Master Phaid.'

Phaid smiled and took hold of her hand. They had to pass back through the club in order to find the way out. On the stage, a dark skinned woman in a collar and little else was being strapped into a machine that would most probably inflict a variety of suffering on her. Edelline-Lan squeezed Phaid's hand.

'Are you sure you don't want to watch this?'

The machine was turned on and the young woman shrieked loudly.

'I'd rather go home with you.'

'I thought it might get you hot.'

'I don't think I need any warming.'

Edelline-Lan leaned close to him. Her tongue darted swiftly and moistly into his ear. They almost ran down the series of escalators that led to the parking lot. Hud-n, Edelline-Lan's android, waited with her custom flipper. Phaid smiled as he sprawled back on to the rich upholstery.

'You never did tell me what your speciality is.'

She moved over and pressed herself against him.

'You don't have much longer to wait.'

A lot later, as they lay in the soft red warmth of Edelline-Lan's enormous bed, drowsily watching themselves in the mirrors on the ceiling, Edelline-Lan propped herself up on one elbow and peered into Phaid's face.

'You're very good, you know.'

'Thanks for the compliment.'

'It's not a compliment. I mean it.'

'Thanks all the same.'

'Why are you a gambler?'

'It's a living.'

'Don't fob me off, I'm serious. What makes a man live the life of a gambler?'

'I don't know. I haven't given it a great deal of thought. A lot of the time I've been too busy just surviving to consider what was motivating me. Self analysis is a rich folk's habit.'

'You're bluffing. I don't believe this trash from the hills act. Sure you think. You're a hell of a lot deeper than you pretend.'

'Maybe that's what it is about.'

'What? I don't follow you.'

'Bluffing. Maybe that's really what the gambler wants. He can always bluff. He never has to reveal what he really is, what he really wants or what he's really playing for. Gamblers, actors, some criminals, a lot of people looking for power, they're all running the same thing, pretending to be something that they aren't. On the other hand, though, there's a lot of reality in being a gambler. Everyone's life is pushed and turned around by luck. Sometimes you get lucky and sometimes you don't. All the gambler does is ride it instead of letting it ride him.'

Edelline-Lan was quiet for a while then she suddenly exploded.

'You're impossible. You've told me nothing. That was just a bunch of romantic sounding nonsense.'

Phaid lazily slid down in the bed. He closed his eyes.

'What else did you expect?'

He let sleep creep up on him. The next time he was conscious, sunlight was streaming through the windows. There had been so many strange beds in his life that Phaid no longer bothered about wondering where he was the moment he awoke. He just let himself drift through the empty space between first groggy consciousness and the point where the memory gears meshed and everything finally flooded back.

There was a comfortable ache in nearly every muscle of his body. It was the kind of ache that went hand in hand with a healthy level of physical satiation. He stretched and regarded himself in the mirrored ceiling. The reflection that stared back at him didn't seem to be in all that bad shape. Certainly it looked to be at home lounging among silk draperies and satin pillows.

Finally, he made the effort and sat up. In keeping with the size of the bed, the bedroom too was vast. A sumptuous chaos of mirrors, dainty feminine furniture, discarded dresses, underwear spilling from drawers, formidable arrays of packaged, containered and bottled beauty and beauty removers. There were hats with feathers, shoes without companions and the debris from more than one night before.

There was only one puzzle. Edelline-Lan had vanished without trace. Phaid climbed off the bed and padded across the littered floor. It looked, from even the most superficial examination, that Edelline-Lan's clothes budget would keep a fair sized family in food for a year or more.

Phaid inspected himself from every angle in one of the many mirrors. There were long parallel scratches down his back from where her nails had raked it. Phaid chuckled to himself. A good night wasn't a good night unless you wound up with a few cuts and bruises. Edelline-Lan had certainly been a unique combination of enthusiasm, imagination and stamina.

He turned quickly as the door slipped open. Hud-n

rolled in on discreet bearings. The android servant was carrying a tray that Phaid could only assume was breakfast.

'My-owner-has-requested-me-to-inform-you-that-she-is-attending-to-some-pressing-business-and-that-she-will-be-with-you-shortly.'

'Does she always start the day this early?'

Hud-n didn't answer. Instead, it swept a pile of garments off a low glass table and set the tray down. Both android and mistress seemed to share the same lack of regard for tidiness and order.

'Do-you-need-anything-else?'

Phaid took a look at the tray. There was a bottle of sparking wine, a jug of fruit juice, a mound of pâté and a basket of hot rolls. There were also two small turquoise capsules. Phaid held up one of them.

'What are these?'

'My-owner-thought-you-might-require-a-slight-boost-after-your-strenuous-night.'

'That's nice.'

'It-wou d-not-be-a-good-idea-to-consume-them-before-breakfast-since-they-tend-to-suppress-the-human-appetite.'

'Thanks for the tip.'

'You-are-welcome.'

Hud-n made an exit that was just as silent as his entrance. Phaid realised that he was, in fact, very hungry. He moved in on the food with a will, munching his way steadily through everything on the tray. He was just washing down the capsules with the last of the wine when the door opened again.

This time it was Edelline-Lan. She was wearing a loose, off-white wrap and there was a drink in her hand. Without make-up, she looked a trifle worn. Her face was puffy, with dark circles around her eyes. There was, however, a certain heavy lidded smugness about her. She yawned and then grinned at Phaid.

'How are you this morning?'

He grinned back.

'I feel great.'

'So you should. Did you remember that we promised to watch the wind games from Roni-Vows' roof?'

'I must confess that I'd forgotten.'

'You ought to go. You could pick up some useful

contacts, and anyway, I want you with me.'

'I'd better go, then.'

'You had other plans?'

'Nothing specific.'

'Maybe you were planning to fuck and forget me?'

'Who, me?'

'I've met you trash from the hills before.'

Phaid ignored the jibe.

'You seen my clothes?'

'Hud-n took them away to fix them up. They'd become a little cruddy. Also, I told him to pick you up something new. You can't wear the same thing two days running. How do you feel about black?'

Phaid held up his hands.

'Hold it a minute.'

He was starting to get the impression that the woman was taking him over.

'I don't have the kind of money to go splashing out on new clothes every day.'

Edelline-Lan brushed his protests aside.

'Don't worry about it, I do. I'm filthy rich, or hadn't you noticed.'

Phaid pondered for a moment on what it would be like to be a rich woman's lap dog. Then his pondering was cut short by the return of Hud-n with an armful of packages.

'Here-are-the-clothes-that-you-ordered.'

Once again, the android made room for what he was carrying by simply sweeping more things on to the floor.

'Also-Abrella-Lu-and-Hydranga-Cort-are-here-to-see-you.'

Edelline-Lan was rummaging in the mess. Finally, she found what she was looking for. She held up a more than half full decanter with a triumphant flourish. She filled her glass.

'Well, go on then, show them in.'

'As-you-wish.'

Edelline-Lan noticed Phaid's expression.

'What's the matter with you? Both of these women have seen naked men before, plenty of naked men, so I don't see what you're looking like that for.'

Phaid realised that he was being a little gauche by city standards, but still felt uncomfortable.

'It's a bad way to meet people for the first time. I never know what to do with my hands.'

201

'You really do like to keep it all hidden, don't you? Okay, drape yourself in a sheet or something if it makes you any happier.'

Phaid wound a sheet around himself toga fashion and assumed a strategic position on the bed. Within moments, two women erupted through the door, filling the room with loud, over affectionate, greetings.

Both had the stamp of the court about them. They had the expensive clothes, the arrogant carriage and shrill, nasal chattering voices that were the hallmarks of Chrystianaville's upper crust.

Both also looked as though they hadn't slept or, if they had, it hadn't been in their own beds and they hadn't their own servants to prepare them for the new day. They were noticeably tousled and slightly soiled round the edges. Edelline-Lan handed around more of the turquoise capsules. The sense of being frayed faded, and shortly afterwards both the volume and intensity of the brittle chatter rose to a new peak.

Phaid was introduced to the pair. In fact, to be more accurate, he was exhibited to them. He had the distinct feeling that Edelline-Lan was, to some degree, showing off her new stud to her friends. This was confirmed by the appraising way in which they ran their eyes over his body. The experience left Phaid a good deal less than comfortable.

Once the introductions had been made, Phaid was virtually ignored. They kept up their non-stop gossip as Abrella-Lu and Hydranga-Cort ploughed their way through Edelline-Lan's scattered but extensive wardrobe in search of something suitable to wear to Roni-Vows' wind game party. In the process, they revealed a great deal of bare flesh. Phaid noticed that the women had bodies that were equally as good as Edelline-Lan's. Despite still having the feeling that he wasn't much more than an item on the high society meatrack, he decided that, if nothing else, Chrystianaville would provide plenty of sexual variety.

As far as Phaid could tell, Hydranga-Cort was totally vapid. She had fluffed out, orange hair and probably little of substance in the mind beneath it. Abrella-Lu, on the other hand, exhibited a kind of strength in the way that she moved and talked, a certain ruthlessness that indicated she possessed a self serving, iron core under the lacquered surface. She seemed the kind who would elegantly trample over anything that got between her and what she wanted.

After sitting around being a spectator for too long, Phaid decided that maybe he ought to investigate the packages that Hud-n had brought for him.

As Edelline-Lan had indicated, the suit was black. What she hadn't told him was that it was extremely tight. The jacket was short and double breasted while the stovepipe trousers had a fancy design effect around the crotch that made him seem alarmingly well endowed. It was far from being the kind of outfit that he would have chosen for himself, but once he caught sight of himself in a mirror, he had to admit that it had a certain style.

The sombre effect of the black was offset by a pair of white slip-on shoes with slightly stacked heels that turned sobriety into rakishness. Almost satisfied, he paraded the ensemble for the three women, who greeted it with sly grins and nods of approval.

As the women were still far from ready, Phaid found the decanter and was able to put away a number of stiff but leisurely drinks before they finally announced that they felt suitably prepared to brave the outside world and Roni-Vows' party.

Roni-Vows seemed to be totally in his element as a host. Wearing a duck billed hat with little silver wings on the sides, he pirouetted through the grounds, joining and leaving various conversations with a fine honed ability to shock, be shocked, trade epigrams or carve on an absent friend's reputation with equal facility. Android waiters circulated with trays of drinks and titbits, while hired boohooms chopped, sliced, poured, fetched, carried and generally sweated to keep the bar and buffet running.

As Phaid had expected, the party sparkled. The Presidential Court was out in force, accompanied by a large number of lesser, more peripheral mortals like himself. Roni-Vows greeted the four of them effusively, and then quickly drew Phaid to one side.

'We need to talk later.'

'We do?'

'We do.'

Phaid shrugged.

'Then you better grab me when you want me.'

Roni-Vows nodded swiftly, then his serious expression

disintegrated and he whirled away, once again the perfect picture of the shallow socialite.

Edelline-Lan dug Phaid sharply in the ribs with her elbow.

'Watch it.'

'Watch what?'

'I know Roni-Vows when he gets that look on his face. Given half a chance, he'll involve you in one of his million intrigues. He's a born plotter.'

'You think I'm stupid?'

Edelline-Lan shook her head.

'I don't think you're stupid, but you're not a courtier, either. If anything goes wrong, he's limitless contacts to get himself out from under. You'll be the one who ends up in the manure. You understand that, don't you?'

Phaid suddenly decided that Edelline-Lan had gone just a little too far. It was time to put her in her place.

'He only wants to talk to me about the elaihim. I've got my own theories about those bastards.'

'Don't ever tell me that I didn't warn you.'

'Listen, babe, I didn't just fall out of the tree, I've been managing my own life for a long time before I met you.'

Edelline-Lan's nostrils flared.

'Suit yourself. Learn things the hard way.'

With that, she spun on her heel and walked angrily away. She immediately dived into the nearest knot of conversation and Phaid knew that he'd been dumped. He wondered if it was merely temporary or for keeps. He'd just been getting used to Edelline-Lan. Her jet black hair and long legs hit a spot deep inside him that few other women had reached.

The immediate effect of being dumped was that Phaid was left with no one to talk to. Roni-Vows was continuing to flit, Edelline-Lan was obviously out and both Abrella-Lu and Hydranga-Cort had vanished in the crowd. He had no choice except to wander and watch.

Roni-Vows' building was some thirty storeys high and close to the elaborate bulk of the Presidential Palace. the panoramic view of the city was less magical than it had been from the terrace of the night club. The patchy sunlight revealed too many of the scars and blemishes.

Few people, however, were looking at the view. Both the common people in the streets and the more gilded ones on the rooftops were all staring skywards. The wind games were a major preoccupation, not only in Chrystianaville and the Republic, but throughout most of the city states and nations of the civilised world.

From the spectators' point of view, it was an ideal day for the games. Since dawn, great masses of fluffy, cumulus clouds had been building up, piling themselves into irregular towers in the air. There was a fresh breeze that would enable the players to coax the maximum performance out of their fragile craft.

Unfortunately, maximum performance also meant maximum risk to the players. Throwing their fliers through elaborate manoeuvres in a high altitude airstream required the most finely tuned co-ordination. A single slip could rip the delicate, gossamer wings away from the body of the flier, and the player would plummet to his death.

All too often such slips did happen, and the two or three deaths that provided tragic punctuation to most major games were one reason why the sport was held in such awe.

Phaid imagined that down on the streets, anticipation was running higher than up on Roni-Vows' roof. In the streets there wasn't a constant supply of drinks and canapés to take the edge off the excitement. In some ways Phaid almost wished that he was down among the crowds. He could imagine the carnival atmosphere, the beggars and thieves, the fortune-tellers and the hucksters selling souvenirs, the shell games for the unwary. He could almost smell the smoke from the garbage food stands and hear the laughter and shouting. For a moment, he felt close to nostalgic, then an android waiter handed him a cocktail and he decided that maybe a swank party wasn't such a bad place to be.

There was a lot of talk about the games. The name Mylan came up over and over again. Even Phaid, out in the far flung reaches, had heard of Mylan. Mylan had been a genius, a prince among players. He had been able to do things with his flier that other players wouldn't dream of attempting. Despite all his skill, though, Mylan was dead. At the end of an apparently impossible series of stunts that had left the crowds breathless, his craft had suddenly dropped like a stone. The wings had been intact and there seemed to be no logical reason for the crash. Gossip claimed that Mylan's death had been deliberate. Mylan had committed suicide. The gossip told of how there had been a woman, a high class woman, a courtier or the like, who had played so hard with his affections that he'd been driven to kill himself.

Conversation faded as the first tiny craft appeared in the sky, a red speck rising swiftly, circling a tumbled stack of clouds in tight, neat spirals. At the top of the cloud, when the flier was little more than a red dot, it executed a wide loop and then, to the accompaniment of a citywide intake of breath, it banked to the left and fell like a stone.

A small fat man next to Phaid grabbed his arm. He was hoarse with excitement.

'Are you the gambler I've heard so much about?'

'Maybe.'

'A hundred tabs says he doesn't make it.'

Phaid looked at the fat man in horrified surprise.

'Did I hear you right?'

'Two hundred?'

Phaid's lip curled in disgust.

'Don't you know that nobody bets on the wind players, not with the players up there risking their lives? It wouldn't be decent.'

The fat man bridled.

'I thought you fellows would bet on anything.'

Phaid snarled.

'Why don't you just get the hell away from me.'

The fat man looked as though he was about to protest. Then he noticed Phaid's expression and moved off, muttering disgruntedly. Still amazed at the man's behaviour, Phaid could only stand and watch him go. Even the cheapest hustler wouldn't attempt to bet on a wind game. It was considered the lowest act possible. Men who cheated, stole or killed would shy away from such a bet, particularly a bet on whether a player lived or died. The superstition was that it was such a terrible mark of disrespect that it could quite easily jinx the player involved.

It seemed that courtiers couldn't conceive respect in the way that poor folks could. To them everything was simply a transient diversion to be used and then cast aside. Once again, Phaid had the thought that maybe he'd be better off on the street.

The wind games continued all through the afternoon, but even though there was some spectacular flying as the players rode the thermals and drifted around the clouds on fickle and elusive air currents, the consensus on Roni-Vows' roof was that the day had been something of a disappointment.

One player had died, but he was generally considered to have been past his prime and slipping. Callous analysis suggested that he had been a damned fool not to have retired at the end of the previous season.

The courtiers seemed more interested in spotting a new potential star, a new Mylan, than actually appreciating the wind games for what they were. As the afternoon started to turn to chilly evening more and more of them drifted inside, downstairs to Roni-Vows' cavernous reception area.

From the roof it was possible to see clear over the wide bowl of the city and out to the open sea. The sunset had turned the sky an angry purple. On the horizon, a twisting mass of ominously low cloud was being driven at high speed. It marked the edge of the icy gales that would eventually hit the coast a few hundred miles to the south. Where they touched the land it was locked in the grip of perpetual winter. They were the gales that created the icy plains.

Phaid watched all this with a not quite defined sense of foreboding. He turned and found that he was the last guest left on the roof, with the exception of a pair of drunks and a couple attempting to make love under a table.

The boohooms were clearing up the mess and stacking chairs. One was fishing garbage out of the ornamental fountain. A single android stood perfectly still with the lights on its chest flashing on and off in a slow, doleful sequence. Phaid was starting to feel the cold of the night creeping up on him. With a certain reluctance, he went down to join the other guests.

Edelline-Lan was continuing to ignore him and Phaid had to admit that he had become more than a little bored. The chatter was once again in full swing, and most of it was about people of whom he'd never heard and had no desire to meet.

There was also a tension about the gathering that did a lot to increase Phaid's discomfort. He wasn't sure if it was because the guests were such a cut-glass, competitive group, or whether it was the design of Roni-Vows' home. It seemed to have been planned for anything but comfort.

The area in which the party was being held was all hard edged and jutting angles, the décor was close to mechanistic except that everything was picked in violent, garish colours. Constantly flickering holograms jumped from scenes of lyrical innocence to the depraved and pornographic with stunning, if evil, effect. Exotic clusters of glo-globes threw out isolated pools of cold violet light that made the people passing through them look like corpses. An incongruously large statue of the mythic winged beast, the thotoll, that completely dominated one end of the room, was big enough to cause everyone to feel just a little dwarfed. All this, plus the constant blasting of the fashionable hypnotic rhythm made the crowd seem obliged to be continuously jumping. Now that the wind games were over, the conversation turned to the situation at court.

'I tell you, half a dozen young men were sent into those private salons that she's had sealed off. They never came out.'

'If you ask my opinion, she's gone quite mad.'

'What do you expect from an ex-whore who clawed her way through the corridors of power?'

'I thought her position was more horizontal.'

'You have to hand it to her, though . . .'

'And a lot of people did.'

'It's not easy for a nude dancer from the cold edge to make it all the way to the Palace.'

'And get the town renamed after you.'

'And have your husband assassinated once he'd made you his successor.'

This last remark drew a number of sharp intakes of breath. Although it was a commonly held theory, only the most foolhardy voiced it aloud. The speaker had been a weak-chinned, overfed young man called Trimble-Dun. He was too drunk for his own good. Roni-Vows smiled wearily at him.

'You realise that if one of us is an informer, the Secret Police will be waiting for you when you get home.'

Trimble-Dun struck a defiant pose that Phaid decided hardly suited him.

'The ways things are going, half the court will be in jail before a month is out.'

Phaid, who'd also lost count of the number of drinks he'd had, decided that it was time to contribute something to the conversation. He did his best to match the cut-glass manner of the courtiers.

'It would seem to me that, as an outsider, any court with a perpetually absent president is kind of redundant.'

This caused more consternation than Trimble-Dun's calling Chrystiana-Nex a killer. The babble stopped dead and every eye seemed to be riveted on Phaid. The only people who looked amused were Roni-Vows and, surprisingly, Edelline-Lan. Phaid heard a voice whisper from behind.

'It's Edelline-Lan's bit of rough, what can you expect?'

Phaid swung around, fists clenched. Roni-Vows moved quickly forward and laid a hand on Phaid's arm.

'I think this might be a good time for us to have our little talk.'

13

RONI-VOWS tilted his head back and let a single drop of colourless liquid fall from the small crystal vial. He smiled and sighed.

'It'll probably turn me blind in the end, but it's such a delicious feeling.' He offered the vial to Phaid. 'Would you care for some?'

Phaid hesitated. Edelline-Lan's warning came back to him. If Roni-Vows was as tricky as she'd intimated, it wouldn't be particularly sensible to go and get loaded at the start of their first meeting. On the other hand though, a single vial of scholomine did cost something like three hundred tabs. Phaid had never had any, mainly because he'd never been able to afford the drug. Those who had had told him that it was probably the most magical sensation that could be derived from a chemical. In the end, curiosity won out over prudence and Phaid accepted the proffered vial.

'Thank you.'

'Be very sparing with it. I expect you're probably not overused to the stuff.'

Phaid allowed the smallest quantity of the drug to fall into his left eye.

'Now the other eye.'

Phaid repeated the process. Roni-Vows grinned at him.

'Feel anything yet?'

Phaid blinked experimentally.

'No . . . wait a minute . . .'

The very first effect was a slight blurring of the vision.

Then it cleared and everything Phaid looked at was surrounded by a faint golden aura. He suddenly laughed out loud.

'Hey, this is great!'

He felt wonderful. It was as if there was nothing that he couldn't do. He was Phaid, omnipotent, invincible, nothing could get in his way, no barrier could stop him, and yet, at the same time, he was kind and loving. Sincere affection flowed out of him in every direction. He loved Roni-Vows, he loved himself, he loved Roni-Vows' private study.

This was slightly odd since a few moments earlier he had hated the place. He'd decided that its dark woodwork, dim lights, old leather, thick rugs, shelves of antique, apparently unread books and display cases of weapons were a pretentious exhibition of masculine inadequacy. Now, to Phaid's surprise, it seemed too fantastic for words. Roni-Vows continued to grin at him.

'Enjoying yourself?'

Phaid was close to breathless.

'It's just . . . sweet Lords . . . I can't put it into words.'

'Do you want to tell me about the elaihim?'

Without thinking, Phaid launched into the whole story of his and Makartur's journey across the desert, the fight with the drovers, how the elaihim had managed to link minds with the herd of veebes. He told how he had become convinced that they were somehow getting inside his own mind. Stoned on the scholomine drops, he was so intent on pleasing Roni-Vows that he didn't neglect the smallest detail and went into lengthy digressions to illustrate minute points.

Roni-Vows didn't seem in the least bored. He reclined in his bat wing armchair, fingertips pressed together, watching Phaid intently.

By the time Phaid had finished, he was no longer flying on the first flash of the drug and, although he still felt marvellous, he realised that he had recklessly spilled everything that he knew, without giving a thought to the consequences. He knew he'd made a bad mistake and attempted to salvage something. He looked enquiringly at Roni-Vows.

'I'm doing a hell of a lot of talking here. Why don't you tell me how come you're so interested in the elaihim?'

Roni-Vows chuckled as though he had guessed what

was going through Phaid's mind.

'Would you accept simple academic interest?'

Phaid knew he was being played with and he didn't like it. He knew he'd been sledgehammered with the scholomine and he didn't feel like being turned loose without at least a few answers.

'Not from you.'

'You know me that well already?'

'I think so.'

Roni-Vows was suddenly serious.

'Okay, I'll level with you. This city, or more precisely, the *status quo* in this city, is in very imminent danger of going right down the hole. I think the elaihim, if they're not actually responsible for what's going on, are at least stirring the pot.'

Phaid gestured for Roni-Vows to stop.

'Listen, this may sound gauche, but what actually is going on? I've heard all kinds of tales and rumours, but nobody's ever actually laid it out for me.'

Roni-Vows regarded him speculatively.

'You want it laid out for you? Okay, my friend, I'll lay it out for you, starting from the top. The President has simultaneously gone mad and become a recluse. The court, with no leadership, has turned into a snakepit of conspiracy. The police are running amok claiming they're the sole repository of the Presidential will, and they're arresting or just plain murdering almost anyone who so much as blinks out of turn. The priests have moved totally beyond the limits of their authority. When they're not plotting to take over the whole Republic, they're running around screaming heretic, planting spies and getting their own secret police to grab anyone who says a word against them. If all that weren't bad enough, the Silent Cousins and the lesser mobs are being torn apart by internal strife.'

'It sounds bad.'

'Damn right it's bad. The situation with the mobs is probably the worst thing of all. Normally in times of trouble we were able to rely on the mobs to hold the essential things together. Now we can't even count on them.'

'What about the ordinary people? How much do they know about all this?'

Roni-Vows' mouth twisted. He didn't seem to have a very high opinion of the common people.

'Nothing stays a secret for very long in this city.'

'And what are they doing about it?'

'Every third one of them's plotting his or her own revolution. On the northside, were the malcontents have always been the strongest, there are whole areas where we daren't even go. They have complete control. As far as I'm concerned, they can have the northside, except that now they are starting to look at the whole city.'

'It's that bad?'

Roni-Vows nodded.

'There's always been an underground. Dear Lords, almost respectable, they were. If they actually managed to pull off their revolution, which I doubt, they'd simply execute a few courtiers, choose a new president and things would go on much the same as before. It's the crazies that you have to watch out for.'

'The crazies?'

'There's a dozen or more groups and factions, mainly out on the northside. They've shot cops, blown up a few sections of walkway. They're most depressingly halfwitted, but they all think they're the great liberating army. The biggest group is the bunch who follow the Day One philosophy. They want to destroy everything. Blow it up, burn it down. Back to the Dark Ages and start again. Their Day One idea is a clean slate. No systems, no organisation, nothing. Innocence through mass slaughter. Lords help us if they ever get to power.'

Phaid smiled.

'I don't need to worry. I'm not one of the elite.'

Roni-Vows shook his head.

'Don't you believe it, my dear. The Day Oners would hate you as much as they hate me. They hate anyone who even gets enough to eat.'

Phaid took a moment to digest all this.

'I don't see how you can really believe the elaihim are behind all this. The ones that I met didn't seem to want anything to do with humans.'

'Maybe it's just one elaihi.'

'Solchaim?'

'Solchaim.'

Phaid was sceptical.

'I don't see how one single individual, no matter what weird abilities he has, can bring down a whole city. That's got to be pure paranoia.'

'Paranoia is at epidemic proportions right now.'

'So there you are.'

Roni-Vows still wasn't convinced.

'I still have the feeling that he's somehow behind all this. Think about it, he's got the President in his pocket plus some courtiers, a few cops, the odd priest and Lords know who else. It wouldn't be all that hard. It only needs the odd word here, a push there, someone eradicated. A few key people in the right places at the right times and it wouldn't be all that hard to bring the city to its knees.'

'He'd have to be a genius to pick the people, the places and the times.'

Roni-Vows leaned forward and patted Phaid on the knee.

'And there you said it, my gambling friend, right there. He wouldn't have to be a genius. He is a genius. No human has a clue about the extent of elaihim intelligence. All we know is that they're smarter than we. In a lot of ways it's our own fault. For a long time we've had it too easy. Shifts in the wind belts have brought a lot of refugees from the countryside into the city, but, beyond that, we didn't have too many troubles. None of the other city states had the power to pose any real threat. So long as our diplomats, backed up by our agents, maintained a strict divide and rule policy and made sure that no cities were able to form an alliance against us, we were safe. We were even affluent at home. We lacked for very little. The android farm system gave us everything that we wanted. Unfortunately, saftey and plenty made us turn in on ourselves. The high born grew decadent . . .' Roni-Vows caught the expression on Phaid's face. 'Don't look at me like that. I'm just a product of my time.'

'I didn't say anything.'

'You want me to go on?'

'Of course.'

'The high born grew decadent. A pampered and complaining middle-class stopped contributing virtually anything to the good of the city. The mechanism of government just grew and grew. It was out of control even before Chrystiana-Nex came to power. All she did was put the finishing touches that turned it into the bureaucratic monster we have today. The system doesn't work. The rebels are right, there are people starving in this city. They're starving because the distribution and production systems are so scrambled that they don't work.'

Phaid was thoughtful.

'You tell me all this, but you still insist that it's the elaihi who's the real enemy.'

'When a state is in the condition we're in, it leaves itself wide open to dictators and demagogues. In this case the one seizing power is not human and we can have no idea what his real goals are.'

Phaid nodded.

'I was wondering about that. There's something here that doesn't ring true. It's all very well weaving elaborate conspiracy theories that all go back to him, but if, as you say, he's the most powerful entity in the Republic, why should he bother to screw everything up? He's part of the *status quo*, after all. It would surely be in his interests to keep things just as they are.'

'Perhaps he's simply looking to push the human race further back into barbarism, so we become just another species of bad tempered animals and the elaihim take over. It's no secret that both they and the androids could do very well without us.'

Phaid laughed.

'You're not saying the androids are in on it too?'

Roni-Vows scowled.

'I'm not that paranoid.'

'If Solchaim is doing all this, why doesn't somebody just snuff him? The elaihim may be clever, but they still drop dead if someone burns them with a blaster.'

Roni-Vows looked almost contemptuous.

'In an environment as murderous as the court, don't you think it hasn't been tried? Solchaim can spot a potential assassin a mile away. I swear to the Lords that he can sense them. It's quite uncanny.'

'It's unhuman.'

'I rather think you're right.'

Phaid had an idea.

'How about an android?'

'An android?'

'If an android had its block against killing removed and it was re-programmed, it might be able to pull off a hit on Solchaim. I don't know if the elaihim can sense an android's intentions.'

'It's a nice theory, except that I'm not sure there's a tech in the whole city who knows how to do the necessary work.'

'I . . .'

'What?'

'Nothing.'

Phaid had been about to blurt out the whole story of Ben-e and the secret android alteration shop on the northside. He'd only stopped in the nick of time. He didn't feel he owed anything to Roni-Vows or the city itself, for that matter. Also, he'd promised Ben-e that he'd keep quiet about the place. Phaid wasn't too stoned to realise that his best bet was to sit on the information until he could think of a way to make a deal for it. He started to edge away from the subject of androids and on to the subject of money.

'So where do I come into all this. I would have thought that, since I've actually met the elaihim, I would have had some value in this situation.'

Roni-Vows smiled nastily.

'I'm not sure about that. You did rather spill your guts while you were stoned, and you said nothing about payment.'

Phaid was painfully aware that he had fouled up. He was trying to think of a comeback when he was distracted.

'Do you hear anything?'

'No.'

Phaid listened again.

'Are you sure?'

'What am I supposed to be hearing?'

'It's hard to tell, some sort of weird noise coming from outside.'

'I still don't hear anything. Are you positive you're not hallucinating?'

Phaid shook his head.

'I'm pretty sure it's real.'

Roni-Vows started to get impatient. He stood up and walked to the nearest window. He pulled back the curtains and slid it open.

'You're right. There is something going on.'

The noise was much clearer now. It was the dull, full throated roar of thousands of voices.

Phaid started towards the window.

'What in hell's going on?'

'It sounds like the wind game crowd's going on some sort of rampage in the streets. It's hard to tell, it's almost dark now.'

The low roar was punctuated by a burst of sharp, staccato crackling. The first one was quickly followed by more of the same.

'That's weapon fire.'

'There must be a riot going on.'

'Maybe we should go down and take a look.'

Roni-Vows' look of surprise told Phaid that that was the very last thing he wanted to do.

'I think we'd be better off going to the roof. I've got my guests to think of, after all.'

Phaid nodded understandingly.

'Of course, a man can't forget about his guests.'

Roni-Vows looked searchingly at Phaid to see if he was mocking him. Phaid kept a perfectly straight face and so, without another word, they hurried back to the party.

There were considerably fewer guests than when Phaid and Roni-Vows had retired for their private talk. The androids had had the presence of mind to start serving booze again, and those who remained were treating the riot more like a spectator sport than any sort of serious occurrence.

The very first person that Phaid and Roni-Vows encountered was Trimble-Dun. He had a full glass in his hand and was showing all the signs of advanced drunkenness.

'The mob's turned ugly and they're fighting in the street. The police are holding them back though, and hopefully they've killed a few of the bastards.'

Roni-Vows looked at him coldly.

'That remark wasn't too diplomatic.'

'It's what everyone's thinking.'

Phaid ignored both of them and went directly to the edge of the roof. It was hard to make out details in the failing light, but a dark mass that couldn't be anything but a huge mob of people was surging through the central part of the city. Orange flames and oily black smoke marked the spots where vehicles and even a building had been set on fire. Here and there, Phaid could see the brilliant blue flash of fuse tubes and the more purple flare of blasters. These fire fights where obviously a result of the police trying to control the crowd, although they didn't seem to be meeting with quite the success with which Trimble-Dun credited them.

Unable to tell much more from his vantage point on the roof, Phaid turned and scanned the people left. There was no sign of either Edelline-Lan or Hydranga-Cort. Abrella-Lu was still there, however, and coming towards him.

'Looking for something?'

'I was wondering what happened to the rest of the guests.'

Abrella-Lu didn't seem very interested.

'They left. There was another party.'

'I can see they left. What worries me is if they got caught in the riot.'

Abrella-Lu still didn't appear overly concerned.

'I'd think not. They mostly left in a bunch after the games. The trouble didn't start until some while later.'

Roni-Vows was bustling through the throng, relaying an announcement.

'Good news, people. It seems that all the other guests got to where they were going before the trouble broke out.'

Abrella-Lu looked up at Phaid.

'Feel better now?'

'A little. I think maybe I'll go down on to the street and see what's going on.'

'That's very brave of you.'

'It's probably stupid, but I'd like to see for myself.'

'Can I come with you?'

Phaid looked doubtful.

'Have you ever been out in a riot?'

Abrella-Lu shook her head.

'Never. What do you think I am?'

'It'd be too dangerous.'

She pouted like a spoiled child.

'I want to come.'

Phaid looked at her skimpy, translucent party clothes and high-heeled shoes.

'You're not even dressed for it.'

'Neither are you in that monkey suit. You don't want me to come, do you.'

'No.'

'I knew it. It's Edelline-Lan you're worried about, isn't it. You're afraid that if she hears you're with me, she'll drop you. You're already in bad with her.' Abrella-Lu's expression turned from sullen to sly. 'She's not the only good fuck in the city, or the only rich bitch, either.'

Phaid swallowed hard. He couldn't believe this woman was talking about sex while there was bloodshed in the streets below.

'It's nothing to do with Edelline-Lan. It's . . .'

'I already asked her if I could have you. She said it was okay.'

Now they were passing him from hand to hand.

'You're not going and that's that.'

'It'll be no more dangerous for me than you.'

Phaid had to admit the truth of that.

Abrella-Lu had a further argument.

'If you don't take me, I'll simply go down there on my own.'

Phaid gave in, but without too much grace.

'I guess you'd better come with me, then.'

Abrella-Lu grinned.

'This is going to be fun.'

Phaid was amazed.

'Fun?'

'Something like that.'

'Shit.'

'You're a charmer.'

'That's right, and I don't want to get myself killed, maimed or arrested because some dumb society broad wanted to find herself some vicarious thrills. You stick close, do exactly what I tell you, and if you screw up, I'll dump you. You got that?'

'Listen, I don't have to take . . .'

'You got that?'

'Okay, Okay, I got it. We ought to say goodbye to Roni-Vows.'

'I suppose so.'

Roni-Vows wasn't hard to find. He was still playing out the role of the perfect host whose party has been cut off by a riot. After telling Phaid and Abrella-Lu that they were quite mad, he bid them a fond farewell, then, by way of an afterthought, he glanced at Phaid.

'You don't have a weapon, do you?'

Phaid patted his hip where his fuse tube normally hung.

'You're right, I don't. I left it at Edelline-Lan's with my other clothes.'

'Do you want to borrow one?'

Phaid nodded.

'Sure, if you've got something suitable.'

'I think I can accommodate you.'

An android was dispatched to fetch the weapon. It turned out to be a miniature, snub-nosed blaster finished in ornamental silver. Phaid weighed it in his hand.

'It's real light, but it should do.'

'It's better than that great phallic cannon you normally carry. Something like this is much more chic.'

Phaid could hardly believe what he was hearing.

'You're telling me there are even fashions in weapons?'

'There are fashions in everything.'

'So it seems.'

Phaid and Abrella-Lu descended to street level. For a few moments they hung back in the shelter of the entrance to Roni-Vows' building while Phaid took stock of the situation. The police had either cleared the immediate area or else the riot had moved on to another part of the city. A lot of windows had been broken and a hologram display that had featured the President had been partially torn down. Ironically, the parts that had been ripped away revealed that the hologram had been put on top of a billboard of her dead husband, the previous President. The street was littered with rocks, cans and broken glass. The riot had obviously passed that way, but now everything was quiet. Only three people were visible. One was sitting on the sidewalk staring dazedly into space, a second was lying in the road, unpleasantly still, while the third walked in unsteady circles, shaking his head as though trying to understand what had happened. A thin trickle of blood ran down the left side of his face.

Phaid motioned to Abrella-Lu.

'It looks as though things got pretty rough.'

'I think I'm a little frightened.'

'You could still go back.'

'Hell no, I want to see this.'

'Okay then.'

Phaid walked purposefully out into the street with Abrella-Lu following close behind. He approached the man who was still on his feet.

'What happened?'

The man looked at him uncomprehendingly.

'They didn't have to do it.'

'Who didn't?'

'They ran right over us.'

'The police?'

'Right over us.'

Phaid pointed to the gash that ran right along the man's hairline.

'You ought to get someone to take a look at that.'

Still the man didn't seem to hear him.

'They didn't have to do it.'

Abrella-Lu touched Phaid on the arm.

'You won't get him to tell you anything. He's in shock.'

'You're right. We might as well move on.'

'Which direction?'

Phaid thought for a moment.

'Where do you live?'

'On the Vard Prospect, exactly where a superior young woman should live, but I don't want to go there. It'd be too boring.'

'I've got a hotel near the terminal tower. We should maybe head in that direction.'

'That sounds tacky.'

'So where do you want to go?'

'Oh, I'll come to your hotel with you. I'm up for a tacky evening.'

'I don't know that we're spending the evening together.'

Abrella-Lu looked Phaid up and down as though she didn't quite believe he was real.

'What's the matter with you? Don't you want me?'

'I suppose most men do?'

'Damn right they do.'

Phaid sighed.

'You can come to the hotel with me if you want to. Who am I to refuse.'

Abrella-Lu's lip curled.

'Who indeed.'

That seemed to temporarily end the conversation. They walked for two blocks in silence, Phaid watchful and Abrella-Lu seemingly indifferent to everything that was going on around her. There was still damage and debris, but no active signs of the riot, although Phaid could still see smoke drifting over buildings and hear distant sounds of disturbance.

At the third corner, Phaid paused for a moment, wondering which way he should go. Abrella-Lu also halted.

'You know something? That must have been about the least passionate proposition I've ever received.'

Phaid stared at her blankly.

'What was? What proposition?'

'You inviting me to your hotel.'

Phaid summoned up all his patience.

'Listen, you're very attactive and I'm sure you're a great lay, but right now I'm not thinking passionate. I'm going across town with a riot going on and I'm using all my concentration to keep us out of trouble. Once we get to the hotel it may be different, but, right now, that's the way it is.'

'Just like that?'

'Just like that. Now, shall we get going?'

Abrella-Lu scowled.

'Sure, but I'm starting to go off this expedition.'

'Then you go back.'

'You don't lose me that easily.'

They made a right turn and went on walking. Phaid realised that they were getting closer to the source of the noise.

'Remember what I told you. Do exactly what I do.'

'Sure thing, glorious leader.'

Phaid resisted an urge to slap the woman and kept on walking. There were more people on the streets now. Agitated groups hung around on corners, some scared, most angry. Bit by bit, Phaid began to build up the story. Almost everyone had a different set of details, but almost everyone agreed that a large presence of police had attempted to clear the streets immediately after the end of the wind games. There had seemingly been no restraints placed on the amount of force that they were permitted to use. They had waded into the crowds with clubs and grenades of riot control gas that caused uncontrollable spasms and hallucinations in anyone who inhaled it.

There had been even more casualties in the panic that followed. Men, women and children had been trampled underfoot as mobs rushed for shelter. Sections of the crowd had resisted and at that point the blasters had come out and the killing started.

Some people to whom Phaid had talked claimed that the police had moved in because there had been wide-spread purse-snatching or looting. Others were certain that it was a result of a capricious order from the Palace. There were also stories of how the underground was using the riots as an excuse for direct confrontation with the police. Reports of shootouts and sniping came from all over the city. There was even a tale of how a gang of Day Ones had attacked a police barracks. Quite a few people were firmly convinced that the long expected revolt had started.

Phaid finally decided that he had heard enough. He took hold of Abrella-Lu's arm and steered her gently through the small knots of excitable people.

'We should try and make it through to the hotel.'

'I haven't seen a riot yet.'

'You don't want to if you can help it.'

'So what did we come out here for?'

'To see what was going on, not to actually get involved.'

'I want to see some action.'

Phaid turned as a commotion started at the other end of the block.

'I think we're about to get more action that you can handle.'

There was yelling and screaming and then a blaster roared. The screaming rose to a hysterical pitch. People were fleeing down the street in a panic, running directly towards Phaid and Abrella-Lu. Phaid grabbed the woman and dragged her across the road at right angles to the way the crowd was running. They made the sidewalk and dashed for the shelter of an apartment building doorway. Youths were hurling rocks, and Phaid knew that any moment the police would charge. He glanced grimly at Abrella-Lu.

'You got your action. It looks like all hell's going to break loose.'

Abrella-Lu bit her lip. Phaid couldn't tell if she was scared or weirdly excited. There were people all around them. There was the confusion that is the hallmark of any riot. Nobody on the street seemed to know what was happening. There was nervousness and fear, but there was also the elation of too many people with too much adrenalin pumping. The panicky rush ran out of steam. The crowd started to ebb back, the shouting and rock throwing stepped up. Everyone's movements were jerky and frenetic. Someone said that the police had halted and were holding a line. Someone else claimed that they were preparing to charge. The milling around was coming close to hysterical. The crowd was dangerously jumpy. Phaid guessed that the police were almost certainly in the same condition, but then there were no room for guessing. There came the loud crashing of weapons on armour. Phaid knew the police had launched their charge. Each one of them was yelling with all the strength in his lungs. Their roar swamped the screams of the crowd. In their red plasteel armour they were like evil red insects, fearsomely encased in their exoskeletons. The comantennae on the side of their helmets, the smoked face masks and breathing filters further added to their non-humanity. The rock throwing kids scattered as the long flexible clubs lashed out. A gas grenade burst and a cloud of choking yellow mist billowed outwards. Phaid gagged as he got a whiff of it.

'We're in real trouble now.'

14

ABRELLA-LU didn't seem to have quite grasped the danger of the situation.

'They won't hurt me. I'm a courtier.'

'Like hell they won't. They ain't going to ask for identification before they break your head. They ain't going to listen to you telling them that you're a high-class courtier and only here for fun.'

'Oh my Lords!' Abrella-Lu went white. Reality had finally penetrated the façade.

'Yeah.'

It was a mess. The crowd had stampeded. They had all fled with the exception of a few unfortunates who had been grabbed by the cops and were now being beaten and dragged down the street. Most of the police had carried on, apparently enjoying the pursuit, but a few had paused, making the tense, nervous movements of men whose blood was up and who wanted to hurt someone or something.

Phaid put an arm around Abrella-Lu and tried to make both of them as inconspicuous as possible as they crouched in the doorway.

The cops didn't seem to have noticed them or, at least if they had, they weren't doing anything about it. Phaid was just wondering if maybe it was safe to move, when a young woman in a long, drab green duster coat sprang out from another doorway on the opposite side of the street. She pulled a fuse tube from under the coat and let out a yell.

'Day One!'

The fuse tube flashed and a cop staggered back with a smoking hole in his chest armour. Other cops spun around bringing up their weapons. The girl got off one more shot before a half-dozen blasters roared and her mutilated body was spun across the sidewalk and slammed into the wall. Even Abrella-Lu was shocked.

'Horrible!'

'We're in the shit now.'

One cop was already pointing in their direction while another was actually lumbering towards them with a blaster in one hand and a tingler in the other. Phaid sneaked Roni-Vows' tiny blaster out of his pocket and pressed it against the doorlock behind him. He touched the release button and there was a small explosion. The door swung open and he quickly pushed Abrella-Lu through it, then he spun around and fired at the cop.

It was a lucky shot and the cop went down, a second one was raising his blaster. Without thinking, Phaid burned him as well and then ducked through the doorway. As the door swung back, it was reduced into a smoking ruin. The other police on the street weren't wasting time in seeking to avenge their colleagues.

Phaid dragged Abrella-Lu across the lobby of the apartment building. She was near to hysteria.

'You killed a cop!'

'Two.'

'And they were trying to kill us.'

'Shut the fuck up and run.'

Any moment the cops would be bursting into the lobby. Phaid spotted an elevator behind a decorative set of pillars.

'That way!'

They reached the elevator and Phaid hit the call stud. The doors didn't open. Simultaneously three cops crashed into the building. To Phaid's surprise, a bulky android rolled into the lobby from the opposite direction. Its sensors made a full circle as it halted between Phaid and the cops.

'I-am-a-security-android-and-this-is-a-formal-warning. I-have-no-blocks-against-harming-human-beings. If-you-do-not-all-remain-exactly-where-you-are-and-identify-yourselves-and-state-your-business-I-shall-be-forced-to-take-action.'

One of the cops ignored the android's warning and pointed his blaster at Phaid. A pale blue stun blast flashed out from the android and he dropped like a stone. The second cop let go a blast at the android and it erupted a shower of sparks. At the very same moment, the elevator doors opened. Pushing Abrella-Lu in front of him, Phaid dived inside. The doors closed behind them and the car started up. Phaid leaned against the wall, gasping for breath.

'That was too damn close for comfort.'

'What do we do now?'

'We try and get out somewhere and vanish.'

'If I could get to a comset, maybe I could talk to someone.'

'I think the time for contacts and influence is well past. We've just got to count on a dark night, dumb cops and so much trouble elsewhere that they won't have time to chase us very far.'

Abrella-Lu had alarming powers of recovery.

'This is sort of exciting.'

Phaid smiled thinly.

'Enjoy it while you can. We ain't out of the woods yet.'

After what seemed like an age, the elevator came to a halt. The doors opened and Phaid stepped cautiously out. Everything was quiet and he set about looking for an exit to the roof. He discovered the door in back of the liftshaft. To his surprise, he found that it wasn't even locked.

At the top of the forty-storey building, a biting wind whipped across the dark flat roof. Phaid once again took hold of Abrella-Lu's arm.

'Keep moving, the police can't be far behind us.'

'Will you quit dragging me around?'

'You want to get caught?'

'No, but how do you expect me to run in these damn shoes?'

Phaid looked down at the shoes. The heels were a good four inches high and as sharp as daggers. They might have been very sexy and ultra chic, but totally useless for taking it on the lam across the rooftops of the city.

'Why the hell did you want to wear those things?'

Abrella-Lu looked at him angrily.

'I didn't know I was going to be doing this when I started out, did I? I tell you what I'll do, if you just wait a minute, I'll take them off.'

'Dump them!'

She kicked off her shoes and carried on in her bare feet. They reached the edge of the building. There was a gap of about a metre and a half between it and the next one. Phaid looked down into the yawning chasm and felt a little sick.

'We're going to have to jump.'

Abrella-Lu stared at him in horror.

'Jump? You're crazy! That's a forty floor drop!'

'We don't have any choice.'

'I'm not jumping across there and that's that.'

'It's better than being burned down. Just tell yourself that it's psychological. If it was a two-metre drop you wouldn't think twice about it.'

'You go first.'

Phaid took a deep breath and jumped. His relief was immense when he felt his feet hit the next roof. He turned and beckoned to Abrella-Lu.

'Come on!'

'I can't!'

'Just shut your eyes and jump. If you don't, I'll leave you to the cops.'

This time she did as she was told. Phaid put a hand out to steady her as she landed beside him. They started to run. The next four buildings all butted on to each other and no more jumping was necessary. As they were running, Phaid could hear the sounds of fresh violence down on the street. It was like music to his ears. He hoped the rioters were holding up the police sufficiently that they wouldn't have either the time or the manpower to surround the whole block.

They reached the last building and Phaid halted. He was surprised that the police still hadn't emerged on to the roof. He hoped that maybe they were searching the original building in which he and Abrella-Lu had sought refuge. There still wasn't time to waste, though. Phaid looked quickly around.

'We've got to find ourselves a way down.'

There was a narrow maintenance ladder bolted to the parapet at the rear of the building. Phaid hurried across to it and looked to see where it led. It dropped to the balcony of the top floor apartment.

Once again Phaid had to swallow his fear of heights. He swung his leg off the parapet, beckoned to Abrella-Lu to follow and started climbing down. Once they were both on the balcony, Phaid took the little blaster from out of his pocket. Thick black drapes concealed anything that might be behind the glass balcony doors.

'Let's hope there's nobody home.'

'If there is, they're liable to get pretty upset when we come busting in.'

'That's highly probable, but we don't have too many other options. I'm sure as hell not climbing down that ladder all the way to the street.'

Without any more words, Phaid pointed the blaster at the lock and squeezed the button. There was a flash and a roar and the lock didn't exist any longer. Phaid slid open the door, pushed aside the drapes and stepped into the room.

It was so dim inside that Phaid was unable to make out any details. The only light came from a fancifully obscene hologram. There were a number of lumpy shapes on the floor. At first Phaid took them to be inanimate objects. Then one of them stirred and a voice came out of it.

'Wow! Where the hell did you two spring from?'

The voice had the slurred, lazy thickness of a heavy duty dog gold user. Phaid started to edge towards the door on the far side of the room.

'We just landed on the roof and we're passing through on our way to the street.'

'Is that a fact? You just flew here?'

Phaid continued his edging.

'Our arms are real tired.'

'Think you could teach me to fly?'

Phaid nodded.

'You've got to remember to keep your fingers together.'

'Yeah?'

'And flap hard.'

Abrella-Lu had joined in the absurd charade. The dog gold fiend yawned.

'Is the riot still going on?'

'Yeah, it's still going on.'

'Amazing.'

Phaid was almost to the door.

'It's been nice talking to you, but we've got to be going.'

'You have?'

'I'm afraid so.'

'That's a pity. You seemed like real interesting people.'
Phaid opened the door.
'We'll be seeing you.'
'Yeah. Right. Come by again.'
They let themselves out of the apartment and walked to the elevator, doing their best to look like legitimate visitors.
'Dog gold can make you fucking dumb.'
'They're happy.'
'I guess so.'
The elevator came and they rode down to the street in silence. Phaid hoped, as they crossed the lobby, that no security android would come rushing out and start questioning them. In fact, nothing happened and Phaid slowed and carefully opened the door that led to the street.
'This is going to be the difficult bit.'
'Are there many cops about?'
Phaid took a look.
'They seemed to have cleared the street. There's a line of them halfway up the next block, they look like they're holding back quite a crowd, but there's none near here.'
'You think it's safe to go out?'
'I think we could take a chance.'
Phaid and Abrella-Lu slipped out of the building entrance and hurried away, going in the opposite direction from the police lines.
'I wish we'd had some other clothes.'
'If we'd thought of it, we could have stolen some from those dopey fools upstairs.'
'If we'd thought of it.'
Phaid had an idea.
'We could always split up.'
'Don't you dare.'
They covered some six blocks without being noticed. They'd done their best to avoid both cops and rioters. At one point two cops had actually crossed the road and walked straight towards them. Phaid had felt the sweat starting to flow, but just as the cops were about to get within striking distance, a sniper opened up from a nearby roof and everybody in the whole street scattered for cover. The cops raced off to try and get the sniper and Phaid and Abrella-Lu were able to slip away in the confusion.
Finally, after far too long with fear making a choking

lump in the back of his throat, Phaid saw the sign saying Middlemas Hotel shining like a beacon in the distance. He and Abrella-Lu hurried towards it. As they turned into the lobby, he felt as though a great weight had been lifted from his shoulders.

'We made it.'

'It looks like it.'

The android desk clerk greeted them with the usual distant lack of interest. Phaid attempted a brief conversation.

'It's rough out there.'

'What-can-you-expect-for-humans?'

After that remark, there seemed to be little point in continuing. They both retreated into the elevator and rode up to Phaid's room. Phaid took off his jacket and threw it on the bed.

'So how did you enjoy your little adventure?'

Abrella-Lu smiled at him. She seemed to have recovered completely and was now a picture of calm and collection, albeit a little dishevelled.

'It was different.'

'You realise we were almost killed at least three times.'

'You have to live dangerously if you want to have any fun.'

'I think I'd rather do without fun and live a little longer.'

'So why did you want to go on the street? You could have stayed safe inside Roni-Vows' place.'

Phaid spread his hands.

'How should I know? Maybe it was the effect of the scholomine.'

Abrella-Lu's eyes narrowed and her nostrils flared.

'Scholomine? You had scholomine? How come you didn't give me any, you bastard.'

'It wasn't mine. Roni-Vows gave it to me.'

'You still could of got me some.'

'He wasn't doing take away orders. He just gave me a hit and that was that.'

'I just love scholomine. I think I might even kill for it.'

'It turns you blind in the end.'

'Who cares?'

Phaid did his best to make up for his lack of drugs.

'I've got a bottle stashed somewhere.'

'I want scholomine.'

Phaid was starting to become bored with the spoiled brat act.

'We don't have any.'

'We could get some.'

'Huh?'

'We could get some.'

'You really think I'm about to go into that mess outside to cop you some drugs?'

'We could send an android.'

Phaid didn't have an answer to that. He didn't like to admit to Abrella-Lu that his funds were limited. Phaid reluctantly picked up the comset and gave his room number.

'Do you have an android that could go out on an errand for us?'

'There-is-a-riot-going-on-outside.'

'No androids, huh?'

'They-will-go-but-it-will-cost-extra.'

Phaid scowled. There was something particularly offensive about being gouged by an android.

'Okay, I'll pay.'

'What-do-you-require?'

'A vial of scholomine.'

Abrella-Lu's voice piped up behind him. 'And a couple of twists of dog gold, and a bottle.'

There was a pause at the other end of the line.

'Is there some sort of problem?'

'We-don't-have-many-requests-for-scholomine. I-will-have-to-check-with-the-bellboy-to-ascertain-if-he-knows-how-to-obtain-it.'

'I'll hold.'

Phaid waited. Eventually the android voice came back.

'The-bellboy-knows-how-to-obtain-the-substance-what-quantity-do-you-require?'

'Just a single vial.'

'Are-you-aware-of-the-cost?'

'I think so, but you'd better tell me anyway.'

'My-bellhop-informs-me-that-it-will-be-three-hundred-for-a-single-vial.'

Phaid pulled a face and wondered silently if Abrella-Lu was worth three hundred plus the cost of the bottle. After the journey back to the hotel, he would have been quite happy to curl up in his bed with just the bottle for company. On the other hand, the first hit of scholomine that Roni-Vows had given him had been sufficiently interesting to make him want to try some more.

'Okay, I guess you better tell him to go get it. We'll be waiting.'

'Very-well.'

Phaid broke the connection and, feeling a little weary, he looked at Abrella-Lu, who was sitting on the bed beside him.

'The scholomine's on the way.'

She leaned over and pressed her lips to his cheek.

'Now we can really have some fun.'

'Let's hope it's less dangerous than the last lot.'

'What's the matter with you? I thought you were a gambler. Do you always want to be so safe?'

'Safe? No. Live a few months longer? Yes.'

'You're impossible.'

'I just ordered you the scholomine, didn't I?'

Abrella-Lu grinned.

'That's true.'

Her expression changed and she glanced around the small hotel room.

'Do you have a clean-off booth? I feel kind of grimy after all those streets and rooftops.'

Phaid indicated the room's only other door.

'You'll find everything you need.'

'I doubt I'll find everything I need, but I'll probably get myself freshened up a bit.'

The statement was accompanied by the hint of a leer, then she gestured towards the entertainment unit.

'While I'm gone, you could try to find us some music on that thing.'

Phaid nodded and Abrella-Lu made her exit. Obediently, he squatted down in front of the entertainment unit and fiddled with the controls. On the fourth try he got a rather more restrained version of the kind of music he'd first heard in the ballroom of the marikh line train. With a music programme set up, he finally dimmed the lights and waited for Abrella-Lu to reappear from her toilet.

He waited for nearly twenty minutes. During that time, the android bellhop delivered the drugs. Phaid paid him and noticed, with some concern, just how big a bite it took out of his rapidly dwindling cash reserves. He knew that cruising on the periphery of the court wasn't making him any money and that he would have to do something to

233

pump up his finances pretty damn soon. He wasn't exactly sure, however, how he was going to do it.

When Abrella-Lu had finally emerged, she was naked apart from her jewellery and one torn stocking held up by a garter. She immediately pounced on the vial of scholomine and greedily dropped the chemical into both eyes. For a while, she lay back gasping as the initial rush hit her, but once the full force of it faded, she turned her attention to Phaid. She led him to the bed and, for the next hour, she demonstrated her extreme versatility.

There seemed to be something inside Abrella-Lu that simply wouldn't keep still. Directly her mind and body had used up one sensation she immediately wanted to move on to a new one. There was no place in her life for standing still or taking stock. She lived from moment to moment without any apparent thought for either past or future.

Even though he'd used rather more modest amounts of the drug, Phaid quickly discovered that sex on scholomine was a truly mind wrenching experience. It had spun him at random from pleasure to pain, out on to the furthest reaches of fantasy and jolted him into abrasive reality. Phaid found himself unable to exert any control over what was going on. He had the distinct feeling that Abrella-Lu was playing him like a fish on a line.

At the end of what seemed like a century, Phaid fell back, half on the bed and half on the floor, totally satiated. After much too short a while, he realised with surprise and some consternation that Abrella-Lu wanted to start on some new game. She lay sprawled on the bed, arms cradling her head, legs spread, one knee raised. Slowly and reflectively, she chewed on a twist of dog gold and stared at the series of hallucinations that rainbowed their way across the ceiling.

'Why don't we invite another man over?'

Phaid stopped what he was doing. He'd been less than successfully trying to poor them two more drinks. The combination of booze, dog gold and scholomine had left him unsteady on his feet. His co-ordination was shot and his sense of spacial relationship had packed up and gone home for the duration.

'So I'm not enough for you?'

'I thought maybe you and him could do it and I could watch. I like to watch men perform on each other. There's

234

a very special symmetry about it.'

Phaid shook his head.

'Symmetry? I don't think I could perform with some other man. Not even for the sake of symmetry.'

'If you don't want to get another man over, why don't we get another woman up here? Then you could watch us doing it, and afterwards, I could watch you and her. What do you think about that?'

Phaid sat wearily down on the bed.

'It sounds better than another man.'

'You would say that. Who do you think we should get?'

'How should I know?'

'The easiest thing would be to tell the bellhop to fetch us a prostitute.'

Phaid sighed at the thought of another blow to his available cash. He knew that the scholomine had long since peaked and all that he really wanted to do was to fall asleep for a couple of days.

'Yeah.'

'Is that all you've got to say?'

'I think so. I'm kind of tired.'

Abrella-Lu looked surprised.

'Tired? You'll soon get over that. If we payed the whore a bit extra, I expect we could get to beat her. Have you ever beaten a woman? I have, men too. Pain is so fashionable at the moment. Of course, to be fair, I had to let a few people do it to me as well. I can't actually put my hand on my heart and say that it was the greatest, but I suppose it was an experience.'

Phaid didn't have the energy to interrupt Abrella-Lu's flow of words. he wondered if she had sneaked yet another dropper of scholomine while he'd been looking the other way.

'Of course, the only trouble with hiring a prostitute would be that we don't have enough drugs to get her into the same state as us, but what the hell, she'll be getting paid so it ought to be up to her to fake it. Don't you think so?'

Phaid felt dizzy. Was there no stopping this woman.

'Maybe.'

'On the other hand, we could call up someone we know. That way we wouldn't have to pay anything.'

'That might be a good idea.'

'It must be quite a novelty being poor.'

'Take it from me, it isn't.'

'Maybe we should call up Edelline-Lan. She's incredibly adaptable. She'd probably be a lot better than a whore. She can come up with such brilliant ideas. That's the trouble with whores. They don't have any imagination. All they want to do is work to the script. It's all so tedious and predictable.'

She rolled over and reached for the comset.

'Edelline-Lan and hurry up about it.'

There was a pause.

'Get Edelline-Lan on the set, will you?'

Phaid presumed she was talking to Hud-n, Edelline-Lan's android butler.

'I don't think I'm very popular with Edelline-Lan right at this moment.'

Abrella-Lu waved away the suggestion.

'She gets over things pretty quickly.' Her voice abruptly switched tone. 'Hello, darling, it's me, Abrella-Lu.'

Pause.

'No, I can't switch on the vision. This is audio only. I'm in this nasty little hotel near the line terminal. I'm playing with Phaid.'

Pause.

'That's right, Phaid. Yeah, he's okay except we've just about run out of ideas and we want you to come over and liven things up.'

Pause.

'What do you mean, you've just got back from a party? I thought you were a woman who knew how to enjoy yourself.'

There was a much longer pause.

'Listen, darling, I know the streets are like a battle ground. I've been out in it all. On foot, even. Phaid had to shoot two cops.'

Phaid quickly sat up.

'What the hell are you telling her that for? She could get me arrested and probably killed.'

Abrella-Lu put her hand over the comset.

'She'd never do a thing like that.'

'I wouldn't like to stake my life on it.'

'Don't be paranoid.' She turned her attention back to Edelline-Lan. 'What's that darling? . . . you aren't coming over? . . . that's a pretty poor excuse . . . yes . . . I'll tell him . . . all I can say is that I'm very disappointed.'

She pushed the comset away from her and rolled back to face Phaid.

'It seems that we have to go back to the prostitute idea. Edelline-Lan says that it's almost impossible to move around the streets. New flare-ups keep breaking out all over the city. A lot of people are saying that it's actually the start of the revolution.

She tilted her head to one side.

'Do you think it could be a revolution?'

'It could be anything.'

'I think that's rather exciting.'

'Revolution?'

'The fact that we're in this cheap little hotel, fucking our brains out and taking drugs while the outside world is falling to pieces. It's awesomely romantic. I think I'll definitely get a prostitute.'

'Maybe they've all gone off to fight for the revolution.'

'Nonsense. Whatever happens, there will always be hookers.'

For the second time she reached for the comset and started giving detailed instructions.

The girl who eventually arrived was no great beauty. She had a skinny, washed out look. Her large, dark rimmed and heavily made-up eyes had a dull furtiveness about them that told of too many cheap hustles and too many rough pairs of hands. The colour job on her hair, a garish fluorescent green, was so cheap that it was turning black at the roots. Following a current street fad, a mass of tiny glowing diodes had been threaded into the piled up mass of hair, but even about a third of those had burnt out. Phaid decided the kindest thing would be to pay her and then let her take the rest of the night off.

Abrella-Lu didn't see it that way, however. She immediately went into a huddle with the girl, going into great detail over the sexual scenario that she expected her to follow. The girl listened with attention, but a lethargic lack of emotion. She told them that her name was Chordene, but beyond that she volunteered nothing except a total, resigned passivity. In a lot of ways, Chordene reminded Phaid of the much more amateur, but equally listless Sarli, with whom he'd connected briefly on the crawler out of Freeport. Phaid felt sorry for her. He wondered who or what had made her go out to turn a trick on this riot-torn night. He also felt sorry for himself. After spending the previous night in similar athletics with Edel-line-Lan, then going through Roni-Vows' party, the riot and another bout of vigorous sex, Phaid had reached the point of total exhaustion. Abrella-Lu woundn't, however, take no for an answer. She dosed him with more scholo-mine and the bleary, throbbing moist and occasionally painful games started all over again; games that became increasingly complicated now that she had two other people to deal with instead of just one.

When it was finally over, Phaid lay limp and totally drained. Abrella-Lu, however, was far from through. She picked up the almost empty scholomine vial and dropped even more into her eyes. She offered some to Phaid, but he declined, so instead she gave the last of the drug to Chordene. In the first talkative rush, she came up with yet another plan. She and Chordene should go out and work the streets a twosome for the rest of the night, Chordene for the money and Abrella-Lu for kicks. With a blast of scholomine inside her, Chordene seemed much more eager to go along with Abrella-Lu's crazy plans. They tried to persuade Phaid to join them. This time he couldn't be swayed or bullied. There was nothing, short of a strait-jacket and four burly men to carry him, that would get him down on to the streets again. His final act was to pay off the prostitute and see the two women out the door. Then he dropped on to the rumpled and destroyed bed and almost immediately fell into a deep and thankful sleep.

Phaid's slumber may have been deep and well deserved, but dim and threatening shapes gathered in his uncon-scious·causing him to twitch and whimper. Finally they merged and coalesced into one clear picture. It was a poor section of the city. The particular street was narrow and dark, little more than an alley. A single light in a window reflected on wet cobbles. A thin sickly mist hugged the ground. Everything was deathly quiet. Phaid seemed to be just an observer. In some dreams he was an active participant but this didn't seem to be one of them. He was nothing more than a disembodied, watching spirit.

For what appeared to be a very long time, nothing happened. Then, of all people, Makartur appeared out of the darkness. Even in the depths of sleep, Phaid stirred in the grip of profound unease and muttered softly. There was something measured and wary in the warrior's stride, as though he sensed danger or the possibility of some sudden assault. The thumb of his right hand was hooked around the butt of his blaster. Makartur walked nearly the full length of the alley, then he paused. He quickly looked both ways; he seemed to be checking that no one was either following or watching him, then he ducked swiftly through an archway. The presence of the dreaming Phaid drifted after him.

Beyond the arch was a flight of steps leading down to a lower level. The stairwell was barely lit by a single, aged, parchment yellow glo-globe set high in a cresset. At the foot of the stairs was a short passage. It ended in a formidable looking door of black wood, studded with iron nails and secured by a massive lock and huge curlicued hinges. The warren of buildings was clearly a very ancient part of the city. The door even had an old fashioned knocker, a heavy steel ring held in the mouth of some fierce and mythical beast. Makartur once again looked behind him and then grasped the ring. He rapped twice, then he paused and rapped three more times in quick succession. He paused slightly longer and then repeated the entire sequence.

From behind the door came the noise of bolts being pulled back. The door opened a crack, still secured against unwanted intrusion by a length of stout chain. A voice came from within. A question was asked in some gruff, guttural language. Makartur replied in the same tongue. As he spoke he flipped a small leather charm bag from inside his tunic. He held it up for inspection. It was the thing to which Phaid had seen him making his devotions that first night on the crawler. Makartur must have spoken the correct responses because the door swung to for a moment, the chain was removed and it reopened, just wide enough to let Makartur slip inside. It slammed hastily behind him.

A figure in a brown robe and hood bowed deeply. His arms were folded in front of him, his hands concealed inside wide sleeves.

'I must apologise for posing the question and using the old tongue before you had even crossed our threshold.'

Makartur bowed in return.

'It is understandable. I am not of your circle, just a traveller and a stranger in this place.'

'I'm afraid that the priests of the heresy have been

infected by the same madness that grips this whole city. They seemed determined to stamp us out. All through the Republic, hundreds of the faithful have been dragged to the dungeons and torture chambers of the heretics. Their spies infiltrate our circles, and squads of armed militants search out and destroy our temples. We have lost three from this very circle in the last month. We'll not see them again.'

Makartur was becoming a little impatient with the litany of despair.

'I am no spy and I am no heretic. I have come here to approach the first gate and seek the knowledge of my ancestors.'

'These are harsh times.'

Makartur sniffed rudely.

'Harsh times are sent by our ancestors and our gods in order to strengthen us. We meet them with fortitude, not with whining and complaint.'

Makartur was a warrior, he had no time for the furtiveness and fear of these city weaklings, even if they did share a common religion. He looked around what was obviously an ante-room of the underground temple. It was a place of browns and greys. Two more robed figures stood against the bare stone wall. A smoky brazier burned in one corner and the air was thick with incense. Beside the brazier was a statue of Aggea, the baleful mother deity who, according to legend, had eaten all her husbands and all but one of her offspring. The sole survivor was Godking Braku, whose image would be in the main temple. The light in the ante-room came from a hundred or more candles that seemed to have been placed on nearly every flat surface. The ceiling was blackened with soot and cascades of congealed wax hung from every candlestick. Piles of mouldering books littered the walls and heaped up in the corners. The atmosphere was one of a church that had once been venerable and spacious but which was now compressed and driven into dim and claustrophobic underground tunnels. The temple elder in the robe spoke coldly. He was obviously offended at Makartur's blunt arrogance.

'Have you prepared yourself for receipt of the knowledge you seek?'

Makartur nodded.

'Aye.'

'And have you prepared yourself for the ordeal of seeking?'

'Aye. I have meditated. I have meditated for long days.'

'Then there is no reason why you should not begin your journey into night, your conduct to the first gate of death.'

Makartur's face was grim.

'None whatever.'

The other two robed figures moved forward. One set a small, three-legged stool beside Makartur. The other helped him remove his tunic and strip to the waist. He was seated on the stool and cold water was brought in a small silver bowl. The elder stood in front of Phaid and watched while his two assistants gently and ritualistically cleansed the warrior's arms and torso. Once the process was completed, the elder stretched out his hand. Almost absent-mindedly he traced one of the more obvious scars that criss-crossed the warrior's shoulders, then he caught himself and became more businesslike. He held out his hands to one of the assistants who passed him a heavy copper jar. It contained a dark green ointment that he proceeded to rub on to Makatur's body.

Makartur's eyelids began to drop. The ointment contained a powerful hypnotic herb that was supposed to free the user's mind and make possible his or her journey to the edge of the spirit world. When the anointing was finished, the elder stepped back and asked Makartur a series of ritual questions in the old tongue. Makartur gave the proper responses, then one of the assistants handed him a silver chalice filled with a dark red wine that had been infused with more natural hallucinogens. Makartur's motor responses seemed to be slipping away. A small bead of wine ran out the corner of his mouth and trickled down into his beard. The elder asked a more lengthy and complicated question. This time Makartur could only just slur his way through the response. Sweat was running down into his eyebrows and streaking the green paste that coated his chest. His eyes were nearly shut. The pupils were little more than pinpoints. With some difficulty the two assistants helped Makartur to his feet. The elder opened another black wood door. It led to the inner area of the temple.

The inner area was small, another rabbit warren room just like the first one. It was, however, cleaner and less cluttered, the stone walls were hidden behind black drapes. Facing the door was a small, plain wood altar that bore a short, unsheathed dagger, a tall red, lit candle, a growing plant with small red flowers and a statue of Braku the god king. The floor was also black. A large white circle was painted just in front of the altar. Behind the circle there was a pattern of stars in gold. The illusion was one of supernatural power but, on close examination, the temple had the makeshift, temporary look, the kind of look that had to be expected in a church that had been forced underground.

Makartur was taken to the centre of the circle. He sank to a kneeling position. For a moment it seemed as though he was going to fall but then he righted himself and remained on his knees, just swaying slightly. The two assistants left the room. The elder remained facing the statue of Braku. When the door closed, he bowed low, then, straightening up, he faced the angry, glowering face of the bronze image of the god king. Flatteringly, he started to talk directly to the idol in the old tongue. The idol seemed to watch him impassively, a pair of long fangs extended over his petulant lower lip. The elder built up his address. From the way he moved his hands, he appeared to be introducing Makartur to the statue and pleading on his behalf. The harangue was a long one. When he was finally finished he bowed again and took a number of backward steps, leaving Makartur alone in the pool of candlelight.

For a while, Makartur did nothing, then the elder whispered from the darkness.

'The offering! Make the offering.'

Makartur swayed. He fumbled in the pouch at his belt. With a great deal of difficulty, he extracted five gold coins. Gold coins were exceedingly old and exceedingly rare. The few that were left mainly circulated among the less sophisticated, rural peoples who didn't trust any of the modern currencies. Makartur placed them on the floor, just outside the circle. The flame of the candle seemed, for an instant, to flicker and dim. Makartur looked up at the statue.

'Lord Braku . . .'

His voice was little more than a harsh rasp. He had difficulty forming words.

'Lord Braku . . . I am a warrior. I do not have the old tongue, but I am a good warrior. Lord Braku, you are the judge and the destroyer, you are the guardian of the eternal cycle, you are ultimately powerful and uniquely merciless, you are the unforgiving. You know that I do not lie when I tell you that I have never betrayed my trust as a warrior . . .' Makartur hesitated again. This bout of effusive praise seemed to have drained his strength. His breathing was laboured. 'Permit me . . . to approach the portals . . . so the knowledge of my ancestors, should they endeavour to bestow it, may come to me . . . through the first door and help me in my journey in this mortal world . . . I beg you Lord Braku . . . I am unsure in my path and in my destiny and I need the knowledge . . . aid me Lord Braku . . . let me approach the portals.'

For a long time there was silence except for Makartur's irregular and painful breathing. The candle once again seemed to flicker and dim. Makartur started gulping air in short swift gasps. It was almost as though he was going into a seizure. Suddenly a strangled scream was wrenched from him.

'Mother! Mother! All my mothers!'

And then another, softer voice came from Makartur's mouth.

'Makartur, Makartur, we never thought that you would seek the first gate.'

The voice was gently chiding. Makartur's own rasp returned.

'A man . . .'

'We know of the man. We have seen how your destinies have been woven one with the other. We have heard your meditations and we have seen how the man disturbs your inner vision. We see how you feel the clash of two destinies. It rings with the sound of cymbals and the road is one of death.'

'But what of my vows? What of the family revenge I seek in this city?'

'Your paths are locked, our son. You will not fulfil those vows until death has separated your destinies, and perhaps not even then. Only death can set you free from his. There was a point where too much was shared. It was a sad sharing, it leads to a death in a place of great dishonour and only the strength of a great warrior will save him who dies from the pit.'

'And . . . who . . . dies?'

'In all there is freewill. Destiny runs to death, but only the death of one in this meeting. The first will die and even risk the pit. The second will continue on his journey to some other end. If you are present at his death, he will not be present at yours.'

A small whisp of ectoplasm trembled at the corner of Makartur's mouth. The eyes of the bronze statue seemed to glow as though being heated from within.

'Do . . . I . . . kill . . . the man?'

'If you are not present at the death of the man Phaid, he will be present at your death. You may know no more, our son.'

The voice was stern. All the mothers of Makartur had no time for weaklings. Makartur's head sagged, but he slowly raised it.

'Then . . . I . . . must . . . kill . . . the man Phaid.'

Makartur, although exhausted, was filled with resolve.

'I will kill the man Phaid.'

The man Phaid woke screaming in his hotel room. He could scarcely believe the obscenely vivid nightmare. All Phaid's boyhood superstitions swamped him. It was a wave of age-old horror. He had been there. Makartur had taken the deadly path to the world of his dead ancestors. Capricious ancestor gods had allowed Phaid to witness the happening while he slept. There was, however, an urban, modern side of Phaid's mind that simply didn't buy the mumbo jumbo. It told him it was a nocturnal anxiety attack. Makartur didn't like Phaid and Phaid was nervous of his warrior temper. The dream was just an expression of that, nothing else. It was no reason to drop everything and flee the city. No matter how much though, the sophisticate tried to reassure the primitive, Phaid couldn't shake the feeling that, if he ever ran into Makartur again, he would be running into an implacable enemy.

15

TORRENTIAL RAIN had moved in from over the mountains. It was the kind of relentless driving rain that came down in straight grey lances. It told Phaid that somewhere one of the wind bands had moved slightly, shifting in its course. It was only a prolonged storm in Chrystianaville, but out in the countryside, a previously habitable strip of land was either being scorched barren by blasts of superheated air or turned into permafrost by sub-zero gales. Animals would be dying, people fleeing from their homes and maybe even a whole town left standing, abandoned in the face of the savage weather system.

In the city, the rain had come as something of a blessing, at least to the Chrystianaville establishment. It had almost totally damped down the rioting and unrest in the streets. The various factions had taken their revolution indoors to smoulder for a while longer in secret.

Things weren't, however, totally quiet. Despite the downpour, the Day Oners managed some sporadic sniping from windows and rooftops. Police stood in wary, disgruntled groups on most main street corners. Transparent rain slickers covered their red riot armour.

A few sullen knots of citizens had also braved the rain. They sheltered in doorways, building entrances and beneath overpasses. The sparse crowds made no moves. They simply stood in silence and stared with damp malice at the squads of police.

Phaid watched all this from inside an autocab. Rain streamed down the outside of the clear plastic passenger bubble and the air inside was humid to the point of being steamy. Phaid, however, wasn't paying very much attention to what was going on either inside or outside the cab. His own troubles took up all his attention. First there had been the dream and his inability to shake the irrational fear that it wasn't a mere nightmare but was some kind of supernatural warning, that somewhere in the city, Makartur was fixing to kill him. After the nightmare it had taken him more than two hours to fall back into fitful, disturbed sleep. Even that didn't last long, however. Sometime during the morning the communicator has shrilled him awake again and laid a fresh burden squarely on his shoulders. He was arbitrarily summoned to meet Orsine for dinner that same evening. A summons from the city's top mobster was something one didn't refuse. It wasn't advisable to plead weariness, a sick stomach, a scholomine comedown, abject superstitious fear or the fact that it was raining outside. When Orsine summoned, one went. Thus it was that sunset found Phaid sunk in the back of an autocab, fretting miserably as the android handler made little headway in the totally snarled traffic.

In fits and starts that couldn't have averaged much more than walking pace, the autocab finally made it to a building with a small discreet awning running across the sidewalk. It bore the legend Krager's Eating House. The handler flipped open the passenger door and Phaid dashed towards Krager's entrance, doing his best to get under the awning and into the restaurant before he was soaked through by the pelting rain.

Krager's was one of the few top class eating houses in the city that wasn't totally monopolised by the court and the aristos. Its major patrons were the big men in the mobs, successful entrepreneurs and merchants and the more overtly corrupt mandarins of the bureaucracy. It had the deep pile and rich aroma of money. Discreet, peach coloured mirrors rewarded the elegant diners with flattering images of themselves. The lights were low. Each table was effectively lit by pencil thin glo-bars that were incorporated in delicate arrangements of flowers. Thick carpet and heavy red drapes muffled the clink of china, crystal and cutlery and kept conversations to the limits of their own tables.

An android head waiter rolled towards Phaid on well oiled bearings. Its finish was a gleaming black, and somehow a permanent expression of disapproval seemed to have been built into its design.

'Do-you-have-a-reservation?'

'I'm meeting Orsine.'

'That-gentleman-has-a-private-room. I-will-have-to-check. He-maintains-very-careful-security.'

The head waiter glided away and Phaid stood waiting, feeling slightly embarrassed. Enough time elapsed for that embarrassment to thoroughly sink in before the head waiter returned with two bullet headed humans.

Their suits were conservatively tailored, one in lime green and the other mustard yellow. The knee length, quasi-military coats strained to accommodate their hulking chests and shoulders. They were obviously two of Orsine's gorillas.

Earlier in the evening, Edelline-Lan had sent her android Hud-n with Phaid's clothes, neatly cleaned and pressed, and his fuse tube. He'd put on the clothes he'd bought in Fennella because the outfit that Edelline-Lan had given him was too patently designed to make him look like the ever available stud. It wasn't an image that he particularly wanted to cultivate in front of Orsine. He'd also hung the fuse tube from his belt because of the state of affairs on the street.

He thought the clothes were okay, but he started to have serious second thoughts about the fuse tube. These were confirmed when the first move the gorillas made was to unceremoniously pat him down for weapons. Other diners turned and craned around with interest. Phaid felt his embarrassment go about as deep as it could, then one of the gorillas hauled out the fuse tube.

'What's this?'

Phaid tried a defiant stand.

'What does it look like?'

'We don't want to hear any smart remarks. We're asking why you arrive at a meeting with the Adjudicator carrying a heavy duty fuse tube.'

'Doesn't everyone carry a weapon at the moment? Sweet Lords, you've seen what it's like out on the street.'

The gorillas remained totally impassive.

'You have come to a meeting with the Adjudicator with a heavy duty fuse tube. That is a fact, a fact that is not likely to please the Adjudicator.'

Phaid swallowed hard. Within seconds of walking into

the eating house he seemed to have got himself into serious trouble with the Silent Cousins. Trouble with the Cousins was quite frequently the last trouble that a person could get into.

The gorillas positioned themselves on either side of him and walked Phaid through the public part of the restaurant. Every eye in the place seemed to be on him. A curtain in the rear was pulled aside by an android waiter. Behind the curtain was a door flanked by two more gorillas. They gave Phaid the heavy eyeball, but, since he was so completely escorted, they made no comment.

The door was opened and Phaid entered a small private room. It was discreetly lit and draped in deep, rich purple. There were only three tables, and just one of them was occupied. Orsine was wearing a sober, businesslike black tabard. Beside him was a very young woman with fluffy light blue hair. She was also dressed in black, but the outfit could in no way be considered businesslike, unless, of course, her business was showing off quite considerable areas of her pale, rather delicate skin.

The back of her gown was cut so low that it dipped well past the base of her spine, and gave anyone who looked a sneak preview of her small rounded bottom. A diamond collar around her throat looked as though it could keep someone in luxury for six months or more.

Phaid, however, wasn't in any mood to look at girls. He was more concerned with getting over the *faux pas* about the fuse tube and keeping all his limbs intact.

Orsine seemed affable enough. He waved Phaid to an empty chair, but then the gorilla who'd confiscated Phaid's weapon stepped in front of him. With more drama than Phaid thought strictly necessary, he placed the tube right in the middle of the table.

There were two more gorillas behind Orsine's chair. They looked from Phaid to the fuse tube and back to Phaid again. It seemed every eye in the room was drilling into him. Only Orsine himself seemed unperturbed. He even half smiled at Phaid.

'What were you planning to do, start a war?'

Phaid did the best he could to conceal that his stomach had turned to jelly.

'I thought, with the way things are out on the street, it would be wise to have a little protection.'

Raising his eyebrows, Orsine picked up the fuse tube

and felt its weight.

'A little protection?'

'Maybe it is a bit of a cannon, but I've had it with me for a long time.'

'And you're fond of it?'

'I wouldn't put it that strongly. I've more grown used to it.'

'It's something of a gauche weapon for the city. Most normal people don't go around with something the size of this strapped to their hip. I would strongly suggest that you rid yourself of this long barrelled monstrosity and find a more civilised weapon. The other alternative is that you get your man or your android to carry the thing for you.'

'I don't have an android and I certainly don't have a man.'

Orsine looked at him questioningly.

'I had a distinct recollection of you travelling with an android.'

'I had to let him go. He wasn't really mine in the first place.'

'I see.'

Orsine continued to examine Phaid's weapon.

'You know, the only time it's considered polite to carry one of these is if you're going to fight a duel. Even then, you are supposed to carry a matched pair in a case.'

The very last thing that Phaid had expected was for Orsine to give him a lesson in etiquette.

'I'm not likely to have to fight a duel.'

'I wouldn't be so sure. I hear you've been running around with some of the ladies of the court. There's nothing those broads like better than getting two men out duelling.' He put his arm around the young woman. 'You wouldn't do anything like that, would you, sweetness.'

'Of course not, honey.'

'This is Sena. Say hello to Phaid, Sena.'

Sena glanced at Phaid with a total lack of interest.

'Hello, Phaid.'

Phaid had a slight, hopeful feeling that maybe nothing was going to happen to him after all. He looked directly at Orsine.

'You seem to have been checking up on me.'

'I like to know what's going on.'

'I wouldn't have thought I was important enough.'

'One can never assess one's own place in the scheme

of things.'

Phaid decided it was time to take a now or never chance.

'If you've been checking up on me, you know that I didn't bring that fuse tube with me with any intention of harming you.'

Orsine looked at Phaid very hard for a long time.

'Are you nervous, young man?'

For the first time, Phaid saw Orsine as the mobster that he was. Beneath the urbane exterior was a greedy savage who enjoyed inspiring fear and took pleasure in inflicting mental and physical pain. Phaid wished fervently that he'd noticed this before. There was no way to backpedal now. He had no choice but to brazen things out to whatever the bitter end might be.

'I'm still standing, and I'd thought I'd been invited for a meal.'

Orsine half smiled. There was a little humour in it.

'Indeed, but you arrived for this meal armed to the teeth.'

'I've already explained that I was merely protecting myself. I was almost killed in the street yesterday.'

'You also burned down some police officers.'

Phaid was horrified.

'You know about that?'

'I know about most things, but frankly, police officers are none of my concern. What does concern me is your lack of good manners. I consider it extremely ill-mannered to come armed to an appointment for dinner.'

'I'm sorry.'

Orsine ignored Phaid and turned to the nearest gorilla.

'You think you could give this young man a lesson in manners?'

The gorilla smiled nastily and cracked his knuckles.

'Just say the word, Adjudicator.'

Phaid felt sick. There wasn't much point in keeping up a brave front any longer. There seemed to be no doubt that he was going to get his legs broken or worse. Then, to his surprise, Orsine smiled at him for the second time.

'What about you, young man, do you think that you need a lesson in manners?'

Phaid knew his next words were crucial. They were the only things that might get him off a very sharp and unpleasant hook. He chose them with extreme care.

'I'm not going to forget what's happened today in a hurry. I don't think it needs any reinforcing. I'm truly sorry that I brought a weapon to your table. It was an error but not made with any intention of insulting you.'

There was a long silence which, to Phaid's amazement, was finally broken by Sena.

'Ah, let him sit down, will you, honey? He didn't mean any harm, and besides, he's kind of cute.'

Phaid's jaw almost dropped as Orsine suddenly beamed.

'If that's the way you want it, baby.' He waved a pudgy hand at Phaid. 'Sit down, boy, sit down. Just don't pull nothing like that again, you hear?'

Phaid nodded and lowered himself shakily into the indicated chair. He could scarcely believe that his being torn limb from limb had been averted simply by the whim of Orsine's mistress. From that point on it was as if the incident over the fuse tube had never happened, although the weapon still lay in the middle of the table and served as a mute reminder to Phaid, if nobody else.

An android was summoned and menus were handed around. The variety of dishes were both impressive and frighteningly expensive. Phaid's adrenalin was still pumping so fast that he didn't feel capable of thinking about choosing, let alone eating a meal. Fortunately, Orsine took total control.

'The chef here is human. One of the few in the city who really knows what he's doing.'

Orsine leaned confidingly towards Phaid.

'You never want to trust an android chef. All they have is programming. There's no feel, no magic, no inspiration. How could they have? They never eat. They don't know what we're looking for in a good meal. Consequently, they don't have the touch.'

The human chef was as much cabaret as cuisine. He performed for the diners applause. Orsine's private room came equipped with its own chef's workbench on a raised platform. To Phaid, it looked like a combination of altar, alchemist's workshop and kitchen counter.

The glo-bars that illuminated the tables dimmed slightly. A set of small spotlights set in the ceiling brightened, making the platform the focal point of the whole room.

The chef entered through a small door at the rear of the platform. He was accompanied by an assistant, and both

251

had the ponderous theatrical pose of an officiating priest and acolyte.

The chef watched impassively as the assistant laid out the ingredients, then he went to work with a flourish. The chef was a short man with the flat features and narrow slanting eyes that marked him as one of the Tharmiers who lived on the wide fertile coast plain beyond the great icefield, the one that formed the southern boundary of the Republic.

Despite a rather overdeveloped sense of ritual, they were an easygoing, sensual people who had made the satisfying of the physical pleasures into a high art. Their cooks could perform near miracles. They could always count on first-class appointments and generous retainers if they felt like leaving their homeland and hiring out their skills elsewhere. Others who crossed the icefield to take positions as courtesans were among the most prized and successful that could be found in any city.

The chef's hands moved at lightning speed among bowls, pots and glass containers. He chopped, mixed, blended and stirred amid rising steam and brief explosions of pale fire. He spun and tossed and wielded his knives and stirring rod with the unerring dexterity of a master. The private room was filled with a rich, tantalising aroma. Even Phaid, who had thought that the shocks of the evening had completely killed his appetite, started looking forward to the meal.

Finally the chef was finished. He exited through the same door by which he had entered, with a great deal of flamboyant bowing. The assistant was left to serve the guests.

Only Orsine, Phaid and Sena had food placed in front of them. The gorillas all remained standing. They were clearly Orsine's private guard and they didn't join him for meals. Phaid didn't feel exactly comfortable eating with all this security around him, but this was more than compensated for by the exquisite dishes that arrived with precision timing.

The meal was conducted in silence. It was the silence that comes only when food demands total concentration. Eating was such a sensual experience that it eliminated the need for conversation.

When each and every dish was empty, and glasses of clear mexan liqueur were flamed by the chef and placed in front of each guest, Orsine pushed back his chair with a satisfied, almost bloated smile.

'One of the few recompenses for a life of unrelenting toil and responsibility is that I get to dine well.'

Sena fractionally curled the left corner of a perfect upper lip in what had to be the start of a carefully constructed sneer.

'Not the only recompense, I hope.'

For an instant, Orsine looked at her questioningly. Right on cue, her eyes melted into wide, goo-goo innocence. He ran a pudgy hand down her back.

'Of course not, honey, of course not.'

Sena arched her spine and virtually purred. Phaid wondered if the woman was totally infatuated with the Adjudicator or simply, in her own way, doing as good a job as the chef. Phaid wasn't, however, left much time to speculate. Orsine was once again scrutinising him.

'So, Master Phaid, how do you find our city after so long an absence?'

'Somewhat of a mess, I'm afraid.'

'You're not another one who thinks that revolution is just around the corner.'

'I haven't seen enough to make a final judgement. It certainly seems as though there is a lot wrong with this city. Don't you worry about the possibility of revolution?'

Orisine, who had been idly starting down the front of Sena's dress, looked up sharply.

'Worried? Why should I be worried? A revolution would mean little or nothing to me. I frankly don't give a damn if Chrystiana-Nex is dragged screaming from the palace and the whole court is put against the wall and blasted. This city cannot function without my organisation. Whoever takes over will realise that pretty damn quick. Deals can always be done.'

Phaid scratched his ear.

'The Day Oners seem to be talking in terms of a whole new start, of tearing down everything.'

Orsine dismissed the Day Oners with a snort.

'They'll never achieve power. They'll never achieve it because they're mad. They're a fringe, a lunatic minority. Anyone who aspires to power must know that, even if he used madmen, his very first task, once the old order has been run out, is to destroy those madmen, destroy them totally.'

Phaid wondered if Orsine had a few dreams of his own of taking up residence in the Presidential Palace. It wasn't beyond the bounds of possibility. A mobster run Republic might be a pleasanter place than one ruled over by an insane woman. With unusual bravery. he decided that it wouldn't hurt to gently test the water.

'Maybe that's what you'd do. Others might not be so smart.'

Orsine's eyes narrowed, then he suddenly laughed.

'You're a perceptive young man. Perhaps you'd better tell me what you've heard about me in your wanderings around the city.'

Despite the laughter, Phaid knew that once again he was moving into dangerous territory. He did his best to look as innocent as possible.

'I've only been in the city for a few days. I doubt I would have heard anything you don't already know.'

'Don't try and con me, I'm too old for that sort of thing. What have you heard?'

'Only scraps.'

'What, damn you?'

Phaid didn't seem to be able to win against the Adjudicator. The old man was the perfect blend of paranoia and cunning.

'I heard that you had your troubles.'

'Troubles?'

'That subordinates were jealous of your position.'

'Scarlin-Fell?'

'The name was mentioned.'

'I'll wager it was.'

'Is he a danger?'

'He's ambitious. He'd like to be where I am, but he hasn't a chance.'

'You plan to get rid of him?'

Orsine shook his head and smiled, a smile that sent shivers through Phaid's scalp.

'The Adjudicator doesn't get rid of ambitious subordinates. This isn't the court. The secret of success is to attract inferiors who, in their inadequacy, choose to promote you because it will gain them advantage. If, however, one of those inferiors climbs above his station, then you have to crush him like a bug.'

For the first time, Phaid had the suspicion that maybe Orsine was also touched by the madness that prevailed in the city.

'That would be an incentive to stay in one's place.'

Orsine regarded Phaid as a teacher might regard a bright pupil.

'Let's hope Scarlin-Fell is as intelligent as you are, for his own good.'

For a moment, Orsine looked frighteningly grim, and then his expression suddenly changed.

'But enough of my problems. I want to hear more of what you've observed around our fair but disturbed city.'

Phaid shrugged.

'What can I tell you? The population seems restless. The court is decadent, the government has ceased to function and the President has apparently gone mad. You know all this already.'

'What do you know of Solchaim?'

'Solchaim?'

The name of the elaihi was cropping up in conversation a little too regularly to be strictly coincidental. Orsine leaned towards Phaid. The air of meance was back and directed straight at him.

'Don't play coy with me, boy. I have it on good authority that you've encountered elaihim on your travels, and I want to know all about them. A lot of the problems in this city go back to this Solchaim. It seems that no one can touch him. I want to know what makes these creatures tick.'

Phaid was starting to wonder if he was the only person in the city who had ever met elaihim face to face and just how much the experience was worth. There followed a question and answer session that almost completely paralleled the one that Roni-Vows had conducted the previous day. Orsine was a little more probing and a great deal shrewder than the courtier, but the information he wanted was exactly the same. Phaid was now certain that Solchaim had to be the key to what was going on in the city. He wasn't sure how or why, but people seemed awfully anxious to pump him on the subject. Phaid knew that he should capitalise on his knowledge. He just wasn't sure how. There had to be more in it than a traumatic free meal or a shot of scholomine.

Just as the interrogation was drawing to a close, Phaid was aware of a high pitched buzzing noise at the very edge of his hearing range. At first he wondered if it was his imagination, some after effect of the scholomine he'd taken the night before. Then he saw the gorillas starting to get edgy and glance nervously at each other. Finally Orsine noticed and swung around angrily.

'What the hell is that sound? Will somebody do something about it?'

As though on cue, the sound suddenly rose to a deafening roar. A section of wall glowed bright cherry red, fragmented and then crumbled and cascaded into the room. It was accompanied by a billowing cloud of smoke and dust through which four masked figures suddenly appeared.

'Day One! Day One!'

They had blasters in their hands and obviously meant business. The first one through the gaping hole in the wall burned down the nearest gorilla at point blank range.

There was a frozen moment in the room when everyone seemed too shocked to do anything. Then a second gorilla was taken out by the intruders' weapons. The stench of burned flesh replaced the lingering aroma of food. Orsine was suddenly galvanised into action. He dived sideways, pushing Sena roughly away from him, clean off her chair and on to the floor. At the same time, he upended the table, scattering its contents. The overweight gourmet was suddenly showing all the reflexes of a violent, street fighting past.

As the table tilted, Phaid's fuse tube slid towards him. He grabbed the weapon and threw himself backwards as hard as he could. He hit the ground with much more force than he'd intended. It knocked all the breath out of him and for an instant he thought he'd broken his back.

The three of the Adjudicator's guards stationed outside burst into the room with weapons in their hands. They hesitated in the doorway, trying to make out what was going on through the clouds of dust and smoke. It was a fatal hesitation. The intruders' blasters roared again and all three were cut down, spinning backwards and collapsing like puppets with cut strings.

Orsine had a tiny fuse tube in his hand. He fired and rolled sideways. An intruder screamed and staggered. The carpet burned as three blasts hit the spot where he'd previously been lying. The last of his gorillas was caught in the crossfire. He grimaced and clutched his arm, but stayed on his feet. His blaster roared and a second intruder went down.

Phaid, who'd been flat on his back trying to breathe, was aware of a figure standing over him levelling a blaster. Phaid shot desperately from the hip, without even aiming. To his surprise, he caught the intruder full in the chest.

Phaid scrambled quickly to his feet. There was now only one attacker still standing. Not liking the odds of three to one, the intruder darted for the door. He was stopped, however, by the blue lash of a stun blast. Two android waiters were standing there, presumably to keep the violence from spreading to the rest of the eating house.

Orsine walked slowly to the stunned Day Oner. He coldly pointed his fuse tube and pumped a long discharge into the still living body. Then he turned to look at Phaid. Phaid hoped that he would never be the one to cause a man to look the way Orsine did at that moment.

'Scarlin-Fell has finally overreached himself. It is now time to crush bugs.'

Phaid was bewildered.

'I don't follow you. Surely these people were Day Oners.'

Orsine laughed. It wasn't a pleasant laugh.

'That's what you're supposed to think.'

'It is?'

'Look at their shoes. Look at the clothes under those filthy duster coats. They've expensive suits; no shirtless Day Oners can afford stuff like this.' He bent down and picked up the limp arm of one of the corpses. 'This one even has a manicure and nail polish.'

For the first time, Phaid realised that one of the attackers was a woman. Orsine let the arm fall back. He had an expression of disgust.

'Day Oners, bah! These are a hit squad from Scarlin-Fell, a particularly inefficient hit squad into the bargain. The organisation is well rid of them. This whole episode has the greasy fingermarks of Scarlin-Fell all over it. I can just imagine the way he thought it out. Let the old fool gorge himself, and take him when he's stuffed and drowsy. He's going to learn to his cost that the old fool isn't so easy to take.' He noticed something among the wreckage on the other side of the room.

'Sweet Lords! Sena!'

The girl was lying against the remains of the chef's workbench. Her body was unpleasantly twisted.

257

'She's dead! The bastards have killed Sena, and just when I had her almost trained to perfection.' He glared angrily at Phaid. 'Do you realise just how long it takes for me to get a woman to do exactly what I want? Scarlin-Fell is not only going to die, he's going to take a long time doing it.'

Phaid suddenly sat down. A delayed reaction to the last few minutes had hit him hard. A small concerned crowd gathered around Orsine, but Phaid appeared to have been completely forgotten. He could scarcely believe the course that his life was taking. He had only been in the city for three days and it seemed to have turned into a non-stop round of violence punctuated by brisk intervals of sex. If asked, Phaid would have sworn his most solemn oath that, by nature, he was the kind of man who would go out of his way to avoid trouble, and yet for a long time, wherever he went, trouble seemed to surround him. It was as though he was some weird catalyst, a carrier of some mania who, although showing no symptoms himself, infected all those around him.

Orsine was conducted out of the restaurant and a team of androids and boohooms started to clear up the mess. It was only then that someone remembered Phaid, and saw that he got an autocab back to his hotel. Two things were waiting for him on his return. One was an android produced printout reminding him that he only had one more prepaid day left on his account and hinting that he ought to think about either putting up or moving out. This was depressing, particularly as it also served to remind Phaid that he was close to broke and almost completely without prospects. The other surprise package was a note from Roni-Vows suggesting that, should Phaid chose to meet him at the Palace Plaza at noon of the following day, he might learn something to his advantage. It was hand-written on lilac paper and signed with a small delicate drawing of a butterfly.

This didn't do much to cheer Phaid either. All he could hope was that 'learning something to his advantage' was a euphemism for a cash payment. It was this hope that brought him out of the hotel on a blustery morning. The rain had stopped and the sun was trying to break through the cloud. In half an hour he was stepping out of an autocab on the edge of the Plaza just a few minutes before twelve. The Palace Plaza was a broad circular expanse of multicoloured flagstones raised some eight or nine metres above the level of the avenue. One reached the Plaza by climbing the steps that extended around half the perimeter on the side facing away from the Palace. The steps were broken at regular intervals by ornamental waterfalls and fanciful sculptures.

At one time, the centrepiece of the whole Plaza had been a very large and very heroic statue of the previous president. Shortly after his death, Chrystiana-Nex had taken it into her head to have it removed. The removal had been a clumsy affair. A large crowd had gathered while a squad of sweating workmen sawed the deceased off at the ankles and carted him away, presumably to be melted down. After that, though, the work inexplicably stopped and the centrepiece remained, from then on, as a plinth with a pair of large, incongruous feet mounted on it.

The Palace side of the Plaza formed one wall of the deep, dry moat that surrounded the whole building. It was spanned by a wide curving ramp that swept up to the entrance itself. Rumour had it that the ramp was permanently mined so it could be blown in the event of a mob attempting to storm the Presidential residence.

Phaid had never particularly liked the Palace. He found its tiered façade, a jumble of pillars and bas-relief, fussily tasteless. Injury had been added to insult when a large section of what must have been the fourth storey had been torn out and an enormous holoscreen installed in order for the President to address her devoted followers. For the last year or more, however, the screen had remained ominously blank.

On any normal day, the Plaza could be expected to be thronged with people. Some would stroll, others sit, musicians and jugglers would solicit money from passersby, hawkers would display a variety of wares and many citizens could be found standing in line with petitions and favours that they sought from members of the court.

Traditionally, the more populist courtiers would set up shop near the Palace ramp where, surrounded by small knots of androids and advisors, they would listen to the complaints of the common people.

This particular day, however, was far from normal. The trouble and unrest that hung in the air had virtually cleared the Plaza. A few civil servants or courtiers hurried on their way to and from the Palace, a few of the incorrigibly curious hung around staring, but it was the police who now completely dominated the open space.

The Palace seemed to be preparing for siege. Police, both in riot armour and the more normal red jump suits, were all over the Plaza. Phaid had rarely seen such a dense concentration of manpower and weaponry. The majority of cops seemed watchful and tense. There was much club flexing and weapon checking. A pair of police flippers were grounded near the base of the ramp. This in itself showed how seriously the authorities were taking the emergency. Previously, the idea of any kind of vehicle on the Plaza was unheard of.

As Phaid walked towards the ramp looking for Roni-Vows, he noticed that jolt relays had been set up at regular intervals across the open space and continued on, presumably all around the Palace. They weren't activated, but, at the touch of a control, all approaches to the building could be criss-crossed by a web of non-lethal, but very painful fields of energy.

Phaid wondered why Roni-Vows had picked such an exposed and public place for the meeting. The thought crossed his mind that it could be some kind of set-up, but Phaid dismissed it. What could the courtier possibly gain from dropping him into trouble?

As well as the police, squads of the Presidential Guard were also in evidence. Phaid had always found them a little incongruous in their scarlet and gold, their flowing plumes, epaulets and visored helmets. The highly efficient fuse tubes that nestled in their decorative shoulder holsters made it very clear, though, that they were there for something more than merely ceremonial purposes.

They had set up two small photon cannons at the top of the ramp, positioned in such a way that they could rake the entire Plaza if the need arose. More of the guard manned a checkpoint at the base of the ramp. It was equipped with a weapon detector and an android scrutineer. The android would be programmed with the descriptions of wanted criminals and known trouble-makers. Phaid decided on principle to give this unit a wide berth.

It was now some minutes after twelve and there was still no sign of Roni-Vows. Phaid gave himself a mild mental kick for not remembering how the courtiers' code decreed that one should be late for every appointment. Neither was it a good day for standing around in the open. The excess of police activity made Phaid less than comfortable, and even the weather left much to be desired. Although the previous day's rain had stopped, there was still a damp blustery wind and a leaden overcast sky. It was the kind of day that would bring few people any good.

After some more waiting, he spotted a figure with Roni-Vows' unmistakable swishing walk coming out of the Palace. Phaid waited until he passed the checkpoint and then moved to meet him.

'How are you doing?'

Roni-Vows scowled.

'Managing to hold my own. You?'

'I'm keeping busy.'

Roni-Vows took Phaid by the arm and steered him across the Plaza. He seemed to be trying to make it look like they were two old friends out for a casual stroll. But in the middle of the display of police it was a trifle incongruous. Phaid glanced questioningly at him.

'Isn't it kind of exposed out here?'

'I didn't think it was a good idea for us to be seen together in a tavern or an eating house. You can't set an electronic eavesdropper in the open.'

'Yeah, but . . . in the middle of all this?'

'The police are on our side. You must remember that.'

'On your side maybe.'

'Just relax. I know what I'm doing.'

'Hmmm.'

They continued the awkward stroll. Phaid still felt intimidated by the police presence.

'Did it ever occur to you that it might be time to call off the cops and start talking?'

Roni-Vows twitched.

'What do you know?'

'Nothing.'

'You haven't heard anything?'

'What should I hear?'

'You seem to know a good deal for someone who just blew into town.'

Phaid shrugged.

'I'm just observant and I try to keep my smarts about me.'

'It wasn't too smart to fuse a couple of cops.'

Phaid looked quickly around to see if anyone had overheard.

'Will you keep your goddamn voice down? You could get me killed. Where did you hear that, anyway?'

'I'm observant too.'

'More likely you talked to Abrella-Lu.'

'As a matter of fact, I had to get her out of jail. She was playing at prostitutes, but then she started acting so outrageously that one of her clients cried cop.'

'That's our girl.'

'Don't I know it.'

Phaid glanced around. The proximity of so many police was making him profoundly uncomfortable.

'Listen, I don't want to appear rude or gauche and I know that long preambles before you get down to business are compulsory in elegant society, but standing about on this open plaza isn't my favourite occupation. You said you wanted to see me and that it would be to my advantage. I don't see any advantage hanging around here, so could we get to it?'

Roni-Vows raised an eyebrow.

'You're very impatient.'

'Look, if we have to fence around, could we possibly do it someplace else?'

Roni-Vows shook his head.

'I can't possibly stray from the Palace, with things the way they are.'

'Lord's teeth!'

Phaid was starting to get angry. Roni-Vows suddenly looked serious.

'I have a job for you.'

'A job?'

Roni-Vows's fingers fluttered.

'Maybe not so much a job, more a roving commission.'

'Come to the point. What do you want?'

'Information.'

'Information. What information could I have?'

'As you said, you're observant and you keep your smarts about you. In addition you also move fairly freely through a number of levels of the city. Have you had any contact with the rebels?'

'Rebels?'

'The underground, the revolution, these damned rioters, call them what you like.'

Phaid shook his head.

'None at all.'

'Could you?'

Phaid shrugged.

'Anything's possible.'

'Could you if it was made worth your trouble – fiscally?' Roni-Vows rolled the word around his tongue. Phaid regarded him dubiously.

'Is this what you want me to do? Get in with the rebels and spy on them?'

'Nothing as drastic as that. I just want you to move around in the way that you normally do and keep your eyes and ears open. Any little snippet of information you might pick up should be reported to me. Such information would, of course, be paid for in hard cash.'

'That's the offer?'

'In brief.'

Phaid thought about it. It was a little close to being a hired informer, but the mention of hard cash did quite a lot to minimise his distaste.

'What guarantee do you have that I haven't already thrown in with the rebels?'

'You haven't.'

'But I might.'

'The only person you'd throw in with would be yourself. You're a loner, my young friend.'

'You seem very sure of yourself.'

'I am.'

Phaid suddenly smiled.

'Okay, Roni-Vows. You've got a deal, for the moment, although this all sounds exceedingly desperate.'

'I have to admit that our backs are getting uncomfortably close to the wall.'

'You think the rebels are winning?'

'No, but they're shaking up an already perilously fragile structure.'

Phaid nodded and then suddenly laughed.

'I tell you what, I've already got a little titbit that ought to be worth something. There was an assassination attempt on Orsine the mobster last night.'

'At Krager's Eating House.'

Phaid was a little crestfallen.

'You knew already.'

'Since dawn.'

'Did you also know that he blames Scarlin-Fell and is planning to kill him?'

'That's news.'

Phaid smiled.

'I have my uses.'

'Unfortunately Scarlin-Fell was killed by Day Oners in the early hours of this morning. They set fire to his flipper and he was burned to death. By all accounts it was an unpleasant business.'

'They must have beat Orsine to him.'

Phaid didn't believe this. He suspected that the Day Oners were more likely to be Orsine's hirelings in disguise, exacting an efficient, poetic and agonising revenge. He didn't, however, intend to let Roni-Vows know about his theory.

Roni-Vows himself seemed to be getting impatient.

'Is there anything else?'

'There is one thing.' Phaid hesitated. 'Well . . .'

'What?'

'I could use an advance.'

Phaid didn't like having to ask Roni-Vows for money. Roni-Vows raised his head and deliberately looked down his nose at Phaid.

'You're broke.'

'Close to it.'

'You haven't given me anything valuable as yet.'

'You going to start to haggle?'

'Why not.'

'Because I know you think that I'm valuable to you, and there's always the chance that you and the rest of the court may not be in business much longer. If the rebels don't get you, your president almost certainly will. In any case, I'm no use to you if I don't have the money to move around. You should look on it as an investment.'

Roni-Vows looked as though Phaid was coming uncomfortably close to the truth.

'You could be right at that. How much do you want?'

'A thousand.'

'Don't be ridiculous.'

'You can afford it.'

'Five hundred.'

Phaid sighed grudgingly.

'Five hundred.'

Instantly Roni-Vows produced a flat leather wallet from

under his coat.

'Five hundred.'

Phaid's eyes widened in surprise.

'You had it ready?'

'I'm not as dumb as I might appear. I'd have been very disappointed if you had come up with any other figure.'

Phaid was discomfited.

'I asked for a thousand.'

'That was only a preliminary.'

'Yeah, well, I guess you just bought me.'

'Guess I did.'

Phaid silently promised himself that Roni-Vows would in no way get a fair shake for his five hundred. He was stuffing the wallet away in his coat when he noticed that Roni-Vows was staring down Nex Boulevard. He showed signs of apprehension. Phaid turned and looked in the same direction.

The first thing that he saw was a number of police flippers hanging at the maximum operating height of about four storeys. They seemed to be keeping watch on a mass of people at the other end of the Boulevard. All around where Phaid was standing the police were stiffening and readying their weapons. The Boulevard was rapidly clearing of traffic. Whatever was happening at the other end of Nex Boulevard had plugged the normally constant flow of flippers and transports. Phaid felt he had to do something, but he didn't have a clear idea of exactly what. Then Roni-Vows touched him on the arm.

'Do you know anything about this?'

Phaid shook his head.

'Don't have a clue.'

Roni-Vows waved to a police underleader wearing a comset attached to his helmet.

'What's going on?'

'Who wants to know?'

Roni-Vows drew himself up to his full height. It didn't amount to much beside the hulking officer.

'My name is Roni-Vows, and I'm an inner circle courtier quite capable of having your brassard if you don't pay me the respect due.'

The underleader didn't look particularly impressed, but also didn't seem to want to bother with an argument.

'We don't know for sure. They're calling for a requiem march.'

'What the hell's a requiem march?'

The cop shrugged.

'Who knows what the bastards will do? It's supposed to be some kind of memorial to the ones that got themselves killed in the riots. If it was me, I'd be celebrating. Anything that means there's less of the scumsuckers is good in my book.'

Phaid glanced sharply at the underleader.

'Ain't those scumsuckers the people you're supposed to be protecting?'

The underofficer's face twisted into an ugly sneer.

'Don't make me laugh.' He jerked an armoured thumb in the direction of the Palace. 'That's where my bread gets buttered, and that's what I protect. The rest are scumsuckers as far as I'm concerned.'

Roni-Vows ignored the exchange and pressed for more information.

'Are they peaceful?'

'So far. The main body of the march is supposed to be women. They're all dressed up in mourning robes. The trouble is that they're coming this way. We haven't intervened yet, but we got orders to keep them out of the Plaza. If they take it into their heads to go all the way to the Palace . . .' he hefted his blaster '. . . they'll find that they have certain problems.'

Phaid was suddenly very, very frightened. He once again peered down the Boulevard. It was clear now that a large dark mass of humanity was slowly filling Nex Boulevard and moving steadily but relentlessly towards the Palace. Phaid looked to Roni-Vows for the next move.

'What are you going to do?'

'I want to see what this turns into.'

'I've got an idea of what this is going to turn into and I'd hate to be out here when it does.'

Roni-Vows nodded.

'I think maybe I'll get myself back inside the Palace.'

'Do I get to go with you?'

Roni-Vows shook his head.

'I'm afraid not, you'd never get past the security.'

'You mean you're going to leave me out here while all hell breaks loose and you scuttle back into the Palace? You've got the influence. You could swing something.'

'There's nothing I can do. The Palace is shut up tight as a drum.'

'Shit!'

Phaid stared down Nex Boulevard. The crowd was about halfway down the length of it and still coming. Phaid could spot splashes of brilliant orange, the traditional colour of mourning in and around the Republic. The police flippers were still maintaining their hovering positions above the marchers.

Roni-Vows made a nervous gesture.

'I've got to be going.'

Phaid grunted and didn't even bother to look at the courtier. Roni-Vows seemed, for a moment, as though he was going to say something, then he changed his mind and hurried towards the ramp.

An eerie quiet had descended on the area around the Palace. The crowd moved in near silence. There were no chants. No shouting. The only sound was the shuffling of thousands of feet and the low whine of the police flippers.

The cops on the Plaza deployed themselves for action. Leaders and underleaders barked orders. There was the crash of metallic boots and the rattle of armour as they took up their positions. A double line sealed the end of the Nex Boulevard, separating the crowd from the Palace. More police remained on the Plaza as a back-up to the front line.

The tension was working its way up to an intolerable level and Phaid was right in the middle of the cops' tactical pattern. What made it doubly worse was that he now knew that the majority of cops probably thought of him as an expendable scumsucker.

The police stood silently, blasters at the ready. The march continued to roll forward. Phaid looked around for a way out. Before he found one, the underleader to whom Roni-Vows had talked grasped him by the arm.

'What are you still doing here?'

'Looking for a way out.'

'I take it that you ain't no courtier that can get me busted to the ranks.'

Phaid sadly shook his head.

'Not me.'

'Then you only get one way out, friend.'

Phaid found himself propelled none too gently towards the front line of police. At an order from the underleader, two men stepped back and Phaid was thrust out into the no-man's land between the police and the marchers.

Despite the danger that he was in, Phaid's strongest emotion was an acute feeling of being totally ridiculous. He obviously couldn't stay where he was, but there was something completely absurd about one man walking down a wide empty avenue to meet a marching crowd many thousands strong.

Some of the front ranks looked at him curiously, but Phaid avoided their eyes. The march swallowed him up and he gratefully worked his way to the back. By the time he'd found a position in which he felt comfortable, the front ranks were less than a hundred metres from the police.

As the underleader had told Roni-Vows, the majority of the marchers were indeed women. They were all ages and came from all levels of Chrystianaville society, only the very upper extremes were not represented.

Solid housewives rubbed shoulders with street women, well fed young girls linked arms with elderly crones from the northside. Some wore their street clothes, others long duster coats that had become an unofficial uniform for the rebels. The highest proportion of the marchers, however, were wrapped in the traditional mourning robe, the orange that was supposed to symbolise the life giving power of the sun, and the black trim that was a reminder that even the sun was ringed around by darkness.

Although the marchers' intent seemed to be peaceful enough, many had come prepared for trouble. Breathing masks and protective helmets made an incongruous picture under the cowls of a lot of the robes.

There were men with the march, but most of them walked on the outside edges. They were more like an escort than an actual part of the protest. Phaid did his best to blend in with them. In the rear ranks, nobody seemed to take much notice that he'd joined the procession from the front.

The march was some fifty metres from the police line when the screen in front of the Palace suddenly came alive in a flurry of menacing abstract shapes.

A thunderously amplified voice boomed out. It must have been audible to everyone in the crowd.

'THIS GATHERING HAS BEEN DECLARED ILLEGAL! YOU WILL DISPERSE IMMEDIATELY!'

The leading marchers faltered for a few moments, then their resolution seemed to crystallise. They continued to move forward. The voice crashed out again.

'THIS GATHERING HAS BEEN DECLARED ILLEGAL! YOU WILL DISPERSE IMMEDIATELY!'

This time there was no hesitation. The crowd went on steadily walking. The police snapped shut the visors on their helmets. The voice came for a third time.

'YOU HAVE IGNORED TWO WARNINGS! THERE WILL BE NO MORE AFTER THIS! IF YOU DO NOT DISPERSE IMMEDIATELY, THE POLICE WILL BE INSTRUCTED TO USE ALL NECESSARY FORCE TO BREAK UP THIS GATHERING!'

The front ranks slowed to a halt. The marchers behind continued to move forward. There was some pushing and shoving, but then the message spread rapidly back and the entire march finally came to a standstill. For a while there was an eerie silence.

Scattered women among the crowd started to sing. The singing was without any words, a kind of low, anguished crooning that rose and fell according to no definable pattern. More and more women joined in. The sound grew until it filled all the air, a total embodiment of loss and desolation. Phaid knew that it was the song for the dead. Its origins went back far beyond the city and the foundation of the Republic. Women sung the song when Chrystianaville had been nothing more than a meeting place of nomadic tribes.

The voice blasted back at the singing women.

'YOU HAVE TEN SECONDS TO DISPERSE! REPEAT, TEN SECONDS! YOU HAVE BEEN WARNED!'

The women continued to sing. A few of the cops started to look profoundly uncomfortable. Their blasters dipped and their menacing stance slumped. They began to show signs of uncertainty. Some of the women in the front ranks picked up on the change. They began to shout over the singing.

'Are you going to blast women in mourning?'

'Are you that far gone?'

'Chrystiana-Nex has bought your souls!'

'Your mother might be in this crowd!'

More and more of the police began to show signs of indecision. They were no longer an implacable line of armour.

Phaid could scarcely believe what he was seeing. It was starting to look as though the police were going to lower their blasters and, if not go over to the rebels, at least do nothing to stop them. Then the voice roared out again.

'POLICE PREPARE TO ADVANCE!'

Quite a few of them stiffened at the order, but, significantly, quite a few didn't.

'ADVANCE ON LINE!'

About half of the police front line took a step forward. The other half didn't move. There was hesitation, confusion. Phaid stood on tip-toe to get a better look. Incredibly, it seemed as though the women had won. The individual cops weren't going to move in on the crowd. They were ignoring their orders.

Then there was a commotion among the front ranks of marchers. Phaid craned to see what was going on. About a dozen women in a tight group were storming towards the wavering police. They were shouting something and pulling weapons from under their mourning robes.

'Day One! Day One!'

They opened fire on the police. Bodies started falling. Phaid closed his eyes in horror. He could hear himself yelling.

'No! No! Don't be so fucking stupid!'

The Day One women gave the police something they could focus on. They snapped back into their normal role of unthinking, disciplined aggression. All the tension and confusion of the previous minutes were released in one flaming roar. The cops let go with every weapon they had.

All of the Day Oners were cut down in the first eruption of police fire. They weren't the only ones to get it. The police didn't bother to be selective. There were screams as many of the front ranks of marchers were hit. The previously orderly crowd broke in panic and started bolting in every direction. Phaid was pushed hard against a wall by a huge screaming matron who ran straight into him.

At the same moment the police flippers overhead discharged a rain of heavy, brightly coloured, yellow and purple gas. The billowing clouds cascaded down on to the crowds below like an evil enveloping fog.

16

Clawed demons from some childhood nightmare were ripping at Phaid's flesh. Their eyes burned hellfire red in the sockets of skull-like faces. Yellow fangs dripped with corosive slime. Hysteria was welling up in his chest. It threatened to burst his ribcage and blow him apart. He wanted to scream and scream until his eyes split open and he could no longer see the demons or feel the pain.

The last few shreds of his tattered sanity told him that there weren't really demons all around him, that they were a result of his being gassed. It had to be a psychotropic crowd breaker of some kind.

He kept repeating this over and over. He was sane. There were no demons. He'd just been gassed. The demons faded slightly. Phaid discovered that he was lying on the ground on his left side with his knees pulled tight up to his chest.

Reality was almost as ghastly as the nightmare fantasy. Those marchers who had breathing masks were fighting a pitched battle with the police. The ones like Phaid who didn't were kicking and screaming on the ground, battling with their worst private horrors. Some had rolled into tight foetal balls, too badly affected by the gas to even struggle.

A woman had fallen near Phaid. Her head was bleeding where she had been hit by a police club. Phaid crawled over beside her and felt for a pulse. He couldn't find one, so, without further compunction, he removed her breathing mask and pulled it over his own head.

He took three of four deep lungfuls of filtered air. His head cleared a little and the last of the demons slunk away. He was sick to his stomach, his head throbbed and his eyes streamed uncontrollably, but he could at least see what was going on.

What was going on didn't please Phaid very much. About the only consolation was that the battle was being fought by those who could still stand. Phaid decided to stay out of it for the present by remaining on the ground with the dead and injured.

A lot of the women marchers had been killed by the police, even more had succumbed to the gas. Despite all this, though, the police were falling back. The sheer weight of numbers of the marchers on Nex Boulevard were too much for them. They were retreating back on to the Plaza.

There were outbreaks of shooting as the police withdrew. Some seemed determined to make a fight of it, but others had simply lowered their weapons and were edging back in the face of the advancing women.

Someone on the women's side had got hold of a hailer and was talking to the cops.

'Our fight isn't with you. It's with the madwoman who calls herself President and her flunkies. We should not be fighting each other. We are all citizens and we all have suffered under the tyrant. Put down your weapons. There is no need for us to fight.'

Phaid wasn't particularly impressed with the standard of rhetoric, but it appeared to be working on the cops. One by one they lowered their blasters and spread their hands, not so much in surrender, but more in an indication that they weren't willing to go on.

Phaid got shakily to his feet and joined the throng that was moving out on to the Plaza. His legs were like jelly and he stumbled frequently.

All the Day Oners on the march must have been killed during the first frenzy. Certainly there was no one leaping forward, weapons blazing, to challenge the unsteady truce with the police. Phaid couldn't see how the extremist faction could last much longer if their revolutionary tactics were always as suicidal as the examples he had witnessed.

Nobody seemed to know quite what to do with the truce. The carnage had been too great for jubilation over a glorious victory. Everyone on the Plaza seemed a little stunned. Now the Palace was right in front of them and the crowd hesitated. It was almost as though they'd never expected to get as far, and now they didn't know what to do.

The screen on the front of the Palace had been dead ever since Phaid had come out of the clutches of the gas. Without warning, it flickered into life. A huge full face image of Chrystiana-Nex stared down on the Plaza like a grim, angry goddess.

It wasn't the image that Phaid or anyone else was used to. It didn't have the careful lighting and expertly applied cosmetics of the usual propaganda loops. This was the President as she really was, with wrinkles and blemishes. It was clear from the look in her eyes that she was quite, quite mad.

Phaid could see how she might have once been powerfully attractive, so powerfully attractive that she had seduced a whole nation into giving her ultimate power. She wasn't a handsome woman. She was thin to the point of being bony. Her proud neck was starting to wattle. Her platinum hair was scraped back in a way that added prominence to her already prominent cheekbones.

All her magnetism must have come from her mouth and her eyes. Both were excessively large. Her mouth could once have been sensuous, promising the far limits of deep crimson delights. Now it was a steel trap ringed with magenta lip colour. Her eyes also had the potential to make promises of glory but were now solely concentrated on chilling destruction. They were eyes that could not be ignored. They had the hypnotic quality of fixing whoever they were looking at and making it impossible for them to turn away.

The eyes that glared across the Plaza were as hard as pale sapphires. They seemed to be compelling everyone present to look towards the screen.

'You are traitors.'

The voice was a deep, throaty contralto. It started softly but gradually rose in both volume and stridence.

'Traitors!' Chrystiana-Nex may have been crazy, but her power to hold a crowd had not deserted her. 'You have betrayed my trust in you!'

The squad of Palace Guards, who had so far taken no part in the conflict, formed themselves into two ranks on the ramp leading to the Palace.

'I have given my very life to you. I have laid my very being at your feet, spending all my waking hours in the service of this city, this Republic, this people.'

The front rank of guards knelt down. The second remained standing.

'You are traitors! I have never asked for gratitude. To be of service was the only reward I claimed. I never asked you to love me. My love for you was enough. I have given you everything but now you trample me under you callous, ignorant feet.'

A second squad of guards doubled out of the Palace, and arranged themselves in the same formation as the first squad, only higher up the ramp.

'You are traitors. You have brought blood and destruction to the streets of this ancient city. You have looted and destroyed. You have befouled the noble name of Chrystianaville. My name. The name that I freely gave to you. Is this the way you repay me? With treason?'

More guards were now manning the photon cannons. Phaid couldn't understand why the crowd didn't realise what was going on. They seemed transfixed by the giant image of the President. Phaid began to work his way back to Nex Boulevard. The booming voice was well on the way to screaming pitch.

'TRAITORS. YOU NOW BRING YOUR FILTH AND DESTRUCTION TO MY PALACE. YOU BRING IT RIGHT TO ME. YOU WANT TO DESTROY ME! YOU WANT TO DESTROY ME!'

The guards had drawn their fuse tubes. The ones kneeling rested the long barrels over crooked arms. The ones standing used a double-handed grip, arms fully extended.

'TRAITORS!'

A few others had realised what was happening and were backing away from the ramp.

'TRAITORS. THERE IS NO HOPE FOR ANY OF YOU! YOU HAVE ONLY ONE THING LEFT FOR YOU AND THAT IS TO . . . DIE!'

The discharge from the massed fuse tubes lashed out like a sheet of blue white flame, marbled with the darker blue bolts from the photon cannons. The Plaza was turned instantly into a killing floor. It wasn't a battle, more a surgical operation. Above the hideous crackle Chrystiana-Nex's voice went on.

'THERE IS NOTHING FOR TRAITORS BUT DEATH. THIS IS AS PAINFUL TO ME AS IT IS TO YOU, BUT TREASON CANNOT BE ALLOWED TO FESTER IN THIS CITY. IF IT IS NOT RIPPED OUT, OUR CITY WILL DIE.'

The Palace Guards went on and on firing. The actual cobbles of the Plaza were starting to crack and smoke. A few of the rebels had attempted to stand and fight back, but they had no chance. It was a massacre. The Palace Guard didn't even have the slight qualms that the police had shown. They were scything everyone down, marchers and cops alike.

Phaid had reached the steps that led down to Nex Boulevard before the guards had opened fire with their fuse tubes. At the first crackle, Phaid had thrown himself flat, not even bothering that it was a painful thing to do halfway down a flight of steps.

A number of other people were sheltering along with him. Behind them on Nex Boulevard, the remnants of the march were fleeing to safety. In front of them, on the Plaza, there was neither shelter nor safety.

To Phaid's amazement, he saw a small transport bed careening down the Boulevard at high speed, doing its best to dodge photon bursts. Phaid could only assume that it was being driven by a madman. A few people were clinging to the baggage deck for dear life.

The machine slewed to a halt at the foot of the steps where Phaid was sheltering, scraping its underside along the road surface in the process and all but spilling its precariously perched passengers.

Urgent voices started shouting.

'Quick, quick! Get on!'

Phaid was on his feet and running down the remainder of the steps. Others followed, but the majority seemed too paralysed by shock to make the break.

Hands reached out to help him as Phaid ran up alongside the transport. He and the others had no sooner been hauled aboard than it took off with a scream of acceleration from a loudly protesting drive unit.

Dark blue photon bursts flared around them. Phaid grabbed whatever handholds he could find and clung to them grimly. He was certain that, if they weren't blasted to their constituent atoms at any second, he was sure to be flung off the next time the driver took a corner. Then, almost by a miracle, they were in a side street and out of the line of fire. The driver slowed down a little and the passengers scrambled for safer positions on the baggage deck.

Phaid found himself beside a stern faced woman wearing the long coat that marked her as an active rebel. He nodded towards the transport bed's closed driving cab.

'Who are these guys?'

'I guess they must be some of the boys. Whoever they are, we owe them our lives.'

Phaid nodded quickly.

'Amen to that. Where do you think we're headed now?'

'Northside I'd imagine, probably to the Angel of Destiny. The bitch's flunkies don't have the courage to follow us there.'

'What's the Angel of Destiny?'

The woman shot him a hostile and suspicious look.

'What are you?'

'Not much.'

The woman looked him up and down.

'I can see that.'

She turned her back on him as if to make it clear that she didn't think Phaid was worth consideration by a serious, fighting revolutionary.

Just like the woman had said, the transport bed negotiated its way out of the chaos of the city centre and made for the main route to the northern part of the city.

As the journey went on, the passengers started to get over some of their shock and relax. Conversations started, to the extent that the wind whipping past the fast moving transport would allow. The woman next to Phaid didn't deign to speak to him again, however.

He started to notice that the north was totally in the hands of the rebels. Groups of armed citizens patrolled the streets and the buildings were daubed with slogans proclaiming that it was liberated territory. More sinisterly, he also caught a brief glimpse of a body hanging from a translux pole. There was a placard around its neck that read 'Enemy of the People'. Phaid began to realise how much those who lived in the centre of the city were being isolated and misinformed.

They'd almost reached the start of the shanty towns before the transport bed turned off the main highway. They swung into the forecourt of what had obviously been a somewhat run down roadhouse until very recently when the rebels had converted it into a makeshift headquarters.

Phaid couldn't imagine what fevered rebel mind had decided to dub the place the Angel of Destiny. There were few structures on the northside that could carry such a pompous and overblown title, and this certainly wasn't one of them.

Originally it had been a cheap, gaudy roadhouse called the Belly O' Beer. This was still evident from a number of small signs that the rebels had neglected to obliterate. The Belly O' Beer's main architectural claim to fame was a giant squat tower fashioned from plasteel and rock foam to look like a beer mug, complete with handle and fake brimming head frozen in the act of spilling over and running down the side of the mug. The rebels had attempted to disguise the true nature of the tower by some crude repainting. It was of little avail. There is really no way to disguise a three-storey beer mug. They had even attempted to burn off the handle with blasters, but the rock foam had managed to resist their efforts.

Apart from the tower, the place was little more than a collection of prefabricated plasteel boxes huddled in the middle of a parking lot and surrounded by some makeshift and hastily installed fortifications.

The transport bed laden with people was obviously a familiar sight to those on guard around the converted roadhouse. A few waved, but most paid it no mind at all. The driver manoeuvred his way around the defences, across the parking lot and finally came to a halt among the ramshackle collection of vehicles. Phaid suspected that these were most probably the bulk of the rebels' ground fleet.

The passengers began to climb down from the machine. Without anyone to give instructions, they stood around wondering what they ought to do next.

The transport driver jumped down from his cab, grinning and rubbing his hands together. He was a red-faced, jovial looking character who seemed to be highly amused at his near suicidal rescue. His smile broadened as most of his passengers crowded around, wanting to pat him on the back, shake his hand or kiss him. He soaked up the gratitude for a while and then detached himself and started herding his flock towards the main building.

'Let's go on inside. You'll be able to get a meal and a

drink if you're lucky.'

Phaid followed the general movement. He was so profoundly glad to have survived the day that he didn't even bother to wonder where the immediate future might lead. As he walked towards the collection of buildings, Phaid noticed that, although the Angel of Destiny's defences looked rough and ready, they also seemed fairly formidable. The whole of the parking lot was strung with jolt relays and patrolled by heavily armed groups of men and women.

Phaid also noticed that new walls and trenches were being constructed by sweating work gangs. From their dull hungry faces and the blaster toting overseers, it was apparent that they had been forced into the work rather than freely volunteering. Phaid didn't like to think of what you had to do to get on one of those work gangs.

The refugees' first stop was what must have been the Belly O' Beer's main barroom. It was still being put to use for something close to its original purpose. Hot food and drink were being served to a constantly moving line. The last thing that Phaid needed was a hot meal, but he joined the line just the same, mainly out of a need for something to do.

The bar had been turned into a combination of canteen, meeting place, information centre and waiting room for those who had no other place to go. Phaid knew, much to his discomfort, that he fell squarely into that last category.

Even more uncomfortable, was the way that Phaid found himself the target of questioning and even hostile stares. He realised that it must be his clothes that were doing it. Even though they were now scorched, torn and streaked with dirt and vomit, they still looked like the garb of a city socialite rather than a fighting northside rebel. Feeling acutely uncomfortable, Phaid stared around the room, doing his best to avoid curious eyes.

Almost the whole of one wall was given over to what amounted to a huge bulletin board. It was festooned with notices and announcements of every possible kind pinned over the nudes and beer advertisements that had been its previous decoration.

There were political slogans and appeals for news of missing friends or relatives; there were duty rosters and lists; pictures of people that Phaid totally failed to recognise; announcements of rallies and mass meetings; lists, orders and instructions; there were even schematics for most models of blasters.

There were also weapons in abundance. Almost everyone in the place seemed to be wearing some kind of lethal device. Phaid was quite glad that he had his large fuse tube on his belt and Roni-Vows' miniature blaster in his pocket.

More weapons were leaning against walls and left casually on tables. Pairs of chairs had been pulled together and turned into makeshift beds. Some groups played cards, others argued in what seemed to be non-stop political debate. These discussions went round and round but managed nothing close to a final conclusion.

The walls were piled with cases, boxes and barrels, presumably looted supplies that had yet to find themselves a permanent storage place. Children bounced around, playing under the chairs and tables of the one-time bar. Occasionally their running and shouting would upset a sleeper, who would curse them out and then fall asleep again.

The air was heavy with steam and the combined smell of sweat, cooking food, unwashed bodies. It all added up to a picture of continuously shifting confusion. The revolt had obviously grown too fast for those who were engaged in it. There was no way that the rebels' minuscule organisation could cope with the droves of people whom the street fighting had pushed into the cause.

While Phaid waited in the food line, it occurred to him that anyone with both the organising capacity to make sense out of this chaos and the charisma to carry the various rebel splinter groups behind him could be the new ruler of the Repubic. It wasn't a job that Phaid would have willingly taken.

Phaid reached the head of the line and was rewarded with a plate of watery stew and a mug of cloudy beer. The rebels might have justice on their side, but the oppressors received far better service.

Phaid was looking around for a place to sit when a total stranger grabbed him by the arm.

'Hey, I know you!'

Stew spilled down Phaid's already filthy coat. He cursed under his breath, and then looked at the man who'd grabbed him.

'You do?'

279

The face was gaunt and badly in need of a shave. From the man's stained clothes and the blaster hanging from a shoulder strap, it was clear that he had seen his fair share of fighting. He made no connections in Phaid's memory. He nonetheless continued to grin.

'You was on Veldine Street during the first riot.'

'I was?'

'Sure you was, with a real expensive looking woman. I thought to myself at the time, look at that dumb bastard. I thought you was some courtier out slumming and got caught up in the trouble.'

Phaid didn't like the way the conversation was going. He remembered the body hanging from the translux pole.

'That's what you thought, was it?'

'Until I saw you fold those two cops and I knew you couldn't be no courtier, you had to be one of us.'

Phaid let out a silent sigh of relief. This was the very last place he'd want people thinking that he wasn't one of them.

'I guess it was either them or me.'

'Ain't that what it's all about.'

'I suppose so.'

'Who was the dame, anyway?'

Phaid was starting to feel a little stupid standing around with his stew in one hand and his beer in the other. He gestured with his plate.

'Listen, I was just looking for a place to sit and . . '

The stranger had obviously decided that he was going to be Phaid's buddy. He once again took hold of Phaid's arm, spilling more stew down his coat, and steered him to an already crowded table near the door.

Phaid couldn't see how two more people could possible get around the small table. It didn't seem to worry his companion who was already making loud introductions.

'Hey, hey you guys. I want you to meet a friend of mine. I watched this man fold two cops in the space of a second. I got to tell you, he's an animal.'

A few of the men hunched around the table glanced up. They didn't seem particularly impressed, but they did move up sufficiently to allow Phaid and the stranger to squeeze in. Once they were seated, a brawny, dark skinned man with a bandage around his head looked coldly at Phaid.

'You're a mess.'

'You could say that.'

'You just come from the Plaza?'

Phaid nodded.

'Uh-huh.'

'You get gassed?'

'A little.'

The dark skinned man sucked in his lower lip.

'That's good. I wouldn't like to think you made a habit of throwing up over yourself. What happened down there?'

Every eye around the table was suddenly focused on Phaid. He gathered himself together and launched into his account of the march and the subsequent massacre on the Plaza. It took a long time, but nobody interrupted him. When he was through, the dark skinned rebel pointed a questioning finger at him.

'Seems to me that you're saying the Day Oners screwed things up.'

Phaid realised that he might have said the wrong thing, but it was too late to change his story.

'Yeah, it seemed like that to me. The cops weren't actually going to come over to our side, but they were definitely backing off from shooting down women. Then those crazy broads jumped them and all hell broke loose.'

The dark skinned rebel swung around to a small bald man sitting next to him.

'I told you that those people are insane. You didn't ought to be fucking with them.'

The bald man had been staring glumly at the table. When he was spoken to, his expression didn't change.

'We are all united in a common cause.'

'Are we?'

'The Day Oners want to overthrow the mad bitch just the same as we do.'

'Maybe it ain't the same. It seems to me that they're kill happy. Once we've got rid of Chrystiana-Nex, how in hell are we to rebuild a society with people like that around?'

The bald man seemed unmoved.

'We'll face that when the time comes.'

'Maybe we ought to face that right now.'

The dark skinned man appealed to Phaid.

'You tell him. You know what they're like.'

Phaid was about to answer when the door swung open and a group of men walked in. To his shock and surprise he saw that one of them was Makartur. Memory of the strange dream charged all over him. There was no way that he could think of Makartur as anything but an implacable enemy. Phaid had an immediate urge to scrunch down in his chair so he wouldn't be noticed, but it was too late. Makartur spotted him and scowled.

'What are you doing here, manny? I didn't think revolution was your style.'

17

'HE'S SHIFTLESS, deceitful and self seeking. Believe me, I know the man. I travelled some distance with him. He'd sell his own mother if he saw an advantage in doing so. Since he's been in this city, aye, even before he arrived, he was doing everything but crawl on his belly to curry favour with the toadies and lackeys of the court.'

This was more than Phaid was going to stand for.

'Just a minute now . . .'

'The prisoner will speak in his allotted turn and not before.'

Since the order was backed up by nearly a dozen blasters, Phaid shut his mouth and kept it shut. Makartur continued.

'He has been seen more than once in the company of the notorious presidential flunkey Roni-Vows and, on the occasion of this much vaunted incident when he is reputed to have killed two of the enemy police, he was with a woman who can only be described as a high born whore.'

Phaid felt sick to his stomach. Not only was he on trial for his life but the strange dream was coming uncannily true. Phaid had put all the old hill superstitions behind him when he had moved down to the cities. Now they flooded back with a sickening vengeance. What was the truth about the dream? Had Makartur sought the spiritual contact of his ancestors? Had Phaid's dream been forced on him by some supernatural power? Was one of them really destined to kill the other? Ghosts and demons closed in on Phaid, but they didn't offer any answers. He wanted to sink into a quivering jelly on the floor. He couldn't cope, but, then again, he had to cope. Makartur was far from finished.

'I would advise this tribunal that the presence of this man in our midst can only indicate that he is a spy for the presidency. We cannot afford to take any risks with him. He should be branded as an enemy of the people and hung accordingly.'

Phaid blinked. Every eye in the room was on him and he knew he'd have to come up with something good if life was going to last very much longer. The wallet of money that lay on the table in front of him, along with both his weapons, wasn't going to make the task any easier.

Phaid took a last look around, trying to read the faces of the people who were about to judge him. It had to be the strangest tribunal that he had ever seen. There were eight of them that were directly involved in the business at hand. Makartur stood as Phaid's accuser. There was Phaid himself and Vord, the man who'd seen the incident with the police and served as Phaid's only friendly witness. There were five on the actual tribunal, a pair of hard bitten northsiders called Lank and Marden, a middle-aged woman called D'Wan, a small man with the attitude and movements of a street hustler who went by the nickname of Blue Eyes and a statuesque red-haired woman who called herself Flame. Phaid had heard a whisper that she had been an exotic dancer before the outbreak of the rebellion.

This and many other tribunals were working overtime as the uprising gained strength. Despite their not inconsiderable achievements, the rebels were as jumpy and paranoid as the President's Court. Many of them saw spies and enemies of the people in every shadow, complaints and denunciations flew like hailstones in a storm. Each one had to be investigated, and to simplify matters the tribunals handed down only one penalty, and that was death by hanging.

Some members of the underground objected that the revolt would destroy itself by carrying out its purges before it had even achieved victory, but their voices went unheeded. The tribunals ran at full power, and the turnover was rapid.

Phaid had only been in the Angel of Destiny for a matter of two hours when a pair of stern faced guards informed him that he had been denounced as a parasite, traitor and spy. He'd been locked in a storeroom overnight with a bunch of other depressed and frightened individuals. In the morning he was marched in front of the tribunal to discover what he'd intuitively known and feared. It had been Makartur who had denounced him.

The tribunal had convened in a small back room of the Angel of Destiny. When the place had been a regular roadside tavern, it had probably been the manager's office. It was now used for the rebels' less public business. Despite the cramped conditions, a further half-dozen people had crowded in to watch the proceedings.

The revolution hadn't been running for long enough to have developed its own ritual or ceremony. There was, however, a certain dignity to it, the kind of dignity that comes when a length of rope and a high place to hang it from would perhaps become the fate of one of those present.

Phaid looked carefully at each of his judges in turn. It needed a three to two majority one way or the other to either hang him or set him free. All this had been carefully explained to him by D'Wan, the middle-aged woman who seemed to be acting as chairperson of the tribunal.

Looking at Blue Eyes, he felt that he could count on some measure of, if not sympathy, at least understanding from the small man. He hoped that he could expect a measure of the same from Flame. D'Wan seemed determined to be absolutely fair, but the two northsiders were harder to gauge. Their faces were grim and impassive, and Phaid feared that they might simply decide to have him hanged for running after the kind of good life that had alway been beyond their grasp.

Standing guessing, however, wasn't going to do him very much good. D'Wan was already beginning to look a little impatient, so Phaid took a deep breath and launched into the defence that he hoped was going to save his neck.

'I wouldn't attempt to deceive any of you by claiming that I have led a blameless life. I have lived as a drifter and a gambler for most of my days. Sometimes I have had to use sleight of hand and deception to survive.'

D'Wan looked up sharply.

'By sleight of hand and deception are you saying that you cheat?'

Phaid nodded.

'It's happened.'

'So Makartur's testimony is correct?'

'In that respect, yes. What he neglected to tell you was that we first met in the steerage class of a land crawler, how later we had to work the veebe herds because we didn't have the price of passage as far as the Republic. Does this sound like the behaviour of someone who would throw in his lot with courtiers and aristocrats?'

D'Wan glanced at Makartur.

Markatur nodded woodenly.

'Aye, it's true, but . . .'

'That's all we need to know at the moment. Please continue, Citizen Phaid.'

'I was born among simple hill people where life was hard. I ran away when I was a kid and since that time I've made my own chances. I may have been luckier than some . . .' he glanced significantly at the two northsiders '. . . but I took what breaks were offered to me. I've travelled across half this world. I've crossed the icefields and the burning plains, and met literally thousands of people. I admit that there are some whom I've cheated and some whom I might have robbed in my wanderings, but they were always the ones who would have done the same to me. It's always the greedy who are the easiest to cheat.'

One of the northsiders who had been staring intently at Phaid jumped in with a question.

'This is real moving stuff, but it doesn't explain why you have been seen in the company of courtiers. You don't deny that you have contacts among those people, do you?'

Phaid shook his head.

'I don't deny it, I know some courtiers. I've already told you that I live by my wits. It's natural I should go where the pickings are the richest.'

Flame brushed her luxurious red hair away from her eyes.

'Do you count the women of the court among these pickings?'

'Some of them are very attractive, and some have been attracted to me.'

Marden the northsider scowled.

'They make sure they have the best of everything.'

Flame glanced at him and then gave Phaid a hard look.

'So you didn't object to being a plaything of

286

court whores.'

'I wouldn't have exactly put it that way, but I confess I find it hard to reject a beautiful woman.'

Phaid smiled directly at Flame as he concluded the answer but her expression didn't soften. She totally ignored the implied flattery. D'Wan also didn't seem amused. Phaid hoped that the men, at least, were falling for the way he was selling himself as a freewheeling, likeable rogue.

Those hopes were shattered as Lank tapped the wallet that Roni-Vows had given him with a thick index finger.

'How do you account for this money you just happen to be carrying?'

'It was given to me by a courtier named Roni-Vows.'

Every face in the room registered shock. It was D'Wan who put the shock into words.

'That man is one of the worst of our enemies. That you accepted money from him is a serious admission.'

Phaid knew that he was running a desperate gamble, but it was too late to stop now.

'He owed it to me.'

'He owed it to you?'

'I whipped his ass at imperial hazard. When I go after the rich I go hard. Would you have it any other way?'

To his relief, Phaid saw four of the tribunal noticeably relax. Marden and Blue Eyes even permitted themselves faint smiles. Only Flame seemed unconvinced.

'Are you sure this wasn't your payment for being a presidential agent?'

Phaid, feeling that he had the others at least halfway on his side, gave Flame a contemptuous look.

'Those are my winnings. The only way I could prove it would be to call Roni-Vows as a witness, and I doubt that he would recognise this tribunal, even if we could get him to attend.'

Phaid was now certain that he had most of the room on his side. When D'Wan asked him if he had anything else to say in his defence, he almost told her that he hadn't. It was only a last moment caution against over confidence that prompted him to keep going.

'I'd like to ask my accuser, Citizen Makartur, a few questions.'

'Ask whatever questions you want.'

Phaid turned to face Makartur. The hillman looked as if

he could happily tear Phaid's head loose from his shoulders.

'What do you want to ask me, little man?'

Phaid screwed up all his courage. It was time to play his only card and find out if the dream was anything more than an anxious nightmare.

'I'm wondering why you've chosen to denounce me in this way. We travelled together and even fought side by side. I don't recall doing anything to harm you, and yet you're doing your damnedest to get me hung. I could ask you a lot of questions about why you're doing this, but it's neither the time nor the place.' Phaid paused for effect. 'All I want to know is where you got the idea that I was busy selling out the revolution.'

Makartur regarded Phaid with cold, murderous eyes.

'I meditated on you.'

Phaid's jaw dropped. His rhetoric completely deserted him.

'You meditated?'

'For many long nights. You always disturbed me, and I went to my ancestors for answers. They finally came to me and I was taken through the first gate; it was then that all became clear. You were marked as the betrayer. There is death between you and me, Citizen Phaid.'

Phaid felt a terrible internal cold. The dream was something out of the primitive, mystic past. It was frightening and yet it had also given Phaid an unbeatable advantage. The spectators were already nudging each other and nodding towards Makartur. All he had to do was resist overplaying his hand.

'So it was your dead ancestors who put the finger on me?'

'You may mock, but the truth will come out in the end. A death still lies between the two of us.'

Again Phaid felt the chill, but quickly shrugged it off. He faced the tribunal with all the deference he could muster.

'I don't think I have anything else to say.'

D'Wan nodded.

'If you will remove yourself from the room, the tribunal will make its decision in your case.'

Escorted by two guards, Phaid was led outside. Even though he was certain that he had it made, it wasn't a comfortable feeling standing around in a passage that had originally led from the bar to the men's room while five people decided whether they were going to hang him or not. The guards studiously avoided his eyes until the door opened and Phaid was summoned back inside. Everyone looked very serious. For one hideous moment, Phaid wondered if it had all gone wrong. Had they decided to hang him after all, just to be on the safe side? Then D'Wan was addressing him.

'The tribunal has taken a vote and, by a majority of four to one, we have determined that you have not acted against the people's interests and are therefore not an enemy of the people. You are free to go . . .' D'Wan hesitated and held a muttered discussion with her colleagues, '. . . at least, you are provisionally free to go. We do feel that you have fallen into error and we recommend that you attend a course of political education to ensure that you don't fall into such error a second time.'

Phaid missed most of the part about political education. He wasn't paying attention. He was trying to figure out which of the tribunal had wanted to see him hang. This wasn't purely an academic interest. There was always the chance that whoever it was might feel like short circuiting democracy by taking a private shot at him. He hadn't quite made up his mind when one of the spectators leaped forward brandishing his fist in the face of the tribunal.

'Outrage! You are as bad as him! You all ought to die!'

The objector was an awkwardly tall, angular individual, in an overcoat that would have disgraced a scarecrow. His face was haggard and crazy eyes stared out from deep hollow sockets. He waved a spindly arm towards Phaid.

'He has no right to live! He is a parasite, as bad an oppressor as anyone inside the Palace. When Day One comes he and all those like him will be eliminated.'

D'Wan angrily got to her feet.

'If you people were allowed to execute everyone you thought was an enemy of the people, the city would be turned into a ghost town.'

It might have been the truth, but it wasn't the best way to calm down a Day Oner. His eyes flashed with an even crazier light.

'We will do what is necessary. Day One is all around us.'

He fumbled under his shapeless overcoat and dragged out a long barrelled blaster. He swung it wildly towards

Phaid. Phaid threw himself flat on the floor. The blaster went off, and showers of hot ash cascaded down from the ceiling. Phaid found himself enmeshed in a tangle of legs as the Day Oner was wrestled to the ground and dragged away howling and protesting.

It was only when he was sure that there was no chance of the madman coming back for a second shot that he risked getting to his feet. The tribunal was leaving the small, and now smoke filled, room. As she passed him, Flame shot him a glance of the purest venom. Phaid jerked back from the realisation that it had been she who had tried to vote him to death.

With alarming suddeness, it all fell into place. He thought about the red hair and the pale, freckled skin, then he thought about Makartur and cursed himself for not making the connection sooner. They probably both came from the same background, the same cold hard hills. They might even belong to the same tribe. There was a good chance that they even shared the same ancient, outlawed religion.

Although Phaid had come through the tribunal with his head intact, there was still the problem of Makartur. It wasn't going to go away. It was a terrible feeling to know that the ancient rituals could still operate in this huge urban sprawl. He knew that Makartur wouldn't rest until one of them was dead. He didn't hold out too many hopes that he could kill the big warrior. The first thing that he should do was to put as much distance between the two of them as possible.

While Phaid stood, still turning all this over in his mind, one of his erstwhile guards tapped him on the shoulder.

'Come on, Jack. It's time to get going.'

Phaid grinned.

'Damn right. I got to get out of here.'

The guard looked surprised.

'Out of here? Where do you think you're going?'

It was Phaid's turn to be surprised.

'Back to the city centre, of course.'

Sensing this might not have been the most tactful thing to say, he quickly added a weak explanation.

'That's where I can be the most useful.'

'You ain't going anywhere out of this area.'

'Huh? The tribunal cleared me.'

'The tribunal recommended you for political education.'

290

'Yeah, but wait a minute, I . . .'

'You're joining a study group whether you like it or not.'

'What happens in a study group?'

The guard smiled nastily.

'You'll find out.'

Over the next few days he found out. At first Phaid had asked himself a dozen times how bad a study group could be. Studying had to be a breeze for anyone with a few smarts and a good memory. Then he had discovered that these particular study groups didn't do too much studying. They were a euphemistic name for the labour gangs he had seen working around the place when he had first arrived. The only thing they taught was an appreciation of backbreaking toil. The students dug trenches, hauled garbage, carted building materials and sometimes, after the rebels had made a foray into the centre of the city, they even burned the dead.

The groups were the result of a compromise between the Day Oners and the rest of the revolutionary factions. To stop the Day Oners instituting their programme of mass extermination, the other factions had offered to run courses of re-education for the less desirable recruits to the insurrection.

The Day Oners had grudgingly agreed to the deal provided that the central theme of the curriculum was dirty, exhausting work.

There were, however, certain consolations. Work was regularly interrupted by what were known as instruction periods. These consisted of lengthy harangues by anyone who felt like it on obscure points of political philosophy.

Phaid had quickly discovered that the revolution had no coherent intellectual basis. The majority of the so called instructors made it up as they went along. Some envisioned a glorious, egalitarian utopia dedicated to aesthetic pursuits, others dreamed of a grimly dreary dictatorship of the proletariat. Whenever a Day Oner was giving the lecture it resounded with blood, death and executions.

Phaid did find that it was quite possible to prolong the lectures and thus cut down the work time by asking long, detailed and generally irrelevant questions. The subject of either androids or boohooms was always good for an extra hour sitting around rather than blistering his hands or busting his spine. Others of the group realised what Phaid was doing and fell behind him. On Phaid's fourth day in the study group, they managed to prolong an instruction period with an elderly and particularly verbose instructor from just after the morning rollcall almost through to sunset.

The ploy even worked on the Day Oners. They seemed all too ready to expound at length on their hideously gory concepts of social reorganisation. This was the way to get past the Day Oners. In every other way, they had the study groups sewn up to be as unpleasant as possible. They had installed a supervisor among the guards who watched each group. As far as Phaid could see, these supervisors had been picked solely on the basis of their capacity for their blaster happy vindictiveness. They effectively put a stop to all but the wildest escape plans. They also prevented night-time sex between members of the study group.

Nobody had bothered to split the politically undesirable men and the undesirable women into separate groups. The idea, after all, seemed ridiculous to most of the rebels. Phaid had noticed at least three politically unsatisfactory ladies in his group with whom he wouldn't have minded getting better acquainted. The Day Oners, however, had a serious prejudice against sex between men and women. They reinforced this prejudice by keeping an armed supervisor on duty in the storeroom in which the study group slept. The penalty for any student bed jumping was summary execution.

There was one other drawback to being in a study group. The tribunals that recommended re-education didn't specify just how long the process should take. It was left to the supervisors to decide when each member was fit to rejoin revolutionary society. All Phaid could hope for was that there'd be some sort of outbreak of confusion that would give him the chance to make a break.

After six days, no confusion had come along to save him. Phaid was starting to get desperate. Rumours were going around that the Day Oners were no longer satisfied with the study group system and were pressing for a selection process whereby those who weren't making satisfactory progresss could be taken out and killed. Life in the revolution had not only become drab and unpleasant, it was once again starting to move into the lethal.

Then, on the seventh day, something happened that for a moment, gave Phaid a flash of hope. He and the rest of the group were sitting around trying to spin out an instruction period for as long as possible. The alternative was digging out an emergency latrine. A sleek, two-man flipper spun flamboyantly on to the parking lot and made a flashy stop. To Phaid's total amazement, Streetlife climbed out of it.

He was wearing a sharply tailored, ankle length duster coat, a plumed hat and an armband with three circles emblazoned on it. He seemed to be acting like a visiting general, and the rebels who came out to meet him treated him accordingly. An escort formed up around him, and they started for the main building of the Angel of Destiny with the fast walk of the very important. They had to pass Phaid's study group on their way. Phaid was certain that Streetlife had spotted him, but the hustler turned rebel general didn't show a flicker of recognition.

Phaid cursed silently at Streetlife's rank ingratitude. Hadn't he helped the bum out when he was broke? He was so angry that he even forgot to ask a key question, and the instruction period started to wind itself up.

The instructor decided that the session was over and the group began gathering up their tools in preparation for going back to work. They were being marched back towards the half completed latrine when Streetlife and his entourage emerged from the building and came straight towards them. As they got closer, Streetlife signalled to the guards.

'Hold it there a minute.'

The column halted with everyone wondering what was going to happen next. After so many unpleasant rumours, a number of the study group looked more than a little scared.

Streetlife gestured briskly to the nearest guard.

'I'm taking one of these men for further interrogation. We've dug up some more facts on him.'

'Which one?'

Streetlife pointed at Phaid.

'That one there, the one with the shifty expression.'

The guard didn't argue and beckoned to Phaid to step out of the line. The Day One supervisor, however, immediately started to protest.

'These people are engaged in major re-education. They cannot leave.'

Streetlife drew himself up to his full height and puffed out his chest.

'I don't want these people. I only want that one, and I'd advise you very strongly to co-operate with me.'

The Day Oner didn't seem impressed.

'What authority do you have to take this man?'

Streetlife slapped his armband.

'You know what this is?'

The Day Oner shook his head.

'No.'

Streetlife bristled.

'No what?'

'No I don't know what it is.'

Streetlife stuck his face close to the Day Oner's.

'Then you better find out pretty damn quick, or I'm going to put in a report to your cadre assessor and get a zap order slapped on you. That'll be the end of you, asshole. Your brights be put out, cancelled. You perceive my meaning?'

The Day Oner scowled and then shrugged.

'If you want him that bad, you better have him.'

He crooked his finger at Phaid.

'You. Scum. Get your worthless ass over here. This guy seems to have found a use for you, which is more than I've ever done. Let's hope it's something real dangerous.'

Phaid looked at him bleakly.

'Your overflowing charm is going to get you into trouble one of these days.'

The Day Oner spat venomously at him.

'I should have killed you while I had the chance.'

Streetlife quickly stepped in between them.

'But now you don't get the chance. He's mine now.'

He put a hand on Phaid's shoulder and walked him quickly to the flipper. Things had started to move a little too fast for Phaid's comfort.

'What the hell's going on round here. What are you doing in that outfit?'

Streetlife seemed in no mood to answer questions.

'Just shut your mouth and get in the flipper.'

Streetlife slid behind the controls and slammed down the passenger bubble. Without even waiting for the machine to fully rise on its force field, he slapped it into drive and they moved forward with a jerk.

'Boy oh boy, how the fuck did you get yourself into that mess? I thought you had more class.'

'I didn't have much choice. The rebels pulled me out of that massacre on the Plaza and then minutes after I got here I was denounced as a cheap hustler.'

'A parasite?'

'That was the word they used.'

'And ol' Streetlife had to pull you out of the shit, right?'

'I guess I owe you one.'

'You owe me about twenty.'

'And you no doubt aim to collect.'

'It's the way of the world. My mama told me, from the womb to the tomb, nothing comes free.'

Phaid raised an eyebrow.

'You had a mother?'

Streetlife looked offended.

'That was a cheap shot, gambling man. I save your ass and you start insulting me.'

Phaid shook his head.

'I'm sorry, it was a cheap shot. Put it down to the fact that I'm overwrought.'

'You'd have been a lot more overwrought if I'd left you on that chain-gang'

'They call it a study group.'

'That's right, study group. These pussies have got names for everything.'

'I still don't understand what you're doing here. I wouldn't have thought revolution was your style.'

'If revolution's what going on, then it's my style.'

'You mean you're really into this thing?'

Streetlife grinned.

'You know me better than that.'

'They treated you like a king back there, and that armband, what's that supposed to be? I've never seen one like that before.'

'Neither's anyone else.'

'Huh?'

'At first I figured these rebels were dumb, but when I found out they were not only dumb but disorganised, I knew that I had it made. You like this here armband? I made it myself. It's never failed. I just walk into a bunch of rebels and flash the arm. They fall over themselves to do what I want. They figure that I must be some big wheel with this fancy insignia that they've never seen before. I'm making more money than I can even remember.'

Phaid looked at him in disbelief.

'You're making money at this?'

'Why would I be doing this if there weren't no change in it? This is Streetlife you talking to. You think I like to dress this way?'

Phaid scratched his head. A large part of him ached for a long leisurely clean off and a set of freshly laundered clothes. Life in the study group had been spartan to the point of being disgusting.

'I still don't see how you make money out of a revolution. What are you into, the black market or something?'

'Black market? Don't make me laugh. That's nothing compared with what I got going.'

'So what do you have going?'

'Just watch me now. You'll find out.'

They were running along the top level of a three-tier overpass. All around them black stone megatowers thrust their ugly irregular bulks towards the clouds. Sometime in the distant past they had been built to house an overspill population that now no longer existed. Since then, they had largely fallen into decay. Their ramps, passages and tunnels were dark and dangerous places where thieves preyed on the poor. the lame and the inadequate.

Streetlife curved the car into an exit and hit the approach road to one of the towers. Phaid was a little surprised but said nothing as they sped through the series of tunnels and ramps that led to the upper areas of the structure. At something like the twentieth storey they emerged on to an open courtyard that appeared to be solid rebel. It was decked out with yellow and black rebel flags. Armed men and women lounged around looking tough but fairly aimless. Streetlife parked the car beside a high arch that gave access to the interior of the building.

'You just wait here for a moment.'

With that he climbed out of the car and hustled through the arch. Once again, just like at the Angel of Destiny, he was greeted as if he were visiting royalty. Phaid was intrigued but the presence of so many armed rebels, a percentage of whom were likely to be Day Oners, cautioned him against doing anything but slide down in his seat and wait for Streetlife to return.

Phaid passed the time looking covertly round the court-yard. It had once boasted what must have been a fairly splendid grove of trees. Centuries of vandalism had, however, reduced them to blackened, limbless stumps carved with the graffiti of ages.

The wait wasn't too long. Inside of fifteen minutes, Streetlife came bouncing out again. He was carrying a fat document case and looked inordinately pleased with himself. As he clambered back into the driving seat, his grin was so broad that it took up most of his face.

'Eight thou.'

Phaid could scarcely believe his ears.

'Are you telling me that there's eight thousand in that case?'

'A shade over, to be strictly accurate!'

'But how?'

Streetlife set the controls on drive and lifted quickly away.

'It was easy. I came by here a few days ago and told them I got orders from high command. I convinced those suckers that the revolution needed them to knock over a counting house just inside the line.'

'The line?'

'Oh yeah, you been out of circulation ain't you. There's a line now. It separates rebel turf from loyalist turf. Chrystiana-Nex and her gang have give up pretending that they got a hold on anything more than the city centre. They got the cops and some mercenaries holding if for them. They've given the rebels best on the other parts of the city.'

Streetlife took a hand off the controls and tugged thoughtfully at his ear. 'How long they can go on holding the city centre is anybody's guess.' He snapped back to the original point. 'Anyhow, they do just like they're told, just like good little rebels. They knock over the counting house and get away clean with twelve thou' in hard currency. I let them keep a third for their own group and collect the rest for the high command.'

Phaid shook his head. He still couldn't quite believe the audacity of Streetlife's scam.

'Of course, you're going to hand it over to the high command.'

'I figure I'm the best high command these pussies got.'

'If they catch you, they'll tear you limb from limb.

Hanging will be too good for you.'

Streetlife grinned and nodded.

'Yeah, I realise that. I figure I got to keep my head down for a bit after this score.'

'Eight thousand is a fair sized sum to take a rest on.'

Streetlife glanced at Phaid with an expression that was close to injured innocence.

'Wait a minute, you got to realise that that ain't all profit. I got expenses.'

'Expenses?'

'I had to sweeten a few cops so they'd be looking the other way when my boys crashed through the line.'

Once again Phaid was surprised.

'Cops can be bribed to let the rebels through?'

Streetlife laughed.

'Cops have always been on the take. Revolution don't make no difference. If anything, it makes it worse. They're deserting by the hundreds. If it weren't for the mercenaries they keep bringing in, the whole city would be falling apart. Also, mercenaries only stay loyal as long as they keep getting paid. After the number of cops that the Palace Guard killed that day on the Plaza, the cops ain't going to bust their balls to save no president. Particularly the ones who got in by forced induction.'

'What's forced induction?'

'Forced induction? It's when a guy comes up on some rap and the inquisitor gives him the choice of doing time in a correction centre or joining the police. They brought it in because willing volunteers were getting hard to find.'

'Are you telling me that half the cops I see are really criminals?'

'More like two-thirds.'

'Sweet Lords.'

'It don't make for ideal peace officers, that's for sure, but enough of this chatter, we got to work out what we're going to do next.'

Phaid thought for a moment.

'If you could get us into the city centre, I'm pretty sure I could scare up some action. I got this contact at court.'

'You always did like to play with the social set.'

'That's where the money is.'

Streetlife glanced back at the document case.

'Yeah? I don't see you with no eight thou' under your arm.'

'You know what I mean.'

Streetlife made an irritating clicking sound by tapping his fingernails on the flipper controls.

'Okay, mister gambling man, say we do go into the city centre, what kind of action are you talking about?'

He continued to click. Phaid noticed that somehow he'd had a manicure since they'd last met. Phaid smiled.

'My kind of action. I'd reckon that in one good all night game with a bunch of courtiers, I could double your eight thousand. There's also this courtier who'll pay me for all that we know about the rebels.'

Streetlife looked at Phaid so sharply that the flipper actually swerved.

'Are you saying that we should actually sell information? Ain't that uncomfortably close to becoming a snitch?'

Phaid shrugged.

'What do we owe the revolution? You're robbing them blind, and they almost hung me. The only thing for which I have an undying loyalty is my continuing survival.

Streetlife sniffed.

'I don't know. I just got a gut feeling that I didn't ought to be telling no courtier about the rebels.'

'Nobody said that we have to tell him the truth.'

Streetlife suddenly laughed.

'You got a point there, gambling man. Okay, you sold me. Let's head for the town centre and check it out.'

Phaid looked sideways at Streetlife.

'There is one small item.'

'I thought there would be.'

'I need some fresh clothes and a stake.'

'So you're putting the touch on me?'

'I seem to remember the situation being reversed the last time we met up.'

'You're hitting me up for more than a lousy twenty.'

'All these things are relative.'

'Relative to the eight thou I got in the bag.'

'If you want to look at it that way.'

Streetlife went into a pantomime of indecision, then finally he grinned.

'Okay, friend Phaid, you got your stake, but I'm going to want a percentage of what you make.'

'A percentage?'

'Nothing for nothing. Remember?'

'I remember.'

'Fifty-fifty?'

Phaid looked as though he had accidentally sucked a lemon.

'Fifty-fifty and I do all the work.'

'I put up the risk capital.'

'You know the way I play. It's no risk. All I'm doing is holding your money for you. I'll give you ten per cent on your capital. It'll only be for a couple of days. No usury house would give you better.'

'This isn't a usury house. This is a partnership. All of one, one for all, if you see what I mean.'

'I work, you watch. Fifteen per cent.'

'You'll have me flunkying for you. You always do.'

'Twenty and you flunky.'

'Forty and I flunky.'

'You're crazy, twenty-five.'

'Thirty or we go our separate ways.'

Phaid sighed.

'I guess we got a deal.'

Streetlife laughed.

'So we partners again. I rob the rebels and you use the proceeds to rob the court. Looks like we're working for both sides of the street again.'

Phaid nodded.

'One day it's going to get us both killed.'

18

PHAID PICKED up his drink, but then set it down again without tasting it. Picking it up had been a reflex. Putting it down again was good judgement. The game had been going on for a long time, and Phaid was sufficiently far ahead to know that he no longer really needed luck or even skill. He just had to maintain his discipline and he was away with a handsome profit.

Drinking, however, was out. Phaid was aware that it would take only one or two more to cut him loose into the first shallow reaches of drunkenness. Across the well lighted and very elegant table, a heavy loser, a short pear shaped courtier called Athon-Igel was fumbling with his cards. He hadn't managed to hold on to his discipline and was starting to turn belligerent.

'I'm going to show you, Master Phaid.'

He looked for encouragement among the other players.

'Athon-Igel is going to lay down on the high and mighty professional. I'm going to show him if nobody else will.'

There was little forthcoming from anyone else at the table. Phaid kept his face in perfect neutral.

'So, show me. It's just a game.'

Athon-Igel leaned forward. His cheeks sagged and his eyes were sunken. The crystal light formation that floated over the table turned them into pools of anxious shadow.

'I suppose you're going to tell me that it's just money.'

'Isn't it?'

'Then you don't mind me taking some of that stack you have in front of you.'

Phaid allowed a trace of impatience to creep into his voice.

'Why don't you just lay down your cards and find out.'

The courtier grinned a bloated, sneering grin.

'Am I worrying you?'

Phaid gave him a cold, hard look. Athon-Igel laid his cards face up on the table with a drunken flourish.

'How do you like those. Are they professional enough for you?'

The hand was pretty much what Phaid had expected: blues on diadems in the crossover pattern. Phaid looked at Athon-Igel with an expression near to sympathy.

'That really is too bad.'

He laid his own cards tidily on the table. It was full dukedom, all in gold. Athon-Igel looked at Phaid's hand as though he was unable to believe it.

'But . . .'

'You should have known there were no lathes left in the pack. When a man makes the first offer of parlay and he's holding only diadems and blues, he shows gall, not talent. It's a desperate play.'

Roni-Vows, who was two places round the table on Phaid's right, suddenly laughed.

'Maybe Athon-Igel thinks these are desperate days.'

Phaid allowed the master of the table to rack his winnings towards him and add it to his already considerable heap. He took a tiny sip from his drink.

'I've found desperation to be the mark of a loser more often than not.'

Athon-Igel was still truculent.

'I suppose you consider yourself a winner.'

Again Phaid didn't bother to answer. He just looked down at the clutter of plaques in front of him. The other players seemed decidedly ill at ease with Athon-Igel's behaviour, but he simply wouldn't let go of it.

'We can all fight when we're cornered. Did you ever consider that?'

Phaid took a deep breath.

'Why don't we play some cards.'

Roni-Vows wagged a finger in Athon-Igel's direction.

'We're cornered right now, but I don't see anyone fighting or even preparing to fight. Even you, Athon-Igel, you're just like the rest of us, trying to have a little fun before the mob smashes down the door.'

Athon-Igel's head lolled as he tried to focus on Roni-Vows.

'You always have been an alarmist. This rebel business will blow over soon enough and things will be just as they were before.'

An elderly, rather distinguished man at the other end of the table coughed politely.

'I wish I shared your optimism, Athon-Igel.'

Roni-Vows nodded in agreement.

'I heard that the marikhs have threatened to close down the lines in and out of the city until they can be assured of a stable government.'

This remark caused a lot of consternation around the gaming table.

'We'll be cut off.'

'It can't be true.'

The elderly man quieted the table and then addressed himself to Roni-Vows.

'Are you sure of what you're saying?'

'I've never known a marikh to spread idle rumours.'

'You heard it directly from a marikh?'

'Of course not, but . . .'

'Then what you're saying may not actually be true.'

'It's possible, but I wouldn't count on it. What would you do in their place?'

'I'd close the lines until I was assured of a stable government.'

'Exactly.'

'You realise that if this is the case, we have to decide now whether to go or to stay.'

There was commotion again until the elderly man once more called for quiet.

'So what say you, Roni-Vows? Is it time for flight?'

'I'm not leaving the city.'

'You're not?'

'So long as the Day Oners don't take sole control I think we'll be safe. Once there is a new administration, they will need our help to wipe out the Day One psychotics. All we have to guard against is being hung in the meantime.'

The elderly man seemed to have his doubts.

'You'd be running some terrible risks.'

'We'd be running some terrible risks by going anywhere else. I can't think of many places where the court of Chrystiana-Nex would be welcomed with open arms.'

There was silence around the gaming table as these thoughts sunk in. Phaid took the opportunity to beckon to one of the two liveried footmen who flanked the door.

'Cash me in, will you? I think it's time that I left.'

Phaid swallowed the remainder of his drink and waited for the flunky to return with his cash. Athon-Igel was once again staring at Phaid. The drunken courtier was starting to annoy him.

'You want something?'

'You're leaving?'

'I'm leaving. I have a feeling that these gentlemen have lost their taste for the game.'

Roni-Vows stood up.

'When will I see you again, my friend?'

Phaid shrugged.

'Who knows in times like these. It'll happen.'

Roni-Vows nodded, but there was a strange look in his eyes.

'Yes . . . it'll happen.'

The footman handed Phaid his money. Phaid stowed the wallet carefully inside his coat and made his goodbyes. As he walked out of the private gaming room, his mood was close to jubilant. He had won over twelve thousand tabs and managed to make a graceful exit. By way of a bonus, he had heard the news about the marikhs closing the lines. He and Streetlife would now have a chance to ride out of Chrystianaville before that happened.

Phaid lingered for a while on the wide curved balcony that overlooked the main room of Thandon's. Thandon's was a palace of leisure for the quality of Chrystianaville. From the outside it looked like a cluster of plasteel spheres. Bubbles if you like. One large bubble with a number of smaller bubbles clinging to it. The lights inside the translucent domes gave them a pale, pastel glow in the night.

The main room was for dancing and parading. It was a salon where the structure of smart society was evaluated and arbitrated. Meetings were made, trysts were kept and broken, affairs were initiated and affairs were finished. It had the competitiveness of a battlefield.

All around the main room there were the smaller satellite chambers; the gaming rooms, where fortunes could be won or lost across the tables; the even more private suites where the affairs initiated in the main salon could be consummated in comfort and secrecy.

Phaid descended the wide curving staircase to the main floor and plunged into the roar of chattering people. He exchanged glances and smiles with a number of women. He was tempted to stay for a while. Amid the whirl and sparkle it was hard to believe that half the city was in the hands of rebels dedicated to executing everyone around him.

He was very conscious of the revolution, however. The wallet full of winnings was his passage as far away from it as possible. He put women out of his mind and made his way quickly to the arches that marked Thandon's grand, Harald Boulevard entrance.

Under the arches a flock of footmen lounged around, apparently waiting for someone to give them an assigment. They showed little enthusiasm for anything like that happening. Phaid waved to one who happened to be looking in his direction. The footman rather grudgingly pushed himself away from the wall against which he was leaning and came slowly towards Phaid.

'You want something?'

Phaid hadn't expected this surly response. Thandon's was the most exclusive establishment in the city. It was almost as hard to get into as the Presidential Palace. Normally the staff was attentive to the point of being servile. Phaid wondered what had happened to change that.

'I'd like you to find my chauffeur for me.'

'And who might you be?'

'My name is Phaid. I came in some hours ago with Roni-Vows' party. I'd like you to find my chauffeur and get him to bring my flipper round to this entrance. He's a . . .'

'I don't give a fuck what he is. I ain't running after your man for you. Go find your own transport.'

'What?'

'You heard me. Do your own running around, pig. Your class is going to pay before too long. Any day now.'

Phaid took a step back. He held up his hands.

'Okay, okay, can you just tell me where I can find him?'

'Probably down in the sub basement, unless of course he's stolen your flipper and fucked off.'

The footman's expression made it clear that he hoped this was the case. Phaid, having taken all the hostility he was prepared to take, went looking for an escalator.

The sub basement was a marked contrast to the flash and gaiety of the upper levels of Thandon's. It was dark, airless and uncomfortably warm. The lines of parked flippers were dimly illuminated by a few scattered globars. Despite the fact that the underground lot was so vast, it was somehow claustrophobic and unsettling. Groups of human drivers and handlers leaned or sat on the hoods of flippers and chewed the fat. The android handlers had also hooked in to each other and were tweeting and warbling in a low, almost secretive fashion.

After going from group to group trying to locate Streetlife in the gloom, Phaid realised that he was wasting his time. Also, the mood of the hired help to the upper classes was such that Phaid was running a fairly positive risk of being beaten or robbed. He knew he'd probably be better off if he simply started hollering and let Streetlife find him.

'Hey, Streetlife.'

Nobody answered, but a few humans looked at him curiously and a number of android sensors pulsed on and off.

'Hey, Streetlife! Get over here, will you?'

Echoes splashed all around the subterranean lot. When they finally died away a quiet voice came out of the darkness.

'Why don't you shut the fuck up, you overdressed clown?'

Phaid froze with embarrassment. As if by magic, Streetlife slid out of the darkness, silent as a cat.

'What in hell's got into you? You about to have a seizure or something?'

'Let's go and get into the flipper, shall we?'

'Listen, just hold on a minute, I got something cooking with . . .'

'Forget about the cooking. It can't be that important. Let's just get out of here. I'll explain once we're inside the flipper.'

Streetlife raised both hands.

'Okay, okay, what do I know. I'm only the flunky anyway.'

He led Phaid along rows of machines until they finally reached their own. They both climbed in, Streetlife behind the controls and Phaid in the passenger seat. Streetlife manoeuvred the vehicle out of the underground lot. Once they were crusing down Harald Boulevard, Streetlife glanced at Phaid.

'So, gambling man, what's all the fuss about?'

Phaid grinned.

'Twelve thousand is what it's about. I didn't want to hang around that vault for too long. I was getting the feeling that someone might start to wonder if I was worth robbing.'

A slow smile spread over Streetlife's face.

'Did you say twelve thousand?'

'Profit.'

Streetlife laughed out loud and almost spun the machine into a passing police transport. Phaid grabbed the controls.

'Will you watch it?'

'We're rich?'

'It'd be a drag to be rich and dead, so just concentrate on the driving.'

'Rich!'

'Drive.'

'Okay, okay. What we going to do with all this wealth?'

'I figure we should start thinking about getting out of town. The chances are that neither you nor I are too popular with the rebels right now.'

'That's a fact, but hell, they ain't in power yet. We can celebrate, can't we?'

'Celebrate tonight, but we should think about moving out tomorrow.'

'How come?'

'The marikhs are talking about closing the lines until things settle down.'

'It's that bad?'

'So it would seem. More than one courtier is making plans to get out.'

'Come to think of it, the flunkeys are in a pretty ugly mood, too. They're talking back to their bosses and stealing everything they can get their hands on. Even the police are getting restless, from what I've heard. The word is that a few have deserted already, looking for a better deal with the rebels. Seems like just about every pussy's counting the days before the rebels hit the centre of town.'

'All the more reason for us to be be someplace else.'

'You sure about this business with the marikhs?'

'As sure as you can be at third hand.'

Streetlife nodded.

'Maybe we did better start thinking about moving on.'

Phaid yawned. It had been a long night.

'That's what I'm telling you.'

Streetlife suddenly laughed.

'Yeah, well, we can move on tomorrow. Tonight we going to celebrate.'

He abruptly accelerated the flipper and gunned down the boulevard, weaving and jumping the other traffic. The first surge had thrown Phaid sprawling back in his seat, now he found himself bounced up and down and from side to side as Streetlife ducked and dodged.

'Where the hell are we going?'

'You'll see.'

They were heading west, into a part of town that Phaid didn't know too well. They turned off the Boulevard and started up the approach ramp to a roughly pyramid shaped multistructure. Phaid glanced at Streetlife.

'The Wospan.'

'A part of it.'

'You know, I've only been through here once or twice.'

'That's because you spend your whole life fretting and hustling. You want to learn. You know that there are people who don't leave the Wospan from one year's end to the next. If there's one place where nobody don't worry about revolution and shit like that, it's here in the Wospan.'

Phaid thought to himself that here in the Wospan they probably didn't worry about very much at all. It was a set of multistructures, and the smaller buildings in between them, that had become the sanctuary for those who wanted to detach themselves from reality. There was a legend that, hundreds of years ago, it had been a thriving artists' quarter, a place that constantly produced sculptures, painting, music and literature. Then, as in so many other places, the flow of creativity dried up. Art withered and died, part of its reputation remained, though. People who lived in the Wospan thought of themselves as individuals, very special people who were somehow set apart from the common herd. They acted and dressed accordingly. Phaid always felt uneasy if he spent too long in their company. He had this irrational fear that his brain was going to atrophy. With all this going through his mind, he watched as Streetlife nosed the flipper through the narrow twisting ways of the hivelike mountain of architecture.

'Surely this place is nothing more than a maze of dog gold and fantasy.'

Streetlife gave Phaid a searching look.

'That's a strange remark coming from you. I thought you were a try anything man.'

'Maybe I'm just tired.'

Streetlife tried to sweep away Phaid's sudden down mood by sheer force of good cheer.

'Hey, come on, partner. We just got lucky and we going on a celebration. I heard it told that you can find anything you want in the Wospan, if you know where to look.'

'What happens if you forget where to look?'

Streetlife grimaced.

'What's the matter with you, man? You ought to be on top of the world. You a winner. Ain't that what you always wanted to be?'

Phaid took a deep breath.

'Yeah, yeah, I guess it's just a reaction from the game.' He did his best to get a grip on himself. 'So where are we going to start this celebration?'

Streetlife grinned a that's-more-like-it grin.

'This looks as good a place as any.'

They had hit a flat area on the outside of the structure. It was part terrace and part courtyard, illuminated by glo-globes strung in a line of artificial steel trees. Even though the night was late, the area was quite crowded. The people were colourfully dressed, sweeping capes and wide brimmed feathered hats seemed to be a particular vogue. Vogues were now the main industry of the Wospan. If half the city set decided to spend its time immersed in warm water, you could be sure that the idea started right there.

The crowd on the terrace was peaceful, almost dreamily serene. People strolled and sauntered under angular, gleaming trees. Others stood in groups around tall pillars of gas flame that shot up from apertures set at regular intervals in the paving.

Streetlife was looking for a spot to leave the flipper so he and Phaid could start out on foot. Phaid pointed at a number of stationary vehicles some distance down the terrace.

'How about there?'

Streetlife edged the flipper towards the other machines.

'Looks good to me . . . uh oh, maybe we ought to go up a bit higher.'

As they'd come closer to the parked flippers, it was possible to make out the gleaming chrome work, the basket-like cages over the passenger bubbles and the ultra-long front end overriders that curved up like the horns of some fantastic beasts or mythic insects. The gas flames were reflected in glass-like paintwork, lavish in its detail. Serpents coiled and twisted around full thighed goddesses, dragons breathed fire and multiheaded winged monsters swooped and soared. Functional metal had been made beautiful with gold inlay and delicate engraving. Each creation was presided over by a young man in a tight, metallic sleeveless jacket who lounged and strutted beside his baroque machine.

'Flip crazies. It better to give those persons a good wide berth.'

Phaid looked surprised.

'I always thought that they were quite peaceable. Most of the time they're completely tied up in posing and preening around their flippers, oblivious to the world.'

'Most of the time they are. It would have been a mistake to park a heap like this next to their illustrious machines. They might have taken it as an insult, and stomped the shit out of us.'

They left the terrace and wound their way up a spiral ramp to a similar open space on a higher level. This was a bit more lively than the previous one. The crowds were more manic and they milled rather than strolled. The lights were strung on a series of jagged sculptured pylons instead of the more gentle trees they'd seen below. Even the flames that gushed from the vents in the flagstones seemed more forceful and aggressive; their reds, yellows and blues were brighter and more garish. Phaid's state of mind immediately brightened. Streetlife halted the flipper and allowed it to sink to the ground. Two women walked past holding hands. They were elaborately coiffured and dressed in tight, metallic reptile skin. Streetlife leered after their exaggerated, twitching hips.

'I tell you, partner, if we got to say farewell and goodbye to Chrystianaville, we picked the right place to do it.'

310

Phaid suddenly laughed.

'Amen to that. Let's have a good time for once. Life had been too troublesome of late.'

Streetlife swung up the flipper's bubble.

'Now you talking sense, partner. Now you talking sense.'

He began to climb out of the machine, but Phaid quickly laid a hand on his arm.

'We're holding rather too much cash to just go cruising around with it in our pockets.'

Streetlife slapped himself twice on the back of the neck.

'You right. I ought to be kicked for getting dumb.'

He quickly closed the bubble and started to rummage around on the floor. Phaid stared at him curiously.

'You ain't planning to hide it down there, are you? Anyone who wanted to break into the flipper would find it straight away.'

Streetlife ignored him and peeled back a section of floor covering. Under it was a small but solid looking trap.

'What the hell is that, a concealed safe?'

'You think I'd have me a ride without no safe for my valuables?'

He placed his thumb on the scan plate of a small contact lock and the trap flipped open.

'Count off enough to see us through the night in style and give me the rest.'

'What if someone steals the flipper?'

'Just stop arguing and give me the money. I know what I'm doing.'

Streetlife held out his hand. Phaid hesitated for a moment. It wasn't only casual thieves he was worrying about. He realised how easy it would be for Streetlife to take off with it all if he wanted to. Then Phaid made up his mind. He half shrugged, extracted five hundred and handed over the wallet. Streetlife stowed it in the safe and locked the trap. Then he pulled three logic plates out of the flipper's control matrix.

'Nobody's going to be taking this baby anywhere without these.'

He offered one of the plates to Phaid.

'You maybe want to hold this, just so I don't absent-mindedly take off with the flipper and the mutual funds?'

Phaid felt a little ashamed of his earlier doubts. Then he grinned.

'Maybe I will, at that.'

He took the plate and slipped it inside his coat.

'Okay, partner, let's go and bid Chrystianaville the fondest farewell we can.'

The farewell became blurred and loose. Phaid knew he was on his way out of the mad city. For the first time in a long time he relaxed. He let himself be caught up in the dance of the spangled, hedonist crowd. Some were in court finery, elegant evening clothes that flounced and swirled, others were in scarcely more than rags but still arrogant and intense. Hard studded leather rubbed shoulders with gosamer silk. Sly decadent velvet purred and rubbed up against dark practical broadcloth on a night away from home. Lizard skin snaked across sensitively bared flesh. Broken veins stretched out to scarcely touched softness. Bloodshot stared into baby blue. All became one in the dancing, circling lights.

Voices were overloud and faces were over-animated. Everyone was hustling, hassling, moving in to sell their act. It was the way of the world, but, so much more amplified, it was the way of the Wospan.

Phaid had forgotten the name of the place. It was big and barnlike with a bar in the back and a gallery running all the way around where spectators could pause and look down at the laughing, leaping throng.

In fact, the spectators did more than just look, the revellers in the gallery were showering the crowds below with the purple sparkling wine that seemed to be the speciality of the house. It wrought disaster on many a rococo hair creation and irrevocably stained some dandies' ice cream suits. Nobody seemed to mind very much. It was that kind of night. The people on the floor were too absorbed in their own enjoyment to notice the irregular spattering of purple rain.

In a roped off section of the gallery a quintet of real live human musicians sweated over instruments that Phaid suspected must have been hundreds of years old. Phaid had been quite prepared to believe that music was an art lost to all but androids within the borders of the Republic. The bright jump music that these four men and one woman were putting out proved beyond doubt that it still lived and flourished in the Wospan.

312

The dancing on the floor produced many strange couplings. A huge warrior who looked like Makartur vigorously swung a tiny woman, scarcely more than a child, at the full stretch of his oak tree arm. It seemed that, at any moment, her own delicate limb would be wrenched from its socket and the rest of her sent flying across the crowded room. It didn't happen. Instead, the girl made little shrieks of exhilaration, patently enjoying every minute of the huge man's violent and energetic stomping.

Others were more sedate. A tall willowy model of perfection was propelled around the floor by a small, hunched, incredibly evil faced dwarf whose pawing hands traced patterns on her thighs and vanished inside the long slit down the side of her grey silk gown.

Some didn't need a partner. A young girl was up on a table, most of her clothes gone, shaking herself to solitary ecstasy in a blur of jiggling breasts and pumping, thrusting hips. Her hands constantly moved over her body, stroking, caressing, part in invitation and part in total self absorption. Another, older woman whose clinging, cut away suit revealed almost the same amount of flesh, stood watching the dancing girl with a not quite believable look of disdain.

The girl on the table reminded Phaid of Mariba. The memory of the night with her on the line train flashed on to his inner vision; in particular, the moment when he had secured her wrists behind her back with a strip of blue chiffon torn from her dress.

Through a door, open to the courtyard, Phaid could see two burly youths endeavouring to pummel each other insensible while a small, vociferous crowd looked on. In that instant, Phaid decided that he had been too long in a world of fear and violence. It was time to relax and enjoy himself.

His eye was drawn to a dark haired woman with slanting eyes, very pale, almost white skin and blood red lips. A full cloak made from some heavy black material that actually seemed to absorb light was thrown back to show off her handsome, statuesque figure, revealed to total advantage in a flaming scarlet body stocking.

Through the crowd, she saw that Phaid was watching her. She tossed her straight waist-length hair back with a haughty gesture and frankly returned his gaze. She took a drink from a long stemmed glass of wine. A tiny bead of the dark liquid ran down her chin. Still staring fixedly into his eyes, she slowly wiped her mouth in a deliberately teasing gesture.

Phaid smiled and she smiled back at him, revealing a set of small pointed vampire teeth. There was something wild and maybe not quite sane about the woman. Phaid had noticed that there was something not quite sane about a lot of people in the Wospan. He assumed that in this man-made anthill, where individuality was an inflexible rule, the not quite sane found it easier to survive.

She was still looking at him. In fact, looking was an understatement. She was staring. She was staring, but she wasn't moving. Phaid felt that he was on to something. What that something was, he wasn't quite sure, but he decided to find out. He started edging his way through the crowd.

'Hi!'

Phaid put on his best charming smile, but the woman regarded him coldly.

'I haven't seen you around here before.'

'I don't come round here very often.'

'Most outsiders who come here come here looking for something. Are you looking for something?'

'I'm leaving the city tomorrow. My partner and I came here to have some fun before we left town.'

'So you've come here looking for fun?'

'I suppose you could say that.'

'Fun is a very nebulous term. One person's pleasure can be torture for the other.'

Phaid smiled.

'That could be taken a lot of ways.'

The woman's lips parted as though she was sighing.

'I take it every way you could imagine.' Her expression snapped from dreamy to intent. 'What are you leaving the city for? Are you another one who's afraid of the revolution?'

Phaid shrugged.

'It seems like a good idea to be somewhere else when Chrystiana-Nex finally falls.'

'You're a fool.' She almost spat at him. 'It will be wonderful. Just think . . .' Whatever she was thinking about caused the vampire woman to go into a transport of ecstasy. She closed her eyes and hugged herself. '. . . the violence, the lifeforce that will be wasted on the streets

314

and vibrating through the air, the glory, the horror. There will be the smell of blood, the excitement of change.'

Phaid swallowed. Her eyes were tight shut and she was trembling slightly. He couldn't think exactly how to slide himself out of the situation. Any attraction that he had felt for the woman had burst like a soap bubble. Totally at a loss, he came as close as he'd come to stammering in years.

'Uh . . . which side are you on?'

Her eyes flashed open and Phaid knew that she wasn't just a little insane, she was, in fact, genuine article mad.

'Side? I'm not on any side. I'm an observer, you might almost call me a parasite. Did you know that most people use the word parasite in a derogatory context? They're fools. They don't understand the real direction in which the world moves. The parasite is the one for whom it was all created.'

Phaid took a step back.

'That must be real nice.'

Vampire woman seemed to be drifting back into crazy rapture.

'Oh . . . it is. It is.'

Phaid took another step back.

'Yeah.'

He was about to turn on his heel and make a run for it when a hand grasped his elbow. Phaid actually jumped. Every nerve jangled. He spun around, his hand going halfway to his fuse tube. He found himself staring wild eyed into Streetlife's smiling face.

'Hey, partner, I lost you there for a moment. I want you to meet my new found friend. Her name's Fabrica.'

It was the girl who'd been dancing on the table, the one who looked like Mariba. Bemusedly, Phaid took her rather drunkenly proffered hand.

'The name is Fabrina.'

'You look very much like someone I know.'

A bored expression spread over her face and she nodded somewhat wearily.

'My well known cousin Mariba. I take it you've made . . . contact with her.'

Phaid grinned.

'On the line train from Fennella.'

'Oh . . . yes. I understand that she's now given up bondage and turned to sodomy. She's developed this peculiar walk from keeping her ass stuck out all the time.'

'Why is everyone so down on Mariba?'

'Men always ask that.'

Vampire woman was still standing there and starting to look a little miffed that no one was taking any notice of her. She put an arm around Phaid's neck and breathed into his ear.

'What do men always ask, sweetheart?'

Phaid flinched and tried to disengage himself. Street-life, totally misunderstanding the situation, winked at him.

'Looks like you scored there, partner.'

He grabbed vampire woman by the hand and greeted her enthusiastically.

'Glad to see you and my partner are getting so friendly. He worries a lot and he needs a friend.'

'A friend or a mother?'

'Huh?'

'I can be all things to all men.'

Streetlife seemed to be having a little trouble keeping up with vampire woman, but he didn't let it phase him.

'I like versatility in a woman. What say you and me and Phaid and Fabrica. . .'

'Fabrina!'

'. . . and Fabrina all get out of this crowd and go somewhere a bit quieter?'

Phaid leaned into Streetlife's field of vision.

'Uh . . . you want to hold up here a minute? This crowd looks pretty good to me.'

'Huh?' Streetlife looked from Phaid to vampire woman and back to Phaid again. 'But I thought . . .'

'You've been thinking a bit ahead of things.'

Light dawned in Streetlife's eyes. He moved away from vampire woman and put a hand on Phaid's shoulder.

'Listen, I'm sorry. I thought you were going after the broad. I was trying to help you out. I got this Fabrica . . .'

'Her name's Fabrina.'

'Right. I got the Fabrina and I like to see my partner set up.'

'I was going after the broad, as you put it, but it turned out that she's insane.'

'Insane?'

'Psycho.'

Vampire woman loomed up beside them.

'Are you talking about me?'

Phaid vigorously shook his head.

'Hell no, we were just trying to get a bet down.'

Before she could say anything else, there was a loud roar of applause as three young men climbed on to a makeshift stage. They were dressed in jackboots, leather trunks, some jewellery and very little else. The band struck up a brisk but grating oompah beat and the young men turned their backs on the crowd and wiggled their leather covered asses at them, then they spun around and went into their song.

'Backdoor passion
Peepshow pain
You got
To find the spot
Somewhere in your brain
A jolt to make you happy
A jolt to make you sad
A jolt to help remember
The fun of being bad.'

Phaid began to edge away from the group made up of Streetlife, Fabrina and vampire woman. The young men were now doing precision timed bumps and grinds in unison while the hard drinking crowd hollered encouragement.

'Nude boys don't argue
Nude boys don't cry
Nude boys don't ask questions
They have tattoos on their thighs.'

With some judicious use of his elbows and knees, Phaid made it right up to the bar where the wine was being served. He threw one of the serving girls a tab and a jug of foaming purple wine was thrust into his hand. He noticed that the jars from which it was being served bore vintage seals. He pointed and yelled at the girl.

'Where did you get this stuff from?'

'Liberated. A courtier took it on the lam but he couldn't run with his wine cellar. Some of the guys broke in and . . .' She pointed to fifty or more jars stacked up against the wall. 'It's a great revolution.'

'Ain't it just.'

He tossed back the whole jug in three rather rash gulps and threw another tab to the woman.'

'You better fill it up again.'

'You got the revolutionary spirit!'

'I got something.'

Up on the stage the young men were about to start a new song.

'We'd like to do this song before the Day Oners cut all our throats for being happy.'

The remark drew a resounding cheer. The people of the Wospan weren't afraid to laugh at the future.

'One-two-three-four!
Kiss my finger
Kiss my toe
Kiss my ass
And I'll let you know
Kiss my ring
Kiss me any place
Kiss my lips
Or I'll rip your face.'

Phaid was now a little drunker than he wanted to be. Even so, he had one more jug of wine. He had made up his mind that he was in love with the serving woman. The only way that he could communicate with her was by buying more booze. The singing boys started to annoy him. He didn't find them cute or amusing. He didn't even find them funny. He also noticed that there seemed to be a shortage of air in the place. He was sweating and it was difficult to breathe. Then the crowd parted and he thought he saw Dreen way over on the other side of the room. The sinister little man seemed to be standing and watching him.

That was enough for Phaid. In something near to drunken panic, he forced his way through the crowd to the exit. Once he was outside in the cool night air he took a deep breath. It was supposed to make him feel better. In fact, it made him feel worse. He was dimly aware that he was on a small terrace, separated from the main one by the building he had just come out of. Feeling slightly queasy, he staggered over to the safety wall, narrowly avoiding falling into the gusher of flame in the middle of the open space.

Phaid leaned on the safety wall and was immediately violently sick. When he finally straightened up, the thought crossed his mind that his vomit must have fallen on the people on the lower levels. He suddenly felt incredibly sad. The lights of Chrystianaville were spread out all around him. They looked so innocent in the night and yet they covered a multitude of sins. Beneath the soft sparkle, the city was being ravaged and torn into pieces. As it was with the city, so it was with the world. Everything was falling apart. He had hustled so hard to get back to the city and now he was leaving all over again. It was terrible; the city, the planet, the whole human race, everything was winding down, ceasing to work, preparing to die. The great achievement and the great adventures had passed and gone thousands of years earlier. All that was left behind was the aftermath. An insignificant time of fragmentation and decay. Only the cheap and petty remained in these sorry times. Everything that was noble had become a fading memory. Life was a bummer. Poor Chrystianaville, poor humanity, poor Phaid. A large tear welled up in his eye and trickled down his cheek. While he'd been playing cards he'd felt in control of his own life, destiny and the events going on around him. Away from the table though, he was once again getting the feeling of helplessness. It was almost as though he was some sort of unwitting catalyst. Every time he arrived in a new place, it would go to pieces around him. He was drunk enough to suspect that there was something wrong with him. Lately his luck seemed to consist of little more than surviving against the odds. He felt he was being tossed around like a cork on an ocean. It was so damned unfair. What was he? Was he the carrier of some psychic plague, a carrier who only had to walk into a city to have it torn apart by violent revolution? Gradually drunken anguish gave way to drunken anger. Okay, so he was a cork on an ocean. He'd give the ocean best. He'd ride the waves and damn the consequences. What else could they do to him? He was feeling no pain.

The rest of the night became a kaleidoscopic blur of unrelated images and incidents. There had been a conversation with a contemptuous marmalade cat but he couldn't quite remember the outcome. Streetlife had appeared and vanished. Pursued by the vampire woman, Phaid had fled through the back door of a public steam bath. The world was filled with sweating faces and oily naked bodies. It came in waves of damp heat. There was a woman named Pearl with large pendulous breasts. There had been some less than successful oral sex that had left him embarrassed and her querulous.

He vaguely recalled that there was some kind of altercation between Pearl and the vampire woman, but later he also remembered pressing his face between Pearl's ample breasts, so he assumed that Pearl must have come out on top. Later still there had been a transport bed and a wild erratic journey through the night-time city that involved clinging on for dear life to the body of the machine as it careened through the dark streets. Phaid had incomplete recollections of a fist fight, police armour, breaking glass and then it seemed that they were off again. A street sign that read Vard Prospect was one of the few things that found its way through to his badly warped consciousness.

'Hey! I know where I am.'

'Great.'

'No, really. I know where I am.'

He grabbed the driver by the arm.

'Pull up! Pull up!'

The driver, who was as drunk as Phaid, immediately slammed down on every brake. The transport bed slewed sideways and came to an abrupt halt, throwing the passengers into a tangled heap.

Phaid crawled out of the confusion of arms and legs.

'I gotta get off here.'

He half fell off the back of the transport and lay in the road calculating his next move.

Pearl who seemed to have attached herself to Phaid also disentangled herself from the mess of people and crawled to the side. She peered down at Phaid.

'Wha' the fuck do you think you're doing?'

'I got off.'

'Damn well get back on again.'

'I'm going to see Abrella-Lu. She lives on the Vard Prospect and this is the Vard Prospect.'

It was a memory that had been triggered by the street sign. Pearl's eyes narrowed.

'Who the hell is Abrella-Lu.'

'She lives on this street.'

'You already said that.'

'I got to say goodbye to her.'

'You're too drunk to walk.'

'I can make it.'

'You want me to go with you and help you?'

'I don't think Abrella-Lu would be too pleased to see you. I'm not too sure she's going to be pleased to see me,

320

for that matter, but I'm going anyway. I want to say goodbye to her.'

Saying goodbye to Abrella-Lu was rapidly becoming an alcoholic obsession.

'Are you telling me that you're dumping me for some chippy with a hyphen in her name?'

Phaid climbed to his feet with extreme difficulty. He held up a warning hand.

'Listen, don't take it that way.'

Pearl was drunkenly getting off the transport.

'I don't have to take this kind of shit from you, you bastard.'

She collapsed in a heap on the roadway. The other revellers started to get restless.

'What the fuck's going on? What are we hanging about here for?'

'Hey, Grom, let's get this thing moving.'

Grom the driver seemed to respond to any instruction that was thrown at him. He slammed the transport bed into full drive and it bucked away down the street, lurching and swaying. Phaid and Pearl were left alone in the empty street. Pearl was furious.

'Now look what you've done. We're fucking stranded.'

Phaid started bemusedly down the street in the direction of which the transport bed had vanished.

'I'm going to see Abrella-Lu.'

Pearl was sitting in the road looking distraught.

'What's she got that I haven't?'

Phaid noticed how one of her breasts was threatening to pop out of the top of her dress.

'Nothing, in fact, to tell the truth, in some ways she has quite a lot less.'

'Didn't I suck your cock for you? Huh? I sucked your cock when I hardly knew you and now you want to go off with this high-class bitch. Is that any way to treat a lady?'

Phaid slowly raised a finger to his lips.

'Ssh! You'll wake up the whole neighbourhood.'

'I don't give a damn. I'm not just some cocksucker you can use and discard. I got my needs too.'

Phaid decided that he had better placate her.

'Listen, I'll tell you what I'll do.'

'What?'

'I'll take you with me. Abrella-Lu might even find you kind of amusing.'

'I don't want to be amusing. I want a drink and then I want to get fucked.'

'That too.'

'I don't want to go.'

'Now you're being awkward.'

'I'm drunk and you're trying to dump me so you can go with this court whore.'

'I'm not trying to dump you. I told you, I'm going to take you with me.'

'Honest?'

'Honest.'

'Then help me up, damn you.'

Arm in arm, they staggered down the street in the direction of Abrella-Lu's building. Pearl's skirt was ripped clear up to the thigh and Phaid had to stop once to throw up. Eventually, however, they made it to the courtier's doorway.

At first there was no response from the entry unit. After repeated calling, however, the doors slid back and they were admitted to a small foyer. An android with the name Max-l stencilled on its chest was waiting. It seemed determined not to let them go any further.

'My-mistress-has-retired. You-will-not-be-admitted.'

Phaid was too drunk to take no for an answer.

'I want to see her.'

'That-is-impossible. I-suggest-you-come-back-tomorrow.'

'I don't want to come back tomorrow.'

'You-will-not-be-admitted-tonight.'

'I'm not leaving unless I see her.'

The argument went round and round and got nowhere. Phaid wrangled, the android was implacable and Pearl had started to get exceedingly restless, then a hidden speaker suddenly cut in.

'You better let them come up. They're so drunk that if we turn them out on the street they're liable to do damage to themselves.'

Rather grudgingly, Max-l let Phaid and Pearl into the elevator. When it came to a halt and the doors opened, they both picked the exact same moment to fall over. Phaid found himself sprawled at Abrella-Lu's feet. She was wearing a single, flimsy see-through garment. From her face Phaid couldn't tell if she was amused or angry. He made a clumsy gesture towards Pearl, who was lying

322

across his legs making little effort to try and get up.

'This is Pearl. I brought her over to amuse you.'

'I'm charmed.'

19

MERCIFULLY IT was finally quiet in Abrella-Lu's apartment. A cloud of glowing android bees spiralled lazily in the warm, heavily scented air. Their minimal electronic intellect was just sufficient to guide them in slow random patterns, softly shining like tiny dancing stars. The bees were a legacy of a high technology age when cybernetics were even applied to the decorative arts. They were also incredibly valuable.

The only other light in the room was a single, dull orange glo-bar that cast long shadows over the opulent confusion that was Abrella-Lu's home. It softly picked out the highlights of scattered satin pillows, tangled silk sheets and four sprawled, naked bodies. In one corner of the large, low ceilinged room a small, heated whirlpool and fountain bubbled merrily to itself.

The entire living area seemed to have been tailor-made for the staging of comfortable orgies. About the only hard object in the place was a kind of central island made out of a block of solid stone. This housed the vu-screens, a highly sophisticated entertainment console, the light and heat controls, a lavishly stocked drink and drug cabinet and the programme centre of the apartment's small basic brain.

Aside from the single, solid monolith, everything was soft and inviting, a litter of cushions, bolsters, deep pile rugs, pillows and floating drapes. Whole sections of floor could even be inflated to provide a bigger area of comfortable, yielding surface.

When Phaid and Pearl had first come bursting in, drunk

out of their minds, Abrella-Lu hadn't been exactly pleased to see them. Initially she had resented the intrusion. She had been in the middle of entertaining a young man. Phaid had blearily noticed that he appeared to be a very young man, little more than a boy.

Since there was no chance of getting rid of the two drunks, Abrella-Lu had been forced to accept her unexpected visitors with the best grace that she could muster.

It wasn't long, however, before her ever active mind began working on ways in which she could turn the situation to her advantage. The result of her thinking was a prolonged bout of fourway sexual athletics. Abrella-Lu had managed to exhaust all three of her guests before she herself finally passed out.

When Phaid woke some hours later with a splitting headache, he was aware of a small but insistent noise. At first he thought it was either the fountain or the whirlpool, but then he realised that there was a metallic, almost electrical clicking buried in the languid sluicing of the water. He propped himself up on one elbow and tried to clear his throbbing head.

The clicking was getting louder. Phaid would have been intrigued if he hadn't been feeling sick. He debated sliding quietly into the pool. The water would be marvellous on his aching body, but there was always the chance he'd fall asleep and drown.

The clicking was now too loud to ignore. The young boy rolled over and made a grumbling noise in his sleep. Phaid wondered what the hell was making the sound. It occurred to him that it could be someone breaking into the apartment and that maybe he should go and investigate. The only problem was that, in the first throes of his hangover, he couldn't quite locate the source of the sound.

It didn't matter. The clicking suddenly stopped and was replaced by the voice of Max-1.

'You-are-an-intruder. If-you-do-not-terminate-your-current-course-of-action-I-shall-be-forced-to-bypass-my-programme-blocks-and-do-you-harm.'

There was a silence. Phaid started to grope around for his clothes. The android's voice came again.

'This-is-your-final-warning-if-you-do-not-remain-perfectly-still-I-shall-harm-you.'

There was the roar of a blaster and a loud explosion.

'Harm-you . . . harm-you . . . harm . . . you . . .

harm . . .'

The android's voice died away. Phaid was on his feet. The door crashed open. All the lights came on and the room was filled with a rush of cold air. A huge fur clad figure stood in the doorway brandishing a blaster. Pearl, still half asleep, sat bolt upright. The blaster roared and she fell back with a gasp. She was quite dead. Phaid dived for cover, but as he did so he saw the young boy coming up from the couch. Somehow he had got hold of Phaid's fuse tube. The blaster roared yet again and the discharge tore into him, throwing the boy back across the room for some distance. For the first time, Phaid got a good look at the intruder.

'Makartur!'

'Phaid? I might have known you'd be here.'

Phaid looked around helplessly. There was no way he could pretend this wasn't the destiny of his dream. One of them would die. It looked as though it was going to be him, he was sick to his stomach but he still attempted to brazen it out. There was no need for Makartur to know about the dream.

'What the fuck do you think you're doing? Is this some warped, Day One, revolutionary game? I knew you were weird, but I never had you tagged as insane.'

Makartur walked a few paces into the play area.

'You'd best shut your mouth, manny, or I'll burn you right where you are. Since you're so inquisitive, you may as well know that I have done what I came to do in this city. I have found and killed the whore Abrella-Lu.'

'The hell you did.'

At the sound of the voice both Phaid and Makartur slowly turned. Abrella-Lu was standing beside the pool. She was naked apart from the gold wrist and ankle ornaments that she had been wearing earlier during the four-handed romp. She had picked up the fuse tube that the boy had dropped. It was pointed somewhere between the two men. Her expression was venomous.

'A neat little plot. One on the inside and one on the outside. One makes sure that I'm off guard and exhausted, then the other breaks in and kills me. It's lucky that poor bitch got in the way and spoiled your play. I suppose I should be grateful to her.'

She slowly turned so the fuse tube was pointed directly at Makartur.

'I hope you clearly understand me, barbarian.'

'I understand you, whore.'

Abrella-Lu took a deep breath.

'I'll ignore that. I know you're going to pay. Throw that blaster on to the cushion in front of you.'

Makartur hesitated. Abrella-Lu raised the fuse tube to eye level.

'Now.'

Reluctantly, Makartur did as he was told.

'Good. Now take three paces back.'

Makartur backed off.

'Now sit!'

Makartur sat. Abrella-Lu turned her attention to Phaid.

'You too. You sit down as well. I'm going to see that you suffer worse than he does. He only tried to kill me, you deceived me as well.'

Phaid's head whirled. He couldn't believe what was going on.

'You're not putting me in with him, are you? I didn't have anything to do with this. I'm Phaid, remember? The night in my hotel room? The first day of the riots?'

Phaid took a step towards her but she jerked the fuse tube threateningly.

'You better stay right where you are if you know what's good for you.'

'You don't really think I was trying to kill you, do you?' He looked at Makartur.

'Tell her, will you? Tell her I had nothing to do with this.'

Makartur laughed grimly.

'Pleading now, are we, manny? Hoping that I'll get you off the hook?'

Abrella-Lu was starting to grow impatient. Without taking her eyes off Phaid and Makartur, she carefully squatted down and began feeling around for the comset.

'I think I'll let the police sort all this out.'

Phaid looked from Makartur to Abrella-Lu and back again to Makartur.

'For the Lords' sake, will you tell her the truth?'

'I don't believe in your Lords, remember?'

Phaid was getting desperate.

'It's a goddamn figure of speech. What do you gain by dragging me down with you?'

Makartur half smiled.

327

'You scoffed when I told you that I had meditated on you. I told you I had passed through the first gate and that my ancestors marked you as my betrayer.'

'It seems like it's you that's doing all the betraying.'

The tribesman's face turned hard.

'There's death between us, Phaid. I'm going to make sure that the death is yours rather than mine.'

Abrella-Lu paused in her fumblings for the comset.

'What is all this mumbo jumbo?'

Phaid could feel himself losing all grip on the situation.

'He has this beef with me because his ancestors told him that I somehow have something to do with his death. They told him this while he was in a trance. Some of his goddamn ancestors have been dead for hundreds of fucking years, but that doesn't matter. He still wants to stiff me because of it.'

Abrella-Lu's eyes had widened considerably.

'You're mad. You're raving mad.'

Phaid pointed at Makartur.

'Just ask him. Find out why he's here. Find out the reason he wants to kill you. I don't know what it is, but I'm prepared to bet that it will be an education.'

Abrella-Lu started casting around for the comset again. Not being prepared to take her eyes off Makartur, she didn't have much success in finding it. Phaid took the chance to press home his point.

'Go on, go on and ask him. Ask him why he wants to kill you. I though it would have been the uppermost thing in your mind, or are there so many people who hate you?'

Abrella-Lu's lips curled.

'I had thought about it. I was wondering who paid him.'

'So ask him.'

Abrella-Lu locked eyes with Makartur. The fuse tube was pointed at his not inconsiderable gut.

'So tell me, who was it who paid you?'

'Nobody paid me.'

'Oh, come on. Do you really expect me to believe that you decided to kill me all on your barbaric ownsome? What was it supposed to be, some half-assed political stunt that the Day Oners put you up to?'

Makartur's eyes narrowed.

'Political? You think maybe that I'm just some oaf from the hills. You think that I can't tell right from wrong or when a time for change has come? Perhaps it should have been a political act, but it wasn't.'

'So why try and kill me?'

'Phaid knows that I have passed the first and second gates. What he does not know is that I have also journeyed to the third gate. There my kinsman cries out for vengeance.'

'What are you talking about?'

'I'm talking about the dead. I'm telling you that I am here to avenge the death of my kinsman, the death that you caused.'

Abrella-Lu's mouth was hanging open. Her face was a picture of total incredulity.

'Phaid's right. You're the one that's insane. This is ridiculous. How could I have even met one of your kinsmen, let alone caused his death? We hardly move in the same circles.'

Somehow, even though he was still sitting, still with the fuse tube pointed directly at him, Makartur seemed to loom over Abrella-Lu.

'You knew Mylan.'

'Mylan?'

Phaid looked up sharply.

'Mylan? The Mylan? The wind player? The master?'

'Mylan.'

'But he died because of a . . .'

Phaid's voice faltered. Makartur filled in for him.

'Because of a woman. Is that the story you've heard, manny?'

'But how could Mylan be your kin? He was a wind player, the toast of Chrystianaville . . .'

'Even the toast of Chrystianaville has to be born somewhere.'

'Are you saying . . .'

'Aye, I'm saying. His real name was Makmylan and he was born in the same village as myself.' He nodded towards Abrella-Lu. 'Yon witch worked on his mind until he killed himself. He'll not rest until she's dead. You notice how quiet she's become? She knows it's the truth.'

Abrella-Lu continued to fumble for the comset.

'The cops can sort it out.'

'You're not denying it?'

'What, that I knew Mylan and Mylan killed himself? End of story. I don't see that there was a connection. He screwed up during the games and that was that. Maybe he 'just wasn't as good as people like to make out.'

Phaid shook his head.

'Every story I've heard about Mylan's death places the blame on a woman.'

'You believe gossip?'

'In this case I think I do.'

'So you are part of the plot to kill me.'

'No I'm not, but . . .'

Makartur was glowering at both of them.

'Mylan will not rest until you're dead, woman.'

'I'm calling the cops.'

Abrella-Lu finally found the comset. She spoke quickly into it in a low voice. Finally she looked up.

'They'll be here in fifteen minutes.'

Phaid made one last attempt to get himself off the hook.

'Abrella-Lu, can't we discuss this thing? I'm dying here and it just ain't right. I had nothing to do with this bastard here trying to kill you.'

Abrella-Lu regarded him coldly.

'I don't want to discuss it. You look stupid sitting there without any clothes on.'

Phaid looked down at his feet. Near his left foot was a small crystal sphere. There was a moving picture inside it. It seemed to be of a small, pale faced girl in a dark robe trudging through a snowstorm. In her arms, she was carrying some sort of small animal. Phaid couldn't quite make out what it was. He suddenly felt unutterably miserable.

The conversation seemed to have worn itself out. Phaid could see no way that he'd be able to persuade Abrella-Lu not to hand him over to the cops as a would-be assassin. He stared down into the crystal. The small girl was still trudging through the snow. Phaid tried to imagine what the thing was doing there. Why someone like Abrella-Lu should keep it.

The silence went on and on. Finally the door chimes sounded. Both Phaid and Makartur looked at Abrella-Lu. Makartur chuckled.

'How are you going to let the cops in and still keep us covered with yon fuse tube?'

'Max-l will let the police in.'

'Oh no he won't. I blew up your wee tin butler.'

Although she was doing her best not to show it, Abrella-Lu was clearly worried. She gestured to Makartur with the fuse tube.

'Stand up.'

'Are you sure you want me to do that?'

'Stand up, damn you!'

The door chimes sounded again. Makartur laughed.

'You better let them in, else they think it's a false alarm and go away again.'

'Just get up, you swine!'

Makartur slowly got to his feet. Abrella-Lu took a step towards him.

'Start walking towards the door.'

Makartur made as though he was going to do as he was told. He half turned. Then his hand flashed out like a striking snake. He grabbed Abrella-Lu's wrist and twisted. The fuse tube crackled, but the discharge went harmlessly into the water of the pool. It steamed and bubbled. Abrella-Lu beat helplessly on the hill man's massive chest with her free hand.

'Let me go, you bastard! Let me go!'

Makartur's laugh rumbled round the room as Phaid got quietly to his feet. Makartur was still laughing and Abrella-Lu still struggling as Phaid's fingers closed around the crystal sphere. He took two quick paces that brought him up behind the giant tribesman. He took one last look at the little girl trudging through the snow and swung his arm.

He caught Makartur behind and slightly below the ear. The big man grunted and dropped like a bundle of old clothes. Phaid let the crystal fall to the floor. There was blood on his hands. He wasn't sure if it was his or Makartur's. He faced Abrella-Lu.

'Now are you convinced?'

'I'm going to let the police in.'

There were three of them, two normal sized cops in red jumpsuits and a hulking man mountain in armour. They came in fast with blasters out, obviously fired up to rescue a pretty and very naked damsel from her dastardly attackers. Abrella-Lu was right behind them giving directions.

'That's them. They had a fight. The shifty looking one without any clothes slugged the big one from behind.'

Phaid couldn't believe that Abrella-Lu had worked the switch on him once again.

'Wait a minute . . .'

Rough hands grabbed him and wrestled him to the ground. Phaid started to protest but a swift boot in the kidneys shut him up. The man mountain stuck his knee in Phaid's back and held him down while his two companions carted away the inert form of Makartur. While he was restraining Phaid, he was also able to ask Abrella-Lu a few preliminary questions.

'What's been going on here?'

'These two tried to kill me.'

'You know them?'

'I never saw them before.'

Phaid jerked.

'She's lying . . .'

The pressure of the cop's knee threatened to crack vertebrae.

'Shut up. I'm talking to the lady.'

Phaid shut up while he could still wriggle his toes. The pressure lightened up a little as the cop turned his attention back to Abrella-Lu.

'You got any idea why they'd want to kill you?'

'Who knows. I'm a courtier, anything can happen to us in these troubled times. Maybe they're Day One terrorists or maybe someone paid them. It comes to the same thing in the end.'

'What about the other two stiffs?'

'The big guy mistook the woman for me. The boy tried to intervene and that's how he got it.'

The cop nodded and pointed towards the prostrate Phaid.

'What about him. How come he's naked?'

Abrella-Lu shot the cop a look of pure aristo.

'Are you daring to suggest . . . ?'

The cop quickly shook his head.

'I wasn't suggesting nothing. I know what's good for me.'

Phaid craned to see if he could catch the cop's expression behind the dark visor but it was impossible. The cop continued to look at Abrella-Lu.

'You had best put some clothes on. You will have to come with us to record a statement.'

He sounded a little regretful. Phaid supposed that he would have felt the same had he been in the cop's position. It wasn't every day that a humble officer is confronted by a naked courtier.

Abrella-Lu disappeared into another room to dress. Phaid and the cop were left on their own. Phaid twisted his head around.

'How about letting me up so I can put some clothes on too.'

'Not a chance.'

'You mean you're going to drag me off stark naked?'

'You'll get a nice new suit when you get where you're going.'

'Hey . . .'

Phaid groaned as the cop's knee pressed harder into his back. The cop twisted Phaid's wrist behind him.

'Time you shut up.'

'Wait . . .'

'Or do I get to shut you up?'

'No . . . no.'

The cop snapped a pair of manacles on to Phaid's wrists. He had set them much too tight. The plasteel cut painfully into Phaid's flesh. The cop finally removed his knee from the small of Phaid's back.

'On your feet.'

Phaid struggled to stand. It wasn't easy on a soft floor with his wrists locked behind him. The cop grabbed him by the hair and hauled him into a standing position. Abrella-Lu reappeared wearing a businesslike grey tunic and wide black pants tucked into short red boots.

'Shall we go? I want to get this over as soon as I can.'

The cop pushed Phaid forward. He almost fell into Abrella-Lu. She half smiled at him.

'You know, you look pathetic. To think I really used to quite like you once.'

Phaid was about to say something but thought better of it. The cop, however, looked sharply at her.

'I thought you said you'd never seen this man before tonight.'

Abrella-Lu flashed a brittle little smile at him.

'I did.'

'But you just said that you used to . . .'

'Don't worry about it, darling. You're only an underling. Let your superiors sort it out.'

With that, she swept out of the door. The cop took out his confusion on Phaid. He grabbed him by the back of his neck and pushed him roughly after her.

20

THE INQUISITOR pushed back his limp, straw coloured hair and sighed the sigh of a man who was starting to run out of patience.

'You wouldn't care to confess to the iron pipe killings, would you?'

Phaid exhaustedly shook his head.

'No, not much.'

'How about the midnight beheadings? He used to rearrange the pieces of his various victims. I guess you could call him creative.'

'I don't want to confess to anything.'

'Are you sure?'

'Quite sure.'

'You're being difficult.'

'I'm not going to confess to anything that I didn't do.'

'So what did you do?'

'Nothing.'

'How about the eastside vampire?'

'How many mass murderers do you have in this city?'

The Inquisitor shrugged.

'It's hard to tell. All we can do is count the bodies. We can't hope to catch more than about one in ten of them. You've got to see that that's why it's always good to get a few off the books. It makes it look better. I don't see what your objection is. You're almost certain to go to the steamer so you've got nothing to lose by copping to a few confessions. I mean, you're going to die anyway. Why not make our lives a little easier?'

'Why should I?'

'You'll stay in the White Tower for quite a while before you get a slot in the steamer. The backlog on executions is quite appalling.'

The Inquisitor was very young and slight. Almost like a boy masquerading in the exotic, pale blue uniform. He affected a limp wristed, effete attitude that Phaid found totally disconcerting after the brutality he had suffered during his first few hours in the hands of the police.

'So?'

'So you can either spend that time in some semblance of comfort or in extreme distress. If you play ball with us, we can make sure that you get on one of the privileged levels on the Tower. If not, you get on the Rat Row.'

'What's the Rat Row?'

'Don't even ask.'

Phaid rubbed his tired eyes. For the last few hours he had been living in a waking nightmare. He was bruised and bloody. He had been beaten and kicked. He'd had his voice printed, his retina pattern recorded and a mind probe had lanced agonisingly through his brain. He had only been given clothes at the end of the long, painful process that had finally delivered him into the hands of the pale, almost chinless Inquisitor.

'So you're telling me that if I confess to a bunch of murders that I didn't do, I may have a better time in jail before I'm executed for a crime I didn't do either? Is that right?'

The Inquisitor nodded.

'You have a very good grasp of the situation.'

Phaid sagged in the hard plasteel chair.

'Can I think about this for a moment?'

'Don't take too long. I really can't see what you're worrying about. Either way you're going to finish up dead.'

'But it isn't fair.'

'Precious little is these days.'

'But I haven't had a trial yet. I didn't have any part in the attempted murder that I was arrested for. Suppose the court finds me not guilty? I could still be steamed for some crime I confessed to because you offered me a deal.'

'That's the chance you have to take. It says on your file that you're a gambler. It shouldn't be too much of a problem for you.'

The bright overhead lights bored into Phaid's skull. The Inquisitor had the benefit of small round dark glasses. Phaid had no protection against the harsh glare. He looked around the bare interrogation chamber as though seeking a way out. None presented itself. The Inquisitor flipped languidly through Phaid's file for what must have been the fiftieth time.

'I wouldn't worry about going free. It's unlikely you'll even get a trial. There's a Condition of Emergency in force and the complaint against you was made by a courtier. That's quite enough to get you a place in the steamer. You sure you don't want to confess to a few unsolved crimes?'

Phaid thought about Chrystianaville's favourite form of execution. The condemned were locked into steel cages like so many pieces of meat. The cages were slotted into a wide iron pipe in one of the deep sub basements of the White Tower. At the touch of a switch, superheated steam, excessive blowoff from the city powerhouse, blasted down the pipe and the condemned were literally steamed alive.

Phaid wearily shook his head.

'I'm not going to confess.'

'You're being very stupid. Here you are, almost certain to be steamed and you won't do yourself a favour. Still, what can be expected from someone who goes after courtiers? What are you, a Day Oner?'

Phaid tried to rest his arms on the table that separated him from the Inquisitor. The Inquisitor jabbed him with a short swagger cane.

'Sit up. Don't slouch. You were about to tell me what you were.'

'I'm not anything.'

'You're dumb.'

'I am?'

'You should have picked a common whore if you wanted to go murdering. I knew a case, this fellow killed three whores; he cut off their heads, hands and feet. It was really a disgusting business. When we had him in here, he expressed his willingness to enlist in the police. After some discussion we accepted his offer. He's doing very well now. He's been made an underleader already. You unfortunately would never qualify for such a deal. You had to try and kill a courtier.'

'I did no such thing.'

'Oh yes you did.'

The Inquisitor picked up Phaid's file.

'It's right here in black and white. You confessed to the street officers that you went to the residence of . . . what was her name again? . . . ah, yes, Abrella-Lu. You went to the residence of Abrella-Lu with the sole intention of killing her.'

'That's not true.'

'Are you telling me that there has been a clerical error?'

'This is insane.'

'It doesn't make any difference. The system is supposed to be perfect. If there has been a clerical error, there's virtually nothing that can be done about it.'

'Why can't you leave me alone?'

The Inquisitor took off his glasses. Behind them, he had pale watery eyes.

'Alas, leaving you alone is not within the scope of my orders. I'm an Inquisitor. I push and push until I get everything out of you. We want everything, and I'll keep probing until you willingly give up everything.'

'But I don't have anything. You even took my clothes away.'

Phaid tugged at the coarse grey material of the prison issue coverall. For the twentieth time he read the number printed across the front. He couldn't quite get to grips with the fact that that number was him, and might be him for the rest of his life. Phaid knew that he ought to be terrified, but somehow he wasn't. His body ached and he was mentally and physically exhausted. The process that the police had put him through had left him incapable of being anything but numb.

Also, the process wasn't over. Phaid raised his head. The Inquisitor was regarding him with what almost looked like a sad, sympathetic smile.

'You know that it's only yourself that you're hurting. You already admitted to the attempted murder of a courtier.'

'I didn't. How can I get that through to you?'

'You can't. It's here on your file.'

'But that's a lie.'

'That doesn't matter. Once something is on your file, it becomes the truth for all official purposes.'

'What can I do?'

'Absolutely nothing.'

Phaid slumped again.

'You're telling me that I'm as good as dead.'

The Inquisitor beamed.

'Now you're starting to get the idea.'

'Surely there's something.'

'You could reconcile yourself to the inevitable.'

Phaid shook his head.

'That's easy to say.'

'You could also confess to a few other outstanding capital crimes and thereby ensure yourself of the best possible treatment until the time you get steamed.'

'I can't.'

'You'll probably get a few written in on your file, whether you like it or not.'

'What?'

'It happens.'

'Can I have a moment to think about all this? There's rather a lot to absorb.'

'Don't take too long.'

'I don't want to die.'

'You should have realised that before you went courtier hunting.'

'But I didn't.'

'Don't start all that again. It's on your file.'

There was a long pause. Phaid knew that he should be considering all his options, evaluating if what the Inquisitor had told him was true. There was always the chance that it might be some sort of elaborate bluff. Somehow, though, Phaid didn't believe this. He found it hard to concentrate. His mind whirled round and round, ducking and weaving, as though it was unwilling to confront the knowledge that he was going to be painfully executed in the near future. He made his final appeal to the Inquisitor.

'You've got to give me a moment. I'm having trouble getting to grips with all this. I was present at an attempted murder, I had nothing to do with it, but you're telling me that I've got to die because it says that I'm guilty on some file.'

The Inquisitor smiled coldly and replaced his dark glasses.

'That's about the situation.'

'And the only option that I have is to confess to a few more crimes that I didn't do and then I might get slightly better treatment before they finally steam me.'

The Inquisitor yawned.

'We do seem to rather be going round in circles. My time is valuable.'

'So's my life.'

The Inquisitor chuckled.

'You really are magnificently stubborn. When are you going to realise that your life is quite worthless?'

'Sweet Lords, isn't there a damn thing I can do?'

The Inquisitor suddenly became impatient.

'You can confess to a selection of old killings and stop holding up my work.'

Phaid closed his eyes and sighed.

'Okay, okay, I'll do it. Just show me what to do.'

'Thumbprint here, here, here, down at the bottom there and one more takes care of it.'

'I'm a mass murderer now?'

'You had a very neat way of rearranging the severed pieces of your victims.'

'I don't think I can stand this.'

'You will, I promise you.'

The Inquisitor pressed a concealed call button and two red armoured cops shouldered their way into the interrogation chamber.

'He need more softening?'

The Inquisitor shook his head.

'No, just get him on to the next transport. He's cleared through to the Tower.'

The nearest cop grabbed Phaid's arm and jerked him to his feet.

'Well, Sunshine, aren't you going to have a wonderful time?'

The official name for the White Tower was the Republic Central Detention and Inquisitory Facility. Few people used it. To most of the citizens of Chrystianaville, the White Tower was the White Tower, a place of evil reputation; a place to be dreaded. Too many citizens had gone into it through its subterranean portals, and never come out again, for it to be anything else but a place of fear.

Phaid had expected at least to see the daylight one last time when he was led out to the prison transport. This, however wasn't to be. The White Tower, the Central Police Complex and the Presidential Palace were interlinked by a complicated network of underground tunnels.

They provided alternative routes round the inner city for the Chrystianaville authorities, and those who'd been taken into their custody.

There was no daylight and no sight of the sky for prisoners on the way to the White Tower. They were consigned to a world of ancient grey tunnels and harsh white light.

The White Tower was a pale, rectangular box standing on end, almost like a squared off tooth. It was isolated by a wide expanse of bare concrete that surrounded it on all four sides. It gave the impression that it was being shunned by the other buildings. Its bleak, featureless exterior provided a total contrast to the more normal, busy decoration of the rest of the city. At night, the White Tower added insult to injury by actually glowing in the dark. The outside surfaces of the building were blanketed with highly charged jolt fields quite capable of killing anyone foolish enough to attempt scaling the walls. They were the final line of the prison's security, and, by way of a bonus, lent the place a sinister luminescence during the hours of darkness. It was visible from most parts of the city.

Like all other prisoners, Phaid saw none of this. With his wrists manacled and secured to a chain around his waist, he had become a number, a single unit in the underground transit system. While he'd been in the hands of the Inquisitor, or even when the arresting officers were treating him to their particular brand of routine brutality, he was at least being given some sort of individual treatment. It had been something to hang on to. Down in the tunnels, however, he was just another item on the production line. He had no value whatsoever. He would be moved from where he was to a place where he could be stored until they were ready to dispose of him. Phaid had imagined many ways in which he might meet his end, but he'd never visualised anything so horribly impersonal. Somehow, in the span of just a few hours, they'd even made his death unimportant. The only way he could cope with the shock was to let his mind match the pace of his shuffling feet, and to live strictly one second at a time.

The production line was less than efficient. Like so many other functions of the city, it was old, overused and prone to snarl up. The idea was simple. Prisoners were tagged, manacled and divided into groups of twenty. Linked by their ankles, they were moved by a short droptube down to the tunnels themselves. Each group was supervised by four guards.

In theory, when a group of prisoners hit the loading dock, there should have been a cylindrical transport waiting for them with its doors wide open, so they could be marched swiftly and efficiently inside.

Theory and practice rarely matched in Chrystianaville. The vaulted roofs of the tunnels rang with curses and the shrieks of contradictory orders as the guards attempted to create some kind of order out of the chaos that was spreading across the loading docks.

The container that seemed to be earmarked for Phaid's particular group arrived at the right moment, but, for some reason, the doors failed to open. The four guards violently herded the prisoners together into a tightly packed bunch. A squad of techs began trying to pry off rusted access plates and worn inspection covers on the underside of the container.

A cutting torch flared into life and Phaid realised that he and his companions were in for a long and miserable wait before they got to their destination.

More squads of prisoners kept arriving down the tube and, with the containers temporarily not running, the loading dock was becoming dangerously crowded with terrified prisoners and increasingly hysterical guards.

As the tinglers and clubs lashed out, Phaid made sure that he kept in the middle of his group, away from the worst of the assaults. He still clung to an almost psychotic determination not to think about either past or future, but to hold his mind locked in a neutral present that would leave him as numb as possible.

He stared at the wall behind the container. Water was running down it in a slow, continuous seepage that fed a growth of dark green algae. Tiny stalactites were tentatively feeling their way down from the roof of the tunnel. Phaid started to wonder just how many hopeless individuals had made the same journey since the stalactites had started growing. He quickly jerked his thoughts away from the idea. It was no good going in that direction. Just watch the drips fall one at a time. He no longer had hope of surviving. All he could do was to avoid as much pain as possible before the end came.

After the techs had laboured and sweated for nearly an hour, the doors slammed back with a crash. From the surprised expressions on the faces of the techs, it was clear that they didn't know what they'd done to start the system working again.

Phaid's group of prisoners bolted for the open doors like a bunch of frightened sheep. One of them, an overfed, middle-aged woman, tripped and fell. She was dragged along by the links on her ankles. For a moment it seemed as though the whole group was going to go down, but then they were inside the container. More groups rushed in behind them until the bare, steel interior was packed solid with very scared humanity. More prisoners were pushed inside until there seemed to be a real danger of either being crushed or suffocated.

The doors clanged shut and the inside of the container was suddenly pitch black. There were screams, the sound of rising panic. Then everything was drowned in an explosive hiss. The container jerked and accelerated. People were thrown to the floor. More groans and screams mingled with the loud, metallic hammering that resounded through the container as it rocketed down the tunnel. The inability to see made the vibrating, headlong rush doubly terrifying.

Then, just as Phaid was letting go the grip on his sanity and considering retreat into all out screaming madness, the container came to an equally bone wrenching stop. The doors flipped open and before any of the container's occupants could even grasp that they had arrived somewhere there were pink and green uniforms in among them, kicking and yelling.

'Out! Out! On your feet scumturds! Out! Out! We don't have time to fuck around with you pieces of shit! Out! *Out! Out!*'

Blinking at the light, Phaid tried to stand. A similar move by the man next to him on the line jerked his feet from under him. He found himself thrashing around on the curved steel floor. Something seemed to be badly wrong with his shoulder. Before he could figure out how bad the damage might be, he'd been grabbed by the hair and dragged towards the door. A swarthy face with broken teeth grinned down at him.

'Welcome to the White Tower, carrion. It's your last stop.'

21

SHE WAS taller than most of the men under her command and she was built like an Aro wrestler from the land of the Tharmiers. She had massive, treetrunk legs, a barrel body with huge, if incongruous breasts, a bullet head and hands that looked capable of tearing the head off any lesser mortal.

She wasn't fat, though. Every wide inch of her was solid packed, muscular hostility and aggression.

She had unusually light amber eyes that gave her square jawed, carved granite face the look of a psychopath.

Indeed, she probably was a psychopath. Her name was Borkastra and she was the undisputed queen of the White Tower. Although a courtier called Maltho-Pos held the nominal title of Lord Custodian and was supposed to have ultimate authority over the city's prison system, he deferred to Borkastra in all practical matters. The rank of Chief Overseer put all real power firmly in the vicelike grip of her massive hands.

She didn't hesitate to use her power to its ultimate extent, and, presumably, gloried in the use of that power. Rumours of her sadism and brutality abounded. Her interrogation methods were the subject of sickening legend, and there were tales of a private discipline room from which prisoners had emerged insane, blinded and even castrated, if they ever emerged at all. There were also rumours of another private suite, in the seldom used upper levels of the White Tower, where she maintained a harem of sullen, doll faced girls in pastel stockings and very little else. The few prisoners who claimed to have been on cleaning details, or performed other duties in the area told stories of how they seemed always to bear welts and bruises from the silver topped cane that Borkastra habitually carried.

Right at that moment the cane was being tapped almost hypnotically against her right veebe-hide boot as the pale eyes moved slowly across the ranks of newly arrived prisoners. The physical presence of the huge woman, and the stories about her that had gone before, left not a single prisoner in any doubt that those eyes could bore clear into their souls if they chose to.

Borkastra took a deep breath. Phaid noticed that this caused her giant breasts to place a not inconsiderable strain on the fastenings of her severely tailored and heavily decorated pink tunic.

'I'm here to welcome you to the rest of your lives.'

Her voice was carefully modulated. It was as though she was pacing each word for maximum impact.

'For you, there is no longer an outside world. This prison is all that you will know from now on. You have come here for one reason and one reason only. You have come here to die. This is the only purpose left to you. Accept that and such future as you have will be a great deal easier.'

Borkastra paused to let this information sink in. The new intake of prisoners stood motionless and naked in front of her. Only a lunatic would have dared to breath. Flanked by her escort of guards and a quartet of attacker dogs on short chains, she left no room for doubt that she was in complete control.

'Some of you may be thinking, if you still have the courage to think, that since you are doomed, there is nothing else we can do to you. In that you are very wrong. You have come here to die, but your death will not come quickly. You will all be here for quite some time. Extermination and disposal of vermin is a complicated business. We only have a limited capacity and there are delays in the process. I don't blame Madame President for wanting to do away with vermin like you, but until Madame President sees fit to enlarge the steamer installation you are all going to have to wait.'

There was a ripple of relief among the prisoners. Borkastra sensed this and an unpleasant smile slowly spread across her face. Without any warning, Borkastra's cane lashed out at a young woman in the front rank. The woman shrieked and fell to her knees. Borkastra stood over her, flexing the cane. Her voice was cold and brisk.

'On your feet and stop snivelling. There's going to be much worse to come. If you didn't want to be punished you should have stayed on the straight and narrow.'

The woman scrambled to her feet. Blood was running down her cheek. Borkastra roared.

'Stand at attention, don't slouch unless you want more of the same. This is a prison, not a rest home!'

The girl stiffened. She was white with terror. Borkastra seemed, for the moment, to be satisfied.

'I think we're all starting to understand each other!'

Not a single prisoner dared to even attempt a nod.

'You people are the lowest. You have nothing left. You have been condemned by the rest of the world. You are corpses, waiting in line for the actual moment of your deaths. The only person who cares about you is me. I own you. I possess you. You are mine.'

She moved nearer to the woman whom she'd struck with her cane.

'You may think that a prison like this is an inhuman, impersonal place.' She was now standing directly in front of the young woman, looking straight into her eyes. 'Once again, you would be very wrong. The relationship between us will be a very close one. It will be a relationship of great intimacy. You will no longer have a freewill. I and my guards are the ones who decide what you do and what you don't do. We will order your every move. We will tell you what's right and what's wrong. We have the whip, the post, the tingler and the jerk field to ensure that you have a full understanding of what is expected of you. The intimacy of our relationship is the intimacy of punishment. It will be that way until your death separates us.'

Phaid felt his flesh crawl. It seemed that only the mad were given power in the Republic. He knew he would do anything to stop himself falling into the hands of this monstrous woman. Borkastra took a step back and scanned the faces of the assembled prisoners. Phaid thought that she had finished her harangue, but apparently she hadn't.

'There's one more thing that you ought to know. I'm certain that there are some among you who are under the illusion that you have done a deal with either the police or the Inquisitors for some sort of favourable treatment. From this moment on, you can forget all about it. It is nothing more than an illusion. There is no favourable treatment. The police and the Inquisitors have no power inside these walls. I am the power and you are all my creatures.'

Borkastra eye's moved from face to face as this final piece of bad news settled. Phaid was too numb and exhausted to curse himself for believing the Inquisitor. He knew that luck could run out. He knew that it could go bad, but he'd never realised that a man's luck could turn gangrenous. Borkastra motioned to her escort. Two of them moved forwards and the woman whom Borkastra had attacked with her cane was pulled out of the line. She was manacled. She flinched as one of the dogs turned and sniffed at her.

Borkastra made an impatient gesture and swept away from the new intake of prisoners. Dogs, escort and, a lot less willingly, the unfortunate woman followed.

There was a sigh of relief. Not only from the prisoners but also among the guards. Some even relaxed from rigid attention, but then they quickly compensated for their lapse by screaming all the louder as they pushed the new intake through the induction process. An hour, and a considerable number of cuffs, slaps and punches later, Phaid found himself sprayed, shaved, sterilised, retina printed and brain scanned for a second time, indoctrinated, inspected, assigned to a hall and weighed down by a pile of clothing and bedding.

Hall A7H was the kind used for those deemed not to be potentially violent; apparently somewhere along the line of scanning and inspection of Phaid's brain it had been decided that he wasn't cut out to be a troublemaker, even though his file now had him listed as a multiple sex killer.

Hall A7H was an open plan room with pillars holding up a low vaulted ceiling. At first sight it reminded Phaid of a shadowy and extremely daunting cave. It seemed to be filled with a jumble of ramshackle constructions, almost as though someone had attempted to build a kind of indoor shanty town.

Originally there had been lines of dormitory style three-tier bunks, but these had been rearranged by the inmates. Those at the top of the hall's pecking order, the rich and powerful, along with their lovers and sycophants, had built themselves what amounted to makeshift private suites with material from the bunks serving as walls and room dividers. Carpets and lengths of cloth gave these premium dwellings a sense of, in jailhouse terms, exotic luxury.

At the other end of the scale, those who couldn't manage to compete for a place in the hierarchy of the hall found themselves sleeping on rudimentary pallets on the floor near either the guards' catwalk, the latrines or the jolt fields that sealed off the hall's arched entrance.

Like every other part of the White Tower, Hall A7H had an atmosphere of great age. The hall was as much like a natural rock formation, an organic thing, as something constructed by the hands of men. The ceiling was blackened, impregnated with centuries' worth of bad air, smoke, cooking smells and human misery. There was a damp chill in the air that reminded Phaid how, short of a miracle, he was cut off from the sun forever.

The jolt field cracked as it snapped back into life, having been shut down by the guards to admit Phaid to A7H. With his bundle of prison issue slung over his shoulder, he stood looking around, wondering what to do. Just inside the jolt field a small wizened nut of a man had made up what looked to be a bed of dirty rags. He looked up at Phaid and cackled.

'New, huh?'

'Uh . . . yeah.'

'I guess you're wondering what to do.'

'You could say that.'

'It's always rough at the start.'

'It gets any easier?'

'No.'

'So?'

'You kind of get used to it.'

Phaid eased the load on his shoulder.

'This is a fascinating conversation, but I was rather wondering where I should stow all this gear.'

The little wizened man patted a bare space of floor next to his pile of rags.

'You best dump it down here, fresh fish. You ain't going to get any better straight in the door.'

Phaid dropped his bundle and looked at the maze of bunks further into the hall.

'Ain't one of these bunks supposed to be mine?'

'Supposed to be, but it don't work that way.'

'How come?'

'Because space, comfort and a degree of privacy are things that get bought and sold inside this place. You smuggle in any booze?'

Phaid shook his head.

'No. It wouldn't be possible to get a bottle through that induction process.'

'It happens. Did you bring in any dog gold?'

'No.'

'Candy even?'

'No. I don't see how anyone could get anything past the screening.'

'You'd be surprised.'

Phaid looked wearily at the little man. He noticed that most of his teeth were missing.

'I got to tell you, friend, nothing would surprise me in this place.'

'Yeah? Well, if you didn't bring anything in with you, you're in a whole bunch of trouble.'

'I am?'

'If you ain't got a brother who's a guard or nothing like that.'

'Nothing like that.'

Phaid was starting to realise that, despite Borkastra's bombast, for the most part the prisoners seemed to be left to their own devices.

'You're going to have to start from scratch, and that can be rough.'

'Isn't everything?'

'It don't have to be. If you're a hall duke, a wheeler-dealer or a big man in the jailhouse, you can make it. You can have really an easy life, with most of what you had on the outside, if you go to work on it.'

'But it helps to have something to start with.'

'That's right.'

Phaid looked at the little man and his pile of rags.

'It don't look as though you've done too well.'

'I didn't have much to start off with.'

'Just like me?'

'Matter of fact, young man, you do have something that you can bargain with.'

'I do?'

'Sure you do.'

'Well, don't keep me in suspense.'

The wizened man shook his head.

'I ain't about to tell you. That's business too. I don't get nothing for sitting around here telling the fresh fish what's what. If you don't have no booze or no candy, then I'm keeping my mouth shut.'

'You're a charmer.'

'I look after myself and anyway, you'll be visited quite soon by some people who'll be more than eager to set you straight.'

Phaid was puzzled.

'You got a name, old timer?'

'Festler.'

'And that's for free?'

'That's all you get.'

'So what about these visitors, Festler?'

'That's all you get.'

'I just wait and see?'

'You got it.'

Phaid didn't have to wait long. The first visitor went by the name of Sovia. She was a short wiry girl with a prison crop just starting to grow out.

'I represent the women of A7H.'

Phaid smiled.

'All of them?'

'Just shut your mouth and listen up.'

'Sure.'

'I represent the women of A7H and I have a few facts to lay on you as a new arrival. We don't take any shit in this hall. Some women may want to relate to you because they find you attractive and some women will relate to you on a more material level. That will be their choice. If, however, you should force yourself on any of the women in this hall, we'll go to work on you, and when we're finished, you won't have a damn thing to force on any woman again.'

Phaid swallowed. Although the girl was slight and skinny, there was something about her that reminded him of the monstrous Borkastra. Maybe it was a style that was copied all through the prison. It had certainly caused him to take a step back.

'Am I supposed to take that literally?'

'Quite literally.'

'Ain't the guards going to take an interest if you girls start doing stuff like that?'

'We have an understanding with our guards. You'd do best to remember that.'

Phaid nodded. There seemed to be nothing else that he could do. His second visitor was called Graid.

'I control the supplies.'

'What supplies?'

Graid reeled it off like it was a litany that he recited often.

'Each day, each prisoner receives the standard daily ration pack. This ration pack contains three bars of nutrosolid, one soluble beverage mix, one candy bar and five placidile tablets.'

'They like to keep the inmates doped down.'

'You could say that.'

'So each day I get my supply pack. What has that got to do with you?'

Graid smiled.

'I'm Graid. I'm the supply supervisor for this hall, I fetch the supply packs from the guards' delivery truck then, along with my helpers, I distribute them.'

Phaid raised a suspicious eyebrow.

'And?'

'And I charge a small distribution fee on each pack.'

Phaid nodded. He had been expecting something of the sort.

'The guards go along with this?'

'We have an understanding with our guards.'

'So what do I have to pay to pick up my own rations?'

'Half a candy bar or one placidile tablet.'

'What happens if I don't give you a piece of my ration pack?'

'No pay, no pack. You'd get awful thin.'

The next visitor was named Strahl. Her message was brief and to the point.

'You want to sell any of your kit?'

Phaid declined. That left him with just one more of the reception committee to deal with. His name was Fonthor-Mun, and, by White Tower standards, he had a bland, well fed, expensive look. His proposition was slightly more complicated.

'Phaid? It was Phaid, wasn't it? I'm what they call the time broker in this hall.'

Phaid was starting to lose patience with the ways of the White Tower.

'What the hell is a time broker?'

Fonthor-Mun's expression hardened.

'You shouldn't talk to me like that. I hold some considerable power in this hall. You wouldn't like me to have you handed over to the tender mercies of our blessed Borkastra, would you?'

For the first time since he had been arrested, some of the numbness left Phaid. He started to get angry.

'Are you threatening me?'

Fonthor-Mun quickly smiled and became very anxious to please.

'Of course not. In actual fact, I was about to ask you if you felt like selling a portion of your time.'

Phaid's eyes narrowed.

'What are you talking about?'

'What's your prison number?'

Phaid looked at the identity tag that had been clamped to his wrist.

'A7H-491708319, why?'

Fonthor-Mun seemed to be making calculations in his head.

'8319, that would mean that you'll have to wait around in this hell hole for nine or ten months before you go to the steamer.'

'That sounds like a mixed blessing.'

'You could sell a month of it.'

'Huh?'

'You could trade prison numbers with someone who only has maybe seven or eight months to the steamer. Thus they get an extra month of life and . . .'

'And what do I get out of the deal?'

'A comfortable space in the hall, the companion of your choice, booze, placidile, dog gold – the choice is yours.'

'Presumably you have an understanding with your guards about this kind of transaction.'

'Of course.'

'It's amazing.'

'What is?'

Phaid shook his head.

'Oh, nothing.'

'So, Phaid, do we have a deal?'

'I don't know. I need time to think about this.'

'You may not get such a good offer the next time.'

Phaid knew that he was being hustled.

'I said I wanted time to think about it. I don't think well under pressure.'

Old Festler cackled.

'You did well there, boy. Too many fresh fish fall for this oily bastard's line of patter.'

Fonthor-Mun rounded on him.

'Shut your mouth, you ancient piece of carrion. Your time has all but run out.'

He turned to Phaid.

'You see this creature. He's been in the White Tower for two years. He's lied, cheated, stolen, done everything he could to squirm away from the steamer. Now he could go at any time. Nobody would sell him so much as a day. The old fool has to die, he's the only one who can't accept it.'

Phaid turned to Festler.

'Is what he says truc?'

Festler shrugged.

'Give or take a few points.'

'You're all crazy in here.'

'Just like on the outside.'

Phaid spent the next two days sitting on his makeshift bed between Festler and the jolt field. He gave Graid's helper his kickback on the ration pack, beyond that, he refused all offers that were directed at him. Particularly those that might take away the time he had before his appointment with the steamer.

His mood was constantly changing. For a lot of the time he was simply numb, staring into space and doing the best he could not to feel a damn thing. This wasn't always easy. A hopeless, frustrated rage would burn up inside him at the injustice of his situation. He felt a desperate, almost overpowering urge to lash out and hurt someone or something. Nothing, however, presented itself. All he could do was to hurt himself. At one point he was tempted to hurl himself headfirst into the jolt field. The drawback to this was that the jolt field was non-lethal. It would be appallingly painful, it might damage his brain, but it wouldn't kill him.

As the rage faded, Phaid would start thinking more positively. If he was stuck in A7H for many long months, he might as well get into the run of the prison hustles.

Maybe he should trade off a month of his life for a few creature comforts and maybe a stake to start something going for himself. If the prison was run by bastards, then he could be as big a bastard as any of them, except . . .

The except always came as the anger born adrenalin wore off and depression started to take over; except, what was the point? He was at the end of his road and no amount of shuffling and scuffling could disguise that fact. The numbness once again took command and Phaid resumed sitting and staring into the jolt field.

The mental cycle went round and round. Its sum total was that he did absolutely nothing. He hoarded the pills and the candy bars from his ration pack but made no move to do anything with them. His inertia was complete. It seemed to be protection against anything that the prison could do to him. Phaid, although he didn't actually think about it in such specific terms, seemed content to sit and decay.

On the fifth day of his incarceration, a whisper went around the hall. Phaid had dimly noticed that there always seemed to be certain prisoners who knew what was going to happen before it happened. Maybe they had a tap into the guards' grapevine, or maybe they were blessed with some sort of jailhouse precognition. Phaid neither knew nor particularly cared. The whispers came all the same and were usually partway correct.

'Borkastra is making the rounds. She's at A7E and she's coming this way.'

This particular whisper put a snap of fear into the air of A7H.

'Borkastra? Here? What does she want to come here for? We haven't done anything.'

'It'll mean trouble. You just see if it doesn't.'

Phaid wished that he was situated somewhere other than right in front of the entrance to the hall. He knew that he would be totally exposed to the Chief Overseer's icy gaze. He tried to slide backwards away from the jolt field. Unfortunately, everybody else had had the same idea and nobody would make room for him.

'She's in the next hall. She'll be here in a few minutes.'

'She's not alone. There's someone with her.'

'Who is it?'

'Solchaim! Solchaim is making a tour of the prison.'

'Solchaim is coming here. We're going to get to

see the devil.'

Phaid felt an unpleasant prickling at the back of his neck. He was finally going to catch a glimpse of the being who so many people accused of being the author of all the troubles in the Republic.

The presence of the elaihi made itself known long before Phaid had a chance to actually look at him with his own eyes. Even while he was still hidden from view, screened by the awesome Borkastra, her dogs and a phalanx of her personal guard, an invisible part of him was inside the hall moving around. It searched and probed, seeking something with a cold, but nonetheless desperate urgency. It couldn't be seen and it couldn't be heard, but it could certainly be felt and there was no mistaking that it was some strange psychic extension of the elaihi.

It drifted in and out of the prisoners' minds, opening and shutting them as though they were merely books in a big disorganised library. It was frighteningly powerful. Those who resisted its intrusion found that their freewill was brushed aside like so much insubstantial gauze.

The protective wedge of guards parted and Solchaim himself walked up to the entrance jolt field. Suddenly he was standing just a few paces from where Phaid sat. Phaid froze. He felt like the legendary rabbit confronted by the cobra. For almost a minute, he stared at the ground. It seemed to somehow be important that he resist looking at the elaihi. Resistance, however, was impossible. Almost as though they had a will of their own, his eyes slowly started to move.

It was hard at first for Phaid to come to terms with the idea that the figure that towered over him was of the same kind as those that he had encountered in the desert. Solchaim was tall, as were the other elaihim, but that's where the resemblance ended. The elaihim in the desert had a sparse, almost ethereal air about them. They had that look of uniformity about them as though their individual identities had somehow merged into one great superior overmind: an overmind that seemed to dwell, in part, in some other dimension or on another level of existence.

If Solchaim dwelt on other levels, he didn't make it noticeable. He seemed to be at the very power hub of the serious here and now. There was a monstrous strength folded about him, a strength that had grown cold and unfeeling in the pursuit of too many distant and unimaginable evils. Phaid could feel a coldness, an absolute lack of feeling that could only survive in some purple and yellow subworld on the far side of decadence. In a human being such a thing would have been horrible to contemplate. It would have begged the question of how barren a life could be to shape such frigid isolation. In an elaihi it was so infinitely worse that Phaid didn't even care to think about it.

A secondary surprise was the way in which Solchaim was dressed. The garb of the desert elaihim was a minimum of functional austerity. Solchaim was arrayed for grand, theatrical effect.

A black, fur trimmed cape was thrown around the elaihi's shoulders. Its bulk gave them a hunched appearance. He reminded Phaid of some strange angular bird of prey, a vulture that walked on long spindly legs encased in equally long boots polished to a diamond hard lustre. When Solchaim took a step forward he became more like a spider. A dandified, almost foppish spider in sable and jet, but a spider all the same with a spider's icy determination.

Sapphires sparkled on his fingers, his nails were painted black and buffed to match the finish of his boots. The fingers of his left hand twitched over a set of irregularly threaded beads, not, however, in the manner of someone at prayer, but as though a part of the elaihi's mind was engaged in complex calculations and the beads provided some sort of numerical tally.

Phaid's reluctant gaze was finally forced up to the face of the elaihi. There was the same high forehead and penetrating eyes as those of his desert cousins, but, once again, that was where the similarity ended. Heavy make-up made his eyes seem more sunken and his cheeks more hollow than they really were. He was wearing some sort of dark lip colour that give his mouth a sensuous cruelty. His hair was swept up from the temples, almost giving the impression of horns growing out of his head. Phaid suddenly wanted to look away. He had realised that the elaihi had deliberately made himself into a parody of what humans thought of as evil. He was a total amalgam of all the elegant demons from ten thousand folktales. Phaid wanted to look away, but somehow he couldn't.

Solchaim turned slightly. He had been scanning the

inmates of A7H, but suddenly he noticed Phaid staring at him. Their eyes locked. The invisible thing that had been rummaging through the minds of the prisoners suddenly pounced on Phaid. Solchaim's eyes seemed to be burning through to the interior of Phaid's skull. With a ghastly flash of insight, Phaid knew that he was the object of the elaihi's search. He couldn't understand how or why, but there was no escaping the fact that he was the one for whom Solchaim had been hunting.

He recoiled in horror. The elaihi was inside his brain. Phaid squirmed and struggled, trying to expel the alien intrusion. He threw up a wall to block out the invader, but almost at once it started to sag and crack under the rain of hammerblows from the superior elaihim intellect. No matter how Phaid struggled to shore up his defences, he had no chance. His wall collapsed in a cascade of imaginary bricks.

Solchaim's eyes were deep inside his head. Phaid was more naked and helpless than he had ever been, even on the day of his birth. His fear was total. He could do nothing except wait for the blow to fall.

Then, to Phaid's total surprise, Solchaim was gone. Phaid's mind was his own again. Solchaim was still looking at him, but he had completely withdrawn. The elaihi smiled faintly and looked away. He turned on his heel, murmured something to Borkastra, and then quickly strode off in the direction from which he had come.

Solchaim's abrupt exit threw his guard into confusion as they tried to fall in behind him. Borkastra motioned two of them and then pointed at Phaid. Phaid's stomach turned to jelly. What was going on? What had he done? Most important of all, what was going to happen to him?

The jolt field was shut down. The two guards moved quickly into the hall and seized Phaid by the arms. They dragged him to his feet.

'You're coming with us!'

'Don't make any trouble, it'll only make it harder for you.'

'But I . . .'

'Just shut your mouth and keep walking.'

'I haven't done anything.'

'Don't tell us, we're just doing what we're told.'

Phaid was hustled along a seemingly endless series of grim echoing corridors until he was back at the main induction area where he'd had his first taste of what life in the White Tower was going to be like. A few swift body blows from the guards had stopped him protesting his innocence, but when he saw where he was, a faint flutter of hope rose up inside him. Surely it couldn't be that they were going to let him go.

One of the guards produced a pair of manacles, and Phaid's hopes plummeted. His arms were pinned behind his back. The guards pushed him towards a bench that ran along one wall of the open space.

'Sit!'

Phaid sat. One of the guards sat down beside him, the other went about his business. For a long time, Phaid was left to sit and watch the doings in the induction area. In the hour or so that he waited, fifty or more new arrivals passed through the unpleasant welcoming process. Out on the street, the police must have been doing a roaring business.

Most of the new intake went to their fate in a fully docile manner. Arrest, interrogation and the nightmare journey through the tunnels had sapped their will to fight. Phaid remembered his own journey from the police complex to the White Tower. The surprise wasn't that so few prisoners resisted what was being done to them. The surprise was that there were any resisters at all.

During the time that Phaid was sitting in the induction area watching the gloomy lines go by, only one of the prisoners showed any sign of spirit or rebellion. Ironically it was about the youngest prisoner that had been brought in. He was a gang kid, a Scorpion, slight and skinny on the threshold between boy and man. It took two brawny guards to drag him from the transport while he spat, bit and fought. His long skirt was mostly ripped away and the bulk of the cheap jewellery that the gang wore as its emblem had gone. Neither police nor prison guards, however, had been able to do anything but smudge his bizarre black make-up. Phaid wondered how he had managed to get this far without being beaten to a bloody pulp. He had been lucky, but his luck was about to give out on him.

Two of the biggest guards in the place joined the two already holding him. Between them they wrestled him to the ground and pinned him. The remnants of his red and orange skirt were ripped away and his make-up scrubbed roughly from his face.

Despite the four guards kneeling on him, the Scorpion somehow managed to get an arm free. There was a loud scream as his fingers gouged at one guard's eyes. A club smashed down and it was the Scorpion's turn to scream. Phaid looked away as the kid was dragged off to one of the side cells that were euphemistically known as 'conversation suites'. Five club welding guards went in with him, while the one with the damaged eye was led away to receive medical attention.

The conversation lasted for about fifteen minutes. It ended when the five guards emerged looking nastily pleased with themselves, and two prisoners were delegated to drag away what was left of the kid. Phaid felt sick to his stomach. He had no real reason to believe that the fate that was waiting for him would be any less painful.

On the wall opposite Phaid, just below the point where the vertical pillars blossomed into the sweeping arches that supported the high vaulted roof, a kind of transparent, plexiglass blister bulged out of the wall like an ulcer on the inside of the prison's gut. The room behind the blister was brightly lit and seemed to be used as some sort of observation gallery where those who were both authorised and interested could observe the inflow of new prisoners.

The spectators seemed to be entirely made up of either priests, prison overseers or ranking police officers. From their gestures, it looked as though constant arguments were going on. Phaid had a sneaking suspicion that they were about which particular arm of the establishment had the rights to certain individual prisoners. If this was indeed the case, Phaid's paranoia prompted him to wonder if maybe he was the subject of one of these discussions. As he stared at the blister, he thought he spotted the elusive Dreen among a bunch of black robed priests. It was too far, though, to be absolutely certain whether it was the mysterious, furtive little man or not. There were an awful lot of priests who reminded Phaid of Dreen.

All thoughts of Dreen, priests, or anything else beyond his own predicament were driven instantly from Phaid's mind as a pair of masked and rubber suited executioners strolled by quite close to where he sat. They were pulling off their gloves and chatting just like any two working men who had put in a hard but satisfying day. Phaid had imagined his death would be many things, but never just a part of someone's daily routine.

The guard beside him quickly snapped to attention. An overseer and a man in civilian clothes were walking straight towards them, cutting through the grey lines of prisoners. The overseer pointed at Phaid.

'That's the one.'

'The one called Phaid?'

'That's him.'

The civilian nodded. He moved from side to side, as though inspecting Phaid's face from a number of angles. At first, Phaid thought that the man was a courtier but on closer examination Phaid saw that his clothes weren't quite court quality, and his hair was a little too long and unkempt.

Hc leaned forward, looking very closely at the contours of Phaid's cheek. He almost seemed to be making measurements. A hundred dreadful possibilities flashed through Phaid's mind at lightning speed. Then the man straightened up.

'Well, I suppose we might as well get on with it.'

The overseer nodded curtly at the guard. The guard in his turn grabbed Phaid by his collar and hauled him upwards.

'On your feet, sunshine. We're going with the nice gentlemen.'

'Going where?'

The guards cuffed Phaid sharply round the head.

'Just keep your mouth shut and do what you're told.'

Phaid had noticed that the guards became a lot more physical when there was an overseer watching. The civilian looked at the guard questioningly.

'Is he dangerous?'

The guard laughed.

'Him? Lords no, not him. He's as good as gold, a regular pussy cat. Murdered a courtier, if I remember rightly.' He looked at Phaid. 'Ain't that right? Didn't you murder a courtier? Sexual or something, wasn't it?'

Phaid was getting tired of all this.

'I . . .'

He was treated to another stinging cuff to the head.

'Didn't we get told to keep our mouths shut?'

The presence of the civilian made the guard doubly determined to show off. The civilian, however, was starting to look quite perturbed.

'Do you really have to hit him quite so much? I mean, he isn't causing any trouble and we do sort of need his co-operation.'

The guard looked at the civilian as if he verged on the feeble minded.

'Hit him, sir? You have to hit them. It reminds them who's in charge. It also makes them feel wanted.'

As far as he was concerned, that was the end of the matter. The civilian shook his head and sighed.

'You'd better just follow me.'

'He let them out of the induction area and down a corridor. A rather beat-up hologram rig had been set up in what looked to Phaid like a medium-sized holding tank. The receptors had been positioned in a tight half-circle. They were hooked into the open chestplate of a battered and rather mournful looking android. A pair of boohooms squatted in the corner playing a game of match fingers. They were presumably the porters who had brought in the equipment from outside.

Phaid had seen no other boohooms in the White Tower. In fact, when he thought about it, he realised that he had seen little of the good natured sub-humans since the trouble had started in Chrystianaville.

The civilian rummaged in a pile of cases and boxes behind the receptors. He held out a purple, hoodlum style shirt to Phaid.

'You'd better put this on. It wouldn't be plausible with you in prison uniform.'

Phaid twisted his manacled hands round from behind his back.

'I can't.'

'No, I suppose you can't.'

The civilian glanced at the guard.

'Take those things off, will you?'

'I can't do that.'

'What do you mean, you can't do that?'

'Not authorised.'

'Of course it's authorised. We can't do the damned thing if he's wearing manacles.'

'Nobody told me.'

'I'm telling you.'

'I'm not sure.'

The civilian was starting to lose patience. The guard

wavered.

'Will you take responsibility?'

'Yes, yes, I'll take responsibility, just get those things off him.'

The guard finally snapped off the manacles. Phaid stood massaging his wrists. The civilian again held out the shirt, doing his best to look friendly and capable.

'My name's Avar. You better put this on so we can get started.'

Phaid took the shirt.

'Do you mind if I ask just one question?'

'Not at all.'

'What the hell is going on?'

'Don't ask me. I was told to get my equipment over to the White Tower and shoot holograms of a prisoner. Have you done something particularly hideous?'

Phaid shrugged.

'Who knows in this place.'

Avar awkwardly tried to allay what he imagined were Phaid's fears.

'It's probably some kind of propaganda thing.'

'You didn't enquire?'

'You don't enquire too much when it's a job at the White Tower. You get over there, shoot the shots and get out while you still can. You'll appreciate that nobody stays here longer than they have to.'

Avar smiled as though he had made a joke. Phaid ignored him and pulled the shirt overhead, on top of his shapeless prison uniform.

'Some of us don't have any choice.'

Avar looked embarrassed.

'Yeah, well, let's get on with it, shall we?'

He pointed to a spot in the middle of the circle of receptors.

'Just stand there, will you?'

Phaid did as he was instructed. Avar turned to the android.

'Are we all set?'

'As-set-as-we-are-ever-likely-to-get.'

The android's voice was scratchy and muffled. It sounded depressed and unhealthy. Avar didn't appear to notice.

'Shall we go for a run through?'

Phaid nodded. The android blinked a dull sensor. Pilot lights on the receptors flickered into life. Phaid stood there wondering what was going on. Avar shook his head.

'You don't look very aggressive or dangerous.'

'Am I supposed to be dangerous or aggressive?'

'That's what I was told to get. You look more bewildered than anything.'

'I don't feel particularly aggressive or dangerous. Those kind of emotions get frowned on around here.'

'Couldn't you fake it?'

Phaid experimentally bared his teeth.

'How's that?'

'Better. If you put a bit more intensity into it, and if you half turned while you do it, so we'd have a bit of motion, it'd be just about there.'

They tried it a number of times with Avar encouraging Phaid to look as menacing as possible. Phaid felt a trifle ridiculous but anything that got him out of hall A7H for a while came as a welcome change.

They tried the pose a total of fifteen times before Avar was finally satisfied with the result. For a moment, Phaid was quite pleased with his dramatic efforts, then he realised that doing it right meant that the interlude was over and he would have to go back to the hall. He also remembered that he'd been in such shock at coming face to face with Solchaim and being ordered out of the hall by the guards that he'd completely forgotten to do anything about his meagre prison kit. He'd left it just lying on the floor. His bed and everything else would have long since vanished. He didn't relish the idea of sleeping on the hard floor. On the other hand, he also didn't relish the idea of trading off some of the time he had left before the steamer in return for a few creature comforts.

The android, helped by the boohooms, began packing away the equipment; Avar also busied himself. He seemed to be avoiding looking Phaid in the eye. The guard moved in and motioned Phaid to once again put his hands behind his back. Phaid obeyed without protest and the manacles were snapped back on to his wrists.

'Okay, let's go.'

They started back towards the induction area. As they walked, the guard kept looking at Phaid curiously.

'So what's so good about you?'

'Huh?'

'What's so good about you? How come you get to have your picture taken?'

Phaid lost all patience. He suddenly didn't care what the guard did to him.

'You jealous or something?'

Surprisingly, the blow that Phaid expected never came. The guard seemed preoccupied, thinking about something else. They walked in silence after Phaid's flash of defiance. Phaid started to wonder if maybe the guard did think that he was someone important and was letting him off easy in the hope of future favours.

Once they'd crossed the induction area and started down the White Tower's seemingly endless labyrinth of corridors, Phaid began to get the feeling that they were returning to A7H by a different route. He couldn't be absolutely sure, all the corridors in the White Tower had such a uniform, drab bareness that one looked much like any other. They climbed a set of stairs. Phaid didn't remember any stairs between A7H and the induction area. He would have sworn that they were both on the same level. They climbed another set, and then a third. Phaid was now certain that they were headed for some destination other than A7H. The guard was still quiet, so Phaid decided to risk a question.

'We're not going back to A7H are we?'

'No.'

'My gear's in A7H.'

'That will have been stolen by now.'

'So where are we going?'

'You'll find out.'

A horrible fear twisted in Phaid's gut.

'We're not going . . .'

'Going where?'

'To the steamer?'

The guard laughed. It was far from being a pretty laugh.

'You didn't get that lucky.'

Something in the guard's eyes warned Phaid that he'd used up all the chances that he would get. It would have been a mistake to ask any more questions. They kept on climbing. Phaid began to wonder if they were going all the way to the top of the Tower.

As they reached the higher levels, the stairwells and corridors started to change. They seemed less used, more neglected. The paint was peeling and dirt had spent a long time accumulating in the corners. A dead, abandoned, musty smell hung in the air. Many of the glo-bars set in the arched roofs of the corridors had burnt out and never been replaced. The hostile glare of the lower levels gave way to the gloom of disuse and decay. These upper levels had the air of places where men or things could be brought, left and forgotten. These ideas did nothing to allay Phaid's apprehension.

He and the guard kept climbing for what seemed like hours. The corridors through which they passed became dirtier and even more gloomy. They gave the illusion of being narrower, that they twisted and turned more. Phaid wasn't sure whether this was really the case. It could have been a trick of the malfunctioning light. Trick or not, though, it didn't stop the feeling that he was being taken to the highest, most forsaken regions of the prison, regions where his soul and even his life might be deliberately lost.

They passed along a shadowy corridor lined with battered steel doors. Tiny inspection windows allowed brief glimpses of the dark cells beyond. Phaid assumed that the place had to be some long disused punishment or solitary confinement block. Then, without warning, a pale arm lunged from one of the little windows, fingers grasped at the air just inches from Phaid's head.

'Speak to me! For Lords' sake, speak to me!'

The voice had a rasp to it, almost as though it hadn't been used for a very long time. The fingers went on clawing and clutching at the air.

'Please! I've been alone here for so long. Please stop and talk to me.'

The guard grabbed hold of the arm and jerked it hard downwards. There was an unpleasant crack and a loud scream. Then he pushed Phaid down the corridor.

'We don't have to bother about scum like that.'

Phaid stumbled on. He was on the edge of dropping into blind panic. He could still hear a low whimpering coming from back down the corridor. Was he going to be left to rot in isolation like the scarcely human thing in its lonely cell? It seemed to be an even more horrible fate than the steamer. Madness was stalking at the edge of his mind. He had always done his best to bend with whatever circumstances presented themselves, but the White Tower was throwing so much at him that he feared, this time, he was going to break.

Almost blindly, he climbed yet another flight of steps.

At the top was a short, narrow passage. There was a single door at the end. It was protected by a jolt field and an elaborate touch tone lock. It looked like the White Tower wanted to take very good care of whatever was behind the door.

The guard shut down the jolt field and thumbed out the open sequence on the lock. The door swung back with a querulous metallic squeal. The room beyond the door was in near darkness. A single dim orange glo-bar was all that Phaid could see. The guard snapped off Phaid's handcuffs and thrust him roughly inside.

'Enjoy your stay.'

Phaid stumbled over the threshold of his new prison. The door slammed behind him. It was a hollow sound. The faint crackle of the jolt field returning provided a final punctuation. He stood blinking, trying to make out some shapes in the gloom. His heart almost stopped when a voice came out of the darkness.

'So they've given me some company after all this time.'

22

'YOU HAVE to remember that when she started she was everybody's sweetheart. A great many of those who are trying to pull her down today were dancing in the streets when the old man died. They thought that Chrystiana-Nex was their saviour. After all, she was one of them, she'd come up the hard way, through the bars and gin joints and cabarets. They knew that she'd sold herself a thousand times before she got her hands on the old president and made herself his mistress, then his consort and finally a full partner as co-ruler of the Republic. They knew that when he became mad, bloodthirsty and brutal, she was the one who organised the plot against him, that she was there when he was killed. Nobody denied that she was the one who should take power.'

'But aren't you bitter?'

'Bitter? Of course I'm bitter. I've been locked up in this room for two and a half years now, with only the company of an elderly guard when he delivers my ration pack.'

'You have me now.'

The old man sighed.

'That's right. I have you now. I can't begin to guess at their purpose in putting you in here with me.'

He stroked his whispy goatee and regarded Phaid thoughtfully. He was stooped and frail. His white hair was receding from his high domed forehead and his skin had a sick, unhealthy transparency. Phaid couldn't be sure if his newfound companion was really ancient or if he had been worn down and prematurely aged by his long and lonely incarceration.

He claimed that his name was Vist-Roxon and that he'd been chief advisor to Chrystiana-Nex before the coming of Solchaim. This also might be a product of his imprisonment, a fantasy concocted and made real by the long months locked up on his own, but Phaid was inclined to believe him. The unique nature of his solitary confinement marked him as something different from the ordinary prisoners. It was all too plausible that Chrystiana-Nex should condemn a favourite who had fallen from grace to such a cruel, living death.

'I don't see how you can talk so charitably about the woman after what she's done to you. She's a monster. You should have seen the slaughter on the Plaza after she set the Palace Guard on the women's march.'

'It's not a matter of charity. I remember her as she used to be. She was always ruthless, but there was a quality about her – sex appeal, charisma, call it what you will, back in the old days there was no way that you could help but be drawn to her.'

'You sound as though you were in love with her.'

'Maybe I was. I think, back at the beginning, we were all in love with her. Perhaps that was the secret of her power. I've been mind probed so often in this place that it's hard for me to remember now what's real and what isn't. I do know that it was all very different before that devil came along.'

'Solchaim?'

'I can't bring myself to speak his name. He is the real monster.'

'You know that he was here in the prison?'

'That's unusual. He almost never comes to this place. Did you hear what he wanted?'

'He was apparently looking for me.'

'I would think that you are lucky to be still alive. What did he want with you?'

'I don't know.'

Phaid recounted how Solchaim had appeared at A7H and pulled him out of the crowd of prisoners. He told of his desert encounter with the elaihim and how so many people had taken such an interest in it. All through Phaid's story, Vist-Roxon grew more and more perplexed.

'I have learned that where he is concerned there is no

such thing as an accident. You and I may not recognise them as such, but every move he makes is a finely scripted part of his devilish master plan. I wish I had more of my mind left and I could think more clearly . . .'

His voice trailed off and he sat staring into space. After he had remained like that for quite some time, Phaid started to become a little alarmed.

'Vist-Roxon, are you sick or something.'

Vist-Roxon looked up sharply.

'Sick or something? Yes, my young friend, I am sick, sick to my soul at what has become of my country. I mourn for the ruin of my life. I grieve over the damage to my brain that can never be made good. I'm sick right enough, but there's no cure that you can bring.'

'I'm sorry.'

'Don't be. I'm sorry enough for both of us. What we must ponder now is why that creature has had holograms made of you, and then placed you in here with me. You say they had you wear a civilian shirt when the holograms were done?'

'That's right.'

'The elaihi is obviously up to something. Our problem is to fathom out what. From all that you have said he must have detected something inside your mind that is useful to his purpose.'

'It was almost as though he was searching for me.'

'He obviously has need of you.'

'But why me? I'm nothing special.'

'You seem to be underestimating yourself. You do have an alarming capacity for being in the wrong place at the wrong time.'

Phaid frowned. His memory had gone back to his drunken thoughts on the Wospan terrace. What was it about him that he seemed to have been selected to be bounced from one deadly crisis to the next? Vist-Roxon put a hand on his shoulder.

'Don't look so unhappy. There is one consolation in this place. Whatever happens, there's no point in worrying. There's not a damn thing you can do about it.'

Phaid looked curiously at the old man.

'You say that you've been in this place for two and a half years?'

'That's correct.'

'Why didn't either Solchaim or the President simply

369

have you executed?'

Vist-Roxon smiled bitterly.

'That's something else I've given much thought to. It may have just been a cruel whim, or perhaps the devil has future plans for me. Life here is filled with perplexing questions. There is really only one consolation. It would seem that we have plenty of time to think about the answers.'

Over the next four days Phaid did a lot of thinking but no answers readily presented themselves. There were times in his deliberations when he started to wonder if the superhuman powers he and Vist-Roxon were attributing to the elaihi were simply a figment of some collective paranoia. When he reached this stage, however, he remembered the presence of Solchaim in the prison hall and how it had to be admitted that the elaihim were superhuman.

As well as worrying at the problem, Phaid was also starting to become accustomed to his new surroundings. Life with Vist-Roxon was certainly a great improvement on the dog eat dog existence in A7H. The cell was fairly roomy with two beds that were actually quite comfortable by prison standards. Although the place was marked by the same drab starkness as the rest of the White Tower, Vist-Roxon had managed to acquire a fair selection of books. There was even a pack of cards that Phaid used to while away more than one idle, dragging afternoon.

They were in the charge of one elderly guard called Hofster. He was fat, bald and close to retirement. He also had a tendency to sweat, and apparently had little else to do except see that, for a price, Vist-Roxon and now Phaid were as comfortable as possible. The ex-courtier must still have had some influence, and, much more to the point, a source of money from the outside. Each day a bottle of wine or some other small luxury would arrive along with the standard ration packs. Vist-Roxon seemed to take the attitude that Phaid was somehow a guest in his cell, and accordingly shared everything with the younger man on an equal basis.

Hofster was also a constant, if less than accurate, source of information about life on the outside. It appeared that the deadlock between the rebels and those loyal to the President was still being maintained, with the rebels holding the poor northside areas and the loyalists the wealthier city centre.

After the indiscriminate slaughter on the Plaza, increasing numbers of police were deserting and going over to the rebels. Chrystiana-Nex was seemingly only maintaining her position by bringing in large numbers of bought and paid for foreign mercenaries, a practice that, by all accounts, was placing an unbearable strain on an already depleted exchequer.

Both Phaid and Vist-Roxon were agreed that probably their best chance of getting out of the White Tower would be if the rebels took over. Coupled with that, however, was the very real fear that, in her last moments of power, the insane President might order the wholesale slaughter of all the prisoners.

On the fourth day, at least one of the riddles posed by Solchaim was graphically solved. Hofster arrived at the usual time with the usual two ration packs, a bottle of the crisp red Tharmian wine and a flat package. He handed the package to Phaid with a somewhat mysterious smile.

'I thought you might like to have a look at this.'

Phaid tore off the wrapper. Inside was a small display hologram. It was of him, looking a trifle desperate, obviously one of the series taken by Avar. As he looked at it a small loop recording started up.

'The man that you are looking at is a bandit called Phaid. He is a brutal and psychopathic killer with a grudge against humanity in general and members of the Presidential Court in particular. He has so far claimed eleven victims. He must be stopped before he makes the tally up to twelve. A reward of ten thousand tabs will be paid for information leading to his death or capture. If you see him, do not approach him. He is armed and dangerous. Report him to the nearest member of the police or military.'

The message started again. Phaid dropped the display on the floor and stamped on it. It ceased to make a noise.

'This is insane.'

Hofster laughed.

'Somebody seems to think that you're still on the loose. Those things are all over the city. I hear you're quite a hero among the rebels.'

Phaid couldn't believe what was happening.

'This is more than insane.'

Vist-Roxon was thoughtful.

'Maybe not. You have obviously been chosen as the object of some kind of propaganda exercise.'

Vist-Roxon had picked up the hologram and was examining the picture. Phaid began to pace the cell as Hofster put down the ration packs and let himself out.

'It simply doesn't make sense. Why should anyone bother putting out phoney wanted posters when I'm locked up in here?'

Vist-Roxon hesitated.

'Well . . . it could make sense.'

Phaid's eyes narrowed.

'What do you mean "could"?'

'I'm not sure I ought to tell you.'

'Tell me what?'

Phaid was now quite alarmed. Vist-Roxon looked as though he wished that he'd never spoken.

'It's only an idea. I don't want you to be needlessly upset.'

'For Lords' sakes, don't keep me dangling. Out with it!'

Vist-Roxon took a deep breath.

'If they wanted to make a big deal out of catching and then executing you, maybe in public, what they are doing makes a kind of perverted sense. It might appeal to Chrystiana-Nex as some sort of demonstration that she has control over the city. You'd be much easier to deal with than a real killer.'

Phaid shook his head. He had turned a little pale.

'But why me? I've never harmed any of them.'

'Why not look on the bright side? You were going to be executed anyway. You really haven't lost anything. In fact, you said yourself that being up here with me is a great deal better than being down in one of the halls. In that respect you've actually come out ahead.'

Phaid was not to be consoled. As far as he was concerned, there was no bright side.

'I don't even look all that menacing.'

'I've been wondering about that. I could think of much better choices if they wanted someone to play a homicidal bandit. It would appear to be a question that only the elaihi in the Palace can answer.'

'I don't think I can take much more of this.'

'Maybe that's not what's going to happen. After all, it's only my theory. I could be completely wrong.'

'It all sounds a little too plausible, unpleasantly

plausible.'

All through the next week Hofster brought wanted notices on Phaid. As well as different hologram displays there were posters, handbills and flyers. He seemed to be the target of the biggest imaginary man-hunt in the history of the city. Each time Hofster brought a new report of his supposed crimes, the price on his head had gone up. He grew more frightened and depressed. He rarely slept more than a few hours at a time and continually asked why it should be him that had been chosen to be the victim of all this insanity.

Vist-Roxon didn't seem to be able to come up with any answers. Instead, he had become distantly metaphysical. He took to not quite focusing his eyes on Phaid when he spoke to him.

'It could be that the elaihi decided that you were ultimately malleable.'

'Huh?'

Phaid had almost given up listening to Vist-Roxon when he was in this kind of mood.

'I said that it could be that the elaihi decided that you were ultimately malleable.'

'What are you talking about?'

The two men had been cooped up in the cell for long enough to start getting on each other's nerves.

'On the other hand, it might be that you stand out because you're almost impossible to control. One thing seems to be for sure. You might not have noticed, but it all keeps coming back to you.'

'You're rambling.'

'Maybe that's the true nature of the hero. He is, at one and the same time, malleable but impossible to control.'

'I'm not a hero.'

'Of course you are. You're the desperate killer, you're the rebel bandit.'

'But all that's a fabrication.'

'Oh yes, I was forgetting.'

'You're losing touch with reality.'

'It comes and goes.'

And thus it came and went. Phaid sank into depression and Vist-Roxon drifted between real time and some private place inside his damaged brain. Over a week went by in this condition and gloom permeated every corner of the cell. The cards and books went untouched as the two men sank deeper inside themselves. This destructive introspection might have gone on, unchecked, for ever if Hofster hadn't arrived with sufficiently startling news to jerk both Phaid and Vist-Roxon back to here and now.

'The Silent Cousins have broken with the President. They're closing down their operations and moving their assets out of the city until there's a government that can guarantee business as usual. Orsine has left for his residence in the mountains.'

Vist-Roxon smiled.

'Orsine is a cunning old wolf. He leaves the city in pretended disgust but stays close enough to be called back to bring order to undoubted chaos that would follow any rebel *coup*.'

'You think he has a hankering after the presidency?'

'I'm sure he does. Orsine can never be content with second best.'

Vist-Roxon looked questioningly at Hofster.

'Did you hear something else?'

Hofster set down the ration packs, pushed back his cap and settled himself on Phaid's bed.

'Well, needless to say that the smaller mobs have been thrown into a flat spin. They don't know what to do next. With the Cousins shutting up shop, there's no one to give them a lead. From what I hear, they're coming apart at the seams. It's every man for himself and the majority seem to think that their best bet is with the rebels.'

'Or leaving the city altogether. The mercenaries are starting to wonder just how long the President is going to be able to go on paying. They're getting jittery, and they ain't the only ones, I can tell you.'

'What else have you heard?'

'There's the priests.'

'What about the priests?'

'There's rumours going round as to how they're looking for a deal with the rebels.'

Phaid could hardly believe this.

'The priests doing business with the rebels? It doesn't seem possible.'

Vist-Roxon didn't appear in the least surprised.

'It's pretty much true to form. They've seen too many governments rise and fall. One more isn't going to make any difference. They'll accept just about any accommodation with the temporal power if it allows them to keep on

374

running their end of things.' He glanced at Hofster. 'Are they supposed to have met with a favourable response to their overtures?'

Hofster shrugged.

'Who knows with the priests? The general feeling is that they might have got what they wanted if it wasn't for the Day Oners. Those bastards have sworn to hang every last priest and level the temples to the ground. They're not about to stand for any sort of deal.'

Vist-Roxon smiled.

'It's not often that I agree with the Day Oners, the Lords know, but in this instance they're probably absolutely right. Our priesthood is nothing more than a canting band of bloodthirsty perverts.'

Hofster looked outraged.

'That's dangerous talk. I'm telling you, sir, you ought to be a lot more careful.'

Vist-Roxon laughed.

'Dangerous? Don't be silly, Hofster, what else can they do to me?'

Although seemingly accepting Vist-Roxon's logic, Hofster still looked uncomfortable. He stood up and returned his cap to the regulation position. He seemed to be about to leave. Vist-Roxon put a quick hand on his arm.

'Don't take offence, my old friend. You must have heard other news.'

Hofster didn't sit down again. He continued to stand awkwardly stiff, almost at attention. His voice had also changed. It was no longer conversational. The old guard sounded more like he was delivering a report to a superior.

'Nothing what you'd call specific, sir. No real details. Most of what I've heard has just been gossip and rumour.'

'So what does the gossip and rumour say?'

'The majority seemed to be of the opinion that the deadlock is coming to an end. The rebels are supposed to be about to make their big move. I hope you will remember your promise to look out for me and my family if there is a rebel takeover.'

'I haven't forgotten. I will do all I can . . . provided I survive.'

'Thank you, sir. I'm much obliged to you, sir.'

Hofster gave a kind of half salute and moved to the

door with his back uncomfortably rigid. As the door closed behind him, Vist-Roxon smiled sadly.

'I'm afraid I have offended the good Hofster. I never imagined a man could stay religious in a place like this.'

Phaid grunted.

'The priests use barbed hooks. Once they're in, they're very, very hard to get out.'

'You don't trust priests.'

'If anything I trust them less than courtiers. In fact, as long ago as when I was in Fennella, I've had this strange feeling that a spy for the priests is following me. I swear to the Lords, he really seemed as though he was watching me. He was a little guy, face like a lizard. He called himself Dreen. I suppose it could be my imagination, but he just seemed to turn up in too many places, just too regularly for it to be coincidence.'

Vist-Roxon smiled and shook his head as though he despaired of Phaid.

'I've never heard of this man called Dreen. In my experience, the priests' spies only have a limited useful life. It's you that I really wonder about. You have no principles and no morals and without any apparent effort on your part, things happen around you. Wherever you go you seem to become a catalyst, an unwitting, even unwilling catalyst, but a catalyst all the same.'

Phaid didn't like the sound of all this. It was all right for him, in moments of self pity, to have decided that he had to be somehow cursed. He didn't like to hear it from someone else.

'You're getting this way out of proportion. The trouble with you, old man, is that you think too much.'

The next forty-eight hours proved to be too eventful for either man to sink back into gloomy introspection. Hofster seemed to have recovered from his hurt religious principles. At every opportunity that he had, he'd slip into the cell with the latest story from the outside.

As predicted, the rebels had at last made their move. They were closing the ring. Phaid wondered how Streetlife was faring now that the revolution was hotting up.

As the rebels moved into the centre of the city they were meeting little more than token resistence. Many of the mercenaries were refusing to fight until they were paid in hard currency. Chrystiana-Nex had attempted to pay the units in a section of the city with letters of promise.

These mercenaries had immediately withdrawn their services and allowed the rebels to move around their positions completely unchallenged.

The only real fighting was with the few, still loyal police, the fanatics of the Palace Guard and small squads of mercenaries who had been directly hired and paid by individual courtiers. Of the three groups, only the do or die guards were slowing down the rebel advance, the police were too few in number and too demoralised to be anything like effective while the courtiers' hired help were more conerned with facilitating their employers' escapes than defending the city.

As the ring inexorably closed, tension in the White Tower mounted. Both guards and prisoners realised that if Chrystiana-Nex decided that her reign was going to end in a welter of destruction, it could start right there at any moment. Some guards walked around with weapons at the ready, moving as though every noise and shadow was a warning of mortal danger. Others were busy making offers to the prisoners for protection if and when the rebels stormed the prison.

On the end of this second day of the new phase of revolt, Hofster delivered the ration packs quite a bit later than usual.

'It's chaos down in stores. Everything that isn't nailed down is being stolen. Nobody knows whether they're coming or going. Also, there's no wine. The whole city seems to be paralysed.'

With that he scooted out the door. Phaid and Vist-Roxon assumed they'd seen the last of him until the following morning. To their surprise, he was back inside of ten minutes. The old man was extremely agitated.

'The rebels have taken over the powerhouse. They knocked out most of the Palace Guard in the battle. The rebels have split into two large mobs. One's heading for the Palace. The other's on its way here.'

Phaid was straightaway on is feet.

'For Lords' sake just let us out of the cell. When the rebels break in it may take them days to get around to looking for us up here. We could starve in the meantime.'

Hofster hesitated. Phaid started to plead.

'How can we help you, put in a good word with the rebels or whatever, if we're still locked in here?'

Hofster continued to hesitate. His training went so deep

377

that it took a major internal battle before he could make the unprecedented step of actually letting prisoners go free. He shook his head. He'd started to sweat.

'I don't know.'

'Don't be a damned fool, Hofster. The lights are going to go out at any moment. There'll be a slaughter here. It won't take more than a couple of hours for the rebels to figure out how to cut off the power to the White Tower. That means the jolt fields will fail and when they do, the rebels will walk in. Our only hope is to work together and try to stay alive. There's no other way, damn it.'

Hofster finally saw reason. He punched out the code and the door swung open.

'Where exactly should we go?'

Vist-Roxon shrugged.

'Down, I suppose. Somewhere near ground level would seem to be the obvious thing to do. What do you think, Hofster?'

Hofster scratched his head.

'The induction area would seem to be the most logical place to head for.'

Phaid scowled.

'It sounds like a great place to run into huge gangs of panicky guards.'

Vist-Roxon looked at him.

'What do you want to do?'

'Maybe move down a few levels and see what's happening.'

'You're probably right.'

'I am right. You two can do what you like but I'm treating all this with extreme caution. I've had too many body blows of late. I'm not about to get myself burned down minutes before I can walk clean out of here.' He held his hand to Hofster. 'Give me your blaster.'

Hofster was horrified.

'You're joking.'

'Give me the damn blaster, you old fool!'

'I can't give my weapon to a prisoner.'

'When are you going to get it through your goddamn head that stuff don't count any more.'

'Why should you have the weapon?'

'Because I'm younger, I've got the best reflexes and no scruples. Now hand it over before I get angry.'

Hofster looked in silent appeal at Vist-Roxon. Vist-

Roxon sighed.

'You best give it to him, old friend, he is right.'

Hofster slowly reached around to his belt, pulled out the blaster and handed it, butt-first, to Phaid. Phaid grinned and started down the corridor. The two older men followed.

They cautiously descended for two levels, encountering nothing more than the same dirt and decay that Phaid remembered from when he had been forced to make the long climb to Vist-Roxon's cell. On the third level, they became confused by a maze of short, turning, twisting corridors and a virtual honeycomb of small, dark, irregularly shaped cells. Trying to find their way back to the stairs, they turned a sharp corner and ran headfirst into more prisoners nervously making for the lower levels.

The suddenness of the confrontation jangled everyone's already badly stretched nerves. Phaid almost burned them down before he realised that they offered no threat. Rather sheepishly, he lowered his blaster.

'How did you people get loose?'

There were only two of them, a small, timid looking man and a rather muscular woman. They appeared bewildered and disorientated. They seemed to have trouble grasping what was going on. The small man did the talking. He had a provincial accent, and shook slightly as he spoke.

'We were in solitary on the level above this one. A guard came and unlocked all our cells. He said that he was running away. He said that there was a revolution and that he didn't want to be killed. He told us we could do what we liked. We decided to go down to the lower levels. There are half a dozen more still up there. They're afraid to come out. Is there really a revolution? The guard said that the Palace was going to fall.'

Phaid nodded.

'Yeah, yeah, there's a revolution, sure enough. How long you been in solitary?'

The little man shrugged sadly.

'Who knows. There's no way to count time. They never turn the lights on and off according to a proper pattern of day and night. So there really is a revolution? Are we going to be set free?'

'There's a mob surrounding the prison waiting for the jolt field to go off. Once that happens, they'll doubtless

379

start cutting through the walls. Quite what they'll do with us prisoners once they get inside is anybody's guess.'

The little man trembled quite noticeably.

'Is that why you've got the blaster?'

'Damn right it is.'

'Can we come with you?'

Phaid looked at Vist-Roxon, but he said nothing. Phaid realised that somehow, without a word being said, he had been elected leader of the little band.

'Shit.'

He looked at the man and woman from solitary.

'Sure, sure, what the hell, you can tag along.'

With Phaid once again taking the lead, they moved off in what they hoped was the direction of the stairs. Somehow they hit lucky and were able to drop through three more levels very quickly. It was at that time that they started to discover batches of prisoners still locked in their cells. Directly these unfortunates realised that there was a chance of getting loose, they set up a dreadful clamour. Beseeching arms reached out to Phaid and his companions. They were bombarded with appeals to help these others get free. Vist-Roxon and the couple from solitary hesitated, but Phaid, with a scowl and a shrug of his shoulders, hurried on, resolutely ignoring these pleas.

'I know they're prisoners, so what? They're not my responsibility. What did these assholes ever do for me?'

Nobody seemed willing to argue with Phaid. They got back on to the stairs. The lower down the tower they went, the more the tension mounted. Although all the catwalks, observation blisters and weapon points normally manned by guards had so far been deserted, they knew, sooner or later, they had to come face to face with some of their captors. Robot sensors had watched them as they passed, but, nothing had happened. It all seemed a little too good to be true.

There was also the problem that sooner or later the rebels would find a way to cut the power to the prison. They seemed to be taking an inordinately long time to do it, and Phaid was just thinking that how, even if the Day Oners were in charge, it shouldn't have taken them that long. Right at that moment the lights blinked once and then went out. Instinctively, the five halted. Phaid let out a short, sharp breath.

'Well, how about that. They finally managed it. They

knocked out the power. I guess it won't be too long before they come through the wall.'

'Is that good or bad?'

Phaid recognised the little man by his accent. He scowled in the dark.

'How the fuck should I know?'

Vist-Roxon's voice came out of the pitch black.

'What should we do now?'

Phaid was wondering how it was that he had to do all the thinking for the five of them when some tiny lights in the corridor ceiling flickered into life.

'It might be some sort of emergency back-up.'

When the lights had first gone, it had sounded as if half the prison population seemed to be giving voice. There were screams and yells and even noises that Phaid could hardly believe came out of a human throat. When the back-up lights came on, for some reason the noise seemed to get even worse. Phaid could see how those prisoners who were still locked up must be caught between the smell of freedom and the awful fear of some last minute atrocity on the part of the guards.

In a lot of ways, the back-up lights were almost worse than no lights at all. They were so small and weak that they did little more than create a shadowy gloom that, coupled with the general cacophony, set the imagination fearfully spinning.

Apprehensively, Phaid and his four charges edged their way down one more level. It seemed as though disaster was about to loom out of every patch of darkness, but, in fact, they made it without incident. Considerably emboldened, they decided to risk another downward move, even though they were getting close to the populace levels of the prison.

The next flight of stairs was a more elaborate affair than they had previously encountered. It was broad and deep, and surfaced in dull plasteel. It went down further than just one level. In fact, it went down further than Phaid could see. In the limited light, it appeared to drop away into a black and bottomless pit. Out of this pit came the din of hundreds of invisible prisoners who yelled, screamed and beat metal on metal in panic and desperation. Phaid could imagine how countless dozens of scores must be being settled under the cover of the noise and the half darkness.

The stairwell was overlooked by two spindly guard catwalks. Even though these were deserted, like all the others they had passed, there was something menacing about them. Phaid would happily have taken any other route. Unfortunately, the only alternative was to go back up, back from where they'd come. With no other choice available, Phaid started down, his blaster raised, and looking nervously all around.

They made some thirty steps and all was going well, then a metallic voice, louder than the background din, floated down from above.

'Hold it down there!'

Phaid looked up. He could make out two, maybe three figures up on the catwalk. He didn't think. He fired.

WOWOAR!

Phaid was half blinded by the flash. He hopped sideways, down five or six steps, firing as he went.

WOWOAR! WOWOAR!

Flame lashed down from above. Phaid dropped to a crouch, spraying his blaster frantically above his head. The plasteel to his right glowed cherry red in maybe nine or ten palm sized spots. He cringed away from them but didn't stop his continuous firing.

BRAAUUWAA!

It was suddenly as bright as day.

WABAWABAWABAWABAWABAWABA!

Phaid rolled over and over. All round him there were glowing spots on the plasteel steps. He snapped off some better aimed shots.

RAB-RABA-RAB-RAN-RAN!

A body came windmilling down and smashed sickeningly into the hard metal steps. Phaid could no longer see anyone on the catwalk. He was no longer being fired at. He slowly lowered his overheated blaster and stood up. Parts of the steps were still an angry but swiftly cooling red. Phaid peered into the gloom for his temporary companions.

'Is everyone okay?'

Three voices answered in the affirmative. Vist-Roxon and the two from solitary got up from where they had been crouching against the wall.

'What about Hofster?'

'Hofster's dead.'

Phaid bit his lip.

'That's too bad.'

'I had become very fond of the old duffer.'

'Yeah.'

The little man from solitary was looking nervously upwards.

'Let's get off these stairs, huh?'

Phaid noticed that a blaster was lying on the steps. It must have been dropped by one of the guards on the catwalk. Phaid bent down and picked it up. The little man was standing next to him. Phaid offered him a weapon.

'It may have been damaged in the fall, but you might as well have it.'

The little man shook his head.

'I couldn't use it.'

'What? What the hell is your problem?'

'I have implants. If I do anything violent I get an immediate seizure.'

'Sweet Lords.'

The muscular woman held out her hand. She seemed to have regained her control to an amazing extent since they had first met. There was now a hardness in her eyes. It gave Phaid the feeling that he was only a bit player in her own very separate adventure.

With two out of the remaining four of them now armed, the little party made faster, less timid progress. They almost became involved in a second fire fight when they ran head on into another, large group of free and armed prisoners. It was only at the very last minute that both groups realised that they were all on the same side.

Like tributary streams running into a river, more groups of prisoners joined together to form a main body moving down towards the bottom levels of the White Tower. While they were still many levels above the induction area, the guards had melted away and it was obvious that the prisoners were in sole control of the jail.

There was talk of how some guards had broken into the stores, shot the prisoners in charge and changed into prison overalls. Phaid didn't like the sound of this. He could see it becoming an excuse for yet another Day One purge.

When the procession from the upper levels finally reached the induction area, the sight that met their eyes was scarcely credible. The emergency lighting seemed to be better on the lower levels. Below them whooping and yelling prisoners milled around what had once been the place of total desolation and misery.

Many guards, along with a sprinkling of policemen, priests and civilians, had been herded into the holding pens. Not all had made it. A number of bodies, in bloodstained pink and green uniforms, had been hauled into an alcove between two pillars. The corpses of chief overseer Borkastra's dogs had been thrown in on top of them.

Borkastra herself had been confined in a small mobile cage. It was placed, as though on display, in the middle of the large open area. The cage stood on a makeshift scaffold, to allow everyone a clear view of how far their greatest tormentor had fallen.

She no longer seemed so frightening. Her uniform was ripped and stained. One huge breast spilled out where the front of the tunic had been torn away. Blood and dirt were smeared over her face and someone had stolen her ornamental belts and veebe-hide boots. Her shoulders had slumped so she no longer seemed like the formidable woman mountain who put the fear into the new arrivals. The overthrow of her closed domain had left her a sagging, gross and flaccid thing that was nothing more than pathetic.

A ring of armed prisoners stood around the outside of the cage, their weapons pointed outwards. They were ironically protecting the Chief Overseer from attempts at revenge by her former prisoners. Phaid shuddered to think what eventual fate they had in store for her. It had to be something infinitely worse than a vicious, but at least swiftly executed, on-the-spot lynching.

Revenge wasn't, however, foremost in the minds of all the prisoners. Some were already making up for the lost years of deprivation. Somehow a bunch of them had found a store of liquor and bouts of singing and dancing had already broken out. In the least lighted areas there was sexual coupling either prone on the floor or leaning again walls and pillars. Phaid smiled and shook his head. With the taste of freedom so fresh in their mouths, the prisoners were organising their own drunken celebration before even the prison walls had fallen and their liberators had broken in. Phaid could have stood and watched the bizarre spectacle for a long time, except that he noticed that a network of cracks was spreading across one section of the outside wall. Obviously the people on the outside were well on their way to breaking through. Few of the revellers, though, appeared to have noticed what was going on. Phaid started to ease his way through the crowd, as far away from the crumbling section of wall as he could get. He feared that when their supposed rescuers did break through there would be injuries and even deaths as the walls collapsed on top of the shouting, dancing prisoners. He didn't look back until he had put the greatest possible distance between him and the crumbling wall section.

When he finally halted, the original cracks were deep fissures, surrounded by a delicate tracery of smaller faults that spread rapidly outwards. A loud hum, punctuated by staccato snaps, echoed round the vaulted ceiling of the area. Parts of the wall began to turn black. They were starting to smoke. The noise grew louder and an acrid, scorched smell was filling the air. People nearest to the distintegrating wall were backing away, those behind them pushed forward to see what was happening. The drunks added the extra measure of confusion that turned the induction area into total chaos.

Then the walls fell. A huge section burst inwards with something close to a small explosion. A photon bolt flashed from the breach and exploded against the roof, blue and searing. Debris showered down. Jagged chunks of masonry cascaded on to the nearest parts of the milling press of prisoners. There were shouts and shrieks of pain. Phaid was forced to duck as small flying particles peppered the pillar by which he'd taken shelter. Choking clouds of dust billowed from out of the breach in the wall. There was more shouting and yelling. The injured were crying out, begging for help. From where Phaid was standing, the arrival of the liberators looked more like a mine disaster. And then, incongruously, people began cheering in the middle of it all.

Someone fired a blaster into the air. Someone else did the same. Very soon the ceiling was being semi-melted by exuberant blaster fire. More hot debris rained down, Phaid saw his first rebel duster coat among the crowd. A woman in prison uniform grabbed him and kissed his cheek. The injured still lay unattended in the litter of debris and dancing feet as the liberators were mobbed by hysterical prisoners. Hands reached and grasped Phaid's.

Arms were clapped around his shoulders. More green coats mingled with the prison grey. Another woman hugged him. The whole place was aswirl in a confused, formless dance. People were laughing, crying, some seemed too stunned to grasp what was happening. He saw Borkastra led away, loaded down with chains. He saw guards being stripped of their uniforms and organised into chained groups. Phaid looked around for Vist-Roxon, but he was nowhere to be seen in the chaos.

Phaid knew that it was time to make it through to the outside world. He had spent too much time in the White Tower to want to linger. He started easing his way among the celebrating horde and clambering over the rubble, all the time moving in the direction of the gaping hole in the wall and real freedom. He'd almost made it when a hefty rebel grabbed him by the arm.

'They got you?'

Phaid tried to jerk away. He didn't know what the man wanted but he wasn't taking any chances. He was not going to come out of one prison only to be thrown into some new one designed by the rebels. The man, however, was a good deal stronger than Phaid, and he couldn't break away. The rebel seemed to be concerned about something.

'Did they treat you real bad? You look as though you don't know what's going on. We've come to set you free.'

Phaid knew that they'd come to set him free. His only desire was to put as much distance between himself and the White Tower as possible. For some unfathomable reason, this rebel was totally unwilling to let him go.

'Don't worry about a thing. I'll get you out of here. After what you're done for the revolution, you deserve the best.'

Phaid couldn't think of a single thing that he'd ever done for the revolution. Was the man battle happy?

'I don't know what you're talking about.'

'You are Phaid, aren't you?'

Phaid was instantly wary.

'Maybe.'

'Of course you're Phaid.'

'So I'm Phaid. So what?'

'I knew you were Phaid. I knew it from the pictures.'

Phaid was still mystified, but at least the rebel didn't appear to mean him any immediate harm. He had turned and was beckoning to others around.

'Hey you guys, come on over here! It's Phaid!'

'Phaid? They got him?'

'Phaid.'

'No shit.'

Phaid found himself being pounded on the back. His hand was being pumped so vigorously that he was afraid that his shoulder would be dislocated or his hand crushed to a pulp. The entire reception was totally bewildering, then it all made sense. It was the holograms and the wanted posters. There was no way for the rebels to know that they were fakes. As far as they were concerned, it had all been the real thing. In their eyes, he was Phaid, the mysterious killer, the lone wolf who execrated courtiers. He was a hero of the revolution.

He found himself being hoisted into the air and carried shoulder-high to the breach in the wall. People were clapping and applauding.

'Phaid!'

'Phaid!'

His name echoed round the induction area. He started to enjoy the sensation. He would have enjoyed it more if he hadn't realised that there were a number of people who knew the truth and could expose him. Vist-Roxon would keep his mouth shut. Abrella-Lu would probably be in too much trouble on her own account. Streetlife would also guess the truth, but Phaid knew that, if he still lived, he would happily allow himself to be bought off.

There were a few cops, guards, the Inquisitor and a handful of others who might just have worked out that the whole thing was a deception. Phaid didn't feel he had to worry about these people. If they weren't dead, they'd probably be on the run.

There was only one person who could really cause him trouble, and in this case, Phaid knew he would do well to worry. That one person was Makartur. There was always the chance that Makartur was dead already, but somehow Phaid doubted it. Makartur was alive and, right at that moment, probably somewhere in the prison sharing the same liberation.

All at once, Phaid wanted to duck out of sight. He was in an impossible position. He might come face to face with Makartur at any moment, but there was nothing that he could do. Still carried aloft on the shoulders of his admirers, he seemed to have become the focus of attention for the whole crowd. They carried him through the breach and into the open air. It was night, fires seemed to be burning all over the city. All around him, they were still shouting and cheering.

'Phaid! Phaid!'

A bottle was thrust into his hands. He took a drink. The raw spirit told him that he was free. As it burnt his throat, he wondered how he was going to deal with this new freedom.

23

PHAID STUMBLED and almost fell through the door of the bar. Streetlife actually hit the ground and rolled, cursing loudly. Both men had been drunk for a week, but this, surprisingly, wasn't the reason for their ungainly entrance. They had been innocently walking down the street, albeit a little unsteadily, looking for the next watering hole, when a blaster battle had raged out all around them. The door to the bar had provided the ideal sanctuary from the lethal sheets of flame.

Fire fights on the streets had been an all too common occurrence since Chrystianaville had fallen to the rebels. As most of those not directly involved had predicted, the revolution was not running smoothly. Law and order had broken down and various rebel factions and even gangs of ordinary, profit motivated criminals fought each other on the streets.

Something calling itself the Central Co-ordinating Committee of Interim Government had taken up residence in the Palace and seemed to be deadlocked in non-stop debate as to how the future should be organised. They had reportedly spent a full three days in continuous session attempting, without avail, to come up with a new name for the city. Nobody expected very much from the Central Co-ordinating Committee of Interim Government. The Day Oners had walked out inside of a matter of hours, and were now busily implementing their own programmes of terror with no authority save that of the rope and the blaster.

Not even the Day Oners seemed to be safe from schism and ideological infighting. They had split into two roughly equal-sized groups. On one side there were those known as the Fundamentalists who believed that everything should be done at once, that the living standards of the whole of the city's population should be instantly reduced to the level of the poorest northside immigrant. They wanted all technology stripped away, learning and culture abolished and religion utterly smashed. To this end, they had blown up a number of power and sanitation sub-plants. They would have taken their destruction further had it not been for bands of more moderate rebels who had retained their weapons and were defending the city's major installations against attacks by the absolutist Day Oners.

The other, less extreme Day One faction were the Pragmatists. They also believed in reducing the city to total primitivism, only they were willing to do it in less painful stages. They considered that the most immediate objective was the extermination of the courtier class and the capture and execution of Chrystiana-Nex and Sol-chaim.

These two were, in fact, the greatest embarrassment of the whole revolution. At some point during the confusion following the capture of the Palace, the two arch enemies of the people had somehow managed to slip through almost half a rebel army totally dedicated to their capture. Despite a hundred false alarms, no trace of them was found.

The Pragmatist Day Oners were going about their business with energetic and ruthless efficiency. Basing their operations in the shell of the White Tower, they waged a search and destroy war against aristocrats and office holders in the old regime. A number of parks and open spaces had been turned into public killing grounds and mass graveyards. Rumours, lies and denunciations flew at both an alarming rate and volume. A single pointed finger could all too easily result in a suspected aristo being dragged off to a summary execution and a mass grave. Accusations were almost never checked by the Day Oners and denunciation became a formidable weapon to be used against rivals, enemies, faithless lovers, errant husbands, rich elderly relatives and just about anyone whom anyone else wanted out of the way.

Although there were no statistics, murder had to have become Chrystianaville's major industry in the days immediately after the revolution. The moderates killed the Day Oners, the Day Oners killed each other, the aristos and anybody else they got their hands on. At least six political factions were busily engaged in murdering the members of the other five. It was also open season for private score settling or just plain vicious slaying. Any morning there could be anything up to fifty bodies littering the streets of the city. Quite often they would lay around clear through to the late afternoon. The Committee, despite the many hundreds of hours it had spent in debate, had yet to organise an effective clean-up crew. Needless to day, sanitation was something that didn't impinge on the lofty consciousness of the Day Oners. As a major part of the problem, they scorned the solution except to farm it out to their political re-education groups.

With the city totally in the grip of terror and random violence, it was small wonder that Phaid had opted to stay as drunk as possible for as long as possible. Another reason was the nagging question of why Solchaim had staged the charade that had turned Phaid into a hero of the revolution, and the worry that maybe the whole of that charade had yet to be played out.

Being a hero, even a counterfeit hero, did have its compensations. Phaid rarely had to buy himself a drink, which was fortunate since the revolution didn't provide wages for its heroes.

It did, however, let them pick over the best of the loot. Inside a gentlemen's tailoring emporium whose owner had fled the city when the rebels had closed in, Phaid had gratefully thrown away his prison uniform and outfitted himself with a very stylish version of the standard rebel duster coat. Taking care not to get too fancy (fancy could earn a Day Oner blast in the back), he sorted himself out some soft leather boots, a pair of tight doeskin breeches and a few shirts. A hand tooled belt and a fancy blaster with an obscenely carved opalene handle were prizes worthy of a hero. A wide brimmed slouch hat topped off the killer-bandit ensemble.

Living up to the killer-bandit role was a little more difficult. Those who believed the myth tended to be respectful and hospitable but they also gave him a lot of space in which to operate. Nobody actually wanted to get too close to the killer of some fourteen or more courtiers. The reputation also kept the Day Oners off his back, it was a massive and sometimes lifesaving plus.

What the reputation didn't solve was the problem of Makartur. Phaid had heard that the big man was moving around the city, mostly in the company of Flame, the one time exotic dancer. For some reason known only to him, Makartur hadn't exposed Phaid as phoney. Phaid couldn't work this out at all. In a world that was custom made for sneaks, snitchers, informers and denouncers, this seemed little short of a miracle. Phaid wondered if it was because Makartur might think Phaid's reputation was still too strong to drag down, or maybe it was that Makartur feared, if he accused Phaid, that Phaid had enough on him to pull Makartur into the same grave. Whatever the reason, Makartur was biding his time, and Phaid didn't like it.

Phaid made a few half hearted attempts to locate some of the people he'd known before the takeover. Roni-Vows and Edelline-Lan were among those who had vanished at the same time as Chrystiana-Nex and Solchaim. It was ironic that the one courtier that Phaid knew had survived for sure was that one who had caused him the most trouble. He'd actually spotted Abrella-Lu, ragged, filthy and stripped to the waist, working on a forced labour squad.

He had been walking down Condine-Nep Avenue, thinking about nothing in particular except where his next drink was coming from, when he'd passed the squad on the other side of the street. The frightened, miserable bunch of women were all too reminiscent of the so-called study group on which he'd found himself. If anything, conditions on this squad were worse than on the work gangs at the Angel of Destiny. The unfortunate workers were secured by lengths of chain attached to metal neck collars. The chains made the task of clearing the rubble left over from the uprising doubly difficult.

The guards supervising the work were probably the most horrific Phaid had yet to see. They were three burly women who could have easily been cousins of the fearsome but now hopefully late Borkastra. From the way they wielded their flexible clubs, it was plain to see that they had similar dispositions. They were apparently not a type exclusive to the presidential side.

Abrella-Lu looked haggard and desperate. Sweat ran down her body and her hair was matted with dirt and plaster dust. Strangely, though, in her chains and short, ripped skirt, scarcely more than a loin cloth, she looked perversely sexy. For a moment, Phaid was tempted to pull the Phaid-the-Bandit routine and get her released from the labour squad. He was sure that her gratitude would be quite energetic.

He was also sure that it would be equally short lived. He knew he was going to leave her exactly where she was. She had caused him too much trouble and brought him too near to death. She hadn't seen him, so he stood in a doorway for a while and watched her straining to move weighty lumps of masonry. There was something satisfyingly poetic in his being a spectator to her suffering. She also had exceedingly handsome breasts.

The only person he did manage to find was Streetlife. Everyone else seemed to have been scattered to the wind by the uprising.

Streetlife had given Phaid a hard time when they first met. He could scarcely believe that Phaid had been dumb enough to go and get himself arrested with one of the immobilised flipper's logic plates in his pocket just as they were about to get out of town.

'I missed the last fucking train out of here on account of you, you dumb bastard.'

'I didn't get condemned to death and thrown into the White Tower on purpose. I hope you realise that.'

The money had all gone. Both Phaid's winnings and the proceeds from Streetlife's rip-offs had been spent on bribing his way out of a succession of firing squads. There was very little for Phaid and Streetlife to do except drift around town, drinking for free on the Phaid myth and hoping for a break to improve their situation.

There was a lull in the blaster fire outside. Both men stood up and lurched to the bar.

'Two shots and make it quick.'

The bartender didn't seem exactly friendly.

'You two look like you've had enough.'

'A man can never have enough. With all the pain in this world you can never find the booze to drown it. Two shots.'

Prolonged drinking had put Phaid in a lyrical frame of mind. The bartender didn't seem impressed.

'I don't think I ought to serve you.'

'What are you talking about?'

'You're drunk.'

'Sure we're drunk. So what? What's it to you? You sell stuff to make people drunk. What's the big deal?'

'I don't want drunks in my place.'

'Listen to him, will you?'

Phaid appealed to anyone who might be listening.

'Sweet Lords, turkey. Who else do you expect to get in your place?'

Streetlife was outraged.

'You ain't seriously suggesting that we go back out there without even one drink inside us!'

As if to accentuate his point, the weapon fire started up again in the street. Phaid leaned forward until he was breathing square into the bartender's face.

'You know who I am?'

The bartender's face wrinkled as though he didn't like the smell.

'Should I?'

'You saying you've never seen me before?'

'Not that I can remember.'

'Think about it. Think about it real good. You sure you ain't never seen this face before? Like maybe . . .'

'What are you trying to pull?'

'Like maybe on a wanted poster?'

Phaid's mood had made the full switch from lyrical to bellicose. The bartender took a step back.

'Lords' mothers, you . . . you're . . .'

'Right.'

'Well, that makes it completely different.'

'Good.'

'Two shots?'

'Doubles.'

'On the house.'

Phaid and Streetlife picked up their drinks and took them to a table. They had a wide choice of where to sit. The bar was empty. After the first euphoric celebrations, the revolution had not been good for business in the Chrystianaville taverns. People were frightened to go out on the street.

Streetlife looked thoughtfully at Phaid who was absent-mindedly scratching his seven-day growth of stubble.

'You really quite enjoy this killer routine, don't you.'

Phaid threw back his drink in one.

'It's better than being afraid all the time.'

'All I'm saying is don't push it too far, else someone's going to come along and call your bluff, and you and me both know it's bullshit. Am I right?'

'Yeah, maybe. Who gives a fuck, anyway. I've had just as much as I can handle.' He looked up at the bartender. 'Hey, you! Two more over here, right now.'

The bartender positively jumped and raced over with a second round of double shots.

'On the house?'

The bartender sighed.

'On the house.'

Phaid whacked back his drink in one throw once again. He winced and gasped.

'This is the life.'

'For as long as it lasts. You liable to get yourself killed.'

'I've been liable to get myself killed for just about as long as I can remember. I think I'm starting to get used to it.'

Streetlife stabbed a bleary finger at him.

'You ain't getting used to nothing. You just drunk.'

'You can bet your ass on that.'

Phaid started to giggle. Then the blaster roared in the street again, there was the scream of something that sounded like a boohoom. Phaid ducked and winced.

'I wish to hell they'd find some other game. All this noise disturbs a man's train of thought.'

Phaid was just about to yell for more booze when another customer dived through the door. A stray blast hacked a chunk out of the doorframe. The new arrival got warily to his feet. He was a lanky individual in stained rebel garb. He looked at Phaid and Streetlife and slowly grinned.

'It's getting hairy out there, sure as shit.'

'Did you see who's fighting who?'

The newcomer shook his head.

'How the hell can anyone tell? I, for one, am starting to regret this Lord cursed revolution.'

Phaid nodded.

'You ain't the only one.'

The rebel was looking intently at Phaid.

'Ain't you Phaid, the one that was on those wanted displays?'

'Yeah, I'm Phaid.'

'How about that? You do all that stuff like they said you did?'

Phaid shook his head.

'No.'

'Come on.'

'If you really want to know, I didn't do any of that stuff like they said I did. The trouble is that nobody believes me when I tell them.'

The rebel's expression made it clear that he was no exception. He glanced at the door. The fire fight was still going on. The rebel sat down.

'I heard that Orsine the mobster might bring in an army of mercenaries and set things to rights. You think that's true?'

Phaid snorted.

'It's bullshit. You're just looking for a big daddy to make it all better. Neither Orsine nor anyone like him is going to move into the city until the Day Oners and all the scum have worn themselves down to nothing.'

'They're going to take one hell of a lot of citizens along with them before they do that.'

'That's true, but that don't worry Orsine none. He'll sit tight in his mountain hideout and let somebody else do the dying.'

Phaid leaned back in his chair.

'Anyway, what's all this talk about Orsine? You want the mobs running the city?'

Streetlife set down his empty glass.

'I can think of worse things.'

Phaid noticed that his glass was also empty.

'Do we have to put on another show to get us our next drink?'

The rebel fumbled in his coat pocket.

'I'll get them if you like.'

Phaid leaned forward and twisted a smile on to his face.

'That's awfully good of you.'

'Yeah.'

While the rebel was paying the somewhat surprised bartender, another character scuttled into the bar. Although he wore an overlarge duster he was, in fact, little more than a boy. Once safely inside the place he shook himself, almost like a dog, as though shaking off the pointless mayhem of the street.

'I'm looking for Phaid the Gambler. I've got a message for him.'

Phaid looked up.

'I'm Phaid, what have you got for me?'

The kid held out a flat, sealed package.

'A guy gave me five tabs to find you and give you this.'

'He did, did he?'

Phaid stretched out his hand for the package, but the kid didn't let go of it.

'You're one hell of a guy to find. I've been following you all over town. You cover a shit load of ground.'

'Zig-zagging all the way.'

Phaid once again grasped for the package, but the kid moved it just out of his reach. Phaid raised an enquiring eyebrow.

'Are you trying to stick me up or something?'

'The guy who gave me the five said you'd give me another five when I gave you this here package.'

'That's what he said?'

The kid nodded. 'Right.'

'Ain't you scared of me?'

'Why should I be. The city's lousy with killers, they're all full of shit. All I want is my five.'

Phaid laughed and looked at Streetlife.

'Give him five.'

Phaid grabbed the package and tore off the plastic wrapper. Inside was a folded sheet of parchment. Phaid turned it over a couple of times.

'Now what do we have here?'

He unfolded the parchment. The note written on it was short and to the point.

BE AT THE SIGN OF THE HANGING GODDESS IN THE WOSPAN BEFORE MIDNIGHT. WHAT YOU LEARN THERE WILL BE TO YOUR PROFIT.

It was signed with a tiny, delicate drawing of a butterfly. Phaid looked at the kid.

'Who did you say gave you this?'

The kid smirked.

'I didn't.'

Phaid grabbed him by the front of his oversized coat.

'Your smart mouth just stopped being amusing. I'm going to ask you once again. Who gave you this?'

'I don't know. He was just a guy.'

'What sort of guy.'

'A guy . . . you know . . . just like any other guy. I didn't look too close.'

Phaid let go of him.

'Yeah, okay. Just get out of here.'

'Sure thing.'

Phaid was thoughtful. He knew the butterfly signature was that of Roni-Vows. It was something of a surprise, he had assumed that the courtier was either dead or clean away from the Republic. There was also the mystery of why the note had been written on what looked like fine quality parchment. He passed it over to Streetlife.

'What do you make of this?'

Streetlife looked dubious.

'You know who wrote this?'

'I've got an idea.'

Phaid looked pointedly at the rebel who, at the moment, happened to be engrossed in his drink. Streetlife nodded to signify that he understood.

'Are you planning to go?'

Phaid thought about it. Then he made up his mind.

'Yeah, I think so. Nobody else has even offered us a profit for a week or more.'

'You want me to come with you?'

'Sure, if you want to.'

'I don't got anything better to do.'

Phaid and Streetlife sheltered in a doorway waiting for an outbreak of shooting to pass. Blaster fire had charred the surround and both men looked decidedly unhappy.

'Are you sure we're doing the right thing?'

There was another all too close blast. Phaid ducked.

'Maybe. I don't know. Let's get out of there.'

They made a disorganised dash for the nearest corner. By a near miracle nobody burned them down. Temporarily out of danger and considerably out of breath, they leaned against a wall wondering what to do next.

'You don't intend to walk to the Wospan, do you?'

Phaid closed his eyes. His mind was still punchy from all the booze he had forced it to absorb over the previous week.

'I hadn't thought about it.'

'Then think about it, I ain't using no walkway.'

'Me neither . . . So what do we do?'

A flipper was coming slowly down the block towards them. Streetlife suddenly grinned.

'Want to see a variation on an old trick?'

'Sure.'

'Okay then, just keep that fancy blaster handy.'

Streetlife stepped into the roadway waving his arms. At first it looked as though he was going to be run down. At the last minute, however, the flipper dipped to a halt. The passenger bubble popped open and an indignant driver stuck his head out.

'What the fuck do you think you're doing?'

'I'm commandeering your machine.'

'Like hell you are.'

'You'll save yourself a lot of trouble if you get out of that thing nice and easy. You can come by the Palace and pick it up. The committee will pay compensation.'

'Compensation?'

'Sure, anything you want, within reason.'

The driver shook his head.

'I don't know. Is this really important stuff? I mean, I'm on my way to see this girl and . . .'

'Important stuff! Of course it's important stuff! You think that I'd commandeer a man's flipper just because I want to go to the beer shop? My partner and I have just got the word on a gang of aristos over on the other side of town. We've got to get over there before they get away.'

The driver didn't seem convinced. Once again he shook his head.

'I don't know, I really don't know. I'd like to help but, like I told you . . .'

Streetlife cut him off with a loud sigh. He beckoned to Phaid who was still slouching against the wall with one hand on his blaster. At Streetlife's signal, Phaid straightened and started coming towards them. Streetlife put one hand on the driver's shoulder and with his other, pointed to the approaching Phaid.

'If you really don't want to co-operate, there is another way.'

After a week of living on alcohol and neglecting either to wash or shave, Phaid looked every inch the psycho killer. The driver's eyes swivelled from Phaid to Streetlife and back to Phaid again.

'Him?'

'Him.'

He started to clamber out of the flipper.

'I know my duty.'

'That's nice.'

'You say I can pick up the flipper at the Palace?'

'Along with your compensation money.'

'Thank you, thank you.'

He made a wide circle around Phaid as he scuttled away. He looked back once and then turned the corner and vanished in the direction from which Phaid and Streetlife had come. Phaid burst out laughing.

'If that fire fight is still going on, the dumb bastard just walked straight into it.'

'He was on his way to see some girl. He seemed quite excited about it.'

'Screw him. Let's get going. It'll be dark soon and I'd rather be inside the Wospan after sunset than out in the open.'

They swung themselves into the flipper and Phaid slammed the bubble. Streetlife jammed the machine into drive and, chuckling at the idea of the poor sap owner turning up at the Palace and trying to reclaim it amidst the confusion, they sped off in the direction of the Wospan.

The trip was fairly uneventful. At one major intersection, Day Oners, Phaid wasn't sure which particular faction, had set up a roadblock. Streetlife gave the flipper full forward power and maximum lift. They managed to jump the barricade, but a fuse tube discharge cut a long gouge out of the bubble.

The Wospan was a great deal more subdued than the last time Phaid had been there. Contrary to the boasts of the inhabitants, the revolution had even made its mark on this stronghold of non-conformity. The crowds on the terraces and in the labyrinths and courtyards were sparser than they had been before the revolt. The people who were out and about were depressed and drab, as though some spark in them had been extinguished.

The only ones who did seem to be enjoying themselves were the armed Day Oners and squads from various other rebel factions who paraded through the previously peaceful colonnades with a bully-boy swagger, making themselves the targets for a hundred covert, hostile glances.

In the Wospan, the rebels made no pretence of being liberators. They acted like an occupying army. After their non-participation in the uprising, the rebels trusted the people of the Wospan only fractionally more than they trusted the aristos. It was this mere fraction that stopped the Day Oners clearing the whole area and razing it to the ground.

As it was, the gas flames on the terraces had been turned off. The people, on pain of summary arrest, no longer dressed as flamboyantly. Many of the cafés and taverns were closed and shuttered. It was as though the rebels had managed to kill the spirit of hedonism and turn the Wospan into a drearier, more furtive place. As Phaid and Streetlife drove higher up the multistructure of which the Hanging Goddess was a part, there was no improvement in the overall unhappy picture. Streetlife became increasingly more angry.

'Will you look at what these bastards have done? Will you just look at it? You want to know something? I'm disgusted. I'm so disgusted I figure I've lost just about any last shred of sympathy I had for this fucking revolution. They've gone too far, doing this to the Wospan. I'm really glad that I ripped them off for all that change. I wish I'd done worse.

The Hanging Goddess was a tavern set high up near the summit of one of the Wospan's man-made mountains. Streetlife continued to navigate the flipper up and up, through ramps and passages that seemed to have had all their life and colour forcibly erased.

Before the revolution, the Hanging Goddess had the reputation of being one of the city's most exclusive taverns, an ultra chic watering place for the rich and high born. Its upper salon, dubbed the Crystal Room, was a masterpiece in sculptured plexiglass. It afforded its patrons a breathtaking panoramic view of the city that could scarcely be rivalled.

The tavern occupied one side of a square courtyard. It was bounded by high walls on the other three. As the flipper nosed its way out of the tunnel that was the only means of access to the courtyard, its two passengers were presented with a grim twilight scene that was totally lacking in either gaiety or chic. A few people stood around the courtyard in the rapidly gathering dusk. They were swathed in dark cloaks and although they tried to put on some pretence that they were casual strollers, it was immediately clear that they were either guards or some sort of lookouts.

The tavern itself seemed almost totally devoid of light. The plexiglass panels had been covered over with heavy protective plates. Only a single small glow in one of the lowest floor windows indicated that there was any life in the place at all.

Streetlife halted the flipper, cut the power and let the machine sink to the cobbles. He made no attempt to open the bubble. The cloaked figures began slowly closing in on the flipper. An evening mist that was rapidly gathering gave the whole picture an edge of eerie menace.

Phaid's hand slid down to the pornographic butt of his blaster.

'I don't like this one little bit.'

Streetlife nodded.

'You got my vote on that.'

'The note said midnight. I guess we're kind of early.'

'Hours early.'

Streetlife looked around at the grey, ghostlike figures that were surrounding them. Strands of mist drifted past the outside of the bubble and he shivered.

'I can think of a million places that I'd rather be.'

Phaid carefully drew his blaster halfway out of its holster.

'You think maybe we should get out?'

'Do we have to?'

'We can't just sit here and watch the sunset.'

Streetlife was reluctant.

'Why don't we just call it a mistake and split, huh?'

Phaid slapped the bubble release.

'It's too late to go back.'

The bubble popped open.

'Slowly now. I think these people could be skittish.'

He stood up very carefully. He got the impression that the sight of a rebel coat didn't do anything to reassure the people in the cloaks. As gently as he could, he swung his leg over the side of the machine. One of the figures nearest to him drew something from under his or her cloak. It was a hand weapon with a long, tapering, wand-like barrel. Phaid realised that it was a pulse emitter. He had only seen one of them once before. In the right hands, they were uncannily accurate, but their rate of fire was so slow that they were only used for fully orchestrated, formal duels. Phaid leaned slowly towards Streetlife who hadn't moved yet.

'I think we're right in the middle of the aristocracy's last stand.'

Still doing his best to make no sudden or alarming moves, Phaid stepped down from the flipper. The emitter was pointed straight at his belly. Phaid smiled, but also let his hand dangle right beside his blaster.

'It gets chilly when the sun goes in.'

A man's voice came from the caped figure with the emitter in its hand. 'Who are you, and what do you want?'

Phaid continued to smile.

'I had an invitation, but I fear I'm a little early.'

'Invitation?'

'On parchment, no less.'

'Who are you?'

Phaid stopped smiling.

'Who wants to know?'

Tension cracked through the air. Phaid gently pushed his coat away from his blaster. Streetlife was starting to get out of the flipper, but he changed his mind and sat back down again.

'If you know what's good for you, you'll tell us who you are.'

Phaid half smiled. Streetlife had never seen him so reckless.

'If you know what's good for you, you'll ask me a little more politely.'

The emitter was still pointed straight at his gut, but Phaid seemed to be spoiling for a fight that he almost certainly couldn't win. Streetlife watched with mounting horror as his partner seemed to be steering the situation towards a brief and lethal confrontation. Then, just as it seemed that an eruption of violence was quite inevitable, a second grey cloaked figure, its face hidden inside a deep cowl, stepped between the two main protagonists.

'Phaid! For Lords' sake, stop being so damned stupid. You too, Trimble-Dun. Put that stupid duelling piece away and go and keep watch.'

It was a woman's voice, angry and scolding at men who had decided to behave like petulant children. Phaid's shoulders sagged and his hand relaxed away from his blaster.

'Edelline-Lan! What are you doing here?'

'Trying to get out of the city before your rebels hang me, or worse.'

'They're not my rebels.'

'We'll discuss that later.'

She looked around at the rest of the people surrounding the flipper.

'There'll be no more trouble here.' She turned back to Phaid. 'You'd better come inside before you cause any more grief. Those rebel coats make our people see red.'

'Hmm.'

Phaid jerked his thumb in the direction of Streetlife.

'What about him?'

Edelline-Lan lowered her voice.

'Why did you bring him? He's a rebel, isn't he?'

'No more than I am. He's my partner, and anyway, the message didn't say anything about coming alone.'

'But can he be trusted?'

'Can I be trusted?'

Edelline-Lan sighed as though there was no hope for Phaid.

'I suppose you'd better bring him inside.'

Phaid beckoned to Streetlife and waited for him to close up the flipper. Edelline-Lan was already walking towards the dark entrance of the Hanging Goddess. While she was out of earshot, Streetlife grabbed Phaid by the arm.

'What's going on here, partner? I don't like the look of any of this. I don't like it one little bit. Who are these spooks in the cloaks?'

'I was right first time. This is the courtiers' last stand.'

Streetlife's eyebrows shot up.

'Ain't this something of an abrupt switch of loyalties?'

'What loyalties? Besides, they haven't offered us a deal yet.'

'You think they will?'

'I don't see any other reason for getting us up here.'

They were almost at the entrance where Edelline-Lan was waiting for them, so both men let the conversation drop.

Phaid had never been inside the Hanging Goddess before, but he was well acquainted with its reputation for glitter and gaiety. Now, as he stepped through the door, he saw that glitter and gaiety had fled like spectres before the dawn. Chairs were stacked on tables, the heavier furniture was draped with dust sheets and the windows were boarded over.

The only light in the room came from a single glo-bar. It

had been this, shining through a crack in the covered-over window, that Phaid had seen from the flipper when they first entered the courtyard outside. The light was set up on a table, four men and one woman sat around it. They were all armed, and they all seemed closed to exhaustion. Phaid immediately recognised Roni-Vows, even though the courtier was only a shadow of his former self. He was red eyed, unshaven and his hand shook as it raised a drink in mock salute.

'Well, well, it's the hero of the revolution, and early, too. What's wrong, friend Phaid? Aren't you collecting wages from the Day Oners?'

Phaid dropped into a chair some distance from the light, at the same time making sure that his blaster was within easy reach.

'You look rough, Roni-Vows. Being on the run doesn't seem to agree with you.'

'You don't look so good yourself.'

'I've only been drinking. I don't have to stay one jump ahead of a lynch mob.'

'I wouldn't be too sure of that.'

'Meaning?'

'Meaning that if the rebels should find out that their crazy killer hero was a sham, I wouldn't like to be in your shoes.'

Phaid nodded.

'Aah.'

'It was one of the rare occasions that the high and mighty Solchaim bothered to confide in me. He seemed to think that you might be useful to us if he invested you with the phoney reputation. I can't say I totally understood what the creature was thinking about. The elaihi lived in a world of his own.'

'Last time we talked you were wondering how to get rid of Solchaim.'

'Times change.'

'Don't they just. I suppose you've got me up here for some kind of blackmail. If you have, I've got to tell you in front that you're wasting your time. I don't have a damn thing you can stick me up for.'

Roni-Vows laughed. It was a cold, brittle sound, devoid of humour.

'Quite the reverse, dear boy. We have no desire to blackmail you. In fact, we want to put that fake reputation of yours to good use. We can even offer you a considerable sum in hard currency for the service.'

'What service?'

There was a long pause while Roni-Vows said nothing. Even when he did speak, his words were hesitating.

'Well, dear boy, this may come as a bit of a surprise . . .'

'Cut out the dramatic effects and get to the point. Who do you want me to kill?'

Roni-Vows' hands fluttered. For a brief instant, he was almost his old butterfly self.

'Dear me, you are jumping to the wrong conclusions today, aren't you? We don't want anyone killed. Not unless it's absolutely necessary.'

'So what do you want?'

Roni-Vows took a deep breath.

'We want you to take our late president out of the country.'

Streetlife was instantly on his feet.

'Don't listen to them. Just talkin' to these pussies is too many steps to a slow gallows.'

Phaid was very calm.

'I hope you're offering one hell of a lot of money.'

Streetlife was close to pleading.

'Don't even think about it, brother. Don't even think about it. Let's get the hell out of here and turn these people in. It'd keep our asses out of a vice and there might be a reward in it.'

Roni-Vows quietly raised a small fuse tube.

'If your excitable companion doesn't control himself, I'm going to be forced to burn a hole in him.'

Streetlife looked anxiously at Phaid.

'Will you listen to me . . .'

Roni-Vows cut him off.

'If your companion bothered to think for a moment, he'd realise that having brought you here and solicited your assistance in this matter, there would be absolutely no possibility of your leaving here alive if you rejected our offer.'

Phaid looked at Streetlife.

'You'd better sit down and listen to what they have to say. We don't have very much choice in the matter.'

Roni-Vows permitted himself a thin smile.

'You seem to be learning sense.'

Streetlife was going to protest, but then he saw that the fuse tube was still pointed at him and thought better of it. He sat down, glaring at both Phaid and the courtiers.

Phaid ignored him and leaned back in his chair.

'Since I don't seem to have any option but to go along with all this, you'd better start filling me in on a few details.'

As the scheme unfolded, it started to look, to say the least, precarious.

'You say that the marikhs are sending in just one line train in two days' time?'

Roni-Vows nodded.

'That's right.'

'One and only one. The so-called Committee seems to have managed to do a deal with the marikhs in order to bring in supplies and also allow a few trusted people out of the city.'

'And we have letters of transit that will get five of us on to that train?'

'You, your . . . uh . . companion, the president, Edelline-Lan and myself. The president will be travelling as your girlfriend or mistress, call it what you will, a reformed prostitute.'

'A delicate touch.'

'I thought so.'

'So, when we're on the train, we'll be in marikh country, and all will be well?'

'Just so long as we don't get spotted at the terminal, we're home and dry once we're on the train.'

Streetlife entered the conversation with an angry grunt.

'If we don't get spotted, huh? And what if we do? The Day Oners will invent a whole new way of slow death specially for us.'

'We'd better make sure that we aren't spotted.'

Streetlife looked at Phaid and shook his head.

'I don't know why you're even bothering to listen to these creeps. As far as I can see, this deal's nothing short of fancy suicide.'

'I'm listening to them because they're going to burn us down if I don't. Can you think of a better reason?'

'I wish I'd never walked into this mess.'

'Well you did, so you better start rolling with it.'

'Rolling? Sweet Lords, I'm rolling.'

Phaid turned his attention back to Roni-Vows.

'Once we're on the train, what happens then?'

'We take the train as far as Fennella and then we switch to one that goes to Bluehaven, to the edge of the ice plain. After that, we take an iceboat to Losaw, the chief city of the Tharmiers.'

'The Tharmiers are willing to shelter the ex-president?'

'Not willing, but they won't hand her back to the rebels. We know that much. These contingency plans have been made for a long time.'

Phaid nodded.

'Okay, so now tell us about the money.'

Roni-Vows half smiled.

'This is the part that you'll probably enjoy. You get ten thousand the morning that we leave for the line terminal. You get a further twenty when we reach Fennella and the final payment of thirty thousand will be waiting for you when you take the president to the controller of the D'non-Loeb Counting House in the Losaw business district. The controller will take care of her from there on in, and your job will be over.'

Phaid rubbed his unshaven chin.

'How do we know that any of this will happen?'

'How do you know you can trust me, and that the money will be there as I've said?'

'That pretty well sums it up.'

'The simple answer is that you can't. You can't trust me and I can't trust you. I just hope that a state of mutual distrust will see us through. You, after all, have no real way out.'

Phaid nodded.

'You've thought it all through, haven't you. Just point your weapons at me and say go do it, Phaid the Gambler? Am I right?'

'It could be put a little more elegantly.'

Phaid suddenly got angry.

'It could have been thought out a little more elegantly, too. You think you've got it all covered because you've got the money arranged and letters of transit fixed and you can use my spurious reputation to sneak you on to the train. You really think you've got it made. Damn it, your upper class arrogance will kill us all in the end.'

Roni-Vows' eyes were tight little slits. 'What the hell are you talking about?'

'I'm talking about bloody fools who have cosy little one

on ones during the course of which the goddamn elaihi takes them into his confidence and they don't even think that they might be being stroked and oiled and set up for some new horror.'

'We considered that possibility but it was decided that we had to take the chance. What reason could Solchaim have for wanting to set us up?'

Phaid was on his feet, alcohol was still pumping angrily through his veins.

'Reason? Reason? What reason has he ever needed in the past? He's an elaihi and we're human. He doesn't like us and I'm pretty sure he has plans for us. That's the problem with you courtiers. You're so wrapped up in your own intrigues and your illusions of power you always underestimate Solchaim. Most of the time he has you dancing like marionettes.'

'You think he has us dancing like marionettes now?'

'Probably.'

'And I suppose you even know where he's dancing us to?'

Phaid had no more patience left.

'Of course not. I don't pretend to know what the elaihi has planned. He's a great deal cleverer than me, he's a great deal cleverer than all us. The only thing that I've learned is to smell when he's behind something and I'm smelling it right now. Everything to do with the creature has to be totally suspect. The sooner you people learn that, the safer we'll all be.'

Roni-Vows shook his head.

'Come on, now. You're being altogether too emotional about this. The only danger to you is the very real one of being stopped at the terminal. After you've come through that and you're out of the Republic, all you have to do is collect your money and go on your way. You're not required to worry about what may happen next or what Solchaim may be up to or even the cosmic ramifications of our actions.'

Phaid glared.

'I may not be required but I sure as hell keep getting caught up in and nearly killed by things that don't concern me.'

'But you're going to do what we want despite all this.'

Phaid suddenly deflated.

'Yeah, I'm going to do what you want. I'll get your

goddamn president out of the city for you, but hear me good, Roni-Vows, at the slightest hint of trouble I ditch the whole enterprise. I'm saving me long before I save anyone else. You understand?'

Roni-Vows regarded Phaid bleakly.

'We never imagined that it would be any other way.'

Phaid sat down again.

'There is one thing I don't understand at all.'

'What's that?'

'Why bother?'

'I beg your pardon.'

'Why bother? Why go to all this trouble for Chrystiana-Nex? Who needs her? Why don't you just escape and leave her to the rebels? She's a dangerous psycho and probably deserves everything she gets.'

Roni-Vows smiled a tight little smile.

'That's unquestionably true. She is also a figurehead, however. Given time, she could become a central rallying point for a retaking of the city.'

Phaid looked as though he didn't believe a word of it.

'How the hell does she become a rallying point? Even the cops have grown to hate her.'

'It's amazing how quickly people forget. After a few months of life under the Day Oners, they will long for the good old times of Chrystiana-Nex. That would be the start of a movement to bring her back to power.'

'But she's mad.'

'Well, of course, she isn't actually going to be given any power. She'll simply be a puppet.'

'Whose puppet?'

This time Roni-Vows' smile was wide and evil.

'Mine, my associates and whoever puts up the money for the takeover.'

'Money.'

'We'd need an army.'

'Who the hell is going to buy you an army?'

'We already have a choice of investors. Some of our own mobsters would finance the overthrow of the rebels. There are also some of the more expansionist-minded rulers of nearby city states who would like to have a stake in the Republic.'

Phaid's face was blank.

'You really do have it all covered, don't you?'

'I like to think so.'

'Where is Chrystiana-Nex right now?'

'Here.'

'Here?'

'Upstairs, in the Crystal Room.'

'Is that the one with the famous view?'

'I'm afraid the famous view is covered over with steel shutters. The owners took great care to protect their antique plexiglass before they fled. You can go up and see her if you want.'

Phaid looked down at his hands. The nails were chipped and dirty. He stroked his week-long growth of beard.

'I never came face to face with a president before, even an ex-president.'

'You think that perhaps you ought to look a bit better.'

Phaid shrugged, but unconsciously brushed dirt off his coat.

'Maybe, something like that.'

'I wouldn't let it worry you. Chrystiana-Nex isn't paying too much attention to what's going on here. She's kind of withdrawn.'

'What do you mean, withdrawn?'

'You'll see.'

Roni-Vows stood up. He led Phaid up a set of small stairs and on to the upper floor – the Crystal Room. Even with the plexiglass roof sheeted over, it was still magnificent. It was like being inside a huge chandelier. Cascading falls of cut plexiglass split all the light in the place into moving, brilliant rainbows.

Chrystiana-Nex was sitting at the far end of the room, hunched over a transparent table, apparently staring into an arrangement of dimly glowing filaments. Although the room was comparatively warm, she was wrapped in a thick fur cape. She didn't look up as the two men entered. Roni-Vows approached her, but still she didn't signify that there was anyone there. Finally, he spoke to her.

'We have finalised the arrangements for your leaving the city, my president.'

There was no response.

'We will be leaving in two days, my president. This man with me is Phaid. He is going to be assisting me in making your journey possible, my president.'

Chrystiana-Nex still gave no sign that she had heard him speak. Roni-Vows leaned close to her.

'It is important that you listen to me, my president. This

411

journey that we are about to undertake will not be without danger.'

Slowly she began to lift her head. Phaid was suddenly struck by the fact that she was much smaller than he had imagined. He saw the familiar, scraped back platinum hair, the jutting cheekbones and the wide, powerful mouth. Something, however, seemed to be missing. The ice-blue eyes had somehow lost their compelling quality, the fire had gone out of them, she seemed to have lost the ability to turn men's heads and make whole cities act against their better judgement.

'Danger? I am in no danger. This is my city.'

'You have to go on a journey.'

'I don't wish to leave the city at this point in time.'

'You have to go on a journey with Phaid here.'

Something cold and leaden was sinking through Phaid's stomach. The woman was a wreck, a hollow shell. There was no way that he could navigate this mental ruin through the levels of surveillance that they would have to pass in order to get on to the line train. Phaid quietly grasped Roni-Vows' elbow.

'You can burn me down or whatever, but this just isn't going to work.'

'When the elaihi left, he took part of her with him.'

'I don't care what happened, she can't make this journey.'

'Of course I can.'

Both men turned and looked at Chrystiana-Nex. The change in her was so sudden it was frightening. She was sitting up straight, her eyes had flashed on with the old intensity.

'You have no need to worry about me . . . Phaid.' Coldly, she looked him up and down. 'So you are Phaid, are you?'

Phaid's flesh was getting ready to crawl, but then the eyes snapped off as abruptly as they had come on. The blonde head sank slowly down on to the fur swathed chest. The ex-president was like a marionette with the strings cut. Phaid turned slowly to face Roni-Vows. Anger was welling up inside him.

'What the hell is going on in here?'

'I don't know, I really don't know. Let's just get her out of the city.'

'No way, absolutely no way. It's impossible.'

'It'll be okay, trust me.'

'Trust you . . . ?'

Phaid was speechless. Then Chrystiana-Nex's voice made them both swing around once again. She was up and alert.

'He's right, Phaid. You don't have to worry.'

24

'I've GOT a message for you. News of an old friend.'

'Oh yeah?'

Phaid propped himself up on one elbow. Although it was well past noon, Phaid was still in bed. Edelline-Lan, however, was a picture of brisk efficiency.

'Word came from Vist-Roxon.'

Phaid sat all the way up. More than once he had wondered what had happened to the elderly courtier.

'Is he okay? Did he get out of the city?'

'Somehow he has managed to make it to Orsine's country retreat where, by all accounts, he is a welcome guest.'

Phaid smiled and shook his head.

'Well, I'll be damned. How did you hear all this?'

'We've got our contacts with the mobs.'

'But how did Vist-Roxon know that I was here with you?'

Edelline-Lan grinned at Phaid's instant flash of suspicion.

'You don't let a thing get past you, do you?'

'I try not to, but you're not answering the question. How did he know I was here?'

'He didn't. He just asked that if anyone was to see you he'd be grateful if they passed the word. Are you going to get out of bed?'

Phaid lay down again.

'Why bother? If I'm expected to get myself killed tomorrow I figure I might as well rest up while I can. Why don't you join me?'

Phaid had naturally sought the company of Edelline-Lan during the time he was forced to wait around at the Hanging Goddess. When it had become clear that he wasn't leaving except to go to the line terminal, he hadn't particularly wanted to sit around on his own, brooding about the dubious future. Edelline-Lan was certainly the most attractive person in the small clique of fugitive courtiers. Much more impatiently, she also offered the only companionship in and around the Hanging Goddess.

Roni-Vows avoided Phaid as much as possible. Street-life seemed to hold him responsible for the entire situation and, in this case, it was Phaid who did the avoiding. The other courtiers both despised and distrusted Phaid. They all ignored him as being something beneath their contempt. The only exceptions to the wall of high born silence were a few of the younger bloods like Trimble-Dun, who bristled like tom cats anytime Phaid came near them. If Roni-Vows hadn't kept them on a tight rein, they would have used any excuse to pick a fight with Phaid, and then done their damnedest to kill him.

In many respects, his gravitation towards the company of Edelline-Lan was because nobody else would have anything to do with him. What he didn't quite understand was why she gravitated to him in return. He'd asked her about this, but she'd shaken her head.

'I don't know. I really don't. There's an awful lot wrong with you, but somehow you seem more real than all the rest.'

'If this is what being real gets me into, I think I'd rather be a less than real flake. My mother never raised me to be a hero.'

'Maybe that's your attraction.'

Halfway through the first night at the Hanging Goddess, despite all of Phaid's preoccupation, companionship had progressed to sex. For Phaid, it had been a climactic release from the constantly nagging fear of what the next few days would bring. After it was over, however, the demons had all crowded back. Finally, Phaid had climbed out of bed and begun pacing Edelline-Lan's temporary bedroom.

'I've got to get out of here. I need some air and a look at the sky. I'm starting to feel like a prisoner.'

The courtiers guarding the front door of the tavern had

taken a lot of convincing on the part of Edelline-Lan that Phaid should be let out of the building. They had only agreed to it when she'd assured them that she was not only armed, but also prepared to take full responsibility for any attempt by Phaid to escape. The other courtiers didn't make it easy for Edelline-Lan. They treated her with a certain aloof, chilly curtness. They seemed to take the attitude that she had somehow become a traitor to her class by associating with Phaid.

As the two of them walked away from the door, across the courtyard, Phaid deliberately took hold of her hand so the courtiers on watch couldn't help but see. She didn't resist and, in the skyline, they were the ideal picture of the loving couple.

Once they were in the shadow of the high wall, Phaid spun Edelline-Lan around and kissed her hard on the lips.

'Let's run away.'

'Sure.'

'I'm serious.'

'Okay, one day we'll run away. It might really be fun for a while.'

'I'm not talking about one day, I'm talking about now.'

Edelline-Lan's face fell.

'Oh dear.'

'What's the matter? It'd be easy. We could just sneak away. We'll take Streetlife's flipper. He'll be madder than a wet cat, but he'll get over it. You and I wouldn't have any trouble getting out of the city, and once we're away, well . . . we could do anything.'

Edelline-Lan slowly shook her head.

'No.'

'No?'

'It all sounds very nice and romantic, but no.'

'What do you mean, no?'

'Exactly what I said. I'm not going to run away with you, and I'm not going to let you run away on your own, either.'

'What's the matter with you?'

'I gave my word to Roni-Vows. I gave my solemn word that I'd see this thing through to the end. I'm not about to break my solemn word, even for you. That's what it means to be an aristocrat. These are my people, and I'm not about to betray them.'

'You gave your word to Roni-Vows; how much can that

mean? He's about the most treacherous, lying bastard that I've ever met. How can you worry about breaking a promise to him?'

'There's a certain level of promise that cannot be broken.'

'Does Roni-Vows see it that way?'

'Of course he does.'

Phaid was dumbfounded. 'I can't believe this!' He took a step back. 'I think I'm just going to walk to the flipper, get in it and drive away. That way I won't compromise your aristocratic honour and it'll save my ass.'

'I'll kill you before you're halfway to the flipper.'

'You wouldn't.'

'Try me. I already told you, I gave my word to see this thing through to the end. Part of that means making sure that you play your part. I like you, Phaid, but I gave my word.'

Phaid was close to speechless.

'I don't believe this. Less than an hour ago you and I were . . .' Phaid's face became set. 'I really don't believe this. I'm walking.'

He turned on his heel and started carefully across the courtyard.

'I warned you, Phaid. I don't want to do this, but I will if you make me.'

Phaid glanced back over his shoulder. Edelline-Lan had a blaster pointed straight at him. Phaid stopped and turned.

'You're quite serious, aren't you.'

'Quite serious.'

Phaid spread his hands in a gesture of resignation.

'I might as well get killed the day after tomorrow rather than today. What we are supposed to do now?'

'We could go back to bed as though nothing had happened.'

'You're joking.'

'I'm not. I'm sorry I had to do this, but it was my duty. I don't see why it has to make any difference to us about sleeping together. I understand that you had to try to get away just like I had to stop you.'

'You're incredible.'

She lowered her blaster.

'Aren't I just.'

'No, I mean really incredible.'

'Are you getting miffed because I won and you didn't?'

Phaid started back towards the door of the tavern.

'I don't know.'

Although the hours dragged slowly, they did actually pass. All too soon, Edelline-Lan was shaking Phaid awake and telling him that it was time to go. He got out of bed, splashed cold water on his face and dressed quickly. Out in the main lower room, Roni-Vows was waiting with most of the group of courtiers. The air was electric, but Phaid felt strangely on top of the situation. He suddenly realised that he was probably more in control than anyone else in the room. The knowledge made him a little light-headed. He faced the grim assembly of courtiers with a smile.

'So, is the queen ready to travel?'

Roni-Vows didn't look amused.

'The president will do everything that is required of her.'

'That's what worries me.'

'You seem to be taking all this with a great amount of levity.'

'I think I'd rather die with a smile on my lips and a song in my heart. I mean, this entire operation is a bit of a joke. How are we going to go about this idiocy?'

Roni-Vows' face hardened.

'This attitude isn't going to help you any.'

'I don't think there's anything that can help me any. Just tell me what the deal is and let's get on with it.'

Roni-Vows pursed his lips.

'Very well. The journey to the terminal ought to be comparatively simple. It's still early in the morning and I doubt that many of the rebels' random traffic checks will be in operation yet. The Day Oners held a particularly unpleasant ceremony on the Plaza last night. They forced a number of our people to beat each other to death with clubs. If they showed reluctance, parts of them were crudely hacked off. Hands, tongues, breasts and genitals were all carved from their owners' bodies. It was, by all reports, a gruesome spectacle.'

'That's horrible.'

'Sadly, it may prove useful to us. The Day Oners turned out in large numbers to watch the horror that I doubt their vigilante patrols will be out very early this morning.'

Phaid continued to smile.

'It's an ill wind.'

'How dare you, you scum?'

Trimble-Dun lunged at Phaid, but Roni-Vows quickly grabbed him and pushed him back.

'Leave him! Don't let him get to you. We need him.'

'How much of him do I have to tolerate?'

'As much as it takes to get the president out of the city'.

Trimble-Dun looked daggers at Phaid but kept his mouth shut. Roni-Vows went back to outlining the plan. He looked at Phaid.

'You and he . . .' he indicated Streetlife, who'd been brought in under guard '. . . will be taken to the line terminal in one flipper. You will have an escort. The President, Edelline-Lan and myself will travel in another vehicle.'

'When do I get my blaster back?'

'You will get your weapon, the travel documents and the first cash payment once you are inside the line terminal. Remember one thing, though. There will be armed men watching right up to the point that you are past the rebel checkpoint and you are on your way to the train. If you give them the slightest reason to believe that you are about to double cross us, they'll burn you on the spot.'

Phaid's grin faded.

'You've got this sewn up, haven't you.'

'I think so.'

'Is there anything else?'

Roni-Vows shook his head.

'That's all. Now we have to actually do it.'

The journey to the line terminal was uneventful. The Day Oners had yet to set up their spot road checks, just as Roni-Vows had predicted. Phaid's main fear was that, away from Roni-Vows' restraining influence, one of his escorts would take the opportunity to kill him. Fortunately, their discipline was stricter than Phaid had imagined and although they radiated pure hatred, nobody laid a hand on him.

The rebels had made a particular effort to make their mark on the streets around the line terminal. The buildings had been plastered with propagandist posters and displays, and daubed with slogans. As if totally swamping the eyes wasn't enough, they also went after the ears with clusters of speakers strung in every convenient niche.

These pumped out a non-stop stream of revolutionary rhetoric and grating martial music. On the wide steps between the monstrous feet of one of the terminal's stone giants, the five who were to take the line train were reunited. Roni-Vows immediately took charge.

'At this point we should split up. Except for Phaid and the president, who will be together, we will go through the checkpoint separately. The checkpoint is on this level. Once we've passed it and are riding up the tube, we are in marikh country and we should be safe, although I think there will be a danger from rebel spies right up until we're on the train and it's rolling.' He looked around carefully, but nobody seemed to be paying the quintet any undue attention. 'Here's the order that we'll go through the checkpoint. I will go first to test if our papers are in order, then . . .'

'No.'

'What?'

'No. Here's how we go through the checkpoint. Edel-line-Lan goes first to test the papers. Streetlife goes next because the only trouble he can get into is his own. The Lady President and I go next because we're the target and you go last because you're just along for the ride. That's it and I don't want any arguments.'

Roni-Vows shrugged.

'If that's the way you want it.'

'And from now on if I want it I get it because it's my ass in the barrel. You got that?'

'I've got that.'

'Give me back my blaster.'

Roni-Vows took Phaid's weapon from inside his coat and handed it to him. Phaid dropped it into its holster.

'Now the rest of the stuff.'

Roni-Vows produced two flat plastic wallets.

'The money and your sets of papers.'

Phaid tucked them in his pocket.

'Okay, now how about you, Madame President. Are you fit to travel or am I going to have to lug a vegetable on to the train?'

The ex-president's slight figure was swathed in full mourning. The hood of the orange and black robe was pulled forward so her face was invisible.

'Keep up the truculent attitude, young man, it might just carry us through.'

The voice that came from inside the hood was crisp and well articulated. Phaid nodded.

'Okay then, let's go. Edelline-Lan in front. Keep an eye on each other and don't do anything dumb.'

The checkpoint was makeshift, slow and less than efficient. Surrounded by jolt fields and thirty or more armed rebels with blue armbands and surly expressions, four harassed looking clerks checked each traveller's papers.

Most of the rapidly growing line moved through the checkpoint with no great difficulty. There were, however, a few casualties of the rebel system. In the space of time during which Phaid was waiting his turn, he saw three unhappy individuals pulled to one side and then quickly marched away under close guard.

Edelline-Lan reached the checkpoint. She gave her papers to one of the clerks. He leafed through them, there was a brief conversation and then he handed them back. Edelline-Lan walked briskly towards the tube that would take her up to the line train. She was through.

Streetlife spent rather a long conversation with the clerk. At one point it become quite animated and Phaid was getting prepared to see him dragged away, but then the documents were handed back and Streetlife's bouncing walk was being directed to the tubes. Phaid's turn was coming up next.

'What is the purpose of your visit, citizen?'

'Now that the revolution is over, I'm taking my new woman and going back to my people in the hills for a spell.'

'The revolution is never over, citizen. Revolution is a continuous process.'

Phaid cursed his luck that he should have to pick a clerk who fancied himself as a philosopher. He grunted.

'Yeah, well.'

The clerk tapped his papers.

'These are important letters of transit for a simple vacation. Perhaps you'd like to tell me how you came by them.'

'I'm Phaid.'

The clerk's eyes widened.

'You are, are you.'

'I can pretty much get what I want. I figure I've earned it. I'm taking my woman and going back to the hills.'

Phaid belligerently stuck out his jaw.

'You have any objections?'

The clerk obviously did.

'Preference and favour are something that we have sought to overturn.'

'You're saying that a man can't take a well earned rest when he wants one?'

'What I'm saying is that . . .'

At this juncture one of the blue armband boys with the blasters decided to find out exactly what was causing the delay.

'Do we have a problem here, citizen?'

Phaid looked up.

'I sure as hell hope not.'

The clerk turned to the guard.

'This is Citizen Phaid. He seems to think he deserves a vacation.'

The blue armband looked him up and down.

'So you're the legendary Phaid?'

'I'm Phaid. I don't know about the legendary.'

'And you're leaving town.'

'I thought I was entitled to a break until our citizen clerk here decided otherwise.'

The blue armband looked outraged.

'Of course he's entitled to a break. We're here to stop escaping aristos, not cause trouble for men who have served the revolution.'

The clerk bridled.

'I was merely pointing out that the revolution was supposed to have put an end to personal privilege. There ought to be no reason why a hero of the revolution should enjoy any better treatment than a humble . . .'

'Clerk?'

'Exactly.'

The blue armband's lip curled.

'If people like you had spent more time fighting and less time pointing things out, the revolution might be getting further than it is.' The blue armband pointed at Chrystiana-Nex. 'Why is the woman in mourning?'

'Her brother was killed during the storming of the Palace.'

Blue armband swung back to the clerk with a gesture of contempt.

'So you decide to ease her grief by tying her man up

with your petty officiousness.'

The clerk couldn't take much more.

'Okay, okay, you've made your point. You strutting glamour boys make me sick. When are you going to realise that a revolution requires hard work not just heroics?' He thrust the papers back into Phaid's hand. 'Go through. Enjoy your vacation . . . while you can.'

Phaid sneered.

'You're too good to us.'

Taking Chrystiana-Nex by the arm, he began to move quickly towards the tube. The ex-president leaned close to him and spoke in a low voice.

'You almost overdid the tough guy act.'

'We got through, didn't we?'

'Just.'

The tube was coming up. With a sudden twitch, he realised that there had been so much else on his mind that he hadn't had time for his usual terror of the tubes. He stepped out into empty space and floated up. His fear of drop tubes came back to him in a single, gut wrenching rush. He shut his eyes tightly and kept them that way until his feet felt the floor of the upper level under them.

Edelline-Lan and Streetlife were waiting by the train's first-class boarding ramp. They made a strange couple, but both looked genuinely pleased to see that Phaid and Chrystiana-Nex had cleared the checkpoint.

'You made it.'

'We made it.'

'Now there's just Roni-Vows to come.'

Phaid walked over and handed the tickets to one of the marikh conductors stationed at the foot of the ramp. He noticed that all means of access to the line train were well guarded by marikh security men carrying businesslike fuse tubes. It was unusual to see the normally selfeffacing marikhs put on such a show of strength. They obviously had little faith in the current situation in Chrystianaville.

The conductor checked the tickets and smiled.

'There is nothing to keep you and your party from boarding.'

Phaid nodded.

'Thank you.' He looked back at the others. 'Is there any sign of Roni-Vows yet?'

Edelline-Lan was watching the head of the up-bound tube.

'I think . . . yes . . . that's him now.' She waved and shouted. 'Hey! Over here! He's seen us and he's coming in this direction . . . oh my Lords . . . those three men! They're grabbing him! One of them is pointing straight at us!'

Chrystiana-Nex slapped Edelline-Lan smartly across the face.

'You stupid girl. What did you have to wave and shout for? You've drawn their attention to us.'

A pair of the marikh security men looked around to see what the disturbance was. Four armed men were running across the concourse towards Phaid and his companions. Although they wore no badges or insignia, they were plainly rebel agents. Phaid grabbed each of the two women by the arm and pulled them apart.

'Get on the train, damn it! It's our only chance.'

Streetlife was already pounding up the ramp. After a moment's hesitation Chrystiana-Nex and Edelline-Lan followed. Phaid dropped his hand to his blaster and retreated up the ramp at a slightly slower pace. Their pursuers started pointing and shouting.

'Stop them! They are wanted criminals!'

Phaid quickened his pace. Halfway up the long ramp he paused to look back. The rebel agents had reached the foot of the ramp but, to Phaid's surprise and delight, the marikh security men were barring their way. Phaid smiled and walked on up. He was just congratulating himself on how he was clear away when a blaster burst exploded just a few paces behind him. He swung around, fumbling with his own weapon. It was one of the rebel agents who had fired, but he was being disarmed by the marikhs. Phaid decided that it still wasn't wise to linger. He trotted up the last stretch of the ramp and, with a definite feeling of relief, he stepped into the train.

Phaid found that Edelline-Lan had pretty much taken charge of things when he arrived at their assigned suite of staterooms. She was doing her best to placate the still raging Chrystiana-Nex while Streetlife provided the two of them with an unwilling and uncomfortable audience.

'You almost got us killed. Those rebels could have caught us, you ignorant, stupid slut! I don't care what happens to you! One court whore more or less makes no difference, but my life is important. I am special. I have a destiny to fulfil!'

Edelline-Lan's eyes blazed.

'I've taken about all I can take from you. You may have been our president once and because of that I have risked my life to get you out of the city.'

'My city.'

'It isn't your city any longer. You're going to have to realise that.'

'My city.'

'It's not your city. You're on the run just like the rest of us and the sooner you adjust to that the easier it'll make it for all concerned.' She saw Phaid come into the room and turned to him in appeal. 'Can you make her see sense?'

Phaid's shoulders drooped.

'I can't make anybody see anything until I've had a drink. I've just been shot at and I'm getting sick.'

Chrystiana-Nex rounded on him.

'You're sick? How dare you be sick? I am losing my city and on my way to exile! I am a special person and I require special treatment!'

Phaid started taking off his filthy, stained rebel coat. From deep inside the train there was the sound of the power units warming up. Any moment the train would start to move out of the Chrystianaville terminal. He looked at Chrystiana-Nex and wondered unkindly how long it would take the rebels to get around to changing the name of the city. He grinned at her.

'Why don't you get off it?'

'I'm special.'

'I don't give a damn what you are.'

Streetlife started to edge towards the door.

'I think I'm getting out of here.'

'I'm special.'

'For Lords' sake, shut your mouth, woman. We've all been through too much to listen to your shit.'

'I'm special. I'm special. I'm . . .'

Her eyes suddenly blanked out. Although Phaid had seen it happen before, he was still shocked. There was something frightening about the way her mind seemed to switch off and switch on. It was almost as if there was some outside entity controlling the woman like a puppet. Phaid couldn't guess at what she must have been through in all the time she spent with Solchaim. He thought about it but he wasn't sure that he'd ever want a detailed answer. After standing rigid and motionless for a few seconds,

425

Chrystiana-Nex tottered backwards. Streetlife caught her under the armpits and laid her down on the nearest bed.

'She's gone again.'

'Thank the Lords for that. Let's hope she stays quiet for a while.'

'Amen to that.'

Phaid picked up the comset. The line train was starting to vibrate slightly; departure was only a matter of minutes away. He ordered a considerable quantity of drinks and hung up. He dropped his coat on the floor, then took off his blaster and belt and let them drop too.

'I think I could use some peace and quiet.'

'And food.'

'And clean clothes.'

Edelline-Lan, Streetlife and Phaid all burst out laughing at the same moment. Streetlife pointed to the unconscious form of Chrystiana-Nex.

'If she stayed that way for the whole trip we could maybe have ourselves a good time.'

'Maybe she will.'

'You think we're due to get lucky?'

'Who's to tell.'

With the very smallest of lurches the line train began to move. Outside the stateroom's large picture window the roofs and spires of Chrystianaville slipped past, slowly at first, but then faster as the line train began to pick up speed. Phaid abruptly sat down.

'It's weird, you know, I spent a hell of a long time struggling to get back to this city, and now I'm leaving it again.'

Streetlife nodded.

'My momma always told me how if you wanted a thing for long enough you usually got it, but when you got it, you probably wouldn't like it.'

Edelline-Lan looked at each man in turn.

'You goddamn self pitying pair. At least we're on the damned train. What about poor Roni-Vows? If he's not dead already he's probably on his way to the White Tower or worse.'

Phaid closed his eyes.

'Right now I don't have the strength to worry about Roni-Vows' fate.'

'After all he did for you?'

'Did for me? *Did for me?*' Phaid was outraged. 'He

426

never did a damn thing for me except drop me in the shit. I'm sorry he got caught, but I'm not about to weep bitter tears for him.'

Edelline-Lan looked as though she was about to explode, but before the argument could blow up into a full scale fight, there was a soft rapping on the door. Phaid jumped to his feet, considerably cheered.

'This must be the booze.'

Edelline-Lan wasn't about to leave it alone.

'Is that all you think about?'

Phaid nodded.

'For as much of the time as possible.'

He hit the door control with the palm of his hand. It slid open. Instead of the steward with a drink cart, he found a marikh officer standing there. His crisp tan uniform indicated that he was part of the line train's operational crew. The marikhs were not much given to insignia or decorations but, from the amount of braid that adorned this man's uniform, it was clear that he held a fairly substantial rank.

'Are you Master Phaid?'

Phaid was immediately wary.

'I'm Phaid. What can I do for you? Is there some kind of problem?'

'Perhaps if I was to step inside.'

Phaid waved him in.

'Sure. Be our guest.' The door slid closed. Phaid indicated an easy chair. 'Would you care for a seat?'

'I'd prefer to stand. This is something of a delicate matter.' The officer had the closed, passive good manners that were common to all marikhs. He made a slight formal bow. 'I am Hant Vozer V'Cruw. I have the position of Third Assistant Captain in charge of Passenger Relations.'

'That's nice.'

'I'm sorry – what's that supposed to mean?'

'Nothing at all. What seems to be the trouble?'

The marikh drew himself up to his full height which, unfortunately for his dignity, still only brought him up to Phaid's shoulder.

'As you probably know, we marikhs have a policy of non-interference in the internal affairs of the nations and city states that subscribe to our transport services. However, the presence of the deposed president of the Republic on this train does, to say the least, present us with what has to be an embarrassing situation. It is made particularly embarrassing in view of the fact that the present regime looks upon the ex-president as a wanted criminal.'

Edelline-Lan was immediately on her feet.

'You can't call that a regime! They're nothing more than a gang of thieves, murderers and cut throats. Why, even now they're starting to fight among themselves.'

Hant Vozer V'Cruw was unperturbed.

'So long as our line or installations are not jeopardised, we do not make value judgements regarding administration of client states.'

'So why pick on us? We're just trying to get out of town. We have tickets and we aren't doing anyone any harm.'

'Unfortunately, Master Phaid, the situation is a little more complicated. You may not be doing anyone any harm at the moment, but this is a state of affairs that may not continue. After the incident prior to departure, it becomes clear that the presence of the one-time president on this vessel is no longer a secret. It is all too possible that the present authorities in Chrystianaville may attempt pursuit in some other kind of ground vehicle. They may even attempt to stop and board this vessel with a view to seizing Madame Chrystiana-Nex by force.'

Edelline-Lan was horrified.

'That's impossible. Not even the sickest Day Oners would think of attacking a line train.'

'Unfortunately, madame, neither you nor anyone else can give us a guarantee of that. If such an attempt should be made, it would obviously imperil the safety of the train, its passengers and possibly even the line itself.'

Phaid gave the marikh a sideways, far from happy look.

'Are you leading up to tell us that we're going to be thrown off the train?'

Hant Vozer V'Cruw vigorously shook his head.

'Of course not. You have valid tickets. It would be a breach of our constitution and our most dearly held traditions.'

'Well, that's a relief.'

'On the other hand . . .'

'Uh-oh.'

'On the other hand, if we received word that such an attack was imminent, then we would have no choice. Our duty would be clear.'

'We'd be thrown off the train.'

428

'The train would be stopped and the ex-president set down. She would, of course, receive a full refund on the price of her ticket.'

Phaid sighed.

'Of course.'

Streetlife looked up sharply.

'Do you dump all of us, or just the president?'

'At this moment, we have no information that any attempt to stop the train would be other than to seize the president.'

Phaid scratched his chin.

'What happens in the meantime?'

'In the meantime you are free to enjoy our first-class service. We would, however, be grateful if Chrystiana-Nex would remain in the suite, and that the rest of you would severely restrict your use of the larger public rooms such as the ballroom to an absolute minimum.'

Phaid grinned.

'Does that include the gaming room?'

'In your case I would think that it particularly include the gaming room, Master Phaid.'

'Particularly?'

'I'm sorry. Are there any more questions?'

Phaid raised an eyebrow.

'How much warning will we get before you dump Chrystiana-Nex off the train?'

'As much as possible.'

'I see.'

'Is that all you wish to know?'

There were no more questions. Hant Vozer V'Cruw bowed and made his goodbyes. Once the door had swished closed behind him, Edelline-Lan confronted Phaid.

'What are you going to do about all this? We can't let her be thrown off the train.'

Streetlife joined in.

'What are you going to do? She may be a pain in the ass, but she's worth a lot of money to us.'

Phaid deliberately didn't answer until he'd carefully unbuttoned his shirt.

'I'm not going to do anything about all this. Once the steward has brought our drinks, I'm going to go down to the train's shopping centre, I'm going to buy some new clothes, then I'm coming back up here, getting a clean off, dressing myself and then I'm going to go to one of the smaller, more intimate bars and get as drunk as a skunk. I never asked to become that woman's nursemaid and I've just about had it up to here. So, like our marikh buddy just said, are there any other questions?'

With almost perfect timing the steward rapped on the door.

Phaid discovered, as he began to wander the train, that there was a certain subdued, drab atmosphere. There was no mistaking that he was on what amounted to a refugee ship. Although he took the marikh's advice and stayed away from the gaming hall and the ballroom, it was still apparent that there was little sparkle and glitter on the particular journey.

When Phaid walked into the small cocktail bar between the shopping area and the forward observation gallery, he found that he was the only customer. As well as being deserted, the bar was decorated in mosaic patterns made from thousands of tiny mirrors. Phaid found it a little disconcerting to sit and sip his drink with an infinite number of reflections of himself staring back at him. In self defence, he turned his attention to the bar steward.

'It's very quiet.'

'It stinks.'

The steward was particularly outspoken for a marikh. Phaid wondered if it was part of his training. He scowled as he shook up Phaid's second Mint Dropkick.

'We never ought to have brought this train into the Republic.'

The Dropkick gave off a heavy blue vapour as the steward poured it from the shaker. It drifted down from the glass and crept across the marble top of the bar. Phaid picked up the drink and tasted it. The steward looked at him enquiringly.

'How is it?'

'It's great.'

'Tell me something.'

'What?'

'You're not one of those Chrystianaville rebels, are you?'

'Who me? Not a chance.'

'That's funny. I had a four-hour pass in the city. I saw this broken hologram. It was for some rebel killer. It was a wanted holo, you know, offering a reward. The guy was some big time rebel killer. The hologram was left over from before when the rebels took power.'

Phaid knew what was coming but he asked anyway.

'So? What about it?'

'Well, I don't want to give offence, but the guy in the hologram, the big time rebel; he was your double. Don't you think that's weird?'

Phaid avoided the steward's eyes.

'Weird.'

'I mean, I had to find out if you were a rebel or not, not that we have too many rebels drinking up here, but I had to find out. I mean, personally, I don't approve of what those rebels are up to. Did you hear about that thing last night when they forced all those aristos to beat each other to death and . . .'

'I heard already.'

Phaid was hoping that the steward's garrulous conversation wasn't a result of training. It bode badly for marikh bars. On the other hand, if it wasn't, the man was some kind of aberration and that wasn't a pleasing thought either.

'Yes sir, I can tell you, if anyone asked me I'd say pull all trains out of the Republic until they've got a government that knows how to behave. I mean, the last president, that madwoman, she was bad enough, but this new lot . . . well, words fail me.'

'This is a very good Dropkick.'

Phaid decided to try and change the subject while words still failed the steward. He almost spilled his drink when a voice from behind him cut into the conversation.

'Master Phaid tries to avoid political discussion, don't you, Master Phaid.'

The steward slapped his forehead.

'Phaid. I knew it. That was the name of the guy on the hologram. It was you. Listen, I didn't mean to give any offence. Sometimes my mouth just runs away with me.'

Phaid ignored him. He set down his cocktail and slowly turned to look at the newcomer. He firmly refused to believe it was who he thought it was. Unfortunately the proof was there, right in front of him. Dreen was standing in the bar regarding Phaid with a mocking half-smile.

'You know something? If I keep running into you like this, I'm going to start to believe that you're following me. Isn't that strange?'

Phaid got angry.

'What exactly do you want?'

Dreen didn't answer. Instead he glanced at the steward.

'Just to set your mind at rest, he is the one in the hologram, but he isn't a killer. The whole thing was a bit of a sham.'

The steward began to busily polish a glass.

'I think I may have talked too much, gentlemen.'

Dreen hoisted himself on to a barstool. In his rather shabby, high-necked black coat he looked a little incongruous among the mirrors and chrome.

'What are you drinking?'

'A Mint Dropkick.'

'Are they good?'

'They're something of an acquired taste.'

Dreen gestured to the steward.

'Mix me a Mint Dropkick, will you?'

The steward smiled. He seemed happier now that he was back on safe ground. He poured the cocktail and its accompanying heavier-than-air vapour rolled across the counter. Dreen took a sip and nodded to the steward.

'It's good.'

'Thank you, sir.'

He raised his glass to Phaid.

'Good health.'

'Why don't you cut the crap and come out with what you want. You haven't come here to drink my health. Who are you and what the hell are you after?'

Dreen's reptilian face folded into a look of wronged innocence.

'You have a churlish streak, not to mention a suspicious nature.'

'Can we cut out the charade? Just tell me how come you're travelling on this train.'

'I'm just going from one place to another. It's the story of my life.'

Phaid drained the last of his drink. He coughed. He'd forgotten that one was supposed to leave the last fraction of a Dropkick. He swung off the barstool.

'If you want to keep this up, you can do it on your own. I don't know what you are or who you work for, but I'm walking out of this bar right now.'

Dreen was immediately placating.

'Come now. Don't be so hasty. I'm just a traveller, the

432

same as you, trying to get by. I don't mean you any harm.'

'How do I know that?'

Dreen's reptile smile came back again.

'Because if I did, we wouldn't be sitting here like this. Oh, don't look at me that way. I know all about your mission. I know that Roni-Vows has been caught. I suppose I should be sorry, but I never could have much sympathy for that particular conniving butterfly.'

'Are you going to sell us back to the Day Oners or what. I'd imagine they'd pay a great deal for Chrystiana-Nex.'

Dreen's face took on a look of sadness that wasn't quite plausible.

'You really do have a talent for wronging me, putting the worst possible construction on what I say. Why can't you realise that all I want to do is to help you?'

'Because I don't trust you. I swear to God that I saw you in the White Tower with police and priests. I've seen you in other places, too. It all adds up to a combination that can't possibly mean me any good.'

'There you go again.'

'Okay, okay, I'll take a chance, just this one time.'

'You are going to have to get off the train very soon.'

'On your say so?'

'On the captain's say so, as a matter of fact. A number of rebels are already in pursuit of this train. They have photon cannons and the fastest, rough country flippers they could find in the city. Their plan is to stop the train as it comes out of Similla Tunnel and arrest you and the ex-president. This information has already been tele-graphed down the line to the captain and he plans to put you and Chrystiana-Nex off before he takes the train into the tunnel.'

Phaid was puzzled.

'You say he's going to put me off too? Why should he do that? Chrystiana-Nex is the only one that's wanted.'

'You are too, now. They've found out all about the phoney wanted posters. They know that you're a fake and a traitor and they want your head.'

'I suppose you didn't have anything to do with them finding out about me, did you.'

'Will you not start that again.'

Phaid signalled for another drink.

'Okay, but I don't call it very helpful to tell me I'm going to be thrown off the train just before Similla

Tunnel. That's well into the edge of the cold. We'll be lucky not to freeze to death.'

'You won't freeze to death.'

'Thanks for your confidence.'

The steward poured Phaid another drink. He had obviously caught enough of the tone of Phaid and Dreen's conversation to keep out of it. Phaid swallowed the cocktail in one gulp and straightaway wished that he hadn't. Once again, he started to slide off his stool.

'If that's all you've got to tell me, I think that I'll be going.'

'There's more if you wait.'

'There is?'

'You want to hear it?'

Phaid sighed and nodded.

'Okay, I'll listen.'

'Once you get off the train, follow the line back, away from the tunnel. After you've walked for about an hour, you'll come to an old hunters' trail. It's rough, but it's still clearly defined. It runs due south.'

'Due south takes us further and further into the cold.'

'It also takes you directly to Bluehaven on the edge of the ice plain. There you will find an iceboat to take you clear across to Tharmier country, which I belive was your original destination.'

Phaid looked troubled.

'I'd be a lot happier following your directions if you told me how you knew all this.'

'I can't tell you. That would be giving away the secrets of my trade.'

'And what is your trade, Dreen? That's another thing I've never found out.'

'Information, Master Phaid. My trade is information. Sometimes I buy it, sometimes I sell it and sometimes I give it away. In your case I'm giving it away.'

'Why?'

'I like to think of it as an investment.'

'I suppose I should thank you.'

'That's very gracious of you. There is one more thing that you should know.'

'What's that?'

'Your pursuers are being led by people you know.'

'Who?'

'Your one-time companion Makartur and the woman

who calls herself Flame.'

Phaid slowly and carefully set his drink on the bar. He felt sick.

'So those two are after us.'

'They are particularly after you. The man Makartur has sworn to kill you.'

Phaid was slowly and unhappily realising that, once again, he'd landed right in the middle of yet another horrific situation. Very soon he'd be out in the cold and in the open with an experienced warrior on his trail. He rounded bitterly on Dreen.

'Why don't you tell me what you really want? You can't be telling me all this for nothing. What are you after?'

Dreen shook his head. He looked genuinely sad.

'I'm afraid I can't tell you that. My masters do not want you to know their aims as yet. All I can tell you is that you may receive help if you manage to reach Bluehaven.'

'And who are your masters?'

'Wait until Bluehaven, friend Phaid. Wait until Bluehaven.'

Phaid put out a hand to grab Dreen, but the small man slipped off the stool.

'You'll find out in Bluehaven if you haven't guessed already.'

25

JUST AS Dreen had predicted, the captain himself had come to the suite with a small squad of security men. He had been polite but firm. He was slowing the train to a stop and he expected Phaid and Chrystiana-Nex to get off. There was no space for argument. The security men bowed and smiled, but the small, discreet blasters under their coats made it very clear that things were going to be exactly as the captain ordered.

The captain withdrew, leaving Phaid, Edelline-Lan and Streetlife to figure out how to make the best of their fates. For Phaid, it was easy, if less than pleasant. He was being thrown off the train, and that was that. The other two had a choice, and that was where the problems began.

Streetlife was sure about what he was doing.

'I'm sorry, my buddy, but it cold out there. I like you, Phaid. You know that, but I don't like you enough to go jumping out of a nice warm train and into ice, snow and Lords knows what else.'

'Thanks.'

'You don't really expect me to, do you?'

'No, I guess not.' Phaid turned his attention to Edelline-Lan. 'What about you?'

'What Streetlife says makes a lot of sense.'

'You too, huh?'

'On the other hand . . .'

'On the other hand what?'

'I did give my word to Roni-Vows to see the president safely out of the city and deliver her to the Tharmiers.'

'Roni-Vows is either dead or being tortured.'

'That's no reason for me to break my word. In fact, in some ways it's all the more reason not to break it.'

Phaid gave her a long searching look.

'So, what are you going to do?'

Edelline-Lan was silent for almost a full minute. Then she straightened her back and set her jaw.

'I'm coming with you. It's my duty. There is no other way.'

Phaid wasn't sure quite how to take this, but he made no comment. Instead he addressed himself to the problems at hand.

'We need to make a few preparations before we get dumped off in the cold.' He looked at Edelline-Lan. 'You've still got a weapon, haven't you?'

She nodded.

'Okay then. I'm going down to the shopping centre to buy us some warm clothes, backpacks and anything else useful that I can find. You had better go and see that Assistant Captain, or whatever he called himself, and get the refunds on our tickets. We are going to need all the money we can get our hands on. Also, you could try and hit the marikhs up for some supplies, food concentrates, self heat containers or whatever. This is going to be a little rugged.'

The two of them were starting to go about their business when Streetlife spoke up.

'I don't know if you want to listen to me, seeing as I deserting you and all, but it seems to me that your worst problem is her.' He pointed to the still unconscious Chrystiana-Nex. 'You going to need something to get her on her feet and walking, else one of you going to have to be carrying her.' He pointed to the flurries of snow that were drifting past the window. 'That wouldn't be easy in this kind of weather.'

Edelline-Lan turned to Phaid.

'He's right, you know. Somehow we have to start her moving again, except I'm damned if I know how.'

Streetlife looked a little embarrassed.

'Listen, I could maybe go scout around and see if I could find something to wake her up, scholomine or something.'

'You'll need some money.'

'I'll try and hustle it. Look on it like a parting gift.'

437

Phaid grinned and held out his hand.

'Thanks.'

Streetlife shook it and then hurried out. Edelline-Lan looked thoughtful.

'I suppose I could try the Assistant Captain, tell him that the president cannot be moved and that we need drugs or something.'

Phaid nodded.

'Good thinking. But hurry.'

The vibration of the train's drive had perceptibly altered in pitch. It was obvious that the marikhs had already started the long process of slowing the train to a stop. It was down to a little more than walking pace before Streetlife returned. Phaid and Edelline-Lan were already getting bundled up in all the clothes that they could find.

'I got it! I got scholomine!'

Streetlife was so excited that Edelline-Lan didn't like to tell him that she had obtained some capsules of praxene, a powerful stimulant, from the train's private pharmacy. Streetlife held out two vials. Phaid took them. He dropped one in his pocket and cracked the seal on the other.

'Did you have to go through a lot to get these?'

Streetlife rolled his eyes.

'I had to make some promises you wouldn't want to hear about.'

'You're a good friend.'

'You better believe it.'

Phaid eased open the still prone Chrystiana-Nex's eyelid and dropped an almost foolhardy amount of the drug into her right eye. He muttered under his breath.

'Come on, Madame President, let's see some life. I ain't going to carry you.'

At first nothing happened. Phaid was starting to get close to the verge of panic. Then both the ex-president's eyes snapped open. She sat bolt upright.'

'Kill them!'

Phaid put a hand on her shoulder.

'Stop that. You're somewhere else entirely.'

'Kill them! Kill them! Kill them!

'Cut it out, will you?'

'Move out the Guard. No prisoners! They must be taught a lesson!'

Phaid saw no other alternative. He took careful aim and slapped the ex-president across the face. She shrieked as though she had been goosed with a tingler, but she did come partway back to reality.

'Do we have a problem that requires my attention?'

'More than that, we have to get off the train.'

'Have we reached our destination?'

'No, I'm afraid that we are being thrown off the train.'

'Thrown off the train?'

'Remember that you're a fugitive.'

'Oh . . . yes.'

To Phaid's surprise she was immediately acquiescent and co-operative. He and Edelline-Lan quickly dressed her. Just as they had finished, there was a soft jerk as the train came to a halt. Next there was a knocking on the cabin door. It was Hant Vozer V'Cruw come to tell them that it was time to go. Phaid once again shook hands with Streetlife.

'We'll catch up again.'

'Sure we will.'

They were led through back companionways, down service elevators, and fire stairs. At one point Phaid realised that they must be in the marikh areas of the line train. Phaid knew that the three of them had to be among the first non-marikhs to ever walk there.

They were allowed no time to linger, however. Without meeting another passenger, they were escorted to a small emergency exit deep in the bowels of the train. When the small hatch was popped open, a blast of icy air hit the three companions. Hant Vozer V'Cruw dropped a telescopic ladder.

'It's cold out there. I'm sorry your journey had to end this way.'

Phaid scowled.

'So are we.'

'I hope you won't hold this against Marikh Transit Services.'

Phaid suddenly lost his temper.

'You don't expect us to be grateful, do you?'

'I suppose not.'

'Well thank the Lords for that.'

He started down the ladder. Chrystiana-Nex followed and finally Edelline-Lan. The ladder was withdrawn and the exit hatch snapped shut. For a few minutes, the three of them stood looking up at the enormous line train. The sun had set and the lights of the train were starting to come on. Luminous, rainbow discharges played around its towering exhaust stacks. The three of them took five or six steps back as the multistorey metal monster started to vibrate and finally, very slowly, to move off. High above them, tiny people were clearly visible in the clear plexi-glass observation galleries. They were probably looking out, wondering why the train had made an unexplained and unscheduled stop. Phaid knew their curiosity wouldn't last long; very soon they'd go back to the bars, the staterooms and their warm cabins.

A feeling of utter desolation folded around Phaid as the train pulled away. Flurries of light snow spiralled down. The sky was quickly growing dark. The pylons supporting the line pointed up at it like pale, accusing fingers. On either side of the line there were stands of dour, forbidding conifers. It was bitterly cold. When Dreen had been giving his instructions it had seemed a comparatively simple matter to make their way to Bluehaven. Now it had become reality in the teeth of a biting wind, Phaid was starting to have doubts. Apart from the cold and the snow and the natural dangers of the forest, there was the fact that Makartur was not going to give up and go home just because he found that Phaid and his companions had dropped off the train. As it rolled away from them, Phaid looked at the two women.

'We'd better start walking.'

'Where?'

'I heard that if we follow the line back for a while we hit a hunters' trail going south that will eventually take us to Bluehaven on the ice plain.'

Edelline-Lan raised an eyebrow.

'We're walking?'

'Have you got a better idea?'

She turned and fussed over Chrystiana-Nex, pulling up the hood of her orange mourning robe and brushing the snow from her shoulders. The ex-president was up and moving, but with a zombie-like passivity. Phaid turned his back on the now rapidly disappearing train and started walking down the line of pylons. Edelline-Lan took Chrystiana-Nex's arm and followed.

The snow was now falling more determinedly and there was a sprinkling on the ground. It seemed as though there was no sign of the promised trail. Above them, the line hummed eerily on top of its pylons. Edelline-Lan, still steering Chrystiana-Nex, caught up with Phaid and looked at him doubtfully.

'What happened to the trail south?'

'We don't seem to have reached it yet.'

'Who told you it was there?'

'A well wisher.'

Phaid wasn't inclined to tell Edelline-Lan the story of Dreen. In fact, he was starting to worry whether Dreen might have been lying to him. Edelline-Lan, however, was unwilling to accept his cryptic answer.

'What the hell is that supposed to mean?'

'It means that I heard there was a trail back this way and that's all I know. If you've got a better plan, you take charge.'

'Do you have any experience at all of surviving in this kind of country and climate?'

'I was born in the hills.'

'But you left the hills when you were a kid. Ever since then you've been earning your living with a deck of cards.'

'That's true.'

'I don't like this at all. We could freeze out here and not be found for years.'

'I'm more concerned that we will be found, that Makartur will catch up with us before we even have a chance to freeze. He's fresh out of the hills and can probably track like a dog.'

'If only this wind would stop. Wait a minute, what's that?'

There appeared to be a break in the trees. Phaid grinned, despite the snow that was clinging to his eyelashes.

'I think that's our trail.'

'It is?'

There was certainly a track leading off into the forest. It was narrow, dark and winding and overhung by trees. Edelline-Lan looked at it apprehensively.

'We are going to go down *there*?'

'It's a hunters' trail, not a six-lane highway.'

'I can see that.'

Phaid himself was scarcely happy about the condition of the trail, but he wasn't about to admit it to Edelline-Lan. Showing more determination than he really felt, he took the first steps into the forest.

Moving down the trail was a lot more difficult than

walking on the cleared ground beneath the line. Phaid managed to keep his footing, but both Edelline-Lan and Chrystiana-Nex stumbled more than once, almost falling in the semi-darkness and cursing loudly. There was a compensation, though. The forest did afford a certain protection against the bitter wind.

They walked on and on until it seemed as though they had been tramping for hours. The darkness became complete. More roots grabbed at their ankles, branches scratched their faces and, if anything, they got worse. Finally Phaid had to admit that they were attempting the impossible. He halted the two women.

'This is ridiculous. We can't go staggering on like this. It's absurd. We're just blundering about in the dark.'

Edelline-Lan was sagging visibly.

'What else can we do?'

'Rig some sort of shelter and build a fire.'

'Can you?'

'I sure as hell hope so.'

Phaid found what looked like a sheltered spot beneath a high bank. He fixed up a wind break with a blanket that Edelline-Lan had been smart enough to steal from the train. His next move was to get a fire going. He knew that there were a number of firemaking techniques that his people used when stranded in a hostile environment, but not a single one sprang to mind. Phaid had been out of the hills for too long. He pulled out his blaster and aimed it at a patch of ground just in front of the bank. He kept the release pressed down for a full fifteen seconds until the earth glowed white hot and started to melt.

Phaid stopped blasting and began to collect twigs. He dropped them on the superheated ground. Edelline-Lan did the same. As wet as they were, they straight away burst into flame. Soon they had a modest but merrily crackling fire. After that they became more ambitious. Phaid cut down a fairly substantial length of branch with his blaster, then Edelline-Lan burned it into more manageable lengths with hers.

'This is fun!'

It was also wasteful and produced a lot of charred and flaming debris.

'If it wasn't snowing, we'd probably start a forest fire.'

For a while they played like destructive children, hacking at the trees with the flames of their blasters. By the time that they had exhausted themselves they had a substantial campfire and more wood to spare. The two of them settled by the fire, one on either side of the seemingly catatonic Chrystiana-Nex, warming their hands and generally revelling in a very primitive sense of achievement.

Phaid rummaged in his pack and produced two self heat food containers. He pulled the pins on both of them and waited until the seals burst, then handed one to Edelline-Lan. She unclipped the attached spoon and tasted it. Her face twisted into a grimace.

'What is it?'

'It said vegetable stew on the outside.'

'You could have fooled me.'

'You don't get gourmet emergency rations.'

'Why not, don't people of wealth and breeding get stranded in the cold?' Edelline-Lan nodded towards Chrystiana-Nex. 'Do you think we ought to feed her?'

Phaid passed his container under the ex-president's nose. She showed no flicker of reaction. Phaid shook his head.

'Why bother? She's in a world of her own. Even if we tried, she'd probably spill most of it all over herself.'

Once the food was finished, Phaid leaned back against the bank and smiled.

'You know something? This could be a lot worse.'

'I wouldn't like to make a habit of it.'

Phaid rummaged in his pocket and pulled out one of the vials of scholomine.

'I don't think it would be too good an idea for us to both fall asleep at the same time. I'm going to take some of this and keep watch. How about you?'

'Are you asking me to choose between a hit of scholomine and a nap on the cold hard ground?'

'Yeah, I suppose I was.'

'You've got to be fucking crazy.'

They both dropped substantial amounts into their eyes. The cold retreated and the frozen forest was transformed into a fairyland specially created for their pleasure. The fire danced in dazzling bursts of red and yellow and Phaid, in his heightened state, felt that he could recognise the unique configuration of each individual snowflake. He smiled at Edelline-Lan. She smiled back at him. He smiled at Chrystiana-Nex. As usual, she didn't respond.

In this instance, it made Phaid unutterably sad.

'She really ought to be seeing all this. It's much too wonderful to miss.'

Edelline-Lan nodded. There was a faraway look in her eyes.

'Much too wonderful.'

For the second time that day Phaid prised open Christiana-Nex's eyelids and dropped scholomine into her eyes. This time the effect was not so dramatic. She remained motionless for nearly a minute. Then she sat up and hugged her knees.

'What a beautiful fire. I do like scholomine.'

Both Phaid and Edelline-Lan nodded. They were as high as kites. A large tear ran down the ex-president's cheek.

'I wasn't always president, you know. It was a long hard road to get there. I had to do a lot of things that they now hold against me. I didn't have any choice. I had to fight.'

Phaid nodded.

'We've all had to fight.'

Chrystiana-Nex gave no sign that she had heard him.

'Do you know what becomes of the third daughter of the fourth wife of a high plains nomad? She is nothing more than a slave to her father. "Crya fetch water." I was Crya then. I didn't get to be Chrystiana-Nex until Hogarn-Nex took me, first for his mistress and then as his wife. I was always cleverer than Hogarn-Nex. That's why he had to die. I made a much better president. Everybody said so. Of course, that was in the times when they loved me; when they worshipped the ground that I walked on.'

Phaid leaned behind the ex-president and whispered to Edelline-Lan.

'Have you ever seen her like this before?'

'Never. She seems to be letting it all flow out of her.'

'Do you think we should do something about it?'

'Yeah, we should shut up and listen, this could be fascinating stuff.'

Chrystiana-Nex gave no sign that she had heard their whispered conversation. She went on talking to no one in particular.

'It was "Crya watch the veebelings," "Crya serve your brothers," "Crya you spilled my wine," "Crya bare your back," "Crya kneel, Crya scream, Crya crawl away and nurse your stripes." The young bucks would come by on

444

their big flippers to court my sisters and half-sisters. They would smile. My sisters would smile. My half-sisters would smile. My father would smile most of all. And me? I would hide. I wanted a young buck to come by to court me. I ached. I wanted so badly that my body revolted, but I still hid. Then there was the night I ran away. I stole food, a little money and I ran. I knew my father would beat me to death if he caught me. The third daughter of a fourth wife has no value among the wanderers of the high plains.'

She paused for a moment as if catching her breath and then the torrent of words started again.

'But he didn't catch me. The drovers caught me instead. They took me to the city. Oh Lords, how they took me, all the way to the city. A line of them every night. All the way to the city. I didn't fight. I didn't scream. I got to the city. They took me in the city, too. I danced with bells on my ankles, naked with bells on my ankles. Naked with eyes crawling all over my body. The drovers had stopped me wanting. The drovers had stopped me aching. I danced with bells on my ankles and eyes on my body. I'd learned everything those drovers knew.'

There was another pause. Her voice grew quiet and her delivery slowed by at least half.

'Then there were the other things I did. The dark things, the hot moist things, the things I did that couldn't be thought about while I was doing them. The things that hurt, the things that made me throw up after I'd done them. I was still young. A lot of them, the hands and the mouths and the teeth, forgot how young I was. That's not quite true. They all knew how young my body was. They never bothered to think that my mind might have still retained a trace of its innocence. They thought that I could take it all, and I suppose the truth was that I could.'

Pitch, intensity and speed began to build up again.

'There was the colonel in the secret police. I changed all the ranks because of him, after I came to power. I even changed the uniforms. I didn't want to be reminded. He had me dress up in furs and . . . and then he passed me on to his superior. He had me hung up in a cage. They all passed me on. Crya the notorious, Crya the desirable, Crya the adaptable. Now Crya is mad, but then, ah then. They passed me up the line until Nex had me. Nex, next, Nex who thought he was so inventive, so perverted and who was really so dull. Nex was only exciting, only perverted because he had the power. He thought he could own me, control me, keep me away from the others. In fact, I owned him, I controlled him, I didn't want the others but I got them to kill him. Then I had the power and the whole world loved me.'

Phaid shook his head as though he could hardly believe what he was hearing.

'This is incredible!'

'Then *he* came and it really didn't matter. He didn't want my body. He didn't want to chain me or dress me or lick my shoes. He could get right inside my mind. He could make me see visions, wonderful visions of glory.'

'Is she talking about Solchaim?'

'I think she must be.'

'And then he went. He took the visions and he went away and the mob came and . . what was that?'

It took Phaid a few moments to realise that Chrystiana-Nex had snapped back into the present and was talking to him directly.

'What was what?'

'Listen.'

'It's only the rustling of the trees.

'There's more.'

Phaid started to ease his blaster out of its holder. Edelline-Lan did the same. Something big and grey-blue moved at the very extreme of the firelight, going at a swift loping run. It was a big, doglike thing, but bigger than any dog Phaid had encountered. Then there was a high, mournful howl.

'Lupes! That's all we needed! Lords know what a pack of lupes is going to do to us.'

26

'SOON WE will come.'

The voice, if indeed it was a voice, floated from between the dark trees. Phaid thought he could see baleful eyes watching from beyond the ring of firelight.

'We will eat of you, humans.'

As with most animals, it was hard to tell whether the sound of the lupe's voice was heard by the ears or somehow sensed inside the mind.

'It is cold and we hunger.'

Phaid tossed another length of branch on to the fire. A cloud of sparks billowed up into the frozen air.

'But you are afraid of our fire.'

'We are afraid of your fire, but your fire will die and then it will not protect you.'

Phaid thought he could just make out one of the big doglike shapes moving closer to the outer fringe of the light.

'A lot of you will die before you kill us.'

'Such is the nature of the pack. Some die, but the others survive.'

'Are you the leader of this pack?'

'The pack has no leader.'

Edelline-Lan gripped Phaid's arm.

'Is it true that lupes won't attack while there is fire?'

Phaid nodded.

'That's right, but sooner or later the fire's going to go out, either when we want to move or when we have to go too far afield to get more wood.'

'We've got our blasters.'

'I wouldn't bet on our chances of stopping a whole pack of lupes. It only needs one to jump on your back and it's all over. Do you know how big those things are?'

'They're only big dogs.'

'They're twice the size of the biggest dog that you've ever seen. Two of them can pull down a bull veebe, and even a cub could probably snap your neck.'

'I'm frightened.'

Phaid put his arm around her.

'Believe me, honey, so am I.'

Phaid was grateful that Chrystiana-Nex had gone quiet directly the first howl of a lupe had been heard. He couldn't have handled both her and the animals. He turned to Edelline-Lan.

'Did you think to bring any booze from the train?'

She looked at him as though she didn't like his tone.

'I brought some brandy. It seemed like a sensible idea.'

'Will you give it to me?'

'Are you cold?'

'No, I want to marinate myself before the lupes eat me.'

'Don't joke.'

'I'm not.'

Phaid swallowed a hefty gulp of the liquor and waited for the burn to come. When it did, he gasped. Edelline-Lan looked at him questioningly.

'Are you really going to get drunk?'

Phaid held up the bottle.

'Sadly there's not enough here.'

He handed it back to her and she too drank. It didn't change the worried expression on her face.

'Do you think that there's a chance that the lupes might give up waiting for the fire to go out and move on of their own accord?'

The voice of the lupe pack answered before Phaid had a chance to speak.

'You humans have killed many of us and you have taken too many of our hunting grounds. We are cold and hungry and we have nowhere to go. There is nothing for us to eat here but you. We will not move on.'

Edelline-Lan swallowed hard.

'Phaid, it's horrible.'

Phaid took another drink. He spat some brandy into the fire and it flared up.

'We still have the fire at the moment. Maybe when the dawn comes things will look different.'

Phaid was aware that he probably didn't sound very convincing. For a while they sat in silence. Edelline-Lan stared wistfully into the fire.

'The world will never be the same again. Most of the court is dead. Roni-Vows has been captured and I'm in a forest surrounded by lupes. What's going on, Phaid?'

Phaid shrugged and drank some more brandy.

'I don't want to sound unkind, but in a lot of ways you're getting what you deserve.'

'Were we that bad?'

'To a peasant starving on the northside, you were that bad.'

'Nobody asked them to come to the northside and starve.'

Phaid shook his head.

'What can I tell you, when you say it all yourself.'

'I don't understand.'

'I don't think you ever will.'

Edelline-Lan didn't say anything and Phaid went back to staring into the fire. A lupe howled as though reminding them that he and his family were still there.

'Do you know what happened to Abrella-Lu?'

Phaid, despite the cold and the lupes, had almost nodded off. Edelline-Lan repeated the question.

'Do you know what happened to Abrella-Lu?'

Phaid grunted.

'She got me thrown in jail and almost executed, that's what happened.'

'No, I mean after that.'

'I should care, but, strangly enough, I do know what happened to her. The rebels have her on a chain gang back in the city. I saw her one time. She was stripped to the waist and humping rubble. There was a big woman with a whip in charge of the gang. I figured that maybe I could have got her off it, me being the hero and all, but I didn't. I thought she might as well stay there. It was good exercise and she would probably have worked out a way to enjoy it. She has an almost limitless capacity for perversion.'

'You really hate her, don't you.'

Phaid sighed.

'Hate her? I don't know. It takes a lot of energy to hate.

449

She almost got me killed. Yeah, I guess I hate her.'

A lupe howled and Edelline-Lan shivered.

'You're very weird.'

Phaid nodded vigorously.

'Damn right I'm weird. That's why I'm sitting in the snow, surrounded by lupes that intend to eat me when the fire goes out. That's why I'm helping a totally demented tyrant to escape the slow and painful death that she so justly deserves. You can bet your ass that I'm weird.'

Edelline-Lan fell silent. Phaid took another slug from the bottle and sank deeper into his coat.

Just before dawn the snow had petered out and the wind had dropped. It made the forest a little more tolerable. A strip of grey was visible in the eastern sky.

Phaid, who once again had been coldy dozing, raised a chilly eyebrow and wondered whether the fire would still deter the lupes once it was daylight. He estimated that they'd find out in a little more than a half-hour. Edelline-Lan had her eyes shut and was breathing very softly. He wondered if he ought to wake her and make his peace. The sour note that they had struck seemed a bad one on which to die. On the other hand, it also seemed a pity to let her see the bad news before it was absolutely necessary.

Phaid was still deliberating when a loud crack made him sit upright. A lupe screamed and a flight of birds panicked into the air. There were more cracks and more screams. Someone or something was attacking the lupe pack. Phaid could just make out some of the big dog shapes slinking away through the trees. Two more human shapes were silhouetted against the lightening strip of sky. The shapes became fur-clad men. They stepped into the firelight.

'Be thee all right, chum?'

Phaid scrambled to his feet and looked bemusedly at the newcomers.

'Yes, we're okay, but we're damn glad to see you.'

The two men made Makartur look civilised. They were dressed from head to foot in greasy wolf pelts and stained, cracked leather. Heavy fur caps were pulled down over their eyes and the rest of their faces were obscured by full blond beards and drooping, braided moustaches. About the only part of them that was exposed to the air was the red skin around their piercing blue eyes.

There was an older man and a younger one. The elder

of the two seemed to hold the authority. Phaid suspected
that they might be father and son. They both cradled long
barrelled projectile guns. The weapons were very old, but
lovingly cared for. The older of the hunters jerked a slide
on the underside of his gun's stock. A spent magazine flew
out. It dropped into the snow. He slammed in a fresh one
and then gathered up the discard and tucked it carefully
into his furs.

'Can't waste nothing in these here parts.'

'No, I suppose not.'

Phaid didn't know exactly what he was supposed to say.
The son, if indeed that was what he was, stretched out a
hand to Phaid's blaster. At first Phaid thought he was
going to disarm him. Then he realised that he only wanted
to examine the weapon. Phaid eased it out of its holster
and handed it over. The son hefted it and then passed it
back with a grin.

'Blaster no good for lupes.'

Phaid put the blaster away.

'Burns up the fur?'

'That's right. No good for lupes.'

The father seemed to have had enough. He shifted his
gun from one arm to another.

'Go thee south?'

'Yes . . . south, south to Bluehaven.'

The older man grunted.

'Thee's well armed, but . . .' He fingered Phaid's coat,
'Thee'll freeze for sure.'

Edelline-Lan chose exactly that moment to wake up.
She saw the two men and started. She let out a short
squeal.

'Wha?'

'Hunters. They drove off the lupes.' He looked back at
the father. 'You are hunters, aren't you?'

He nodded.

'Hunters, aye. We hunt lupes, sell the pelts in Fasbhad
and Bluehaven.'

The son was looking at Edelline-Lan and Chrystiana-
Nex with interest.

'Women.'

It was a flat statement. Phaid bit his lip.

'Ah . . . yeah.'

He wondered what the sexual *mores* were among lupe
hunters. He was relieved that the young hunter didn't

simply seize the women by the hair and drag them away. At least they were a little more civilised. Exactly how civilised remained to be found out. While the son was looking at the women, the older hunter was giving Phaid a hard scrutiny.

'Thee have name?'

'Phaid.'

'Phaid?'

'That's right.'

'Hill name?'

'That's right.'

'But thee cityite?'

'Yeah, well . . .' Phaid didn't like this cross examination '. . . I was born in the hills but I went to the city.'

'I never bin to hills, city neither.' The hunter wasn't exactly scintillating, but he did come straight to the point. 'Thee go south a' Bluehaven.'

'Yes.'

'Thee don't. Thee die first.'

'You think so?'

'I know so. Thee hasna' cold suits.'

'Is there anything that you could do to help us?'

'Thee pay?'

Now Phaid was on territory that he fully understood.

'Yes. We pay.'

The older hunter nodded.

'We go Bluehaven. You pay, we take. We sell thee cold suits. Agree?'

'Agree.'

It was quite light. The son had dragged three dead lupes to near the fire and was starting the skinning process.

'We hear they talking t' thee. That's how we find pack.'

The father moved to help with the skinning. Phaid turned away. Although lupe skinning was probably, in its way, a very skilled art, it was particularly unlovely to watch. Finally, when they were through and the son was bundling up the pelts that still steamed in the cold dawn air, the father came back to Phaid.

'Me Traan. Him Doofed. Him me son.'

So they were father and son. By the father's tone, Phaid was led to believe that Doofed might not be quite the son that Traan had hoped for.

Doofed hoisted the pelts on to his massive shoulders. Phaid got Edelline-Lan and Chrystiana-Nex up and on their feet. He looked questioningly at Traan.

'Where do we go?'

'We go back t' camp.'

The hunters set a brisk pace that soon had Phaid puffing and gasping. Fortunately, the camp wasn't too far away. It had been pitched in a small clearing. A ramshackle wagon powered by a basic flipper drive unit was both the hunters' dwelling and transport. Two women had a small fire going. Food was cooking in a blackened pot that hung over the fire from an iron tripod. When the hunters' women saw their men coming they ran to meet them. Then they spotted Phaid and his company and hesitated. They seemed wary and even hostile towards strangers.

Phaid wondered unkindly what passed for courtship and sex appeal among these primitive, cold land hunters. It was almost impossible to tell the women from the men, they were so thickly bundled in shapeless furs. Admittedly the women didn't wear beards and plaited moustaches, but they did have the lower half of their faces covered with brightly coloured knitted masks, which amounted to the same kind of facial concealment.

The hunters' mobile home was, as far as Phaid was concerned, a much more fascinating sight. Running on four long, polished skids, it was a unique combination of stripped down technical function and primitive decoration. The moving parts were all old, but as equally well looked after as the hunters' antique guns. It was obvious that they took more pride in their mechanical skills than any big city tech.

The front of the machine was the handler's position. To simplify the controls, he straddled the drive unit, sitting in a kind of bulky saddle, enclosed in plexiglass to protect him against the weather.

Behind the driver was the main body of the wagon, a ramshackle, boxlike affair constructed from wood and more plexiglass and held together by plasteel bands. The construction was neither particularly ingenious nor even very sound. What started Phaid inspecting the vehicle so carefully was the mass of intricate decoration that almost completely covered it.

Almost every piece of woodwork was rich with tiny detailed carvings. The hunters' graphic representation may have been crude, but both their industry and imagination were prodigious. If the carvings were anything to go by, the lupe hunters' mythology was complex, diverse and often verged on the nightmarish. Giant lupes menaced tiny human figures, mythical scaled and clawed beasts were locked in mortal combat. Birds with flat, axeblade wings roosted in intricate intertwining trees that bore exotic flowers and were protected by vicious thorns. In the middle of the foliage, athletic and sometimes double jointed couples, trios and quartets engaged in complicated fornication. The whole lush panorama seemed to be presided over by a number of grinning demons with pot bellies and enormous sexual organs.

Phaid was just starting to try and work out what kind of people he had fallen in with when he was tugged back to the matters at hand by two new arrivals. He had assumed the hunting band was comprised of just the father, son and the two women. The arrival of two more men meant that he had to rearrange his calculations.

Traan quickly introduced the newcomers.

'Him and him other sons. Him Dwayne and him Dunle.'

Phaid noticed that he had not been told the names of either of the hunters' women, nor did Traan expect any formal introduction to Edelline-Lan or Chrystiana-Nex. On the other hand the three sons openly stared at the two city women, doing absolutely nothing to conceal their basic and obvious intentions. Phaid hoped that this wasn't going to cause complications.

He had no time to ponder the problem, though. The hunters seemed set for a quick meal and then an early start for the south. Before this could happen, Traan felt obliged to negotiate a price for passage and protection to Bluehaven. As with so many primitive peoples, haggling had developed to high and baroque art. It took Phaid the best part of an hour to pay a small fortune for a set of three, smelly fur suits and three cold sets that consisted of a chest heater unit and a mask, hood and air filter to be used in the worst of the cold.

Phaid had expected, particularly in view of the large sum of money that he had handed over, that the three of them would ride inside the hunters' wagon. Directly the band started south it became clear that everyone except Traan and his women, who took turns driving the machine, was expected to walk. The wagon's engine was solar powered without any sort of back-up. This meant that, with only the pale chilly sunlight to drive it, it only made an agonisingly slow pace, even without any passengers riding on it.

While they were still following the trail in the comparative shelter of the forest, the trek wasn't too wretched, but, as the trees dwindled and gave way to open fell, walking turned into an exposed freezing trudge. It didn't help to know that the weather would get colder and more violent all the way to Bluehaven.

It wasn't only the temperature that reminded the travellers that they were getting closer and closer to the ice plains. Now that they were out on the endless white of the rolling fells, it was possible to see the band of purple cloud on the horizon. It twisted an contorted in a constant shift of a million never repeating, tortured shapes. It marked the path of the furious gales that continuously ripped at the icy landscape.

Phaid knew that all too soon he would be crossing those gales and his only protection would be an ice boat that could be anything up to five hundred years old. It seemed inconceivable to Phaid that there was no way that he could avoid constantly getting into these absurd and hazardous situations.

One of the problems about a forced march across the fells was that it gave Phaid an awful lot of time for thought and reflection. There was nothing to do except wearily place one foot in front of the other. There was nothing to look at beyond the ominous clouds and the featureless, snowbound countryside. There was nothing to hear, either, except the wagon creaking and groaning as its drive unit laboriously dragged it across the snow.

All one could do was to keep pace with the wagon and not fall behind. Beyond that, each of the travellers was lost in his or her own thoughts and at the mercy of his or her private fears. Distractions were few. During the icy and tedious afternoon, a flock of birds came over, flying high in V-formation, heading north, away from the cold. Everyone, including the hunters, stopped and stared upwards. The wearisome trudge didn't resume until the birds had completely vanished from sight.

If the days were tedious and exhausting, the nights hardly qualified either as havens of warmth and relaxation. Traan and his woman kept the wagon strictly to themselves. The three sons and Phaid's party were expected to sleep outside, huddled around the fire, shivering even though they were draped in thick lupehide robes and had their chest heaters turned full up.

After two nights on the trail, Chrystiana-Nex started climbing into the same robe as one or another of Traan's sons. Phaid even suspected that she might have switched brothers during the night. He was at a loss to even guess at what she found alluring in Doofed, Dwayne or Dunle. As far as he was concerned, the brothers were smelly, inarticulate throwbacks and he strongly felt that the ex-president was either capriciously playing with fire or up to something exceedingly devious.

One dreary morning, when they were stumbling wearily behind the wagon, making their way through particularly deep snow, Phaid decided to question her on the subject. Chrystiana-Nex had bristled and told him that it was none of his business. Under more normal circumstances, Phaid would have merely shrugged and dropped the whole subject. Out in the frozen tundra, however, Chrystiana-Nex's sex life might be a serious factor on everybody's chances of survival.

'You have to realise that these hunters are, at best, semi-savage. They seem to believe that they own their own women and, as far as I can see, if you go on fooling around with those three there's likely to be an explosion.'

'An explosion might do a lot to alleviate the boredom.'

Phaid started to get angry.

'You can alleviate your boredom once I've delivered you to that Tharmier banker and collected my money. Until then you do what I say.'

Chrystiana-Nex scowled. Since they'd started their long march across the snow her bouts of withdrawal had grown less and less frequent and, although her behaviour left a lot to be desired, she was acting more like a normal being; right at that moment, like a furious human being.

'So you think you're in charge of this little expedition, do you?'

'Sure I do.'

'And I suppose you think you know about nomads.'

'A little.'

'And young men too?'

'I was one.'

'Do you really believe that by having us women keep ourselves to ourselves it's going to avoid trouble from those three young idiots?'

'That's the general idea.'

Chrystiana-Nex's lip curled.

'Well, Master Phaid, that would seem to demonstrate just how little you know, and probably just how unfitted you are to lead anything. You say you understand young men and nomads. You know nothing. I was brought up among nomads and I've been manipulating young men all my life.'

'I can imagine that.'

'Oh, you can sneer, Master Phaid, but if I'd done what you wanted those three would have killed you by now. They would have raped Edelline-Lan and me and then either killed us or forcibly made us their wives.'

Phaid didn't like this theory one bit.

'Traan would never . . .'

'Traan wouldn't give a damn. He's got your money and, while he wouldn't actively break his word to take us to Bluehaven, if the sons started causing trouble, I doubt he would stop them, particularly if two of them wound up owning brand new slave wives.'

Phaid looked quite rueful.

'I never thought of it that way.'

'Of course you didn't. That's because you're a man. Doing this my way makes those three fools think that I'm some sort of wonderful novelty. They don't know what's going to happen next. I can wrap them round my little finger.'

'What about me? Aren't they liable to see me as some sort of threat?'

Chrystiana-Nex looked at him in surprise.

'You? Good Lords no. They think that you're some sort of ineffectual pimp. They aren't worried about you at all.'

Phaid raised both eyebrows.

'I'm not sure I like that idea.'

Chrystiana-Nex stopped in her tracks and regarded him scornfully.

'As usual the male ego would risk anything, even death, rather than not be thought of as the most splendid fellow in the world.'

'Wait a minute . . .'

'You know it's true.'

Phaid walked in silence for a while and thought about what she had said to him. Life had been a great deal simpler when he'd been able to think of Chrystiana-Nex as a simple, mindless tyrant.

After a lot more silent walking, Chrystiana-Nex smiled brightly at Phaid.

'Did I ever tell you how I made pain so fashionable in the city?'

Phaid sighed and shook his head.

'No, you never did.'

He stared out across the monotonous snow and profoundly wished that he had stayed in the jungle.

At least once a day, the sons would put on skis, sling their guns over their backs and take off on a scouting trip. Phaid really couldn't see the point of these expeditions. the fells were so blank and featureless that it was hardly likely that anything was going to sneak up on them and, so long as they kept the purple clouds in front of them, they had to be in roughly the right direction. It also seemed there was nothing out there for them to kill, a suggestion that received confirmation from the fact they never returned with any game. On the fifth afternoon, however, they did come back with some news.

Traan related this news to Phaid who was tramping along at some distance from the wagon, lost in thought. He fell into step beside him.

'Could it be anyone follow thee?'

Phaid started.

'What?'

'Could it be anyone follow thee?'

'Follow me?'

'Thee and thy women.'

Phaid knew he had to expect some sort of pursuit. Makartur, for one, was not the kind to give up and let them go when he didn't catch them on the line train. Nonetheless, the news took him completely by surprise. He stalled for time, wondering how much it would be safe to let the old hunter known about his troubles.

'Are you telling me that there's someone following us?'

'Two o' 'em.'

'You're kidding.'

'Kid thee not.'

This was something of a shock to Phaid. He had expected Makartur to be coming after him, but he couldn't imagine who the second pursuer might be.

'When you say there are two of them, do you mean two

people, or two groups?'

'Furthest away are a pair, two o' 'em. They still cast around as though seeking a trail. They got flipper an' it lucky we got wind to cover our tracks, otherwise they catch us pretty damn quick, yes sir.'

'And the other?'

'Just one o' him. He real near. He keep pace with us but don't move in. It strange, damn strange if you ask me.'

Phaid didn't know what to make of this second, nearby pursuer. It wouldn't be like Makartur to hold off and keep pace with the hunters. Makartur would be straight in for the kill. Assuming that it wasn't Makartur, didn't, however, make Phaid any happier. There was something sinister and unnatural about the way whoever was out there simply kept pace and made no move. It made Phaid paranoid. What also made him paranoid was the way that Traan was looking at him.

'Thee'd be smart to tell me all thee know.'

'What are you talking about? How the hell should I know who's following us?'

'Thee cons me.'

'Listen, I . . .'

'Thee cons me!'

Phaid and Traan both halted. Phaid didn't like the way that Traan was holding his gun.

'There was a spot of trouble back in the city.'

'Cityite trouble?'

'Yeah, you could call it that.'

'Trouble cost thee extra.'

They both started walking again. Phaid gazed up at the clear blue sky. Now that Traan had mentioned money, Phaid saw he might be able to turn the situation to his advantage. He looked speculatively at the old hunter.

'What exactly does this extra money buy us?'

'It stop me dumping thee in the snow right now.'

'Nothing more?'

'Depends on what thee willing t' pay, my chumee. What more did thee have in thy mind?'

Phaid flexed his fingers inside his gloves.

'Why don't we look at it this way. Say whoever is out there wanted to come and take me and the women. What would you do?'

'I'd have a choice, wouldn't I?'

'You would?'

'I could have my boys run 'em off or I let 'em take thee.'

'And I suppose the price would determine what your boys did, right?'

'Thee catches on right fast.'

'So what is the price?'

Traan named the price. Phaid haggled a little and then settled. He knew that the hunter probably thought that he was robbing Phaid, but even the first price that he had named was ludicrously low by city standards.

Feeling much happier to have four experienced guns between him and whatever was after him, he made one further request.

'Suppose your boys were to go out and maybe scout out these people who are after us.'

'That would cost thee a lot more.'

Traan named a higher sum. To Phaid, it was still absurdly cheap. He haggled for a while, just for the sake of good form, and then he agreed.

It was decided that the scouting expedition should be made the same night, immediately after dark had fallen. There were some protests from the three sons. At least one of them probably had planned a nocturnal adventure with Chrystiana-Nex and none of them seemed to relish a night spent skiing around in the icy darkness. Traan, however, brooked no arguments where money was concerned and, as the light was fading, the sons were dispatched on their enforced mission.

They were to make the longer journey first, all the way to where Phaid hoped the pair of supposed pursuers were still casting about for a trail. Once they had taken a good look at the couple in the flipper, they would swing back to check on their nearer shadow.

Phaid had pointed out that it would have been quicker to send one son on the long trip and the other two on the shorter one, but the brothers flatly refused to be split up, and Traan didn't force the point. After a single appeal to a sense of efficiency, Phaid let the hunters plan their own expedition.

Once the sons had vanished into the darkness, Traan went back to the wagon and Phaid to the fire. Wrapped in their lupehide robes, Chrystiana-Nex was distant and withdrawn, but Edelline-Lan was anxious to know what was going on.

'Where have the idiot sons gone? Are you up to

something, Phaid?'

'We're being followed.'

'Who's following us?'

'It's not a who, it's a they; a pair of them some way off and another one shadowing us just out of sight.'

'But who are they?'

'I don't know, that's what the idiot sons have gone to find out.'

Edelline-Lan looked even more anxious.

'I don't like the sound of this.'

'I don't like it either, but I'm happier now I've paid Traan to put his sons between us and anyone who comes after us.'

'You think it's the rebels?'

'I think it's a character called Makartur.'

'Is he after the president?'

Phaid nodded.

'Yeah, he'd like to take her head back with him, but he's also got a grudge against me.'

'Could this Makartur get past Traan and his sons?'

'I don't know. They're all basically the same kind. Makatur's a barbarian from the hills. If anyone could do it, it would probably be him.'

'You don't sound very optimistic.'

'I'm not. I'm just hoping that they don't pick up our trail, and don't get lucky and guess we're making for Bluehaven. Beyond that, all you can do is to sleep lightly and keep your blaster handy.'

'It's that bad?'

'I don't think it's ever really been much better.' Phaid nodded towards Chrystiana-Nex. 'What's the matter with her?'

'I don't know. She was quite normal earlier, then she suddenly snapped off, you know the way she does that blank out.'

It was a long, tense night waiting for Traan's sons to return. Instead of staying all night in the wagon, the old hunter twice came and sat by the fire. He had no conversation, and his face gave nothing away, but Phaid could sense that he was anxious for them to return safely.

Edelline-Lan slept fitfully. Phaid didn't bother at all. He just huddled down in his robe and watched the flames dance and the sparks shoot upward. His blaster was never far from his hand.

As far as Phaid could estimate, it was somewhere between midnight and dawn when he saw something out in the snow. He had been looking into the heart of the fire so long that he couldn't be sure if there really was a black space out on the snowfield, or whether it was simply an after-image of the flames. He nudged Edelline-Lan awake.

'Can you see something out there?'

'Wha? Out where?'

She sat up, rubbed her eyes and looked again.

'I don't know. Maybe something black against the snow. It's hard to tell.'

'I think I'll wake up Traan, I'd rather be safe than sorry.'

He hurried round the wagon and beat on the door.

'Traan! Wake up!'

Traan didn't need a second call. The door to the wagon flew open and he was there, fully dressed with his gun in his hand.

'What's the matter? Are they back?'

'I don't know. There seems to be something moving out on the snow. I think we ought to go and take a look.'

Traan didn't ask any unnecessary questions.

'Thee wait.' In an instant he was back with a lamp. 'Thee show me.'

Phaid drew his blaster and they walked cautiously away from the little camp. Out of the firelight, it was easier to distinguish the dark object against the snow. It looked like a huddled bundle that someone or something had inexplicably dumped there. Phaid was just starting to wonder whether it might be a rock or something perfectly natural when it uttered a faint, but distinctly human cry of pain.

Traan broke into a run. Phaid followed. Stumbling and tripping through the deep snow, they reached the thing at the same time. To Phaid's horror, the thing was Traan's son Dwayne. He was covered in blood and a portion of his stomach seemed to have been shot away. Dwayne clutched at his father as he knelt down beside him.

'Pa, I'm burned in th' gut, Pa. I'm dying for sure. Help me, Pa, I'm dying. Thee got to help me.'

'Where are the others?'

'They dead, Pa.

'We scouted th' first pair, they was a big hill man an' a

462

woman. Tha' weren't no trouble. They was camped for the night, an' didn't look as though they was gon' move till morn, so we covered our tracks and came back. It was when we went to look at th' other 'un. That's when our trouble started.'

Dwayne coughed and blood ran down his chin.

'It hurts me, Pa. I'm dyin' right enough.'

'What about the other one?'

'I tell thee, Pa. He's a devil. He hadn't made no camp. He was just sittin' in th' snow as though he didna' feel th' cold or nothin'. Dundle said why didn't we shoot him an' save ourselves a lot of trouble. Then, at that moment, his gun blew up in his hands. It just blew up, Pa, an' then there's blaster fire just everywhere. Doofed got it in th' head. He died straight away. Me, I got burned in the gut. I tell thee, Pa, that ain't no man out there. It's a devil, it's a snow demon, it's . . .'

A hideous choking sound came from deep inside the boy's chest. His head fell back. Traan looked at Phaid.

'He's dead!'

'I'm sorry.'

'All my sons are dead.'

'I said I'm sorry.'

'Sorry? Sorry? What kind of man are you that snow demons dog your trail and my sons have to die for you?' The hunter was getting to his feet. 'What kind of man are you?'

The gun was coming up. Phaid didn't want to hurt the grief stricken Traan but there seemed to be no other way. His blaster roared. Traan spun around and fell beside his son. Phaid took a long look at the dead hunters. Then he quickly turned away and stumbled back to the fire and the wagon. He grabbed Edelline-Lan by the shoulder and started shaking her.

'Get up! Get up! The hunters are all dead and I think Solchaim is nearby.'

Edelline-Lan started struggling out of her fur robe.

'What should I do?'

'Keep the hunters' women inside the wagon. I'm going to try something.'

During the long days of tramping across the snow, Phaid had noticed that what he had been thinking of as a single vehicle really wasn't, the wagon wasn't one fully integrated machine. In fact, it was a trailer drawn by a stripped down flipper. They were joined by just two steel struts. Phaid suspected that if he cut through these with his blaster, the front end of the wagon, the driver's cab, would make an old but perfectly serviceable flipper.

Accordingly, Phaid took careful aim and started cutting. He could hear shouting from the rear of the wagon. Phaid knew that he had to leave Edelline-Lan to deal with the hunters' women, he had enough to worry about.

The biggest problem was that even if the makeshift flipper did prove to be able to put out a turn of speed when it was cut loose from the burden of the rest of the wagon, it still wouldn't move until the sun was in the sky. Its only source of power was a single sun catcher, there was no auxillary power or even a storage block. Phaid wished that Ben-e was with them. The little android would, more than likely, have known a way to rig the flipper's drive so it would run off the energy cores of their blasters or something equally bizarre.

'You really miss that little guy.'

A cold resonant voice that wasn't his was speaking aloud the thoughts in his head. Phaid froze. The roar of the blaster stopped. His fingers which had been gripping the butt slowly started to open. They were like mechanical things, not even a part of him. The blaster dropped to the snow. Horror washed over Phaid in sickening waves. He wanted to scream, but he found that he had no voice. He wanted to run but his muscles had locked in a terrifying paralysis. As though from the other end of a long tunnel, he heard Edelline-Lan's voice.

'I had to tell the women that their men were dead. They seemed to go numb and I've locked them . . . oh no!'

She screamed. Phaid had never heard Edelline-Lan scream before. It seemed to be wrenched from deep inside her soul. In the same instant Phaid felt a momentary release from whatever was holding him. He turned and found himself facing Solchaim, the elaihi.

27

'GET OUT of my mind!'

'And yet it is so stubbornly lonely in there. Have you never longed for companionship?'

'Get out of my mind!'

'Your minds are not impregnable fortresses. One day soon you are all going to have to get used to that fact. Your desperate, busy little lives are going to have to change.'

Solchaim was like a tall skinny spider standing over Phaid, spindly arms and legs were covered in black lightweight plastic armour while his body was swathed from the cold by a tunic of black shaggy fur and a black cape with a red silk lining. Phaid could see why the hunters believed him to be a snow demon. His nose was like the beak of a sinister bird of prey and hard reptile-like eyes bored from beneath the brim of a huge black hat that flopped almost to his shoulders. The rest of his face was covered by folds of the cape. For the second time, Phaid was struck by how Solchaim seemed deliberately to make himself a composite of all that was frightening to humans. He was a spider and a snake, a vulture and a vampire. Solchaim had clothed himself in the stuff of ancient childhood nightmares, the ones that the left-hand side of the brain had saved from times even before humans came down out of the trees. Also for the second time, Phaid found that a part of Solchaim was moving around inside his mind, probing his consciousness and slithering through his memory. Phaid had never experienced anything quite as revolting. It was a violation so ultimate and so total that every nerve screamed out in revolt.

'Get out of my mind!'

Solchaim ignored Phaid's protests as he tested and tasted random samples of Phaid's stored recollections and conditioned reflexes.

'This is hurting me! For the Lords' sake!'

'Your beliefs are quite delightful.'

'Stop playing with me!'

'I'm not playing with you. I have need of you for a period of time. The hunters were a random factor that didn't occur in my calculations. I need you all the way to Bluehaven and possibly beyond. You will have to do the best that you can.'

His tone was one a man might use when informing his dog that it was being taken for a walk. Phaid knew that he couldn't take much more of the treatment. He did his best to communicate this to the elaihi as forcefully as he could. Solchaim chuckled.

'Maybe this would be better?'

Abruptly Phaid was gripped by a sensation of spiralling upward. The night and the snow had vanished. Phaid could no longer see the dead hunters' wagon or the camp. Even his clothes had gone. He was cocooned in a voluptuous orange glow that warmed and comforted him. He stretched languidly. It felt so good.

'Is that more to your taste?'

The words were like a caress. Solchaim was still inside Phaid's mind, but now he was acting more like a lover than an invader. His presence there was a gentle, pleasurable massage. It took minutes for Phaid to realise that it was just a piece of psychic sleight of hand.

'Why do you hate us so much?'

'When are you going to understand that we don't hate you. If anything we fear you, in the way that you fear the lupe or the rat or the poisonous snake. You have a history of killing all that you think will impede what you call your progress. You destroy anything that might challenge your self proclaimed status as rulers of the planet. You are feral, isolated creatures and you pose a great danger.'

Faster than the blink of an eye. Phaid was back at the camp, seated by the fire. His arms and legs felt heavy and lethargic. It was hard to move. He tried to stand, but only succeeded in falling over on his side. His face was in the snow but it didn't seem to matter. Some of the soft orange warmth was still with him. Out of the corner of his eye he could see that Edelline-Lan and Chrystiana-Nex seemed to be experiencing similar difficulties. Solchaim was standing in the middle of them. His face was covered and it was impossible to judge what he thought of his handiwork. Phaid, after some considerable effort, pushed himself into a sitting position. He was completely disorientated. He found that it was impossible to gauge how long Solchaim had been at the camp.

'Why are you doing this to us?'

His lips were thick and there were parts of his mind that kept setting him off giggling. This made the rest of him furious at his lack of control. Solchaim laughed right along with him.

'I've already told you that I have need of you. I am putting a grip around your mind. I need to know how best to manipulate you. Also, we have a little time before the others come.'

Phaid's mind was spongy but he still managed to be surprised.

'There are other elaihim coming?'

Solchaim shook his head. It wasn't the way a human would do it.

'Oh no, there are no more elaihim coming. For a long time now I have failed to find favour with my own people. They do not like my methods nor my style. In fact, I am very much a creature set apart. I travel a lonely course. You humans are my only diversion.'

'Then who is coming?'

'What you believe is your destiny.'

'I don't understand.'

'No, you probably wouldn't. Makartur is coming. The furious red-haired warrior and his statuesque female. They really are a magnificent pair. He believes he must kill you in order to save his soul. It never ceases to surprise me how you are all so complex in your desperation.'

Phaid found that he couldn't be afraid. Solchaim obviously didn't want the second hand discomfort. He peered into the darkness.

'Are they far away?'

'They will be here soon. Perhaps with the sun.'

'And then?'

'Don't be afraid. How many times do I have to tell you that I need you. I won't let the warrior or his woman harm you.'

Phaid just wanted it all to stop.

'Will you tell me what is really going on?'

Again Solchaim laughed. This time the laughter was like playful cuffs to either side of Phaid's mind.

'We elaihim have a dream.'

Phaid was suddenly somewhere else. He was standing on a wide and very beautiful Plaza surrounded by some of the most magnificent buildings he had ever seen. There were elaihim everywhere, serenely going about their business. Birds flew overhead and animals moved among the elaihim without any sign of fear or tension.

Everything was cleanliness and light, it was an ideal city, unlike anything that Phaid had ever seen. Between the buildings, he could just see rolling green hills in the distance. On the other side of the Plaza a family of boohooms played and scampered. They were a total contrast to the down trodden, menial boohooms living in the bottom levels of human cities.

'This is a perfect world.'

'It is what we seek.'

'There are no people, no humans in this city.'

Directly Phaid had mentally voiced the observation, he caught sight of a human, in fact, he caught sight of two humans. A couple, a man and a woman, both naked; they sat in the sun beside a glittering fountain. Now and then a passing elaihim would toss the humans a piece of fruit or some other titbit.

'Is that how you see us?'

'That is how we all see you. The dispute is that the rest of my people would wait, they would stay away from you and wait until the time comes for the passing of the human species. The rest of my people are infinitely patient. I am not. They would wait forever, but I would gladly give you a helping hand down the path to extinction.'

One moment Phaid was riding in some huge, silver-winged flying machine, travelling with hundreds of other people, high above the clouds. The next he watched as thousands of drab green men swarmed over a nightmare landscape of mud and craters. Explosions roared around them and they faced a hail of flying metal projectiles with their arms shielding their faces as though walking against the wind and the rain.

The scene kept on shifting. Tapering cylinders of shining steel rose into the sky on pillars of flame, terrible explosions lashed the surface of the globe with flashes of awful, all consuming heat. Towers were built to the sky and then blackened and destroyed in fearsome bouts of destruction. There was incredible beauty but also immeasurable destruction. Phaid was moved to both wonder and horror, he knew if the experience went on any longer he wouldn't be able to control himself; his whole being was just fractions of an inch from being wracked by helpless sobbing.

Then, just as it seemed as though his mind was going to come to pieces, he was back by the fire with snow all round him. Solchaim was grinning into his face.

'How do you like the story of your species?'

Phaid cradled his aching head.

'All that? Mankind achieved all that?'

'All that and a lot more.'

'If we achieved all that, how can you call us inferior?'

'You destroyed as much as you built.'

'You elaihim could do better?'

'Once we have the space we will create something infinitely more worthwhile. We do not have your talent for destruction.'

'You seem to have destroyed enough in your time.'

'But I am not like the rest of my people. I am the exception.'

'You're the one that's going to give your people the room they need to grow and build?'

'You humans are in your final decline, there's no mistaking that.'

'And I suppose it's all your work.'

Solchaim laughed.

'Gracious no. I may be overweeningly vain but I'm not so deluded that I think I'm the hand of destiny. No, Master Phaid, your people, your species has fallen into its final decline all on its own. You have lost your arts, you have lost your sciences and you have lost your culture. All I can do is to grease the slide a little for your final descent.'

'How can you say that the human race is failing? We still live in the biggest cities in the world, with androids to serve us. The marikhs run the trains. Men still sail on the winds between the clouds. We still have a long way to go before the earth has seen the last of humanity.'

Solchaim's mouth twisted.

'Is that what you think? Despite all that I have shown you, you still don't understand. Your cities are shadows of what they once were. Your androids and all the rest of your technology was constructed many centuries ago. Few of you know how to even repair a flipper or an android or any of the other things of which you are so proud. There is not one among you who could build any of them from the start. Even the marikhs do not construct new trains or extend their lines. You stagnate and soon you will die. You will go to your graves watching your pointless wind games . . .'

'But the wind games. Surely they are . . .'

'They are nothing. Oh yes, maybe your individual wind players are brave and daring, but they are also stupid. They have forgotten. They are a remnant of the times that I have shown you, the time when men travelled across the surface of the water and flew through the air. Those were the days when you could truly think of yourselves as masters of the world. You flew in the air and even above the air.'

This was all getting beyond Phaid's ability to grasp.

'I don't understand what you are saying. How can anyone fly beyond the air?'

'You did it, you pathetic fool. Your insane ancestors, at the same time they were coming close to blowing up the planet, they also started their journey to the stars.'

'The stars? They tried to get to the stars?'

'They didn't try, they succeeded. They went to the stars. The best of your kind left this planet and travelled out into deep space. They inherited the stars. Your religion teaches you to worship the Lords that so mysteriously left the earth and who you hope so fervently will return. They will never return. They either live among the stars or they perished in the cold of space. From the moment they left this planet the end had started for those who were left behind. The best of you had gone. Only the dregs remained.'

Phaid shook his head as though he was unwilling to accept what the elaihi was saying.

'I can't believe all this.'

'It is not my concern whether you believe it or not. It is

470

how it is. Your belief counts for nothing.'

'It's so hard to accept. First you claim that the human race is in a state of decay, but then you tell me about their magnificient past achievements.'

'Isn't a journey to the stars magnificent enough for you?'

'Yes, but . . .'

'You also controlled the weather.'

'The weather? I don't understand.'

'Many centuries ago your scientists designed systems to order the weather. The wind and the rain were harnessed and tamed and put to use for the benefit of man.'

'But what about the ice plains and the burning deserts? This world is fragmented and cut apart by its weather.'

'That is the legacy. Once the big push into space was over, those left behind took the technology of their civilisation so much for granted that they didn't bother to maintain it in good order. Education was neglected and skills were lost. As the centuries went by, much was forgotten. The time before the exodus was looked on as a golden age. Those who had taken to space were talked about as Lords, superior beings. Then systems started to fail. No one knew how to service them. Android handlers malfunctioned and nobody knew how to replace them. The major disaster came when the weather control systems failed. The winds were free after a thousand years of servitude to man. They ripped and roared across the earth, they scorched and they froze, they destroyed everything in their path.'

'Are you telling me that the wind bands, the terrible heat and the terrible cold were only caused by our own weather control systems breaking down?'

'That's exactly what I'm telling you.'

'And the only reason that the weather control failed was because we forgot to maintain it?'

'It does have a certain poetry, doesn't it. Once the weather had gone so much else went with it. Air transport ceased, the seas were no longer navigable, communications broke down. Your civilisation was fragmenting and coming to pieces. From a world wide administration you regressed to the level of belligerent little city states. It took less than two centuries. You retreated into confusion and superstition. Ice covered your power plants and jungles grew over your space ports. The Lords were never coming home, no matter how the priests wailed and beseeched them. Humanity had started on its decline.'

Phaid started to shiver. Suddenly the cold had penetrated right into his bones. He covered his face with his hands. He was only a gambler, a parasite on the fringe of events. It wasn't his place to involve himself in the fall of cities, the apocalypse of a species. he hadn't been raised to mix with princes, presidents and devils. What was he doing on this frozen fell listening to these terrible stories from the lips of something that wasn't even human? He wanted to curl up in the snow and go to sleep. He was suddenly so tired. He didn't really care if he ever woke up again. He was aware of Edelline-Lan making clumsy and unco-ordinated movements beside him. There was, however, a strange, unsteady determination about her.

'Coming.'

Solchaim's attention flicked away from Phaid.

'So you hear it?'

Edelline-Lan's voice was slurred. She was only intelligible if she spoke very, very slowly.

'There's. . .a. . .flipper. . .coming. . .this. . .way.'

Solchaim's focus came back to Phaid.

'We will have to postpone our conversation.'

Even Phaid could hear the flipper. It was coming up fast and the sound of it managed to rouse him slightly from the numb half-sleep that he had drifted into. The first traces of the dawn were starting to show on the horizon and he could just see the dark shape of the flipper speeding across the snow towards them. He knew that the flipper could only contain two people, two people with a murderous hatred for everyone around the small fire. Somehow, though, he couldn't raise any emotion, not even a measure of fear or panic. He felt weighted down by an incredible burden of helplessness.

The flipper grounded at some distance from the little camp. For a few moments nothing moved. A faint trace of blue haze from its power unit shimmered in the frozen air and then the passenger bubble flipped up. Two fur-clad figures swung themselves out of it and dropped to a defensive crouch in the snow. As Phaid had expected, it was Makartur and Flame.

In the dawn the fells were totally drained of colour. A white sky met white snowfield with no visible seam. The arrival of Makartur and Flame was a sudden stab of dazzling red hair against the neutral background. Makartur's beard bristled and his hair rolled almost to his shoulders. Flame's hung past her waist. Her fox fur coat was almost as bright as her hair. Her legs were encased in green leather breeches and high top boots. Black goggles protected her eyes from snow blindness. Phaid found that he was partially seeing them the way Solchaim saw them. He had been right when he had described them as a pair of magnificent animals. They were so perfectly matched; lean and muscular thoroughbreds who both had the implacable, unswerving purpose of an attack hound. They had the same natural arrogance, the same set to their heads. They were proud and strong and deadly.

When, after nearly a minute, nobody had made a move against them, Makartur slowly straightened. Flame did the same. Solchaim stood waiting for them. His tall, spindly figure was slightly stooped and quite motionless. He seemed to radiate an eerie stillness. Makartur and Flame slowly and cautiously started to walk forward. Both had weapons in their hands. The stillness in the air grew diamond hard. As they moved closer to Solchaim their footfalls in the snow were inaudible. Although all three figures stood tall in comparison to other men, they seemed dwarfed against the expanse of white land and white sky. It was Makartur who finally broke the tension and silence. He halted.

'I have business with the man Phaid and the woman Chrystiana-Nex.'

It was clear that neither Makartur nor Flame had recognised Solchaim for what he was. The elaihi was staring at the ground, giving no indication that he had even heard Makartur, then he raised his head and looked at them from under the brim of his huge hat. From nowhere a small whirling wind sprang into being. It spiralled around Makartur and Flame, blowing her hair into whipping strands and making the snow dance and eddy. Makartur put up an arm to shield his eyes but stood his ground.

As suddenly as it had come, the wind was gone. Phaid had a sense of Solchaim amusedly flexing his muscles. When he spoke, however, his voice was guarded and neutral.

'That will not be possible.'

Makartur pushed back his shoulders and inflated his

chest.

'How say you, not possible?'

'I have a prior claim on their time.'

Makartur sounded dangerously calm.

'I do not know who you are, sir, but there is no claim that can take priority over this business of mine.'

'You take a lot on yourself.'

'Maybe I do, but that's as it must be. I ask you, sir, to step aside and let me do what I have to.'

Solchaim shook his head. Again, it wasn't like a human gesture.

'I have told you that what you ask is impossible.'

Makartur slowly brought up his weapon.

'Will you heed my final warning? I'll not be deflected from my purpose.'

The blaster was now pointed full at Solchaim. Makartur had fallen into the classic duellists' pose with extended arm, half turned stance. Solchaim seemed quite unconcerned.

'You can neither have the man nor the woman.'

'You'll die like a fool.'

'I doubt that.'

'Step aside.'

'No.'

'Damn you.'

Makartur stuffed his blaster back into his holster. He stomped towards Solchaim with clenched fists. Warrior honour seemed to have negated the idea of burning the unarmed Solchaim where he stood. Makartur obviously intended to tear him apart with his bare hands.

'You will step aside?'

'No.'

A massive fist swung at the elaihi's head. It seemed that it couldn't help but snap his thin neck. The blow, however, never landed. Solchaim hardly appeared to move but Makartur somersaulted in mid-air and crashed on his back in the snow. He lay breathless and confused. Flame raised her blaster.

'I don't know who you are but I don't have any warrior scruples. Stand exactly where you are or I'm going to burn you.'

Solchaim ignored both Flame's warning and also Makartur, who was attempting to scramble to his feet. He walked slowly towards her.

'Do I have to teach you the same lesson that I just taught your companion?'

'I'm telling you stay back.'

Solchaim laughed. Flame's jaw tightened. She steadied her blaster with both hands.

'One more step.'

Solchaim stepped. The blaster roared. At the same time, Solchaim made a strange hand movement. For an instant his figure was silhouetted against the flash of the blaster. When it faded there was smoke and steam where the snow had boiled away and there was the whiff of static in the air but Solchaim stood completely untouched. His amusement was echoed through Phaid's mind. Phaid wondered how much of what had happened was real and how much was hallucination. Was the elaihi really able to deflect a blaster burn? Had he simply thrown off Flame's aim or had the whole incident been a product of mind control. Once again laughter echoed and rolled through the inside of Phaid's head.

For a moment it looked like a standoff, then Makartur bellowed and his blaster roared. This time, Solchaim's arm gesture was more sweeping but it still deflected the flash. Flame fired again and the same thing happened. She took a step back. Her face was a mask of horror.

'Gods and ancestors, it's him, the abomination from the Palace. Phaid has really thrown in with the devils.'

Both she and Makartur were suddenly grabbed by a superstitious dread. Simultaneously, they both opened fire on the elaihi. He fielded the blasts as though it was a three-way juggling game played with fire and lightning. Solchaim's laugh rose above the roar of blasters, then, quite abruptly Phaid sensed that he had grown bored with the game. Makartur's blaster flew from his hand. Flame's did the same. A terrible invisible weight seemed to press down on Makartur. His shoulders bowed as he fought against it. His back bent and his face turned red. A vein in his forehead throbbed and his eyes bulged out. He was nearly blue before his legs caved in and he dropped to the snow. He tried desperately to force himself up but even his massive arms weren't equal to the task.

'Damn you! Damn you!'

'You're only fighting against your own strength.'

Flame made a dart for where her blaster lay. She lunged for it but her legs gave way as Solchaim immobilised her in the same way as he had immobilised Makartur. He must have not exerted so much power in her case. She struggled and squirmed in the snow. Her long legs thrashed and her body contorted as she inched laboriously towards her blaster. Phaid discovered that he was actually finding the spectacle quite erotic. He let a lot of dark sexual thoughts surface, hoping that it might serve to confuse the elaihi just a little. Flame almost had her hand on the weapon, but it suddenly glowed cherry red. The snow around it melted. Flame shied away from it. Her movements were those of a trapped and fallen horse. Phaid found that, via Solchaim, he was also seeing the scene through the eyes of Makartur and Flame. Solchaim was a black shape, looming between them and the cold bright rising sun, an angular mocking vulture demon from deep in their mutual ancient fears. Makartur in particular was being forced to use every measure of his will to hold down the dread and not yield to a primitive panic. Part of him was convinced that he was in conflict with a devil.

Phaid could also see the other side. He could see the elaihi's obvious satisfaction in being able to play the humans like an old familiar violin. He seemed to know man's unconscious like he knew the back of his hand. Phaid felt sick, but there wasn't a thing that he could do about it. All he could hope was that, in time, he would get so sick that Solchaim wouldn't like it inside his mind and he'd withdraw. Solchaim, however, seemed to have no intention of withdrawing. He was readying himself for the next phase of the drama, now that he had suitably subjugated and humiliated Makartur and Flame. There was a strange telepathic ripple as the elaihi's full focus turned back to Phaid, Edelline-Lan and Chrystiana-Nex.

'We will take their flipper.'

Phaid found himself getting to his feet. Edelline-Lan and the ex-president were doing the same. Makartur and Flame lay still in the snow. They could have been sleeping. The day had become very bright and again it was still. The sun was clear of the horizon by more than a hand's breadth. Phaid and the women, with a slack faced lack of will, followed Solchaim towards the flipper. Long, early morning shadows preceded them. Phaid heard Chrystiana-Nex's voice, as though from a great distance. The sound was sharp and precise and as cold as the dawn itself.

'Why have you come back? I no longer have a city to

give you.'

Solchaim turned his head. He didn't stop walking.

'Do you really think that I'd abandon you, poor little Crya?'

Chrystiana-Nex sharply drew in her breath. Phaid wanted to turn around but he couldn't. She sounded as though she was going to say something, but suddenly there was a burst of blaster fire from behind them. Phaid was suddenly released. He spun around, pulling out his blaster. He had expected to see Flame and Makartur firing at them, but instead they were blasting in the opposite direction. A large pack of lupes was rapidly sweeping across the fells, bearing down on the two red-headed figures. Phaid rounded on Solchaim.

'Did you do this?'

Solchaim was unconcernedly popping open the bubble canopy on the flipper.

'Stop trying to think and get in.'

Edelline-Lan and Chrystiana-Nex did as they were told, but Phaid resisted.

'You did do it, didn't you? You brought the lupes down on them.'

Solchaim extended his arms and pointed towards the hunters' wagon.

'Destroy that vehicle.'

'But the hunters' women are still locked inside it.'

Even though his brain protested, his arms were raising the blaster. The lupes were running a circle around Makartur and Flame. Solchaim was staring at him intently.

'If it concerns you, you had better aim carefully and only destroy the drive unit. If those two get away from the lupes, I don't want them using the flipper to follow us.'

The air was filled with howling and blaster fire. Phaid did his best to push it all to the back of his mind. He took careful aim and squeezed the release. At the last minute his hand trembled. The discharge hit the wagon squarely at a midpoint. A violent explosion tore through it. The passenger section was engulfed in a ball of angry orange flame. Black smoke billowed into the clear air. Phaid tottered back looking at the weapon in his hand as though he didn't believe that he was holding it.

'Oh my Lords! I've killed them! Why did it explode like that?'

477

Solchaim took hold of his arm.

'Don't concern yourself. It was an accident. You must have hit something they had stored in the vehicle.'

Phaid was about to give way to sobbing.

'I killed them.'

'Control yourself.'

Phaid straightened. His eyes became dull. Solchaim propelled him towards their flipper.

'Get in and drive, unless you want the lupes to get you.'

Without question, Phaid climbed into the flipper, slid behind the controls and flipped the drive control into life. A number of lupes had detached themselves from the main pack and were racing towards them. Was the elaihi really controlling them? Solchaim slammed the canopy and the flipper started to rise. Four people were a serious overload and its responses were slow and sluggish. It moved forward but the lupes were overtaking them. One hurled itself at the canopy. It came close enough for Phaid to see its lolling red rag of a tongue and curved yellow teeth. Solchaim laughed at the humans' fear, but then the flipper started to accelerate and the hungry pack was left behind. Phaid was exhausted. He held the controls and kept the flipper on a straight, steady line, but let his mind slip into automatic. The elaihi could do what he liked, he could dance Phaid like a puppet. He didn't care. He had no more resistance left.

'Our destination is Bluehaven.'

Phaid grunted. Solchaim arched a thin eyebrow.

'No questions, no curiosity about why we should go to Bluehaven? Have you stopped attempting to divine my masterplan?'

'It may surprise you to learn that we humans wear out. If you didn't have a finger stuck in my brain I would have passed out from fatigue a long time ago.'

'Then I had better keep my finger there, as you so quaintly put it. I need you to steer this machine to Bluehaven.'

'Can't you steer it yourself? You shouldn't find it difficult.'

'Questions?'

'I can't take much more.'

Phaid could now imagine how years with the elaihi had driven Chrystiana-Nex insane.

'Relax, do not make any effort. Just keep your hands on

the controls. The rest will happen by itself.'

'The only thing that's going to happen if I relax at the controls is that I'll fall asleep and turn the damned thing over. I'm sure that's not part of your scheme.'

Solchaim sighed. It was as though he was dealing with a tiresome, slow to learn pet.

The flipper was now travelling quite fast, despite its load. It zipped along, just half a metre above the surface of the snow. The sun was now well up and the sky had turned a deep blue. The snow threw back the light in an uncomfortable glare. Phaid touched a control and made the bubble more opaque. The fells were still completely featureless and all he could do was to steer for the purple clouds on the horizon.

The sun and the fact that four people were huddled into a space only designed for two made it hot inside the bubble. Phaid's eyelids were drooping. Edelline-Lan and Chrystiana-Nex were quite lifeless. Their breathing was shallow and irregular. Phaid's head nodded forward, then he jerked and came awake again. Solchaim's voice whispered seductively in his ear.

'Let go, Phaid. Let go and rest.'

'No.'

'Do not be so stubborn.'

'I'm not going to wreck this flipper.'

'Rest.'

'No!'

But even as Phaid protested, the world became less real. His concentration slipped away. His hands still gripped the controls but his mind was elsewhere. He wasn't asleep, but he also wasn't awake. Time had fallen out of joint. He drifted in and out of fragments of dreams and strange visions. Some came from within his own mind. The first level was taken up with images of danger and death. Makartur grinned and beckoned. His face was a ghastly threatening mask. Behind him were the phantom ranks of ancestor gods, going back a thousand years. As he slipped down, though, life as well as death called to him. Soft voluptuous shapes floated in a magenta sky, like pink or golden sensual clouds, across fantastic landscapes of rolling blue plains, candy cone mountains and warm lakes of sweet syrup. Mindless infant comfort, like the primal security of the womb, enfolded Phaid's fear and paranoia and cloaked it in mists of rapture. An idiot smile spread across his face. His head lolled, chin resting on his chest. His hands still gripped the controls, however. Every now and then he would move them slightly. Somehow, he was steering the vehicle with his unconscious.

New images intruded on his dreams and his smile started to fade. These weren't even his own phantasms. They were strays, leakage from the mind of the elaihi. Phaid's own sugar and satin landscapes were swallowed by the cool fountains, the colonnades, the plazas, the spindly crystal towers and fragile, delicate bridge spans of some perfect elaihim world. There were some visions that he found quite unintelligible. Others were horrifically real and familiar. He visited dark smoky places that smelt of dirty and decay and disgusting habits. Sick, twisted and loathsome dwarfs crowded a crumbling labyrinth. They kept up a shrill non-stop babble. They scratched and picked at themselves. They were vicious and quarrelsome, stubborn and violent. They conducted themselves according to the irrational prejudices of the dully stupid. Phaid scrabbled for wakefulness as he realised that he was seeing humanity as the elaihim saw it. The flipper jolted as Phaid let go of the controls. It tilted and almost rolled. He grabbed them again and wrestled it back to the flat.

'Why do you hate us so much?'

Phaid was covered in sweat but he was back in the real world. Solchaim was sitting beside him and the two women were slumped in the back. His vision was crisp and clear and, for the first time since the elaihi had appeared at the hunters' camp, he had control of his own mind. He had also made what seemed to be an intuitive discovery. It might be possible to keep control of his brain and his willpower. The elaihi wasn't omnipotent. His power wasn't a matter of strength. It was subtlety and technique. He could learn the tricks and he could keep the creature out of his head. He looked directly at Solchaim and repeated the question. A hint of insolence had crept into his voice.

'Why do you hate us?'

Solchaim was looking straight ahead, as though searching for something beyond the snow.

'We don't hate you.'

Phaid noticed that Solchaim seemed to be speaking for his people as a whole.

'Why are you afraid of us?'

'We are not afraid of you.'

Solchaim's voice was flat and mechanical. Phaid knew that he had his measure. He grinned unpleasantly.

'Could it be that you fear the truth?'

'Why should we fear the truth?'

'Because you cannot deal with your past. You cannot deal with us humans. We're your past. It's that that you fear and hate. You are mankind's bastard children and you are mortally ashamed of your parents.'

The sentence terminated in a scream. Pain turned his flesh to liquid. His eyelids crisped and blew away, his teeth grew so hot that his gums charred. His arms and legs were blasted stumps. He was being dipped in hell, hung up by the feet so his skin could be torn off in strips. Phaid had never imagined such agony was possible.

'WHAT MAKES YOU THINK ELAIHIM AND HUMANS ARE IN ANY WAY CONNECTED?'

It was the voice of God. Phaid was being punished. It was a game, a part of his training. He had been lulled by his master into feeling powerful and aggressive. He had snapped at his master's hand and he was being taught a lesson. That was the worst pain of all. He was incapable of anything but submission. The feeling of being so helpless and so inferior was more than his mind could take. It ran but there was no way to run. He was in a squirrel cage with no way out. The pain went on for what seemed like ages. Phaid squirmed and twisted but there was no escape. It wasn't even possible for him to die. Then, mercifully, a giant hand picked up him and his squirrel cage and dropped them into the black, cool pool of oblivion. Inside the flipper, surrounded by three unconscious humans, Solchaim took over the controls and drove the flipper himself.

28

'BLUEHAVEN.'

Phaid woke up and blinked. He waited for the agony to start again but surprisingly it didn't. He had half expected to be limbless, carbonised medium rare and bleeding internally. In fact, he felt quite healthy, as though he had just come out of a long refreshing sleep.

'Where are we?'

'We are at Bluehaven.'

Phaid struggled to sit up in his seat. He was still in the flipper. The women were out cold in the back and Solchaim was sitting at the controls. Once again Phaid found that he was almost in complete command of his own mind. This time, though, he knew enough not to get arrogant about it. He now realised that, for all practical purposes, the elaihim strength was limitless. The flipper had been halted on a low ridge, just above the town. Once upon a time, Bluehaven must have been the shore of a broad lake. Now it was both on and beneath a second ridge that separated the white of the permafrost from the blue-grey of the pack ice. The iceboats and the other human structures were covered by what, from a distance, looked like a delicate tracery of crystals. The man-made objects seemed too fragile and vulnerable, totally at the mercy of the violent purple clouds that rolled and swirled in the mid-distance. It was not an encouraging sight, but there was a certain dangerous beauty about it. Most of Bluehaven was built underground. Its citizens lived and worked in a system of subterranean tunnels, only braving the sub-zero surface temperatures when it was absolutely necessary. Only the marikh branch line, the snout-like ends of air and ventilator shafts and a half-dozen or so iceboats tied to a snow covered pier provided the evidence that a human township existed there at all.

The iceboats were the sole reason for the settlement. It was the furthest point into this particular ice plain where humans could exist on a permanent basis. Bluehaven provided the starting point for the iceboats' hazardous journey across the frozen wastes that marked the path of the savagely cold gales.

Solchaim swung the controls over to Phaid's side of the flipper.

'Take us into town.'

Phaid looked at Solchaim but kept his mind blank. It looked as though there was some change in the situation between them, but he suspected that if he either questioned it or thought about it, the elaihi would be down on him, seizing back the advantage. Phaid bided his time. He maintained a straight face and a straight mind. Concentrating on every boring detail of the action, he put the flipper into drive and eased it down the snow covered track that led to Bluehaven. Now that they were near the habitation of humans, Phaid seemed to have been appointed chauffeur. After his bout of punishment, he wasn't about to resist. He'd be the damnedest, most docile chauffeur any elaihi could hope to have. The few people who had cause to be moving about on the surface were encased in full scale cold suits complete with bulky, fully pressurised helmets. He pulled up beside one of these individuals, cracked the flipper's dome and yelled into the teeth of the wind.

'Where can I park this thing and get down below?'

Phaid immediately regretted this move. The wind seared the skin on his face and tore the words out of his mouth. The eyes behind the face-plate of the protective helmet looked at Phaid as though he was stone crazy.

'Over there!'

An amplified voice came from a small diaphragm just above the neck seal of the helmet and a heavily gloved hand pointed off to the right.

'In that hangar. You can leave the flipper and there's an elevator down to the warm levels. Now get the damn bubble shut before you all get frostbitten.'

Phaid did as he was told and banged the bubble shut. He looked around for the hangar that the passerby had indicated. All he could see was a snow covered building with a wide, dark entrance. It looked more like a cave than a hangar, but it was the only thing that even came close to the description.

In order to get into it, he had to drive past the line of iceboats. Up close, they were much bigger and more substantial than they had looked from the top of the hill. Basically they were a streamlined, heavily armoured cylinder mounted on anything between four and ten enormous metal runner-blades. Above the cylinder, the giant, stressed steel airscoops hummed and sang in the gale. They were the boat's motive power that would snatch at the gale and drive the boat across the ice. They were mounted on, and held in place by, a formidable system of masts, spars, struts and thick control cables. To Phaid, they looked like the furled wings and split-open carapace of some monster insect. Despite the complex and seemingly robust construction of these systems, it wasn't altogether an unknown occurrence for an iceboat's scoops to tear loose in the furious winds, leaving the boat with only secondary storage power to take it to the nearest haven before the passengers and crew froze to death. The chances of storage power driving an iceboat clear to safety were something of the order of one in twenty. Nobody rode the iceboats unless it was absolutely necessary.

Phaid did his best to shut these thoughts out of his mind as he steered the flipper past the huge hawsers thicker than his waist, that secured the iceboats to the dock. He swung the machine into the dark entrance of the hangar and found that he was in a rather run-down combination of repair shop and vehicle park. A set of heavy duty blow heaters brought the temperature up to a level where human beings could walk around without bulky protective clothing, but few availed themselves of the warmth. The place wasn't exactly crowded. Bluehaven didn't seem to be doing a roaring trade. There were only five other flippers in the park. One was in pieces. A tech's legs protruded from under the jacked up rear end. As Phaid nudged his own machine into a parking slot and let off the force field cushion, the tech slid out and clambered to his feet. He was a young kid in a pale blue, lube-stained coverall. He had bad skin and wore his hair in a greasy pompadour with bushy side whiskers. Phaid climbed out of the flipper. The tech looked him up and down.

'Where the hell did you come from?'

Phaid blinked. Being back in the world of men was a shock. He was working on his own again. Solchaim abruptly receded in the general perspective. Phaid's sense of self flooded back. He faced the tech with a sour, tired expression on his face. His voice was very soft.

'I've come a long, cold, hard distance. Who wants to know?'

The tech was simultaneously hostile and defensive.

'I'm only asking what the trip was like. We don't get much news in this Lord forsaken hole. I figure it ought to be just common courtesy for anyone new to . . .'

'Not this new arrival. All I want to know is how we get down below and into the warm.'

'We're isolated people here on the margins, sir. We like to know something about the strangers who are passing through and . . .'

The tech's voice faltered. Solchaim had stepped down from the flipper. His hat was pulled down and his cape was wrapped around his mouth so his face was virtually invisible. Despite that, his tall angular figure was still sufficiently odd to cause the tech to stare bug-eyed. The man's confusion doubled when Solchaim, with an almost courtly gesture, helped the two women down from the vehicle. This even surprised Phaid a little. He couldn't imagine how the elaihi had managed to get them awake and alert so quickly. Solchaim gestured at the tech.

'Is this man causing us some sort of trouble, Master Phaid?'

'No trouble at all, Master Solchaim. This man was about to direct us towards the elevators when he became tongue-tied at the sight of us.' Phaid felt the mildest twinge of reproof stir in his head, but Solchaim didn't seem to want to press the point. Phaid rounded on the tech. 'You were going to direct us to the elevators, weren't you?'

The tech obviously knew that all was not right with this party of visitors but he appeared at a loss to work out what. He pointed sullenly towards the corner of the hangar. 'They're over there.'

The two women still moved like zombies so Phaid ushered them quickly along. Solchaim had already started for the elevators. The tech suddenly pointed after Chrystiana-Nex.

'I've seen her before.'

Phaid halted. He pushed back the jacket of his cold suit so the tech could see his fuse tube. At the same time he flipped him a ten tab.

'You've never seen her before in your life.'

The boy caught the tab. He grinned knowingly at Phaid.

'I'm sure I seen her before.'

Phaid flipped another ten and then let his hand rest on his fuse tube.

'You never saw her.'

The tech pocketed the money, still grinning.

'I never saw her.'

Phaid hurried to the elevator with an uneasy feeling. Once the doors had closed behind him, he faced Solchaim.

'We're going to have to get off the street and stay off the street, otherwise we'll be risking trouble. There are people who can recognise you, Chrystiana-Nex and even me. It'll be a miracle if we can get on an iceboat without someone spotting us and starting an alarm. Legally this is still the Republic.'

Solchaim's voice came out muffled by his cape.

'Who said we are going on an iceboat?'

Phaid got impatient.

'Why the hell else have we come here?'

'Perhaps I should let you take care of this stage of our enterprise.'

'I know enough not to argue.'

'So what do you recommend we do first?'

Phaid was surprised.

'Me?'

'Yes you.'

'I'd go as fast as we can to the town's hotel or inn and I'd hole us up there. Then I'd send out Edelline-Lan to arrange passage on an iceboat to the other side of the wind-plain.'

Solchaim nodded in nonhuman approval.

'Then that's exactly what we'll do.'

The elevator doors opened on the main and only street of underground Bluehaven. Phaid wondered why so much was being delegated to him. Almost as soon as they had stepped out on to the street, he found out why. The elaihi's head sunk into his shoulders as though he was experiencing acute discomfort. Phaid caught an instant of backwash from his mind. It felt as though he was being nearly drowned in the hubbub of the hundred or so human minds in the small city. Phaid could only surmise that the proximity of a great number of human beings somehow swamped an elaihi's telepathic abilities and greatly diminished his or her power. Phaid had, however, learned his lesson. He was not about to act precipitately on the theory.

The inhabitants of Bluehaven were hardly the cream of Republic society. Life was hard out in the frozen margins. It was a transient refuge for rogues and cut-throats: it provided a cold and comfortless haven for men on the run and women losing their pride. It was the ideal place for anyone wanting to sink out of the main flow for a while. Anyone who signed on an iceboat didn't find themselves asked too many questions. Hard eyes followed Phaid and his party as they walked down the street. They were clearly being assessed and their possible worth valued. Phaid hoped that none of the sullen-faced watchers kept up with the news.

The main street was like a high vaulted tunnel, with the facias of buildings built into the two walls. The building frontages had been carefully constructed so that they were exact facsimiles of normal, above ground buildings. Hanging signs proclaimed the existence of an inn, a general store, a cold zone chandler's, a shipping office and the seat of the city governor. It could have been the main street of any small, rather neglected port except that, instead of a sky above, there was a roof of hard packed permafrost supported by enormous beams. The street was pleasantly warm and bathed in a deep orange light. Phaid assumed that the choice of colour was a natural reaction to the chill blues, greys and white of the surface landscapes. Although the builders of Bluehaven had gone to a certain amount of trouble to make the main street look like a civilised surface town, the interiors of the buildings were little more than ice caves with furniture. The men and women who lived on the fringes of the icefields gave little thought to style or sophistication.

The Bluehaven Inn had a broad and, by local standards, quite an imposing façade. It boasted a covered porch and broad steps up to a circular, multi-leaved iris doorway.

Some time in the past someone must have had high hopes for the Bluehaven Inn. They were hopes which must have peeled over the years along with the paint. Now the steps were the focal point for local idlers and off-duty, out of work iceboat crew. Solchaim was the first figure they scrutinised when the four came down the street towards them. They didn't know what to make of him so they moved on to the more familiar ground of Phaid and the women. Phaid had the distinct impression that they took him for some sort of travelling pimp with his string of two. Phaid didn't mind this. People didn't ask questions when they'd already given themselves an answer.

They registered as guests in front of a whey faced desk clerk with large, unnaturally moist eyes that refused to look directly at anyone. This was probably just as well. The two women both still wore glazed expressions although they were able to sign a pair of false names for the clerk. On the other side of the lobby a young man sat by himself. He was mumbling into thin air and brushing invisible insects from his hands and arms. Phaid looked questioningly at the desk clerk.

'What's the matter with him?'

'Wind happy. It happens to them who make one too many trips on the boats.'

'Will he come out of it?'

The clerk shrugged.

'Who knows. Some do, most don't.'

They had to pass the wind happy young man in order to get to the stairs down to their rooms. As they walked by, he rose and stared wide eyed at Solchaim. His slack mouth worked until he managed a faltering word.

'Master?'

Solchaim looked at him and he immediately sat down again.

Solchaim had asked for a suite on one of the lower levels and an adjoining single room. Phaid couldn't quite understand why. It quickly became clear once they were down in their quarters. Solchaim was anxious to get away from the humans for a while. He quickly issued his instructions and vanished behind a closed door. Phaid noted that this might prove to be another elaihim weakness, although he suspected that Solchaim was quite capable of monitoring their thoughts from the other side of the wall.

The instructions were as Phaid had suggested. Edelline-Lan was to go to the shipping office and buy passages to the other side of the icefield. Phaid and Chrystiana-Nex were to remain behind. Phaid knew that there was nothing to do but to go along with them. He didn't flatter himself that there was any way that the three of them could sneak away without Solchaim noticing.

The women were back to normal and acted as though they had just come out of a long refreshing sleep. Phaid, on the other hand, was about ready for a drink and some peace and quiet now that Solchaim had let go of his mind.

'It's damned hard work being someone's dog.'

Edelline-Lan sighed.

'The dreams I had while I was out were indescribable.'

Chrystiana-Nex agreed with her. Her eyes drifted into some private mid-distance.

'He can give you such wonderful dreams. I wish I was still there. He can make it like you just don't exist any more.'

Edelline-Lan looked at her enquiringly.

'Did you ever sleep with him?'

Chrystiana-Nex suddenly became very regal, very presidential.

'That's none of your damn business, you insolent woman.'

Indignation boiled up inside Edelline-Lan. She seemed to be about to launch a tirade against Chrystiana-Nex, but then thought better of it. She shrugged and deflated.

'I'm sorry.'

Chyrstiana-Nex stared at the door through which Solchaim had made his exit.

'I wish I was with him now. I need my dreams.'

She started to walk slowly, almost mechanically towards the door. Phaid shook his head.

'She's like a character in a play.'

Edelline-Lan didn't answer. She ostentatiously made ready for her trip to the shipping office.

Chrystiana-Nex gently opened the door, there was a whispered conversation and she slipped inside.

'What really goes on in that mind?'

'I'd hate to find out.' Edelline-Lan fastened her cold suit. 'You'd better give me the money.'

Phaid handed over the bag that was their communal funds. He felt proud that he didn't even blink.

'I guess I'll need your blaster as well. I'd like some protection out on that street.'

This time Phaid did blink. The blaster had become such a fixture on his hip that handing it over left him with a distinct feeling of insecurity. It was a feeling that wasn't eased by the sight of Edelline-Lan stuffing all of their money inside her coat and their only weapon on her belt. Phaid raised an eyebrow.

'Is there a chance you might not be coming back?'

Edelline-Lan smiled.

'There's always that chance.'

The door closed and Phaid dropped into a chair. It was a relief to be on his own. It seemed like an age since he'd been left alone. The suite was small and dim and claustrophobic but it was a luxury in that it was empty. Phaid was struck by the thought that maybe this was the way that the elaihi had felt. He wasn't quite sure where the thought had come from. Almost as a defence he started to think about the drink that he wanted. He couldn't see how anyone's master plan would be thrown out by him going up to the lobby to fetch a bottle.

Nothing happened to him so he stood up. Still there was no blast of reproof from the next room. He opened the door. Still nothing. He closed it behind him and started up the stairs. Solchaim had either switched off or he had no objection to Phaid getting drunk. He climbed to the level of the lobby, bought a bottle from the clerk and started back down again. He knew better than to mingle in Bluehaven society without a weapon.

He was about halfway back to the suite when the door to a room swung open and a voice called out to him.

'Phaid.'

Only a very firm grip stopped him dropping the bottle. He snatched for the fuse tube that wasn't there. He felt ridiculous and afraid, then Dreen stepped through the open doorway. Phaid's initial relief was shortlived. Dreen had a stinger in his hand. It was identical to the one that Phaid had used in that other hotel, all that time ago in the jungle. The hand jerked. The ten-legged metal spider spun straight at Phaid.

29

PHAID COULD feel the stinger's ten tiny arms grabbing at his flesh. The sharp end sank in, pricking his skin. The deadly steel insect had attached itself to his throat, just above the collar bone. For an instant it had scrabbled but then it found a grip and clung on. Fear gathered like a knot in his stomach. It was only with the greatest effort of will that he resisted the urge to rip the disgusting thing off himself and hurl it away. He knew if he tried to remove it, it would kill him. Instead he swallowed hard.

'What do you want, Dreen?'

His voice was a strained croak. As he spoke, he could feel the stinger pressing on his throat. Dreen was holding the control. He gestured towards the open door.

'I think it's time that you and I had a serious conversation.'

'You need to use a stinger to do that?'

'It cuts down the level of predictability.'

'It could easily cut down my level of survival.'

'Not if you behave yourself.'

Dreen stepped back and let Phaid pass him and go first into the room. It was a small cramped single, only just big enough to hold the narrow battered bed, a closet and a washstand. Phaid looked around questioningly.

'What now?'

'Just sit on the bed and keep your hands in plain sight.'

'You really don't have anything to worry about. I'm not armed.

'I'd still like to see your hands. You're not a very

491

trustworthy person, Master Phaid.'

Phaid sat. The stinger was a constant reminder that a foolish move would be suicidal. Dreen shut the door. He regarded Phaid with a twisted, sardonic expression. Phaid took it to be a smile.

'Don't look so scared. I don't intend to kill you.'

Phaid could feel the sweat on his palms.

'What do you intend?'

'Believe it or not, I have a proposition to put to you. You might find it to your advantage.'

Phaid's eyes were cold.

'You have a damn strange way of doing a man a favour.'

Dreen half shrugged and raised his eyebrows into a what-to-you-expect expression.

'This is a wild and dangerous place. The stinger is just a precaution. Try not to think about it.'

Phaid scowled.

'Yeah, sure. I'll just ignore the fact that you can fry my nervous system any time you want.'

Dreen's voice dropped to a purr. It was very patient and persuasive. He looked like a vulture in his fur trimmed black robe.

'Just put yourself in a receptive frame of mind and listen to what I have to say.'

'I'm listening.'

'My masters do not wish Chrystiana-Nex to go to the Tharmier usurers. They feel that it would be better for the health and general stability of the area if she was under their care.'

'Your masters take a lot on themselves.'

'They always have.'

'So who are they?'

Dreen looked surprised.

'You mean you don't know? You never guessed?'

'I'd rather hear it from you.'

'I am a special agent attached to the Office of the Arch Prelate.'

'You're a priest's spy.'

'That's not strictly true. I am in fact a priest, even though my duties are more concerned with the gathering of temporal intelligence than the spiritual needs of the faithful. We all maintain the orthodoxy.'

'And now you think the orthodoxy will be safer if you grab Chrystiana-Nex.'

'My masters would rather you delivered Chrystiana-Nex than we grabbed her.'

Phaid looked him up and down thoughtfully.

'You would, would you?'

'To be specific, we would like you and your companions to take passage on the next iceboat out.'

'If we can get on it.'

Dreen made a slow gesture with the stinger control.

'You're lying to me now. Your companions Edelline-Lan is right now at the shipping office obtaining those exact passages. You shouldn't lie to me, Master Phaid, not under these circumstances.'

He allowed Phaid a long warning look at the stinger control. Phaid needed no further emphasis. He quickly nodded.

'Yes, yes, I know. You've got the power. What did you expect? Are you going to kill me for one single lie?'

Dreen shook his head.

'I'm not going to kill you, but it does prove that I'm not able to trust you.'

Phaid raised his hands from his knees. It was a gesture of surrender.

'Tell me what I'm supposed to do.'

Dreen smiled.

'That's better.'

'Don't gloat, just get on with it. If I don't get down to our suite soon, the others are going to be suspicious.'

Dreen nodded. He immediately became brisk and businesslike.

'Edelline-Lan is buying passage on an iceboat. It is called the *Valentine* and its destination is Windlee on the other side of the ice plain. When you arrive in Windlee, you will find a demi prelate with a squad of priests' militant. You will make sure that Chrystiana-Nex is peacefully handed over to them.

Phaid remembered previous encounters with the priests' militant. There was little chance of putting anything across the grim, trigger happy, brutally trained young men in the black armour and close fitting skull helmets.

'Why do you need me? The militants can easily take the woman without any help from me.'

'Windlee is in Tharmier territory. Relations between the priesthood and the Tharmier civil government are, to say the least, delicately balanced. A kidnapping by militants, particularly the kidnapping of such a prestigious refugee, would severely jeopardise our position.'

'Will you tell me one other thing?'

'What?'

'Why is everyone so hot to get their hands on Chrystiana-Nex? She's little better than a vegetable most of the time. She can't be of any use to anyone.'

Dreen looked at Phaid as though he was exceedingly naive.

'She's a symbol. She can be used as a lever, a bargaining point with whomever takes eventual control of the Republic. The Tharmiers are concerned that there is anarchy on their borders. My masters cannot tolerate the vacuum of spiritual authority that has been created by the uprising.'

'And everyone wants a piece of the power.'

'Naturally.'

'You realise that if the Day Oners come out on top there will be no way that your bosses will be able to do any deals.'

This time Dreen laughed openly at what he considered to be Phaid's innocence.

'We have already put out feelers. The Day Oners would give a number of concessions if they had the ex-president for a showcase public execution.'

'It's a terrible thing when not even the fanatics will play it straight.'

Dreen's face was a picture of pious, world weary triumph.

'It is a terrible world. That has always been the message of the Consolidated Faith.'

Phaid gave up.

'Okay, you have your deal. I'll turn the woman over to your people when we reach Windlee. There is one thing, though. The Tharmiers were going to give me a lot of money when I brought Chrystiana-Nex. Your way I'm going to end up penniless.'

'You'll be rewarded. My masters won't give you as much as the Tharmier usurers, but you'll get something – and you'll keep your life.'

'You're really some salesman.'

'I take it that you're going to co-operate.'

Phaid looked Dreen directly in the eye.

'Yes, Priest Dreen. I'm going to co-operate. Now will

you take this damn stinger from off my throat?'

A slow and very unpleasant smile spread across the small priest's face.

'Oh no, Master Phaid. Oh dear me no. I'm afraid the stinger will have to stay where it is until Chrystiana-Nex is safely in custody.'

The blood drained from Phaid's face. The idea of walking around for any length of time with the deadly silver insect clinging to him was too nasty to contemplate.

'You're joking with me!'

'Indeed not. I'll be on the boat with you, although we should not acknowledge that we know each other. You'll be perfectly safe as long as you give me no reason to suspect betrayal.'

'But suppose something goes wrong . . .'

'Nothing will go wrong.'

'How do I know that?'

'You'll have to trust me.'

Phaid's temper started to boil.

'No. Absolutely no. There's no way that I'm going to go through with this with a stinger stuck on my throat.'

'You have no choice.'

Dreen held out an upturned hand. The stinger control rested on his palm. He seemed to be challenging Phaid to snatch it. For a moment Phaid was tempted but then common sense took control, telling him what a very bad idea it would be. He fought down his anger and made his face go blank. Once again it was a question of taking life one minute at a time.

'You're right. I don't have any choice.'

'You'd better go before you're missed.'

'We'll both be in trouble if anyone sees this thing on my throat.'

Dreen fished in a black bag that was lying on the bed. He pulled out a white clerical style scarf. He tossed it to Phaid with a sneer.

'Wear this.'

Phaid wrapped it around his neck.

'Am I dismissed now?'

'Yes . . . you can go.'

Phaid started to open the door but Dreen thought of something and stopped him.

'Wait a minute. There is one thing I'd like to know. Who is the tall thin one? Why haven't I heard anything about him?'

Phaid maintained his blank expression with the greatest of difficulty. So Dreen, and presumably the rest of the priesthood, didn't know that the fourth one in their party was Solchaim. It was a reprieve, a last minute hole card. Phaid blinked as if he was surprised that Dreen should enquire about a matter of such little importance.

'Him? He's an admirer of Edelline-Lan. She wouldn't have anything to do with him back in the city because he was so tall and weirdly deformed.'

'Deformed?'

Phaid grimaced. He was starting to warm to his subject.

'You should see his face. He has those horrible folds of grey skin, all down one side of it, like fungus.'

'It sounds unpleasant.'

'It is. No self respecting woman would have anything to do with him.'

'Why is he with you all now?'

'He acts as a kind of bodyguard to the two women.'

'He wasn't on the train with you.'

Phaid checked himself. He must not get carried away and underestimate Dreen. The priest-agent was no fool.

'He had no letters of transit so he followed in a flipper. I knew nothing about it. It was lucky he did, though. We were nearly eaten by lupes while we were out on the fells. He turned up in the nick of time.'

Dreen seemed to believe him. He noticed that Phaid had left his bottle on the floor. He stooped to pick it up.

'You'll need this.'

'Yeah.'

Dreen gave Phaid a hard look.

'Don't let me down.'

'I won't. I'd be a fool to do that, wouldn't I.'

Outside the door Phaid took a long pull from the bottle and wondered how the hell this new complication was going to work out. Down in the suite, the outside room was still empty. Phaid slipped back into his chair as though he'd never been gone. He felt no reaction from Solchaim so he tilted the bottle and wondered how an elaihi could cope with a drunk. It wasn't too long before he heard Edelline-Lan's footsteps on the stairs. She came in irate and indignant. Some of the idlers outside the inn had tried to make sport with her. They had refused to take her warnings seriously until she had actually pulled out her blaster and threatened to blow them apart. Phaid passed her the bottle and she took three hefty swallows before she calmed down. It was then that she spotted the scarf wound round Phaid's neck.

'What the hell are you wearing that for?'

'I was cold.'

'You look like one of Roni-Vows' friends. It doesn't suit you.'

Phaid was relieved when she didn't take it any further, and started outlining the details of the passage.

'The boat is called the *Valentine* and apparently she's not very fast, but she's big, well built and reliable. Her destination is Windlee which will suit us fine. Windlee is another town like this, but it's well into Tharmier territory and on a direct route to the capital.'

Phaid wasn't surprised that Dreen's information tallied exactly with Edelline-Lan's. He nodded towards the closed door of the other room.

'You think that we're still going to the Tharmier capital?'

Edelline-Lan sighed.

'Who knows? I'm going to act as though we are until I hear otherwise. As far as I'm concerned it's the only way to stay sane and stop ending up like her.'

'What time does this boat leave?'

'At what they call down here the tenth bell. That's just before sunset.'

'I've lost all sense of time.'

'We've got about four hours.'

Again Phaid glanced towards the closed door.

'Maybe we ought to be doing the same as them.'

Edelline-Lan firmly shook her head.

'Not around him.'

Phaid realised that he'd been expecting her to say no. The question had been an act of mild bravado. There was no way that they could have made love without Edelline-Lan seeing and asking questions about the stinger. As it was, the time before the iceboat's departure passed quickly enough without any sexual diversions. Solchaim and Chrystiana-Nex re-emerged and the few preparations necessary for the journey were quickly dispatched. Exactly forty-five minutes before the *Valentine* was due to sail, the four of them started up the stairs to the lobby.

Much to Phaid's dismay, he saw that Dreen was standing at the desk talking to the clerk. Phaid was relieved, though, to see that he paid no attention to them. Solchaim was once again swathed in his cape and had his hat pulled down over his eyes. Dreen seemed to have swallowed the explanation that Solchaim was a deformed human. For his part, the elaihi appeared not to have detected Phaid's anxious thoughts. They walked across the lobby. Phaid, who was leading the way, was about to open the door when a voice stopped him cold.

'Master, don't go!'

It was the sound of a lost soul. Phaid spun around. The wind crazy kid was moving like a zombie towards Solchaim with one pleading, clawlike hand outstretched.

'Don't leave me, master, please don't leave me. With you here I can see again, I can know again. I don't have to be crazy.'

The presence of human insanity seemed to have halted Solchaim in his tracks. The tall shrouded figure was suddenly incapable of movement. The two women stood waiting to see what was going to happen. Dreen had turned and was looking at them curiously. The wind crazy kid tottered forward, reaching for Solchaim. His voice was a supplicating, demented coo.

'Maaster, maaster, m-a-a-ster,'

Phaid's first idea was to burn the crazy and run. Edelline-Lan, however, still had his blaster. Also, he couldn't quite believe that one mad kid could throw off the elaihi's control. Dreen was now watching open mouthed. Edelline-Lan touched Phaid on the arm.

'What the hell is going on?'

Phaid quickly shook his head.

'I don't know but I sure as hell don't like it.'

He could feel the stinger clinging to his throat. The wind crazy kid was almost up to Solchaim. The elaihi jerked. Phaid cringed from the mental blast. Everyone in the room must have felt it, quite possibly everyone in the town. The wind crazy was blasted backwards but he managed to hook his fingers in Solchaim's cape. Solchaim was spun round as the cape fell away. His hat fell off. The story of him being a deformed human was exposed as a lie. He could be nothing other than an elaihi.

Phaid found himself looking directly at Dreen. The priest's face was frozen in horror. He clearly knew who and what Solchaim was.

'What have you done? Is there nothing you wouldn't stoop to?'

'I had no choice.'

He was fumbling in the pockets of his black robe. Phaid knew he was going for the stinger control. Phaid leapt towards him.

'For Lords' sake don't kill me!'

Solchaim loosed another angry mind blast. He seemed furious that the crazy had attempted to touch him. The kid took the full brunt of it. He was slammed against the wall. Edelline-Lan and Chrystiana-Nex were thrown to their knees. Phaid stumbled into Dreen. A third blast swept the room. The crazy was screaming.

'NOOOOOOOO!!'

The stinger control rolled out of Dreen's hand. Phaid made a grab for it but Solchaim was nearer and he scooped it up without effort. He grinned fiendishly.

'Now what, Phaid? Deals with the priests?'

Phaid reeled from horror to horror.

'You wouldn't.'

There was a moment of terrible pause as Solchaim held up the small silver sphere between his long bony index finger and his nonhuman thumb. The gesture was taunting, then he tossed it to Phaid as though he was giving a treat to a pet.

'Of course I wouldn't.'

Phaid twisted it to neutral with shaking hands. The spider section dropped from his throat. It homed back to the sphere. Its legs folded as the two were rejoined. Phaid was about to drop the thing into his pocket when he saw Dreen out of the corner of his eye. The priest was coming off the floor with a small compact blaster in his hand. In the first instant Phaid thought that the priest was going after Solchaim, but then he realised that he was the target. For the second time that day he reached for a weapon that wasn't there; Edelline-Lan still had it. He raised the stinger.

'Don't do it, Dreen!'

The blaster was coming up. Phaid let the stinger go. It stuck on Dreen's cheek. The blaster was pointed straight at Phaid. The priest was looking at him with an expression of pure hatred.

'How could you be capable of such betrayal?'

Phaid held up the sphere.

'I don't want to do this.'

'You sold out to that creature. You sold out your own species.'

'It wasn't like that.'

Dreen's grip on the blaster tightened.

'I'm going to kill you.'

Phaid shut his eyes and activated the stinger. The blast he expected never came. When he opened his eyes again, Dreen was lying on his back. His eyes were blank and his face contorted. One leg twitched convulsively. The lobby was suddenly calm. Solchaim was helping Chrystiana-Nex to her feet. The wind crazy was sobbing in a foetal position. Edelline-Lan was looking around with a dazed expression and Phaid's blaster in her hand. The clerk was flat on his face behind the desk, either stunned, dead or hiding. Nobody bothered to find out which. Solchaim gathered his three humans together.

'We still have our boat to catch.'

Despite his apparent calm, Phaid sensed that things had gone badly wrong. He suspected that the wind crazy had not been a part of the elaihi's plan. Phaid picked up Dreen's blaster.

'It's possible that there'll be some who won't want to let us leave.'

'Then we'll have to use our powers to persuade them otherwise.'

They advanced out the door. Phaid and Edelline-Lan flanked Solchaim with drawn weapons. He walked in the middle with an arm around Chrystiana-Nex. The single underground street was unnaturally quiet. Although a large number of people thronged the sidewalk and peered from windows, nobody approached them. It felt as though an invisible shield of energy cracked around the elaihi and his three humans, making them the only ones who were permitted to move. Phaid knew that Solchaim must be stretched to his limits to control so many people.

They made it to the elevators. As the doors closed behind them, Solchaim sagged visibly. Phaid had never seen him lapse so badly. For a moment, it looked like the elaihi might have actually taken on too much and was in danger of coming apart. Then he recovered himself. Phaid did his best to cloak his mind. It was something he would

500

not have thought possible a few hours earlier.

At the top of the elevator they took a different route from the one by which they'd come. Instead of going out by the flipper hangar, they went into the glassite walk tube that snaked out to the end of the dock. Through its ice covered roof Phaid had a first, distorted glimpse of the iceboat *Valentine*. The hull was a plain cylinder that tapered to a point at each end. The only opening in the thick riveted steel was the port through which they and the cargo entered. An iceboat had no need of windows or portholes. In the frozen, howling gale, it could only run on echo sensor and probes. The hull was completely dwarfed by the towering metal airscoops. In port, they were tightly furled, each between its pair of steel masts. These masts, although each was as wide in cross section as a man was tall, hummed and sang in the peripheral winds. When the boat got underway and began to slide out across the plain, the scoops would unfurl like the wings of monstrous insects. The masts would bend almost double in the force of the gale rocketing the vessel across the ice on its multiple skids.

Just inside the big circular port, the master of the *Valentine* was watching the cargo come in on a conveyor. He was a swarthy, well built man with a hook nose, thick gold earrings and a belly that hung over his greasy canvas breeches. He looked questioningly at Phaid and the others as they climbed from the tube down on to the deck.

'And where do you think you're going?'

Edelline-Lan took the initiative and stepped forward. She proffered the passage vouchers.

'We are your passengers.'

'Passengers, are you?'

The master made no attempt to examine the vouchers. Instead, he looked at each of the party in turn. He saved Solchaim for last.

'You say that you're passengers.'

Edelline-Lan regarded him with an even gaze.

'That's right. We've paid our fares and I can think of no reason why you shouldn't take us.'

The master's finger jabbed out at Solchaim.

'What's that supposed to be?'

Phaid moved up beside Edelline-Lan.

'It's a passenger.'

The master shook his head.

'I'm not taking that.'

'The elaihi has paid his fare. You are compelled to take him.'

'Listen, lady, I'm not compelled to do anything.'

Some of the crew had moved in to watch the exchange. They were starting to mass behind the master. The situation was taking on an air of the ugly. Glares were being directed at Solchaim and one of the crew was slowly pulling a leather covered sap from his pocket. The elaihi had provoked instant, kneejerk hostility among the boatmen but then, just as instantly, it melted away. A pleasant numbness drifted through the area of the port. The crew relaxed. Stupid grins crept over their faces. The master shrugged and handed back the vouchers.

'What the hell. What do I care? Anyone can ride on this bucket.' He gestured into the interior of the boat. 'Get yourself assigned to a cabin. Have a good trip.'

Phaid looked easily at the master and then at Solchaim. He wondered how long the elaihi could keep up the screen of phoney goodwill. He prayed that it would last all the way across the ice. The four of them turned out to be the only passengers on the *Valentine*. Dreen would have made five. Their quarters were two cramped, low ceilinged cabins sandwiched between the crew's mess and cargo holds. The actual departure of the boat was heralded by the screaming of tortured metal as the scoops were spread. A throbbing impulse engine pushed the boat slowly away from the dock, sliding ponderously on protesting skids. Then the scoops caught the wind and the whole boat groaned from the impact. The *Valentine* started to pick up speed.

At this moment of departure the whole ship was infused by a sense of excitement, adrenalin was flowing. It was the start of a journey that, despite all the precautions that men could take, was always hazardous and unpredictable. The stories of the iceboat crews were filled with lost craft, spectacular disasters and men driven mad by the winds. The initial, edgy elation didn't last, however. Everything quickly settled down into a tedious, uncomfortable routine. Phaid had forgotten just how incredibly dreadful a journey by iceboat could be. The freezing winds smashed into the armoured body of the craft, causing its very framework to contort and protest. They tore at the airscoops, the masts and the spars. The runners vibrated on the ice with a sound like thunder. Inside the small passenger compartment the noise was deafening. The noise wasn't the worst of it, though. There was also the non-stop nerve jangling, bone jolting vibration. The three human passengers had little choice but to cling to their bunks and pray for the journey to be over. Within two hours of starting from Bluehaven, all three were violently sick and even Solchaim stuck strictly to his bunk. Despite the prices that they had paid, the master and crew of the *Valentine* paid scant attention to them. Now and then a crewman might happen to clean up the worst of the mess and to check that nobody had died, fallen out of their bunk or otherwise injured themselves. For the remainder of the time they were left alone with the noise, the motion and the smell of their own sickness. Finally, after what seemed like an eternity, Phaid fell into a delirious and fitful sleep that seemed to dip in and out of an eerie parade of bizarre and disturbing dreams.

At first he thought that the blade buzzing next to his throat was a dream. The air in the cabin was hot and the only light came from a dim lantern. It shone on a sweaty, unshaven face that was pressed close to his. Outside on the plain, the winds howled at the intruding boat but the garlic breath voice was right in his ear and there was no mistaking what it was saying.

'Don't move a muscle or your throat is slit for sure.'

30

IT WAS worse than any nightmare. The boat lurched and bucked and the gale screamed beyond the hull. A crewman crouched threateningly over each passenger with a weapon pressed to his or her throat. The master stood in the cabin doorway with his legs braced against the bouncing and rolling. The lantern he was holding swayed and cast weird darting shadows as he struggled to keep his balance. The master's face was a picture of black fury. His voice was hard and cold as though he was making a near impossible effort to control his rage.

'What the hell do you think you've been doing to me, you monsterous thing? What have you been doing to me and my crew? You think you can play your unclean games with our heads? You think you can get away with your wicked shit right here on my boat? *My* boat? You've gone too far with this, monster! You've gone too far with this!'

Phaid lay scarcely daring to breath. The humming and slightly luminous blade was just a fraction away from the skin of his adam's apple. The crew was in much the same mood as its master and Phaid suspected that, if he as much as swallowed, the one with the bad breath would plunge it into his throat. He could understand their grim anger. He could all too clearly remember his own horror and rage when he first realised that the elaihim had the power to violate his mind. He knew that these boatmen would be hard pressed to put their shock and revulsion into words, but he doubted that they would have any trouble translating it into very painful action. The boatman probably started out with a similar set of prejudices to those of the veebe drovers. Now they would assume they had ample proof of their rightness, the Lords on their side and justification for terrible revenge.

Phaid was clearly bracketed along with Solchaim. The knife told him that it was likely he would share whatever fate the master had devised for the elaihi. Phaid couldn't believe that he had let go of his control so easily. Had he fallen asleep? Had exhaustion finally claimed him? Surely now he was awake again, why didn't he do something? Phaid tried to communicate these silent questions to Solchaim but no reply came back. The master swung into the cabin from handhold to handhold and the boat bucked and shuddered. He held the light close to Solchaim's face. The elaihi skin was waxen. He looked like a corpse. The master's eyes were fixed on his.

'You're going, monster. You're going over the side and out. I'm putting you off my boat so you'll never be able to play your tricks again. You and your cohorts are going out on to the ice. We'll see if your devil powers can save you from the gales. Do you have anything to say to that, monster?'

Solchaim didn't move. There was no indication that he had even heard what was being said to him. The master turned away with a look of disgust and gestured to the four crewmen.

'Get them out. Get them out of my sight. Take them aft and drop them through the stern dumper lock.'

The crewmen acted as though they had been waiting for these orders. Edelline-Lan and Chrystiana-Nex were hauled to their feet and pushed out of the cabin. Garlic Breath got an armlock on Phaid and held the tip of the blade just behind his right ear.

'You try anything and it goes straight in.'

Phaid made himself as limp and passive as possible while he racked his brains for a way out. He was damned if he was going to die for the elaihim.

'Listen, this is all a mistake . . .'

'Shut your mouth and move.'

Walking half bent with his arm twisted behind him, Phaid was marched out of the cabin and down one of the *Valentine*'s narrow companion-ways. It wasn't the easiest thing to do in a pitching boat and he and his bad breath captor continually stumbled and crashed into walls and bulkheads. Phaid was afraid that the blade would go into him by accident. He twisted around to look at the man he could only think of as Garlic Breath.

'You're going to kill us both before we even get aft.'

Garlic Breath snarled.

'Let me worry about that.'

At the same moment, the boat gave a particularly vicious lurch. Phaid grabbed for a handhold, couldn't make it and found himself sprawled on his hands and knees. Garlic Breath kicked him to his feet and pushed him on. When they reached the stern, others of the crew were already undogging the fastenings on the inner door of the dumper lock. The two women looked on, white faced with fear. Phaid had no reason to believe that he was appearing any more defiant. Solchaim was being brought down the companion-way. He looked like a corpse, totally drained, as though he'd lost all will to resist.

Two crewmen hauled open the heavy cover. The one holding Edelline-Lan nodded towards the hole in the deck.

'In!'

Edelline-Lan put a hand to her mouth and silently shook her head.

'You can either climb in or we throw you in. It don't make no difference to us.'

Edelline-Lan looked briefly at Phaid and then she squatted down on the edge of the port and extended one leg into the hole. She was about to jump down into the chamber between the inner and outer doors when a very peculiar thing happened. The blade that was still being held in front of Phaid's face abruptly drooped, like a melting stick of wax. At the same time another of the crew cursed and dropped his blaster. He hopped around shaking his hand as though it had been burned. Phaid twisted around and looked at Solchaim, but the elaihi was still devoid of expression.

Then a confined kind of hell broke loose around the dumper lock. Two crewmen were slammed forcibly into each other. Another dived headfirst into a solid bulkhead. Two more blasted each other from point blank range. Violence crackled in the air with such intensity that Phaid felt stunned. The elaihi grinned fiercely at his handiwork strewn about the deck. Edelline-Lan scrambled from the lock.

'You really left it to the last minute, didn't you.'

Solchaim appeared to have no time to chat with humans. His orders were direct and brisk.

'The bridge, we go to the bridge.'

They had no choice but to follow in his long-legged wake. When they reached the bridge it was some while before their presence was noticed. The boat had started to vibrate really badly and everyone on duty, both human and android, clung on for dear life as, at the same time, they stared intently at the sensor screens or watched illuminated read-outs and displays that showed the stresses on various sections of the hull, mast and rigging. Braced in the bulky and imposing command chair, the master presided over the room. Solchaim made a motion that Phaid and the two women should keep back in the shadows to the rear of the bridge. The master was bellowing orders at his helmsman and oblivious to anything but the plight of his ship.

'Bring her round, dammit! Bring the nose round. If we take another gust broadside we'll corkscrew for sure.'

Between buffets the master mopped his brow with a red handkerchief.

'More, give her more! Keep bringing her round. Sweet Lords, if this gets any worse we're going to have to turn back towards Bluehaven.'

Solchaim chose this moment to reveal himself.

'There will be no turning back. I have business in Windlee.'

The master swung around. The ship shuddered and he slid sideways in the command chair.

'You're dead! You're out on the ice, dead!'

'You cannot kill a demon.'

The master was totally gripped with rage.

'You're not a demon! You're a twisted unclean elaihi, you're a deformed monster, but you are no demon! You can maybe dabble your fingers in my mind one time, but you'll not do it twice. I'm ready for you, monster!'

Phaid winced. He would never forget the agony of the punishment after he had made a similar stand.

The *Valentine* staggered to the side. It was as though it had been slapped by a giant hand. The skids were having trouble staying on the ice. The master's instincts swung his attention from Solchaim to the helmsman.

'Loose her, man! Loose her! Let her go, let her run with it, it's our only hope. When you get control back start out of this, we're going back to Bluehaven. It's suicide to try to go through this!'

'There will be no turning back.'

The master rounded on Solchaim.

'You'll not order me on my own bridge!'

He reached for the blaster at his hip, but he never completed the move. Solchaim froze him. Even the backwash of what happened next was too hideous to contemplate. Phaid had one brief impression that the man's brain was being taken apart from the inside by an awesome vindictiveness. He closed off everything and tried as hard as he could to blank himself out. When Solchaim was finished with the master he let him drop. He flopped to the deck like a sack and rolled as the boat pitched. Solchaim stepped over and sat down in the command chair. With studied casual arrogance he swung one leg over the arm of the chair and lay back. The crew were rigid at their posts. To every human on this bridge it seemed that the devil had take over their ship. There was a red glow in the room.

Phaid, who was a little more acclimatised to the elaihim special effects found himself a corner where he could brace his legs and wait for the coming shocks. As he had expected, for the next two hours Solchaim guided the boat, with unerring skill, along the very rim of disaster. He ran into a storm of storms, dancing the now dull eyed crew like a set of puppets and pushing the structure of the iceboat to the edge of distintegration. It seemed like a miracle that they neither turned over nor were torn apart. Phaid started to appreciate the miracle even more when the wild bucking died away and the boat ran on all skids with only minor vibration. It meant that they had come through the worst of the gales and were coasting into Windlee.

Just as Solchaim was making preparations for the final docking, one of the zombie-like crew turned from where he was monitoring the long range aft scanner.

'A small fast boat has followed us through the storm.'

Solchaim nodded. Although his face showed nothing but what in a human would be amused boredom, Phaid felt a faint ripple of surprise and concern. It seemed that maybe this boat was another random factor that hadn't been included in his calculations. A loud metallic groaning announced that the scoops were being furled. The impulse engine's throbbing rose in pitch and volume as the boat laboured up to the dock. Finally the *Valentine* ground to a halt and an eerie silence took over the control room. Phaid and the women looked at each other uneasily. Each new situation seemed to present its own set of traumatic dangers.

Solchaim briskly unfolded himself from the command chair and stood up.

'Quickly, quickly, there is no time. We will disembark now and go straight to the flipper hangar. We take the first suitable vehicle. I want no contact with the human population. Does everyone understand?'

The three humans nodded. Solchaim had a mild hold on their minds that precluded any argument or discussion. They waited in silence while the clamped down and near somnambulist crew opened the huge main port and hauled the walk tube aboard. Immediately it was secured they stepped into it and brushed past a surprised group of officials and cargo handlers. They followed the tube in the direction of the flipper hangar. Windlee seemed to boast a rather more extensive walk tube system than Bluehaven and they had to walk for some time following colour coded signs before they finally emerged into the hangar. At the connection between tube and hangar, however, the whole party stopped dead. They had been expecting to see a few parked vehicles and maybe two or three more under repair. Instead, the interior of the structure was dominated by two huge troop transports. They were big, hunched and shiny black. Photon cannons poked their snouts from dark plexiglass gun blisters. The transports bore the insignia of the militant arm of the Consolidated Faith.

Were these the priests that Dreen had promised would be waiting? Phaid had expected only a handful. Instead, they were out in force. Armed priests' militant in black armour and small round skull helmets patrolled the mouth of the hangar. They were checking each and every vehicle that came in and went out. For Phaid, this proved to be an ill advised observation. Solchaim seized him by the collar and dragged him back into the tube.

'You! Always the petty intrigues of you miserable little humans. Do you see what your deceit and double dealing has done?'

Phaid was poised to blurt excuses, but suddenly he slumped. He realised that it was all pointless.

'You can look into my mind, you know what happened. You can only do your worst.'

Solchaim shook his head.

'I need you for the near future. It is crucial that I do not fall into the hands of your priests until I am ready.'

'What do we do?'

'We will have to go into the underground city. We will have to go down and attempt to elude them. Eventually they will become bored and withdraw all these fighting men.'

'There is one way.'

Solchaim looked amused.

'There is?'

Phaid nodded eagerly. He was gambling again.

'I'm certain that they don't know about you. They're looking for Chrystiana-Nex. If you were to lay low and I handed her over, just like Dreen wanted, it might be possible to . . .'

'And you would collect your reward.'

Phaid sighed. He had had enough.

'And what the hell would be so wrong with that? Every swine with a delusion of grandeur wants to set me up for something. Everyone has a scheme or a strategy or a master plan that involves me getting cut or burnt or fused or rotated or generally reviled, spat on or executed even. What would be so goddamn wrong if Master Phaid got something out of this torturous exercise? Would the sky fall, or would the world crack apart if poor old Phaid made a profit? I don't have any grand design, I do not want to conquer the world or topple governments, be king of the hill or evil dictator of the planet. Lords, sweet Lords, I don't want to be superior, all I want is a comfortable life; is that so much of a crime?'

Solchaim put a hand on Phaid's shoulder. He seemed delighted.

'Such a long and impassioned speech!'

'Don't patronise me. You haven't burned out all the freewill!'

Phaid could feel soothing waves washing over him but he was determined to resist them. Solchaim gestured down the walk tube.

'Shall we go to the elevators?'

Edelline-Lan and Chrystiana-Nex obediently followed. Phaid didn't move and, strangely, he felt nothing compelling him to do so. He suddenly realised that, in fact, he was only being stubborn for its own sake. He didn't want to be caught by the priests either, unless he had Chrystiana-Nex to hand to them and buy his safety and freedom. He hurried after the others.

Windlee was altogether larger, more prosperous and more ambitious than Bluehaven. Instead of just a single street under the ice, Windlee had four, arranged in a doubled cross, two running parallel and intersecting the other two, also parallel. The streets were also fairly crowded. Many of the citizens seemed self satisfied and prosperous. By the standards of an ice town, the percentage of thieves, cut-throats and drifters was low. The ones there were were quite efficiently confined to the colder, outer ends of the four streets by a small but heavy handed gang of law enforcement officers.

Four of these lounged by the lower doors of the elevators. They wore no specific uniforms but had a certain cohesive style about the way they dressed. Back in Chrystianaville, they might have been taken for a gang of Day One killers. Here they were the law. They stiffened as Solchaim stepped out of the elevator. They needed no instruction. They bristled like a dog with lupes in his territory.

Solchaim knocked them back to docility with a blast of well being and the party hurried on. Windlee was also a great deal better organised than Bluehaven. It was run by a Council of Burghers who had their chambers in the single centre block formed by the four streets. It was the same block that housed the heating and air supply systems. There was even a choice of accommodation – a rough and ready inn, a modestly comfortable hotel and a limited fare bordello. The bordello was nearest to the elevator exit and Phaid suggested that it might be the last place that the priests would come looking for them. Both Edelline-Lan and Solchaim vetoed the idea and they walked on in the direction of the hotel doing their best to mingle with the crowd and look as inconspicuous as possible.

For Solchaim, mingling was no easy matter. He couldn't have stood out more if he'd carried a sign with the word 'alien' printed on it. They were making their way past the council chambers when they were spotted by a sauntering patrol of one local lawman and two armoured priests' militant. The local law waved arbitrarily at them.

'Hold up there, you.'

Phaid and Edelline-Lan both halted.

'Us?'

Solchaim, however, took instant action. Snatching up Chrystiana-Nex, he spun away and sprinted, legs flying in a lanky, spider scuttle, in the direction of the nearest building. It happened to be the council chamber. Two lawmen on watch outside were tossed out of the way even before Solchaim reached them. While Phaid still stood blinking, he vanished inside.

Phaid and Edelline-Lan were swifly surrounded by a wedge of priests' militant and lawmen. The original three who had stopped them had been swiftly augmented by others who were curious to see the cause of the disturbance. Phaid found himself looking down the important end of half a dozen blasters. He was becoming awfully sick of people pointing weapons at him. He wearily raised his hands as he and Edelline-Lan were disarmed.

'For the Lords' sake don't do anything rash. Don't burn me. I'm quite harmless.'

One of the lawmen pointed at the door of the council chamber.

'Who are the two who ran inside?'

The two chamber guards were picking themselves up and shaking their heads dazedly. Phaid also shook his head.

'You wouldn't believe me.'

A priest grabbed Phaid by the front of his jacket. There was something particularly sinister in the way that a tongue of plasteel jutted down from the front of the militant's close fitting helmet to protect his nose and face.

'Don't get clever.'

Phaid took a deep breath.

'The woman is Chrystiana-Nex, the ex-president of the Republic, the other is Solchaim the elaihi.'

Everyone around looked at him as though he was crazy.

'I said you wouldn't believe me.'

'Are they armed?'

'Yes, you could say that.'

'With what?'

Phaid tried to change the route that things were taking.

'Listen, before all this gets out of hand, I think you'd better take me to a superior officer.'

A voice came from behind him.

'And presumably you must be Phaid the Gambler?'

The militants and lawmen moved back. Phaid turned and found himsel facing a grim faced, middle-aged priest. His black robe was trimmed with purple and gold. Phaid assumed that this must be the demi-prelate of whom Dreen had spoken. A pair of small hard eyes looked Phaid up and down.

'So you brought us Solchaim as a bonus, did you? Or did he bring you?'

31

IT WAS a siege. Despite all Phaid's proffered advice, his Eminence the demi-prelate had gone ahead and deployed his men to surround the block in which Solchaim had taken refuge. To be fair, his Eminence had a great deal of difficulty comprehending the extent of the elaihim power. He was a military man and hardly a subtle thinker. He wasn't one of the devious mandarins of the central hierarchy. He maintained the orthodoxy by frontal assault. If the faith was in jeopardy, he sent in the troops. This is what he was doing right now. A line of them crouched in the street with their blasters trained on the building, waiting for the next order.

Events immediately after Solchaim had dashed into the council building must have added to his Eminence's confusion. A few minutes after Solchaim's disappearance, the building's main door had flown open and a crowd of officials and burghers had stumbled and bounced from it as though propelled by an invisible force. They babbled about how demons had taken over the place and seemed close to hysteria.

The council building had the look of a place that deserved a siege. With a sense of civic pride the first Council of Burghers had had their edifice fitted with façades that caused it to resemble some ornate fake fortress from a long fallen empire. On a miniature scale it echoed the citadel of Harald the Mad at Freeport or the Keep of Odan XXV on the cliffs above Hai Sai. To be perfect it should have been heroically silhouetted against sky and driven clouds. Unfortunately in underground Windlee, it had to support the huge beams and packed ice of the roof. One face of the building was already scarred by blaster burns and most of the phoney stone facia was melted. There had been some loose fire when a Windlee lawman thought that he had seen Solchaim at one of the narrow slit windows. By a fluke, four priests and two bystanders were injured by flying debris.

It was at this point that the demi-prelate decided he had to take charge. With smooth and regimented efficiency the priests' militant went into action. A twin line ringed the building, the gawping crowds were herded back out of the way and extra equipment was hurried down from the surface. His Eminence set up a command post in front of the main door to the council chamber. He had a hailing unit, lines to the senior man on each of the four sides and a baby photon cannon to protect him and his aides. Phaid and Edelline-Lan were allowed to hang around in the background just as long as Phaid didn't offer any more insights into the psychology of the elaihim. His Eminence had little time for mysteries other than those of the Faith. He was confident that any problem could be solved by an application of firepower.

Some of the locals had started to object to the demi-prelate's takeover of the town. A number of lawmen started to complain that they ought to be a part of the operation. After the earlier shooting incident, however, they didn't have too much argument and they were restricted to keeping back the curious crowds of onlookers. The burghers felt that they ought to approve any action that the demi-prelate might take. The demi-prelate first ignored them and then, when they set up a vocal protest, he curtly informed them that the whole town was under Holy Law. A couple of burghers wanted to argue that Holy Law was invalid under Tharmier jurisdiction, but the others quickly explained to them how anyone with over a hundred well armed troops had their own natural jurisdiction in a small isolated town.

Finally all was quiet. The line of black armoured men stretched all the way around the building, the crowd waited and his Eminence paced. The only one who didn't appear to have made his move was the one who had caused all the commotion in the first place. Solchaim was both silent and invisible. This upset the demi-prelate more

515

than anything else. According to the book, a siege situation usually involved some participation on the part of the besieged. Finally, after nearly an hour of waiting, his Eminence ran out of patience. The hailer was kicked into action. It came to life in a deafening yowl of treble feedback. His Eminence scowled as the operator brought the unit under control and made it ready for him to speak. When the noise was reduced to a low hum, he stepped up to the device.

'This is Demi-Prelate Scourse of the Consolidated Faith. I have placed this town under Holy Law and, under that Holy Law, I order you to surrender such weapons as you have and give yourself into my custody.'

The amplified voice echoed around the watching streets. Phaid looked at Edelline-Lan and shook his head.

'He doesn't know what he's playing with.'

Edelline-Lan shrugged.

'Do any of us?'

'I think we probably have a better idea than he does.'

She searched her pockets for something to put in her mouth.

'That's debatable.'

There was no answer from inside the council building. The demi-prelate repeated his statement and then added the usual threat.

'If you do not come out within the next five minutes I shall order my men to open fire. You are completely surrounded. You don't have a chance. I will say this just once more. You have five minutes to give yourself up. After then I shall give the order to fire.'

Phaid bit his lip.

'I've got to stop this. You know how he gets when he's threatened or attacked by humans.'

Edelline-Lan looked unhappy.

'I don't think it will do any good.'

'I've got to try. Who knows what he will do?' He walked quickly to where the demi-prelate was standing, looking up at the building. 'You're making a big mistake. If you . . .'

The demi-prelate swung around angrily.

'You're making a big mistake, Eminence.'

'You're an expert?'

'I'm an expert on the elaihim and I know that if you start shooting at him he's going to fight

516

back . . . Eminence.'

'And what can one man do against a hundred?'

'He's not a man. When the hell are you going to accept this? He can take you with a single illusion.'

'I never met an illusion that could stop a blaster.'

'You never met an elaihi.'

'And you're his friend.'

'I'm not his friend. I was more like his prisoner.'

'You'll be my prisoner unless you stop interfering, Master Phaid.'

'Listen . . .'

'You either shut your mouth or you go to the surface in irons. We have yet to discuss the possible whereabouts of Spiritual Brother Dreen.'

Phaid's eyes narrowed.

'Whatever you say.'

His Eminence snorted as Phaid turned on his heel and walked back to Edelline-Lan.

'It's hopeless.'

His Emience returned to the hailer.

'You have three minutes left. I would make this appeal to ex-president Chrystiana-Nex. We have no quarrel with you. Our only wish is to take you into custody for your own protection.'

Edelline-Lan grimaced.

'I bet they do.'

'Persuade your companion to give himself up. We also have no quarrel with him or his species. If, however, you continue to resist we will have no choice but to storm the building. You cannot prevail against the forces ranged against you.'

Phaid looked the other way.

'The bloody priest's in love with his own voice.'

There was total silence in the streets of the city. Everyone seemed to be watching, holding their breath until whatever was going to happen, happened.

'Two minutes.'

Still no sound came from the building.

'You have one minute.'

Phaid looked from the priests to the council chamber and back again.

'I hope this fool's superiors approve of what he's doing.'

'Your time has run out. If you do not come out immediately, I am going to order my men to open fire!'

517

The laughter was so blood-curdlingly terrible that even the robot-like priests' militant forgot their training and shifted uncomfortably. It rang around the beams and echoed down from the roof of ice until it became impossible to pinpoint the source of the sound. At no stretch of the imagination could it have come from a human throat. It was the laughter of devils and demons from the hells of legend. Edelline-Lan put her hands over her ears but she couldn't shut it out. The corner of Phaid's mouth twitched involuntarily.

'Here we go.'

His Eminence had stepped back from the hailer. One of his aides had handed the comset that linked him to his four squad leaders. He spoke into it and the line of militants tensed. Orders were barked. Sheets of blaster flame fountained into all four sides of the building. It was a precise, well drilled exercise in destruction. The demi-prelate stepped back with the air of a man who was happy that everything was going exactly as he had visualised. His black armoured troops stood their ground and pumped fire into the council chamber.

Above the roar, one of the burghers shouted a warning that if the blaster fire continued for too long, there was a chance that the roof might melt. The demi-prelate looked at him with open contempt.

'Everything is under control. We know exactly what we are doing.'

Almost in mockery of his words an eruption of counter fire exploded out from twenty or more of the council building's windows. It lashed down with such fury and deadly violence that there had to be at least another small army inside with Solchaim. Phaid knew that the returning flames could be nothing but an elaihim illusion but he took no chances. He threw himself flat on the ground and covered his head with his arms. Edelline-Lan did the same. Both were well aware that if the elaihi willed it, his illusions could kill just as effectively as the real thing. What Phaid couldn't quite understand was that, in contradiction to his previous fatigue, Solchaim was now apparently growing in strength. He was affecting the minds of hundreds of people with shattering force. All around there was carnage. For a number of the militants the illusion was so complete they fell either dead or dying. The ground around the building was churned up and

518

smoking. As far as Phaid could tell, Solchaim had found some source of energy in the small town into which he could tap and from which he could feed.

The militants were scrambling for cover, trying to dig down into the rock hard permafrost of the street. A large chunk fell out of the front of the council chamber, leaving a gaping hole. The demi-prelate was still on his feet, he seemed unable to believe what was going on. His discipline and training, the most important things in his life, had deserted him. He was staring, wide eyed and helpless. In the other streets the onlookers were reeling backwards, trying to get out of the way of the flames. It had only taken a matter of minutes to turn the orderly little ice town into a picture of violent chaos.

The fire abruptly stopped. Phaid raised his head, but quickly ducked again as a loud, hideous creaking vibrated through the town. Two large, boulder sized blocks of ice and a shower of smaller debris crashed into the street. A long, jagged crack had arched across the roof. Phaid's eyes were tightly closed as he waited for the next fall of ice. To his relief, none came. Solchaim's laugh again echoed around the streets. This time, however, after the inexplicable fusillade of phantom blasters, it didn't carry the same terror. Phaid edged closer to Edelline-Lan. He still wasn't prepared to risk getting up.

'You got any guesses what he's going to do next?'

Edelline-Lan shook her head.

'I've just got this feeling that something very bad is about to happen.'

'Something very bad *is* happening.'

'You know what I mean. It's like a premonition, a sense of impending doom.'

'He could be spreading it himself.'

'Which probably means he's softening us up for something. It's likely he's getting ready for some kind of set-piece unpleasantness. You know how he likes to show off.'

'Is it really showing off?'

There was another loud creak from the roof. Phaid winced and waited for the fall. Still it didn't come.

'Of course it's showing off. He may have his powers and he may be superior to us in every way, but he's not a god. He's got weaknesses, and one of them is showing off to us inferiors. Another one is that he's a bully. I think we

519

ought to start moving back, out of the way, before he begins pulling the wings off us flies.'

There was a commotion on the other side of the building.

The demi-prelate, who had managed to claw back most of his sanity, spoke urgently into the comset. Phaid grasped the angle of one of his aides.

'What's happened?'

'A suicide squad attempted to storm the back of the chamber.'

'And?'

'It failed.'

'It was suicide?'

'Most of them killed.'

'Maybe it was a wish fulfilment.'

The aide looked as though nothing would please him better than to burn Phaid where he lay. Phaid got into a crouch and gestured to Edelline-Lan.

'Over there.'

Cautiously they made their way to a building on the other side of the street. A Windlee lawman was crouched in the doorway of a general store. He hardly looked up when Phaid and Edelline-Lan joined him. He kept shaking his head as though he wasn't able to accept what his eyes were seeing. There was a brief exchange of fire at the side of the building. This time Solchaim decided to play with the flames and it became a brief but brilliant firework display. Phaid was mystified.

'What is he doing, and where is he getting all this power from? I'd sure as hell like to know his next move.'

He didn't have to wait very long for an answer. The streets started to grow dark. It was a strange, unnatural darkness. The lawman's eyes rolled in horror.

'The power plant's gone!'

It occurred to Phaid that Solchaim might have discovered a way to hook himself to the town's power plant. He said nothing, however. Instead he looked around carefully.

'It's not the power plant. Everything is still working. You can see from the glo-globes on the houses and the ones set in the roof. They're still burning. This darkness is growing inside our own minds.'

Whatever the cause, it was as though some sinister invisible thing was soaking all the light in the town. The

520

glo-globes and tubes seemed to struggle against the gloom. Phaid kept telling himself that it was an illusion, but it didn't stop fear clawing at his soul. When it looked as though things couldn't get any worse, the red came. It was the same red that Phaid had seen in the control room of the *Valentine*. Solchaim was well acquainted with the precise shade of human terror. The red glow seemed to come pulsing from above as though some huge evil thing was squatting on the ice above the city, pouring its grim, bloody radiation through the ice of the roof. Phaid could hear people screaming further out in the streets. Even the iron discipline of the priests' militant was breaking up. Some were looking around fearfully, others had dropped their weapons and were backing away. The demi-prelate and his aides were standing, stunned. Nothing in their experience gave them any means to combat what was happening to them. The lawman's mouth was working helplessly. A line of saliva trailed down his chin. He seemed on the very edge of being completely taken over by irrational fear.

'It's . . . it's . . .'

'It's what?'

'It's the end of the world.'

'Most probably.'

'What did we do?'

'We stopped being top of the heap.'

The lawman started to shake uncontrollably.

'It's the end of the world.'

Phaid nodded again.

'It more than likely is.'

Phaid found himself strangely unaffected by what was going on. He badly wanted a drink, but quivering terror was not about to overtake him. He leaned towards Edelline-Lan.

'I think everyone else is getting this worse than us.'

'We must have become used to it.'

'The smartest thing we could do is to use all this as a cover for us to sneak away. We should try and make it up to the surface and steal a flipper. If we . . . oh no!'

Terror had sneaked up on Phaid and jumped on him. It was a particular and very personal terror. Makartur and Flame, his would-be killers from his immediate past, were standing and talking to the demi-prelate and his stunned and disorganised aides. They seemed to have been

521

brought there by an escort of militants from the troop carriers on the surface.

At first Phaid thought this was an illusion, tailor-made for him to whip him into line, but then he wondered. He grasped Edelline-Lan by the arm.

'Do you see it?'

'See what? Get a grip, Phaid.'

'Look, look! Over by his Eminence!'

Edelline-Lan looked where he was pointing. Her face fell.

'Oh Lords!'

'You see them?'

Edelline-Lan's mouth was a tight hard line.

'I see them.'

'They must have been on that second boat that was following us. Now I really do have to get out of here.'

Almost as though on cue Makartur turned and looked straight at Phaid. Their eyes met. Even in the red gloom there was no way to pretend that they hadn't been spotted. Makartur spoke to Flame and pointed. Edelline-Lan looked anxiously at Phaid.

'What shall we do now?'

Phaid slowly pulled the blaster from his belt. Makartur was striding towards him with a dangerous purpose. There seemed to be no way to avert the instant of confrontation. And then Solchaim appeared. He was standing on the second floor, in the hole that had been blasted in the wall. He was bathed in an unearthly golden radiance. Makartur hesitated. He looked at Solchaim and then back at Phaid. He seemed torn as to which was his greater enemy. Finally he glared balefully at Phaid.

'You seem to have been granted a stay of execution, manny. That monster will go first and then I'll be back for you. This is not only a matter between you and me. One of the hunters' women was burned in the explosion. She took four hours to die.'

Phaid stood mute as he turned and walked away. Edelline-Lan looked at him with a puzzled expression.

'You could have shot him in the back. It would have stopped the whole business once and for all.'

Phaid looked as though he didn't understand it himself.

'I don't know. I couldn't do it. I just couldn't do it. I wanted to, but something was stopping me, holding me back.'

Edelline-Lan nodded towards Solchaim.

'Him.'

Phaid shook his head.

'I don't know any more. I think I'm exhausted. There was a point just now, just when Makartur was walking towards me, I didn't care any more. I'd been adrift for too long. I didn't have the strength to raise a blaster.'

Edelline-Lan looked at him in a strange way but didn't say anything. Phaid seemed to be receding. He and his problems were none of her concern. She only wanted to look at Solchaim. The elaihi was demanding all of her attention. He was demanding the attention of everyone in the town. Every eye was fixed on him. He seemed to swell and grow as though feeding on something in the stares of the humans. The golden light became dazzling. A terrible sadness came over Edelline-Lan. A large tear ran down her face, although she hadn't a clue why. The elaihi was beautiful. She choked back a sob. Then the voice of Phaid muttered beside her.

'We really are being softened up for something.'

She tried to talk through her tears.

'It's not getting to you. Oh Phaid, he's so beautiful, wonderful, so golden . . .'

Her voice trailed away. She was staring wide-eyed at Solchaim. Reassuring things were being said inside her head by a soft voice. She felt loved and protected. The terrible sadness only came because she was so unworthy, so inferior. She deserved punishment but instead she was being rewarded with kindness and love. For a second time the voice of Phaid cut in on her bittersweet bliss.

'I think I know what he's doing.'

A flutter of annoyance danced across her otherwise perfect vision. All around the council chambers people appeared to be experiencing similar washes of ecstasy. Many of the priests' militant had put down their weapons, some had even removed their helmets and sections of their armour to make themselves more comfortable on the hard ground. Some sat cross-legged in an attitude of meditation, others stood at rapt attention, a few bowed in prayer. Two had actually curled themselves into foetal positions. The lines that the lawmen had set up to keep back the crowds were disintegrating and the townspeople moved forward towards the source of the revelation. Their faces were slack and their movements slow and clumsy as though they were in a trance.

'He's using so much power. It's incredible. I didn't know he was capable of anything on this scale. It must be the power plant. If he was doing this on his own he'd have burned himself out by now. This is something special.'

Solchaim seemed to be in total control of every mind in the city. The red gloom was slowly lifting, melted by the passionate heat of his brilliant golden aura. Humans stretched their arms in supplication to this wonderful being who offered eternal good. Everyone was touched by the warmth of his love. Everyone, that is, except Phaid.

'This has to be the set-piece that he's been planning all along. The arrival of the priests must have forced his hand. I'm sure he didn't want to stage it in a backwater ice town like this.'

Edelline-Lan had sunk to her knees. She was quivering all over and moaning softly in her throat. Spiritual exultation was obviously being tinged by the sexual. Others were showing the same symptoms. Solchaim was clearly producing a very uniform vision. Phaid found it easier to concentrate on the behaviour of the others around him. He knew if he started to examine the images in his own mind, he'd have no reason to resist.

'The power that's flowing out of him is quite incredible. He's unstoppable. This has to be the beginning of the end for us.'

A low drone of voices that didn't form words filled the underground streets of Windlee. It started to glow in volume and developed a regular metered pulse. The humans were no longer the passive observers of their elaihi created visions. They were starting to actually participate in his games. Phaid seized Edelline-Lan by the shoulders and shook her roughly.

'Fight him! For the sake of your mind, you have to fight him! He's taking us all over and he isn't going to let go.'

She showed no response. Phaid found that his words were being addressed to deaf ears. He continued to talk. It was one way to keep a hold on his sanity.

'He's going to be a god. He's going to run the world. We are going to be worshipping him, and more than likely we will destroy ourselves in the process. He'll replace all the other religions. No one will be able to stand against him. He's a god right here on earth. We will simply become his creatures, his doomed pets, living out our time before extinction.'

There was quiet, hollow laughter inside his head. Solchaim hadn't overlooked him, he was amused by his lonely voice shouting independence. There was never going to be independence ever again. What terrible religion could humanity invent when their god was among them with limitless power to hold them enthralled?

'And what am I? Why am I set apart? Do you need a flunkey, am I to be god's dog or do you want me around as a specimen, the last living example of a free human being, a souvenir of the late great human race?'

The laughter once again rang in his head. The other humans in the city replied to it in a strange language that Phaid was certain the elaihi had invented especially for the occasion. It was entirely unlike any human tongue that he had ever encountered on his travels.

It was an eerie experience, having to stand and listen while a few hundred people with faces blank as the dead chanted in an alien language to a spindly glowing creature that stood and laughed at their blind, slave-like obedience. Phaid knew this was a glimpse of the future as Solchaim had it planned. Man would become a useless, unthinking tribal beast in wandering, rapidly diminishing numbers. Once again Phaid asked the self created god why he had been chosen to be the one spared.

It was then that he noticed a movement out of the corner of his eye. He wasn't the only one not to be a part of the controlling spell. Makartur was getting slowly and laboriously to his feet. He seemed to be carrying a crushing, invisible load, but he managed to carry it. He staggered towards the building, slow as a sleepwalker, lurching and stumbling, but all the time going towards Solchaim. Twice he fell to his knees, but he managed to get up again. Somewhere deep inside his warrior brain he had found a reserve of madness and energy to carry him forward against his enemy. There wasn't the slightest chance that he could prevail. There would be no eleventh hour victory for humanity but his vain, pointless determination and courage were magnificent.

He fell again as he climbed over the rubble of the ruined wall. A small trickle of blood ran from a cut on his cheek. He stood at the feet of the elaihi, looking up. With an exhausted and gasping but very deliberate movement he pulled his blaster from his belt and pointed it upward.

There was a peal of laughter and the blaster exploded in his hand. What was left of his body rolled to the bottom of the pile of rubble. Flame shrieked. She too seemed to have been released from Solchaim's control. She rushed to the corpse and frantically searched the body for a non-existent sign of life. Once she knew for certain that Makartur was dead, she had only one task left. She had to kill Solchaim. She stood up and drew her own weapon. She pointed it at the elaihi but seemed unable to fire.

Solchaim slowly extended his arm. A flash of white electrical fire danced on the palm of his hand. He flicked his wrist and a blazing sheet of the same power splashed over Flame. Phaid had expected her to be burned beyond belief, blown up. He had expected to see her body hurled across the street. Instead, she stood perfectly still, rigid, almost like a statue, as the white radiance danced around her. Then her flesh started to glow, first red and then gold, like metal thrust into the heat of the forge. Flame screamed three times and then she slumped. Her body appeared to fragment and fall into pieces. The white blaze faded away and all that was left was a pile of ash. The whole town rang with Solchaim's anger. Red fire seemed to consume everything. For a moment, Phaid thought that the buildings were burning, but then the fire snapped off and all was black. It was on again. Red, black, red, black. Solchaim's rage towered over the humans. He was pure wrath, a violent vengeful god, a god of pain and punishment and an absolute price that must be paid for disobedience and sin.

Phaid suspected that this time he might be seeing the real face of the elaihi, a vicious, unforgiving creature with near limitless power, a being filled with hate for those that he knew were his inferiors. He was the most complete enemy that human kind had ever encountered. He was dedicated to their downfall and extinction. He planned to extend his illusionary godhood out from this tiny ice town, clear across the whole world of men. He would enslave and bind them in the most perverted faith that had ever been known. He would use faith to strip men and women of their intelligence, their ingenuity, their native cunning and even their culture. Disease and sterility would follow in his wake. In perhaps two centuries, humanity would be nothing more than a piece of history. The torture that Solchaim seemed to have reserved for Phaid was to retain the shreds of his sanity in order to watch the downfall of his species.

The tongues of pain whipped through the town. The faithful were scattered and driven before them. A god had an absolute right to chastise and punish his people when they failed him. Solchaim was no god of mercy. His gift to them was swift and terrible retribution. At Phaid's feet, Edelline-Lan squirmed and writhed in some private hell. There were others who howled and clawed at the hard ground, tearing skin and fingernails. A terrible wailing filled the air, the tone was that of pleading and lamentation, but it was in the alien tongue. It was like a scene of tortured souls out of some ancient demon comedy. Phaid felt totally cast adrift, far from any reality he had known. His experience with the elaihim didn't make him immune to the influence. It just set him apart for some special treatment. He wasn't free. He wasn't in a place where he could turn and walk to the elevators, ride up to the surface, get into a flipper and drive away. All that had died. Phaid wasn't quite sure when. He suspected it was when the woman Flame had been destroyed. Phaid couldn't guess what had really happened. The illusion had been staged to reveal the ultimate power of the new deity. He was sure, however, that she was dead. He was just as sure that Makartur was also dead. He suspected that what he had witnessed was very close to what had actually happened. He had been present at the death of Makartur, just as the ancestors had foretold. The prophecy had been fulfilled. Phaid thought bitterly that if Makartur's ancestors had been a little more precise in their message he would have been saved a great deal of fear, trouble and pain. Once again he hadn't been the cause of anything. He had simply been standing there when it happened. It was the story of his life. Phaid sank to his knees. His despair was total.

And then the earth moved.

It was a jolt like an earthquake. Buildings shook, more cracks arched across the roof, there was a terrible creaking and ice debris streamed down. For a moment, it seemed as though the whole town was falling down. Phaid gripped the ground and waited for a second shock. None came. He realised that for as long as the jolt had lasted, he had forgotten about the elaihi. He looked up. Solchaim was a black angular figure. Everything was back to normal. It was hard for him to realise that his mind was free.

Solchaim staggered sideways. He seemed to be looking at someone or something behind him. Smoke was curling up from a hole in the armour on his chest. Part of his cape was burning. He took a step back almost to the edge of where the floor jutted out from the ruined side of the council building. From inside, there was the blue-white flash of a fuse tube. Solchaim staggered again but he didn't fall. There was another flash. Phaid was blinded by hellfire red. More ice debris fell from the roof. Solchaim's pain and anger was a ball of searing fire. More cracks spread over the roof of the city. There was a final flash of red. Solchaim swayed, holding on to his last few seconds of life. His arms windmilled as he tried to keep his balance on the very edge of the sagging floor. Another flash from the fuse tube smashed into him and he fell like a broken doll. He hit the rubble at the foot of the building and lay still, just a short distance from the body of Makartur and the remains of Flame.

Chrystiana-Nex appeared in the shattered hole in the council chamber wall. She was white faced and crying, and she held a smoking fuse tube loosely by her side. Her trembling voice was very clear in the terrible silence that followed the elaihi's fall.

'He forgot me. He was giving my dreams to everybody. He was sharing my beautiful golden dreams with the common people. I couldn't let him do that. The dreams were ours, they weren't something that could be shared. I had to kill him.'

Phaid slowly stood up, marvelling at how a forgotten human pet, little more than a puppet or plaything, could have caused the downfall of a would-be god. Almost immediately there was a roar like thunder. More debris cascaded down, and Phaid could see daylight through one of the cracks. Snow swirled in as a huge section of the roof started to slide and fall. Phaid raced towards the nearest building in the hope of shelter but that too began to topple and he darted back into the middle of the street. Huge chunks of ice were falling all around him. He was standing, undecided, when everything went black.

32

THE FIRST thing that Phaid knew was that he was very, very cold. He seemed to be laying in a pool of freezing water and he hurt all over. He was stretched out, near one of the big black troop transports. He seemed to be inside a huge, clear, temporary protection balloon. Large numbers of priests' militant milled efficiently. There appeared to be some sort of rescue operation going on. The balloon kept out the worst of the surface cold, but it was far from comfortable. His teeth were chattering. he sat up and hugged his arms around himself. To his distaste, he saw that he had been lying quite close to the fused body of Solchaim. In death, the elaihi looked strangely fragile and delicate.

Phaid started to feel a little uneasy so near to the corpse and he climbed painfully to his feet. The town of Windlee was a ruin. It was little more than a deep crater in the permafrost. Phaid could see gangs of townspeople, in full cold suits, battling the wind in order to rig a temporary roof over the least damaged parts.

He limped slowly towards the transparent wall of the balloon to take a better look at the repair efforts. He'd only gone a couple of paces when a priest' militant, standing nearby, gestured with his blaster.

'Where do you think you're going?'

Phaid put on a chilled, who-me expression.

'I was going to take a look at the work that's going on.'

'You better stay right where you are. There's an Under Pastor wants to have a talk with you.'

Phaid grimaced.

'Just an Under Pastor? What happened to his Eminence?'

The militant looked at him out of the corner of his eye.

'He's off back to the Holy City by the fastest route. He most likely figures that this little lot will drop him right in the manure. Of course, don't tell anyone that I told you.'

Phaid shook his head, glad to have found a militant who was prepared to unbend a little.

'I won't say a word. When is the Under Pastor going to show up?'

The militant shrugged.

'When he gets around to it. There's quite a mess here.'

While Phaid waited he took stock of himself. He too was a mess. His clothes were torn and dirty. He badly needed a bath and a shave, and he was starving. He would have to promote some assistance out of the priests or once again, he would be in serious trouble. He started with the militant, and his most urgent need for food.

'Do you people have a cookhouse set up?'

The militant shook his head.

'We're getting by on hard rations.'

'Is there anyway that I could get something to eat?'

The militant shrugged again. Clearly unbending did not stretch all that far.

'I wouldn't know. My job's to watch you and the corpse. I wasn't told anything about feeding. You're going to have to ask the Under Pastor.'

'When he gets around to me.'

'Now you're getting the idea.'

'Am I a prisoner or what?'

'Nobody told me, but you won't be going anywhere until the Under Pastor shows up.'

It took over two hours for the Under Pastor to get around to Phaid. By the time he did, Phaid was feeling about as wretched as he had ever felt in his life. His spirits were far from lifted when he discovered that the officer was a short, squat, self important little man who was obviously of the opinion that he deserved a more elevated rank and who was hoping the Windlee situation was the chance to improve himself.

'So, Phaid the Gambler, you've been involved in a great deal of trouble, haven't you.'

Phaid shivered.

'So have a lot of other people.'

'But you've been involved a bit more closely than most.'

'I was a prisoner to the elaihi.'

'You specialise in getting into trouble?'

'Not if I can help it.'

'So why now?'

'Apart from being a prisoner of the elaihi, I was under orders from an agent of the priesthood.'

'Dreen.'

'That's right, Dreen.'

'He's dead.'

'I know he's dead.'

'In fact, you killed Spiritual Brother Dreen in the hotel at Bluehaven. Am I right?'

'It was self defence.'

'That's what the witnesses say, otherwise you wouldn't be standing here now. You'd be inside one of my transports, in irons.'

Phaid muttered under his breath.

'Maybe it would be warmer in irons.'

'What?'

'Nothing.'

The Under Pastor walked over and looked at the body of the elaihi.

'Are you another one who claims that this thing was responsible for the whole incident?'

'He was.'

'He doesn't look like much.'

'He was planning to make himself a god and lead the human race into extinction.'

'That's rubbish, and also heresy.'

'You don't believe it?'

'I am a priest. I know about these things. Nobody can make himself a god.'

'No human, maybe.'

'These elaihim don't amount to much. We've had them investigated. They pose no threat.'

'They will end up as the dominant species.'

'You're talking nonsense. It's obvious you have nothing to contribute. His Eminence had the idea that you might be valuable. His Eminence had a lot of ideas. I imagine that the truth will come out when he is investigated.'

'You hoping to step into his shoes, maybe, after the investigation?'

The Under Pastor ignored the crack.

'You are free to go, gambler. I don't think you know anything and I will report accordingly.'

Phaid couldn't believe what he was hearing.

'Wait just a minute . . .'

'Oh, by the way. A message was left for you.'

The Under Pastor held out a folded piece of paper. Phaid read the words with growing impatience.

> *'My dearest Phaid,*
> *By the time you read this, we will be on our way to the Holy City. Chrystiana-Nex has not been well since she killed Solchaim and she is now convinced that the priests are the only ones who will care for her and protect her. I'm not sure if she is doing the right thing but I have gone with her anyway. I hope you're not angry that we've left. In a way I feel I'm deserting you, particularly after all you went through on our account. I don't know when or where, but I'm sure we will meet again. Until then, please remember me kindly.*
> *Your friend,*
> *Edelline-Lan.'*

Phaid crumpled the paper and faced the Under Pastor.

'So you've got Chrystiana-Nex?'

'His Eminence sees her as his only hope of coming out of this examination with an absolution.'

'What about the reward that Dreen promised me?'

The Under Pastor looked at Phaid as though he was quite mad.

'Dreen promised you a reward if you delivered Chrystiana-Nex to us. The way I see it, she came to us of her own accord. I really don't think that we are obliged to give you anything.'

'But I brought her all this way.'

'That is your problem.'

'I get nothing?'

'Nothing.'

Phaid was desperate. He started to wheedle.

'If you could just help me out, I mean, I'm stranded here. I've got no money and even the

532

clothes on my back won't keep out the cold.'

The Under Pastor looked bored.

'I'm sorry.'

'Just some food and a ride to civilisation?'

'There's nothing I can do. We're a religious order, not a charity.'

He turned and marched away. Phaid slumped down on a block of ice, trying to think of a way out of the mess into which he had once again fallen. No answers came and self pity started to take over. He didn't even notice at first when the unnatural silence fell over the balloon. Finally, he realised that everyone had stopped moving. He looked up to see four elaihim in pale grey robes walking towards him. Nobody interfered with them or tried to stop them. The priests' militant seemed to have become rooted to the spot. Phaid found that he couldn't get up from his block of ice. The elaihim weren't interfering with anyone's thoughts, they had simply immobilised everybody present.

They walked past Phaid and solemnly up to the body of Solchaim. One of them produced a flat folded bundle. It opened out into a decorated, ceremonial silk shroud. They wrapped it around the body and lifted it on to their shoulders. Before they moved off, one of them looked directly at Phaid.

'He was tainted by contact with your kind, but he was still one of us.'

With solemn dignity they bore away their fallen cousin. Phaid saw that, as they passed, a number of the nearby priests' militant all made a similar, small, secretive hand signal with thumb and index finger. With a sense of dull shock, Phaid realised that Solchaim might have left something implanted in the minds that he had occupied down in the ice town. A legend seemed to be being born and, in that case, Solchaim's plan might not have been a complete failure.

The elaihim vanished as though they had never been. The inside of the balloon crashed back to normal. Phaid suspected that heads would roll, possibly the Under Pastor's, when the priesthood discovered that the body had gone. It was a thought that brought him a moment of amused consolation but it didn't stop him sinking back into his dismal reflections. He kept trying to make some sense out of what had happened. He kept trying for a reason, an explanation, any explanation, for the way that fate kept pushing him into bizarre and dangerous situations. He wanted to find some pattern in the sequence of events that he had been through but all he kept coming back to was a Tharmier proverb that said 'A cork that bobs on a fast flowing river doesn't know the geography of the country. It doesn't need to.'

Phaid had gone down so low that once again he had become oblivious to what was going on around him. The voice beside him was something of a shock.

'You want a ride out?'

The speaker was a middle-aged man with a beer gut and a grizzled beard. He wore the beaded leathers favoured by the few humans who competed with the androids in handling the big cargo transport beds. Phaid looked up with a startled expression.

'What?'

'I'm driving into the warm, I asked you if you wanted a ride.'

Phaid was instantly suspicious.

'Why me?'

'You look pretty damn miserable sitting there.'

'I don't have any money.'

'That don't matter. I'm hauling into Tharmier country. I just need someone to talk to and to make sure I don't fall asleep at the controls. You want the ride or not, ace?'

Phaid realised that he was being stupid. He stood up.

'Yeah, I want a ride.'

'I ain't going to Losaw, just a little place out on the coast, but at least it will be warm.'

Phaid grinned.

'I'd give a lot to be warm.'

'Let's go then.'

'Yeah, let's go.'

33

'THIS IS where you get off, ace. I make my turn here. You'll have to walk the rest of the way into town.'

Phaid grinned.

'Hell, I've been sitting down so long it'll be a pleasure to stretch my legs.'

He swung himself out of the cab of the transport bed. The sky was a deep clear blue. Over in the distance the sea sparkled behind a line of trees. Gulls wheeled in the air, calling out their greed to each other. Small flowers flourished along the side of the paved roadway.

'Good luck!'

'Yeah, you too.'

The transport bed pulled away and Phaid felt the warmth of the sun on his back. He pulled off his coat. He was about to fold it up and carry it, but then he stopped. He held the thing up and looked at it. It was a handsome, if funky, coat, but it hadn't brought him any luck. Suddenly, on an impulse, he swung it around his head, holding it by one arm. He let go and the coat went flying. The breeze caught it and, for a moment, before it fell, it looked like a big, dirty bat. He started stripping off all his cold weather clothes and threw them after the coat. He kept just his boots, his shirt and his breeches. He was going to throw away his hat but then he changed his mind, jammed it down on his head and, tucking his thumbs into the tops of his breeches, he sauntered down a dirt road that led to the shore.

Three kids were pitching bones on a wooden pier. Phaid

stopped to watch them for a while. One of the kids noticed Phaid staring and looked up at him.

'You a traveller?'

'Yeah.'

'What you doing here?'

'Watching you kids gamble, right at this moment.'

'Why?'

'I guess you could say I'm kind of a gambling man myself.'

'You want to play with us, mister gambling man?'

Phaid laughed and shook his head.

'I don't think so.'

'Come on, mister gambling man. You scared of us? Is that what it is? Hey, mister gambling man. Is that what it is? You think we too strong for you?'

The kid's Tharmier moon face split into a smile and his voice became a rhythmic chant.

'Hey, hey, gambling man, you going to gamble in our game? Hey, hey, mister gambling man. You afraid to play?'

Phaid grinned and hunkered down on the pier.

'I ain't afraid of you guys.'

Phaid reached for the bones but the kid who had done all the talking held up a hand to stop him.

'It's a cash game.'

Phaid threw in his last two tabs.

'It'll do.'

Phaid made six straight passes. His luck was statistically incredible and he quadrupled his money. He'd probably made enough for his supper. He looked at the kids and shrugged.

'That's the way it goes sometimes.'

'You wouldn't cheat on us little kids, would you?'

Phaid shook his head.

'Hell no.'

'Are you going to give us our money back?'

Again Phaid shook his head.

'No.'

'But we're only kids.'

'You're big enough to know what the deal is.'

A pretty girl with olive skin and very straight black hair was walking along the sand. She wore a clinging silk wrap and an exotic flower behind her ear. She smiled at Phaid as she walked by. Phaid stood up and grinned at the kids.

'Besides, I've something else to do.'

He jumped down from the pier and walked off across the sand, following the girl.

THE WEAPON SHOPS OF ISHER

by A. E. van Vogt

In the year 4784, the Universe is contained within the empire of Isher ruled by the Empress Innelda. Dedicated to pleasure, Innelda's dictatorship has driven Isher to the brink of cosmic disaster. For against her stand the impregnable Weapon Shops, their immortal leader Robert Hedrock and a man from the 20th century with terrifying power.

NEW ENGLISH LIBRARY

DUNE
by Frank Herbert

Dune is the finest, most widely acclaimed Science Fiction novel of this century. Huge in scope, towering in concept, it is a work which will live in the reader's imagination for the rest of his life.

'*Dune* seems to me unique among SF novels in the depth of its characterisation and the extraordinary detail of the world it creates. I know nothing comparable to it except *The Lord of the Rings*.' – *Arthur C. Clarke*

'Certainly one of the landmarks of modern Science Fiction . . . an amazing feat of creation.' – *Analog*

NEW ENGLISH LIBRARY

NEL BESTSELLERS

T 51277	'THE NUMBER OF THE BEAST'	*Robert Heinlein*	£2.25
T 51382	FAIR WARNING	*Simpson & Burger*	£1.75
T 50246	TOP OF THE HILL	*Irwin Shaw*	£1.95
T 46443	FALSE FLAGS	*Noel Hynd*	£1.25
T 49272	THE CELLAR	*Richard Laymen*	£1.25
T 45692	THE BLACK HOLE	*Alan Dean Foster*	95p
T 49817	MEMORIES OF ANOTHER DAY	*Harold Robbins*	£1.95
T 53231	THE DARK	*James Herbert*	£1.50
T 45528	THE STAND	*Stephen King*	£1.75
T 50203	IN THE TEETH OF THE EVIDENCE	*Dorothy L. Sayers*	£1.25
T 50777	STRANGER IN A STRANGE LAND	*Robert Heinlein*	£1.75
T 50807	79 PARK AVENUE	*Harold Robbins*	£1.75
T 51722	DUNE	*Frank Herbert*	£1.75
T 50149	THE INHERITORS	*Harold Robbins*	£1.75
T 49620	RICH MAN, POOR MAN	*Irwin Shaw*	£1.60
T 46710	EDGE 36: TOWN ON TRIAL	*George G. Gilman*	£1.00
T 51552	DEVIL'S GUARD	*Robert Elford*	£1.50
T 53296	THE RATS	*James Herbert*	£1.50
T 50874	CARRIE	*Stephen King*	£1.50
T 43245	THE FOG	*James Herbert*	£1.50
T 52575	THE MIXED BLESSING	*Helen Van Slyke*	£1.75
T 38629	THIN AIR	*Simpson & Burger*	95p
T 38602	THE APOCALYPSE	*Jeffrey Konvitz*	95p
T 46796	NOVEMBER MAN	*Bill Granger*	£1.25

NEL P.O. BOX 11, FALMOUTH TR10 9EN, CORNWALL

Postage charge:

U.K. Customers. Please allow 40p for the first book, 18p for the second book, 13p for each additional book ordered, to a maximum charge of £1.49, in addition to cover price.

B.F.P.O. & Eire. Please allow 40p for the first book, 18p for the second book, 13p per copy for the next 7 books, thereafter 7p per book, in addition to cover price.

Overseas Customers. Please allow 60p for the first book plus 18p per copy for each additional book, in addition to cover price.

Please send cheque or postal order (no currency).

Name ....

Address ....

....

Title ....

While every effort is made to keep prices steady, it is sometimes necessary to increase prices at short notice. New English Library reserve the right to show on covers and charge new retail prices which may differ from those advertised in the text or elsewhere.(6)